D1380824

SANDRO OF CHEGEM

Fazil Iskander, who was born in 1929, is one of the Soviet Union's most popular writers. A native of Abkhazia, an autonomous republic in the Caucasus, he has lived and worked in Moscow for over two decades, though he returns frequently to his homeland. He is widely considered the preeminent example of a non-Russian writing in Russian and making a permanent contribution to Soviet multinational literature.

Iskander began his career as a poet, but it is his fiction that has won him fame. *The Goatibex Constellation*, the best known of his novels published in the USSR, was published in the United States in 1975. *Sandro of Chegem*, the major work of Iskander's career, has been fully published only outside the Soviet Union.

SANDRO OF CHEGEM

Fazil Iskander

Translated from the Russian by
SUSAN BROWNSBERGER

LONDON · BOSTON

First published in Great Britain in 1983
by Jonathan Cape Ltd, London

This paperback edition first published in 1993
by Faber and Faber Limited
3 Queen Square London WC1N 3AU

Printed in England by Clays Ltd, St Ives plc

A CIP record for this book is
available from the British Library

ISBN 0-571-16782-9

2 4 6 8 10 9 7 5 3 1

FOREWORD

I began writing *Sandro of Chegem* as a comic piece, a gentle parody of the picaresque novel. The concept gradually became more complicated, overgrown with details; I tried to break away to the wide-open spaces of pure humor, but I couldn't do it. This is one more proof of the old saying that the writer merely follows a voice, which dictates the manuscript to him.

The book you are reading is in fact only part of the epic *Sandro*. Further episodes of the novel will be published in the future.

I have wanted the images of the people I portray in these chapters to reveal the might and beauty of the moral sky under which the people of Chegem lived. The history of a clan, the history of the village of Chegem, the history of Abkhazia, and all the rest of the world as it is seen from Chegemian heights—that is the concept of the book, in broad outline.

Increasingly, as the book developed, my inspiration has been the poetry in the life of the people. That is what matters.

Kenguria is a fictitious district in eastern Abkhazia.

Enduria is an even more fictitious district in even more eastern Abkhazia.

The Endurskies are the mystery of ethnic prejudice.

Every people perceives its own way of life as the greatest one of all. This perception seems to reflect a nation's instinct of self-preservation: Why should I imitate another people's way of life if mine is the greatest? Hence ethnic prejudice; it is inevitable, for the time being. To pretend that it did not exist would be cowardly and vulgar. Ironic mockery of another people's way of life is the most peaceful form of ethnic prejudice. That is all I make of it. In portraying that irony, and in speaking ironically about it, I have tried to be true to life and true to the natural principles of equality among nations.

Following the traditions of classical Russian literature, which revealed the value of the inner life of the so-called little man, I have attempted to reveal, to the best of my abilities, the significance of the epic existence of the little nation.

In my childhood I caught fleeting glimpses of the patriarchal village life of Abkhazia and fell in love with it forever. Have I perhaps idealized a vanishing life? Perhaps. A man cannot help ennobling what he loves. We may not recognize it, but in idealizing a vanishing way of life we are presenting a bill to the future. We are saying, "Here is what we are losing; what are you going to give us in exchange?"

Let the future think on that, if it is capable of thinking at all.

—FAZIL ISKANDER

CONTENTS

SANDRO OF CHEGEM

SANDRO OF CHEGEM

UNCLE SANDRO has been around for nearly eighty years, so that even by Abkhazian standards he may confidently be called an old man. Considering the many occasions in his youth—and not only in his youth—when people tried to kill him, we may say that he has been downright lucky.

The first time he took a bullet was from a young reprobate, as he invariably called him. It happened while he was cinching up his saddle girth before leaving a prince's courtyard.

At the time he was the princess's lover and had been hanging around her day and night. Thanks to his extraordinary knightly virtues, he was her foremost, indeed her only, lover.

The young reprobate was in love with the princess and had also been hanging around her day and night, exercising his rights as a neighbor, I believe, or a distant relative on the husband's side. He did not, however, as Uncle Sandro himself used to say, have the extraordinary knightly virtues that Uncle Sandro had. Or maybe he did, but he could find no opportunity to make use of them, because the princess was mad about Uncle Sandro.

Nevertheless, he had hopes, so he never moved a step from the princess's house, or even from her side, as long as she would have him there. Possibly she refrained from banishing him because he spurred Uncle Sandro to ever more inventive feats of love. Or perhaps she kept him around just in case Uncle Sandro suddenly became disabled. Who knows?

The princess was of Svanian extraction. That may explain certain of her erotic eccentricities. Among her good points, in addition to those of her fair exterior (Uncle Sandro used to say that she was as white as milk), I think we should note that she was an excellent rider, not a bad shot, and when the occasion required it, she could even milk a buffalo.

I mention this because milking a buffalo is hard—you have to have very strong fingers to do it. So the question of her being effete, infantile, or physically degenerate simply does not arise, despite the fact that she was a full-blooded descendant of the princes of Svanetia.

I don't think that this statement runs contrary to historical materialism if one considers the specifics of societal development under the alpine conditions of the Caucasus, not to mention the splendid air that she and her forebears had breathed. Uncle Sandro used to say that sometimes this amazon was not averse to pinching her beloved at intimate moments. But he bore it and never once cried out, because he was a truly gallant knight.

I suspect that her husband, a peaceable Abkhazian prince, was forced to bear cruder expressions of her despotic temperament. So, just in case, he tried to keep out of range.

At one time the young reprobate tried to enlist the husband's support (come to think of it, he must have been a relative rather than a neighbor). He had little to gain by this ploy, however. Even though the husband also hung around the house a lot, he was not around so much as Uncle Sandro because he passionately loved to hunt ibex, an avocation that requires a great deal of energy and forays lasting many days.

It may have been that the prince needed someone to stay home during his lengthy hunting trips—some dynamic and brave young man who could amuse the princess, receive guests, and if necessary, defend the honor of the house. Just such a young man, in those days, was Uncle Sandro. According to Uncle Sandro, the princess's husband loved him no less than the princess did. To the importunate young reprobate the prince therefore replied once and for all, "Don't get me mixed up in your intrigues."

This remark, perhaps, was what made the nameless young reprobate feel so lonely and bereft that the only remedy he could find was to shoot Uncle Sandro.

In any case, this was how matters stood that day, when Uncle Sandro was briskly cinching up his saddle girth and his inconsolable rival was loitering mournfully in the middle of the courtyard with a decision ripening in his mind, the decision—frivolous even for those days—to shoot Uncle Sandro.

He had just tightened the front cinch when his rival called his name. Uncle Sandro turned, and the shot rang out.

"F--k your mother," Uncle Sandro screamed furiously, "if you think you can do me in with one bullet! Shoot again!"

But just then the princess's servants came running, and the princess herself flew out to the terrace.

They got Uncle Sandro to his feet. With the bullet in his stomach, he kept on swearing for a while, but finally he collapsed.

At first they put him to bed in the princess's house, but then that began to seem improper, and a few days later his relatives took him home on a stretcher. The princess rode along behind and stayed at his bedside night and day, which was no small honor, since his father was a simple peasant, although fairly well off.

Uncle Sandro had a very bad time because the young reprobate's Turkish pistol had been loaded with something like iron splinters. A celebrated doctor from the city was called in to save his life; he performed an operation and treated him for about two months. For each day of treatment he took one sheep, so that subsequently Uncle Sandro's father used to say of him that this "goat" had cost him sixty sheep.

No one knows how much longer the treatment would have lasted if Uncle Sandro's father had not returned home unexpectedly from the fields one day. He had broken his hoe and was coming for a new one. As he entered the yard he saw the doctor dozing peacefully in the shade of a walnut tree instead of treating his son or at least brewing herbs for him. He may be asleep, but I daresay his sheep are busy getting fat in the pasture, the old man thought as he went into the house.

He was even more surprised when he went into Uncle Sandro's room, because Uncle Sandro was sleeping, and not alone. This was going too far for any sister of mercy, even if she was of princely lineage. The thing that made the old man maddest was that he didn't know on which of the sixty days she had joined Sandro in bed, she being the first to realize that he was well, or at least that the method of treatment could be revised. Had he known a little sooner, he might have been able to avoid giving that lazybones the last ten sheep. Anyway, he poked the princess.

"Get up, Princess, the prince is at the gate!" he said.

"I guess I must have dozed off shooing the flies away from him," she yawned, stretching and hiking herself up a bit.

"Oh sure, from under the covers," the old man grumped, and he left the room.

At this point, Uncle Sandro, who out of modesty had been pretending to be asleep and wanted to keep on pretending, could not stand it any more. He burst out laughing. The princess started laughing too, because as a true patrician, albeit of alpine lineage, she was not particularly embarrassed.

The doctor was banished to town that very day, along with the sheep that were due him. The princess stayed on for several more days as Uncle Sandro's guest, and when she left, like a true princess, she gave his sisters gifts from among her silks and pearls. Everyone was happy—everyone except the young reprobate. After his ill-fated shot he was utterly bereft because the princess had moved to Uncle Sandro's, and despite his considerable effrontery, he did not dare make an appearance there. More than that, he had to get out of our part of the world altogether. He was not hiding from legal retribution so much as to avoid a bullet from one of Uncle Sandro's relatives. While he might still have had some hope in the princess's house, some occasion to demonstrate his more extraordinary knightly virtues (if he had any, that is), he was now forced to suffer from afar.

Besides this incident there have been many other times in Uncle Sandro's life when he could have been killed, or at least wounded. He could have been killed during the Civil War with the Mensheviks if he had taken part in it. In fact he could have been killed even though he did not take part.

Apropos, I will relate an adventure of his that I consider typical of the troubled time of the Mensheviks.

Uncle Sandro was returning home from a feast of some sort. Before he noticed, he was overtaken by darkness. It was a dangerous period, Menshevik detachments forayed everywhere, and he decided to ask to spend the night under the nearest roof. He recalled that a certain rich Armenian with whom he was slightly acquainted lived somewhere nearby. In his time this Armenian had fled from the massacres in Turkey. Now he raised high-grade tobaccos and sold them to the merchants of Trebizond and Batum, who paid him, Uncle Sandro claims, in pure gold.

Uncle Sandro rode up to the gates of the Armenian's house and shouted in his resonant voice, "Hey! Anyone home?"

There was no answer. But he saw the light go out in the kitchen, and wooden shutters closed over the inside of the windows. He shouted again, but there was no answer. Then he bent down to open the gate himself, and rode into the yard.

"Don't come any closer or I'll shoot!" came the owner's none-too-confident voice. Times are bad, thought Uncle Sandro, if this tobacco grower has taken up arms.

"Since when do you shoot at guests?" Uncle Sandro shouted, using his quirt to fend off the dog that leaped out to meet him. He heard women's voices, and the voice of the owner himself, coming from the kitchen. Apparently they were holding a council of war.

"You're not a Menshevik?" the owner asked finally, his voice imploring Uncle Sandro not to be a Menshevik, or at least to call himself something else.

"No," Uncle Sandro said proudly, "I'm just myself, Sandro of Chegem."

"Then why didn't I recognize your voice?" the owner asked.

"Out of fright," Uncle Sandro explained. The kitchen door opened cautiously, and the old man came out carrying a rifle. He walked up to Uncle Sandro and finally recognized him, only then calling off the dog. Uncle Sandro dismounted, his host tied his horse to an apple tree, and they went into the kitchen. Uncle Sandro noticed immediately that the man and his family were glad to see him, although he did not understand the true reason for their gladness until much later. For the moment he took it at face value, so to speak, as a modest tribute of thanks to him for his feats of gallantry, and it made him feel good. Incidentally, the man's family consisted of his wife, mother-in-law, and two teenage children—a boy and a girl.

In Uncle Sandro's honor the man sent his boy to slaughter a sheep, got out some wine, and although the guest, to be polite, tried to restrain him from the bloodletting, everything was done as it should be. Uncle Sandro was happy that his choice had fixed on this house, that his already sensitive nose for the possibilities of finding hospitality among people he barely knew had not betrayed him. In later years, with continuous practice, he developed this sense to the point of absolute pitch. It was largely responsible for his becoming a celebrated tamada, or toastmaster, in our part of the world—at once the merriest and the saddest star, as it were, in the firmament of marriage and funeral feasts.

When he sampled the wine, Uncle Sandro was convinced that the rich Armenian had already learned how to make good wine, even though he had not yet learned how to defend his house properly. Doesn't matter, Uncle Sandro thought, in our part of the world one learns everything eventually. So they sat past midnight by the fireplace fire at a bounteous fine table; the host constantly directed the conversation to Uncle Sandro's feats, and since Uncle Sandro, not being bashful, moved in this direction with satisfaction, the table was animated and instructive. Among other things, Uncle Sandro recounted for him a famous episode from his life, the time he shell-shocked a certain horseman by the sheer force of his voice, sweeping him from his mount as if with a sound wave.

"In those days," he added, when telling me the story of his adventure with the rich Armenian, "I had such a voice that if I gave a sudden shout in the dark the rider sometimes fell right off his horse, though sometimes he didn't."

"What did it depend on?" I probed.

"His blood," he explained confidently. "Bad blood curdles from fright, just like milk, and the man falls in a dead faint, though he doesn't die."

But to go on with the story. The talk and the wine flowed with a peaceful murmur, the logs crackled in the fireplace, and Uncle Sandro was perfectly content. True, it struck him as a bit strange that his host did not send his mother-in-law and children off to bed, because the wife could have taken care of the table alone. But then he decided that the children would profit by hearing tales of his feats; after all, it wasn't every day that they had a guest like Sandro of Chegem.

But now the dog barked again. The host looked at Uncle Sandro, and Sandro at him.

"Hey! Anyone home?" came a shout from the yard. Uncle Sandro listened intently, and from the way the sound kept shifting around, he determined that the dog was barking at five or six people, at least.

"Mensheviks," his host whispered, looking hopefully to Uncle Sandro. Sandro did not like this, but he was ashamed to retreat.

"I'll try my shout on them," he said. "If that doesn't work, we'll have to defend ourselves."

"Hey in there!" someone's voice called again, over the dog's barking. "Come on out, or it'll be all the worse for you!"

"Get away from the doors," Uncle Sandro ordered. "They'll start shooting through the door in a minute. Mensheviks shoot through the door first," he explained. No sooner had he said it than pow! pow! pow!—bullets struck the door, blasting splinters into the kitchen.

All three of the women burst into tears, and the rich Armenian's mother-in-law even set up a wail, just like our women at funerals.

"Why don't you have a chestnut door?" Uncle Sandro said, surprised to see that the door wasn't holding up worth a damn.

"Oh, Allah," his host cried out, "I know the tobacco business, but I don't know about things like that."

He had completely fallen apart. In Uncle Sandro's words, he was holding his old flintlock like a shepherd's staff. You might at least have brought a decent rifle with you from Turkey, Uncle Sandro thought with irritation. He realized that there was no point in depending on this tobacco grower for help.

"Where does that door lead?" Uncle Sandro asked, nodding at the other kitchen door.

"To the storeroom," his host said.

"I'm going to shout now," Uncle Sandro announced. "Have the women and children hide in the storeroom, or they'll ruin my shout with their bawling."

The owner herded his family into the storeroom and was ready to go in himself, so that no one would be in Uncle Sandro's way, but Uncle Sandro stopped him.

He ordered him to stand by one of the shuttered windows while he went over to the other one himself, his rifle at the ready.

"Open up in there, or it'll be all the worse!" the Mensheviks shouted, and again started shooting up the door. More splinters flew. One of these struck Uncle Sandro's cheek and clung there like a tick. Uncle Sandro ripped it out and turned on the rich Armenian in a rage.

"If the Turks never told you about chestnut doors," he said to him, "you could've at least put in oak."

"I don't know about these things, and I don't want to," the rich Armenian lamented. "All I want to do is sell tobacco to the merchants of Trebizond and Batum."

At this point Uncle Sandro inflated his lungs with air and shouted with his incredible voice.

"Hey you!" he shouted. "I've got a full bandolier, and I'm going to defend the house! Look out!"

With these words he opened the shutter a bit and peered into the yard. The moon was shining, but Uncle Sandro saw nothing at first. Then he stared into the dark shadow of the walnut tree and realized that they were hiding there. He was surprised that they had not walked right into the rich Armenian's house—they could scarcely be afraid of him—but then he surmised that they had noticed a strange horse tethered to the apple tree and had decided to bide their time.

They appeared to be talking things over, discussing his ominous warning.

Maybe they'll go away, he thought, and then suddenly, I just hope they don't take my horse. He froze at the window, peering intently at the men standing in the shadow of the walnut tree.

"Well, did they fall off their horses?" the old tobacco grower asked. He was too distrustful of the Mensheviks to open the shutter a crack and look out.

"Where would those ragtag Endurskies get horses?" Uncle Sandro muttered, continuing his surveillance.

In those days he believed all Mensheviks came from Endursk. Of course he knew they had a bunch of local stooges around here, but in his opinion Endursk was the true motherland of Menshevism, its hornet's nest, its ideological queen bee.

Now Uncle Sandro saw one of these scoundrels run quickly across the yard and stop in the shadow of the apple tree near his horse. Uncle Sandro could not make out what he was doing there, because he was on the far side of the horse. All the same he didn't like it.

"Hey," he shouted, "that's my horse!" His voice made it clear that the man who was shouting and the man who owned this house were far from one and the same.

"And who are you—Noy Zhordania?" came the answer from beside the horse, where as Uncle Sandro now guessed the fellow was rummaging through his saddlebag. Although the saddlebag was empty, Uncle Sandro did not like this kind of thing in the slightest. If a man dips into your saddlebag, it means he's not afraid of you, and if he's not afraid of you, he might kill you.

"I am Sandro of Chegem!" Uncle Sandro cried proudly, and his desire to blast the fellow's head off was so great that it was all he could do to restrain himself. He knew that if he shot one or two of the men the rest would flee, but they would come back later with a whole detachment and do their worst.

"We'll kill you and the owner both if you don't open up," the fellow said, continuing his search in the saddlebag.

"If you kill me, Shashiko will swear blood revenge!" Uncle Sandro called out proudly. When they heard this, the men standing in the shadow of the walnut tree talked briefly among themselves and called back the one who was over by the horse. Uncle Sandro surmised that word of the famous Shashiko had spread even to Endursk.

"What's he to you?" they asked.

"He's my cousin," Uncle Sandro replied, although Shashiko was only his neighbor. Shashiko was a well-known Abkhazian abrek, a rebel outlaw, and he was worth any hundred good Mensheviks, as Uncle Sandro explained to me.

"Have him open up—we won'tlook for his gold," one of them shouted.

The old tobacco grower started nervously. "I don't have any gold anyway," he said.

"What kind of rich tobacco grower are you if you don't have any gold?" Uncle Sandro asked in surprise.

"They already took it!" the old man shrilled, throwing down his flintlock and starting to beat his brow.

"You already took his gold!" Uncle Sandro shouted angrily.

All the Mensheviks started shouting at once, so that it was impossible to make out what they were saying.

"Just one of you do the talking," Uncle Sandro shouted. "We're not at a bazaar."

"It wasn't us, it was another detachment that took the gold," one of the Mensheviks shouted in an injured voice.

"Then what do you want?" Uncle Sandro asked in surprise.

"We'll take a few animals, that's all—since you're Shashiko's cousin," one of them answered.

"So shall I let them in?" Uncle Sandro asked, because he did not feel much like risking his life for the tobacco grower, especially since the door was about as bulletproof as a pumpkin.

"Let them in, let them rob me," the old tobacco grower said in despair. "I'm leaving this place anyway."

Uncle Sandro opened the door and walked out, holding his rifle at the ready. The Mensheviks also came out of the shadows and walked toward him, not taking their eyes off him. There were six of them, and along with them was the village clerk, who shrugged his shoulders faintly when Uncle Sandro glanced at him. His shrug intimated that they had forced him to get involved in this distasteful affair.

Looking around warily, the Mensheviks walked into the kitchen. From the way they stared at the table Uncle Sandro could tell that these ragtags did not have dinner every day, and his contempt for them increased, although he did not let on.

"Where does that door lead?" their senior man asked. He wore an officer's uniform, but without epaulettes.

"That's the storeroom," the owner said.

"There's someone in there," one of the Mensheviks said. He aimed his rifle at the door.

"That's my family," the old Armenian said. His mother-in-law set up a low wail to show that she was a woman.

"Have them come out," the officer said.

The owner stumbled to the storeroom and, in Armenian, began trying to persuade them to come out. But they balked and raised all sorts of objections. Uncle Sandro understood everything they said in Armenian, so he suggested a way for the owner to smoke them out.

"Tell them they have to fix the soldiers some grub. Then they won't be afraid," he prompted in Turkish.

The owner spoke to them about the grub, and they did in fact come out and stand by the door. One of the soldiers took a lamp and peered into the storeroom to discover whether there were any armed men in there. No armed men turned up, and the Mensheviks relaxed a little.

The Armenian's mother-in-law threw some fresh logs on the fire and began washing a kettle in which to boil the remains of the sheep. As soon as she started cooking she ceased to fear the soldiers and began reviling them, albeit in Armenian.

"Let's sit down at the table," Uncle Sandro said. "Pile the rifles in the corner."

The Mensheviks very much wanted to sit down at the table but did not want to let go of their rifles. Although they were not afraid of the owner, they realized that Uncle Sandro was not to be trifled with.

"You put yours down too," the officer said.

"You're guests, you have to go first," Uncle Sandro said, explaining basic etiquette to the soldiers' ignorant leader.

"But you're a guest too," he protested. However, it was pointless to argue with Uncle Sandro in such matters, even then.

"I arrived first, so I'm a guest in relation to the owner, and you arrived after me, so you're guests in relation to me," he said with finality, instructing this upstart how to behave before sitting down to a good table in a decent house. Vanquished, the officer understood once and for all that Uncle Sandro was no ordinary man, and he stood his rifle in the corner first. The others followed suit, except for the clerk, who had none. Uncle Sandro stood his rifle separately in another corner of the kitchen. The owner's flintlock lay by the window. No one paid any attention to it.

They all sat down facing Uncle Sandro across the table, each ready at any moment to dash for his rifle, realizing that the main thing was not to let the other get ahead of him. Actually, Uncle Sandro still had a pistol in his pocket, but he pretended that he was now unarmed.

"Usually," Uncle Sandro said to me at this point, interrupting his story, "before I went into a house where there might be danger, I hid a rifle or a spare pistol somewhere nearby. But I hadn't hidden anything here because this was a peaceable Armenian."

"Why would you hide a gun?" I asked, knowing that he was waiting for the question.

He smiled slyly. "If someone suddenly attacks you and disarms you," he said, "there's no better method. He goes off with your gun, he's exulting, he's lost control over himself, and now you catch up with him and take away your gun and everything he's got. Do you understand?"

"I do," I said. "But what if he's hidden a gun too, and now he catches up with you and takes away his gun, your gun, and everything you've got?"

"That couldn't happen," Uncle Sandro said confidently.

"Why not?" I asked.

"Because this was my secret." He smoothed his silver mustache haughtily. "I reveal it to you because you not only have no use for my secrets, you can't even use your own."

After this small lyric digression he went on with his story.

In brief, they sat at the table the rest of the night—drank wine and finished up the sheep. They raised toasts to the happy old age of their host, to the future of his children. They drank, with sidelong looks at the rifles, to the flowering of Abkhazia, Georgia, Armenia, and to a free Federation of Transcaucasian Republics, led, of course, by Noy Zhordania.

At dawn the officer thanked the owner for his hospitality and said they should get down to business, because it was time for them to go. With these words he took from his pocket a sheet of paper which told how many goats, sheep, and cattle the Armenian had. When the officer took out the paper, Uncle Sandro gave the clerk a look that made him cringe.

"I corroborated that Shashiko was your cousin," the clerk said in Abkhazian, under his breath.

"Shut up, scab," Uncle Sandro replied scornfully.

"You're not at home in Chegem," the clerk snarled, evidently made bold by drink.

"I don't have to go to Chegem to squash a toad," Uncle Sandro said, with a look that instantly made the clerk sober up and hold his tongue.

The leader of the detachment haggled with the owner a long time, and at last they reached an agreement that the old man would give him twenty rams and three oxen.

"No, I'm not staying here, I'm leaving for Batum," the old man lamented, crying out loud.

"It'll be the same in Batum," the one in the officer's uniform, but without epaulettes, promised honestly.

"The Turks slaughtered us for being Armenians, but what are you doing it for?" the old man asked.

"To us, all nations are equal," the officer replied importantly. "This isn't stealing, it's aid to the people."

Then they all got up from the table, took their guns, and went outdoors together. It was early morning, and the old man's household was still asleep.

"I'm leaving, I'm leaving, I'm leaving," he keened as they walked to the barnyard. Still cursing this "equality" as the work of the devil, he led the oxen out of the barn. They were strong, purebred oxen. Uncle Sandro felt bad that such fine oxen had to be given to these Endursky thugs. He noticed there was one more ox standing tethered in the barn. "You can't plow much with one ox," Uncle Sandro thought, pitying the owner. Then he remembered that he himself had recently lost an ox at dice, and his mood darkened. The debt still hung on his honor and kept him from having a good time.

The detachment leader agreed with the owner that they would not select the sheep but would simply count off the first twenty head that came out of the pen. Cracking a whip, the clerk climbed over into the pen and began driving out the sheep. After the sheep were driven into the barnyard it turned out that one of them was lame, barely dragging along.

"Defective," the officer said.

"Oh, Allah!" the tobacco grower implored. "We had an agreement, *I* didn't drive the sheep out."

"But will it be able to walk all the way?" the leader said pensively.

"What do I care!" the owner exclaimed. "Have one of your men carry it on his shoulders."

"To hell with that," the soldiers said. "It may be contagious, too."

"What do I care," the owner repeated, closing the pen to indicate that the haggling was over.

The clerk was unable to restrain himself. "If you don't need it, give it to me," he said to the leader.

"Take it, damn you!" the leader said. He was glad he would not have to force the soldiers, because he feared they would not obey him, and he would be ashamed before Uncle Sandro.

With greedy joy the clerk caught the sick sheep, hoisted it to his shoulders, and started for the road. Like a dog with its bone, Uncle Sandro thought, looking at him.

"One scab loves another," he said as the clerk went by.

The clerk made no reply but purposely, in order to enrage Uncle Sandro, squished loudly through the mud, cautiously exulting under the weight of his booty. As soon as he had walked a little way off, the sick sheep craned its neck to look back at the pen and bleated so pitifully that Uncle Sandro felt quite uncomfortable. When the soldiers followed the clerk with the rest of the sheep, the sick one calmed down. Yet Uncle Sandro knew that when the clerk turned off toward his own house and the soldiers kept on going, it would begin crying again, and he felt sorry for the hapless sheep, the old tobacco grower, and himself.

When the Mensheviks disappeared from view, Uncle Sandro said, without looking at the owner, "Even at that, they're not going to leave you in peace; give me that ox . . ."

The owner looked at Uncle Sandro and silently began beating his brow. Uncle Sandro felt mean talking to him about the ox, but the damned clerk with his sick sheep had completely undone him.

"Take it, take everything, I'm not staying here another day!" the owner shouted finally, still beating his brow as if carrying out the gloomy mourning ritual of *shakhsey-vakhsey*.

"No," Uncle Sandro said, restraining his own sobs, "I'll just take the ox, I owe it to a man."

With these words he went into the barn and began to untie the ox.

"Take everything," the old tobacco grower shouted after him, "just leave me the rope!"

"What do you need the rope for?" Uncle Sandro asked in surprise.

"To hang myself!" the old tobacco grower shrilled gleefully.

Uncle Sandro did not like his glee, and he began to shame the old tobacco grower for his faintheartedness, reminding him that he had a family and children.

"Batum, I'm leaving for Batum," the old tobacco grower muttered, no longer listening to him.

"Listen here," Uncle Sandro said impressively, "if you go alone, you'll be robbed ten times on the way. I give you the word of Sandro of Chegem that I will accompany you right to the boat, just let me know when you're leaving."

With these words he gave the ox a slap to make it walk ahead down the road while he himself returned to the front yard and went over to his horse. He quickly tightened the saddle girths and was about to mount when he remembered that the soldier had rummaged in his saddlebag. "Maybe he planted a bomb," he thought, and he thrust his hand in the bag and quickly felt around the inside. It was empty. Uncle Sandro jumped on his horse and rode out of the yard. The ox was walking slowly ahead of him along the edge of the old tobacco grower's land. When he caught up with the ox, Uncle Sandro could not refrain from looking back at the owner. The old tobacco grower, bent over the wattle fence around the pen, was carefully straightening some stray twigs, as if it was through this hole that all his wealth had escaped.

Uncle Sandro kept his promise. Inside of two months the old tobacco grower sold everything he could sell, hired a carter, and set out for the city. Uncle Sandro accompanied him on horseback right to the dock. To look at the emigrant's beggarly goods and chattels, no one would have believed that this had been a rich Armenian, purveyor of high-grade tobaccos to the merchants of Trebizond and Batum.

"If the door had been made of chestnut, you could have held out," Uncle Sandro recalled as he said good-bye.

"I don't even want to hear about it," the old tobacco grower said in despair. Thus they parted forever, and Uncle Sandro never encountered him in our part of the world again.

"Because of the Mensheviks, our country's best people were forced to abandon her," Uncle Sandro said at the end of his story. He opened his eyes wide and nodded significantly, as if hinting that the consequences of this waste of personnel were still being felt and would long continue to be felt, both in an administrative and in a purely economic sense.

UNCLE SANDRO AT HOME

ONCE WHEN I was getting ready to leave the mountain village of Chegem, where I had been visiting relatives at my grandfather's house, they told me there was a man wanting to see me.

I came out of the house and saw an old man beating off the dogs with a stick as he entered the yard. In one hand he held a rather weighty jug. I called off the dogs and went over to him.

Looking at the old man I thought I had seen him somewhere, but couldn't remember where. More accurately, it was not the old man himself but the zestful spite with which the dogs attacked him, and the unabating fury with which he beat them off, that reminded me of a familiar scene, but I simply could not recall when and where it had been.

Only later, on the bus going back, did I remember that it had been right there, by my grandfather's house. Evidently I had to leave the place in order to recall the half-forgotten scene.

I remembered that when I lived with my grandfather as a child, during the war, this man used to pass our house occasionally; the dogs always attacked him with that same zestful spite, and he always beat them off with that same unabating fury, neither quickening nor slowing his step.

Back then we used to chuckle and say that he'd have to walk all the way to the city, because buses were infrequent during the war and it was none too easy to get on them.

It was odd, or rather something of a marvel, that he should be the only one the dogs went after that way, because he came by here fairly often. They could have gotten used to him, as they got used to everyone else, but for some reason they had no desire to. So, without going outdoors, we could tell by the way the dogs barked that it was he going by on the road.

Usually, of course, someone came out to quiet the dogs, but this didn't always happen, and besides he did not seem in the least afraid of them. He walked on by, with a sack or without one, at his stubborn gait. If he was returning from the city he even managed to shout the war news through the dogs' barking, and went on without stopping. But as I say, I remembered all this on the way back, when I was already on the bus.

. . . I exchanged greetings with the old man. He lifted the jug and asked me—keeping a furiously scornful eye on the dogs all the while—to take this small present to his brother Sandro in the city.

I shot a glance at the jug. The proposition was not appealing, to lug that thing ten kilometers to the bus and then go looking for some Sandro in the city. But I was also embarrassed to refuse outright, and the old man took advantage of my hesitation. He had caught my sidelong glance at the jug, and he forestalled my refusal by saying that he would see me to the bus.

"All right," I agreed, "but where does he live?"

"My granddaughter wrote a paper," he answered. Thrusting his staff into the ground—with another sidelong look at the dogs, as if to let them know that he could still grab it if need be—he put a stiff old hand in his pocket to get a sheet of notebook paper. On it was an address written in large, childish letters. Again I regretted having agreed to this, but it was too late. His brother lived in a suburb. Granted, there were regular buses out that way, but all the same, who wanted to chase after this Sandro? Laziness is resourceful, and it occurred to me that he might work somewhere in town, in which case it would be more convenient to take the jug to him at work. I asked the old man.

"Sandro isn't an ordinary man, he's a watcher-over," the old man said, with what struck me as covert mockery of my ignorance. In Abkhazian the word "watcher-over" also means "leader."

I tried to ascertain what he watched over. The old man again looked me in the face with covert mockery, and I now realized that his meaning was that I could not help knowing the watchers-over; there weren't all that many of them, and if I didn't move among them it still did not mean that they didn't exist or that I hadn't heard of them.

"He goes to gatherings where worthwhile people gather," he explained patiently, but in a manner which made it clear that I would not manage to outwit him.

Half an hour later I said good-bye to my relatives and set off. Incidentally, they had reminded me that this was the Sandro who before the war had lived not far from Grandfather's house. Later on, after our first meetings in the city, I remembered—as one often does—much connected with his life in the village, but what my relatives told me meant almost nothing to me at the time.

The old man proved to be a very obliging and uncommonly taciturn traveling companion. Along the way he made several attempts to take my pack, and when the path went through wild hazelnut bushes he held up the overhanging branches and let me go first.

When we had descended to the river and were standing on the bank waiting for the ferry, he stuck the jug in the water for some reason and kept it there until the ferry approached. Why he had to cool the honey was a mystery to me. He must have known that honey does not spoil, and such a brief period of cooling would not have done any good anyway. The sun was scorching hot, and I finally decided that he had plunged the jug into the cold mountain river simply to make things nice for the honey, or even for the jug itself.

"Don't lose the jug, I need it for something," the old man said when I got on the bus.

"I won't," I answered, knowing full well what he meant by this ostensibly abstract interest in the jug. He stood beside the bus, patiently waiting for it to leave. I told him he should go home, but he stayed and waited, wearing an enigmatic smile, as if I were again trying to outwit him in something. He seemed to want to make sure that the jug of honey started off in the right direction, at least.

"Tell Sandro I'll bring nuts and corn as soon as I can manage it!" he shouted after the bus started. He was nodding his head, as if to reveal his deeper meaning: yes, indeed, and I'll check up on how you fared with my commission.

The next day, with some difficulty, I found the plot of land allotted to Uncle Sandro, as I later called him. But that was what practically the whole town called him.

Planted in fruit trees and mandarin oranges, the allotment was situated on a steep slope. As I climbed the narrow path to the door, it occurred to me that here, near the city, my host had chosen himself a spot that replicated in miniature the terrain of the mountains. The warm autumn day was nearing sunset. The smell of overripe figs and the subtle aroma of citrus hung in the air. I came up to the house.

A trim, sweet-faced old woman was standing on the steps, calling the chickens in a caressing voice and scattering handfuls of corn evenly, as if sowing seeds. When she saw me she gathered the last handful of kernels from her hem and scattered them, and as she shook out her apron she gave me a cordial smile.

"Is the master in?" I asked.

"For you," she said, turning toward the veranda.

Hearing her voice, I suddenly remembered her name—Aunt Katya!

"Who?" asked a controlled but powerful male voice. The veranda was open, and I was surprised that I could not see who was speaking. I decided the master was lying on a couch.

"I haven't met him," the old woman said, flashing me a smile, as if in apology for having to explain herself in front of me.

"Have him come up," the voice said from somewhere down low.

I mounted to the veranda and caught sight of Uncle Sandro. He was sitting on a little low bench, washing his feet in a basin.

"Welcome," he said, and got partway to his feet, indicating that the basin prevented him from making a more expansive gesture of hospitality, while at the same time seeming to suggest that I could be sure of his potential expansiveness. After that he settled down more comfortably on his seat, rubbing one foot against the other, and eyed me with polite curiosity, making it appear that his curiosity was wholly absorbed in my spiritual essence and in no way extended to the jug.

"I see by your appearance that you're from the city," he said, cracking his strong, flexible feet as he rubbed them.

I gave my name, explained to him the purpose of my visit, and sat down. The old woman had set a chair for me, flicking an invisible speck from it with her apron. Uncle Sandro cocked an eyebrow at the jug and said to his wife in an undertone, "Take it away."

Giving me a smile that meant a man of my caliber shouldn't be bothered over a little thing like honey, the old woman took the jug and carried it out to the kitchen.

Astonished that I had grown so much since those prewar days—although it would have been more astonishing had I stayed the same—Uncle Sandro lamented how swiftly life flowed. Then he regained his calm and began questioning me about my relatives and the prospects for the harvest this year. As I answered, I looked him over.

He was an uncommonly fine-looking old man with a head of short silvery hair, a white mustache, and a small white beard. His pink, pellucid face shone with health, almost indecently youthful for his age. Every time he raised his head, a fatty fold showed on his thoroughbred neck. But it was not the heavy, hardened fold one sees on aged gluttons. No, this was a light, almost transparent fold; high-calorie fat, I would say, the sort probably stored up by a very healthy body which manages its usual functions without special effort, and in the time remaining amuses itself, this invulnerable body, by making this fat, as, let us say, women who are not too busy amuse themselves by knitting.

In short, he was a handsome old man with a noble, almost coinlike profile—if, of course, a coin profile can be noble—with rather cold, slightly prominent blue eyes. In his face the beneficent spirit of Byzantine perversion coexisted with the rhetorically ferocious expression of an aged lion.

While we made small talk he went on washing his feet, from time to time pouring warm water over them from a pitcher as if adding fragrant oils to the basin.

When he finished washing his feet, he placed them wide apart on the rim of the basin, with careful symmetry. Without breaking the flow of our conversation, he said to his wife, "Bring it."

The old woman went to the kitchen and brought out an old but clean towel.

He took the towel from her hands and lightly lifted both feet, indicating that she could remove the basin, which the sweet-faced old woman did. She picked up the basin and splashed the water over the railing.

Uncle Sandro rested the heel of one foot on the floor and, holding the other in midair, began carefully wiping it with the towel. He dried one foot with one end of the towel, then the other foot with the other end, as if to give each foot, as well as anyone standing around, a lesson on fairness and impartiality in the use of the good things of life.

All the while he kept up a conversation with me, sometimes glancing at the doorway as if expecting someone, sometimes giving his wife a trifling domestic order. When he did, he would lower his voice, and the order sounded like an aside in the theater, which the spectator supposedly does not hear.

"The stretch socks," he said suddenly, and the old woman brought his socks. He put them on with satisfaction, thoroughly smoothing out all the wrinkles. The old lady set some galoshes beside him on her own initiative, but the venture was unsuccessful, because Uncle Sandro immediately corrected her.

"The new ones," he said, on account of my coming, I imagined. The old woman carried out the old galoshes and carried in new ones with a shiny black finish and turned-up toes.

Uncle Sandro put on the galoshes and lightly stood up. On top of all his other virtues, he also proved to be a tall, well-built old man, broad-chested and narrow-hipped, a fact that somewhat diminished the iconlike serenity of his face and simultaneously strengthened the spirit of Byzantine perversion, possibly in part because of the galoshes with turned-up toes.

"Set this one," he said to his wife, going over to the table that stood at the end of the veranda. I tried to refuse, but Uncle Sandro would not let me. The old woman put a clean cloth on the table, then brought cheese, *lobio*, greens, bread, yogurt in frosty jars, and saucers filled with fragrant honey.

Over supper, Uncle Sandro asked me where I worked. I said I worked at the newspaper.

"A writer?" he asked, pricking up his ears.

I told him that I sometimes did my own writing, but more often put in order what others wrote.

"Then you watch over the ones who write," he surmised, and subsided.

Uncle Sandro was thoughtful for a while, and then, looking me in the eyes, asked how much it cost nowadays to hire a newspaperman to write a satirical article. I told him one didn't have to pay anything for this.

"Then why do they take money to announce a relative's death?" he asked.

I explained the difference to him by saying that satirical articles were written about swindlers, parasites, and bureaucrats.

"Then do you have to hire a lawyer first to prove that the man is a swindler or a bureaucrat?" he asked.

"What are you getting at?" I said.

"I have an enemy in the city soviet," Uncle Sandro explained, "a small-time engineer from Endursk, though he hides his origins. I'm supposed to get money for the landslide and he won't give it to me."

"What landslide?" I asked.

"I had a landslide here on my allotment, and the house is insured. The bastard doesn't want to sign the form. I'd love to intimidate him with a satirical article," Uncle Sandro said. He shook a clenched fist at the engineer from the city soviet.

Just then a woman came up on the veranda. When she saw us at the table she stopped in confusion.

"My dear Uncle Sandro," she said, blushing and stammering, "forgive me for reminding you, but you haven't forgotten . . . ?"

"How could I!" Uncle Sandro exclaimed. Half rising, he gestured her to join us at the table.

"Oh, please don't get up," she said, clasping her hands. "I can only stay a minute."

"He doesn't forget things like that," Aunt Katya put in, half in sorrow, half in scorn.

"Quiet," Uncle Sandro said pacifically. He added in a businesslike way, "Where is the wine from?"

"It's a Lykhny wine, goes down like lemon fizz," the woman said. She added, "They say they're bringing a man that's a real prodigy, they say . . . He's planning to make all our folks get drunk—"

"Who's that?" Uncle Sandro asked, aroused.

"A relative from the Shlarba clan," the woman explained, "a real prodigy, they say. What if he puts us to shame, Uncle Sandro? Please try to—"

"Oh, I know him, I've sat with him," Uncle Sandro remembered. He thrust out his lower lip in scorn. It was as if he had riffled through a mental file of places he'd occupied at festive tables, pulled out the right card, and assured himself that his rival offered no danger. "You tell your folks: whatever he drinks I can pour in my ear," Uncle Sandro added. He slapped his ear for emphasis.

"You're our great fortress, Uncle Sandro," the woman said. She backed to the doorway and made to hurry away. "Then I'll go along, Uncle Sandro, there's still so much to do."

"I'll be over in an hour," he said. He set to work on the yogurt.

"You're our great wall!" The woman's voice floated up from the path.

"The meat—don't overcook the meat!" Uncle Sandro roared, suddenly remembering. She had already disappeared in a thicket of mandarin oranges.

"Don't worry, Uncle Sandro, we'll try!" she answered from somewhere down below.

"Don't forget, you're an old man," Aunt Katya said with futile sorrow.

"How could I forget, with you around," Uncle Sandro said. He turned his attention to supper, dipping his spoon first in the honey, then in the yogurt.

"They're letting a son-in-law into the family," he explained. Easily, I should say elegantly, he was dispatching the spoon to his mouth. "They want me to be the tamada. I couldn't refuse—they're neighbors."

"Everyone in the city is a neighbor to you," his wife said with the same futile sorrow, peering at the road that passed below their allotment.

"And you can be proud of it," Uncle Sandro remarked, with a look at me.

"You're quite something," I said.

After supper we washed our hands, and Uncle Sandro spent a long time carefully rinsing his big yellowish teeth. Then he pulled on some light Asiatic boots and donned a cherkeska, mildly reproving his wife because the rows of cartridges sewn across the chest were badly polished. He polished them with a clean handkerchief and cinched in his wasplike waist with a Caucasian belt.

"Come and I'll show you what the landslide did," Uncle Sandro said, and we started down. Uncle Sandro walked with an easy, light-footed gait, and again I could not help admiring this silver-haired, incredibly well-preserved old man.

He pointed to the cement piles supporting the house. On two piles there were indeed some cracks, not too catastrophic to my eye. Getting ahead of my story, I can tell you that his house still stands, although several years have elapsed since then.

"All the same, we could put a scare into him with a satirical article," Uncle Sandro said, noticing that I was not greatly impressed with the cracks on the piles.

"We'd have to get some advice," I said vaguely.

I said good-bye to the old woman, and Uncle Sandro and I went down the path to the gate.

"Don't drink too much, don't forget you're an old man," the old woman called after him, stubborn in futility. It was as if she had been trying for decades to inculcate this thought in him.

"That woman," Uncle Sandro muttered. Without looking back, he jerked his head in his wife's direction, implying that she deliberately simplified the complex circle of his social obligations.

As we climbed down the path Uncle Sandro asked me whether I happened to know a reliable runner who could be trusted to deliver fruit to Moscow. I said I did know some runners, but they were most likely swindlers.

"Those I don't need," Uncle Sandro said. He thrust his hand between the fence boards and closed the latch on the inside of the gate. We went out to the road.

We were to go in different directions, but Uncle Sandro lingered as if he wanted to ask about something important and couldn't bring himself to do it. He did ask me whether I happened to know anyone who would like to buy fresh fruit straight from the tree. I could tell by his tone that this was not the question he wanted to ask; rather, it was an approach to the other one, which he had decided to postpone. I told him I did know people who would like fruit.

"Then bring them over," he said, "or take some yourself."

"All right," I said.

"Think about that engineer," he reminded me cautiously.

"All right," I said briskly, which obviously pleased him. His eyes lighted up.

"It might even be better not to print it," he added, "just show him and give him a scare . . ."

"I'll think about it," I said earnestly.

"We're from the same hometown, we have to help one another," Uncle Sandro observed as we parted. "Drop by again."

It was obvious that he was satisfied and had decided that that was enough from me for this time. He set off, and I stood there admiring his majestic and somewhat operatic figure. By his ironic air he seemed to acknowledge this operatic quality and at the same time, with a vindicating smile, lay the blame on the secret buffoonery of life itself.

That was how I began frequenting Uncle Sandro's. Had it not been for his tales of the adventures he had survived, which I listened to with pleasure, we would have met much more seldom. I am a good listener, because I know how to turn off when a story enters a tedious phase. When I do that, I ask a specific question from time to time, seizing on the tail of the last sentence, a device that so far has helped me maintain my reputation.

Only once in my life have I been caught. In my student days I used to go to a literary house where they held poetry and short-story readings. There were usually pretty good refreshments afterwards, especially if the host was reading.

He was the one who read that day. After prefacing his reading with the melancholy observation that we would never see this story in print, although we had never seen his other stories in print either, he began reading an unbearably boring story about an official from the fish inspectorate who was doomed to turn out to be a well-concealed poacher in the end. He was so painstakingly disguised that this was clear from the very beginning.

To put it briefly, I fell asleep, in the grossest sense of the word. Goodness knows, it doesn't matter any more; I resisted with all my might and at last, as happens at meetings if you sit anywhere in the back rows, I decided to lean back a moment in order to awake with my mind refreshed.

Nothing like this has ever happened to me either before or since. When I woke up, there was no one in the room. At first I couldn't understand. Then, hearing from the other room the clatter of dishes and the bright voices of my comrades, I understood all and was horrified. While I slept, they had had time to hear the story, had maybe even discussed it, and had then gone to the other room, leaving me to sleep. Of course I could have plucked up my nerve and said, "Great trick I played on you," and sat down at the table. But that was risky because they might ask who had said what during the discussion. Humiliated and insulted, I went quietly to the foyer, grabbed my raincoat, and hurriedly left the house.

At any rate, I always listened to Uncle Sandro with unflagging attention. I do not remember ever being distracted, even for a minute.

Gradually, through these stories, I began to discern the outline of the quasi-fantastical life he had led in his youth, and his rather strange, or at any rate unusual, old age.

Uncle Sandro first moved to the city at the invitation of Nestor Apollonovich Lakoba himself, back in the early thirties. In those days he was famous for being one of the best dancers in the renowned Abkhaz Song and Dance Ensemble, directed by Platon Pantsulaya. At the same time that he danced in the ensemble he had a job as superintendent at the Abkhazian Central Executive Committee, where Nestor Apollonovich had taken him on. He already danced almost as well as the star of the ensemble, Pata Pataraya, or at least he was breathing hotly down Pata's neck, and who knows, Uncle Sandro might have kept on dancing long enough to feel the first soloist's jealous breath on the back of his own neck, had it not been for the insane events of that insane year.

After Lakoba's death, when the mass arrests began and the director of the ensemble, Platon Pantsulaya, was seized, Uncle Sandro had the perspicacity to realize that they were hauling in all the best people. First he developed a limp, and then, retiring from the ensemble, he returned to the village for good.

Poor Pata, spoiled by fame, could not do that and paid dearly. They seized him, charging that during a sword dance at one of the concerts he had cast an evil look toward the government box, involuntarily betraying a secret plot. Of course he confessed all and got ten years. Telling about it, Uncle Sandro declared ruefully that those swords couldn't cut a cabbage, let alone anything else.

The second time Uncle Sandro left the village was after the war. This time, most likely out of caution, his halfhearted flight ended in the suburbs. He stopped at the spot where the collective farms ended and the city had not begun.

Over this time he continued to gain in fame as one of the finest adornments of the table, a wise and merry tamada. By the time I met him, his reputation had achieved impressive dimensions, although I knew nothing about it then. I had lived in a different sphere, and once I emerged from it, I began to encounter Uncle Sandro or hear his name quite often.

In the years of the liberalization he began calling on officials, sometimes on the strength of his having met them repeatedly at the table, sometimes simply walking in with administrative suggestions. I know for certain that he went to one high official with the suggestion that he restore to the local rivers, mountains, and valleys their ancient Abkhazian names, mistakenly changed during a time which in its turn was also mistakenly named, the erstwhile "time of the cult." The cult, without question, existed. No one denies it. But it existed outside of time, and so cannot be called the "time of the cult," although it existed in space, and a large space at that.

But let us return to Uncle Sandro. Unfortunately, they did not act on his suggestion of restoring to local rivers, mountains, and valleys their ancient

Abkhazian names. They might as well have, because after certain events in Abkhazia the renaming had to be accomplished posthaste, which led to some confusion and disorder.

Incidentally, according to Uncle Sandro, the official to whom he took this suggestion did not stand up when he came into the office and did not stand up when he left, either. Possibly, Uncle Sandro said, he meant to imply that he sat as solidly in his job as in his chair.

Nevertheless, after a while this same official was forced to leave his job, supposedly in connection with a transfer to another one, as our newspaper reported. At the time this report came out, he himself was yelling bloody murder, telling the whole town he did not want to leave his job. Later he even burst out sobbing in the office of the regional committee, an act that unquestionably proved his true affection for the job he was leaving.

After all that, Uncle Sandro said the reason they fired the man was that in his time he had received him, Uncle Sandro, with a degree of rudeness impermissible by Abkhazian custom. I started to snicker at this hypothesis, but then I decided the remark did contain a kernel of truth. After all, private rudeness to Uncle Sandro may have been a sign of the official's degeneration into universal rudeness, of a degree impermissible not only by Abkhazian custom but even by the generally accepted All-Union norm.

When the fad of defending doctoral dissertations set in, many young scholars came to Uncle Sandro with the request that he explain the outward causes of the prerevolutionary, and sometimes postrevolutionary, civil strife among the princes. Uncle Sandro willingly explained the outward causes to them, whereupon they in their dissertations revealed the inner causes and analyzed the disintegration of the Abkhazian nobility. In the bibliography Uncle Sandro would be cited as an aged eyewitness to this disintegration.

When I first began visiting him, I usually found him in a public orchard, which he was guarding. The orchard was located near his house and belonged to a tobacco factory. In it grew apples, pears, plums, and persimmons. The first time I went, the orchard was already mostly harvested, although the persimmon trees glowed with their lanternlike fruit and a few late trees were still hung with Abkhazian winter apples, if such a term can be applied to a local variety.

In this orchard Uncle Sandro grazed his quasi-legal cow, holding her on a long rope. Usually he sat on an old saddle blanket, neatly dressed, with a proud expression, as if what he had on the tether was not an ordinary cow but a smallish wild aurochs, tamed by him personally. Sometimes he carried around his neck a pair of fine Zeiss binoculars—a personal gift from Prince Oldenburgsky, as I later learned.

I noticed that from where he sat he had a good view of the road, and if anyone appeared who looked suspicious to him he drove the cow behind a big spreading blackberry patch, which had seemingly been grown in the orchard expressly for this purpose.

The cow was evidently so accustomed to this that as soon as Uncle Sandro stood up, or even if he did not stand, just gave the rope a twitch, she ambled behind the blackberry patch of her own accord and peered out, waiting for the suspicious person to pass. Incidentally, I never once heard this cow moo.

I don't mean to say that Uncle Sandro trained her to silence, or that she herself understood the illegality of her being in the suburbs. Still, it was rather strange to see an animal so inarticulate.

The first time I visited him at the orchard an amusing thing happened. A policeman appeared on the road below, a local man, to judge by the loaf of bread he carried under his arm. Uncle Sandro stayed put on his saddle blanket, assuming a dignified air.

When he drew even with us the policeman stopped by the fence, cast a melancholy glance at one of the apple trees, then said to Uncle Sandro, "Grazing your cow?"

"I am," Uncle Sandro said firmly.

"Fine tree you assigned me," the policeman sighed. He again examined the apple tree, on which, as I now noticed, there was indeed practically no fruit. It was a tree of the local variety.

"You chose it yourself," Uncle Sandro replied enigmatically.

"Fine favor you did me, real neighborly," the policeman said. He settled the loaf of bread more firmly under his arm and went his way, continuing to grumble.

"What was that about?" I asked.

"Because of the cow, I allotted him an apple tree," Uncle Sandro said. "As you see, it didn't produce a crop this year. He's angry."

"Have you been doing this long?" I asked.

"This is the sixth year," Uncle Sandro said. "I used to keep a goat. Every spring I let him choose a tree. This year he was unlucky. I gave him an early plum to make up for it but he's still not satisfied."

I asked him why he kept an eye on the road if he had worked out a business relationship with the policeman.

"And the district soviet?" Uncle Sandro said.

"Allot them a tree too," I suggested.

"You can't take care of everyone," he answered, somewhat irritated, I thought, by the uncalled-for levity of my tone.

When I came here, I usually sat down beside him and we chatted, although Uncle Sandro warned me not to sit on the bare ground, for that was what caused the majority of illnesses, in his opinion. You should sit on a stone, he maintained, on a log, on an animal skin, or in an extremity, if you had nothing else, on your hat. According to him, in his whole long life he had never once sat on the ground.

"And as you see, I'm pretty well preserved," he would say, stroking his face with his palm. There was no denying that.

Apropos of almost anything, he would remember incidents from his stormy life; or he would ask me to tell him what was going on in the world. He would listen attentively, but would not be too surprised, as if everything that happened now was a variation on what he had long known or had lived through himself.

When I told him about the murder of President Kennedy and how they had found the murderer, he heard me out calmly and then turned to me as if giving me a piece of friendly advice. "If you're planning to murder a man, you ought to do it in such a way that they don't find you. Any fool can murder the way he did."

Achievements in space seemed to leave him cold. He irritated me somewhat, the way he would first question me about everything in great detail and then, after hearing me out, wave his hand as if to say, That's all lies.

"A man from our village," he said after one of my periodic space stories, "drove a stake in his vegetable garden and then told everyone it was the middle of the earth. Try and prove it!"

I was stung, and I got rather worked up trying to show that this could not be any kind of fraud.

"Listen here," he said, and stroked his silver mustache with dignity. "A shepherd, when March was over—that's the rainiest month, the most disagreeable one for shepherds—the shepherd said, 'Thank goodness this stinking March is over, now I can get some rest.'

"March heard him and took offense. Well, says March, I'll show *him*. March asked April, 'Lend me a couple of days, I'll take revenge on this beggar for the insult.' 'All right,' says April, 'I'll give you a couple of days, as a neighbor, but don't ask for any more, because I'm short of time myself.'

"March took two days from April and brewed up some weather that was so bad you wouldn't set foot out of doors for a call of nature, much less lead the flock out. What to do? The hungry goats were crying, the kids were upset, they'd all die soon without milk. Anyhow, the shepherd found a way out. He put a cat in a goatskin bag and hung it from the beam in the barn where he kept the goats. The cat cried inside the bag and rocked it back and forth over the heads of the goats. Goats, as you know, are curious, like women. The whole two days they clopped around under the bag, trying to guess why it was rocking and crying in a cat voice, and they forgot their hunger. That's how our shepherd outwitted March."

"Now, that's going too far, Uncle Sandro," I laughed.

He was pleased. "You can't fool me," he smiled. "Sandro of Chegem has seen something of the world. I met Prince Oldenburgsky, I was like a close relative to Lakoba, twice I sat with Stalin the way you and I are sitting now. How could I be surprised at anything you might say?"

"Tell me about it," I begged.

"At the right time, in the right place," he answered, pensively staring into the distance.

Below us lay a picturesque slope with houses showing through the verdure of orchards and vineyards. The houses were very diverse: ordinary village houses on high pilings; nearby, hovels hastily knocked together by homeowners just getting started; and beyond, the big, tasteless, two-story houses of flourishing suburbanites.

Glancing out over the settlement, Uncle Sandro remarked on the rise or fall of individual owners. That was when I first heard about Tengiz, whom he usually referred to affectionately as "my Tengo."

"That boy will go far," he said, pointing out his house. On the veranda side it was cozily planted with a wall of grapevines, while the other side was still in construction scaffolding.

"What does he do?" I asked.

"He watches over all the vehicles traveling the Enduria road," Uncle Sandro said.

"A car inspector, is he?" I asked. Perhaps he sensed in my question a lack of respect for his pet, because his eyes suddenly blazed, and the ferocious expression of an aged lion now struck me as more than rhetorical.

"You can call him a garbage man, but he watches over the moving vehicles and has a government pistol—"

"I'm not arguing," I put in.

"How could there be any argument?" he remarked, subsiding. "If they've trusted him with a pistol it means they trust him to shoot when necessary. They've trusted you"—he suddenly poked a finger at the cap of the fountain pen sticking out of my coat pocket—"with a toy gun that shoots ink, and you're afraid even to put a scare into an engineer from the city soviet."

From then on I was more circumspect when the conversation got around to Tengiz, and tried as best I could to make my face express admiration for his pet.

Sometimes I encountered Uncle Sandro on the seashore, where he would sit on a bench telling his beads and admiring the endlessly wheeling seagulls. Other times he strolled importantly along the shore, occasionally shading his eyes to peer at the horizon like a disguised admiral waiting for a secret transport. Or I would find him sitting by the shore with a newspaper in his hands, and at these times he looked startlingly like a prerevolutionary professor who had successfully grown into socialism and was therefore well preserved—if, of course, one disregarded his exotic attire or the fact that, unlike a professor, he still spelled out the words.

He would sit in the coffeehouses surrounded by a noisy group—often composed of young people, by the way. Evidently he told them funny stories, because bursts of laughter would go up from time to time. Occasionally I caught him just as he was coming in, and sat down with him at a separate table.

"I met the Lamba brothers at the bazaar," he began once at the coffeehouse, without any preliminary. "I've been wanting to have a talk with them for a long time but never had an opportunity.

" 'Let's go to the coffeehouse,' I say. 'There's something I want to talk to you about.'

" 'Let's go, Uncle Sandro,' they say.

"We go in and sit down. I order coffee at my own expense, cognac, Borzhom water. The waitress serves us. I say nothing. I think, Let her go away. She goes away. I look at them, these two lunks sit across and look at me.

" 'Can you guess,' I say, 'why I invited you?'

" 'No,' say the lunks, exchanging glances.

" 'How come you're so slow?'

" 'We don't know,' say the lunks, and they exchange glances again.

" 'Maybe,' I say, 'it's your parents' fault?'

" 'No,' they say, 'we're just that way.'

" 'Then your parents aren't to blame?'

" 'No,' they say.

" 'Including your father?'

" 'Including our father.'

" 'Then pay attention to me,' I say. 'I knew your father well. He was killed forty years ago by Prince Chachba's lackey. The Soviet authorities dealt with the prince somehow but to this day the lackey walks our earth and laughs at you to himself, and sometimes openly. Over these forty years of the Soviet regime,' I say, 'the most primitive shepherds, from the most primitive, isolated mountaintops, have seen the world; and some have even become deputies. Can you really still be so benighted that you don't know—sons must avenge their father?'

"And how do you think they answered my pure, fine words?" Uncle Sandro asked me.

"I don't know," I said.

"Then listen, if you don't know," Uncle Sandro observed. "Well then . . .

" 'But Uncle Sandro,' says the lunk that's older, 'they'd arrest us for that.'

" 'Goathead,' I answer him. 'Of course they'll arrest you if they catch you. But think: as the Twentieth Congress disclosed, even good Party men have done ten years, fifteen years, for nothing—and you're refusing to do time for your own father? Do you renounce him?'

" 'We don't renounce him,' answers the lunk that's younger, 'but maybe our father was to blame in this affair?'

" 'What are you,' I say, 'a judge?'

" 'No,' he says, 'I'm a store manager.'

" 'Then you do your job,' I say, 'and the judge will do his. He'll decide who was to blame.'

" 'No,' he says, 'don't drag us into a thing like that, Uncle Sandro—'

"I couldn't take that. I'm reminding him of his honor, I'm treating him to cognac at my expense to awaken courage in him—and I'm to blame!

" 'May I buy you a coffin,' I say, 'in your own store! Get out of here, and don't set foot in the bazaar or any other public place as long as I live!'

"They didn't say a word—got up, went out. What's the use—men have forgotten conscience, turned into swine . . . True, I made a mistake, I should have talked to them separately, but I was relying on their conscience . . . Their father was an eagle," Uncle Sandro added after a silence, as if he had been mentally reviewing all possible causes for the fall of the Lamba brothers, "but on the mother's side I think their blood was tainted by an Endursky admixture."

He finished his now-cold coffee in several big gulps and regained his composure.

"By the way, my Tengo helped me with the landslide," he said. Perhaps this recollection of his thoroughbred racehorse had been prompted by the slightly tainted store manager.

"They paid you, then?"

"No, they ran a concrete conduit at the city soviet's expense—I'll settle for that."

After this encounter I didn't see him for about a month, and I learned indirectly that Uncle Sandro had been in an accident. He was riding in a truck with friends from home, on the way to a big funeral in the village of Atary. A truck bringing people back from the same funeral came hurtling toward them. The driver of the oncoming truck, out of inexperience, had drunk too much at the funeral banquet. In short, the trucks collided. Luckily no one was killed, but many people were hurt. Uncle Sandro got off comparatively lightly: he dislocated his foot and lost one tooth.

"We almost arrived at the funeral with our own dead," he told me the next time we met. He pulled back his lip with his finger to display a single gap, obviously forcible, in a mouth that even without the missing tooth was overfilled with strong, yellowish teeth.

He was sitting in the orchard on the same saddle blanket, only now he had a staff, thrust upright in the ground beside him. He had taken a liking to it after the accident. The cow grazed on a long tether, from time to time tearing herself away from her juicy pastime to raise her head and glance at the road.

At that time it so happened that the pension program was undergoing review. Either Uncle Sandro found out about this, or he decided that a truck accident was none other than an industrial trauma, but anyway he began asking for help in wangling a pension. In some abstract sense he had indeed suffered a job-related trauma, but the social security office would hardly want to understand that.

He showed me two long forms listing his modest services in the economic and cultural development of Abkhazia (the years spent in the song-and-dance ensemble). The forms were addressed to Khrushchev and Voroshilov.

"What do you think, will Khrushchit help?" he asked, pronouncing the name in the Abkhazian manner.

"I don't know," I said, returning the typed copies to him. Evidently the originals had already been sent to the government.

"Well, do what you can, apply some pressure," he requested, secreting the papers in his pocket.

"Uncle Sandro," I said, "you don't have any work record."

"I've spent six years watching over this orchard—may it burn," he said, without special enthusiasm. Evidently the question had already come up.

"Not enough," I said.

"Some people fabricate records," he grumbled. "You'd think they'd been feeding me all these years. If a man hasn't robbed or killed, then he's lived by his labor. But what if you ask around on behalf of an aged kolkhoz worker?"

I started to laugh.

"But my brothers work in one," he said in answer to my laughter. "They pay all their taxes on time—"

"That's not likely to help," I said.

"We'll see," Uncle Sandro said. "I'll ask my Tengo's advice. Did you hear what he did?"

"No," I said, watching my step.

"He brought up water on his allotment with an electric pump, that's what he did!" Uncle Sandro exclaimed.

"An unusual man," I said, and looked him firmly in the eye.

"In the good sense," Uncle Sandro corrected, and looked firmly back at me.

Again the policeman appeared on the road. Uncle Sandro tidied up a little, waiting for him to draw even with us. When he drew even, the policeman again stopped and shot a glance at his tree, as if in the scornful hope of finding that fruit had unexpectedly appeared on it, although by now there was not a single fruit on any of the other trees, either.

He shifted his gaze to Uncle Sandro. "Grazing the cow?"

"I am," Uncle Sandro answered with dignity.

"May you have as much luck with that as I've had profit from your tree," the policeman said, and he walked on.

"Next time choose summer apples," Uncle Sandro shouted after him.

The policeman stopped and turned. "Summer apples," he said, drawing the words out mournfully. "You'll get what's coming to you, Sandro, worse than what's already happened," he added, and walked on. By this enigmatic phrase the policeman appeared to mean that the accident had been a subtle hint from Him who watches over our acts from on high and occasionally inflicts a blow to remind us of His existence.

"Go on, go on, you fool," Uncle Sandro said skeptically, but not very loud.

"Why doesn't he like the summer varieties?" I asked.

"Our local variety is good because it's thick-skinned. You can sell them in spring."

I think this observation on the profitably thick skin of the local apples concluded our visit that time. In later years, apparently having lost hope of using me to deal with the bureaucracy, Uncle Sandro merely commissioned me to pick fruit if I came to him in season.

"You can eat a bellyful," he would say, standing under the tree and handing the basket up to me when I had clambered onto the bottom branch.

By the way, he did receive a pension, that very winter. A small one, to be sure, something like two hundred rubles in old money, but still a pension. I don't know how he got it, on the basis of the accident or what. Perhaps people who have reached his age have a right to a pension regardless of their work record.

"No," he said, as if mildly disagreeing with someone, "the authorities aren't all bad, they come halfway to meet a man."

"How did you get it, anyway?" I asked curiously.

We were sitting at a little table in the same seaside café. Trying to expiate my guilt over not taking part in his pension quest, I ordered a carafe of cognac, Borzhom water, and coffee—the kindling for our talks.

It was one of those marvelous December days when the sun does not flood down untrammeled but delivers its warmth in a noble, measured dose. Uncle Sandro was in an excellent mood. As he listened to my question he stroked his mustache, looking around at the other tables in benevolent distraction. Then he tipped his head back a little and touched the soft fold in his neck.

"Do you know what that is?" he asked, his eyes merry.

"Fat," I answered, simplifying.

"Callus," he said, with humorous pride.

"What from?" I asked, trying to penetrate his well-constructed but not quite intelligible syllogism.

"You may think it's easy to be a perpetual tamada." He threw his head back still farther to show that when you drink you have to hold it in that position all the time. He touched the fold in his neck again and even slapped it encouragingly: it would serve him a while longer.

That was the meeting at which our conversation touched on divine providence. At the time the newspapers were full of talk about the abominable snowman, and I told him something about it.

He listened with interest and then asserted calmly that it was all true. As a young man, up in the mountains, he himself had seen a forest woman, as he called her in our idiom. Before his eyes she had jumped out of a thicket, her knee-length hair flying, and run down into the hollow, all the while beating her brow as our women do during lamentation.

"You weren't frightened?" I asked.

"No," he said simply, "I had a gun. I even tried to overtake her, but she suddenly darted into a rhododendron thicket, vanished in a flash."

"What did you want—to catch her?" I asked.

"I don't know myself," he shrugged. "I don't want to embroider. In general, when a woman runs, it makes me feel like giving chase. We were tending the flock in the mountains at the time, and I hadn't seen a woman in several months. In those days a lot of us saw forest people, but it was very seldom a woman. There was another time in the mountains that I really was scared. But He contrived that Himself," Uncle Sandro concluded, jerking his chin toward the sky.

"What do you mean, He?" I asked him to repeat because I had never heard Uncle Sandro allude to the heavens before.

"He or one of His people," Uncle Sandro said more precisely. He gave me a significant look.

"So tell me," I begged.

"Let's have another coffee and cognac," Uncle Sandro acquiesced, glancing at the waitress. "I don't tell this story very often, but I'll tell you . . ."

I called the waitress over and ordered. Uncle Sandro, while I gave the order, sat calmly facing me, his hands folded impressively on the staff he had taken up after the accident. I waited for him to begin the story, but Uncle Sandro said nothing, merely glanced at the waitress, who was clearing the table. The story was not meant for the ears of the uninitiated.

Then he began to speak, and I realized for the first time that he was just as good at tales of an epic mold as he was with everyday subjects.

"It was the year before the Great Snow," he began, taking a sip of coffee from his demitasse, "and the year after our popular hero Shashiko killed the constable and went into the forest. They hunted him fifteen years and couldn't catch him. No police officer could get through from Chegem to Tsabal, on foot or on horseback. Shashiko's sure bullet was waiting for him everywhere. But why go on about Shashiko—the story's not about him, may he rest in peace. As always, they tricked him into coming out of the forest, they promised an amnesty and then kilied him and his brother in prison.

"But that's another story. I want to tell you what happened to me. That summer my father kept his cattle on Bashkapsar. In those days the wild animals up there were unafraid, and roebuck sometimes came to play with our goats.

"One time one of our horses got lost. We started looking for him early in the morning, and when the sun had risen to the height of a good-sized beech, we came on his tracks. We followed the tracks for two hours until we saw him on a ledge he couldn't get down from by himself. That happens with domestic animals, especially when they're hungry and come across some good grass. This horse had only just been driven up from the village. We sweated blood dragging him out of there and driving him back.

"Well, we were getting near our camp, but we decided to stop and rest on a hillside by a stream. You'd never find a better place to rest.

"A mile or so below us in the hollow lay our camp. There was smoke over the shanty—the shepherds were fixing dinner. On the slope to the right the cows were grazing, higher up the horses, and higher still the goats. On the left the firs and the cedar forests, breaking each other's ribs, stretched their heads to the sky. And the sky was clear—not a cloud. The air was strong and flavorful, like buffalo milk. We don't have air like that, abundance like that, any more. Even in the mountains the air is spoiled now, because the planes fly everywhere.

"So it was that kind of place where we squatted by the stream, drank our fill, and decided to stop and rest. My comrade, a man from our village, I won't tell you his name because he's still alive, decided to soak his moccasins in the water. They had gotten too dry. I saw him take them off his feet and stick them in the water right where we had drunk.

" 'What are you doing?' I say. 'Don't you know you're not supposed to do that? Since you've drunk here, you have to go downstream if you want to bathe your feet or soak your moccasins or wash out a handkerchief.'

" 'Oh, nothing will happen,' he says. 'We've already drunk our fill and people don't come here—'

" 'Maybe nothing will happen,' I say, 'but why violate the custom? We didn't invent it.'

" 'Those who invented the custom,' he answers, making a joke out of it, 'are long gone, and we won't tell anyone . . .'

"I didn't like that, but what could I say? He was too easygoing, and besides I was young. I thought we'd get away with it. So he stuck his moccasins in the brook and even weighted them with a stone so they'd soak up the water better.

"So, then, we were lying in the honeyed alpine grass. The sun was warm, the brook babbled, drowsiness came over us . . . Such a sweet place—you couldn't help falling asleep. I was probably having my second dream already, and moving on to my third, when I felt in my sleep that something bad had happened.

"I was still asleep, but I thought to myself, What could have happened? Could the broadpaw—a bear, that is—have killed one of our flock? I wanted to guess what had happened while I was still asleep, because I thought by the time I woke up it would be too late. But I got the feeling that I simply couldn't guess in my sleep. No, I thought, I have to wake up and look at everything with my own eyes; then maybe I'll understand what's happened. I raised my head and looked around.

"I looked down—the shanties were still there, the smoke was rising, the shepherds were fixing dinner. I looked to the right along the slope. I saw the cows grazing, higher up the horses, and way high up the goats, like white rocks. No, I thought, nothing's happened up there—the flock would have taken alarm. My comrade was sleeping peacefully. Then why was something itching my soul? And suddenly I listened and my heart stood still—the brook had stopped babbling. I looked at it and felt—God forbid you should ever have such a feeling! To make a long story short, the brook had dried up. The water lay in puddles here and there, like on a road after a rain. You couldn't have scooped up so much as a handful.

"I shook my comrade and said, 'Look what you've done!'

"He was so scared he couldn't pull his moccasins on. His arms dangled as if they were broken, his lips whispered, 'Allah have mercy . . .'

"That summer during a thunderstorm, his buffalo cow was driven mad by the big hailstones and fell off a cliff and died. I had a yearling calf killed by a bear. After that we never went back to those grazing grounds."

"Uncle Sandro," I said, "what if a big stone fell somewhere, up high, or an avalanche dammed up the brook?"

"I just knew you'd say something like that," Uncle Sandro answered with a grin. "So you think an avalanche had been waiting day and night for my comrade to wash his moccasins in this brook and then said to itself, 'Aha, now's the time to fall and dam up the brook!' "

"All sorts of things could have happened," I said.

"Then answer me this," Uncle Sandro said, his eyes flashing. "Why did He take a buffalo from him, and only a yearling calf from me?"

"What do the buffalo and the calf have to do with it?" I asked blankly.

"Just this," Uncle Sandro replied: "He punished us, like a good judge. He took the buffalo from my comrade, the main culprit, and a yearling calf from me because I didn't stop him."

"Uncle Sandro," I said, "didn't He see any other sins in you?"

Uncle Sandro looked at me calmly and said, "He doesn't chastise all sins. If you sinned at the risk of your life, He takes that into account. But if you sinned without risking anything, you can't escape punishment. And I do have that kind of sin."

"Tell me about it, Uncle Sandro," I begged, pouring the last of the cognac.

"There's nothing to tell," Uncle Sandro said. He rinsed his mouth with the cognac and swallowed. "At Tatyr Khan's wedding I slaughtered twelve oxen with my own hand, and now in recent years my right hand's been hurting."

Uncle Sandro held out his right hand and wiggled it, as if hearkening to the effect of ancient sin. Even at the time, he remembered, the wrist had hurt the same way. It was stupid, he agreed.

He became thoughtful, and for the first time I thought I saw a sentimental expression in his slightly prominent eyes.

"Yes," he said, "twelve defenseless oxen . . ."

I thought he was about to burst into sobs. But just then a young man came over to us, full of exuberant respect.

"Uncle Sandro!" he exclaimed. "I've been looking for you all over town—"

"Well, what do you know!" Uncle Sandro said, reviving. "I completely forgot. I'm getting old, getting old, my friend."

"How could you, Uncle Sandro, everyone's waiting for you!" the young man exclaimed. "No one wants to touch a thing."

"I'm coming, my boy, I'm coming!" Uncle Sandro stood up and straightened his cherkeska.

The young man turned to me. "Sorry, friend, but we have company expecting us," he said pacifically but firmly, as if letting me know that it would be a senseless waste to squander the great tamada's precious strength on one man when the thirsting masses were waiting.

"So you're staying here?" Uncle Sandro asked, as if he had been trying to persuade me to go with him but I had refused.

"Yes," I said, "I'll sit a while longer."

Tapping his stick and nodding to acquaintances, Uncle Sandro walked among the tables like a rakish prophet, and disappeared down the street.

It always hurts a little when someone you have been with goes off to make merry, even if you never meant to accompany him. I sat a little while longer, pondering Uncle Sandro's story, and then went home in a rather melancholy mood.

I remember thinking, in a desultory way, that not only do men create gods in their own likeness, but each man individually creates a god in his own personal likeness. Then again, I may not have thought of that at the time, but somewhat later, or maybe earlier.

PRINCE OLDENBURGSKY

PRINCE OLDENBURGSKY stood lost in thought, looking out over the pond in Gagra Park like Peter over the waters of the Baltic Sea. His huge body, still sinewy despite his age, leaned lightly on his cane.

Alexander Petrovich was in a bad mood. Beside him on a park mall as long and broad as a Petersburg boulevard stood his retinue, which with the aide-de-camp numbered six men, their posture expressive of their readiness to rush to fulfill his every order, or conversely, to scatter in all directions.

The retinue watched the prince in silence. The prince himself was watching a black Australian swan glide noiselessly toward him over the water. It looked like a small pirate frigate fearlessly attacking the imperial cruiser—that is, the prince himself.

It was a fierce old male, spoiling for a fight with a young rival who sat on the water two paces away from Oldenburgsky. Foolishly unconcerned, the young swan curled its boneless neck to dig under its wing with its Easter-red beak.

It was a marvelous sunny day in early October. The prince's shadow fell lightly on the water. The young swan sitting in his shadow continued to dig under its wing with its beak. Alexander Petrovich suddenly had the thought that the reason the young swan was so unconcerned just now was that it felt itself in a fatherly shade. That may have been true.

The old troublemaker, meanwhile, its ringlike head arched, was approaching the shore. The scum, he's going to peck him, the prince thought. The swan, without slowing down or changing its warlike intentions, swam into his shadow. With unexpected agility Prince Oldenburgsky stooped and slapped his cane on the water, right in front of the old male. It stopped and looked up indignantly. Then, without moving forward, it stretched its neck to reach its insouciant rival. Prince Oldenburgsky swatted its neck with his cane, and with difficulty pushed back on its heavy, stubbornly braking body. Then he slapped his cane on the water again several times more, and the old swan, somewhat cooled down by the mercurial spray that spattered on him, turned back to get a running start for a fresh attack.

The pink pelican Fedka dozed on an artificial island, with the heavy sword of its beak resting on its wing. Sometimes it opened an eye and without any special curiosity watched what was happening—the way a wise, self-respecting dog will sometimes keep an eye on the puppies' squabbles as it dozes.

Attracted by the noise of water, a huge white swan known for nipping approached cautiously and swam past the prince. There was a strange incongruity between the snow-white grandeur of its majestically gliding body and the expression of greedy curiosity in the foolish eye that crowned its divine neck. The chaos of worldly folly, and the cruel folly of all womankind, peered out of that eye.

The swan that the prince was defending went on digging voluptuously under its wing, never noticing the danger.

Alexander Petrovich straightened up and sighed. He remembered now with particular longing what it was he had missed in recent weeks. He remembered the soft, strong fingers of his masseuse, Eleonora Leontievna Kartukhova—or Kartuchikha, as she was usually called by the people of Gagra, and by the prince himself when he was in a jovial mood or, conversely, a wrathful one.

Nearly a month ago he had placed her under house arrest and ordered her not to appear on the streets of the town under any pretext on pain of exile to distant provinces, because she had been discovered in outrageous perfidy.

At the time the prince had been busy with efforts to prepare a hotel for Empress Alexandra Fyodorovna's maids of honor, who were arriving from Petersburg. Around the same time, a veteran of the Preobrazhensky regiment who traded in rat poison and diuretics in the town unexpectedly went on a bender, or rather, went on a bender of unexpected scope. When one of his drinking companions asked how come he had so much cash, he blabbed that Kartuchikha had bought a lot of rat poison from him to poison the arriving maids of honor, who, incidentally, never did arrive.

The Preobrazhensky veteran blabbed in his cups, his drinking companion informed in a hangover. Although Alexander Petrovich did not quite believe that Kartuchikha was really planning to poison the empress's maids of honor, or at least the one whom he was allegedly planning to seduce, the very attempt to blackmail him in this manner drove the prince into a legitimate fury.

In the past Kartuchikha had been the prince's masseuse and mistress; the two roles grew naturally one into the other. But with increasing frequency in recent years she had had to confine herself to massage, because passion was peacefully dying out in the aging prince. He was well past seventy.

Kartuchikha, thinking that the prince had grown cool specifically toward her, was madly jealous. She massaged him with special refinements in an attempt to restore her second role.

Never before had Prince Oldenburgsky felt himself so brisk and refreshed after her massage—not for amorous delights, by any means, but for government activity, as the foolish woman (without whom he could not manage) could not understand at all.

Alexander Petrovich had never been either a playboy or a libertine and could not endure such men. He and Kartuchikha had become intimate out of physical necessity, because his once passionately beloved wife, Princess Evgenia Maximilyanovna, had been paralyzed for many long years now and was dragging out her existence feebleminded.

Never mind her, this Kartuchikha; she was only a woman. But would they understand him in Petersburg? The czar, whom Alexander Petrovich loved so tenderly despite all his weaknesses, was constantly misled by court intriguers. So many fine and timely undertakings had been spoiled because the people around the czar placed their own personal interest above the interest of the empire—a fact adroitly utilized by the Socialist Jews in their propaganda.

When he went to the czar at the beginning of the century with a scheme to create a health resort on the Black Sea coast, meaning eventually to turn it into a Caucasian riviera, the czar had agreed to the suggestion with unexpected alacrity. Alexander Petrovich later surmised that Petersburg was simply using this as a way of getting rid of him. He knew that he was considered a crank at court because he always—without regard for rank, with all the candor of a loyal subject—spoke his thoughts on ways to save the czar and the Russian state. All the Oldenburgsky princes had been like that, and all were considered cranks.

The princes Oldenburgsky belonged to the Holstein-Gottorp line of the house of Oldenburg. They were direct descendants of George-Ludwig Holsteinsky, who had been called to serve in Russia by Emperor Peter III. Under Catherine they went into something of a decline, and some even seem to have returned to Germany, thereby demonstrating their loyalty to Peter III, but later they were always in view and always considered eccentric. Since those long-ago times they had become more Russian than the Russians, but they continued to be cranks.

Thus Alexander Petrovich's grandfather, Prince George, although he was governor-general of several provinces and an efficient one at that, wrote poetry. What was worse, he also published his poems for all to see, invariably dedicating them to his own wife, Grand Princess Ekaterina Pavlovna, which was practically indecent.

Alexander Petrovich had not forgotten how the court had snickered at his father, Peter Georgievich, when he proposed to the late Alexander III that he should declare in a solemn manifesto that a copy of the code of laws would henceforth be preserved under the same bell jar with the imperial crown and scepter.

But what was so ridiculous about this most noble and useful proposition, gentlemen? It would have been a great manifesto, signifying that henceforth the code of laws was just as sacred within the borders of the Russian Empire as the imperial crown. Was it not because of lawlessness and abuse, which have no place in an autocracy truly grounded in the idea of the people, that Russia had faltered? Was it not these vices that gave poisonous food to the Socialist loud-mouths?

Prince Oldenburgsky advanced a very effective argument for the creation of a Caucasian riviera: moneyed Russians would come to Gagra instead of squandering their rubles on the Mediterranean coast. But even this important consideration was merely a subtle tactical maneuver. In truth, the prince's burning dream—for the time being diligently concealed from everyone—was to create here on the Black Sea coast, within the Russian Empire, a small but cozy oasis of ideal monarchy, a realm of order, justice, and a complete confluence of the monarch with the people, and even the peoples. (As if on purpose for the convenience of the experiment, the coast was rich in the diversity of its nationalities.)

And now palaces and villas had grown up on the wild coast; on the site of the swamp a huge "park with plantings," as it was called, had been laid out; a port, a power plant, a hospital, hotels, and finally, the prince's pride, a workers' dining room with two departments: for Muslim and Christian workers. In each department of the dining room, the kitchen was divided from the public hall by a glass partition so that the slovenly cooks were within the workers' view at all times.

This was the prince's personal invention, a thing that might also seem ridiculous there in Petersburg. But do not forget, gentlemen, the mutiny on the battleship *Potemkin* began in the kitchen!

But the prince's crowning accomplishment here was the finest fire station in Europe. Each piece of equipment was numbered, and the town's bravest and strongest inhabitants were provided with special nameplates with corresponding numbers, so that in the event of a fire they would not cast about, seizing whatever came to hand, but would run to the scene of the disaster with their own implements.

The town's most costly buildings were equipped with perforated piping, placed in the middle of the ceiling of every room. In the event of fire, according to the plan, water was to be pumped through these pipes under great pressure, so that the flame would not only be attacked from without but destroyed from within, as if by a sudden cavalry raid behind enemy lines. A hereditary member of the Preobrazhensky regiment, a participant in the Turkish campaign, the prince knew what was what in such matters.

Admittedly, fires were as rare in Gagra as in a Turkish bath, but that's what public safety measures are for. Public safety is a great thing! It was not in vain that in his time Prince Oldenburgsky had headed a commission on plague.

Needless to say, the town flourished under the vigilant fatherly eye of Alexander Petrovich. On holidays, in the park with plantings, he was always in the thick of the crowd, illumined by the flare of fireworks, which were held frequently and offered no danger of fire, since they were aimed strictly at the sea (the mightiest fire-fighting element). On days of misfortune he was always with the people, inspiring the distraught and the weak in spirit by his personal example. Thus, not long ago, when a flood burst the dam on the Zhoekvara, had he not been the first, with his loyal Preobrazhensky company, to cast himself into the water, so that there was nothing for his retinue to do but follow him in?

Yes, only by personal example can one inspire a nation, as Peter the Great, himself a tireless toiler on the throne, taught us and continues to teach us. But Prince Oldenburgsky frequently reinforced his personal example with his personal cane, whose direct Petrine heritage destined it to wreak havoc on the backs of police chiefs, bureaucrats, and insolent engineers. Sometimes this truly democratic cane reached even to generals.

But of course it was not only the common people whom Prince Oldenburgsky tried to influence by his personal example. No, his activity was intended as a reproachful yet inspiring nod in the direction of Petersburg. Unfortunately, the true point of his work was not yet understood there.

Even the tenderly beloved czar, when he passed through on a cruiser and visited the health resort in 1911, stayed only two hours. The czarina did not even deign to disembark on the hospitable Gagra shore.

The czar spoke very approvingly of the park with plantings, but for some reason declined even to inspect the fire station and the workers' dining room. Worst of all, he gave no indication that there would be any gradual but universal dissemination of the Gagra experiment.

The prince's true design was understood by precisely those who were trying to destroy and break down the Russian state—that is, the Socialist Jews. As early as 1903 he had received an anonymous letter, evidently from one of the scoundrels at court. The writer enclosed an underground newssheet with a challenging, inflammatory name—*The Flame*, perhaps, or *The Bonfire*. In it was an article against Oldenburgsky entitled "Crowned Thief; or, The Royal Dowry." The article was a mélange of monstrous brazenness and equally monstrous ignorance. He was particularly struck by one passage which said that "the seizure of the Gagra woodland caused a whole storm of discontent among the Abkhazians, the aborigines of the region, and two companies of infantry were called to Gagra on their account."

In the first place, why the "seizure" of the Gagra woodland, when the czar had approved the explanatory note concerning the matter of the Gagra woodland, the ministry of finance had examined and studied it, and finally, the project had been undertaken in full compliance with all laws, according to the ministry of finance's report? What kind of seizure was this, Socialist Jews? Now, your doctrine that everything on earth belongs to the proletariat—that's seizure, that's robbery and brigandage, whereas this was an absolutely legal act, and most importantly, one advantageous to the fate of the empire.

As regards the two infantry companies—more lies. No one called up any infantry companies at that time, inasmuch as there was not and could not have been any storm of discontent among the aborigines of the region.

True, some workers did get stirred up two years later, but they weren't aborigines, just your usual tramps. At that point an infantry company was indeed requested from Novorossisk (one company, not two, Jews!), and they didn't send it because they were having troubles of their own.

When he received the letter with this inflammatory newspaper, Alexander Petrovich not only did not go berserk, as the anonymous scoundrel evidently expected, but felt enormous satisfaction. Ah, yes—it was the enemy who were the first to guess the meaning of his design and sound the alarm.

As for the aborigines, he had the best of relationships with them. He often defended them against swindling contractors who tried to hire them for public works, and against bureaucratic scribblers.

Certain customs of theirs delighted him by their primordial wisdom. In their exceptional respect for old age—or rather, for seniority by age, which naturally culminated in the greatest deference for the oldest man—he took scholarly joy in divining a biological monarchism, a precursor to the harmonious ideal of the Christian autocracy, now unfortunately defiled in many respects by aristocratic parasites and no-goods.

Like Peter the Great, Prince Oldenburgsky organized a curio house in Gagra with marvels live and dead. The point was to develop an inquisitive spirit among the aborigines. The prince gave generous rewards for interesting exhibits. To avoid bureaucratic routine in this matter, Alexander Petrovich issued a special order that people with interesting finds should be directed to him personally.

The curio collection contained local minerals and ores, a huge ancient Greek amphora with a pancake of wine coagulated in the bottom, some arrows and feudal swords that were not yet too badly rusted, a woman's saddle the size of a camel's hump, entitled "Saddle of an Unknown Amazon," and many other things that were no less curious and instructive.

Live nature was represented in the form of stuffed local eagles gazing with hatred on their live fellows, a cornstalk with fourteen ears, Abkhazian ginseng roots, a totally white albino wild boar, a fern tree the size of a cherry tree, a wild water buffalo, captured in the mountains but subsequently recognized by its owner and acknowledged to be a domestic one run wild.

Besides all this, Prince Oldenburgsky experimented a good deal with the beautification and development of nature itself, although along with his successes in this sphere there were disappointing failures.

Thus he turned loose half a hundred rose-cheeked Angolan parrots bought in a Berlin zoo. At first all went well, the little parrots acclimatized and would even come to the park, but then they were rather speedily pecked to death by the overwrought native hawks.

Despite the assurances of specialists that monkeys could not survive the local winter, Prince Oldenburgsky turned loose ten marmosets of both sexes. The question of the African marmoset's ability to acclimatize remained open, because local hunters shot them all before winter set in.

The first slain marmoset was brought to the prince by the hunter himself, who knew nothing of the experiment and demanded a reward. Then a whole delegation of elders from neighboring villages appeared and rather firmly declared that in the future Abkhazians would not tolerate the defilement of their ancestral forests with creatures resembling human beings. The prince swallowed his pride and gave up on monkeys for the sake of his larger goals. He was tireless in his hope that wise expediency would make Russian protection appealing to people of other nationalities.

The process of civilizing the area was in full swing, although it sometimes stumbled against unexpected obstacles. Just today, a series of outrageous incidents had spoiled his mood.

At exactly 6:00 A.M. Alexander Petrovich had waked to the bugler's call and immediately left his bed. In theory, the silver sound of the bugle that echoed over Gagra at 6:00 A.M. was to summon the inhabitants of the town to creative labor. In reality, the only ones who got up at the sound of the bugle were the prince himself and the workmen in the repair shops, whom, incidentally, despite the theories of Socialist Jews, he loved above all other inhabitants of the town.

Today the prince decided to begin his rounds of his domain with the repair shops. The rows of busily humming machine tools, the figures of the workers bent over them in concentration, always put him in a joyful creative mood.

This morning the prince's spiritual condition was insufficiently serene; he was still bothered by a bitter aftertaste of yesterday's outrage. Yesterday morning he had visited the barracks near Gagra, where the Austrian prisoners who were building the railroad were housed. The prince found the general condition of the barracks unsatisfactory. It especially bothered him that despite the huge capacity of the barracks they had only one door each, which would lead to panic and loss of life if there was a fire at night. Prince Oldenburgsky ordered the chief engineer of the district, Engineer Bartmer, to summon all carpenters forthwith and have doors cut through every third window in all barracks by five o'clock in the evening. At exactly five o'clock Oldenburgsky's Benz limousine again stopped in the Zhoekvara Gorge, not far from the barracks. By this time three doors remained to be cut and hung. Chief District Engineer Bartmer was given a month's arrest with performance of duties.

Since the beginning of the World War, in addition to all his numerous official duties, Prince Oldenburgsky had been appointed chief of the Public Safety and Evacuation Service, and among his direct responsibilities was supervision of the maintenance of prisoners.

Alexander Petrovich attached great significance to the humane treatment of prisoners. Today he's a prisoner, thought the prince, but tomorrow he'll return home, and it's up to us what he'll be when he gets there, a booster of the empire or a detractor. So Peter the Great taught us. As Pushkin says of him, "He comforts the glorious captives . . ." Engineer Bartmer, with his limited practical intelligence, did not understand this—which was why he was being punished.

That was what had happened yesterday, and why a certain blight still lay on the prince's soul. It was to restore his serenity of spirit that Alexander Petrovich had decided to begin the day with the repair shops.

. . . The golden-green morning sky promised a fine day. The Benz limousine, driven by a leather-clad Italian chauffeur, carried the prince, his sleepy retinue, and his fool of an aide-de-camp to the workers.

"Hello, chaps!" The aristocratic German accent echoed through the workshops, and Prince Oldenburgsky strode lightly between the rows of busily humming machines, accompanied by the foreman. Sometimes he stopped at a machine and asked the foreman who was doing what, and why; each time he received a clear, mollifying answer. His mood improved. He felt like living and working. What touched him most was the beautiful, concentrated faces of the workers, who continued to labor without a particle of servility or trickery even when he stopped by their machines. After thanking the workers for their service, Alexander Petrovich got back in the car with his retinue and drove on to inspect the town's other establishments.

"Turn off the machines," the foreman said, watching the departing car from the window. The machines not needed for the day's work were turned off then and there. It had been noticed that the prince liked to have all the machines working.

Cheered by the repair shops, Alexander Petrovich bowled along the Gagra Highway, which was clean and clear as a pane of glass. Suddenly, near the police station, the car came to a dead halt: in the middle of the road lay a crushed watermelon. When they had driven by half an hour ago, there had been nothing there, and someone had already managed to make a mess.

Prince Oldenburgsky slowly turned purple. Hearing the car stop, the assistant chief of police ran out of the station, his boots clumping. The aide-de-camp and the retinue woke up a little and slid forward on their seats in anticipation of an entertaining hide-warming. The humor of the situation was heightened by the fact that the assistant chief of police had run up from behind the car. When he drew even with the seated prince, he stopped without even noticing the crushed melon.

"What is that?" Alexander Petrovich thrust out his cane and jabbed it in the direction of the outrage. Casting a doomed glance at the cane, the officer cautiously peered over the radiator.

"A watermelon, Your Highness!"

"Who?" roared the prince.

"Begging your pardon, I don't know, Your Highness!"

"Remove it!" The cane, raising a plume of dust, landed on the instantaneously stiffened back of the guardian of the law. The Benz limousine picked its way fastidiously around the outrage and tore off.

At breakfast that morning the prince learned of fresh outrages. As usual while breakfasting, he was going over the day's mail. Letters requiring immediate reply were placed in a neat stack, the rest were tossed on the heap of throwaways or items not requiring prompt reply.

Alexander Petrovich's attention was caught by a letter from a certain very rich landowner who had recently spent two months vacationing at Gagra. The landowner wrote that he missed this heavenly place created by the prince's hands, he dreamed of Gagra at night, and he could not settle down on his ancestral estate.

On the one hand, Alexander Petrovich was pleased by the impression his brainchild had made on this surfeited epicurean who had seen the world; but on the other, he would have liked Gagra to inspire such people to more creative thoughts, not these sentimental sighs.

Now there's an eccentric, thought the prince; do as I do at your own place, and you won't miss mine. Undecided whether to remind him of this or whether it was worth starting a correspondence with him, Alexander Petrovich tossed his letter between the heap of throwaways and the stack of urgents.

Next there was a letter from a student named Dadiani, a relative on the Georgian side of the family. He wasn't much of a relative, a cousin ten times removed, but he was among those whom the prince helped. Alexander Petrovich helped poor students from good noble families.

The student reminded him of his need in respectful tones, but the letter itself was written in vulgar modern orthography—without a single *yat*—which made an exquisite mockery of the respectful tone. The letter was crumpled up and thrown away: the Social Democrat contagion had infiltrated even here!

"The blackguard—not one kopeck!"

The bailiff, with a slight bow and a nod, let it be known that the disposition had been noted, and not without personal satisfaction.

Still another piece of correspondence arrested the prince's attention. It was a copy of a telegram from Engineer Bartmer to the management of the company in which he served. Engineer Bartmer complained of the barracks incident—stating the facts with absolute accuracy, however. That is his right, the prince thought, setting the telegram aside.

"Your Highness," the bailiff said, "the telegraph operator wants to know whether or not to send the telegram."

"Within the Russian Empire," the prince answered severely, "everyone has the right to telegraph where he wishes and to whom he wishes."

The bailiff froze, sensing that Alexander Petrovich had mounted his favorite hobbyhorse.

"And if it's a criminal, Your Highness?"

"Even if an attempt on the person of the reigning house is being plotted," the prince pronounced in a voice terrible with inspiration, "he is obliged to forestall it loyally by informing the police, but without stopping the telegram."

What do you do about secret letters, the bailiff thought, but he held his tongue, as if stunned by the tragic beauty of the independence of Russian laws.

Now it remained for the bailiff to report two more outrages, an especially difficult task considering the nature of these and the prince's high dudgeon. But one way or another he had to report.

The first outrage was that early this morning a certain Abkhazian had broken the head of the watchman at the Hotel Alpine with a gun he had snatched from the watchman's hands. The criminal, who offered no resistance, had been seized by the hotel servants and sent to the police, along with his horse. In self-defense he claimed that the watchman had insulted him with an obscene noise, purposely emitted while the aborigine was drinking from the fountain by the hotel.

Whether the watchman had made the obscene noise, and made it on purpose to offend the aborigine, was not known, because he had been taken to the hospital unconscious and there were no other witnesses.

The second outrage was that one of the three black male swans—the prince's favorite, in fact—had disappeared during the night. Rumor had it that drunken voices of unknown people had been heard in the park that night, and the park watchman had collapsed with a tropical fever the day before.

"Find out who knew the watchman was sick," the prince ordered, but this did not help any, because everyone knew the watchman had taken sick.

The prince ordered his aide-de-camp to tour the sea around Gagra in a motorboat, in case the swan had simply fled from its persecutors. Sometimes the swans flew out to sea by themselves, but they always came back later.

The swan hunt by motorboat ended without result. Nothing was known about the drunks except that a belt without identifying marks was found on the bank of the pond, from which one could conclude that the drunks, or at least one of them, had undressed and tried to catch the swan right in the pond.

Without giving vent to his personal sufferings, Prince Oldenburgsky adamantly pursued his daily routine. He ordered the criminal brought to the park by eleven o'clock; he would be there inspecting the scene of the night's event.

The vanished swan usually defended the young one from the old warrior's attacks. It was partly for these chivalrous qualities that Prince Oldenburgsky loved him. He very much loved all the birds he raised, but was especially partial to the pink pelican and this vanished swan for their beauty and nobility.

Next to being massaged by Kartuchikha, blast her, and inspecting the repair shops, feeding the pelicans was third in its power to soothe Alexander Petrovich.

The pink pelican still dozed on the little island, and three black female swans, because of whom the old male gave no peace to the young one, were calmly feeding at the far end of the pond. To all appearances, the old male was so absorbed in the process of enmity that he had forgotten the reason for it. Now he approached his rival again.

The prince drove him away again. "I'm just going to stand here," he muttered, brandishing his cane.

"They're bringing him already, your Highness," the aide-de-camp responded, irrelevantly as usual. He nodded toward the park mall, at the end of which appeared three figures—the chief of police, an interpreter from the prince's staff, and the criminal Abkhazian. The aide-de-camp even raised the binoculars that hung on his chest and peered at this group, out of a parasitic idleness that the prince considered characteristic of him. He was still carrying the binoculars on his chest after his fruitless search for the lost swan.

Alexander Petrovich did not like his aide-de-camp, considering him a scapegrace and a ne'er-do-well. He would have fired him long ago, but since he suspected the aide-de-camp of watching him and occasionally denouncing him to Petersburg, he kept him on purposely, out of pride.

Prince Oldenburgsky went over to his retinue and looked down the mall. They were drawing near. The one in front, evidently, was the criminal himself—a well-built young man in a cherkeska and the soft Asiatic boots. In one hand he gripped the traveling *khurjin* slung over his shoulder. Alexander Petrovich could not help admiring his elastic, lynxlike gait.

About thirty paces away, the criminal looked back and asked the interpreter in Abkhazian, "Which one is he?"

"The one with the cane," the interpreter answered quietly.

The young man—alas, it was Uncle Sandro—stopped about five paces from the prince and bowed slightly, murmuring a greeting in Abkhazian. No one replied to his greeting, and he fell silent, trying to moderate the natural vivacity of his eyes, which might at this moment, and not without reason, be taken for a sign of boldness bordering on insolence.

The awkward silence lasted for several seconds, because Alexander Petrovich felt uncomfortable at having to conduct a court of law standing up. There was a sort of violation of order here, and he silently moved toward a bench that stood ten paces away under an oleander. Everyone followed him.

At last the prince sat down. Symmetrically divided, the retinue stood on either side of the bench.

"How did it happen?" the prince asked, hunching forward and examining Uncle Sandro from under his brows. This habit lent his posture a threatening impetuosity and impressed his fellow conversationalist with the necessity of getting to the truth by the shortest possible path.

Uncle Sandro understood this immediately. Sensing that the shortest path to the truth would be the one most perilous for him, he decided not to give in, but to force his own path to the truth on the prince. He had already embarked on this path back at the police station, where he had pretended not to understand Russian.

The interpreter translated the prince's question. Uncle Sandro nodded his thanks for the translation and began to present his version of the event. Prince

Oldenburgsky sensed that Uncle Sandro was deviating from the shortest path to the truth and interrupted him by poking the *khurjin* with his cane.

"What's he got wiggling in there?" he asked the interpreter.

Uncle Sandro nodded and began to untie the *khurjin*. To the great surprise of the entourage and of the prince himself, he pulled out a black swan, somewhat smothered and smeared with its own droppings.

The prince started. "Where did you get him?" Lightly jumping to his feet, he took his favorite bird from Uncle Sandro.

"It may dirty you," Uncle Sandro warned, but the interpreter did not dare translate.

"I brought it as a present," Uncle Sandro added.

Carrying the swan in his arms, Prince Oldenburgsky went over to the pond and set it in the water. The swan sat there dully for several seconds, but then suddenly started and swam with a cry to the middle of the pond, a triangular ripple rolling from its breast.

"Why didn't you say so immediately?" the prince asked, staring at Uncle Sandro in surprise. Uncle Sandro's brazen charm was beginning to work on the prince.

"I was bringing it as a present, but since the other happened, I decided, Let them punish me first, then I'll give it to him," Uncle Sandro replied.

"Nobly said," the prince nodded, sitting down again on the bench. In actual fact Uncle Sandro had been depressed to see several black swans in the pond, thinking that the prince already had some and his find would not be of any great value.

"Where did you find it?" the prince asked, leaning back on the bench and looking benevolently at Uncle Sandro, as if allowing him to lengthen the path to the truth somewhat. Uncle Sandro understood this immediately. Sparing no words, he told the story of the capture of the black swan.

Early that morning Uncle Sandro was riding from Gudauta to the village of Achandary, where he planned to stay several days with a relative, in anticipation of a memorial feast that was to be held in a neighboring house. In our part of the world the fortieth-day memorial repast is not celebrated very precisely; it is adjusted for the weather, sometimes for other domestic considerations, so that Uncle Sandro had decided that it would be better not to take any chances, and to wait on the spot rather than miss a good funeral repast.

So there he was, riding along the coastal highway, and suddenly he saw a long-necked black bird, unknown in our part of the world, sitting not far from shore.

He had never heard of Oldenburgsky's swans, though he had heard plenty about the prince himself, but he had never seen him.

So Uncle Sandro was curious about the bird, and he rode cautiously down to the shore. The bird noticed Uncle Sandro too and perhaps was curious about him, because it stretched its long neck and began to watch him. Uncle Sandro was very surprised by this strange reception and decided to shoot the bird and take it to his relatives for breakfast, if it didn't stink too much of fish. According to him, it was bigger than a good-sized turkey.

Without getting down from his horse, Uncle Sandro drew his Smith & Wesson, aimed, and fired. The bird was sitting on the water within thirty meters of the shore, but Uncle Sandro missed it. Oddly enough, the bird did not fly away, merely swam off twenty meters, not out to sea but along the shore. Uncle Sandro moved forward a bit, and when he drew even with the bird, took careful aim and fired again. Again he missed, and oddly enough, the bird did not fly away, merely swam along the shore, about the same distance out. Highly provoked, Uncle Sandro again drew even with the bird and fired at it. Again he missed. Either the Smith & Wesson was not accurate at that range or the bird was bewitched. "If I'd had more cartridges," Uncle Sandro used to say, "I'd have driven it to Gagra, because it kept on swimming in that one direction." Uncle Sandro had five or six cartridges in all, and having fired them in vain, he was so infuriated that he decided to swim after the bird, since it was not flying away.

Without thinking twice he drove his skewbald courser into the sea. Uncle Sandro had never tried her in the sea before, but the horse had managed the rivers of Abkhazia and Mingrelia.

Nevertheless, she did not like the sea and balked for a long time. Uncle Sandro forced her into the water. As soon as the horse was swimming, she immediately became obedient, because there was nothing to dig her heels into. The cursed bird let her get quite close, but as soon as she did, the bird moved off, again toward Gagra.

Either it's wounded or it's an hallucination, Uncle Sandro thought. Although he was soaked through, he was so inflamed that he did not notice the cold. Oddly enough, Uncle Sandro used to say, the horse went after the swan like a good bird dog on the trail of a wildfowl, but even so she could not catch it.

God knows how it would all have ended if they had not luckily come out in a shallows. Feeling the bottom under her feet, the horse quickened her pace. The bird, as Uncle Sandro used to say, could not quicken its pace, "because although it had a neck as long as my arm, its legs were short, especially compared to a horse." At the last minute it tried to dive, but Uncle Sandro managed to grab it by its black tail and lift it out of the water.

Uncle Sandro was horribly disgusted and enraged by this strange bird, especially after he fingered it and ascertained that its body was hard as a board and much inferior to a turkey. He wanted to smash its head then and there but remembered that nearby in Gagra lived a Prince Oldenburgsky who bought odd items out of boredom.

Maybe he'll buy it, Uncle Sandro thought, and he thrust the bird into his *khurjin*. With the *khurjin* strapped to his saddle, he started for Gagra.

Two hours later Uncle Sandro was in Gagra. His clothes had dried out some, but he was still chilled to the bone and very much wanted a drink to warm his blood. He had nothing to drink and nothing to buy it with.

In the town he met another Abkhazian and asked him whether the prince still accepted odd items.

"If he likes the odd item, he accepts it," the Abkhazian answered. Then Uncle Sandro asked to be taken to the prince. But the man refused, citing the fact that the prince had been in a bad mood since yesterday.

"What happened yesterday?" Uncle Sandro asked, beginning to feel irritated.

Gleefully, but in great secrecy, the Abkhazian told him that the doors hadn't been cut yet in the Austrian prisoners' barracks and the prince was very mad about it, especially at Engineer Bartmer, who if you thought he was dead you wouldn't be far wrong.

Uncle Sandro's face darkened still more, and then the Abkhazian said that there lived in Gagra a certain Greek who bought up presents for the prince and then presented them to him, either himself or through his relatives.

"Built his house by doing that," the Abkhazian boasted of his friend the Greek, and offered to put Uncle Sandro in touch with him. Uncle Sandro refused. Then the Abkhazian asked Uncle Sandro to show him his present for the prince, but Uncle Sandro refused that too.

"It's nothing, a trifle," he said.

"Keep in mind," the Abkhazian said, eyeing the *khurjin* and trying to guess what was in it, "if it's an eagle you might as well give it to the dogs; he doesn't take eagles any more."

"Oh, sure, an eagle!" Uncle Sandro said, rejoicing over his bird. "It almost pecked me to death, and my horse too."

The Abkhazian went his way. Uncle Sandro, left alone, darkened again.

"So when will they cut the damn doors?" he shouted after the Abkhazian.

"No one knows!" the Abkhazian said gleefully over his shoulder. "All I can say is I wouldn't want to be Engineer Bartmer, not for a million rubles."

The Abkhazian waved and disappeared around the corner, still rejoicing that he was not Engineer Bartmer.

Uncle Sandro rode on. He came to the Hotel Alpine and caught sight of the luckless watchman. Uncle Sandro asked him if he couldn't see Prince Oldenburgsky, for whom he had brought a small curio. To this the watchman replied that he could not see the prince and, like the Abkhazian, began telling him again about the unhung doors and the Austrian prisoners, although he said nothing about Engineer Bartmer.

You can imagine what it was like for Uncle Sandro, hearing all this a second time. On top of that, the watchman wanted to know what kind of present he was bringing Prince Oldenburgsky.

"Stone or animal?" he asked.

"It's not an eagle, anyway," Uncle Sandro replied, barely restraining himself.

Realizing that he would not succeed in seeing the prince because of the foolish unhung doors, Uncle Sandro lost hope and asked the watchman how to find the Greek who bought odd items for the prince. The watchman made no reply to this, merely gave him a suspicious look and became sternly reserved, as if alluding to his job.

Uncle Sandro swallowed this insult, but lest the watchman think he was intimidated, he got down from his horse and began drinking water from the fountain in front of the hotel entrance, although he was not thirsty.

Bending down, Uncle Sandro had taken five or six gulps from the fountain, when suddenly he heard an obscene noise emitted by the watchman's infidel ass.

Disoriented by the strange goings-on in Gagra, tormented to exhaustion by the bird, Uncle Sandro had reached his limit. He let go of his horse, leaped at the watchman, grabbed his rifle, and struck him on the head with the butt. Spurting blood, the watchman fell to the ground beside his hotel. The servants emerged from the hotel, seized Uncle Sandro, and sent him off to the police station.

Uncle Sandro told the prince all this, discarding unnecessary details along the way, and, conversely, dwelling on the useful ones. Thus, he decided the Smith & Wesson was not worth mentioning, while the distance from the shore to the black swan he boldly enlarged to a half-mile.

"But how could you have seen it from the shore?" the prince asked in surprise.

"We Chegemians have sharp eyes," Uncle Sandro explained modestly.

Prince Oldenburgsky glanced meaningfully at the aide-de-camp.

"He found it up near Gudauta," the aide-de-camp reminded him.

"And the binoculars?" Alexander Petrovich asked, to which the aide-de-camp could find no reply.

"You mean," the prince said, turning to Uncle Sandro, "all Chegemians have sharp eyes?"

"Yes," Uncle Sandro said without blinking his sharp Chegemian eyes. "It's our water."

"I wonder what the water's like," Prince Oldenburgsky said thoughtfully. "I'll have to send a man up for a sample."

Uncle Sandro looked at the prince, his clear gaze expressing his readiness to supply all specifications regarding the Chegemian springs.

"I'm giving you a present for your inquisitive spirit and keenness of vision," Prince Oldenburgsky said, and he nodded toward the aide-de-camp's binoculars. The aide-de-camp silently took them off and handed them to Uncle Sandro. Uncle Sandro thanked the prince and hung the binoculars around his neck.

"Lucky stiff," the interpreter said in Abkhazian.

Uncle Sandro passed over the incident with the watchman rather lightly, trying not to spoil the good impression made by the rest of the story. He said that while passing the hotel he had decided to slake his thirst, and when he dismounted and began drinking from the fountain, the watchman, for no reason at all, blasted a fart at him, which in Abkhazia is considered a dreadful insult. That he couldn't take.

A savage, Alexander Petrovich thought, but what a sense of dignity.

He nodded to his interpreter. "Ask him how he knows the watchman meant to insult him."

"There was nobody else there," Uncle Sandro replied.

The retinue burst out laughing. The prince frowned: his retinue was beginning to be infected by his own not-quite-legitimate sympathy for this young man.

"And if the watchman dies?" the prince asked, trying to grasp the psychology of what the young aborigine had done.

"Well, it was in the cards," Uncle Sandro replied. To make himself quite clear he tapped his index finger on his forehead.

"Then we'll banish you to hard labor," the prince said, still trying to force this stubbornly unreflective young man to an awareness of the full tragic absurdity of his act.

"I know, to Siberia," Uncle Sandro corrected him. He added, "Well, that's fate."

"But if he did it unintentionally?" the prince persisted.

"He should have said immediately, before I had time to get insulted, 'No offense meant, it was an accident!' " Uncle Sandro answered joyfully, indicating that in the absence of malice aforethought one could always find a common language.

Prince Oldenburgsky became thoughtful. Uncle Sandro, sensing that the interrogation was over, turned his *khurjin* inside out and squatted down by the pond to wash it.

A savage, but how freely he behaves, Alexander Petrovich thought. They haven't known serfdom, that's why . . .

At that point a wheeled chair drawn by a little donkey passed along the park mall. In it, her withered head bobbing, was Princess Evgenia Maximilyanovna. The donkey's bridle was held by a cossack. A second cossack steadied the carriage from behind. The retinue bowed. Noticing nothing, the princess rode past like a terrible dream.

"Who's that?" Uncle Sandro quietly asked the interpreter when he caught sight of this dreadful spectacle.

"His wife," the interpreter replied, just as quietly.

"What a wife," Uncle Sandro sighed, pitying the prince.

"Your Highness, what shall we do about this?" the police chief asked, sensing that it would be both unseemly and dangerous to take up any more of the prince's time.

"If the watchman comes to, let him go, and if anything happens, we'll try him," the prince said.

Uncle Sandro started back with the interpreter and the police chief. His escort could barely keep pace with him now; he wanted to catch up with the carriage and look once more at the face of the dreadful princess.

The police chief was having trouble thinking through the prince's remark, trying to penetrate to its hidden meaning, to guess whether there was a trap, a secret trial. He sensed that the prince had liked the criminal for some reason, but on the other hand, it pleased him—the prince—to execute the laws rigorously.

"They haven't known slavery, that's one good thing about the Abkhazians," the prince said significantly, addressing the retinue. The retinue sighed, and several faces seemed to express a certain belated guilt for the prolonged slavery of serfdom in their native land.

The boom of a muzzle-loading cannon resounded from the pier, officially proclaiming midday. Prince Oldenburgsky cast a sidelong look at his retinue. The retinue was pointedly immobile, expressing complete confidence in the accuracy of the muzzle-loading cannon. It used to be that as soon as the cannon went off someone would glance at his watch, as if hoping the cannon might be mistaken. But the cannon could not be mistaken, because it was connected to the clock-tower by an electric wire.

Twelve o'clock was when dinner break began at all the working places of Gagra. Furthermore, it was time to feed the pelicans and herons.

The pink pelican had charged into the water when it heard the shot and was now rocketing across the pond.

In a few moments the harbormaster appeared at the pond carrying a wet landing net full of horse mackerel. Prince Oldenburgsky demanded the very freshest fish to feed the pelicans, which is why the harbormaster always kept on hand a net full of fish, submerged in the sea. Fish kept that way were like fresh-caught, at least for twenty-four hours.

When it spotted the harbormaster, the pelican came out of the water and ran toward him, clucking and spreading its enormous wings. No matter how much of a hurry it was in, the pelican stopped at the edge of the mall where the green turf ended—it knew that one did not go farther. The female pelican, more reticent, came waddling along behind, and then the herons, who in their extreme modesty stopped somewhat short of the mall.

The birds had adapted better than other people to the social order Prince Oldenburgsky was inculcating with such energy. The birds and the workmen in the repair shops—which was why he loved these two above all.

The feeding began. Alexander Petrovich took a large horse mackerel from the net and threw it to the pelican. Opening its monstrous bill, the pelican caught it adroitly on the fly, like a dog. For a moment one could see the fish sliding, falling, down the trough of the lower jaw. The mouth slammed to with the authoritative sound of a shut umbrella. Alexander Petrovich threw a fish to the female pelican. The same noble bony sound with metallic overtones, only a smaller umbrella. This was repeated many times over, and the mouths of the pelicans kept clacking away, seizing the fish.

Sometimes Alexander Petrovich purposely threw a horse mackerel that had been beheaded. Both pelicans, with an angry toss of their unopened bills, would rebuff this attempt to slip them a low-quality mackerel. Each time, the headless fish was detected unerringly and on the fly, to the sorrowful admiration of

Alexander Petrovich. Oh, if only the rulers of Russia, and her peoples, were this accurate in grasping high-quality ideas and rejecting faulty ones!

At last the pelicans were full. The female walked away, and the male stood immobile—pink marble wings outspread and primitive bill jutting forward—poised like a mysterious heraldic device. The herons modestly dispatched the remains of the fish, including the headless ones.

Alexander Petrovich felt his inner harmony returning.

"Let's go see if they've cut the doors to the barracks," he said to his retinue, wiping his hands on a clean towel proffered by the harbormaster.

As he was getting into the car beside the leather-clad chauffeur, he thought, If all goes well, I'll drop in on Kartuchikha after dinner. Actually, he thought, it wouldn't be an infringement on my order. The order placing her under house arrest, which still had two days to go, in no way precluded daily massage. He had canceled the massage as a sign of his personal disfavor, although it was he himself who had suffered thereby.

"Say that I shall come after dinner," he told the aide-de-camp. By sitting down next to the chauffeur, the prince had blocked his attempt to get into the car. He had to make the point that the aide-de-camp's fruitless tour of the bay in search of the black swan would not go unpunished. The aide-de-camp put on a penitent expression, although he was glad he would not have to stand around at the stinking barracks.

The Benz drove along toward the Zhoekvara Gorge. An occasional pedestrian would stop and stare at the prince's conveyance and at Oldenburgsky himself. He lay back on the seat as if he had complete trust in the impetuously speeding motor and could therefore allow his own impetuous drive to rest. His hand lay on his chest, the thumb hooked through the catch of his full-dress uniform. The curved handle of his famous cane now hung over his bony wrist—a reliable sign that his spirit was serene.

Half an hour later the jolly Abkhazian that Uncle Sandro had met that morning lost his mythical million: Engineer Bartmer was forgiven, in view of the fact that the last door in the last barracks (order: every third window in each facade) had been hung by the time the prince arrived.

At six o'clock that evening the prince's huge back received a deserved dose of bliss. The prince lay in Kartuchikha's bedroom on the low divan, in which, over the years, his big body had worn a comfortable hollow. Kartuchikha worked over him the way a tenant farmer, wearied with longing, works over his own little plot. Alexander Petrovich slept. The last waves of bliss flowed down to his feet and up to the back of his neck. Kartuchikha covered him with a light blanket and stole out of the bedroom.

A moment later, slamming the gate, she went down the street to her neighbor the Turkish coffee chef, ostensibly to buy coffee. Actually she wanted to show people that the phase of great anger had given way to grace. Although Prince Oldenburgsky had not lifted his punishment, she knew from experience that once

Alexander Petrovich's back had tasted massage it would intercede for her itself and in the end would mitigate the severe precision of his order.

On the street Kartuchikha encountered an orderly running from the hospital to the police station.

"Where are you going, Serafim?" Kartuchikha asked, stopping him.

The orderly looked at her in a daze. "The watchman came to and asked for water," he said. "I'm off to the police."

"Ah," Kartuchikha said. "Run along, then."

The orderly hurried on. When he heard the orderly's report, the deputy chief of police, executing his chief's order with precision, personally opened the door to Uncle Sandro's cell and released him, saying, "Get the hell out of here while the watchman's still conscious. If I had my way—"

Uncle Sandro did not wait to find out what his way might be, although he surmised that it promised him no good. He hastily led his horse from the police stable and rode out to the street.

Uncle Sandro didn't make it to that memorial feast in the village of Achandara, because, not having much confidence in the watchman's health, he decided to take no chances and go home to Chegem. The binoculars dangling on his chest weighed pleasantly on his neck, a reminder of his amazing encounter with the amazing Prince Oldenburgsky.

I should add that after the revolution Prince Oldenburgsky moved to Finland, where, according to rumor, he busied himself with civilizing some little town, which he named New Gagra for old times' sake. Whether he continued his experiments because he was counting on the prompt fall of the Soviets, or whether his energetic nature simply could not endure stagnation remains unknown. Nor is anything known of his later fate, either to me or to the owner of the splendid binoculars.

"He wished people well," Uncle Sandro used to say with a sigh. "But more than a few of them turned out to be sons of bitches . . ."

GAMBLERS

FOR THREE DAYS and three nights, in the grand salon in the mansion of the famous tobacco merchant Kolya Zarhidis, a major game had been under way.

They were playing *nard*. Three times that night fresh candles had been put in the candlesticks, and one by one the players had dropped out, moved to cosier corners where they drank wine and played cards for small stakes. Several people were clustered around the low table in the middle of the salon, like a corps de ballet with two principle soloists—the master of the house and an Endursk cattle dealer.

Uncle Sandro knew Kolya Zarhidis because Kolya bought tobacco from his father, and besides he owned several plantations in Chegem as well as in other villages. In summer, Kolya Zarhidis' relatives, especially those who were worn down by the then-prevalent Colchian fever, were often guests in Uncle Sandro's house. Kolya, too, had been there.

Whenever he came to the city, Uncle Sandro observed the highland tradition of mutual hospitality by calling on his friend, who valued in Uncle Sandro his fleetness of foot when it was a matter of dangerous adventure, and his firmness on his feet when drinking.

In spite of his solid prestige as a prominent tobacco merchant, Kolya Zarhidis was notorious in Abkhazia for being a hard-drinking gambler. Or to put it more exactly, in spite of being a notorious drinker and gambler, Kolya Zarhidis had not lost his inherited nose for tobacco and flair as a merchant.

Preparations for this game had been made well in advance. Among those present were several secret confederates of the cattle dealer, and an even larger, none-too-secret contingent of Kolya's. Prominent among his friends was Uncle Sandro, whom Kolya had forewarned and invited. Anything could happen in a game like this, he had to be ready for all eventualities.

Kolya Zarhidis had been counting on winning a bundle in this game. But providence saw fit to arrange otherwise. For three days and three nights, with only short breaks, the small, pale Greek sat across from the sprawling, broad-shouldered cattle dealer, who had the tufted brow and keen eyes of a wily old boar.

Lucky Kolya was losing this time. If he succeeded in taking *oin*, the cattle dealer answered with *mars*—that is, a double game. The cattle dealer played boldly and expansively, left himself open and let his stones be taken. The captive stones would unexpectedly break through the Greek's defense and end by capturing his stones and dragging them off.

Four times the Greek changed the dice, but nothing helped; they fell the way the cattle dealer wanted. He was in good form, and every time, from a dozen possible combinations, he almost unerringly chose the one that would keep his game going best. In the same way, from a herd of soft-eyed calves, he could divine and put his brand on the one that would some day be the mightiest, the sternest-browed bull.

Besides, he was lucky, as cattle dealers all over the world are lucky. And nothing so inspires, so sharpens facility, as luck, while nothing so facilitates luck as inspired play.

Over these three days and nights, the protagonists had had several unpleasant squabbles in connection with the appraisal of certain plantations, but everything turned out all right, because on this last night the Persian merchant Ali Khan, as a representative of a solid neutral nation, had been invited to arbitrate.

Ali Khan kept a coffeehouse and bake shop called the Idler, where he sold Eastern sweets that he made himself, hard and soft drinks, and, of course, Turkish coffee.

After all the plantations had been lost, Ali Khan was told he could go home, but for some reason he stayed on and began helping the young hostess, the tobacco merchant's mistress, as she made coffee and served the guests. This round, sleepy girl, an ox-eyed beauty named Dasha, was someone Kolya Zarhidis had stolen, or rather borrowed, from an officer friend of his at the garrison, a high-roller like himself. Kolya had liked Dasha for quite a while; he might even have fallen in love with her if he had had more time. But Kolya had no time, and that was why, one night, when he and his friends were returning by phaeton from an out-of-town carouse (Dasha and the officer were riding in the same carriage with him), he asked the officer, "What would you say to Dasha coming with me?"

"I'd say 'Whew!' " the officer replied.

Dasha was from Ekaterinodar. The officer, returning from leave in Russia, had stopped there to visit a friend. Almost in jest, for laughs, he had secretly abducted her from the house, promising to show her Moscow and to marry her there.

Only in Tuapse, when she caught sight of the sea, did Dasha guess that they were heading not for Moscow but, indeed, in the opposite direction. She stood up to get out of the diligence, which was now rolling along beside the sea, but the diligence was going too fast, and besides there were strangers in it. Suddenly shy of the strangers, Dasha sighed and sat down. Two days later, when they were already approaching Mukhus, she regained her calm and said that the sea reminded her of the steppe, except that you could walk on the steppe but not on the sea.

The officer had lived with her four years now. He whipped her, to arouse her interest in life or get at her sleeping soul, or at least break her of recounting her dreams in the mornings, dreams endless as roads on the steppe, their monotonous landmarks her erotic mirages.

As he saw it, he was tolerating Dasha while he waited for a felicitous marriage, when he would be able to get out of the army, out of the Caucasus, out of this malarial hole with its extravagantly mediocre provincial binges. But there was no good match to be had here, and in Moscow he lacked sufficient furlough time and useful acquaintances. While stationed at the garrison he had become enough of a Caucasian that he could share a meal or a toast with the local tobacco merchants, but not enough so that any of them wanted to have him as a relative and allot him a share of the family hoard, much less take him on as a partner.

Dasha flourished on the easy life of the Caucasus, and as is typical of the Slavic nature, she quickly adapted to alien forms of bliss. She took part in her lover's carouses, disturbing his table mates with her youthful abundance and slumberous bloom.

Best of all she liked to drink Turkish coffee, washing it down with famous Logidze Brothers lemon fizz. She learned to tell fortunes; after drinking her coffee she would turn the cup over and let the coffee grounds drip out, then peer into them. The readings of the coffee grounds she correlated with scenes from her dreams, amalgamated them, mentally projecting the crooked line of fate.

"Something's going to happen," she would say with a sigh when she finished her divinations.

The readings of the coffee grounds, underwritten by the dreams, actually did come to pass, because there is always something happening in life.

So now, when she heard her lover's conversation with Kolya, Dasha realized that what was happening was what had to happen, and she said nothing. She only bit her lip in chagrin and tied her kerchief more securely around her neck, as if she felt on her face the wind of fate. Besides, she was hurt that her lover had replied with a sigh of relief, and she realized with sad resignation that she could never forgive him for it.

From this moment on, her flickering consciousness turned to Kolya. She recalled that she had always liked the impetuous little Greek, she had felt an almost motherly tenderness for him. The only trouble was that his endless flitting about used to make her head spin; she always wanted to slow him down, although she did not know how. Here, in the fact that even before tonight she had wanted to calm Kolya Zarhidis, Dasha divined a hint of long-ordained fate, and finally regained her composure. She began to think how she would tangle him in an enveloping tenderness, swathe him in caresses, croon to him.

He'll probably slow down, she thought, trying in advance not to omit—and most importantly, not to forget—the new dreams she would have in her new place.

Early the next morning, while Dasha diligently slept in her new place, Kolya got up (disentangled himself after all) and went as usual to the coffeehouse, where over *khash*, brandy, and Turkish coffee he sobered up and obtained the latest commercial data.

Kolya had gone out, but his numerous kin remained at home. When his mother went into his bedroom—as she habitually did in the morning, to tidy it up and determine by the smell of it where her son had been drinking and how much he had had—she suddenly found a woman in her son's bed. The old woman let out a shriek. It had never happened before that her one and only son, Kolya Zarhidis, had brought a Russian woman into an honest Greek house. At her shriek the kinswomen came running, a dozen bowlegged and tradition-bound dependents.

Dasha opened her eyes and tried to get up, smiling the dazed smile of a high school girl remembering her first school dance. Actually she was trying to remember that night's dreams. The women's expressions and the ruckus they were making gradually brought Dasha around to the hostile waking world. She made one more attempt to stand up and did in fact sit up in bed, amazedly looking around at the women and listening to their hostile alien babble.

"Kolya and I decided," she began, clasping the blanket to her, and suddenly she sank into a reverie, flooding the women with the delightful contagion of the sin she had incurred in her sleep.

"*Diabolos!*" they screamed. Tripping over each other's feet in the doorway, they dashed out of the room.

That evening all the relatives, among whom were a good many respected merchants, gathered for a family council at the Zarhidis house. Kolya's grown-up married sisters raged like hungry tigresses. Several times during the council they burst into his bedroom, where Dasha awaited her fate, in order to beat her up. Fortunately their husbands intercepted them in time and dragged them back with an exaggerated display of zeal.

When they had been subdued, the sisters proposed that Kolya be declared insane and placed in custodianship. But this method must have struck sophisticated people as archaic even then, because the respected merchants raised objections. They asserted that the other tobacco dealers would promptly take advantage of it to undermine his commercial reputation. Kolya's mother, too, found it offensive to declare him insane and she did not support her daughters.

Kolya himself laughed at his relatives openly and insolently, because he was sure of his trump card: he was his father's only son, and there was no possible way to carry on the glorious Zarhidis line without resorting to his necessarily voluntary services.

In the end, on the advice of the eldest male relative, they decided to wait until Kolya tired of Dasha, because, as he explained, a man will get tired of any woman if no one tries to take her away from him.

Pursing her lips, Kolya's mother dolefully agreed to this decision, but the sisters demanded that Kolya say exactly when he would tire of her.

"How should I know!" Kolya exclaimed, gleefully throwing up his hands.

As they departed, the sisters cast wrathful glances at the door behind which Dasha awaited her fate. Their husbands, envying Kolya, lingered thoughtfully on the marble staircase.

The decision to wait until Kolya tired of Dasha proved fateful. The end was quite the opposite—quiet, slumberous Dasha outlived the dozen warlike and noisy Greek women.

As in all southern houses, early morning was a scene of furious activity in Kolya's mansion. The numerous kinswomen grabbed their twig brooms, scrubbed furiously with their floor rags, and rattled their pails as they ran for water. All these dependents, at the full-throated direction of Kolya's mother, creaked their market baskets, banged table legs around, scraped the melted wax from candlesticks and the layer of organic excrescences from mussels, picked over mountains of rice seeking defective grains, quarreled with the fruit vendors who rode into the mansion's courtyard on their donkeys, leaned over windowsills and balconies to batter innocent mattresses with sticks, whispered with Greek matchmakers, lived in constant anticipation of unknown guests, and listened with horror to the news from Russia, where, according to rumor, the workers had no mercy on Greek merchants or even on their own czar, having left him and his wife and children without so much as a crust of bread.

And now what? Amid this mighty affirmation of family life, of home and hearth, walked a slumberous, ox-eyed woman, padding across the wet floor in her bare feet, trying to tell people her dreams of the steppe, as incomprehensible and needless to them as felt boots to a Cypriot.

And this woman had captured the heart of the only son, who was to carry on the glorious Zarhidis line! Where was justice, where was the divine plan? The gods had truly turned their backs on Greece and on every Greek individually.

At dinner one time Dasha refused to eat the mussel pilaf.

"Why?" her mother-in-law asked mildly, against her will.

"They're disgusting, they're like snails," Dasha said, not suspecting that snails were even more of a national dish than mussel pilaf. For the Black Sea Greeks, at any rate.

"Borsch ees better?" Kolya's mama asked, with the same mild curiosity. The household dependents stared at Dasha wide-eyed, trying not to make any noise with their jaws. A storm was brewing, but Dasha did not understand.

"Of course," Dasha said. "Mama made such good borsch—"

"Go back mama, I geev you money," Kolya's mother suggested caressingly.

"I can't," Dasha sighed. "Papa might kill me."

"I keell too," the old woman said distinctly, and she got up from the table. The dependents followed her, frightened to death.

That same day, a lugubrious little procession led by Kolya Zarhidis' mother left the mansion, walked across town, and hid in the house of one of Kolya's sisters. True, there remained at home a devoted maidservant, whom the old woman had ordered to keep a sharp eye on this Russian *diabolos* who dreamed of ruining her son, to the delight of competing tobacco merchants.

She was sure that the officer had been bribed by the tobacco merchants to palm Dasha off on her unsophisticated son. By degrees, through reliable people, she undertook to discover how much the officer had received for this operation so that she would not overpay him by too much when she attempted to unload Dasha. It is said that she met with him, but there were no witnesses present, so no one knows for certain.

Day after day Dasha sat on the balcony of the mansion in a short-sleeved dressing gown, glancing at the street, sipping coffee and washing down every swallow with famous Logidze Brothers lemon fizz. If anyone she knew passed by in the street, Dasha would hail him and ask, "Have you seen Kolya?"

"I have, at the coffeehouse," the passerby usually answered.

"Send him home," Dasha usually ordered, taking a sip of coffee.

If the passerby answered that he had not seen Kolya, Dasha was not distressed.

"Send him home if you do," she would request, and immediately forget about the man she had just spoken to. He would stand there, shifting from one foot to the other, expecting something further; finally, sighing for some unknown reason, he would go his now-dim way.

That was how she usually spent her day, unless she was puttering about in the mansion's courtyard, where she laid out a row of sunflowers among the laurels that Kolya's father had planted.

Once when Dasha was sitting on the balcony drinking coffee as usual, her ex-lover came riding up to the house. He reined back his horse, looked up, and said, "Riding high, Dasha?"

"I don't mind that you beat me," Dasha answered, still holding the demitasse in her hand and resting her bosom on the balcony railing. "What I mind is that you said 'whew.' "

"You've had your fling and it's over," the officer advised in a conciliatory tone. "His mama has run away from you."

"I love Kolya now," Dasha answered, "but I can't respect sea snails . . ."

With rising irritation the officer began to harangue her, switching from recollections of their love to threats and back. Dasha listened to him quietly. Laying her head on the railing, she stuck out a round, ungainly arm and dripped the remains of the coffee grounds out of the cup, trying to hit the horse's twitching ear. Finally she did. Rattling the bridle, the horse tossed his head.

"Then you don't want me?" the officer asked. Ox-eyed Dasha, her cheek still resting on the railing, quietly shook her frowsy head.

"Obviously I didn't beat you enough, Dasha," the officer shouted. Striking the horse with his whip, he galloped away toward the sea.

"Obviously not," Dasha repeated, and she burst into tears, still lying with her cheek on the railing. The overturned cup dangled forgotten in her hand.

So Dasha stayed on for good with the dissolute Kolya Zarhidis. That evening Kolya's eldest sister tried to break into the mansion to settle Dasha's account with her own hand. Fortunately Kolya was home. He chained the front door shut, but she broke in through the courtyard entry. Kolya barely managed to intercept her. By way of pathetic revenge she felled all the sunflowers in Dasha's flower bed, which grieved Dasha deeply. That same night Kolya personally boarded up the door to the courtyard and ordered Dasha not to open the front door until she had looked from the balcony to see who was there.

"I'm always on the balcony anyway," Dasha said.

Ten days after his visit to Dasha, the officer, her ex-lover, shot himself. He had been drinking heavily the whole time, but that morning, according to his orderly, he was calm and absolutely sober. Sitting at his table and looking into the mirror, he gave himself a careful shave, then told his orderly to bring him a towel soaked in hot water. The orderly brought the towel, helped him with his hot compress, after which the officer handed back the towel and said, "Thank you, old chap."

As he went out with the towel, the orderly glanced back and saw the officer—who was peering sidewise into the mirror as if to even off his sideburns with the razor—carefully raise the pistol to his temple, look into the mirror, and fire. Some people said this was a covert case of the D.T.'s, others said there was a woman mixed up in it. Curiously, no one thought of Dasha, because everyone knew how he had treated her and how he had unkindly said "whew" when he turned her over to the Greek.

Under cross-examination the orderly repeated his story; only he confessed that the officer had not said "Thank you, old chap" before firing. He had thought that part up himself to lend beauty to the misfortune.

When he sent in his report, the garrison commander wrote that the officer had laid hands on himself during one of his recurrent bouts of tropical fever—thereby ennobling the delirium tremens version of the story.

That was how matters stood in the life of the trim little Greek when he and the hulking Endursky settled down to play to the death at the low game table in the middle of the salon.

The game continued. Pale petals of fire quivered on the candles when the cattle dealer shook the twittering dice in his hand. He threw them to the board, then beat his breast with the same hand, as if taking an oath.

Spinning madly, the two little cubes rolled over the varnished surface of the game board.

"*Shash-besh!*"

"Johan, I beg you!"

"*Du-se!*"

"Johan, I beg you—please?"

"*Charu-se!*"

"*Du-yak!*"

"Johan, I beg you as a brother!"

"*Dort-char!*"

"Johan—one! Johan—two! Johan—three! Johan—four!"

The click of the stones being moved, especially when they were laid on top of ones that were being taken, was like the crack of a jailer's whip. Despair vibrated in Kolya's voice when he announced the roll of the dice or called out the roll he desired. The cattle dealer, because he was winning, played noisily, spoke familiarly to fate; he called his dice with laughter, with humorous catch phrases, which unnerved the Greek and gave the Endursky an added psychological advantage.

"*Shash-besh*-hey!" he said. "Bear 'em away!"

"*Du-bara*-dubrinsky," he reported, "dances the *lezginky!*"

Kolya Zarhidis continued to lose. The plantations and the two tobacco warehouses were long gone. The mansion had already been put into play, and game by game the Endursk cattle dealer was gobbling it up, in big slices like a Christmas pie.

It was getting light. Uncle Sandro paced nervously up and down the salon. He was looking for a way out of the situation and could not find one. Two of the guests exchanged glances and quietly left. Uncle Sandro surmised that these men had connections with the other tobacco merchants, who were vitally interested in being the first to know the final outcome of the game. He had to save Kolya, had to stop the game and turn it around, but how could he do that and still preserve the proprieties?

From an excess of energy Uncle Sandro took a look in the kitchen, where the Persian merchant, with suppressed excitement, was trying to prove something to Dasha. From the next room came a low funeral chant; Kolya had locked up the maidservant so that she wouldn't spy on him and meddle in the game.

It struck Uncle Sandro that the Persian merchant was already trying to persuade Dasha to run away with him. In any case, at the sight of Uncle Sandro the merchant fell silent and shrugged his shoulders, to let him know that he had said nothing of the kind, and even if he had he could take back his words then and there. He lowered his long lashes—too long for a man his age—to extinguish the urgent glitter in his eyes, which did more than any words to betray the secret strivings of this Khorasanian voluptuary. Uncle Sandro said nothing and left the kitchen. He did not take this seriously, the danger lay elsewhere.

Uncle Sandro went back to the table to follow the next game. The cattle dealer looked up and surveyed the ceiling of the salon in a proprietary way. All of a sudden, with a silent nod to Uncle Sandro, he pointed to a corner, where the paint of an ornamental design was peeling a little from dampness.

It was as if the new master of the house had summoned an artisan and pointed out the work that needed doing. It cost Uncle Sandro great effort to restrain himself. He forced himself to become absorbed in the game, especially since Kolya was winning this one.

But when the cattle dealer turned even this game around—reentering all his captive stones from the bar and capturing his opponent's stones too along the way, which inexorably led the Greek to his next loss—Uncle Sandro could stand no more. He seized a silver fruit knife lying on the table and struck the table with such force that the knife broke. The blade went whistling past the cattle dealer's head and hit the wall. The cattle dealer didn't bat an eye. He merely ran his thumbnail along the gouge the knife had left on the surface of the table and said, "The finish . . ."

Uncle Sandro had noticed that the more the cattle dealer won, the more insolently he stared at Dasha. When he accepted coffee from her hands he would take a sip and smack his lips. Then, staring at her magnificent bosom, he would pay her an ambiguous compliment: "That's nice cream, very nice . . ."

This time, when Dasha had collected the empty demitasse cups and departed sleepily to the kitchen, the cattle dealer beckoned one of his men and whispered something in his ear. Uncle Sandro took it all in but pretended not to notice anything. Presently the man reappeared and came over to the cattle dealer. Uncle Sandro quietly went to the kitchen.

Dasha stood by the stove with downcast eyes. The Persian merchant excitedly paced the kitchen, from time to time throwing up his hands under the explosive pressure of an angry but silent soliloquy.

"What happened, Dasha?" Uncle Sandro asked.

"They're inviting me to Enduria; they say that Kolya's poor now," Dasha said pensively.

"What kind of people are they!" The Persian merchant clasped his hands and turned to Uncle Sandro with a look that summoned him to end the merchant's distress by taking action.

"What will you do?" Uncle Sandro asked.

"Me? I'll do as Kolya says," Dasha replied.

When he heard that, the Persian merchant again clasped his hands and said, "What kind of people are they!" His tone indicated that this time he included a broader circle of nations in his exclamation.

"As long as I'm on your side, you have nothing to fear, Dasha," Uncle Sandro said mysteriously, and he left the kitchen.

No one knows what plan Uncle Sandro would have conceived at that early hour if Dasha had not come into the salon again with another steaming tray. At the sight of her the cattle dealer abruptly leaned back in his chair and shifted a leg to one side. Gazing smilingly at Dasha, he suddenly sang out:

Bazaar is big,
Many people today.

Here come Russky girl,
Make way, make way!

"Singing!" thundered Uncle Sandro, and he flew out of the salon as if shot from a sling. All sound suddenly ceased in the salon. They could hear the grandfather clock ticking in the dining room, and the funeral chant coming from the maidservant's room.

Everyone scented mortal danger in the air. The cattle dealer, who had just this minute taken coffee from the tray, carefully lifted the cup. The Greek's supporters froze, and the cattle dealer's too, avidly watching his hand to see whether it would tremble or not. But the cattle dealer's hand did not tremble, he had the nerves of a buffalo. He drank off the coffee, licked his lips, and set the cup on the table. Then he said with a nod toward the door, "He's gone to get his guitar . . ."

The cattle dealer's supporters cheered up.

"Sandro doesn't do anything without a reason," one of the Greek's friends observed, not too confidently. The words were hardly out of his mouth when the Persian merchant came running into the salon and shouted, "Sandro's coming up!"

Almost at the same moment they heard the clatter of metal on marble, getting louder, the bronze sound of fate. The guests jumped up, not knowing what to prepare for, but the little Greek and the cattle dealer did not stir. They continued to sit at their table. And now everyone noticed the blood slowly beginning to drain from the cattle dealer's face, while the Greek's face, which had grown gray over these three days, began to turn pink, as if the two men were linked like communicating vessels, as if an invisible pressure differential had reversed the flow of their common blood.

The antique clop of hooves on marble intoxicated the little Greek's soul with forgotten valor. The Persian merchant was still standing by the doorway, and when the clopping came near he suddenly kicked open both leaves of the door and darted aside like a scared rabbit, right under the fire-breathing muzzle of the horse.

Uncle Sandro pranced through the salon at a controlled jog-trot, his wrathful glare never leaving the cattle dealer. He rode the length of the salon, opened the door for himself, and trotted out to the next room.

"Play!" Kolya shouted to the cattle dealer, who had tarried.

The cattle dealer gave the dice a limp toss, still listening to the departing hoofbeats.

"Kolya, what happened?" came a heartrending cry from the incarcerated servant.

"Sandro's walking his horse!" Kolya shouted, emboldened.

"Is he gone?" the cattle dealer asked when the clop of hooves fell silent in one of the back rooms. The Greek's friends gleefully informed him that Sandro couldn't go anywhere even if he wanted to, Kolya having been forced to board up the other exit because of his eldest sister's misbehavior.

"What's his sister got to do with it," the cattle dealer frowned, and everyone sensed that his nerves were giving way.

Uncle Sandro rode through all the rooms of the mansion. Freeing his foot from the stirrup as he went, he pushed or kicked aside the tables, chairs, and anything else that might impede the horse's movement. In the dining room, when she saw her own reflection in the big wall mirror, the horse neighed and tried to ride into it. Uncle Sandro turned her with difficulty and urged her back.

This time he charged into the hall, quirting the horse, and jumped over the gamblers' table.

"Bravo, Sandro!" the Greek's supporters shouted in one voice. The Endursky laid the dice down on the board in protest.

"Play!" Kolya ordered. He took a pistol out of his pocket and laid it on the table beside his cigar case.

"Tell him not to jump," the cattle dealer begged. "I'm not used to playing underneath a horse."

"Get a grip on your nerves and play," the Greek ordered again. He rapped the muzzle of the gun on the table, like a teacher with a pointer.

It was a ticklish situation. On the one hand, by the unwritten and therefore hard-and-fast rules of the game, the man who was winning had to play as long as the one who was losing had anything left to lose; but on the other hand, the devil only knew what Uncle Sandro was up to. The cattle dealer consulted his supporters, but, overwhelmed by Sandro's boldness, they decided he had to go on playing, provided that Sandro jumped over the game table with equal risk to both gamblers—that is, over the middle of the table.

"Why? Why does he have to jump?" the Endursky objected.

"Fate," they answered.

Again the Persian merchant was chosen to arbitrate, as a representative of a solid neutral nation.

They stationed him by the wall so that he was in a straight line with the doors and the middle of the table and could see exactly how far Uncle Sandro's horse deviated in her flight.

Play was resumed. Uncle Sandro jumped only in one direction, because there was not enough room for a running start in the other direction. So he usually ambled out of the salon, not forgetting to cast a wrathful glance at the cattle dealer.

Every time he heard the approaching hoofbeats the Endursky ducked, pulling his head into his shoulders, and froze until the horse had cleared the table. As soon as the horse completed the jump, he looked hopefully at the Persian merchant. But the latter shook his head sadly, meaning that Sandro had not faulted this time either.

Sometimes when Uncle Sandro galloped up to the table he would unexpectedly turn aside, as if he had miscalculated his approach, and go back for a fresh start. These false attempts flustered the cattle dealer still more.

With Uncle Sandro's every jump the little Greek became ever more confident, more cheerful—his erstwhile luck was returning to him. One time he raised his coffee cup and took a gulp just as the horse's belly flew over with a whoosh of hot air. "Bravo, Kolya!" the Greek's partisans roared, applauding.

The cattle dealer's spirits flagged.

"The horse is getting tired," he said worriedly after the tenth jump.

"It's all right, she's been standing too long," Uncle Sandro answered, patting her neck, and he rode out of the salon to get ready for the next leap. A moment later there was a fearful crash from the depths of the house. It sounded as if both horse and rider had bitten the dust.

The cattle dealer jumped up and shouted joyfully, "I told you so, the horse is tired!"

But now the hoofbeats of the approaching horse rang out anew. The cattle dealer, who was still standing, began pulling his head into his shoulders as he slowly sank into his chair.

"Sandro, what happened?" the other guests shouted in one voice when he appeared in the doorway.

"She thought there was another horse coming toward her," he explained when he landed, stroking the excited horse's neck to calm her a little. "What she doesn't know is that there's not another like her in all Abkhazia."

In fact, although of a local breed, this was a horse of a rather strange color—a bay, but brightly dappled like a lynx. Uncle Sandro used to say that horse thieves had twice run from his father's stable on suddenly spotting her among the other horses. Although it is hard to be sure why the horse thieves ran, Uncle Sandro's story is that they mistook his horse for a wild beast stationed to guard the ordinary horses.

"I couldn't hold her head at all," continued Uncle Sandro, on his way out of the salon, shaking off fine splinters of the mirror like drops of water.

"Why?" the Greek's supporters asked in delight.

"The neck she has," Uncle Sandro said, already at the doorway, "she could lift a steamboat." He rode out of the salon without a backward glance.

"That horse suits him," Dasha said, looking after him thoughtfully.

It goes without saying that the cattle dealer lost game after game, about one loss for every four jumps.

"Well, how's it going?" Uncle Sandro would ask as he took his horse over the players.

"I've got *oin*," the Greek would answer joyfully as he set up the board, if the game was over.

This extraordinary tournament went on for two and a half hours under the belly of the flying horse. During this time Kolya Zarhidis succeeded in winning back all his losses, plus all the cash the cattle dealer was carrying and the carriage in which he had arrived from Enduria.

The Endurian slaughterhouses would probably have been put into play if the horse had not actually tired. After the fortieth jump, Uncle Sandro did not head out of the salon but rode right up to the table and made the horse rear. For several soul-shattering seconds he stood over the players, with the horse wheezing and dripping bloody foam on the game board.

As soon as the horse lowered her hooves, the cattle dealer stood up.

"I'm the loser, and I quit," he said, the words tumbling out in a strange rush. Suddenly everyone noticed that he was no longer an all-powerful cattle dealer, just a broken old man.

"As you wish," Kolya replied, concealing the pistol in his pocket. The correctitude of the prominent tobacco merchant had returned to him.

Still aroused, Uncle Sandro rode out on the balcony. He unbuttoned his shirt and bared his chest to the cool morning breeze.

Peasants from neighboring villages were walking to market, driving donkeys laden with huge panniers of greens, fruit, red-cropped turkeys. Dockhands, hunched against the cool of the morning, trudged toward the port, and little bands of alcoholics hailed each other brightly as they hastened purposefully to the *khash* shops and coffeehouses.

Uncle Sandro looked out over the morning city with an air of weary triumph.

"Sandro, I ask you as a brother!" Kolya shouted. "Someone will see and tell my mother about the horse."

"You should kiss my horse's ass," Uncle Sandro said, riding into the salon.

"I will, I swear by the dust of my father," Kolya replied.

The servant, now released, carried out a pailful of broken plates. Uncle Sandro's horse had poked a hind foot through the dining-room sideboard. Aside from the mirror and the sideboard, and a chunk of marble the size of a fist, which the horse's hoof chipped from the staircase when he was leaving the house, Uncle Sandro's jumping and racing inflicted no damage on the mansion.

The cattle dealer was allowed to go as far as the Hotel Oriental in his own carriage. From there he set out for Enduria that same day in the local diligence.

They say that his affairs went to rack and ruin that year. Another cattle dealer emerged as his competitor in Enduria. He secretly bought wholesale a huge lot of starving cattle in Kuban and drove them to summer pastures in the alpine meadows. In the fall, hordes of fattened Kuban cattle charged the markets of Enduria and ruined the old cattle dealer.

They say that after two such blows the old man was unhinged. Kolya Zarhidis, to give him his due, when he heard about this, dispatched a famous city psychiatrist from Mukhus to Enduria with orders to treat the old man at Kolya's expense until he returned to his right mind.

Strange as it may seem, it was not the psychiatrist that cured him but the October Revolution, when it really took hold in Transcaucasia. The day the old man learned that the new authorities had confiscated all of the young cattle dealer's property, he ordered fifty candles the height of a man, made of the most fragrant Tsebelda wax, to be placed in Illori Monastery in honor of Lenin. In addition he arranged a people's feast at which he fed his last ten bulls to the beggars of Enduria.

The old man was so much improved that he eventually took a job as a butcher in one of his former shops, where he worked to the end of his days.

The shock of the famous game with Kolya stayed with him in the form of a small idiosyncrasy: when he heard the clatter of a horse's hooves, even if it was an ordinary cabby's dray, the old man pulled his head into his shoulders and froze in the position in which the soul-shattering sound had caught him. His customers became used to this idiosyncrasy and did not badger him, waiting until he came out of it by himself.

After the famous victory, the feasting in Kolya Zarhidis' house and the neighboring restaurants lasted almost without interruption right up to the October Revolution (in its Transcaucasian variant), which, according to the false teachings of Trotsky, should also have developed permanently. That would have been dreadful and therefore undesirable.

Malicious tongues assert that Kolya Zarhidis rewarded Uncle Sandro by way of Dasha, but others say that this could not have been, because it was so anyway. Uncle Sandro himself rejects both these propositions with indignation to this day.

From the standpoint of the keeper of a European gambling house, Uncle Sandro's intervention in this famous game (although the only reason it is famous is that he intervened in it) may seem like impermissible pressure on a gambler's psyche. Nevertheless, I am inclined to view Uncle Sandro's deed as historically progressive.

At any rate, he helped preserve Kolya Zarhidis' property, which, with the exception of the wall mirror, the broken sideboard, and other trifles, passed intact into the hands of the Soviet authorities.

"I told you something was going to happen," Dasha reminded him when, in accordance with the decision of the local soviet, they were ordered to abandon the mansion, which they did. True, Kolya Zarhidis' mother again contrived to leave behind the maidservant, who now worked at the mansion as a cleaning woman and lived in one of the outbuildings in the courtyard. This time Kolya's mother left her to keep an eye on the Soviet authorities, a task which was undoubtedly much more complex. The mansion housed local government agencies.

Although Kolya was ruined, of course, his life was much simplified. In the first place, his mother became reconciled to his mistress, whose designs on his wealth could not harm him now. She even insisted that Kolya marry Dasha, which he did, speedily registering for the unceremonious Soviet wedding of those days.

At first they were rather hard up. Then, during the era of the New Economic Policy, the Persian merchant opened his coffeehouse and bake shop again—this time cautiously naming it the Idle Proletariat—and took on the former tobacco merchant as partner, while still trying to realize his Khorasanian designs on Dasha. Although Kolya showed up at work, all he did day in and day out was drink coffee and brandy at the expense of his former friends, and sometimes even at the expense of his former employees at the tobacco warehouses.

Apropos of this last, certain duly authorized persons used to sit down near him on purpose to try and find out whether he was stirring up his former workers. As it turned out, Kolya was not stirring up the workers, and he was left in peace to be forged anew or to wither away with the New Economic Policy, in accordance with the course of history.

Sometimes when living it up with his former friends, now déclassé drinking companions, he shouted for Ali Khan to send over a couple of bottles at his expense. Ali Khan stood at the counter, day in and day out, making coffee in *jezves* and pouring drinks.

"What expense?" Ali Khan would invariably reply when he heard this insolent shout. Spreading his hands, he would raise his round eyebrows in amazement. Nevertheless, he always sent over the bottles as requested, because Dasha was nearby. Sleepily, slowly, she carried the orders to the tables, and no one minded, because this was why they had come to the coffeehouse—to dally, to idle, in keeping with the name of the coffeehouse, to rest up from times that hurtled and rattled like empty freight cars on the rails.

But fate was once more pleased to elevate Kolya Zarhidis. Against all expectation, he was summoned to see our remarkable revolutionary, the permanent (until Beria poisoned him) president of the Council of People's Commissars of Abkhazia, Nestor Apollonovich Lakoba.

The country needed currency. Abkhazian alpine tobaccos were still remembered in the world markets. It was essential to resurrect the old trade ties and establish new ones.

Nestor Apollonovich invited Kolya into his office, located in the former Zarhidis mansion. He told him the gist of the story and ordered him to work honestly with the Soviet authorities. In return he promised to get him a decent apartment and restore to him all that could be found of the requisitioned furniture.

"Agreed," Kolya said, "but don't bother about the furniture."

"Why not?" Nestor Apollonovich said, leaning across the desk with a hand cupped to his ear. He was hard of hearing, Nestor Apollonovich. With a wicked smile (every Greek has something of Odysseus in him), Kolya nodded at the grandfather clock standing at the people's commissar's back. Nestor Apollonovich glanced behind him and said with his sweet, disarming smile, "It has a good loud chime, and I don't hear well . . ."

They did not return to the question of the furniture again. Afterwards, unlike others, Nestor Apollonovich never tried to take revenge on him for that bold gesture, because, again unlike others, he was a clever man himself and valued quick-wittedness in people.

Apropos, a small example of his quick-wittedness. Once at a conference at Tbilisi one of the speakers said that Abkhazia, in spite of repeated directives, was still slow to build highways.

"Evidently," he added, none too tactfully, "we aren't speaking loud enough about this, and Nestor Apollonovich doesn't quite hear us."

"I hear you," Nestor Apollonovich cried in the creaky voice characteristic of people with impaired hearing.

"Then by all means," the orator requested. He yielded the rostrum and limped to his seat with the gait of a man who had been lame since birth.

In his response, Nestor Apollonovich gave a clear account of road construction in Abkhazia, spoke of our shortcomings and achievements in this matter. At the end he added that although Abkhazia had built and would continue to build highways as the Party taught us to, we could not, of course, especially under our mountainous conditions, lay out a highway on which this particular comrade would not limp.

But I am digressing. Kolya Zarhidis found himself back in business. The next year he organized the purchase of tobacco from the population, its processing and subsequent sale abroad.

Nestor Apollonovich trusted him to go with the tobacco to Istanbul, from where he presently returned bringing gold. A year later Kolya Zarhidis took a still larger shipment of tobacco to Istanbul and obtained for it still more currency. Two years later he took nearly a whole boatload of fragrant alpine tobacco to Turkey and did not return. In Istanbul they gamble right in the coffeehouses, and Kolya evidently could not resist . . .

This perfidy (voluntary or involuntary) deeply grieved Nestor Apollonovich. Kolya Zarhidis' deed may well have grieved everyone but the Persian merchant, which is rather eloquent testimony to his apoliticality. He got what he wanted—Dasha remained with him.

But life was not sweet for him—the New Economic Policy ended, the state took over the economy. To start with, Ali Khan was ordered to separate the coffeehouse and bake shop and freely choose one of the two: either the coffeehouse or the bake shop. Ali Khan thought it over and chose the coffeehouse. After a while he was ordered to discontinue the sale of hard liquor in the coffeehouse and at the same time broaden his assortment of soft drinks. Ali Khan consented, but dissembled, continuing to sell hard liquor under the counter. Since the trend was toward complete suppression of the private sector, he was ordered to discontinue the sale of coffee in the coffeehouse but keep the soft drinks. This time Ali Khan did not consent and closed the coffeehouse down completely.

Ali Khan held on. He acquired a vending cart from which he hawked "heavenly sweets" that he made himself: Turkish delight, *kozinaki*, halva, sherbet. Pointlessly stubborn, he went on calling himself a merchant.

At this stage my father brought him into our courtyard. He moved in with us along with his unkempt, slovenly wife. Around the yard people called her sometimes "the former beauty," sometimes simply "the former"—evidently for short.

Day in and day out, I dimly remember, she made coffee for herself on a Turkish brazier, ordered the tall, thin old man around, and shouted after him when he went out of the yard wheeling his cart with its little showcase of the Mohammedan heaven.

Later on he stopped selling Eastern sweets for some reason and switched to roast chestnuts. The grown-ups said, unintelligibly, that he had become a morphine addict. A few years later he and his wife moved to the Crimea, and the smell of roast chestnuts gradually aired out of the yard.

Sometimes in the evening Uncle Ali Khan would sit on the doorstep of his little room, soak his corns in warm water, smoke, and sing Persian songs. I remember the chestnut vendor's glassy stare, his spellbinding melody, sweetly bitter with the meaninglessness of life and endless as a caravan trail to nowhere.

"*Bismillah irrahmani irrahim!*" Blessed is He who is blessed . . .

THE BATTLE OF THE KODOR OR THE NOY ZHORDANIA WOODEN ARMORED CAR

ONE CARELESS STEP in the barnyard is all it takes to land you in a cowpat, and that's how it was in those days, Uncle Sandro used to say: you couldn't poke your nose out of doors for fear of ending up smack in the middle of a historical incident.

This particular day, Uncle Sandro was staying with a friend of his in the village of Ankhara, situated on the picturesque bank of the Kodor. In this large and prosperous village a Menshevik detachment had been stationed for about six months now. The Reds were stationed on the other bank of the river. This was the site of what was then the only bridge over the Kodor. From this side the Mensheviks guarded the bridge against the Bolsheviks, while from the other side the Bolsheviks guarded the bridge against the Mensheviks.

At that time there was, or seemed to be, or else they pretended there was, a balance of power. At all events, both the Menshevik unit and ours were bored. Having nothing to do, and wanting to vary the soldiers' fare, they used to stun fish.

They stunned the fish about two kilometers above the bridge, and dead trout came floating downstream belly up. Sometimes a fish stunned by the Mensheviks ended up with the Bolsheviks, sometimes vice versa.

As soon as the explosions went off, little boys appeared on both sides of the river, because the soldiers and the Red Army men, no matter how hard they tried, could not net all the fish—the current was very swift, even here in the lower reaches of the Kodor.

Since it was not yet clear who was going to attack—the Bolsheviks or the Mensheviks—both sides, by mutual agreement and understanding, stunned their fish far enough above the bridge so as not to damage it. Thus there were explosions of a comparatively peaceful nature nearly every day, partly because both sides were trying to prove they had grenades and other ammunition sufficient to meet the enemy in the event of war.

When the Mensheviks first took up position in the village, they declared it a Closed City, so that the Red scouts could not spy on them. They were also somewhat afraid of the Partisan guerrillas, although, as later became clear, there weren't any Partisans around here because anyone who wanted to fight on the Bolshevik side could simply swim the Kodor and join up.

As soon as the Mensheviks declared the village a Closed City and began restricting the right of entry and exit, the villagers began to chafe. What particularly galled them was the forced separation from their friends and relatives. They could not rest until their relatives should come to town or they themselves should go and visit them.

What were they to do about the necessity, sanctified by ancient tradition, of attending a wedding or any other clan celebration? And the vigil at the bedside of a sick relative? And the anniversary of a death, or the fortieth-day memorial feast? Not to mention the funeral itself!

In brief, a murmur went up. The command, reluctant to complicate its relationship with the local population—especially as the detachment was being fed largely at their expense—and at the same time trying to save face, reversed the order and declared the village of Ankhara an Open City for everyone but the Bolsheviks.

At that the villagers subsided and began to find the separation from their friends and relatives less painful. No one was too insistent about inviting anyone, and no one went anywhere without special need. Everything was done in moderation, as dictated by custom and personal inclination.

That was how things stood in the village of Ankhara until the early days of May 1918—the very days that Uncle Sandro was visiting his friend, an inhabitant of the village. Before his eyes, history took off and went rolling down the Black Sea Highway.

Uncle Sandro's friend was named Mikha. According to his description, Mikha was a stately man, pleasant-looking and wise. Lightly spreading his arms and surveying his own impressive build, Uncle Sandro said of him, "See me? Well, he wasn't much worse."

As Uncle Sandro told it, this friend of his had gotten rich on pigs. Every fall he drove his pigs into the thickest chestnut and beech groves and kept them there until the first snow.

In those days the chestnuts and beechnuts in these groves lay knee-deep on the ground. The pigs fattened with incredible speed, so that by the end of the fall some of them could no longer stand on their feet. Crawling on their bellies, they kept on foraging and fattening. At last, when the first snow fell, the pigs were driven home, and from there to market.

The ones that succeeded in getting fattest had to be taken on donkeys, because they could not move by themselves. Of course a certain proportion were destroyed by wolves and bears, but even so the proceeds from the sale of the pigs covered this shrinkage and spillage owing to beasts of prey.

No one before him—or since him, apparently—had thought of driving pigs to autumn pasture in the chestnut forest, the way they drive herbivorous animals to summer grazing grounds.

However, all this has no bearing on the point of my story. Or rather, almost none.

Granted, it was an anxious time. And when, on the roads of Abkhazia, people began meeting pig-laden donkeys—spitefully squealing, ponderous wineskins of fat, riding on patient long-eared beasts—many, especially the old men, saw the spectacle as a dark omen.

"You'll bring disaster," they said to Mikha, standing still on the road and following this curious caravan with their eyes.

"I don't eat them myself," he would explain as he passed. "I only sell them to the infidels."

So that morning Uncle Sandro was sitting at the table having breakfast with his friend. They were eating cold meat with hot, thick cornmeal mush. Uncle Sandro would cut a neat chunk of meat, spread it with fiery *ajika*, put it in his mouth, and send after it a slice of mush, not forgetting to dip it in cherry-plum sauce. From time to time his host poured more red wine.

The talk was about how the Abkhazian highlanders, as compared to the Abkhazian lowlanders, were more conservative and still did not want to raise pigs, whereas this was a very profitable business because the mountains were full of beech and chestnut groves.

The host let it be known that he appreciated the broad-mindedness displayed by Uncle Sandro as a representative of the Abkhazian highlands, especially since right in the village of Ankhara there were many people who couldn't resign themselves at all to the fact that Mikha, just like that and all of a sudden, had gone and got rich on pigs.

Mikha's neighbors envied him, but since they could never catch up to him in wealth, there was nothing left but to shout after him that he was a bad Abkhazian.

Uncle Sandro complained that he didn't have time to take up pigs, and his father wouldn't consent to raise them out of a foolish Muslim stubbornness. Mikha promised he would speak to Uncle Sandro's father about it when he had the chance, although he couldn't see why Uncle Sandro had time for every table of any note (within the confines of Abkhazia), but not for raising pigs. While he talked with his guest, out of habit Mikha kept listening for the peaceful grunting of the pigs in the pen and the dull blasts from the direction of the river. Today the explosions carried more distinctly, and the conversation involuntarily turned to the latest news, which had led to the intensification of these unpleasant noises.

The night before last the Mensheviks had received reinforcements, and they had begun preparing to storm the bridge. They were trying, insofar as possible, to conceal both facts from outside eyes. They did not succeed in concealing either, of course, and the other shore knew all about it.

In any case, immediately after the reinforcements arrived—that is, the next morning—the Bolsheviks became the first to break the agreement. They began stunning fish right next to the bridge, thereby demonstrating that they knew about both the newly arrived reinforcements and the projected assault.

By stunning fish near the bridge they demonstrated that they now had no reason to guard the bridge, over which the Mensheviks were about to attack. On the contrary, they even had an interest in blowing it up. Nevertheless, they were not blowing it up. Why not? Because they were confident of their strength.

Incidentally, after the reinforcements arrived, the Mensheviks had taken over a large barn belonging to the local prince, who ordinarily used it for community meetings (read "banquets") in bad weather.

They posted a reinforced guard and began building something inside the barn. What it was, no one knew. All they knew was that the Mensheviks were buying ten carts from the local population but using only the wheels. Why they were not using the rest of the wooden parts was unknown. Moreover, they had bought chestnut beams and boards from the local peasants, and to give credit where it's due, they bought generously, at a good price.

In short, it was clear that something was being built in there, that this something was on cartwheels, but what this something was, no one knew.

Some said the Mensheviks were building a huge bomb, and they would use the wheels to get it to Mukhus. There, by rolling it off the knoll of Mount Chernyavskaya, they would shoot it at the city and blow it up. Others said they were building not a bomb but a wooden armored car named after Noy Zhordania. Granted, no one was able to give any definite answer to the question of what would serve as the draft power for this armored car.

Next to the barn lay a green field, the communal pasture, and some peasants were worried that while the weapon was under construction it might blow up and maim the cattle or some of the people.

That day, which we are now describing with a pen free of prejudice, an assembly had been called in front of the village elder's office. The attendance of the adult male population was required.

Although a forced mobilization was improbable, it was not to be entirely ruled out. Therefore Mikha did not hurry to the assembly but waited for the news from it, especially since he had a fairly good excuse for not showing up—he had a guest in the house.

After his wife came running back from the neighbors' and said there would be no mobilization, because they were persuading the assembly but not surrounding it, Mikha decided to go on over, along with Uncle Sandro.

True to his rule of not neglecting small personal pleasures for great social affairs, Uncle Sandro carefully scraped the marrow out of the bones lying in front of him, lightly spread it with *ajika*, and popped it all into his mouth, with a gesture indicating to his host that he was now ready to go to the assembly.

Uncle Sandro and Mikha went out on the veranda, where they washed their hands and rinsed out their mouths. They descended to the yard. Here the host's ten-year-old son met them, everything about him indicating his readiness to carry out any commission.

It occurred to Uncle Sandro that in spite of being a pig farmer his friend still raised his children right, the Abkhazian way. He looked approvingly at the boy and commissioned him to catch his horse and drive it into the yard. He wanted to be ready for anything.

"With these fellows you never know whether to chase after them or run away from them," he said to his friend—to which the latter nodded knowingly.

"Same with the other fellows," Mikha added.

Uncle Sandro and Mikha walked out to the village road. A fresh breeze was blowing in from the sea. Below, at the bottom of the steep slope, lay the Kodor delta, with all its branches gleaming yellow. The sun played on green leaves so downy that it made you want to stop still by a young wild hazelnut bush and gently nibble at it.

Uncle Sandro realized that this was not the time for such thoughts. Flicking his quirt against the soft top of his boot, he stepped out jauntily, as if capering to the heavenly music of this flowering and anxious day.

When he was dismounted, Uncle Sandro liked to walk this way with his quirt. He felt that a man with a riding whip always made a favorable impression on others. Holding his quirt in his hands, tapping it against his boot top as he strolled, Uncle Sandro had a growing sense of masterly readiness to subdue his neighbor, whereas the same quirt, in Uncle Sandro's view, often evoked in his neighbor a growing readiness to be subdued. In some people, Uncle Sandro had noted, the flick of the quirt even brought to their eyes a look of timid yearning to be subdued.

That Uncle Sandro liked to stroll with his quirt was not due to any striving to subdue his neighbor. It was a sort of military stratagem, a self-defense. If you look like a man who strives to subdue his neighbor, Uncle Sandro used to say, then at least others won't strive to subdue you.

Of course, in some cases people were irritated by the sight of the quirt, but Uncle Sandro felt this was simply envy or jealousy of his masterly readiness to subdue his neighbor.

Along the way, they began to encounter villagers riding or walking to the assembly. Some were hurrying, some were not. After a while the two friends overtook a cart loaded with sand. They slowed down because they realized the cart was headed for the barn where the Mensheviks were building their secret weapon. It seemed they needed sand for the weapon, and they had hired peasants to cart it.

Everyone knew that they did not allow the carters to bring the sand right into the barn but ordered them to go off to one side. They led the cart into the barn themselves, unloaded it themselves, and then led the empty cart to its owner to go back for more sand.

When he drew even with the cart, Uncle Sandro immediately recognized the carter. It was Kunta Margania, who at one time had worked as a shepherd and lived in their house.

Kunta was glad to see Uncle Sandro and jumped down from the moving cart. They embraced. Now Kunta walked beside Uncle Sandro, from time to time waving a long stick over his buffaloes.

"*Or! Khi!*"

The cart creaked mercilessly, and the buffaloes, bowing their horned heads, pulled as if trying to go off in different directions.

Talking with Kunta, Uncle Sandro glanced at him and reflected that he had grown old before his time. He wasn't past forty but already he looked to be almost an old man. Small in stature, big in the arms, his back worn out and very stooped, he was like a hunchback. The noiseless way he walked along in his rawhide moccasins made Uncle Sandro think of his own childhood, so far away and so sinless.

Kunta was a kind man, and to be blunt, a foolish one. He was almost unable to run his farm on his own—he kept going broke. Afterward he usually hired himself out to someone as a shepherd. He would make a new beginning, stand on his own feet for a few years, and go broke again. Still, people said, now that he had a grown son to help him, Kunta was able to cope with his modest farm.

After the usual questions about the health of friends and relations, Kunta suddenly brightened.

"Have you heard?" he asked, looking into Uncle Sandro's eyes.

"What about?" Uncle Sandro said.

"The Mensheviks are accepting volunteers," Kunta remarked importantly.

"Everybody knows *that*," Mikha said.

"They say," Kunta added cunningly, "if they take Mukhus they'll allow us to clean out the shops of the Bolshevik merchants."

"Supposing you capture Mukhus, what do you want to take?" Uncle Sandro asked, poking fun at Kunta and winking at Mikha.

"You aren't allowed to take all you want," Kunta said, unaware that they were mocking him. "You're only allowed what one man can carry away on his person."

"But what do you want to carry away?" Uncle Sandro asked.

"Cloth, nails, salt, rubber boots, halva," Kunta enumerated with satisfaction. "Everything you need to run a farm."

"Listen, Kunta," Uncle Sandro said seriously, "stay home and eat your mush, or you'll get in trouble."

"So much turmoil," Kunta sighed. "A lot of people get rich in times like this."

"Stay home," Mikha said with conviction. "We don't know now which end is up."

"That's fine for you to say—you've got the pigs," Kunta said, as if he were speaking of reliable hard currency. After a moment's thought he added, "I won't go myself, I'll send my son."

They emerged on the green in front of the office, and immediately the hum of the crowd reached their ears. Three or four hundred peasants stood under a big spreading mulberry tree. Those who had found room in the shade of the tree were sitting right on the grass. The rest crowded around behind them, standing up. Conspicuous among them were a dozen or so men on horseback who simply did not care to dismount. The tails of a hundred horses switched at the hitching rack.

Kunta said good-bye to his friends and jumped lightly onto the cart.

"Wait," Uncle Sandro said, remembering about the Mensheviks' secret weapon. "Do you know anything about it?" He nodded toward the barn.

"They don't let us get close," Kunta said.

"But try, play dumb somehow," Uncle Sandro requested.

"All right," Kunta agreed cheerlessly. Swinging his stick, he fetched a blow along the back of first one buffalo and then the other, so that two columns of dust flew up from the animals' powerful backs.

"Poor fellow, he doesn't have to play at being dumb," Mikha remarked.

Uncle Sandro nodded with the expression of warm agreement with which we all nod when the subject is the mental weakness of our acquaintances.

"*Ertoba! Ertoba!*" was the first thing Uncle Sandro made out when he and Mikha came near the crowd. The words were unfamiliar to him. He and Mikha walked over to the crowd and cautiously peered into it.

Right at the foot of the tree, several men were sitting at a long table. The table had been set into the ground a long time ago to meet various community needs. Now, out of respect for the proceedings, it was covered with a Persian carpet that belonged to the local prince.

The prince himself, a trim middle-aged man, was also sitting at the table. With him were two officers, the one from the detachment and the one who had arrived with the reinforcement. Uncle Sandro could tell just by looking that both were real gamblers, night owls.

Next to the prince, obviously snoozing, sat a huge, decrepit old man in a cherkeska, with a long dagger at his belt and a turban like a janissary's tied crookedly on his big mustachioed head. His mustache was long but not thick, as if eaten away by time. This was Nahar Bey, who had been a famous cutthroat in his day.

Although he was of simple peasant origins, he was respected for the unheard-of daring and savagery of his reprisals against enemies—respected almost on an equal footing with the most venerable scions of princely families, a fact which in turn gives some clue as to the nature of the merits that once removed the ancestors of present-day princes from the crowd of ordinary men and made them into princes.

People said that Nahar Bey had taken part in the campaigns of Shamyl, but he himself now remembered only dimly the bloodshed of his blossoming youth and sometimes confused the Avarian Shamyl with the Abkhazian Shamyl, a notorious abrek of that era. The local bosses, trying to get ahead in big-league politics, supported first one version of the story and then the other. Right now the Avarian version was in ascendance, because the Mensheviks' struggle against the Bolsheviks fitted rather conveniently with the Avarian Shamyl's heroic struggle against the czarist conquerors.

Nahar Bey dozed, bowing his head over the table, in his sleep sometimes catching an overhanging mustache in his lips. Now and then he opened his eyes and looked at the orator with a threatening sclerotic glare.

The orator stood tall at the end of the table. No one knew who he was, but Uncle Sandro, appraising the proceedings, decided that he was the Menshevik commissar. He was a man with a pale yellow face, hands that gestured too sweepingly, and glowing eyes.

He spoke good Abkhazian, but sometimes inserted Russian or Georgian words in his speech. Every time he put in a Russian or a Georgian word, old Nahar Bey opened his eyes and focused a dim and hostile gaze on him, and his hand gripped the handle of the dagger. But as he did so, the orator switched back to Abkhazian, and the old Dzhigit's eyes filmed with sleep, his head fell on his chest, and the hand that gripped the dagger unclasped and slid to his knee.

From time to time the orator reached for a glass and took several swallows. When the water in the glass was gone, the clerk sitting next to the orator obligingly poured some for him from the carafe. The sound of pouring water or the clink of the carafe against the glass also woke the aged Dzhigit, but not for long.

A notebook lay open in front of the clerk. As he listened to the orator he tapped his pencil on the table, holding it with its long sharpened point up. Looking around at the peasants, he let it be known by his gaze that he would be glad to enter this splendid speech in his notebook, but only if fruitfully transfigured as a list of volunteers.

Now and then during his speech, the orator flung his arm forward and seemed to point with glowing eyes toward some important object that had appeared in the distance. Uncle Sandro already knew that this was done for no particular reason, just to make the words fine and persuasive, but many peasants were still unaccustomed to the gesture, especially in conjunction with glowing eyes, and they glanced back now and then, trying to discern what he was pointing at. Those who were used to the gesture chuckled at those who were still looking back.

To Uncle Sandro's right was a peasant he did not know, sitting on a horse. The horse, coming in contact with Uncle Sandro's quirt, became restive and kept trying to move aside, but there was no room to move, and his master, not understanding the cause of his restiveness, swore softly. Somehow he lumped the horse's restiveness together with the orator's fidgetiness.

The next time the orator flung out his arm, and many peasants glanced back in the direction he was pointing, the horseman looked at Uncle Sandro with a satisfied smile and said, "The first time I saw that, I thought, What's he pointing at? I thought maybe the cattle had gotten into the field and he was pointing at the damage. How is it, I thought, he notices it from where he is but I can't see it from my horse?"

A cornfield could be seen beyond a wattle fence at the end of the green. The horseman, glancing at Uncle Sandro and simultaneously squinting at the field, gave him to understand that his field of vision was much greater than the orator's, and there was probably no way the orator could see anything he couldn't see from his horse.

After this, he unexpectedly pulled down one of the branches that hung over his head and began tossing wet oblong clusters of mulberries into his mouth, slurping and smacking his lips.

"Hey, shake some down!" said someone sitting up front. The horseman got a tighter grip on the branch and shook it several times. A black rain of mulberries showered down. There was a slight commotion up front, and the clerk, when he noticed it, directed a censorious glance at the horseman. Uncle Sandro noted with a grin that the clerk was trying to make his own eyes glow like the orator's. The peasants gradually quieted down until the only sound was from the horse, breathing noisily as he stretched to reach the scattered berries.

Meanwhile the orator continued to speak, trying to warm the gathering up and raise it to the level of a meeting. But the gathering in no way came up to that level. For some reason the orator himself was bothered by the sporadic blasts from the river, as well as by the peasants, who asked all sorts of questions that detracted from the meeting.

As soon as the next blast went off, the orator stood still, turned his pale mobile face to the river, and said, "Hear that? They're destroying it themselves, and then they'll complain that we attacked!"

Uncle Sandro could not imagine who the Bolsheviks would complain to if the Mensheviks did start to attack. Actually there was a lot he did not understand in the orator's speech, and he attributed this partly to his late arrival at the assembly, partly to universal folly.

The orator must have explained before Uncle Sandro's arrival why the Menshevik regime was good and the Soviet regime bad. Now, proceeding from this premise, he was dwelling on the profits to be gained by the peasants under the Menshevik regime, precisely because it was good and not the contrary. That being so, he said, the peasants must manifest political awareness by entering the ranks of the volunteers. In this difficult time, he said, everyone who was not over thirty-five years of age and had not yet lost his conscience under the influence of the Bolsheviks must enter the ranks of the volunteers.

For those who were over thirty-five and yet had not lost their consciences under the influence of the Bolsheviks, he explained, the command would make an exception and would accept them to the ranks of the volunteers. So he explained, although no one asked him for an explanation.

"*Ertoba! Ertoba!*" he shouted at every convenient opportunity.

"What's that word?" Uncle Sandro asked his companion, who was almost as good as Uncle Sandro in all respects and was even better in respect to the Russian and Georgian languages—again, as a man who traded in pigs, that is, who did business with Christian peoples.

"*Ertoba* means unity," Mikha answered. "He wants us to be at one with him."

To Uncle Sandro's left stood a peasant he did not know. Uncle Sandro noticed that every time the man didn't hear or didn't understand the orator he opened his mouth slightly, as if switching on an instrument that would amplify both the sense and the sound of the orator's speech. Now he turned at Mikha's words.

"I can be at one with a relative," he said, crooking a gnarled finger and nodding toward the orator with a stupid smile, "at one with a neighbor, at one with a fellow villager, but how can I be at one with this Endursky when I'm seeing him for the first time?"

"The trouble is he's talking nonsense," the horseman responded, bending another branch down and looking it over to find where the berries were thickest. "A man who's standing will never point at something he doesn't see himself."

". . . Tomorrow we attack," the orator declared. "Whoever is with us, sign up by six in the morning. After six, though you shower us with gold, we'll not take a single man. Hurry to the ranks! *Ertoba! Ertoba!*" He shouted and waved his arms as if calling on a whole orchestra to play in unison.

"*Ertoba!*" a few voices repeated after him, but even they faltered, embarrassed at being alone.

Seeing that people were shilly-shallying, the orator decided to help them out. He said that if some were ashamed to sign up right now in front of close friends whose relatives had gone over to the Bolsheviks, they could drop by the office later and sign up in secret, because the command, in contrast to *them* (a nod in the direction of the river), respected family feeling.

The clerk, scanning the crowd and silently resting his glance now on one, now on another, offered to enter them in his notebook, but those on whom he rested his glance mostly turned away. If they did not turn away in time, they folded their arms on their chests and refused, softening the refusal by this gesture of gratitude for his confidence.

All the same, fifteen or twenty men signed up. At the suggestion of the prince, the first to be enrolled as Esteemed Volunteer was old Nahar Bey. At this everyone raised a joyful noise, the clerk wrote him down in the notebook—slowly, as if to prolong his pleasure—and the orator meanwhile assured the assembly that the spirit of Nahar Bey would shield the righteous cause of the Mensheviks.

The aged Dzhigit himself, hearing his name accompanied by too loud a noise, bit his mustache and fixed the orator with such an immobile and prolonged stare that the latter was seriously discomfited. But here the prince leaned over to Nahar Bey and whispered something in his ear. He nodded his mustachioed head and subsided.

"Are there any questions?" the orator asked, emboldened by the fact that someone, at least, had enlisted. Then he added, with an allusion to those across the river, "*We* are not afraid of questions."

He looked triumphantly around the gathering. Pouring his own glass of water this time, he began to drink it in big gulps.

"He works like a mill—on water," said someone in back.

"He may work like a mill but you won't see any flour," added someone else.

"Sonny," said someone from the crowd, addressing the orator, "they say that if you take Mukhus we'll be allowed to clean out the Bolshevik merchants. We'd like to know, is that true?"

The orator was still drinking water when the question came, but on hearing it he quickly set aside the glass and began waving his arm.

"I never said any such thing and don't even have the right to say it!" From this disavowal, which was somehow too peevish, many understood that that was how things would be, only the command didn't want to come right out and say so.

"Look here," the man who was standing to Uncle Sandro's left shouted suddenly, "what will happen to us if we go with you and the Bolsheviks win?"

Immediately an awkward silence fell. They could hear the horses at the hitching rack clicking the iron in their mouths and swishing their tails as they brushed away flies.

On the one hand, everyone could hardly wait to find out what the orator would say, but on the other hand, the question seemed too audacious for this hospitable country. The Mensheviks, after all, were guests, in a way, even if uninvited.

"An interesting question," the orator said, and he looked at those sitting next to him at the table. Both officers shook their heads scornfully, indicating that the outcome of the impending battle caused no anxiety.

"An interesting question," the orator repeated, and he added, "but the Communists will never beat us, especially since . . ."

The orator stopped and nodded significantly in the direction of the barn, from which they could hear the muffled thud of axes.

"Who knows," Uncle Sandro's neighbor observed pacifically. Though he had posed the question, he was glad that he had somehow gotten out of it.

"Why don't you say what you're doing there in the barn," came an irritated voice from the back. Evidently people were still arriving. Uncle Sandro did not see the speaker, but from his voice he guessed that the man was standing in the sun, maybe even without a hat.

". . . It could blow up," the irritated voice continued, "but we have cattle grazing, our women go by there . . ."

"It can't blow up, we won't let it . . . But I have no right to divulge a military secret," the orator replied. He added, "Tomorrow you'll see for yourselves."

"And what are you going to do," someone shouted suddenly from the crowd, "about Abkhazians who take advantage of the uproar and go all-out raising pigs?"

"What pigs?" The orator was disconcerted.

"Yes, yes! What about it?" People who envied Mikha came to life on all sides. The orator was disconcerted, but not Mikha.

"I don't eat them myself, damn you!" he shouted loudly. "I only sell them to the infidels!"

"And I corroborate that, as his guest!" Uncle Sandro added in a stentorian voice.

Everyone turned to look at him, many in surprise, because this was the first time they'd seen him.

"Sandro of Chegem!" The words rustled through the crowd like a warm breeze caressing the ear.

"You're a guest, you may not know everything," was the snappish but weak rejoinder of the man who had shouted about the pigs.

"Ask the man about the subject at hand," the prince interposed, "and we'll investigate our pigs ourselves."

The prince was also an opponent of pig farming. He felt that if pig farming were introduced into the pure life of the Abkhazians, it would bring with it a disastrous disrespect for seniority, the laconic boorishness characteristic of other nations that were simpleminded in comparison with the Abkhazians. But it was inappropriate to take this up now.

"How long will the campaign last?" said a voice from the crowd.

"About a month, I think," the orator said rather confidently.

"Oho!" said the same voice in loud surprise. "How can I go if I have to hoe the corn in two weeks and my tobacco's getting ripe?"

"Have your relatives—" the orator began, but he did not finish, because the sound of the blasting came again from the river.

"Look what they're doing!" he said, gesturing abruptly in the direction of the blasts. "They're destroying it themselves, and then they'll say that we were the first . . ."

"I'd like to know," said a voice, "how far we're going to carry the war—Gagra or Sochi?"

"Sochi, or even farther—"

"Why farther? Farther is Russia—"

"To gain a conclusive victory over Lenin we must go even to Russia!" the orator shouted. "But to do that we need three things . . ."

He fell silent. Compressing his lips, he fixed the crowd with a glassy, brazen stare, trying to impress them ahead of time with the importance of what he was about to say.

"The Russians themselves couldn't beat Lenin, who are you to do it?"

"Quiet, he's saying the things he needs—"

"A horse, a saddle, and a rifle—that's three things for him . . ."

"*Ertoba, Ertoba, Ertoba!*" The orator discharged the words at last, looking as if he'd said something new.

"I'm sick and tired of his unity . . ."

"Mark my words," the horseman observed again as he looked the mulberry tree over in a businesslike way and moved his horse forward slightly so as to reach a better branch, "a man who points at something he can't see is tetched."

"You may be gorging yourself on mulberries," remarked the peasant standing to Uncle Sandro's left, "but why did we bother to come?"

"Sh-h-h! One of our own is going to speak."

An old man made his way through the crowd, emerged from the front row, quietly set his staff into the ground, placed both hands on it, and said that he would speak on behalf of many, though not all.

He said that some were willing to serve in the Menshevik army, but on condition that they guard the stores, prepare food, look after the horses. But these many, though not all, in whose name he spoke were not willing to shoot, because among the Bolsheviks were many of their relatives and fellow villagers.

Therefore, he said, if our volunteers began shooting at the Bolsheviks now, the possibility could not be ruled out that one of them would hit one of our own men, and the spilled blood would call for vengeance and many innocent people would die. It was especially unpleasant, he said, that the Bolsheviks and the Mensheviks would either make peace or (he added with a sort of tiresome impartiality) conquer each other, while the blood feud would go on for years.

Therefore the many, though not all, in whose name he spoke had decided that our volunteers could go on the campaign but they should be relieved of shooting. With these words he pulled his staff out of the ground and, walking backward respectfully but with dignity, returned to the crowd, which supported his speech with approving shouts, perhaps from the many, though not all, in whose name he had spoken.

"When the issue is freedom, we will not bargain," the orator remarked, making a sour face. Evidently he was not altogether happy with the old man's speech.

"We'll bargain!" the man who had talked about the barn shouted spitefully. Uncle Sandro, recognizing his voice, was surprised that he was still standing in the sun.

". . . The Bolsheviks say they won't bargain, you say you won't bargain," came the heated voice of the man who was standing in the sun, and perhaps without a hat, "but we're cut off from the city: there's no salt and no cloth!"

"You took me wrong!" the orator cried, but now the people would not let him speak.

"We took it that way because there's no lamp-chimneys either," someone shouted, and for some reason that struck everyone funny. The crowd started moving and broke up into groups. By now neither the orator nor the prince, who seemed stunned by the disrespect of his countrymen, could stop them. Some started over to the hitching rack, and others who had come on foot walked off, calling loudly to their relatives and road companions.

The last thing the orator managed to shout was that the relatives of those who had gone over to the Bolsheviks should not prevent their fellow villagers from enlisting in the volunteers.

"We're not propagandizing you, don't you propagandize them," he shouted, flinging his arms out with his palms thrust forward, as if hinting at the necessity of keeping their chances even.

Uncle Sandro and his friend went out to the road, where Kunta would have to pass. During the assembly Uncle Sandro had glanced at the road occasionally so as not to miss him. Finally Kunta appeared on the road.

"I played dumb, but nothing came of it," he said as he drew even with his friends. He stopped the cart and started to get down.

"Fine then, go on," Uncle Sandro said, not letting him get down from the cart.

"You could drop in," Kunta asked uncertainly, looking into Uncle Sandro's face. "We could find a chicken for you—"

"Thanks, Kunta, another time," Uncle Sandro said, thinking his own thoughts.

Kunta creaked on, flicking his switch now and then and humming a cart driver's song. Mikha and Uncle Sandro looked back at the mulberry tree. By now there was almost nobody there. The prince and one of the officers were sitting across the table from each other, setting up the stones for *nard*. Several kibitzers had gathered around, and some who perhaps wanted to take part in the game.

From the prince's manor, which adjoined the green, came three women dragging baskets of refreshments and wine. At the now-empty hitching rack two of the prince's men exchanged shoptalk as they packed the aged Nahar Bey's horse.

"What did you think of the assembly?" Mikha asked when they turned off toward home. Uncle Sandro did not answer for a long time, and Mikha waited patiently, knowing that Uncle Sandro's dictum would be worth it.

"That's no ruler," Uncle Sandro said, spanking his quirt against his boot top. Loudly, as if trying to overcome Mikha's social deafness, he said again, "Mark my words, Mikha, that's no ruler!"

"What should we do?" Mikha asked, listening for his pigpen. "Buying off the guards will take time, and it starts tomorrow . . ."

"I have an idea." Uncle Sandro nodded in the direction of the barn that had been placed off limits. "Let's give it a try."

Judging from the way Mikha seized Uncle Sandro's thought on the wing, we may conclude that he had quickly overcome his social deafness. Let us not forget that all the while he was still listening—albeit unsuccessfully—for his pigpen. He found it much pleasanter, however, to listen to a pigpen, even if unsuccessfully, than to anything he might hear at the meetings and assemblies of those days.

And if you think about it, was social deafness generally characteristic of the man who was the first Abkhazian not only to gamble on pigs but also to think of driving them to chestnut and beech groves in the fall? No, I think not.

Even now, on his way home, he continued to listen for his pigpen with a sort of angry perplexity, as if everything about him meant to say, "Are we ever going to get to the grunting zone, or are we going to keep on babbling in this godforsaken place?"

Or maybe that was not what he meant, maybe he wanted to say, "Did I go deaf at the assembly listening to that gibberish or what, that I can't hear my own pigs?"

No; as long as this grunting (bleating, neighing, mooing) zone exists, there can be no question of social deafness. That will come later, much later, along with "Anh, the hell with this—may it burn! Anh, up yours!" And finally, the calm and therefore unconquerable cry quietly taken up by the whole country, a cry like a new prayer, like a Buddhist call to self-contemplation: "Smo-o-oke break!"

Two hours later Uncle Sandro lay motionless in a fern thicket, watching through his Zeiss binoculars to see what was going on in the off-limits barn.

From time to time he saw a cart drive up to it and stop. The carter jumped lazily down and walked under the sparse shade of a cherry-plum tree, one of 22 soldiers climbed onto the cart while another opened the barn door, and he could see . . .

Uncle Sandro had guessed at the possibility of peeping into the barn when he was inspecting it from the square. But to make use of the five- or ten-minute interval while the cart went through the open door, one had to be directly opposite it, on the communal pasture, which was open to view from all sides.

There were thickets beginning at the end of the common, about half a kilometer from the barn. It could not occur to the sentries that anyone would observe the barn door from that distance. Who would think that in this village there could be a man with a magnificent pair of binoculars, which had once belonged to Prince Oldenburgsky and had now become the property of someone unknown to the Mensheviks, or to the Bolsheviks either—Uncle Sandro?

But what did he see? He saw a wooden structure almost taller than a man, a gigantic box, slightly raised above the ground by its wheels. The wheels were fastened inside and barely stuck out below the side wall of the structure.

Uncle Sandro immediately guessed that it was made this way in order to defend the wheels from enemy bullets. He was surprised at the military astuteness of the Endurian Mensheviks.

As he continued to watch, Uncle Sandro came to the conclusion that the sidewalls of the contraption were double, because a soldier was standing on one of them without much difficulty, doing something with a shovel. As soon as Uncle Sandro guessed that the walls were double and that that was why the soldier was standing on the wall so easily, he immediately realized that the soldier was leveling and tamping sand, which had been poured between the walls.

Now Uncle Sandro finally saw through the purpose of this fortress on wheels. He understood that the Mensheviks were going to try to cross the bridge, using it as cover. That's the Endurskies for you, Uncle Sandro thought, lowering the binoculars, and all our lives we took them for fools.

He turned over on his back, with difficulty stretching a leg that had gone to sleep in an uncomfortable position, and began looking at the blue sky. A little breeze rustled through the bushes and Uncle Sandro smelled the still-damp earth, the dry stalks of last year's ferns, heard high above him the song of the larks, and suddenly thought: Why the Mensheviks, why the Bolsheviks, why am I lying here at all, spying out this wooden monstrosity?

Afraid to move his numb leg, he looked at the sky and thought of the transitoriness of human effort. Was it worth it to make any kind of effort, he thought, if from up there, above, the Chief Tamada was watching through His heavenly binoculars to see that every man did as he had been ordered in accordance with His grand design?

So thought Uncle Sandro, as he felt his leg gradually recover and begin to obey him. Uncle Sandro moved it a little and felt the last prickles run down it and disappear, along with his enervating thoughts about the transitoriness of human effort.

Just as my leg, after momentary numbness, became obedient to my design to move it, Uncle Sandro thought, so must I, after momentary weakness, obey His design, which most likely consists of having me lie in these bushes and keep an eye on the Endurskies' preparations. Otherwise, why would I be here, Uncle Sandro decided. He turned over on his stomach and raised the binoculars.

Now there was only one thing puzzling him: What force would pull this huge and ponderous contraption? A motor? But if it was a motor from the automobiles that nowadays ran snorting and stinking along the coastal highway, then why had no one heard it? And if it was a motor from a steamboat, then where was the smokestack? No steamboat could move without a smokestack, Uncle Sandro knew that for sure. True, some people said that the wooden armored car could be moved by buffaloes hitched up inside it, but Uncle Sandro doubted that.

Carts were still driving up to the barn. The door opened and closed, but he did not succeed in seeing anything more than he already had. Then one of the soldiers came out of the barn and went off somewhere, and after a while about forty soldiers approached the barn and they all went inside. Uncle Sandro guessed that they had been brought by the soldier who had left the barn.

The sentry who stood at the door immediately went into the barn with them and shut the door after him. Uncle Sandro even began fidgeting with impatience, he was so curious to find out why they had locked themselves in.

A cart approached. One of the soldiers came out of the barn and led it inside as usual. The carter, as usual, went off and sat down in the shade of the cherry plum. Perhaps because there was no sentry at the door just then, they forgot to shut it after the cart went inside.

Uncle Sandro trained his binoculars on the open door. Even the carter, who was sitting in the cool shade, when he noticed that no one was watching him this time and the door had been left open, cautiously got up and walked over to a spot from which he could see what was going on inside.

Uncle Sandro smiled. It was amusing to spy from afar through his binoculars on someone who was spying. He remembered the Chief Tamada again and thought, Perhaps it's as amusing for Him to watch me through His heavenly binoculars as it is for me to watch this carter? That's how we live, by watching each other, Uncle Sandro thought. No longer distracted, he watched what was going on in the barn.

Incidentally, friends, some of Uncle Sandro's observations seem rather curious to me. No, I'm not referring to what he said about how we live by watching others, although that is rather curious too, but his thought that it was amusing to spy from afar through his binoculars on somebody who was spying. From afar—not from close up.

It is always odd to watch from afar while a man dissembles. One may watch from afar as a man sleeps, eats, works, kisses, and none of it, my friends, seems at all peculiar.

Yet one has only to see from afar how a man dissembles, argues something, evades, or in an extreme case, just plain cheats, and it all seems somehow odd, improbable, even fantastic. But, you have every right to ask, what's improbable about it? What turns this ordinary sight into an extraordinary apparition? Space, distance—that's what, my friends! Our eyesight seems to be so designed that the farther we are from our fellow observee, the more agreeable it is for us to see him display traits that are common to all mankind—historically authorized, so to speak.

When we observe a man from a distance and guess that he is dissembling, or phrase-mongering, or in an extreme case, just plain stealing the glass from a soft-drink dispenser, we feel with particular keenness that these are surely not displays of the human traits we consider historically authorized. But since these traits, regardless of historical authorization, are nevertheless unfolding before our eyes, we begin to find in all this a subtle mystical significance, I might say a certain connection, albeit a weak one, with the snares of the devil.

But the same human traits displayed in close proximity, although disagreeable, seem quite tolerable. Now, there's the significance of distance!

To put it another way: Directly opposite my house, behind a high stone wall, there is some sort of enterprise, perhaps a furniture factory, perhaps a secret plant. In the daytime something squeaks over there, and there is always a watchman standing at the entrance gate. In short, I don't know whether this enterprise is secret or semisecret; all I know for sure is that drinking is not allowed there during working hours.

The reason I think not is that every day I see the same scene from my window. On the way back from their break, two workmen approach the corner of the wall, and one of them climbs on the other's shoulders. After that, both of them, staggering, straighten up and make a rather high—though structurally (and morally) unstable—pyramid, with a bottle at the vertex of an outstretched arm.

The bottle is carefully placed on the wall, after which the structure collapses without any precautions and again assumes the form of two separate workmen, ostensibly independent of each other, and disappears through the entrance gate.

After a while I see a head appear on the other side of the wall, from which I conclude that on the other side of the wall there is an earthen bank or something of the sort.

Well then, the head of a man appears, but not so that he can seize the bottle immediately and jump down to the ground or into the arms of his friends (what I don't know, I don't know). He, the owner of this head, for some reason first looks from side to side as if observing an unexpectedly discovered landscape, and then, somehow distractedly sliding his eyes along the wall, discovers the bottle. After picking it up he surveys the scraggly little public garden for a few moments, as well as the windows of our house, as if to ask, somewhat censoriously, "Who put the bottle here?" And as if he had received some sort of answer to his silent question but was not quite satisfied by it, he disappears with the bottle.

Now picture to yourself the situation of a man who from some cosmic distance observes all humanity at once and each man individually. I have in mind the Chief Tamada, as Uncle Sandro would call Him.

How is He to look on all this? What a tragic contradiction there is in His situation! On the one hand, according to our nearly proven hypothesis, the very vastness of the distance from the observer in the heavens to the earth creates in the soul of the Chief Tamada an incredible longing for a man who consoles His gaze by the nobility of the traits he displays. On the other hand, the merciless keenness of vision intrinsic to the All-Seeing leaves Him no illusions with regard to the character of such extrahistorical displays.

But that's enough, long enough for our indiscreet stare to linger on these too-intimate trivia of our existence. We had better return to Uncle Sandro, especially since he is obviously disturbed by something.

He settles his elbows more comfortably and freezes, observing. What has happened?

Before Uncle Sandro's eyes, the contraption began to move and went off into the depths of the barn. He saw a multitude of feet, up to about the ankle, protruding below the side wall. The monster seemed to have come to life and crawled away, moving its many short legs.

Then it stopped in hesitation, stood still for a moment, and moved forward again. Then it moved back again and finally stopped directly opposite the door. The soldiers came pouring out of the monstrosity. They crawled up on the side walls and jumped to the ground. One of them led the cart up to the rear wall of the monstrosity and began shoveling sand into it with some of his comrades.

Now it was all clear to Uncle Sandro. He understood that the soldiers themselves would push their fortress from within. That's the Endurskies for you! Aren't they the sly ones, Uncle Sandro thought, noiselessly abandoning his hidden post. But once an Endursky always an Endursky: he'll hide his head but his tail sticks out. You can see their feet, that means you'll be able to shoot their feet.

Meanwhile the soldiers started to come out of the barn, the carter hastily went back to the cherry-plum tree, and the empty cart followed the soldiers out of the barn. The barn door was closed, and the sentry stood by it, as usual.

Fool, Uncle Sandro thought, he might as well not stand there any more. Still, he felt somewhat jealous of the carter, who had managed to find out what was going on in the barn even without Uncle Sandro's clever scheme. Working his way through the bushes, he circled around and returned to his friend's house.

That night, after waiting for the moon to rise, Uncle Sandro rode out of his friend's yard and headed for the Kodor. He had decided to ride to a point several kilometers above the bridge so as not to encounter the Red sentries, and cross the river there. Mikha accompanied him as far as the river.

"The bottom may be a little better here," Mikha said, stopping by a neglected wooden landing. There must have been a ferry here once, but now it had been moved to some other spot. What remained of the ferry was a rusty iron cable strung across the river, with posts on both banks.

In the ghostly moonlight the waters of the Kodor rushed toward the sea. The river was swollen and turbid with the spring runoff from melting snow. The water roared ceaselessly; they could hear the dull thudding and clacking of rock against rock, tumbled together by the current. Mikha reminded him once again how to find the house where the commissar was staying.

"Don't forget to put in a word for me," he shouted through the din of the water. "Good luck!"

Uncle Sandro nodded to him and quirted his balking horse into the water. Mikha cheered him on from behind with shouts and whistles.

Uncle Sandro had made an agreement with Mikha that in the event of a Red victory he would try to convince the commissar that Mikha had always sympathized with the Reds. Moreover, if things went very well, they had agreed that while Uncle Sandro was there on the left bank he would point out his friend's house to the commissar, seeing as how it stood on an elevated spot and had two cypresses growing near it, so that the commissar would warn his soldiers to shoot a little more circumspectly during tomorrow's battle and protect the home of the left-leaning pig farmer.

Cautiously pawing the ground, shuddering and stopping every time her hoof slipped off the stones, the horse moved forward.

Suddenly through the roar of the river Uncle Sandro heard Mikha's voice and looked back. Mikha was pointing upstream and shouting something. The din of the water prevented Uncle Sandro from making out the words, but he sensed danger and looked upstream. A huge, heavy branch—now heaving up out of the water, now submerging—was rushing down on him.

The end, he thought, at the same time doing the only thing he could. He stopped the horse and pulled his feet out of the stirrups. Not understanding why he had stopped, the horse tried to turn, but Uncle Sandro tightened the reins and held her back.

He shifted the quirt to his left hand so that the right would be completely free. Uncle Sandro decided that if the branch ran into them he would try to fend it off with his right arm, but if it struck the horse anyway and knocked her down he would have to be ready to abandon her.

In these few seconds the fate of the horse and rider was determined. The moments fixed in his memory forever as the black branch rushed down on him wet and gleaming, plunging and surfacing, and flecks of moonlight rocked nearby on the murky water, leaping madly about, and the horse trembled under him lightly and ceaselessly.

About ten meters away from him the branch plunged under the water and Uncle Sandro froze, concentrated all his willpower, as he stared into the water trying to forestall any surprise. But even so he had no time to act.

It surfaced right in front of the horse's muzzle. The wet fine branches lashed the horse and Uncle Sandro with terrible force, so that Uncle Sandro was momentarily blinded from pain and surprise. The horse tossed her head, Uncle Sandro barely managed to hold on to the reins. The next moment he saw the tail end of the branch surface farther down the stream and realized that this was not a branch, it was a whole tree that had been washed away by the water. If it had hit them, of course, there was nothing he could have done.

"*Chou, annasyni!*" he shouted, and urged the horse on. The horse started off, and he felt the first scalding touch of the icy water, beginning in his boots, then higher and higher.

"*Chou, annasyni, chou!*" Uncle Sandro shouted, and urged the horse on so that she would not stop for even a second. Now only the heads of horse and rider were above water. Uncle Sandro felt the animal's body tense as she was knocked sidewise by the powerful current, and he kept shouting and shouting at her, so that the power of her fear of a man's will might break the power of her elemental fear of water. On and on she went, and by now Uncle Sandro's head was spinning from the sickening glut of rushing waters and the obsessive dancing of the murky flecks of moonlight on the murky surface of the river.

Suddenly the horse snorted and sank into the water, her hoofs lost the bottom, and Uncle Sandro felt the current carrying them away. The icy water rolled over his head. The back of his burka—his wide felt cloak—instantly puffed up in a bubble, and the bubble lifted him off his horse and began floating him away from her. Uncle Sandro convulsively gripped the horse's belly with his legs, and at that moment they were carried above the water again.

"*Chou, annasyni!*" he shouted with all his might. The horse lunged forward with an antediluvian amphibious leap and felt her feet strike the bottom. Her hoofs clattering on the stones, ever more confident, more furious, more triumphant, she carried him out into the shallows by the other bank. Uncle Sandro looked back and waved at Mikha. Still aroused by a sense of mortal danger, he urged the horse up the sloping bank.

About an hour later he rode up to the house where the commissar was staying. The owner of the house was an Abkhazian who was even more unusual for that time than Mikha, because he made his living wholly by trade. He kept the village store, which stood right in his front yard.

The Abkhazian spoke good Russian, and his house on its high pilings looked imposing and handsome even to Uncle Sandro's exacting eye. So, considering that the house was right on the way to Mukhus, the commissar had all the conveniences handy: an interpreter was nearby, his house was well-to-do, and it was the closest of any to the main road.

These thoughts ran through Uncle Sandro's mind as he opened the gate for himself and noted with surprise that in this clean little yard, with its grass showing pale blue in the moonlight, there was no sign of a dog. He also had time to think, after he had swung open the gate and was riding into the yard, that both the Bolsheviks and the Mensheviks, although they differed in their attitudes toward rich and poor peasants, still preferred to live in a good, substantial house. Uncle Sandro did not condemn them for this; on the contrary, he was glad to find in it confirmation for the fact that both sides often had some clear point, agreeable to everyone, concealed behind their many strange doings.

On entering the yard he noticed in the thick black shade of a cherry-laurel two Russian horses with cavalry saddles. Even before that, he had noticed a sentry sitting on the front steps. Since the sentry did not hail him, Uncle Sandro surmised that he was asleep.

Uncle Sandro jumped soundlessly down from his saddle and tied his horse next to the others, which were huge, and to his eyes awkward. One of them stretched to nip at his horse, but Uncle Sandro—taking care that the sentry did not notice, even though he was asleep—fetched it a blow with his quirt.

Flicking his quirt against his boot top, trying to wake the sentry with this peaceful but sufficiently independent sound, he walked over to the steps. The soldier, a Red Army private, was sleeping on the veranda floor, his feet blocking the top step, his arms clasping his rifle, his head propped against the railing.

Uncle Sandro, coming up close to him, was struck by his youth. His close-cropped little head was round like a money jar, and his thin neck, all worn out, drooped under its weight.

What if he shoots half asleep, Uncle Sandro thought. He touched his quirt to the man's shoulder.

"Hey," he called, and cautiously added the new word, "*tovarish* . . ."

The sentry did not wake up. Uncle Sandro looked around the veranda, stared into the blank dark windows of the rooms, noted that over the veranda railing hung an unfamiliar object—as Uncle Sandro guessed, a small water tank for washing up, with a small plug stem sticking out of it. A towel hung next to it on a nail. Uncle Sandro had seen big marble washstands in rich houses, but he hadn't seen anything small and convenient like this. He decided the commissar had brought this washtank with him.

What won't the Russians think of next, Uncle Sandro thought with surprise, surveying the washtank. He felt like poking the plug stem with the tip of his quirt to make the water run, but he resisted the impulse, out of fear of the owner.

Uncle Sandro again touched the quirt to the private's shoulder. The private mumbled something in his sleep, his throat working as if he were making an effort to wake up. He did wake up, and looked him over sullenly—but without fear, which surprised Uncle Sandro unpleasantly.

"I want the commissar," Uncle Sandro said simply and significantly, so that the soldier, still half asleep, would not doubt his love of peace.

"I've got orders not to wake him," the private answered sullenly. He got a cozier grip on his rifle and went back to sleep.

Uncle Sandro suddenly became aware that his wet burka was weighing on his shoulders with unaccustomed heaviness and his benumbed body was barely obeying his will. He poked the private with the quirt again, this time much more decisively.

"I said I've got my orders, so that's it," the soldier said angrily, and immediately closed his eyes.

Suddenly Uncle Sandro noticed a light go on in the kitchen and heard people whispering. He realized the owner was in there. He was on the point of going in, but the kitchen door opened and a man came out. Shading his eyes with his hand for some reason, he started uncertainly toward Uncle Sandro, trying to recognize him from a distance, as if testing whether this man was even capable of recognition.

"I see from your appearance that you're one of us," the man said, mildly regretful that he recognized him only at the most general ethnographic level.

"Yes," Uncle Sandro said, "I'm Sandro of Chegem."

"Welcome," the owner said, glad to hear his native tongue and surprised to have a visitor, "but what brings you from Chegem at such a time?"

"I didn't just come from Chegem, I came from over there," Uncle Sandro said, nodding in the direction of the Kodor. He threw a sidelong look at the private, but the latter slept placidly on.

"And you're all wet, I see. Hey!" He looked back toward the kitchen. "Poke up the fire a little, the man has to get warm. Let's go in," he added, turning to Uncle Sandro. Secret embers of curiosity lent his voice a furtive note.

"I need to see the commissar, but this fellow won't let me," Uncle Sandro said.

"They've spent all day getting ready for tomorrow," his host observed. With a nod toward the sentry he added, "This lad galloped to Mukhus twice today. If his horse survives, there's not a thing in life I understand."

"Yes, times are like that," Uncle Sandro drawled vaguely. The cracks between the boards of the kitchen wall showed bright, and Uncle Sandro knew that the fire on the hearth had caught. He was on the point of going in, but just then a door creaked and a man in an undershirt came out of his room onto the veranda. His bare feet slapped along confidently as he walked over to the railing. It was the commissar. The instant the door creaked, the private jumped up and stood ready with his rifle.

"What happened?" the commissar asked as he leaned over the railing, scratching his hairy chest.

"I came from over there." Uncle Sandro nodded in the direction of the Kodor.

"So?" the commissar asked. He stopped scratching, lightly pushed the stem of the washtank, and passed a wet palm over the woolly stubble on his face.

Uncle Sandro, who had expected a more fitting reception, maintained an injured silence.

"Maybe you're going to tell us about the wooden armored car again?" the commissar asked, taking his time and reveling in Uncle Sandro's dismay, or so it seemed to Uncle Sandro. The commissar pushed up the plug stem again with the palm of his hand, splashed water on his face, and looked at Uncle Sandro more thoughtfully.

"That's what I came for," Uncle Sandro said. Trying to appear independent (even though he had come here), he spanked his quirt against his boot.

"These people," the commissar grinned. "This is the sixth man to come here with this nonsense and ask me to bear his services in mind . . ."

This was very disagreeable for Uncle Sandro to hear. It was not just that others had forestalled him (the damned carter not only had not kept his secret to himself, but, as later became clear, he had even done a little bargaining with it that night). Especially disagreeable was the fact that Uncle Sandro had indeed been expecting a reward from the commissar, if only a modest one. Well, let's say, only a promise to protect his friend's house during the battle.

". . . You tell your friends"—here the commissar hesitated, because Uncle Sandro gave a particularly deft and independent flick of the quirt to his boot top—"that we're not scared of any Menshevik bugaboo and no one's to come here about it any more," he concluded, looking now with hatred at the hand in which Uncle Sandro gripped his quirt.

Perhaps out of irritation, he struck the plug stem of the washtank too hard and knocked it up into the tank. A stream of water started flowing unchecked. Wonder what he'll do now, Uncle Sandro thought.

The commissar did nothing, but unexpectedly stuck his head under the stream, thereby implying to Uncle Sandro, or so it seemed to him, that nothing surprised the Reds and that he, the commissar, had foreseen this unchecked stream, just as he had the Mensheviks' armored car.

Uncle Sandro could have sworn that a moment before hitting the plug stem the commissar had foreseen no such thing, but he couldn't prove it. The commissar held his head under the stream, breathing noisily and wiping his neck with his hands. Uncle Sandro waited, expecting that either the stream would stop or the commissar, without waiting for it to stop, would raise his head anyway.

"He says they'll manage as it is," the host explained in Abkhazian, to ease the situation. He added quietly, "Don't flick your quirt . . . They don't like it . . ."

Uncle Sandro was insulted by his reception but still felt he had to see the affair through to the end, especially since he had not yet expounded his main point to the commissar—namely, how to fight this mobile fortress. Nevertheless, as a sign of his resentment over his poor reception, he decided not to speak to the commissar any more in Russian.

"Tell him," he said to his host, still flicking the quirt on his boot top despite the danger, "to put machine guns right under the bridge."

The host translated, darting dreadful looks at the flicking quirt, but Uncle Sandro preferred not to take the hint.

At this point the commissar raised his head and the young sentry plunged his hand into the tank and groped around, trying to thrust the plug stem into place. Finally, with a clank of the valve, the stem snapped back into the outlet. The commissar, now that he had raised his head, began drying off with the towel. The sentry went back to the steps.

As he listened to the translation, the commissar watched Uncle Sandro more and more intently.

"Why should I change the weapon emplacements?" he asked, without moving his eyes from the flicking quirt.

"Tell him you have to shoot at the fortress from the side and below, because the soldiers' feet stick out just to the ankles," Uncle Sandro said. He ran the tip of the lash across his boot again to indicate how far the Menshevik soldiers' feet stuck out from under the wooden armored car.

"You'd better put your quirt away for a while," his host managed to say, but by now it was too late.

"Get out of here!" the commissar roared in a terrible voice, and Uncle Sandro heard his hand rustling in search of his holster.

Never had Uncle Sandro been so frightened. He felt his body being ever more tightly constricted by his skin, as if his very flesh were trying to make itself smaller, change its swaddlings, pull in tight, squeeze itself down to the size of a cocoon and hide in it.

Simultaneously, out of the corner of his eye, he saw the commissar's hand continuing to grope at his side. He had time to decide that as soon as it pulled out the pistol he would have to leap under the house (the house stood on high pilings), run underneath it, jump the fence, and then hightail it through the vegetable patch. Out of the corner of his eye he had time to notice a huge winepress lying under the house with an old wooden plow leaning up against it, and he thought, Suppose I trip over it. He noticed the dog, or rather, guessed that the shapeless gray spot lying by the winepress was a dog, and suddenly for a split second recalled from his childhood how the dog was forever taking his rawhide moccasins and would hide in under the house like this to chew on them for hours. And suddenly this recollection clicked with another more important realization, that the commissar was without his belt and therefore without his pistol, and however much he might fumble at his side he would not be able to shoot at that moment—but after that, we would see.

"Comrade Commissar, let me get him," the Red Army man said, and he raised his rifle. But just then the host came to himself and rushed forward to barricade Uncle Sandro.

"You can't, boy! He's a guest! A guest!" he shouted, glaring at the soldier and desperately waving a hand in his face.

"Forget it." The commissar waved away his sentry and turned to the host. "But tell your guest not to butt in."

"All right, my friend," the host said. He drew Uncle Sandro into the kitchen.

"Playing with a whip!" the Red Army man sighed, regretful that he couldn't express his annoyance in more decisive fashion.

In the kitchen a big fire was already burning on the hearth and Uncle Sandro was soon seated beside it. The host ordered brandy, and in a moment his wife, swift and silent as a bat, brought a bottle of pink *chacha*, two small wineglasses, and a plate of broken-up *churkhcheli* for a snack.

Only after he had drunk six or seven glasses in succession did Uncle Sandro feel the life returning to him. His host suggested that he wait and have some cornmeal mush, something more solid, but Uncle Sandro stood up.

His host led him out of the yard and saw him to the very edge of his property. Uncle Sandro crossed the yard cautiously. Neither the sentry nor the commissar was on the veranda, but a light burned in one of the windows.

When Uncle Sandro mounted his horse, he sensed that his host was lingering somehow awkwardly. "I think you want to say something?" he asked him.

"You're not mistaken," his host agreed. He added, "You see yourself how times are. I'm afraid the Mensheviks will be here tomorrow . . . Suppose my family suffers because the commissar stayed with me . . ."

As he said this the host looked into his eyes so intently that Uncle Sandro understood what he had in mind. What he had in mind was this: Put in a word for me with the Mensheviks, and I in turn will hold my tongue about your coming here with a military secret.

"Good luck," the host said. He let go of the reins, which he had been holding while he talked to his guest.

Uncle Sandro raised his quirt and hurried off to the left bank. The moon was no longer to be seen, the gray dawn was breaking. Uncle Sandro went at a very rapid trot, because this time he did not want to risk fording the Kodor. He had decided to go upstream to the ferry.

Later on, when he recalled this meeting with the commissar, Uncle Sandro did not conceal that he had been good and scared, but he found this explanation for his condition.

In the old days, as he put it, you had much more time between the anger of the authorities and the seizing of a pistol, and you could always think of something.

"But it turns out the Bolsheviks take off at a gallop," Uncle Sandro said. "I didn't know that then, and I lost my head . . ."

The next day dawned just as clear and fine. From early morning, all over the village, the cows and the calves kept calling to one another, the buffaloes and buffalo calves, the ewes and the lambs, the goats and the kids. Only the donkeys cried out in solo; their voice was as lonely as the voice of a prophet.

Many eyewitnesses now claim that the livestock of the village of Ankhara had a premonition the battle would begin that morning, although this claim is hard to authenticate because, by order of the command and by the peasants' own wish, the livestock were kept penned up.

If they had been turned out to graze on the common as usual, perhaps they would not have cried out. But since hungry animals who find themselves penned up always make themselves heard, it is difficult to establish now whether they actually had a premonition of bloodshed or not. Especially since the blood to be shed was not that of their peers but of people—that is, the very ones who slit their throats, dry their hides on stretchers, and boil their flesh in huge kettles. So no one knows why they—the livestock, that is—should have had a premonition of human bloodshed and been anxious on that account.

The fact that the livestock ceased to cry out as soon as the shooting started doesn't mean anything either. In the first place, animals might well take fright and fall silent in reaction to anything as noisy as an exchange of shots between two armies. On the other hand, the possibility cannot be ruled out that the animals did not fall silent, people just ceased to hear them over the din of the battle. In the end, the animals may have fallen silent out of common sense, that is, the realization that while people were talking to each other with their flyswatters and rattles, perhaps they'd be better off to keep quiet, because no one would hear them anyway.

For all these reasons, I do not think there is any serious scientific basis for the claim of some eyewitnesses that the livestock of the village of Ankhara displayed mass clairvoyance and foretold the battle.

So, at exactly eight o'clock in the morning, the Mensheviks opened heavy machine gun and rifle fire on the Red positions. Our boys returned it, although, according to doleful eyewitness accounts, their firepower was inferior to the enemy's on this occasion.

Half an hour later, in view of the whole village of Ankhara, the wooden monster crawled out of the barn and started for the bridge. At first, as it passed through the village, it moved steadily and threateningly, but then on the slope down to the bridge it gathered too much speed, bumped into the side rail and broke it, and almost fell into the river.

They say that human shrieks could be heard from inside the monster as it lost direction and careened into the railing. It may have maimed some of the Menshevik detachment before it ever had time to stun the Reds.

When the monster first came out toward the river, the firing stopped on both sides. The size of the contraption apparently made a strong impression on the Reds. If the Reds ceased fire out of amazement at the world's first, and perhaps last, wooden tank, the Mensheviks probably ceased fire in order to let the Reds reflect in tranquility on the horror of their situation. Psychologically this was a sound move, at least according to connoisseurs of military tactics.

But then, when the tank (the monster? the armored car? the fortress? Uncle Sandro was always calling it something different)—when it rolled away and broke through the railing of the bridge and almost a third of it hung out over the river, but especially when they heard the cries and realized that it had crushed its own soldiers, the Reds came to. Laughter and hooting—rather offensive to the Mensheviks—resounded from the other bank. This was especially offensive to the Mensheviks because both the laughter and the hooting were clearly audible to the villagers of Ankhara.

But it shortly became clear (fortune is fickle in war) that the laughter and hooting were premature. The soldiers within the fortress managed to control themselves, back up, and level their machine. Then, remembering the mocking laughter and especially the hooting, they charged the Red positions with redoubled fury. According to Uncle Sandro, the Endurskies might have borne the mocking laughter, but the hooting made them incredibly savage.

The Reds met the oncoming tank with machine gun and rifle fire, of course, but that was like shooting a buffalo with a slingshot. The wood of our chestnut tree is hard as iron. Besides, as we know, the Mensheviks had not procured their building materials through any official supply channels but fresh, direct from the source.

It should be said that the monster not only drew near but peppered the Red positions with rifle fire. Peepholes had been made between the beams for this purpose. As it approached the other end of the bridge, the Reds shuddered, especially when they remembered their mocking laughter and hooting. The inexperienced soldiers ran first, because of their inexperience, and then the experienced soldiers shuddered and started fleeing in fear, precisely because they were experienced and yet had never seen anything like this.

True, the commissar and the commanding officer succeeded in halting the soldiers and creating a new line of defense. Who knows, maybe in these moments the commissar regretted that he had not heeded Uncle Sandro; maybe if he had talked to him nicely Uncle Sandro would have told him quite a lot that was interesting about the Endurskies' ways—in particular, might have let him know that when handling the Endurskies hooting must be totally ruled out, if only in time of battle.

Maybe the commissar regretted all this now, although maybe he didn't either; in the hubbub he may not have remembered Uncle Sandro's suggestion that he had to shoot at the monster from the side and below because the Endurskies' feet were exposed up to the ankles.

When they noticed from the right bank that the Reds were running, the Mensheviks dashed after them with cavalry and foot soldiers. Perhaps because their surge of feeling was so great, or perhaps because it was dangerous to move via the bridge anyway, many cavalrymen rushed into the river and began to ford it, seeing as it was somewhat wider and shallower here than where Uncle Sandro had crossed it.

At this point some were killed by the Reds, of course, and some were swept away by the water and drowned. Still, the majority reached the other bank. Incidentally, at the very end of the bridge, one rear wheel of the wooden tank went through the planking and stuck there, refusing to budge.

It was this hitch that gave the Reds time to throw up a new line of defense, but by then the Mensheviks were on the other bank.

They say that when the horsemen were fording the Kodor, a terrible human cry suddenly rang out over all the rifle shots and the crackling of machine guns. It was Kunta's wife.

Kunta's son was on a white horse and everyone watching the battle from the village saw him. Uncle Sandro saw him too, as he watched this interesting battle with Mikha from behind one of the cypresses that adorned his friend's yard. Since Uncle Sandro was watching the proceedings through his binoculars, he could see better than the others.

Kunta's son had descended to the Kodor delta along with the rest of the horsemen and had crossed one of its small branches when the horse in front of him suddenly veered, threw its rider, and went galloping back.

The infuriated rider jumped up and grabbed the tail of the white horse, who happened to be within his reach. The man was a soldier, not a volunteer, because, as Uncle Sandro said, a volunteer would have run after his own horse, he wouldn't go grabbing the tail of someone else's.

Through the binoculars Uncle Sandro saw Kunta's son turn to the soldier and begin to quarrel, while the horse wheeled, scattering pebbles, between the main riverbed and the branch. Evidently they reached an agreement, because Kunta's son stopped the horse and the soldier dragged himself across her rear. The horse started forward, and after they were already in the water the soldier managed to fling his leg over and sit up at the rider's back.

They had crossed the worst of the rapids when suddenly the horse and both riders disappeared beneath the water. The village cried out with one voice, but now the horse's head and two human heads reappeared above water, much farther downstream. After a moment they all disappeared again, and then one human head appeared above water. People could see how the man was struggling with the current, how it was carrying him farther and farther down.

He swam out right under the bridge, and when he crawled up on shore everyone knew by his clothes that the survivor was the soldier. It was then that Kunta's wife's terrible cry rang out. She must have hoped until the last moment that her son would be the one to swim out.

That day the fighting shifted conclusively to the other side of the river, and when evening was still two or three hours away, the villagers of Ankhara decided to turn their starving livestock out to pasture.

There were stubborn battles in this area for about a week. So say the history books, citing eyewitness accounts, and so also say the eyewitnesses, partly citing the history books.

Then the Red defense was finally broken and the Mensheviks rolled through all Abkhazia. The Abkhazian Revolutionary Military Council was forced to wire Lenin for help, after which soldiers of the glorious Tenth Army smashed the enemy and thrust them back from the borders of Abkhazia.

But unfortunately that was a long time off, both on the day described and on the following day, when Uncle Sandro encountered Kunta on the village road.

Kunta was walking along with a wet, swollen saddle over his shoulders. When he saw Uncle Sandro he stopped wordlessly and gazed at him in bewilderment. Uncle Sandro and Mikha, who was seeing him off, dismounted and went to him to express their sympathy.

Kunta said nothing. Looking at his reddened eyelids, his mournful swollen nose, his big-veined fists gripping the saddle girths, Uncle Sandro could hardly keep from bursting into sobs like a woman.

The body of the horse had washed up a few kilometers from the village. Kunta had removed the saddle so that it would not be stolen. Now he was carrying it home. From there he planned to go out with his fellow villagers in search of his son's body. He said that as soon as he buried his son he would go catch up with the Mensheviks, to meet the lad who had gotten on his horse with him.

"Why?" Uncle Sandro asked.

"Maybe my boy said something to him before he died," Kunta said, and he began crying, just his eyes. Tears flowed down his face along with the sweat, and from time to time he wiped them with his fist, still tightly gripping the saddle girth.

What could Uncle Sandro say to him? He silently embraced Kunta, and the latter set off down the road with the wet old saddle on his shoulders.

"The way he was yesterday, and the way he is today," Mikha sighed, looking after him.

Uncle Sandro made no answer, and they mounted their horses again.

Having accompanied Uncle Sandro to the far end of the village, Mikha stopped and asked him, "What did you think of the Red commissar?"

"A ruler," Uncle Sandro said quietly. After a moment's thought he added, "He's the one, you'll see."

At this the friends parted. Uncle Sandro started back to Chegem, and Mikha returned home, dispiritedly wondering how to adjust to the new living conditions and still preserve himself, his family, and his pig farm.

CHEGEM GOSSIP

ONE HOT JULY NOON Uncle Sandro lay resting under an apple tree in his yard, as is fitting at that time of day even if you have not been doing anything. It was all the more fitting for Uncle Sandro because he had spent the whole morning hoeing his corn. Admittedly he had not been knocking himself out, but still he was doubly savoring the pleasure of rest.

Lying on an oxhide, with his head on a *murtaka* (a special bolster that in our part of the world is put under the pillow at night, and is used instead of a pillow in the daytime if we feel like napping)—with his head on the *murtaka*, he gazed up into the crown of the apple tree, where still-green apples peeped out of the green foliage and cascades of grapes drooped here and there with careless generosity, unripe but already lightly streaked by the sun.

It was very hot, and in Uncle Sandro's view the little puffs of wind that sometimes reached the foot of the apple tree were rare and sweet as the caress of a capricious woman. This view was less than appropriate, considering that his two-year-old daughter Tali sat within two feet of him on the oxhide, and his wife's voice reached him now and again from where she was puttering in the vegetable garden.

Of course Uncle Sandro could have moved over under the mightier shade of the walnut tree, which stood more open to the wind and caught the distant sea breeze more often, but there were more flies over there and it smelled slightly of dung on account of its proximity to the goat pen.

So Uncle Sandro lay under the apple tree, enjoying the relatively rare but clean breaths of coolness, looking now at the crown of the apple tree and now at his own daughter, listening now to the rare whisper of the wind in the apple tree and now to his wife's voice from the vegetable garden, a voice which, unlike the miserly puffs of wind, buzzed ceaselessly on the air. His wife was loudly reproaching a hen, and the hen in turn, to judge by her cackling, was reproaching her mistress. Aunt Katya, after what she thought of as lengthy and subtle maneuvers, had tracked down the hen, who turned out to have laid her eggs behind the garden, where she had made herself a nest in the elder bushes, instead of laying them (like a decent body, as Aunt Katya said) in the baskets set aside for the purpose, where all proper hens laid their eggs.

Having finally discovered her just now at the scene of the crime—if hatching one's own eggs, even if in the elder bushes, can be called a crime—having caught her in this sub-rosa occupation, she drove her off the eggs, transferred all fourteen into the hem of her skirt, and was now returning through the vegetable patch to the yard with this trophy.

Holding up her hem with one hand, she scrutinized the garden as she went. Now she would pull up a mighty weed that had impudently grown up between the rows, now she would alter the pernicious direction in which a pumpkin or cucumber vine was growing. Continuing with her main theme, that is, the unmasking of the ungrateful hen, she would manage to address a venomous aside to the weed, too—"Did I manure this bed and weed it for *you*?"—and put the pumpkin vine in its place: "No good stretching where you're not invited . . ."

All this time the hen followed her, loudly and futilely demanding the return of her unhatched eggs. When a particularly hysterical note appeared in the hen's cackling, Aunt Katya interrupted her monologue to say, "Yes . . . yes . . . you're scared . . . I'm going to put your eggs out for you now . . ."

Uncle Sandro lay under the apple tree and listened to her slowly approaching voice. He was amazed at his wife's inexhaustible capacity for conversing with inanimate objects—plants, birds, animals.

Now off on a new tack, she was saying how if you're an honest hen but don't want to lay your eggs like the others, then don't come running ahead of the rest when your mistress calls the chickens to be fed, go feed in the woods like the other wildfowl, risking every minute that they'll fall into the clutches of the fox, the hawk, or somebody like that. Here she started on a new ramification of her theme and began to voice a guess as to how and why it was that the fox hadn't gobbled up these eggs before now, along with this little fool of a hen, and came to the conclusion that the fox was evidently waiting for the chicks to hatch.

Uncle Sandro could not take any more. Without waiting for yet another ramification of the theme, he shouted to her to shut up and maybe then the hen would quiet down too. Better yet, go get some fresh water from the spring and take the loudmouth with you, and the two of you talk yourselves out on the way, and with you gone we may get some rest around here.

Before he could finish, Aunt Katya, who had just mounted the stile in order to get over into the yard, cried, "Hush! Someone's coming up from the spring!"

"What do you mean?" Uncle Sandro asked, raising his head slightly from the *murtaka*-bolster. He scrutinized the upper Chegem road, as much of it as was visible through the gaps between the trees, but saw nothing there.

"There's a stranger coming up from right by the spring!" Aunt Katya said. Already angry at her hen, who continued to cackle on about the old subject without realizing that her mistress was now busy with something else entirely, she shouted, "Oh shut up, may a hawk get you!"

"What do you mean, a stranger?" Uncle Sandro was surprised at the absurdity of the suggestion that a stranger might be coming up from the spring. Never in his born days! A stranger might appear on the upper Chegem road or the lower Chegem road, but he wouldn't come popping out of the spring cave.

"Just get up off your backside!" Aunt Katya shouted fromthe stile, and then Uncle Sandro actually did get up and see a man ascending by the path that came from the spring.

"Whoever he is, he's coming with bad news," Aunt Katya said, still standing on the stile holding up her skirt with one hand. The hen had already flown over the wattle fence and was cackling at Aunt Katya from the yard.

"It's Shashiko's nephew!" Recognizing him, Uncle Sandro was suddenly alert. "Only what's he doing at the spring?"

"Well, it's all clear now," Aunt Katya said, still standing on the stile. "Poor Shashiko, they've finally ambushed and killed him."

"How do you know he's a messenger of woe?" Uncle Sandro said. He scrutinized the gloomy figure of the nephew of the notorious abrek Shashiko. Clearly the lad was not bringing good news.

"Are we going to keep on standing here with your skirt hiked up?" Uncle Sandro asked his wife, who was still standing on the stile.

Aunt Katya hastily got down from the stile. Trailed by the clucking hen, she headed for the rear of the kitchen, where baskets meant for laying eggs hung in a row. Into one of these she put the eggs she had gathered in the elder bush.

The hen started cackling even louder, expressing her unwillingness to fly up into the basket.

"You'll do it," Aunt Katya answered spitefully. "May I live to see your wings broken . . ."

"May you get the chicken plague," Uncle Sandro responded from under the apple tree, his tone indicating that he made no distinction between the hen and her mistress, he was so sick of both of them.

Meanwhile, Azrael's gloomy messenger was already crossing the barnyard, and Uncle Sandro went out to meet him. Assuming an expression of sorrow befitting the moment, he opened the gate and let him into the yard.

Aunt Katya too crossed the yard and approached the supposed messenger of woe, from a distance mouthing repetitive fragments of a funeral lament, with the sense intentionally obscured because of her total lack of information. Small disjointed snatches stuck out: Poor Shashiko . . . His poor, poor mother . . . He's been killed by mad dogs . . .

Uncle Sandro invited the young man into the house, but he flatly refused. Then Uncle Sandro realized that this was something else again. As a scaled-down version of hospitality he invited him in under the shade of the apple tree, and the man followed him there, none too willingly.

Uncle Sandro seated him on the oxhide. He himself sat down beside his daughter on a sheepskin and began waiting quietly to hear what his guest would say. But while the guest was collecting his thoughts, of course, Aunt Katya lost patience and asked, "But how did they kill our poor Shashiko?"

"Shashiko's alive," his nephew answered. "I'm here about something else. Please God it will end well . . ."

"What is it?" Uncle Sandro asked sparingly, as is proper, because too great an interest in an unknown matter might evoke in the bearer of the news an undesirable impression of excessive interest.

In a sorrowful voice the lad reported that rumors had reached Shashiko that Uncle Sandro had told someone that one of these days, when Shashiko came to his house, he was planning to betray him and turn him over to the authorities, dead or alive. I shall not conceal, the lad added, that Shashiko is terribly angered, and lest blood be shed, Uncle Sandro must find convincing proof of his innocence.

"What's he doing, flinging himself on his own people like a mad dog?" Aunt Katya wailed, forgetting that a moment ago she had used the image of the mad dog in a completely opposite sense.

"Did he ever wonder," Uncle Sandro added in a calm voice, "why I should need to betray my relative, the bravest abrek in Abkhazia?"

"Yes, he did," the nephew answered. "They told him that in exchange for this betrayal the authorities would forgive your house for sheltering him and other abreks so many times."

"Pretty clever," Uncle Sandro agreed, "but the authorities haven't made me any such offer, and what's more, I haven't made any to them."

"Then tell him so," the nephew answered, trying to show good will toward Uncle Sandro and at the same time represent his famous uncle's interests adequately.

". . . He's waiting for you under the walnut tree over the spring," he added after a pause.

"Fine," Uncle Sandro said, getting to his feet. "Go ahead, I'll be right along."

"Sorry, Sandro," the youth answered, also getting to his feet, "but my uncle ordered us to come together."

"Oho!" said Uncle Sandro. "Then he's already arrested me?"

The nephew shrugged, which meant, So he has, but I daren't speak the words.

"All right," Uncle Sandro agreed. Pointing to his bare feet and rolled-up breeches, he added, "I'll go change and be right out."

With that he went into the house. He changed his shirt, put on another pair of pants, and tucked his old Smith & Wesson inside them, checking the hammer first.

"Hey, you," he shouted to his wife, sticking his head out the window, "find me my new pants!"

His wife realized from his voice that he was up to something and came hurrying in.

"You aren't really going to that murderer, like a lamb to the slaughter, are you?" she lamented in a whisper as she entered the room. She sensed that her husband wanted her to help in some way.

Uncle Sandro indicated to her with a nod that he approved of her lamentations, that they were useful now and might even be more sonorous.

"You'll go to the barn," he said quietly, "and tell my brother to take his rifle and come out opposite the spring by way of the woods, without being seen. I'll be talking to Shashiko. Tell him to keep Shashiko in his sights the whole time, and if I can't persuade him and he goes for his gun, tell Isa to shoot. Only Father's not to know anything."

"Maybe it'd be better to tell him?" his wife put in. She began a new lamentation.

"You'd ruin everything," Uncle Sandro answered. "It all has to be decided right now."

Uncle Sandro realized that if his father got wind of anything he would come to the spring, cuss Shashiko out, maybe poke him in the butt with his rifle, and Shashiko would not dare answer back. Such was the force of a patriarchal upbringing: respect for old age. But then when Shashiko went back to the forest his resentment would accumulate drop by drop, and one fine day he might kill Uncle Sandro, this time without warning.

Uncle Sandro went out on the porch, washed his feet, and put on his boots. As he went down the steps, which were made of three great stone slabs whose every pockmark he remembered from his childhood, he suddenly thought: Will I really never see all this again?

That can't be, he told himself. Springing lightly down the steps he seized his little daughter, who was now chasing a butterfly around the yard. He tossed her up in the air, kissed her, set her on her feet, and nodded to the abrek's waiting messenger: "Let's go!"

"Valiko, I beg you as a brother, do what you can," Aunt Katya lamented, accompanying them to the gate.

The nephew softened for a moment. He turned and said, "Don't worry, Aunt Katya, Shashiko's very angry, but he hasn't lost his reason."

As soon as they disappeared beyond the gate, Aunt Katya—evidently not counting much on the abrek's reasonableness—ran to the barn, where old Khabug and his son Isa were making brandy from wild pears. At this moment the old man was not in the barn. Uncle Sandro's brother was nodding drowsily as he sat by the still and watched the brandy drip through the straw into the bottle.

Aunt Katya squatted down beside him, shook him, and repeated all that her husband had asked her to tell his brother.

"It's running strong as a mule," he said when she finished. He nodded at the alcohol dripping down through the straw into the bottle.

Perhaps from his long tour of duty by the still, perhaps from his endless testing of the first-shot (the potent first runnings), Uncle Sandro's brother was somewhat obtunded. He did not seem to grasp what Aunt Katya was saying. He even let some brandy drip into a glass for her to taste.

"Did you understand what I said?" Aunt Katya shouted at him, knocking away his hand with the offering.

"What's to understand," Isa replied. "I've been sick of your Sandro's doings ever since he was a kid. Watch that the coil doesn't overheat."

He drank off the glass of brandy that Aunt Katya had rejected, then got to his feet and went out of the barn. He would have to go to his own house, which was on top of the hill, and then down through the copse to the spring. It was about as far to the spring from his house as it was from the Big House.

While Uncle Sandro and Shashiko's nephew are moving toward the spring from one direction, and Uncle Sandro's brother is hurrying home to get his gun and go down there under cover of the woods, we will try to give a brief account of the history of Shashiko, the famous abrek.

I wondered for quite a while whether I should tell how and why Shashiko became an abrek. Wouldn't it tarnish in the telling, that romantic image that I had heard so much about ever since childhood?

Yet, after hesitating at length and weighing the pros and cons, I have decided that though his image tarnish, we will remain faithful to the truth. But what's the big deal, why should I care so much for the truth—especially in our business, where we heighten things for effect, discard things, generalize things?

Yes, we may generalize and heighten and omit, but only if we have a lively feeling that in so doing we are furthering the cause of truth. When I feel that I have lied, even if only by keeping silent, I lose all desire to write and tell stories. But why?

Every man to whom it is granted to lift himself above the vain bustle of the world, if only for a moment, realizes the solemnity of the gift of life that fate has given him. He cannot fail to understand that this gift is limited in time and he must use it as best he can.

Incidentally, fast livers are not men who have given up on the gift of life but men who understand the value of life in this way and are therefore seeing to it that they accumulate this value.

Thus a man who realizes the solemnity of the gift of life that has been granted him, its secret temporariness, tries at all costs to balance the scales by weighing this terrible realization against a serious life design.

To live is the attempt to accomplish a serious design. The more weighty the terrible realization that the solemn gift of life is temporary, the stronger is the intention to balance the scales with a most serious lifework. And so nature grants man the drive to escape from dust, annihilation, nonexistence, by means of a serious lifework.

But if we have undertaken to make the story of life our life's work, the most unconditional and obvious measure of our intent is the veracity of the story. Thus the storyteller's veracity is necessary first of all to the storyteller himself. It is a form of his struggle against his own disintegration; it is, one might say, the divine egoism of his own being.

What I have been getting ready to say is that Shashiko became an abrek after he killed an unfortunate tailor from the village of Dzhgerdy, where he lived. I myself learned this disagreeable fact long after I learned about all his other feats, and it did not fit his stern romantic image at all.

But, for the reasons which I have just set forth, this too must be told.

So, when Shashiko was a sixteen-year-old boy—already well-grown for his age, it is true, and tall and handsome—he ordered a cherkeska from the local tailor in the village of Dzhgerdy.

The story goes that the tailor, knowing that his customer was hard up for cash, took his time making the cherkeska. After three or four unkept promises, the proud and hot-tempered youth returned home, fetched his father's rifle, went to the tailor's house, and shot him.

That was how it all began. He went away to the forest, where he joined up with an old, experienced abrek. Time passed, and after a few years he himself became an experienced abrek. On several occasions police details tried to surround him, but he always escaped from them, leaving two or three of them wounded, if not dead.

From constant danger and living so long in the deep forest, he turned wild and became incredibly sensitive to smells and sounds of every sort. They say he could catch the scent of a man in the woods at two or three hundred meters.

One time Uncle Sandro crossed the Caucasian crest with him and stole a large flock of sheep from a rich Adygean. On the third day, they had already made it back to Abkhazia and were walking along a rocky mountain path when Shashiko suddenly stopped, listened to something, and with the cry "Get down!" threw himself to the ground. Uncle Sandro flopped down after him and almost simultaneously heard several bullets chirr overhead. Only after that did they hear the shots. It seems their pursuers had overtaken them and come out ahead. They barely managed to get away, saving part of the stolen flock.

Anyone who thinks that a man hiding in the woods turns into a pantheist is deeply mistaken. The sensation of constant danger, the realization that they can hunt you down, bring you to bay like a wild animal, induces a nervous exhaustion that develops into relentless fury.

Once Shashiko fell into an ambush. He had sneaked home in the night to wash and change, and was sitting over a home-cooked supper.

Suddenly came the voice of a police officer at the gate: "Shashiko, surrender! The house is surrounded!"

The house was so situated that one end of the veranda hung over a precipice overgrown with impassable thickets of blackberries and blackthorn. It was the only way out of the ambush. That was what Shashiko was counting on.

"Shashiko, surrender!" the police officer's voice boomed again. Shashiko had already put out the lamp and was standing by the door, his army rifle at the ready.

When the officer's voice boomed out the second time, he kicked open the door with one blow, shot by guesswork at the voice in the dark, raced crouching to the end of the veranda, and without breaking stride leaped fearlessly down the precipice.

The moment Shashiko opened the door and fired, almost simultaneously, the officer's shot rang out. He was evidently a good marksman and had the door in his sights.

His bullet hit Shashiko on the thumb of his right hand, but Shashiko's shot, it turns out, killed the officer. As soon as the first shot rang out, a hail of bullets fell on the house. Shashiko's father, deciding that his son had been killed or wounded, came out of the room and was immediately killed by a fresh volley. Shashiko, meanwhile, escaped from the ambush by successfully leaping down the precipice, which no one dared descend even by day.

His pursuers waited until morning and descended the precipice by a roundabout way, confident that he was lying there riddled with bullets or at least with a broken neck.

After a while they came on a bloody trail and followed it lustily, but were rather quickly disappointed because the trail led not to the abrek's body but to his thumb. The thumb, shattered by the bullet, had been dangling from his hand. Shashiko cut it off with his knife, bound up the bleeding hand with his turban, and went on.

With this curious trophy, obviously not equal in value to the officer's body, the pursuers returned to Kengur. At the police station the thumb was placed in a bottle of alcohol, either for public viewing so that the police, gazing at the abrek's dead thumb, might become accustomed to feel their living superiority over it; or for the sake of precision in the face of higher authorities, as proof that they had managed to seize at least this corporeal fragment from the elusive abrek.

By that evening, striding through the most impassable thickets, Shashiko had covered about forty kilometers and made his way to the same princely house where Uncle Sandro had once loved and been loved by the princess. By this time, according to Uncle Sandro, his love had become a peaceful friendship.

In those days it was considered a matter of honor, even for a princely house, to take in a wounded abrek.

The wound healed quickly, and the princess just as quickly—or perhaps even more quickly—adopted the young abrek in Uncle Sandro's place.

To conceal from her entourage the suspicious presence of the no-longer-wounded, quite healthy abrek in the honorable prince's house, she arranged a match for him with one of her young relatives, who had fallen passionately in love with him. A semiclandestine marriage took place, after which the young couple stayed on in the prince's house for their honeymoon.

It is not known how long or in what proportion they shared the honey, but in the end the young abrek's pregnant wife went back home, while the abrek himself was detained by the princess, who behaved even more madly and incautiously than in Uncle Sandro's time, forgetting that Shashiko, unlike Uncle Sandro, was a state criminal.

But who knows the secrets of a woman's passion? Maybe the threat of death hanging over the young abrek called forth waves of extra tenderness in her, a desire to use her body to shield him a little more closely from the police bullets, to hug, defend, and hide him in her loving womanly bosom.

People began to whisper to the prince. One fine day he left for a protracted hunting trip, but he returned the next day unexpectedly, at an ungodly hour, and caught Shashiko in his bedroom.

Shashiko said later that he had sensed the danger. An hour before the prince arrived he had wanted to slip away from the house to his secret lair in the woods, from which he made his sallies to the prince's house. But the damn princess wouldn't let him go, and, burning with shame, he was forced to abandon forever the hospitality—and more important, the safety—of the prince's house.

Besides, the relatives of Shashiko's young wife—specifically, her brothers—heard rumors of what had happened, of course, and were insulted. These proud and quite vengeful men were added to the abrek's numerous enemies.

No words can convey the shame, pain, and bitterness of the young wife who had fallen in love with him. As with all pure people, incapable of perfidy and treachery, it had never entered her head that this woman, almost twice as old as her husband, could seduce him and then marry him off to a relative in order to conceal her crime. Incidentally, the prince finally exploded with unexpected force, as happens with very peaceable men. He turned the princess out of his house and she was forced to move to Mukhus, to her sister's.

It is true that she later returned to the village two or three times and tried to reestablish herself by storming her own house, but the prince, with the support of his sons, who were already quite grown up, boldly beat off these tragicomic attacks. Soundly defeated, the princess was forced to return each time to the city, where in the end she subsided for good.

When my mother got married and came to the city, accompanied, as is our custom, by several men and women from among her closest friends and relatives, she says she found the princess waiting for her with the wedding party at my father's house, convinced that Shashiko would surely use this opportunity to come to the city and see her. According to Mama, the princess was absolutely crushed when she saw that he was not in Mama's entourage.

What kind of love was this, even considering her natural frivolity, to expect an abrek who had been hunted for more than ten years to appear in the very center of Abkhazia, in Mukhus? Or did she think that once beyond the borders of the Kenguria District he could not be touched?

Poor princess, let us forgive her her sins. After all, for the sake of her mad love she lost her peace of mind, and her good name, and a social position that was high by our local standards. That's obviously an exaggeration about her good name, but the rest she really did lose.

It is interesting that Uncle Sandro, when he recalled the princess's lovers, including himself, always admitted that she loved Shashiko best of all. He spoke of this with the epic indifference of Homer. But Uncle Sandro would not have been Uncle Sandro if he had not introduced a modicum of doubt into his statement at this point. While he gave her stormy temperament its due, he more than once hinted, expressing himself in contemporary language, at a certain sexual illiteracy on her part. So in the end, what it came to was: Take it any way you want.

Now that we have given some picture of the young abrek's life, we will return to the beginning of our tale, where he had spread out his burka and was sitting above the spring at the foot of a huge walnut tree, with a hand on the butt of his army rifle. In this pose, which presaged no good, he waited for Uncle Sandro.

Uncle Sandro and the abrek's nephew approached, but although he heard their steps the abrek did not turn, thereby perhaps expressing an added measure of scorn for Uncle Sandro.

"Well be you!" Uncle Sandro said as he approached the seated abrek, mentally noting where his brother might lie in ambush in order to shoot in good time.

Shashiko was sitting on a green mound directly above a precipitous slope about fifteen meters high. From under it flowed the spring, enclosed by a wattle fence so that cattle would not drink where people got their own water. Above him, the green mountainside sloped up toward Isa's house, with a thick brambly forest on the left. That was where Uncle Sandro's sharp-eyed brother could hide.

"Well be you." Uncle Sandro repeated his greeting and walked around the seated abrek to stop before him in a pose that was sufficiently respectful but would in no way block the target in case a shot from the woods was needed.

"We shall see whether you greet your guests well or ill," the abrek said, casting a brief sidewise glance in his direction without turning his head. Uncle Sandro was standing slightly below and to the left of the abrek and realized how easy it would be for Shashiko, if things came to that, to raise his rifle and kill him. Have to play for time, Uncle Sandro thought, sensing that the hope he placed in his brother was reinforcing his spiritual strength.

"Did you really mean to sell me out because of the prince's bitch?" Shashiko asked at last, glancing up at Uncle Sandro, but with such a sense of superiority that he seemed to be looking down on Uncle Sandro from somewhere high above.

"My dealings with the princess ended long before you," Uncle Sandro replied with dignity. "And you needn't insult the princess, especially since she's suffered because of you—"

"Then how dare you say what you said?" he asked. In his eyes glinted the fury of an animal hunted to exhaustion.

"I never said any such thing," Uncle Sandro replied, as calmly as he could. "They've deceived you—"

"You did say it!" Shashiko roared. "The man who told me so wouldn't dare lie. You, the son of Khabug, a man famous for his hospitality—you let me into your house, seated me at your table, so that then you could kill me, like they kill a sick dog after they've stuffed him with food?"

"Take it easy," Uncle Sandro said, mustering all his strength. "That's slander."

"Slander!" Shashiko repeated threateningly. He nodded to his speechless nephew: "Go get him!"

The nephew silently descended the precipitous slope and started down a little path leading into the forest. Wonder who they've got hidden there, Uncle Sandro thought, looking after the departing nephew.

Twenty minutes later, the nephew reappeared on the path in the company of the local forest warden, Omar, a cranky man with an evil tongue.

During the First World War Omar went into the Wild Division as a volunteer. When he came home from the war with the Cross of St. George and the ability to speak and read a little Russian, they named him forest warden here.

He was also famous for sleeping with the wife of his younger brother, Kunta, a rather stupid man, whose fellow villagers often asked him, for laughs, "Why doesn't your brother get married?"

"He likes 'em used," Kunta would answer readily and loudly, "since being in the army, see."

And now here came Omar escorted by Shashiko's nephew, climbing up the precipitous slope, frightened out of his wits, while Uncle Sandro thought, What will happen if Shashiko believes this son of a bitch? Or if he doesn't believe him, and takes a notion to finish him off? And if Omar, just like me, has warned his brother in case of an evil outcome, and now the brother's hiding in the woods? Will they all shoot each other?

Omar came up quietly and stood near Shashiko, hanging his guilty head.

"Repeat what he said," Shashiko demanded.

Omar, pale as the trunk of a beech tree, hung his head still lower.

"Well?" Shashiko fidgeted on his burka, picked up his gun and dropped it again on the burka.

Omar quietly shook his head.

"Have you lost your tongue?" Shashiko bellowed.

"Sorry, Shashiko," Omar said softly, "I just imagined it."

"Imagined it!" Shashiko echoed in a furious whisper.

"Imagined I heard it," Omar explained, without raising his head.

"Imagined you heard it!" Shashiko repeated. Without looking he felt for the rifle with his right hand, shifted the barrel to his left, and started to rise. Slowly getting to his feet, he straightened up before the little warden, who had fought on many fronts in the war but now lacked the strength to move before the huge abrek with wild blue eyes and an Austrian rifle in his hand. On its worm-eaten stock were fourteen notches, scratched with the sharp edge of a cartridge case.

"So you know what you'll get for this?"

"I know," Omar whispered, without raising his eyes.

"What?" Shashiko asked. He began slowly raising his rifle.

"Death," Omar said softly, without raising his eyes.

Well, if his brother's in ambush, Uncle Sandro thought, he'll start shooting now, and he'll stupidly hit me too. He took an inconspicuous step sideways, farther from Shashiko.

"Hey, you!" Aunt Masha's voice suddenly rang out. Her house was directly opposite the spring on a small rise.

She was standing by the wattle fence that surrounded her yard, looking toward the spring. Since Shashiko and the participants in the scene at the spring were hidden by alder thickets, she could not see them, but she had vaguely heard people talking. Shashiko was a fairly close relative of hers and she had recognized his voice.

Without waiting for a reply, she shouted again, "Am I deaf or do I hear Shashiko?"

"Yes, it's me!" Shashiko answered unexpectedly. He lowered his rifle.

"You've gone wild in the woods," Aunt Masha chirped, "turned into a wild animal . . . If you've come to drink at our water hole, come on up, we'll treat you to something stronger than water."

"We'll be right up," Shashiko said suddenly, with a look at Uncle Sandro. "I just have to finish something here."

"Finish and come on up!" cried the hospitable Aunt Masha. She went inside her yard.

"Turn your back," Shashiko ordered. Omar quietly turned.

"To the end of your days, thank Masha for your life," Shashiko added, and he kicked Omar in the butt so hard that he flew several meters through the air. He crashed to the steep slope, grunted, rolled to the foot of it, jumped up, shook himself off like a dog, and with hasty steps disappeared on the forest path.

"Hardy as a hound," the abrek said in surprise.

"The whole clan's like that—sons of bitches," Uncle Sandro explained.

"Is it all forgotten?" Shashiko said, turning to him.

"What's to remember?" Uncle Sandro shrugged, indicating that he attached no significance to what had happened between them.

"Chick, chick, chick, chick, chick!" From the yard came Aunt Masha's peaceful and peace-inducing voice, calling the chickens, obviously in order to catch one of them and kill it, because of her invitation to Shashiko.

A big red rooster, hastening from the cornpatch at her call, jumped up on the fence in order to fly over into the yard. He was just taking off, it seems, when Shashiko suddenly raised his rifle and fired. The cock's body shot upward and then, scattering a fountain of golden feathers, tumbled to the ground.

Immediately the chickens set up a mad cackling, the turkeys gobbled, the dogs howled, Aunt Masha lamented her rooster, and in a few seconds Aunt Katya's anxious voice resounded from the Big House, asking what was that shot—had Shashiko killed her husband?

Aunt Masha, meanwhile, gathered up the slain cock and looked toward the spring, where Uncle Sandro, Shashiko, and his nephew were coming single file down the path.

"Your cock's alive, alive!" Aunt Masha shouted, shooing away a dog that was sniffing at the slain bird. "It's my cock he's killed, the fool."

Uncle Sandro and Shashiko laughed when they heard Aunt Katya's cry and Aunt Masha's answer. Masha was on her way to the kitchen with the cock in her hand. They started down toward the spring so as to climb up from there to her house.

Suddenly Shashiko turned. With a wink at Uncle Sandro and a nod toward the forest, he said to his nephew, "Tell his brother to come out of there and bring us some of his first-shot."

"How did you know he was there?" Uncle Sandro asked, laughing.

"Sit in the woods as long as I have and fear will wash your ears clean," the abrek replied.

The nephew turned and went to the forest while Uncle Sandro and Shashiko climbed up to Aunt Masha's house. Her two powerfully built little girls popped out of the kitchen and rushed to meet them. Shashiko stooped to pick them up. One of them settled on his shoulder while the other simply hung on him, gripping his hair with her strong little hands. The abrek's face, slightly distorted by a grimace, did not express pain so much as a voluptuous pleasure—evoked, as Uncle Sandro understood, by a yearning for home, for his own hearth.

Evidently he's been coming here and I didn't even know, Uncle Sandro thought.

"How come you're inviting men into the house when your husband's not home!" Shashiko shouted humorously as he entered the kitchen. Bending down, he carefully shook off the little girl clutching his hair and set the other one down. He threw off his burka and tossed it in a corner, then unslung his rifle, carefully leaned it against the wall, and sat down next to it, beside the fire. The children again rushed to pester him. It occurred to Uncle Sandro that children have a good feel for people who are hungry for them.

"It's all right," Aunt Masha answered after a moment. Taking the rooster out of a pot of boiling water, she set about plucking it. "My husband's brothers are around . . . protectors."

He knows both that we're making brandy and that Masha's husband isn't home, Uncle Sandro noted to himself, settling down beside the abrek near the fire. Good for the nephew, Uncle Sandro thought—put on the seriousness of a messenger of woe, but he'd gone all around the houses in the family settlement first and found out which of the men were home and what they were doing.

Soon Aunt Masha had grilled the rooster and boiled the cornmeal, and now the nephew arrived, leading Uncle Sandro's somewhat embarrassed brother, who was holding a bottle of pear brandy in each hand.

At first his embarrassment was understood as the natural embarrassment of a man who has been sitting in ambush waiting for a convenient moment to shoot at a man with whom he now must sit and drink. During the meal, however, it became clear that his embarrassment had a more complicated cause, which Uncle Sandro found mortifying.

It seemed that when Shashiko's nephew went into the woods opposite the spring to get Uncle Sandro's brother, he found him there peacefully asleep—alas—with his head pillowed on his gun.

What most infuriated Uncle Sandro was that his brother had not been wakened by the shot that killed the cock. That shot, if things had turned out a bit worse, might have killed the foolish warden, or if things had really turned out badly, Uncle Sandro himself. Uncle Sandro's brother said in self-defense that at first he had carefully watched all that was happening and had kept our distinguished guest in his sights the whole time (why hide the fact!). But then, when the nephew left, he decided that nothing terrible was going to happen and went to sleep. Besides, he added, he hadn't closed his eyes in days beside the still. They had a good long laugh over Uncle Sandro's luckless brother, taking the measure of his peaceful slumber now one way, now another.

"That would've been a laugh," Shashiko said, stretching the limits of humor somewhat, as an abrek, "if I'd killed our Sandro and laid his body next to his sleeping brother."

Uncle Sandro laughed along with everyone else, although to tell the truth the idea didn't strike him all that funny. They were still laughing at this dark joke of Shashiko's when Uncle Sandro's wife came into the kitchen. After listening to the burst of laughter (patiently, but without any attempt to join in) she turned to her husband and said in a sanctimonious voice, "You'd better finish hoeing that field, now that he didn't kill you."

Her remark lent fresh humor to Shashiko's joke, and now Uncle Sandro laughed with the rest of them in complete sincerity. He kept saying, "What have I done to make you all thirst for my death."

They laughed at Aunt Katya's remark for an especially long time. The funniest thing was that she herself had no idea what they were laughing at, and her face was set in mourning as if she were still wearing the expression she had assumed right after the shot. At the same time, in light of Uncle Sandro's last exclamation, her mournful expression might have been construed as regret that the shot had killed the wrong cock. But the final humor of her pose and her remark lay in her uncertain attempt to put Uncle Sandro back to work now that the threat of death had passed, whereas in Uncle Sandro's understanding—everyone knew this, including her—the passing of a threat of death immediately disposed him to a long, boisterous session at table. The laughter of those around the table was a gay unmasking of her naive stratagem.

In a word, they drank gloriously of pear brandy that day. Shashiko came again to the Big House more than once, to eat, change his clothes, and wash, and nothing threatened him there except the fear of bumping into old Khabug. Uncle Sandro's father was not overfond of abreks himself; he had given his word to the elder at an assembly many years ago that he would not allow abreks into his house, and he formally kept his promise. His tacit agreement with his household was: Do what you want, but don't let me lay eyes on them.

To make a long story short, the famous abrek never again suspected Uncle Sandro of perfidious plots. Two years later the authorities declared amnesty for all abreks of prerevolutionary standing.

After fifteen years of life in the forest, Shashiko returned home to his mother and younger brother, who by this time had managed to get married and raise children.

Shashiko lived at home for about six months, and according to neighbors who saw him, there never was a peasant so eager for work. For days on end he busied himself in the vegetable garden, dug around the fruit trees and pruned them, hoed the corn, chopped shingle in the woods, replaced the dilapidated roof of his father's house, and kept saying, whenever he got the chance, that true happiness was to live in your own home, work in your own field, and sleep in your own bed.

Once he went to the village where his poor wife lived, to ask her forgiveness and take her and her son back home. But her brothers flatly refused to have anything to do with him, and they secretly took the son away to another village, fearing that the father would try to kidnap him. They knew that he was very lonesome for his son.

Shashiko insisted on meeting with his wife himself, but when he entered the yard of her parents' house, where she lived, they loosed the dogs on him, and he went away, enduring this humiliation in silence.

Who knows what his wife felt when he entered the yard and they loosed the dogs on him, when, turning ghastly pale at the insult, he walked backwards toward the gate?

Was she watching him from somewhere, perhaps from behind a window curtain? Could she *not* have watched?

Who knows what she felt? The satisfaction of revenge for insulted love? Or a desire to rush after him—her beloved husband still, in spite of everything—and with an all-forgiving caress restore to life his wild wolf heart?

But Shashiko was not fated to live and die peacefully in his own home. Six months after his return home, the chief of the Kenguria district police was killed. He was killed by one of the abreks who was still hiding in the woods.

On account of this murder many former abreks received a summons to report to the Kengur police station. Shashiko too received a summons. He said at home that he would not go to the police station, because he felt in his heart that he would never get out of there alive.

For two whole days his brother tried to persuade him to go to the police, thereby proving that he had nothing to fear, that he had taken no part in the murder. The brother assured him that the Soviet authorities had issued this summons as a way of establishing who was too frightened to appear and therefore still had ties to the abreks who had not surrendered.

Shashiko finally consented, against his will, when his brother promised to go with him to the police. Neither of them ever came home.

The authorities had decided to deal sternly this time with the most famous abreks, in order to put a scare into the rest. From the Kengur police station they were marched to the prison, fifteen of them in all, and from the prison transferred to Mukhus, where they were evidently given a very speedy and closed trial. By night, bound in twos, they were taken down to the sea and shot by the ruins of the Great Wall of Abkhazia.

It is curious that in all times and in all lands where men have shot those sentenced to death, for some reason they have always tried to shoot them by a wall. One might wonder, what difference does it make where they shoot a man who is incapable of resisting?

But it does seem to make a difference. It must be harder to shoot a man in a wide-open space. A wide-open space links the man sentenced to be shot with the idea of freedom, it makes the killing of a man a too patently criminal act.

But a man standing by a wall has already been driven into a blind alley; the executioner knows ahead of time that the doomed man has no way out. He merely completes, with a last fiery stroke, the final scene, which has already reached its climax before he enters, with this wall, erected before his time and without his knowledge, and with this man, standing at the wall as if he has voluntarily agreed to play his role in this final scene.

Executioners also worry about the comfort of their souls. Since there's a wall (it's the main culprit, actually, but we didn't build it), since there's a man standing by the wall (we didn't sentence him), why not shoot him? After all, he has nowhere to hide—the wall, a blind alley, the end . . .

The man stands at the wall, and the executioner raises his rifle almost automatically; he has prepared himself to raise his rifle that way. But although he has blunted his guilt pangs over pulling the trigger, he has changed nothing for his soul, he has simply stretched out the murder in time, beginning it at the moment when he first sought justifying circumstances.

And what does the wall mean to the man being shot? That is not worth discussing . . .

No one knows what Shashiko's brother paid for, although it is quite possible that Shashiko had gotten him involved in something. It is equally possible that the authorities decided to get rid of the second brother so that there would be no one to avenge Shashiko. If there had been yet another brother left at home, they would most likely have let this one go, because killing two brothers would have increased the chances of the third brother's taking up arms.

Those who punished in the name of the law and those who sought blood revenge at the behest of custom differed little from each other in their sense of justice—in those days, let us add, lest there be false rumors.

When the arrested abreks were being taken from the Kengur prison to Mukhus in the paddy wagon, my mother was riding from Mukhus to Anastasovka in a phaeton, on her way back to Chegem. The two carriages met on the Enduria road.

Shashiko evidently had his eyes glued to a crack that revealed a little piece of freedom to him; he caught sight of Mama and was terribly gladdened. Mama was about as near a relation to Shashiko as Uncle Sandro was. Later, through some people who had been in prison with him, Mama heard that he had seen her ride off to Chegem. One can imagine how his yearning heart reached out after her phaeton.

It pleased fate for Shashiko's shadow to touch our family once more, this time through my father. Next door to us lived an official in the Cheka, the secret police. Every morning when my father left the house, the Chekist was standing on the porch cleaning his boots. The day after the abreks were taken, he stopped my father and said, as he straightened up, "Your Kenguria relatives—none of them's in prison?"

"I don't think so," Father said.

"They brought in a dozen abreks yesterday," the good-natured Chekist went on. "Looks like they're going to liquidate them. So if any of your folks are among them, act before it's too late."

"I don't think so," Father repeated, mentally reviewing the relatives who might turn up in this company. According to him, his first thought was of Shashiko, but he was sure that if anything like this were threatening Shashiko, people would surely have brought word. They had asked for help in much more trivial matters. But as it turned out, the arrestees had been taken away from the Kengur prison under great secrecy and no one knew that they were already in Mukhus.

"If not, so much the better," the Chekist said. He went back to his boots, and my father went his own way, which usually took him to the coffeehouse.

Two months after the execution of the abreks, when Shashiko's relatives found out for sure that the brothers had been shot, and found out that they had been shot by the ruins of the Great Wall of Abkhazia and buried there, they came with Uncle Sandro on horseback to Mukhus, bringing a pair of extra horses to take home the bodies.

According to Abkhazian custom a dead man must be committed to the earth in his family burying ground. If he died or was killed very far from home, one must bring him home at any cost. If he was killed by the authorities, and they are guarding his body, one must steal the corpse or seize it by force, even at the risk of one's life. Such is the law of the mountains, the Abkhazian's code of honor.

And no matter how many years have passed since the loved one died or was slain, when an Abkhazian learns where he was buried, even if it is a thousand kilometers away, even if he has to sell all his property to do it, he must move his relative's remains. For Abkhazians believe that the bones of an Abkhazian in alien soil are waiting, they must be committed to their native soil. Only there will they find rest, and release the souls of their relatives.

The ruins of the Great Wall of Abkhazia were situated a few kilometers from the city on the seacoast, in what was then a wild, desolate place.

During the day they learned that the abreks' burial place was guarded by four soldiers, with one officer in charge. The guards all lived in two tents right near the fortress wall and took turns guarding the burial place against any relatives attempting to seize the criminal corpses of their abreks.

This was their plan for seizing the bodies. The cavalcade of relatives would approach the environs of the fortress by night. They would dismount, tie the horses, and lie low about a hundred meters from the fortress. One of the relatives would dash along the shore past the fortress, riding Dzhigit-style, shouting and shooting in the air, while the relatives lying in wait nearby would shoot at the fortress wall so that the guards would feel the bullets' closeness. As the Chegemians imagined it, the guards would flee in all directions when they saw this massed attack. They reasoned that the guards were Russians by nationality, and Russians could not have any great interest in risking their lives to guard the Abkhazian dead. According to rumor they did not even value their own dead very highly and buried them wherever they had to.

The plan was put into action. One of Shashiko's relatives dashed past the fortress, whooping, shooting in the air, and scattering beach pebbles, while the remaining participants in the sortie, who were lying in wait in the bushes, showered the ancient wall with a hail of bullets. But the Russian guards, instead of scattering, jumped out of their tents and joined the sentry on duty to form a line of defense around the Great Wall.

The guard unit steadfastly defended the bodies entrusted to them. An exchange of shots took place, which fortunately ended without bloodshed.

Some of the relatives were disconcerted when they sensed the stubbornness of the guards, but two, the most fiery, suggested that they openly storm the fortress wall. Uncle Sandro very much disliked this idea. He recalled that in actuality Shashiko wasn't even a cousin, but a much more distant relative. Before, when Shashiko had been famous throughout Abkhazia as a great abrek, he had been accustomed to think of him as a cousin. Although he continued to respect the memory of the great abrek, he now recalled with unaccustomed clarity that in actuality his relationship to Shashiko was very distant and very tenuous. An entirely different plan came to his mind. His thought was that since everything in this country could be done through bribery, why not ransom the brothers' corpses?

The next day Uncle Sandro sought out the right man, and through him quickly found a common language with the officer of the guard unit. The bodies of Shashiko and his brother would come to five hundred rubles plus two good skins of wine. They agreed to show up with the tribute at the wall that night, it being very strictly stipulated that those approaching the wall would first surrender their arms to the man who was to stay with the horses.

That day one of the relatives galloped to Chegem for the tribute, and the next night Uncle Sandro rode with Shashiko's relatives to the ruins of the Great Wall of Abkhazia. They dismounted, surrendered their arms to the lad who was to stay with the horses, and walked up to the fortress, led by Uncle Sandro, who held a skin of wine in each hand.

By the light of a pocket flash held by one of the guards, the officer counted the money and put it in his pocket. After that he began to open the wineskins, and Uncle Sandro suddenly noticed that the officer himself recalled an enormous wineskin.

"If people treat us right . . ." the officer said as he lifted a wineskin. Addressing himself to the mouth of it with gusto, he took a long swallow to check the quality of the wine and pulled away, working his lips and attending to the effect of the life-giving liquid on his mouth and throat, then expelled a noisy breath of air and set the wineskin on the ground. Lifting the other one, he added, ". . . then we treat them right, too . . ."

Again he pressed his lips to the mouth of the wineskin and again took a good swallow, breathed out noisily, set the wineskin on the ground, and then concluded his three-tiered thought, layered with winey pauses: ". . . but you won't take us by shooting, we're used to shooting."

Conversing with the officer, Uncle Sandro learned that seven abrek bodies had already been ransomed by relatives. The officer, when he realized that Uncle Sandro was a good sort, asked him to tell the remaining bodies' relatives, if he met them, that they could ransom their dead this way, peaceably. Uncle Sandro promised.

The guardsman who stood next to them picked up the wineskins and carefully carried them over to the tents, where another guardsman was spreading a tarpaulin right on the shore. The first guardsman left the two wineskins on the tarpaulin and came back. The second guardsman brought glasses from the tent and set them out on this military tablecloth. The glasses gave off a faint, appetizing glint in the moonlight. Then he spread out on the tarpaulin slices of cold meat, *khachapuri* bread, greens—the remains of the last tribute, thought Uncle Sandro.

Suddenly Uncle Sandro got the feeling that here, by this sinister wall on the shore of a sea that breathed the coolness of waves, he would have no objection to holding a memorial supper with these kind swindlers, who so bravely defended their strange, otherworldly booty.

He was immediately ashamed of this blasphemous wish and humbly extinguished it (though it continued to smolder perfidiously for some time). Finally he quieted himself with the thought that he'd only had the idea, and that didn't count.

The officer personally led Uncle Sandro and the other relatives to the foot of the wall. After pointing out the spot where they were to dig, he handed Uncle

Sandro his own flashlight. Uncle Sandro tried to refuse, gesturing toward the moon, but the officer thrust the flashlight at him.

"It'll come in handy," he said, and Uncle Sandro guessed that the bodies must be already badly spoiled by time.

"Two," the officer said distinctly, reminding the remaining sentry. To be quite sure, he held up two fingers.

"Right," the sentry answered. The officer moved toward the wineskins.

Uncle Sandro was once more made aware that bodies were kept under strict control here, and no one would succeed in seizing unransomed bodies along with ransomed ones. Of course, neither Uncle Sandro nor Shashiko's other relatives had any such intention.

The sentry went to the end of the wall, which was overgrown with blackberry bushes. Bending down, he pulled out two shovels that had been hidden in the bushes. He brought the shovels over and silently tossed them at the strangers' feet.

Uncle Sandro wanted to know if these shovels were used to dig the hole after people were shot by this wall.

"Nah," the sentry said, shaking his head. "They liquidate 'em themselves and bury 'em themselves. We're from the army base, we don't have anything to do with them."

Uncle Sandro turned the flashlight on the spot the officer had pointed out, thereby indicating that the others would have to take up the shovels. The relatives—now and then changing places, and never ceasing to marvel at a sort of peculiar stoniness, a sort of unpleasant foreignness, un-Chegemness to the soil, its suspicious Endurishness—dug a rather large hole.

Although Shashiko's body was disfigured by decomposition, they recognized it by the hand with the missing thumb. They pulled the bodies of the brothers out of the hole—the two had been shot still tied together—and after untying the rope they separated them from each other.

They put the earth back in the hole over the remaining bodies. While they were wrapping the brothers' bodies in burkas and strapping them on the horses, the sentry carefully leveled the earth so as not to leave tracks, and just as carefully hid the shovels in the blackberry patch.

When Shashiko's relatives, holding the frightened horses, had strapped the burka-wrapped bodies of the slain brothers to the saddles, Uncle Sandro returned the flashlight to the sentry and mounted his own horse. The sentry quickly headed for the tents, where his comrades were already sprawled out after their late supper.

Holding the horses with the bodies of the slain on a short lead (until they should feel at home with their unaccustomed burden), the cavalcade carefully made their way out to the road. That night they carried the brothers' remains as far as the Kodor, where they carefully washed them, and the next day they buried them in the family burying ground.

Shashiko's wife, when she learned he had been captured, came to the Kengur prison with a parcel and her son. She hoped to visit him, but it was not allowed, although the parcel was accepted.

For many days she came to the prison gate with her son and waited patiently, hoping that Shashiko would notice her from his window. Some of the prisoners called back and forth to their relatives, who, like her, stood outside the prison gate.

But Shashiko could neither call to her nor see her, because even before she arrived all the abreks had been transferred to Mukhus.

Later, when she learned that Shashiko had been shot, she could not bear it and hanged herself. One of her brothers took her son to bring him up—the brother who had most adamantly rebuffed Shashiko's attempts to become reconciled with his family. But can we condemn him, insulted as he was for the honor of his beloved sister?

May God soften our hearts, may He moisten our dry eyes that ever thirst for revenge!

THE STORY OF THE PRAYER TREE

IN THE EARLY THIRTIES, the wave of collectivization rolled over the mountain village of Chegem, rolled over it and broke, washing away the granaries and cattle pens and hurling everything in its path into the common pot—a buffalo, a pig, a sheep, whatever, grab it by the tail and hurl it in. On the big farm it will all come in handy!

Uncle Sandro's father, old Khabug, was considered one of the most prosperous men of the village. He had about a thousand goats, a dozen cows, a few buffaloes, a few saddle horses, four donkeys, and five mules.

This demanding and laboriously accumulated property he controlled and operated with Sandro and his four other sons.

Just as sometimes happens in the mountains during a thunderstorm, when there may be a downpour all around, but here, on a hillock for some reason untouched by the storm, the sun peeps out from time to time, so the Chegemians hoped that the kolkhoz epidemic, with its foolishness of scholars in tussah tunics, might somehow pass them by.

After all, the commune had passed. All that remained of it were memories of the communal dinners, like feasts every day, and great black scars from the fires in the village soviet yard, where the food had been prepared, and assorted jokes about that brief but merry epoch. So now the Chegemians waited, conjectured, marked time.

But by all indications the authorities were not joking this time. The very poorest farms joined the kolkhoz first, then the strong, independent ones began to come over.

Khabug was invited to join too, but he kept laughing it off, making excuses, pretending that he had some special information on this score, his own news, his own *khabar*, which was on the point of being corroborated—things would soon take a different turn. But the *khabar* was not corroborated, and in the end the chairman threatened to deprive him of his voice in government.

"You'd do better to deprive my donkey of his voice, he's the one that's too loud," replied Khabug, who did not yet understand about the right to vote. He had decided that the chairman meant to keep him from speaking at peasant assemblies; but after all, everyone could speak at assemblies, so long as the peasants were willing to listen.

All sorts of officials kept arriving from the city. Khabug was encouraged that they held with time-honored tradition by staying at his house, but they too advised him to join the kolkhoz, because, they said, there was nowhere else to go.

The chairman of the kolkhoz applied special pressure to Khabug, because among the Chegemians he commanded the unforced and therefore abiding respect that is accorded to experts in all realms of life—especially in a realm as open to view as farming, where every ear of corn strives to resemble the farmer, and the fatty tail of every ram slaps his rump with the weight imparted to it by his owner. The chairman knew that many people who were undecided would go over to the kolkhoz if Khabug joined.

Rumors had already reached Chegem that certain rich peasants were being sent to Siberia. Rich peasants were very few in Abkhazia, but still there were some, and Khabug knew it. Knew and pondered, because there was much the old man could not understand.

He could not understand where the kolkhoz would keep the livestock if they collected them from the whole village. Why weren't they looking ahead, building big cowsheds and covered pens for the sheep and goats? And what force would make the peasants work hard on a communal field, when some of them worked indifferently even on their own farmsteads?

But the big question, which could not be expressed in words and which tussah clerks would never understand, was who would want to work, or even live on this earth, if they were going to profane the age-old Mystery of Love, as inexplicable as the mystery of sex—the mystery of a peasant's love for his own field, his own apple tree, his own cow, his own beehive, his own rustling in his own cornfield, his own bunches of grapes crushed by his own feet in his own winepress. And although the wine might then be guzzled and drained by Sandro and his wastrel friends, the Mystery would remain with him; there was no way they could guzzle that or drain it dry.

And if he made money on his cattle or tobacco, the point was not just the money, although that was also necessary in farming; the point was that these coins—as none of the tussah scholars would ever understand—these coins were the basis of the Mystery's sweet magic. Perhaps the nicest thing about them was that by fingering them one could always touch the Mystery.

People promised a life of prosperity in the kolkhoz, and it might well be true, if they got the cowshed built and put knowledgeable men in charge of the livestock farm, and worked the soil in good time. Yet it would all be wrong and would come to nought because the Mystery would be profaned—just as surely as if some work brigade foreman ordered you when to go to bed with your wife and how much to sleep with her, and if he watched through a special peephole to see how zealous you were being for the good of the fatherland ("Entrust, but check up!"), and then reprimanded you in front of everyone, or even more disgusting, thanked you on behalf of the workers of all nations. People were not far wrong when they said, "Wait till they collectivize the goats and cows, then they'll collectivize your wives. Next thing you know the whole village will be sleeping in one barracks under a single hundred-meter blanket."

Although this was probably an exaggeration, the peasants understood it correctly. The point was not your wife herself, the point was the living farm, which you loved and to which you were bound, as to your wife, by the Mystery.

No one takes his wife to bed with the arrogant idea of overtaking and surpassing in population another village, much less a city. Similarly, when a peasant goes out to the field it does not occur to him to compete with anyone out there, as if it were a horse race or shooting match or any other holiday game.

And it most certainly does not occur to anyone that by turning over the soil with his plow he is helping the Chinese or the Africans or what have you. How could you be helping outsiders, people you don't even know? They may have thought up some plot against you, and here you are helping them. After all, you can't read their minds, you can't know what they're plotting against you!

Nor did it mean anything that in some of the kolkhozes in the valleys young people were actually competing to get phonographs and things of that sort as rewards. Such childish games could not make a real peasant work hard, because the Mystery could not be converted into a Game. A game is bound up with holiday excitement and is over along with the holiday, but the Mystery is bound up with life: perhaps it abandons the peasant when life does, or perhaps he carries it with him to comfort him in the next world too, if there actually is another world.

The *kumkhoz* is coming! The *kumkhoz!*

Among the innovations made by the new authorities, there was one that pleased old Khabug: in the village of Chegem, as in many other mountain villages, they had opened a school. Let our children and grandchildren learn to read, he thought, let there be some of our people among these tussah tunics, so that perhaps in the end they'll open the eyes of these loudmouth speechifiers and teach them what it really means to be a peasant.

Whatever the peasants might say at assemblies, they did not say what was most important, because they could not convey it in words, because they did not talk about it with anyone, because one of their own would know anyway and you wouldn't tell an outsider, because the reason the Mystery is a Mystery is that it is bound up with shame.

Although old Khabug understood that by the time they were needed among the tussah tunics, our children who were now studying in the schools might forget about the Mystery or pretend it did not exist, and the tussah tunics might not be issued to them anyway until it was determined that they had definitively broken with their own people, still . . .

Still, old Khabug hoped that one of them, at least, would not forget the sorrow of his fathers, would hide it in the depths of his heart, pretend to remember nothing, and for this reason he would be issued a tussah tunic ahead of all the rest . . .

And perhaps he would force his way up to the topmost echelon, and some day he would find himself in the inner office, face to face with the Big Mustache. He would spill out the whole truth to him, at the same time unbuttoning his tussah tunic and tearing it off. The Big Mustache would grow thoughtful and say, "I think we've made a lot of mischief here. You know what—put that tunic back on and go see to your peasants on our behalf. Let them live as they like, so long as they pay their taxes on time. I'll see to my workers, and we won't get in each other's way."

If only the Big Mustache would say that, we'd try hard for him, we'd bury him in wealth right up to his mustache. But would he really say it?

Yes, old Khabug would ride high in his dreams, but when he woke up the toothache came back: "What can we do? The *kumkhoz* is coming! The *kumkhoz!*"

One summer morning, old Khabug caught the fluffiest, whitest kid in his flock, tied its legs, and hoisted it to his shoulders. Then he stuck an ax in his belt and went out of the yard.

He had arranged with his household that they would not see him off but would all come to the Prayer Tree two hours later, when everything would be ready.

The Prayer Tree, a gigantic walnut, grew in Sabid's Hollow by the cattle trail.

In the summer, when they drove their flocks to alpine pastures, the shepherds would make an offering to the deity. They would slaughter a goat or a sheep, cook and eat the meat, and hang the head on iron hooks driven into the tree trunk. If the hooks were full, they cooked and ate the head as well. It had been noticed that in recent years, since they had begun driving flocks up from the kolkhozes in the valleys, some of the shepherds, when offering a sacrifice, would eat the sacrificial head even if the hooks were not full. We may just get away with it, they reasoned; we still don't know how the deity who protects the four-legged feels about the kolkhoz flock.

This walnut tree had been worshiped from time immemorial. It was huge, and half withered by a lightning bolt that had once set it on fire. Part of the branches were withered, but part were still green and continued to bear fruit. A thick grapevine wound around the tree and untwined at the crown to spread over all the branches. The grapes on the withered branches were especially luxuriant and sweet, as if to console them for having been struck by lightning.

The trunk of the walnut was hollow almost to the very crown, and when it was struck hard it gave off a vibrating sound that hung on the air a long time before dying out. It rang and hummed like a gigantic string stretched from earth to heaven.

Protruding from the trunk, besides the hooks, were some arrowheads and the blade of a crude ancient ax, stuck so high that a man on horseback could not have reached it. Perhaps because of this blade, the inhabitants of Chegem figured that giants had once lived in these parts.

At the foot of the tree, in the hollow, a kettle was kept for cooking meat. It was used by those who came to pray for forgiveness from the deity, as well as by shepherds who were simply overtaken by night in the vicinity. It was a convenient stopping place—there was water nearby, and a shelter made of fallen branches, so dense that the rain hardly soaked through even in bad weather.

The old man went to the tree trunk. Carefully lowering the kid from his shoulders, he placed it at the foot of the tree and mumbled the few words of incantation that had come down to him. Then he took the ax from his belt and, in accordance with accepted custom, sank it with all his strength into the resilient trunk.

An oddly familiar sound, reverberating in the hollow body of the tree, ascended to the crown and melted away in the sky. Stunned by a sudden conjecture, old Khabug listened until the sound had died away. Then with one strong stroke he pulled the ax out of the trunk and sank it into the tree again.

"*Kum-khozzz!*" The word rang out from the trunk and, like a light, humble sigh, fell silent in the infinite sky. The old man was at a loss. He had expected the deity to give a more complex, more mysterious reply, which he would have to interpret over and over. This was too clear, and therefore terrible. The old man pulled out the ax and struck the trunk again.

"*Kum-khozzz!*" the tree sang out, sadly and distinctly.

"You too?" old Khabug roared. He pulled the ax out and began hitting the trunk over and over with the butt.

"*Kum-khoz! Kum-khoz! Kum-khoz!*" The word rolled in waves up the body of the old tree.

The old man stopped, wiped the sweat from his forehead with his sleeve, and plunged the ax into the trunk. He listened one last time to the hopeless sound and picked up the kid.

He slit its throat with a knife, let the blood flow at the foot of the tree, then hung it by the foot from one of the hooks that had been hammered into the trunk. When he had skinned the little carcass, he took it down from the hook and impaled the kid's head, with its open mother-of-pearl eyes, its horns like two odd little plants sprouting over the white down of the forehead.

The old man pulled the kettle out of the hollow tree and put the kid's meager meat in it. Descending to the spring, he carefully washed both the kettle and the meat. Then he put some water in the kettle and climbed back up, straightened the stones of the open fireplace, set the kettle on them, gathered some dry branches, and lit a fire.

Two hours later old Khabug's whole family sat on a carefully spread carpet of green fern fronds to eat the kid's steaming meat, which had been laid out before them on the ferns.

A subdued Uncle Sandro sat next to his father like a prodigal son unready to give up prodigality, driven home by circumstance and forced to be humble at the table.

The next day the old man went to the village soviet and registered in the kolkhoz. He turned over to the kolkhoz half of his four-legged property.

One of his sons, the one in charge of the goats, brought the whole flock into the village soviet yard. Together with the Komsomol activists he counted it and separated five hundred head.

By this time a great many peasants had gathered at the village soviet to see Khabug join the kolkhoz. The old man behaved with dignity and gave no sign of how he felt about the proceedings.

When his son, who had been in charge of the goats since adolescence, approached the Komsomol activists conducting the count, one of them held his nose and turned away. The shepherd, over many years of tending his flock, had been permeated through and through with the smell of goats.

"You should have turned over all your stock, Khabug," one of the Komsomol men joked. "Come next year, the goat smell might've aired out of your son!"

Many people laughed at his joke, but old Khabug thought a moment and replied without haste, "The day will come when you'll be looking all over, trying to sniff out a goat."

Many people laughed at his rejoinder; others became thoughtful. The chairman was displeased with Khabug's words but kept silent.

Some say that as Khabug's son walked out of the yard with his halved flock, they saw him wipe away tears with the trailing end of his turban. He kept on walking, still wiping away tears—a detail that strikes me as a figment of the imagination of peasant mythmakers, perhaps preparing their listeners for what happened next.

As soon as Khabug's son and his diminished flock walked out the gate, the goats that had been left behind dashed bleating after him. Despite the Komsomol's efforts to restrain them and drive them back, they charged through this line of defense. They began leaping the gate and finally broke it down. According to eyewitness accounts, the goats did not so much melt into the rest of the herd as try to hide in it, crowd into the very middle. The whole scene made a grave impression on the assembled peasants. They decided that the animals did not want to go into the kolkhoz because they had a presentiment of their death.

All this was especially annoying to the chairman. It seemed to him to have been cooked up ahead of time and staged by old Khabug in cahoots with his son, if not with the goats themselves.

"You'll answer for this," he said, nodding toward the gate the goats had rushed.

Khabug stood watching his goats breaking though the gate of the village soviet yard. "Let him answer first," he said.

"Who?" the chairman asked, pricking up his ears.

Still watching his goats, Khabug pointed a finger to the sky. "Him," he said. Everyone understood that he meant the Big Mustache, although it could not be proved.

Khabug's son had to drive the flock back into the yard, count and halve it again. There may have been a higher justice in this, as it gave each goat that had been singled out for the kolkhoz one more chance to stay with the master's half (at the expense of its fellow goats, naturally). This time Khabug's son remained in the yard with the half that were being given to the kolkhoz. He stood there, shouting to soothe the agitated flock, until one of the Komsomol men had driven his half a suitable distance away.

The chairman of the kolkhoz—his name was Timur Zhvanba—was a man of that All-Russian type, the savage semiliterate, which was then being plucked from the masses in great numbers by the magnet of time.

Before coming to Chegem he had taught botany in the Kenguria district school, although by temperament he was better suited to zoology. Nevertheless he made some successful speeches at meetings and openly set his sights on the principal's job—in full view of the existing principal, who did in truth bear an absurd resemblance to a prerevolutionary intellectual—and came close to getting it.

But he did not get it, because in class one day he suddenly boxed the ears of a pupil who had confused the laurel tree (*Laurus nobilis*) with the common cherry-laurel. Naturally this punishment displeased the boy's father, who was a commanding officer in the border guard. The latter circumstance made it impossible to dismiss the boy's ear as belonging to an alien class. District-wide clouds began to gather over the temperamental botanist.

The principal, with the tacit consent of the city education department, took advantage of the situation and packed him off to Chegem on the pretext that he had an intimate knowledge of nature. Because they viewed their little city as an important cultural center, Party activists were generally unwilling to leave Kengur, especially for what they viewed as the desolate mountain village of Chegem. Thus Timur Zhvanba became chairman of the Chegem kolkhoz.

The Chegemians received him tolerantly at first, but then it turned out that if he had any knowledge of nature, it was not the nature found in the environs of Chegem. The main problem was that he suffered from acrophobia, as they discovered one time when he took a notion to go down to the mill. He came to a dead stop at a point where the path took a hairpin turn over a precipitous slope, at the foot of which, far below, stood the mill. He was so frightened he could not even climb back up. Mighty Gerago, the miller, had to climb up to him, hoist him to his shoulders, and carry him up to a point where he could no longer see the chalky scree of the precipice.

It is said that the first person to see him there on the path was Khabug, who was coming down to the mill, his mule laden with sacks of corn. At the time, Timur was sitting on the path, clinging to a dogwood bush.

"What are you doing here?" Khabug asked in surprise.

"Just looking around," the chairman said, keeping a tight grip on the dogwood bush.

As Khabug told it, he immediately saw something untoward in the chairman's posture and the fact that he was hanging on to the dogwood like the bridle of a restive horse. But he went on down to the mill without saying anything more. Four hours later, returning from the mill with his freshly ground corn, he was very surprised to find the chairman still trying to tame his dogwood. He realized now that the chairman was badly scared.

"Are we going to just sit here?" he asked, halting beside him.

"Go on by," the chairman barely whispered, pale as the chalky scree at the foot of the precipice, which he could not take his eyes off.

"Grab hold of my mule's tail, he'll get you out," Khabug offered. The chairman's only answer was to shake his head as if he could not accept help from an independent farmer.

"Well, sit here then," Khabug said, and he urged his mule upwards.

"The chairman's tetched," he announced when he rode into the village with this story. Everyone in the vicinity left what he was doing and went to get a look at the chairman. He was still sitting there, and nothing they said could sway him, until mighty Gerago climbed up and carried him in his arms to a safe place.

When they learned of the chairman's mysterious illness, the Chegemians were gravely offended, not so much at him as at the Kenguria District Committee. They decided the committee had sent them a chairman who had been rejected elsewhere as defective.

"We don't want him either," they said to the chairman of the village soviet. They ordered him to convey their opinion to the district committee.

Makhty, as the chairman of the village soviet was called, knew well the mysterious subtleties of Chegemian stubbornness, for he was a Chegemian himself. He realized he would have to go. Incidentally, this was all kept secret from Timur Zhvanba, because the Chegemians considered it an impermissible breach of the laws of hospitality to say right to his face that they did not want him.

Makhty was forced to ride over to the district committee and tell them all this, albeit in softened form. He did everything in softened form, because he was a soft man by nature and wished no harm to anyone. His philosophy was, May things go all right for everybody, and if that's impossible, well, may they go all right for me, at least.

"He's politically sound, but he has an unfortunate illness," he mildly informed the secretary of the district committee. "The people are upset."

"What sort of illness?" the secretary asked in surprise.

"I'm ashamed to say it, but he can't look into an abyss," Makhty confessed, turning red. "He gets dizzy like a pregnant woman."

Here he was forced to relate the incident at the mill.

"Why the devil did he have to go to the mill?" the secretary asked with irritation.

"Nothing special, decided to stretch his legs," Makhty replied, as if insisting on the chairman's total blamelessness in what had happened.

The secretary was beginning to lose patience. "Tell me, can he get down the steps at the village soviet?"

"Easily!" Makhty said joyfully. He explained that the chairman could handle even steeper descents, so long as there were no gaps, chasms, or precipices, especially none with chalky scree, within his range of vision.

"Seems this illness dislikes white stone," he elaborated. This was enough to push the secretary to his limit.

"That will do!" he interrupted. "Tell the chairman not to set foot in the mill, and tell the Chegemians to quit fooling around and get to work."

"He can't set foot in the mill as it is," Makhty persisted in his mild, stubborn way. "And you can't talk to the Chegemians that way, you have to find the right approach."

"Then find it," the secretary said as he stood up, thereby indicating the conversation was over. "That's what you're there for."

Makhty started back, seeking the right approach as he rode. And he found it. He said that the district committee had requested the Chegemians to wait until they could find a suitable replacement; before sending anyone to Chegem they would drive him down the most goatlike of goat paths in order to check his innards for their suitability to Chegemian conditions.

"All right," the Chegemians said, mollified. "Let the poor fool stay on for the time being."

But the chairman did not think of himself as a poor fool at all. As it turned out, he learned about the Chegemians' secret complaint and came down hard on them at the next meeting, full of malice and irritation.

"Well, who won, you Trotskyites?" he said, grinning savagely.

Not only did the Chegemians make no effort to dispute their membership in this dangerous political movement—whose existence, however, they had not even suspected—they simply did not know where to hide for shame.

That first year, the Chegemians still perceived their village as their home, which was why they found all this so awkward. Later on, they and the chairman grew accustomed to each other, and the Chegemians ceased to perceive their land as their own and consequently ceased to perceive the chairman as a guest on the land, albeit uninvited. Only then did the Chegemians begin to answer his favorite political tags with boldly colorful curses, in which the threat of bloody carnage was often inventively balanced against the accusation of incestuous carnality. I am sure that they perceived even the political tags as four-letter words, only expressed in an educated way. Perhaps because of its unintelligibility, his language struck them as even smuttier than their own curses, the obscene expression of a paper-pusher's murky perversions.

Incidentally, the chairman worked in Chegem for about thirty years. During this period, it is true, he withdrew several times for a year or two, but without going out of the village soviet yard. He would set himself up in the village school, where he taught, besides botany, military science as well. There he would excoriate the pupils just as he had the kolkhoz members. From time to time as he marched them around the yard he would switch to Russian and call the pupils by a new political label, Bukharinites.

Later on, in my time, Timur Zhvanba successfully retired and even received the little-known title Honored Citizen of the Village. But then something extraordinary happened, which quite precluded him from wearing this high, though little-known, title, or even ordinary civilian clothes. But that happened much later, and we will tell the story in some more appropriate place.

The news that the Prayer Tree in the village of Chegem replied "*Kumkhoz!*" to every blow of the ax—indeed, to any blow, and the weightier the blow, the more distinct the reply—quickly spread through the neighboring villages.

Drawn by doubt, people came on horseback and on foot. Each was able to convince himself that the tree answered the insistent question honestly, whether you struck it with a stone or hit it with your head.

Uncle Sandro hung around at the walnut tree for days on end, because there was nothing to do now anyway and he still could not bring himself to work in the kolkhoz. Peasants from neighboring villages began bringing not only sacrificial kids but skins of wine as well. Life became gay and interesting.

Although it was hard to discern anything harmful to the regime in what the Prayer Tree said, the chairman of the kolkhoz did not like these pilgrimages. He was somehow disquieted by this swarming around the walnut tree, these comings and goings, conversations and rumors.

The old hunter Tendel now added fuel to the fire. He returned one day from the hunt and told how he had seen a vixen in a forest glade suckling a cow from the Chegem herd, smacking her lips and tugging on the teats. The cow not only did not resist, but seemed not to notice her, and went on munching grass with a strange, furious intensity. Tendel fired, but evidently he only broke the vixen's tail, because she ran away trailing it on the ground.

"When you see a vixen with a broken tail," he said, "that's the one, the she-devil—kill her on the spot."

"But where would we see her," the Chegemians replied, unnerved. Although they did not usually believe Tendel any more than the other hunters, what he had told them this time seemed like a sinister omen.

"So now we have to feed the foxes," they said.

In order to dissipate the impression Tendel's story had made, Makhty went around reminding the Chegemians of the hunter's long-ago adventure with the bear.

Once when he was a young man, Tendel claimed, he was resting in the woods, leaning back against a chestnut tree, when a bear stole quietly up behind him. It peered warily around the chestnut, snatched his gun, and with one blow smashed it against the trunk of the tree. Tossing away the broken gun, it grabbed Tendel by the nose with its paw and started to take him off somewhere—but where, Tendel didn't know, and there was no one to ask.

The bear only wheezed, flooding Tendel with its fetid breath whenever it glanced at him. Only when they had gone about a quarter of a mile did Tendel realize with horror that the bear was leading him to the very spot where he had killed a she-bear two years before.

He had already said farewell to life when the bear happened on a good clump of cherry-laurel. Bending the branches down with one paw, it began to stuff its mouth with black clusters of cherries, its favorite treat. Gradually it got so carried away that it let go of Tendel's nose and even waved a paw encouragingly as if to say, Have a treat before you die. It began raking up the cherry-laurel bushes and moving forward. As soon as the bear went off a few steps Tendel took to his heels and ran all the way to Chegem, grabbing his broken gun on the way.

Naturally, very few people believed this story. The only detail corroborated by the old-timers was that once in his youth Tendel had gone hunting with his nose whole and returned with both his nose and his gun broken. His nose had been crooked ever since.

"So why do you believe this story," Makhty admonished, "when you didn't believe that one?"

"That was then, and this is now," the Chegemians answered, in no way cheered by Makhty's admonitions.

In the end, Timur Zhvanba got fed up with this and asked the Kenguria District Committee to help him take steps against the hunter's tale and the Prayer Tree. The Kenguria District Committee replied that he should attach no importance to the representations of the aged hunter. With regard to the Prayer Tree, they promised to send a commission to make an on-the-spot decision whether it was a perversion of the Party line or, on the contrary, an accidental, but favorable, natural phenomenon.

Several days later a two-man commission arrived in Chegem. Uncle Sandro personally demonstrated, with blows of his ax, the one and only word that could be elicited from the tree. What softened the hearts of the commission most of all was that the tree pronounced the magic word with a pure Kenguria accent.

"Poor thing, it speaks our language," they said. They listened to it happily, true patriots of their district.

Uncle Sandro had selected for the commission members the most resonant, you might say the choicest, places, which were now known to him alone. He gave them each a chance to hit the tree, showed that they could strike with the butt of the ax and the tree would still utter the same word, only in a slightly lower register.

For the sake of completeness, one of the commission members peered into the hollow, lit a match, and for some reason shouted "*Kumkhoz!*" The match went out, but this did not occasion any suspicion.

"What did the tree say before collectivization?" one of them asked.

"A meaningless ringing sound," Uncle Sandro replied.

"Very good," the commission members said. They exchanged satisfied glances.

Uncle Sandro took them home for dinner, where over a well-laid table he demonstrated his own talents.

The commission members left old Khabug's house in a very good mood. Passing the village soviet, they encountered Timur Zhvanba and advised him to refrain from decisive measures for the time being, inasmuch as the walnut tree was doing something useful for us, on the whole.

"People are coming from all over," the chairman began, trying to undermine Uncle Sandro, but the commission members did not let him finish.

They advised him to choose a politically literate man to keep an eye on what was happening at the Prayer Tree and explain the Party's policy on collectivization to the people who came.

Incidentally, they said, Sandro, Khabug's son, was just right for this task, especially since he was the one who lived closest to the Prayer Tree.

"I don't trust him," Timur said, barely able to restrain his fury.

The two commission members, on horseback, exchanged surprised glances. Their swaying figures radiated a hazy glow from the hospitality of the Big House, as Uncle Sandro's father's house was called.

"The commission of the Kenguria District Committee trusts him," said one of the commission members.

"And the Kenguria District Committee trusts its commission," added the second. They rode away.

"It'll be a while before they dry out," said the former clerk, now secretary of the Chegem Village Soviet. The clerk knew the habits and mores of the Kengurians better than Timur did, and there was nothing for the chairman to do but submit, hating the Big House and all its inhabitants more deeply than ever. He reconciled himself to the fact that the Prayer Tree would continue its strange political agitation, and he put Uncle Sandro on the payroll as night watchman at the kolkhoz cucumber and melon plantation, although he worked only in daytime, if this could be called work.

Uncle Sandro came to life and felt himself in his element. He put up a rather capacious cabin beside the Prayer Tree, so that bad weather would not inconvenience people who had come from a distance. Then he laid in a supply of firewood, cleared a briar patch to make room for a hitching rack, and began to receive guests, sitting in the shade of the walnut tree and looking like a modest horse trainer.

In bad weather he sat in his cabin by the fire. The moment he heard the clop of hooves he came out and watched the path, trying from afar to determine who it was—a skeptical pilgrim or simply a passing horseman.

Once a celebrated wit known as Bad Hand came from the village of Ankhara to listen to the talking tree.

Uncle Sandro was sitting in the cabin, passing the time of day with three pilgrims from Tsebelda. When he heard the clop of hooves, he put down his glass and went outdoors.

They exchanged greetings. Even though Bad Hand had not brought any offering, Uncle Sandro tried to be quite polite with him—you never knew what to expect from Bad Hand. He could slap you down with a word, you were lucky to escape with your hide intact.

Bad Hand pulled up and surveyed the tree. "I was going by and thought I'd look in."

"Dismount," Uncle Sandro said, his invitation implying a light repast in the cabin.

Bad Hand took in Uncle Sandro, the tree, and the cabin in one glance. Then, as if he had weighed the possibilities of this makeshift hospitality and decided it was not worth very much, he turned away from the cabin and looked at Uncle Sandro. "You're guarding it?" he asked.

"Not guarding it, watching over it," Uncle Sandro corrected him mildly. "People come from all over. Don't want them to gossip too much."

"Then let's hear it!" Bad Hand said impatiently, as if he were doing Uncle Sandro a favor by listening to his tree. And in essence he was, because Bad Hand's word could boost the flow of pilgrims or dry it up.

"How do you want it—with the ax or the mallet?" Uncle Sandro asked. By this time he had adapted a corn-threshing mallet for use in hitting the tree.

Bad Hand twitched impatiently. "Hit it with a crowbar for all I care!"

Uncle Sandro struck the trunk several times with the mallet and turned to Bad Hand. He was listening with his head down, like a boar.

"It does talk well," Bad Hand agreed. "Now, suppose you hit it and some corn showered down from the hollow—"

"What kind of corn?" Uncle Sandro asked, not understanding.

"Ordinary corn," Bad Hand said brightly. "If you hang a bag of corn up inside the hollow and make a little hole in it so that every time you hit it—'*Kumkhoz!*'—a handful of corn falls down too—"

"I don't use tricks," Uncle Sandro said. "A commission from the district committee looked at it—"

"How much do they give you for this?" Bad Hand interrupted.

"Half a day's pay," Uncle Sandro said.

"Not the kolkhoz—them!" Bad Hand jerked his chin up, toward the universal authorities.

"They don't give me anything," Uncle Sandro said warily.

"Teach your tree to say 'Buy a bond,' " Bad Hand began, turning his horse, which immediately set off at an impatient trot. Now giving vent to his inner fury, and seeming to find justification in the increasing distance, he shouted, " 'Buy a bond! Buy a government bond—or else!' That'd make the boss happy! Get him under your Prayer Tree and rastak his mustached ass! Screw him . . ."

Bad Hand's voice was lost as he rode into the beech grove, continuing to disgorge unintelligible curses. Uncle Sandro listened a while to his fading voice and the occasional flare of sound as hooves struck against stones. Then he dropped the mallet by the cabin and went in.

"Who was that?" asked his surprised guests.

"No one, just a man," Uncle Sandro said as he sat down.

"Wonder where he meant to rastak him," one of the guests asked after a brief hesitation.

"In the tree hollow, I think," Uncle Sandro said, taking up his glass.

"Yes, probably the hollow," the second pilgrim agreed, taking up his glass.

"All we have to do," the third pilgrim said, taking up his glass, "is drive him into the hollow."

"So drive him in," the first pilgrim said. "I'm afraid that while we're doing it to him in words, he's screwing us in deed."

"What can you do, when even the tree yammers the same thing," the third agreed, and they drained their glasses.

All summer Uncle Sandro continued to watch over the Prayer Tree. People kept on coming, although there were fewer and fewer. Timur Zhvanba said nothing, waiting his hour. It came.

Early that fall the government launched a campaign against religious superstition. The *Kenguria District News* published an article entitled "Deprive the Priest of His Forum," proposing that the surviving churches, in accordance with the wishes of a majority of the populace, should be closed—which would have been very difficult, even quite impossible, inasmuch as there had never been any churches at all in the Kenguria district.

I remember when they closed the church in Mukhus. It was located not far from our house and was called the Greek church. I dimly remember the sad peal of its bell, fruitlessly hammering the air. I remember its cozy little courtyard, filled with crowds of worshipers and gawkers on holidays, with the inevitable beggars comfortably disposed along the fence, greeting everyone who came in with a restrained entreaty and a tenacious gaze.

I remember one time a workman, tied in ropes, sat on top of the dome and tried, with methodical blows of a heavy hammer, to knock down the massive copper cross. Evidently the cross did not yield readily (old-time workmanship), because the workman struggled with it for several days, and afterwards, when the cross was gone from the dome, you could make out a gouge on the top as if he had extirpated it, torn it out by the roots like a tree.

The church was taken over as a student dormitory for a technical school. A year or two later the students moved from the church/dormitory to other premises, and the church was hired out as an archive for the NKVD, or so said the people on our street, whispering mysteriously.

By this time I was already passing it on my way to school, and I used to see the mountains of files, or rather the tops of them, through the stained glass windows. It must be supposed that these were case files on enemies of the people, and the possibility cannot be fully ruled out that the Lord God Himself flew down from where He was represented on the ceiling of the dome and dug in the files at night, looking for their sins. Finding none, it must be supposed (otherwise He would have taken some sort of action), He carefully flew up and cemented himself in again, flattened Himself on the ceiling so that He Himself could not be hooked somehow and pulled down to earth, to be hauled in under some appropriate article of the law.

Then during the war they opened it and began calling it the Greek church again. Strictly speaking, it had never ceased to be called the Greek church, although not in the proper sense of the word, simply as a habitual landmark.

"Where can I get kerosene?"

"By the Greek church!"

One fine day I again saw a workman tied in ropes on the summit of the dome; it may have been the same workman, but this time he was fastening a cross on top of the dome. Even a child could see how ill-suited this cross was to the architecture of the building. The old cross had been massive, thick, and shining, and by comparison this was but a puny offshoot of that mighty tree. No, this cross had not grown in that other earth! I think they dug it up in the Mikhaylovskoe Cemetery, took it from some well-to-do prerevolutionary grave.

At all events, the church started functioning again. Its courtyard again became a beggars' exchange; long-haired priests again entered the churchyard with businesslike gait, eluding the female devouts like a district soviet clerk eluding the visitors who try to catch him on his way to his office. There was one thing we did not understand—where the priests had been kept all this time and how they had managed to conceal their long hair.

It was called the Greek church, as before, and continued to be called that even after 1948, when all the Greeks, along with their old people and children, Party members and non-Party members, were raked up in one heap and resettled in Kazakhstan. Later, after the Twentieth Party Congress, when they were allowed to return, along with their miraculously spared old people and grown-up children, along with the former Party members, who had become non-Party members, those who returned—but an insignificant minority returned—well, those who returned could be sure that in our city the church was called Greek as before, if by that time they had not lost interest in the church and in everything else on earth, which, it must be supposed, is also quite possible.

But let us return to the Chegemians. The custom in our country is for every government campaign to be supported and developed in the provinces. Naturally the antireligious campaign was no exception. The difficulty this time was that the Abkhazians—whether they consider themselves Christians or Muslims—do not attend either churches or mosques, because there are practically none in Abkhazian villages. In the Kenguria district, there had never been a single mosque or a single church. But since the campaign had to be waged, everyone did what he could.

The chairman of the Chegem kolkhoz, after consulting with his active members, decided to burn down the Prayer Tree as an object of superstitious worship. The village Komsomol carried out this decision joyfully. That very day they piled deadwood in the hollow of the tree and ignited it.

Even so, the mighty tree survived, although smoke continued to rise for several days from its broken crown, as from the crater of a volcano. On the hollow side, the trunk was charred and black for several meters up, but the other side was hardly even scorched; it was simply too big for the flame to encompass and overwhelm it.

Evidently the symbolic act of committing the Prayer Tree to the flames was more important to the Chegem Komsomol than its total annihilation. At all events, the tree survived; not even the grapevine was harmed.

"He whom heavenly fire has spared, earthly fire cannot kill," a Chegemian named Siko pronounced the next day. He stood at the foot of the Prayer Tree and looked it over along with some of his fellow villagers. They had gathered there from the neighboring field, where they had been hoeing corn.

Kunta, while raking ashes out of the hollow with his hoe, discovered the remains of the iron kettle the shepherds had used to cook meat. It had split, evidently unable to withstand the fire.

A short time later, to the great surprise of the gathering, Kunta raked out still another kettle, of completely unknown origin. No one here had ever seen this kettle. It was covered with a thick layer of soot, slightly dented, but completely intact. They could not understand, in the first place, how it had gotten here, and in the second place, how it had survived, being copper, when the iron one had not withstood the fire and had split.

They could find only one more or less sensible explanation for this miracle: it was decided that the god of the four-legged had surreptitiously placed the kettle here so that the peasants would not fall into confusion and would continue to believe in the Prayer Tree's powers of protection against all evil. While the kettle put here by the deity was not new, it was perfectly good for cooking meat.

They had scarcely finished marveling at the propriety of this miracle when something completely inexplicable occurred. The tireless Kunta raked out of the hollow tree some slightly scorched bones of unknown origin, and a skull came rolling out after them. Although it was clearly a human skull, which explained the origin of the bones, it did not explain its own origin.

"Where did this poor devil come from?" was all the Chegemians could say. They passed the skull from hand to hand. Besides its natural orifices the skull had an extra hole right in the cranium. Some people tried to peer through this hole into the eye socket; others, by contrast, peered through the eye socket into the hole; but neither group could explain the origin of the skull and bones.

Finally someone thought to strike the trunk with an ax. To the still greater bewilderment of the gathering, the tree did not answer "*Kumkhozzz!*" but gave out an unpleasant visceral sound. No matter how hard they hit it, they could not get it to resonate; all they got was this disagreeable and even threatening sound.

"Why?" the Chegemians asked, crestfallen.

"What do you mean, why?" replied Siko, who was the eldest of them. "You burn it, and it's supposed to dance for you?"

"But that wasn't us!"

"We shouldn't have let them come here," Siko answered, surveying the bones and the huge burned-out hollow.

The Chegemians were bewildered. "Then why did it put the kettle here?" Even Siko had no answer to this.

"Put everything back carefully," he said, indicating the skull and bones. "Cover them up well with ashes so the animals don't pull them apart."

Kunta had just buried the mysterious remains in the ashes when a shot resounded from the depths of Sabid's Hollow. Everyone was unnerved.

"Could the abreks be up to mischief?" someone asked.

"I told you this wouldn't be the end of it," Siko reminded them, although he had not said so, only thought so.

"Sh! I think I hear someone shouting," Kunta said, and everyone listened. Indeed, from the depths of Sabid's Hollow they could hear an almost ceaseless human shout. The sound seemed to be getting nearer. Finally the figure of a man emerged from the thicket.

Shouting over and over, "A miracle! A miracle! It's kingdom come!" the man started up toward the Prayer Tree. It was Tendel, the famous hunter. He kept on shouting as he scrambled up the green hillside. In his hand dangled the light flame of a fox carcass.

"What happened?" they asked, when he reached the tree.

"A miracle!" he gasped. Throwing the fox carcass at the foot of the tree, he told what had happened.

He had seen her in a forest glade. Stretched out at full length, she was lying under a rock watching some horses graze nearby. It struck Tendel as strange that the fox should watch the horses so closely. Then he noticed that among the horses there was a mare with a foal. A strange conjecture flashed through his mind—this was the she-devil, the vixen who had once suckled at the udder of a cow. And now she was sneaking up on the mare.

He took careful aim and fired. The fox, which had been lying motionless, went on lying there. Killed outright, he thought, and went over to his kill. Lifting the carcass, he was surprised to find no trace of blood on it. He was still more surprised when he could find no hole on her body where the bullet had entered or exited. Now he was thoroughly convinced that this was the selfsame she-devil who before his very eyes had suckled at the cow's udder, brazenly smacking her lips and tugging impatiently at the teats.

When they heard this, the others told him in their turn what they had found in the Prayer Tree. As they talked they inspected and fingered the carcass, hoping to find the bullet's entry and exit holes.

"Maybe she was already dead?" someone said.

"Not likely," Tendel answered. "She's still warm even now."

Indeed, the carcass was still quite fresh.

"Where did the bullet go?" the Chegemians asked, bewildered.

"In the mouth and out the rear!" Tendel declared. "There's no other way through her."

"Maybe it stayed inside?" the peasants asked, holding the carcass upside down and shaking it, in hopes the bullet would fall out.

"That's the point—it didn't!" shouted the agitated Tendel. "I found where it went into the ground. Kunta, get your hoe and we'll go dig it out."

For some reason everyone found it natural for Kunta to do the dirty work, which has to be done even to demonstrate a miracle. Kunta shouldered his hoe and everyone went down the hill. An hour later they returned with Tendel's disinterred bullet.

They were surprised and horrified to discover that the fox carcass had disappeared from where they had left it at the foot of the Prayer Tree. Tendel stood stock-still with the disinterred bullet in his hand. Then someone noticed that the kettle, which had been standing in the tree hollow in a normal position, was now turned upside down.

"I swear by the god of the four-legged!" Tendel exclaimed. "She's turned it over on herself!"

He ordered Kunta to tip the kettle up carefully while he himself stood ready to shoot as soon as she jumped out. But he did not have to shoot, because it turned out there was nothing under the kettle. Then they raked out the ashes again to see whether the remains of the unknown man were in place. Yes, they were, but the fox carcass was gone. Everyone was now thoroughly convinced that this was the selfsame she-devil that had suckled the milk from the cow, smacking her lips and tugging at the teats like a calf.

"Fools! We're fools!" Siko said, and he beat his brow by way of acknowledging his stupidity. "Obviously we shouldn't have dug up the bullet. That's what was pressing her to the earth, making her dead."

Now it was quite obvious to everyone that the bullet should never have been dug up, and everyone, including Tendel, looked reproachfully at Kunta, who had wielded the hoe.

Kunta was embarrassed and suggested that everyone go back to the cornfield and finish hoeing the section they had been working on since morning.

"What are you, out of your head!" Siko exclaimed. "Go home now, quietly, one by one!"

Shouldering their hoes, the Chegemians climbed back up to the village. With an injured expression, as if offended by the forces of the other world (why can't they let you work in peace!), they scattered to their homes.

Word of what had happened was all over Chegem in an instant, and inside of a day the neighboring villages knew as well. The Chegemians were most shaken by the fact that the tree had ceased to say "*Kum-khoz!*" and by the story of the fox. The discovery of the unfamiliar kettle and the human skeleton also startled them, but not so greatly.

True, toward evening it did develop that the carcass had been appropriated by Khabug, who passed the Prayer Tree at just that time. He was returning from the forest, where he had been checking his traps. If there had been anything in his traps, the Chegemians said pacifically, he might not have taken this fox, but as it was he couldn't help himself and just picked it up.

Tendel ran to get his fox, but Khabug wouldn't give it to him, asserting that the fox had been killed not by Tendel but by his, Khabug's, mule. He even pointed out a crack in the fox's skull, which no one had noticed. Tendel argued with him, saying that once Khabug got his hands on the dead fox he could perfectly well have bashed her head flat.

Khabug based his own argument on the fact that mules, being animals incapable of producing descendants, cherish a very tender affection for foals. If a foal appears somewhere nearby, the mule tries not to leave his side even for a minute and defends him with unheard-of fury against real or imagined danger.

"Last year he laid out two rabbits," Khabug said of his mule. "This year it's a fox."

"Then why didn't you say so right away, if it was your mule killed the fox?" Tendel said, trying to trap him.

"I wanted to hear who'd say which stupid thing," Khabug replied.

"We'll check the tracks," Tendel threatened.

"Go ahead," Khabug replied.

He was so sure that the fox had been killed by the infuriated mule that he made no move to go down and find the hoof marks. Other people did go, and they corroborated that there were indeed mule tracks near the rock. At this point the Chegemians were so disenchanted with Tendel that they not only ceased to believe in the fox that smacked its lips at the cow's udder, and in the bear that had led him by the nose—they hadn't much believed that before, either—but ceased to believe even that he had once gone to the forest with his nose whole and returned with it broken.

"Seems to me his nose was always crooked," said Siko, who was the first to renounce him, since he was an older man and could remember Tendel's youth better than the others.

Tendel himself and the whole hunting clan now perceived a sort of genetic insult in this humiliating version and demanded that Siko henceforth phrase his remarks in more seemly fashion.

"They're offended?" Siko exclaimed when he heard about this. "Let them look at their noses!"

Since he had been an eyewitness to the incident with the fox and one of the first to narrate it, Siko felt like a fool after the triumph of the more plausible story of the fox's death under the mule's hoof. He could not forgive the hunter for this, especially as Tendel's clan was indeed distinguished by a tendency to big noses.

In reply to his audacious sally, the hunter's relatives asserted that one could find himself with a crooked nose even if he didn't have a big one to start with, as they would attempt to prove in the very near future.

To this threat Siko replied, after meditating overnight, that judging by the marksmanship of the best hunter of their clan, their bullets had the property of flying in the mouth and out the rear, and he had therefore arranged for Kunta to follow Tendel with a hoe and dig the bullets out of the ground.

At this point Tendel's relatives fell silent, and this was such a bad sign that Khabug himself intervened. He said for all to hear, as one of the oldest inhabitants of the village, that he well remembered Tendel in the days when he had a perfectly decent nose (for his clan), in no way damaged. As for the fox, he added, if you stretch out a fox properly, you can shoot right through it both in that direction and backwards, especially if it's lying on a slope and has first been killed by the hoof of a jealous mule.

Khabug's intervention seemed to mollify the hunter's relatives somewhat, although they were not quite satisfied with some of his wording.

While the Chegemians were still wondering what the miracles in the hollow of the Prayer Tree might mean and how Siko's quarrel with the hunter's clan would end, they began hearing rumors from the village of Ankhara, where Bad Hand lived, about the mysterious disappearance of the kolkhoz bookkeeper.

It seems the bookkeeper had started back to the village from the district center with money for the kolkhoz, but he had not reached the village and had not returned to the district center. For that matter, he had no reason to return to the district center.

The chairman might not have thought to correlate these several strange facts if the secretary had not whispered something to him. He whispered that the day before the Prayer Tree was burned, people had seen Sandro receive a strange man at his cabin. The man had struck people as strange because he himself was bald, while his horse, tied at the hitching rack, had too long a mane, just like a lion.

Timur pricked up his ears. "Not a word to anyone," he said. He sent the secretary to the village of Ankhara to obtain more accurate information on the horse and the bookkeeper himself, and while he was at it, find out if the bookkeeper had brought a copper kettle with him from home.

"The horse did have a long mane, and he himself was bald as the palm of your hand," the secretary said when he returned, "but no one knows anything about the kettle, because all the kettles and pots are accounted for."

"Sandro must have planted the kettle there on purpose to mix us up," the chairman said. Then and there he sent the secretary to Kengursk for the police.

This was his version of the story: Sandro had killed the bookkeeper with the motive of robbery and had hung the corpse inside the tree hollow, intending to select a convenient moment to cart it off to the woods and bury it. But then the Komsomol unexpectedly descended on him and burned the body along with the tree.

That night Timur ordered the watchman from the village store to hide in the briar patch near Sandro's house and watch to see that nothing was carried out of the house. He was convinced that after killing the bookkeeper Sandro had led the horse somewhere into the woods and was keeping it there, and had most likely hidden the saddle at home. But now that there were rumors about the bookkeeper's disappearance, Sandro would fear a search and therefore carry the saddle out of his house and hide it somewhere else.

Early in the morning the watchman from the village store returned to the kolkhoz office, scared off by a shot from Khabug. The old man had fired twice from his balcony, shouting loudly that the damned rabbits were destroying all his lima beans. Evidently the dogs had caught the watchman's scent.

"Did they carry anything out in the night?" the chairman asked.

"No," the watchman answered. It was a lie, because Khabug's wife had brought him some chicken and *churek* bread in the night. She begged him to sit in his hideout as quietly as possible, or else if her old man found out his house was being watched, God forbid, he'd give everyone a thrashing.

"All right if I sleep?" the watchman asked.

"That'd be the best idea," she answered, and the watchman fell asleep on the spot, succumbing to a long-standing habit of sleeping under any and all conditions.

That day, almost simultaneously, a Kengur policeman rode up to the kolkhoz office from one direction, and two of the bookkeeper's relatives, led by Bad Hand, rode up from another. One of the relatives, an older peasant, was wearing a long felt burka and a turban. The other was in the flower of his strength, as they say, and his clothes hinted that he belonged to the Party administration, although he had no connection with it at all. He was dressed in a tussah tunic, wide riding breeches, and boots. Judging by his clothes, one might have said that from head to waist he represented the legislative branch and from the waist to his boots, the executive.

At the sight of these guests, the chairman of the kolkhoz and the chairman of the village soviet came out of the office. After some vacillation, they split up to greet them. Timur went over to the policeman, and Makhty to the bookkeeper's relatives.

"You burned the bookkeeper, you could at least send the horse back!" Bad Hand shouted by way of greeting. Dismounting quickly, he tied his horse to the hitching rack.

"Wait a minute, Bad Hand," the elder relative remarked, handing his reins to Makhty.

"Our problem's not the horse," Timur said importantly as he came over and shook hands with everyone. He spoke in a sorrowful voice and nodded his head as if intending a political allusion. The policeman also nodded his head, as if affirming the well-known rectitude of the chairman's intellectual tendencies.

"What do you mean, the horse isn't your problem!" Bad Hand said in surprise. "Did he burn her up with our bookkeeper?"

"Why, no!" Timur frowned, because Bad Hand was confusing the high with the low. "Our Komsomol burned the walnut tree in accordance with the decision of our active members."

Here he set forth the version of Sandro's crime as he had represented it to himself or wanted to represent it to others. He said that Sandro apparently killed the bookkeeper and hid him in the hollow of the tree, intending to select a convenient time to bury him later, somewhere farther off, where the village dogs or the jackals around there couldn't dig him up. Then the next day the Komsomol committed the Prayer Tree to the flames, and the crime was discovered.

"Where's the horse?" Bad Hand interrupted.

"I think he's keeping the horse somewhere in the forest," the chairman said.

"*We* think so," Makhty corrected him. He already had to remind people that he too was an authority, but in Chegem, as throughout the country, this was forgotten.

"We need to interrogate Sandro and inspect the place where the bookkeeper's bones were found," the policeman said by way of summation.

"Let's go to the walnut tree, it's just a stone's throw from there to Sandro's," Makhty said.

The chairman said good-bye to everyone and went indoors.

Makhty saddled his horse, which was grazing in the village soviet yard, and all five of them rode out toward the Prayer Tree.

"I ask just one thing," the elder relative said, riding up close to the policeman. "Do not profane the bones of our relative—don't go fingering and measuring and pawing them over."

The policeman halted, taken aback.

"But," he said, "I'm planning to take away the bones, along with Sandro."

"Are you from Russia or from Kengursk?" the elder relative asked, and he also stopped. The younger relative pulled up beside him. Now everyone had stopped.

"From Kengur," the policeman said, watching the younger relative's right hand out of the corner of his eye. The younger relative shifted the reins to his left hand.

"And you don't even know that an Abkhazian does not strew his relative's bones around!"

"I do know that, but the law requires the bones in order to establish the body."

"You mean you want to shame us twice?" the elder relative asked.

"Three times!" the younger relative corrected him. "Killed him—one. Burned him—two. Carry off his bones—three."

"Yes, three times," the elder relative agreed, after hearing him out. He looked at the policeman.

"Not counting the horse," Bad Hand added over his shoulder. He was ahead of them.

"Not counting," the elder agreed patiently.

"The court," the policeman said. He spread his hands.

"Yes," Makhty added, as if sympathizing with the relatives. "That's their custom, to show the bones to the lawyers."

He turned his horse and they all started off.

"Can you really believe," the elder relative said after deep thought, "that we would allow that?"

"What?" the policeman asked.

"Allow you to ride off to Kengursk, rattling our relative's bones?"

"If we tie them up tight—," the policeman began

"Not another word!" the younger relative interrupted, lightly jostling his horse.

"And can you really believe," the elder relative continued, "that we'd allow the government to try him, instead of us?"

"Why not?" Makhty responded pacifically. "The government runs good trials now."

"I don't argue with that," the elder relative agreed. "The government doesn't do badly. But he killed our relative, not the government's."

They emerged from the beech grove, and when the path started down the side of the mountain a reddish cornfield came into view far below them. From up here, on the path, they could just make out the figures of some peasants picking corn.

Makhty checked his horse and puffed up his neck in an alarming way. "Eh-hey, Kun-taa!" he shouted.

They could see how slowly the sound carried: it was quite some time after Makhty finished shouting before the people in the cornfield stopped work.

"Eh-hey, what do you want!" one of them responded finally.

Makhty poised himself again, puffing up his neck, and shouted, "Come to the Big Walnut Tree! The Walnut! The Wa-al-nu-ut!"

"Why do we need him?" the policeman asked.

"He raked the ashes out of the tree," Makhty explained.

They stood on the path and watched as, far below, the little figures stopped, evidently discussing something among themselves. Then all together they began to climb up the path. As they walked along, those who had taken off their shirts to work put them back on and tightened their belts.

Makhty spat. "Damn! Wouldn't you know they'd all come trooping up."

He cleared his throat again and shouted that only Kunta was to come. The rest, after some hesitation, reluctantly turned back.

"There they go; he'll be along," Makhty said, and they rode on.

An hour later, the five horsemen arrived at the Prayer Tree. They dismounted by the hitching rack, and Bad Hand, taking his horse by the bridle, went down to the spring.

"My horse wants a drink," he explained with the unconcealed egocentricity of an old horseman.

"Here's where his bones lie," Makhty said, extending an arm to point his quirt at the cavernous hollow.

Both relatives assumed a mournful, dignified air and went quietly over to the hollow tree. The elder silently removed the turban from his sweaty head and began to inflict symbolic, and therefore quiet, blows on his brow. Acting out the ritual of lamentation to come, striking his brow with his palm, he intoned in a soft recitative the words of mourning, which sounded in part like a vow of vengeance.

After a moment the younger relative, who had been standing behind him, gently turned him by the shoulders and led him aside. With his back to the others, the old man wiped his supposedly moistened eyes and blew his nose unexpectedly loudly, with apparent relief. After this he decisively put his turban back on, to mark a transition from the world of sorrow to the world of action.

"The witness will be here soon to show us how everything was," Makhty said pacifically, lightly putting the brakes on his decisiveness.

"We have no right to touch even one little bone until he gets here," the policeman explained. He never tired of marveling, and calling upon others to marvel, at the mysterious ritual of investigation.

"Isn't it time for me to go get Sandro?" Makhty asked.

"No," the elder relative said, "we have to take counsel first." He turned toward Bad Hand. "Are you here to do business or water your horse?"

"Coming," Bad Hand called. He led his horse up the slope to the hitching rack and tossed the bridle over one of its branches.

"What do you want to do with him?" the policeman asked.

"We're about to decide," the younger relative said.

"Don't forget, I'm responsible for him," the policeman said.

"The blood calls," the younger relative said, shrugging his shoulders.

The two relatives went off twenty paces with Bad Hand and began to talk, and then to argue, now and then glancing over at the policeman. It was plain that the younger relative was still in a warlike mood. The policeman paced back and forth in agitation by the tree, now and then glancing over at them.

"I swear by Allah, they're going to do something stupid," he muttered. "It'll mean the end of them and me both."

"Maybe they're not," Makhty said reassuringly.

The argument became heated. Bad Hand, no longer mindful that people were listening, slapped his good hand loudly on his thigh and shouted, "Can't do it! Not with the policeman watching!"

"I swear by Nestor Lakoba," the policeman said nervously as he listened to this talk, "these people will be the death of me!"

"But the blood calls!" the younger relative said implacably.

In the end, Bad Hand managed to soothe him by giving him to understand that it was never too late to kill Sandro if it turned out he was guilty.

"If he's to be arrested, go find him," the younger relative said.

"All right, go get him," the elder relative agreed, turning to Makhty.

"I'll be right back," Makhty answered. He hurried down the path, still afraid that the relatives might change their minds.

A moment later he disappeared around the bend in the path, and Bad Hand settled down with the two relatives and the policeman on the grass at the foot of the walnut tree.

"There's one thing in his favor that bothers me," the elder relative said, coming out of his reverie. "If he killed him, why didn't he hide?"

"Exactly," the policeman said. "We'll get it all straight in Kengur, we'll take—"

"Him or the bones?" the elder asked.

"Both him and the bones," the policeman replied.

"We don't agree to the bones," the elder said after a moment's thought.

"Both Sandro and the bones—aren't you getting a bit too much?" the younger added.

"Back to square one!" The policeman slapped his knee. "You're letting me take Sandro in alive: why?"

"Because we're not sure he killed him," the elder said.

"If you're not sure Sandro killed him, why are you so sure these are your bookkeeper's bones?"

"That's true too," the elder agreed.

"What if your bookkeeper ran off somewhere with the money?"

"God grant it's true," the elder said.

"What a dumbbell," Bad Hand sighed. "I *told* him—sell me the horse."

"Look on the bright side, Bad Hand," the younger relative said. "Maybe he really did run off."

"Then we'll never see the horse again," Bad Hand sighed. "But if Sandro killed him, the horse is around here somewhere."

"No," the elder relative said with renewed stubbornness. "That's too much, to let you have both Sandro and the bones."

"Back to square one!" The policeman clapped his knee. "Did we make an agreement?"

"What if he killed him?"

"We'll find out when we get there," the policeman said. "The doctors we have in the city now are so sharp they can look at any human bone and tell you right off the first and last name of its former owner."

"I know, I've heard," the elder agreed, "but I'm afraid they'll profane the bones."

"Nothing will happen to your bookkeeper's bones," the policeman said.

"Then you do think it's him after all?" the elder said, starting up.

"Oh, Allah," the policeman sighed. "I don't think anything."

People appeared on the path. In front came Kunta with his hoe on his shoulder, behind him came Uncle Sandro flicking his quirt, and behind him, the chairman of the village soviet.

"I met them on the way," Makhty said, trying to guess how the bookkeeper's relatives would behave.

When they saw Sandro, they both stood up in a pose expressing warlike inflexibility.

Kunta smiled genially. "I decided that you'd need Sandro anyway, so I went by for him."

"Stop, Sandro, there's blood between us!" the elder relative said. The younger thrust his hand in the pocket of his riding breeches.

"I swear by the hospitality of my father," Uncle Sandro said solemnly, "and his hospitality, as you know, is worth something—"

"It is beyond price," the elder relative corroborated.

"—so I swear by his hospitality that there is no blood between us."

It was very quiet. Everyone waited to hear what the elder relative would say.

"We believe you for now," he said. The younger relative took his hand out of his pocket.

"That's good," the policeman said joyfully. "That's our way, the Soviet way. Now," he said, turning to Kunta, "tell us how it was."

Blinking his birdlike eyelashes over pale blue eyes, Kunta stood looking at Bad Hand.

"Kunta looks like he's thinking of exchanging his hump for my bad hand," Bad Hand said.

"This is from God, this you can't change," Kunta answered seriously. "But I didn't recognize you at first."

"I belong to the kumkhoz now!" Bad Hand shouted. "They say my hand will come to life in the kumkhoz. What do you think, Kunta?"

"They say it's for the better; we'll see," Kunta answered, as seriously as ever. He swung his hoe down from his shoulder.

"Stick to the point!" interrupted the chairman of the village soviet.

"We came here," Kunta began, resting his hand on the hoe as if it were a staff, "we wanted to see what had become of our giant. We get here and it's still smoking. So Datiko sits down and says, 'Kunta, rake out the ashes, let's see what's become of the kettle, did it melt or crack?' And Siko settles down where Bad Hand's standing now. He starts rolling a cigarette and he says, 'What I like about this kumkhoz is the smoke breaks.' "

"Get to the point," Makhty interrupted again.

As he continued his story, Kunta began poking through the ashes in the hollow tree and raking out the bones that he turned up. The policeman bent down and cautiously began to assemble a skeleton from the bones, loudly explaining his actions and sometimes changing the arrangement of the bones. Kunta carefully rolled out the skull and the policeman fitted it in place.

"Look like him?" he asked. He got partway to his feet and for some reason looked Uncle Sandro in the eye. Uncle Sandro withstood his gaze and shrugged. The relatives also shrugged.

"I don't know, I don't know," the elder said. He stuck his lip out squeamishly as a sign of the skeleton's alienness and at the same time made mournful eyes, just in case. Bad Hand stooped and picked up the skull.

"Careful, don't break it," the elder relative said.

"Why would I do that," Bad Hand answered peering into the skull with gimlet eyes. "I swear by Allah, except for his baldness he's got nothing in common with our bookkeeper."

"God grant it's true," the elder relative said.

At the policeman's request Uncle Sandro now related everything he knew about the bookkeeper. Then he invited everyone to his house. The elder relative was inclined to be difficult, but Bad Hand again proved more stubborn than he.

"We won't go into the house," he said, mounting his horse. "We'll accept hospitality in the yard and ride on."

"And if the blood calls?" the elder relative asked.

"If it calls, we'll hear it," Bad Hand replied as he rode out to the path. "We're not deaf, thank God."

Now they all climbed up the path. In front was Bad Hand; behind him, Uncle Sandro and the policeman, who was holding his horse by the bridle; then the others. Kunta brought up the rear. In one hand he held his hoe, and in the other the policeman's cloak, in which they had put the bones of the unknown man.

On the way, to clear his conscience, the policeman tried to shake Uncle Sandro's story, but Uncle Sandro could not be tripped up. He answered all questions, calmly flicking his quirt on his boot top.

"Don't be offended, Sandro, but I have to take you to the district center," the policeman told him. "The chairman suspects you."

"I'll be glad to go," Uncle Sandro replied, "especially since I suspect him too."

"Of what?" the policeman asked.

"I think he either planted the bones there himself or got his Komsomol people to do it."

"Sandro," Makhty exclaimed, "how can you say such a thing about the chairman in front of me? Don't you see the position you're putting me in?"

"I'll say it to his face," Uncle Sandro replied. Quickening his step, he opened the gate into his front yard. Everyone crowded around the gate while they decided who would enter first. Finally the elder relative rode into the yard, then Bad Hand, then the rest. The chairman of the village soviet meant to resist, but then weakness won out and he assented. He sensed that from a class point of view it would be unbecoming to accept refreshments from Uncle Sandro now, but he had worked up such an appetite, and they really knew how to entertain in this house, so he rode in. Never mind, he thought, if worst comes to worst I'll tell the chairman that I wanted to fully ascertain what their plans were.

From an excess of feeling, Bad Hand raced around the yard and made his horse rear. Watching him, the elder relative shook his head mournfully, to remind him that he was forgetting the funereal and punitive motives, if not the whole point, of their little expedition.

As a token that the meal was to be taken on the run, they set the table outdoors and brought no chairs out—they ate and drank standing up.

Have no fear of the seated guest, the saying goes—fear the guest who is standing. Especially one who drinks standing up, for the belly of the standing guest, like a well-stretched wineskin, becomes a great deal more capacious.

The sun had already set behind the mountain when the guests left the table.

Sandro's mother gave the policeman a *khurjin* in which he laid the bones of the unknown man, wrapping each one separately in bunches of hay. In accordance with a suggestion from the elder relative, the skull was not only wrapped in hay but firmly stuffed with it too, for strength.

"Doesn't this mean," Bad Hand said, with reference to the method of packing the skull, "that you're profaning our bookkeeper?"

"It does not," answered the elder relative, who was not given to levity on this subject.

The mother, sisters, and two younger brothers accompanied the guests to the fork in the path. There the policeman and Uncle Sandro set off down the path leading to Kengursk, and the rest headed home to the village of Ankhara.

"Sandro, don't forget to bring back the *khurjin* when you come," his mother said in farewell.

"Don't break into a trot, I beg you!" the elder relative shouted, turning back.

"Don't worry," the policeman answered, clapping a hand on the *khurjin* strapped to his saddle. They were already on their way when Bad Hand suddenly turned.

"Sandro," he shouted, "if you see a hollow tree on the way, knock on it, and maybe you can knock something out for the authorities."

They laughed and went their separate ways. To look at Uncle Sandro's tall, well-proportioned figure, tightly buttoned into his cherkeska, one would never have guessed his true social relationship with the little policeman at his side. What he most resembled was a cavalry officer, perhaps from the Wild Division, riding alongside his orderly.

At the district center, despite his vocal protests, Uncle Sandro was put in the local prison, which had been created out of the local fortress. He was summoned several times to be interrogated by the police investigator, but had nothing useful to say about the bookkeeper's murder. He insisted that the kolkhoz chairman had violated the decision of the district committee's commission by burning the Prayer Tree. After the unlawful burning of the tree, he said, the chairman himself had probably planted the bones in the hollow by night, or had his Komsomol people do it.

"Then tell me, where's the bookkeeper?" the investigator said, trying to trap him.

"I don't know," Uncle Sandro replied. "He sat with me an hour or so and left."

"Then tell me, what did he talk about?" the investigator insisted.

"He said," Uncle Sandro replied, "that he'd grown bald over his books but hadn't found happiness."

Several times the investigator interrogated Uncle Sandro in this fashion, wrote his answers down all over again, and sent him back to the prison. When he realized that his answers benefited only the investigator and were of no benefit to himself at all, Uncle Sandro clammed up.

The investigator did not take offense at Uncle Sandro's refusal to talk to him.

"Well, you can just stay a while, then," the investigator told him, "and I'll be slowly building my case against you."

"Can't you do it quickly?" Uncle Sandro asked.

"What's the hurry?" the investigator replied.

"Oh, I'm in no hurry," Uncle Sandro said, "but I feel awkward in front of my relatives."

"Why?" the investigator asked in surprise.

"I left my horse with them," Uncle Sandro explained. "They don't know whether to wait for me or send the horse back."

"All right now," the investigator said slyly. "This question isn't about the bookkeeper . . . Tell me where to find his horse, and I'll tell you what to do about yours."

"I don't know," Uncle Sandro answered, refusing to be tripped up.

"Then stay here a while," the investigator concluded.

In those years, according to eyewitness accounts, things weren't at all bad at the Kenguria District Prison. True, conditions changed drastically a few years later, but back then it was not an impossible place to live.

For example, you could simply talk back and forth with your relatives through the embrasures. They weren't allowed to get near, but from twenty meters, or thirty, you were welcome to talk all you pleased—if your relative wasn't hard of hearing, of course. But the hard of hearing knew better than to come by themselves, and if they were impatient to talk to their arrestee, they brought along a relative with better ears and talked back and forth through him.

You could receive parcels whenever you wanted. Because the whole prison staff had a generous share in them, parcels were encouraged. If there was a good guard on duty, you could even receive wine, but only if it was in skins, not bottles. Not even milk could be received in bottles, because bottles were prohibited as sharp objects.

Technically, of course, wine was altogether prohibited. But what the warden actually prohibited was only its distribution to brawlers who did not know how to drink. One time, under the influence of a denunciation written by one of the brawlers, he totally prohibited the distribution of wine; but then the relatives stopped putting it in their parcels, much to the displeasure of the guards, who ceased to receive their share. The warden gave up and merely ordered all the envious brawlers moved into the same cell, so that they would not torture themselves with pointless envy.

In brief, a prison was not an impossible place to live, back then. Not the Kenguria prison, at any rate. All the same, after a month Uncle Sandro was mighty bored, because a jail is a jail, even with Kengurian conveniences. Besides, his cellmates had begun recounting incidents from their meager lives a second time, and Uncle Sandro realized he would have to do something.

He did not have to rely entirely on his own wits in deciding what to do, because one day when he was especially bored a guard came to his cell with some news. He said that the bookkeeper's horse had returned home; at this moment she was standing at his parents' hitching rack and they couldn't take their eyes off her.

Uncle Sandro was very excited at this news and demanded a meeting with his investigator.

"Oh, yes," the investigator agreed, "we already know about that, but you're accused of murdering the bookkeeper, not his horse."

"If the horse has been found, the bookkeeper will be too," Uncle Sandro answered confidently.

"When he's found, then we'll see," the investigator reassured him evasively.

They took Uncle Sandro back to his cell. The next day the same guard brought him still more joyful news. It seemed that two days after the horse arrived, an Adygean shepherd had followed the tracks to the village and begun demanding the horse. They lured him to the kolkhoz office, and there disarmed him and locked him up, after which he confessed that he had bought the horse from a bald man—by all indications, the kolkhoz bookkeeper.

"Then where'd our bookkeeper disappear to?" they asked him.

"Went down to Russia," he answered.

Uncle Sandro became excited again and demanded to be taken to the investigator. But the investigator refused to receive him, although he ordered the guard to inform him that he already knew all this.

A week later the same irrepressible guard, who might more correctly be called a herald, brought still more remarkable news. It seemed the bookkeeper had been found in the railroad restaurant in Stavropol with an unknown woman, who after interrogation confessed that she was a maid at the Krasnodar Kolkhoz Workers' Club.

"They're bringing the both of them here," the guard said. "Now you've got it made."

Uncle Sandro again demanded a meeting with the investigator, but again his lawful request was refused. Then he decided to act through the power of the people. He broadcast at large a request for some solid citizen to put a good scare into the investigator.

The choice fell on Bad Hand. Whether this was because he really was a respected man who enjoyed the confidence of the community, or because he had already played a part in Uncle Sandro's fate, is no longer known. Most likely it was both.

One fine day he showed up in the district center on the bookkeeper's horse, and whenever he met people he knew he said he had been commissioned to find a new investigator.

"What about the old one?" they asked him.

"He's beginning to smell a little," he answered, squinting up at the sun. "We need someone fresher."

When the investigator was first told that Bad Hand had showed up in town and was saying these strange things, he shrugged it off and said, "Let him talk." But when several other people told him the same thing and added the fact that Bad Hand had come to town not on his own horse but on that of the arrested bookkeeper, the investigator was unnerved. He realized that this was a hint, and a dangerous one at that.

"What are they saying at the district committee?" he asked the man who had last met Bad Hand.

"They don't seem to know yet," he answered.

"Where's Bad Hand now?" the investigator asked, still hoping to avert disaster.

"He's headed for the prison," he answered.

The prison was on the road out of Kengur, and the investigator did not know whether to rejoice or to launch into action: either Bad Hand had gotten restless and left Kengur, or he had thought up something new.

At this point the police chief telephoned, and when the investigator picked up the receiver he turned pale. It seemed the prison warden had phoned the police chief to say that Bad Hand had just ridden past the prison. After shouting in his thunderous voice, "Hold the fort, men!" he had galloped away toward his village. The warden had advised the police chief to send a detachment of mounted police in pursuit of him, to detain him and find out what he meant by this. The police chief had declined the warden's suggestion, but since he knew that Bad Hand had come to town on the bookkeeper's horse, he upbraided the investigator for his slipshod management of the case.

The investigator promptly summoned Uncle Sandro to be interrogated.

"Just don't say it wasn't you who sent Bad Hand!" he burst out in great agitation as soon as he saw him.

"I'm not saying anything, for now," Uncle Sandro answered calmly. Either he had been reassured by Bad Hand's heartening slogan, or when he saw the agitated investigator he realized that the truth was going to triumph.

"What did he mean?" the investigator wanted to know, but Uncle Sandro was calm and unbending.

" 'Don't lose heart'—that's what he meant," Uncle Sandro replied.

"And if this is interpreted as a call to resist the authorities?" the investigator said, amazed at Uncle Sandro's firmness and calm.

"It won't be," Uncle Sandro answered dryly, and the investigator realized that he would have to adopt a more conciliatory approach.

The interesting thing is that Bad Hand should have forgotten this episode. Many years later, when he was called to account for transplanting a tung tree from the kolkhoz field to his own fictitious grave (as I have related in the story "Bad Hand," although I didn't mention this particular fact), they reminded him of the incident, but Bad Hand pretended not to remember a thing.

"I know you didn't kill the bookkeeper," the investigator said to Uncle Sandro, adopting a more pacific tone, "but put yourself in my position."

"You put me in prison, and I'm supposed to put myself in your position?"

"But still, they did find some bones in the hollow of your tree."

"The chairman planted them," Uncle Sandro said, holding firmly to the line he had taken. "Either that or he had his Komsomol do it."

"That remains to be proved," the investigator said.

"Release me and I'll prove it," Uncle Sandro promised.

"That's the trouble, I can't," the investigator sighed. "I would release you, but this has already been written up in the newspaper. Somebody came from the *Kenguria News*. He wrote that you killed the bookkeeper because you're the unpacified son of a pacified kulak."

"But the bookkeeper's still alive?" Uncle Sandro said in surprise.

"That's true," the investigator sighed, "and we'll convict him of embezzlement. But if we release you now, it will come out that the newspaper made a mistake."

Crafty as Uncle Sandro was, this craftiness was beyond his comprehension.

"How many copies of this paper do they put out?" he asked.

"Ten thousand," the investigator replied.

"And it says that in all of them?" (Later, in recounting this incident, Uncle Sandro said he had been playing dumb; it is hard to say whether that was true, but in any case he does not look like a zealous newspaper reader even now.)

"All of them," the investigator answered.

"How much does the paper cost?" Uncle Sandro asked.

"Two kopecks."

"My father will pay five kopecks a copy! We'll collect them all and burn them!" Uncle Sandro said with a great burst of enthusiasm.

The investigator shook his head. "You can't burn newspapers."

"But you can burn the Prayer Tree?" Uncle Sandro asked.

The investigator made no answer. For a while they were both silent, and the ghost of truth hovered between them. But then the door creaked, and the ghost of truth disappeared. The policeman on duty stuck his head in the office, just to remind them he was there, and shut the door again. This was his third reminder in the course of the interrogation. According to our custom, a man whom a policeman has taken to be interrogated must stop somewhere on the way back and buy him a drink. So, he kept reminding them he was there.

"Sandro," the investigator said after some thought, "placate Bad Hand and I'll do everything I can for you as soon as the talk about this affair dies down."

"I can placate him, of course," Uncle Sandro answered. "If you treat us right, why not?"

With these words he went out of the office to the corridor, where his escort greeted him with a protracted sigh.

"I've been suffering and made you suffer too," Uncle Sandro said in answer to his sigh.

"It's not that; they might close," the policeman answered modestly, and they started for the exit.

No one knows how this would all have ended, or whether Uncle Sandro would soon have left the hospitable walls of the Kenguria prison, if it had not been for the aid of chance, or rather, the tireless inquisitiveness of Nestor Lakoba.

Nestor Apollonovich had arrived in Kengursk that day and was glancing through the register of prosperous peasants who had joined the kolkhoz in the district. In the register was Uncle Sandro's father. He attracted Nestor Apollonovich's attention. According to the data in the register it appeared that along with all his other wealth Khabug had turned over to the kolkhoz four camels. Nestor Apollonovich attempted to ascertain from the local leadership how this resident of the Abkhazian highlands happened to have camels. The district leaders were unable to make any intelligible reply. They said that thy themselves had not seen the camels, because they had had no reason to take an interest in them, but the Chegem lists had been certified by the chairmen of the kolkhoz and the village soviet.

Nestor Apollonovich disliked all ambiguities and ordered that a man be dispatched to Chegem at once to ascertain how the camels got there and, if possible, drive them to Kengursk, so that someone could then drive them on to Mukhus, since they were animals uncommon in our parts.

They dispatched the mounted policeman again, the same one who had brought in Uncle Sandro. The policeman was already outside Kengur when he was overtaken by a relative of Uncle Sandro's, mounted on Uncle Sandro's horse.

"I ask you as a brother, take this horse back for me," the relative said as he rode up.

The policeman was extremely reluctant to take Uncle Sandro's horse back. He had not actually been intending to go by his house. He had intended to go to the village soviet, find out about the camels, and come back. Somehow it didn't seem quite right—he took away the rider, brought back the horse. He was so very reluctant to carry out this commission that he immediately conceived of a way to avoid it.

"I'm not actually going there," he said to the relative, and went back to the police station.

He went back to the police chief and said that since Sandro was sitting there in prison, they didn't have to go to Chegem at all, they could just ask him about the camels.

The police chief communicated with the district committee, and the comrades from the district committee informed Nestor Apollonovich that Khabug's son was in the local prison, accused of murdering a bookkeeper who had subsequently proved to be a live embezzler and was now in custody.

"Bring him over!" Nestor Apollonovich said.

Uncle Sandro was promptly taken before the police chief, issued civilian clothes, and informed that Nestor Apollonovich himself wanted to see him. Why he wanted to see him was not mentioned, so that he would not have time to invent anything if he took a notion to lie.

Uncle Sandro responded with a loyal ultimatum. "Until I've washed my hair and shaved and put my clothes in order—I'm not going!" he announced decisively.

"Very good," the police chief assented, and turned to his assistant. "Attend to him."

And they did. While Uncle Sandro washed his hair over the police chief's own washbasin and the assistant poured hot water for him, they urgently summoned the best barber in the district, who shaved and barbered in the homes of real live big shots and the distinguished deceased.

An hour later, with his cherkeska buttoned up and his boots gleaming, Uncle Sandro stood before Nestor Apollonovich, deferential but self-contained.

Nestor Apollonovich at this point was dining with friends and associates in the only private room in the only restaurant of what was then an unimportant district center. It is said that he was quite taken by Uncle Sandro's appearance.

"Even in prison a true Abkhazian behaves like a falcon," Nestor Apollonovich said, looking at him.

"Especially when he's been imprisoned unjustly," Uncle Sandro put in.

Nestor Apollonovich looked questioningly at the police chief. The latter bent quickly and whispered something in his ear.

"The newspaper . . . the newspaper . . ." was all Uncle Sandro could catch. Judging by the expression on Nestor Apollonovich's face and his gracious nods, however, nothing bad awaited him.

"I think we can help you," Nestor Apollonovich said, pulling away from the police chief and looking at Uncle Sandro, "if you'll tell us where you got the camels."

"What camels?" Uncle Sandro asked, trying to think what he meant.

Lakoba frowned. He was developing a distaste for the whole incident. "The register says your father gave the kolkhoz five hundred head of goats, five cows, and four camels."

"Four mules!" Uncle Sandro guessed joyfully. "We had five mules—Father kept one because he's accustomed to ride it."

"Then why does it say camels?" Nestor Apollonovich asked in surprise.

"Probably," said Uncle Sandro, "the Komsomol man who made the list didn't know how to spell *mule* in Russian, so he put them down as camels."

"Ah-h," said Nestor Apollonovich. "Tell your chairman he's a camel himself, and now sit down and have dinner with us."

"I certainly will tell him," Uncle Sandro assented joyfully. He added, just in case, "He'd do better to check the list than go planting bones."

But Nestor Apollonovich paid no attention to this remark, or perhaps he didn't quite hear. Or perhaps Chegemian affairs had begun to weary him, and he merely took advantage of his slight deafness to pretend that he didn't quite hear.

That night they did some hefty drinking, sang more than a few folk songs and Partisan songs, and when the dancing began Uncle Sandro's fate was sealed, because they invited him to dance.

For his Soviet native land, for Nestor Apollonovich, for all his dear guests, Uncle Sandro danced. And how he danced!

"Such talent is not for us alone, but for the whole nation to enjoy," Nestor Apollonovich said. He ordered him to go home, get some rest, and then come to Mukhus and drop by to see him immediately. He promised to get him a place in the Abkhaz Song and Dance Ensemble.

The next day Uncle Sandro saddled his long-unridden horse, rode over to the police station, and rapped on the chief's window with his quirt. The chief popped out onto the balcony, where several policemen were already standing, and invited him to dismount.

"Thank you," Uncle Sandro said, "but I came by for the *khurjin*."

"Bring it here," the chief ordered loudly. Turning to Uncle Sandro he added, "I was actually opposed to your arrest."

"So was I," Uncle Sandro agreed with restraint.

One of the policemen brought out the *khurjin* and was about to hand it to its owner, but the chief stopped him. "Strap it on for him," he ordered. Turning to Uncle Sandro again, he added, "I'm sorry to return it empty."

"That's all right," Uncle Sandro said. "It's not as if I'd been visiting my father-in-law."

According to Abkhazian custom, when you return a dish, a basket, a bag—any sort of container—it is considered good form to put in some kind of treat, and if you have nothing to put in it, you apologize. This custom might be designated as gratitude for a container or, on the contrary, as apology for an unfilled volume. It is practiced among neighbors, and the police chief, in his effort to be agreeable, had clearly gone too far.

"What happened to the bones?" Uncle Sandro asked curiously as he turned to go.

"They're in the fireproof locker, for the time being," the chief answered.

"Good thing it's fireproof," Uncle Sandro agreed. "They couldn't stand another fire."

With that he set off at an easy trot toward Chegem. Inside of a week Uncle Sandro was in Mukhus, where he was accepted into the Abkhaz Song and Dance

Ensemble under the direction of Platon Pantsulaya. He was also earning a little extra at a second job as superintendent at the Abkhazian Central Executive Committee. Nestor Apollonovich knew how to attract and hold gifted people, capable of adorning our little republic. Precisely what might adorn our republic, of course, was something for him and his closest associates to decide.

That fall something else happened in Chegem. One fine day Khabug found a tree with a wild bees' nest in the forest. He was pleased to have the free honey and decided to take it home, but he had nothing to put it in. He was not eager to go all the way home for a vessel, and he remembered that it would be much closer to go up to the Prayer Tree and get the copper kettle from the hollow; the god of the four-legged probably would not be offended.

And then, as he told it, when he had climbed up the mountain to the Prayer Tree and fished the copper kettle out of the hollow, he suddenly remembered something, but exactly what it was he could not determine. He descended to the spring and began washing out the inside of the kettle, and when he finished, it struck him still more forcefully that there was something he ought to remember, but he still could not think just what it was. He thought if he scrubbed the kettle again with sand he might remember whatever it was more clearly, but he was tired of washing the kettle, and he splashed the water out and returned to the honey-bearing chestnut tree. Khabug built a fire at the foot of it, threw some scraps of rotted wood into the flames to make the smoke thicker, hitched the kettle and an ax to his belt, and climbed the tree.

And then, when he had chopped an opening into the hollow and had begun to scrape out big, delicate slices of fresh honeycomb with his knife, and the smoked-out bees were circling above him with a furious drone, he remembered that Kunta's father, who had mysteriously disappeared twenty years before, had disappeared during the summer of what the Chegemians called the year of the War of the Wild Bees and the Carrion Crows. That summer, the Chegemians watched as a swarm of wild bees, who had nested in the uppermost opening of the hollow, waged war with some carrion crows that suddenly attacked the Prayer Tree.

The bodies of several crows fell near the tree, but the bees lost out and abandoned the Prayer Tree forever. It was after that time the shepherds had begun to build fires right in the hollow, if they were overtaken by weather that was too cold and windy: they would have supper, rake apart the half-burned logs, thrust their feet in the warm ashes, and sleep.

Now Khabug felt certain that Kunta's father must have been trying to get at the honey by climbing up through the lower part of the hollow, when he was stung to death by the bees and simply got stuck there forever. Of all the Chegemians, in Khabug's opinion, only he, a man of impure blood (an Endursky admixture), could have brought himself to commit such blasphemy. That was why he had disappeared without a trace—because he had not told anyone, even at home, about his criminal plan.

And now after many years his dried-out bones had been shaken loose by Sandro's mallet, the Komsomol had scorched them with their impious fire, and they had showered down like overripe nuts.

Later that day he told Kunta about all this, sitting at home by the kitchen hearth with his huge bee-stung hands spread to the fire. Submissive as usual, Kunta heard out his story, from time to time glancing at the copper kettle that stood by the fire, now all scrubbed and polished by Khabug's wife. She, too, sat in the kitchen now. She was shelling corn into her lap; whenever her skirt filled up she poured the corn into a pan.

"If I'd known that day that it was my father's bones, I'd've taken them home," Kunta sighed after hearing out Khabug's story.

"That's right." Khabug nodded toward the kettle: "You'd have put them in that and taken them. And my Sandro would be sitting at home instead of making his living dancing like a gypsy."

"What's Sandro got to do with it?" Kunta asked, not understanding Khabug's train of thought.

"It was because of these bones that he got arrested, and that was how he met Lakoba, and Lakoba lured him away to the city."

"True." Kunta nodded in agreement.

Khabug's wife, who missed her son, sighed. They were silent a while. The only sounds were the rasp of the corn being shelled and the squelching of lima-bean soup in a clay pot standing by the fire.

"When I think," Kunta said, staring into the fire, "that my father's bones hung twenty years in that damn hollow, it's strange."

"Why strange?" Khabug smiled.

"I was there almost every day. The deity could have hinted somehow."

"Your family profaned it, and it's supposed to give you hints?"

"That's true too," Kunta agreed. "But if this isn't Father?"

"It's him," Khabug declared confidently. He nodded toward the kettle: "You recognized the kettle?"

"The kettle's ours," Kunta agreed hastily.

"Perhaps there's some bit of his clothing stuck up there," Khabug suggested, but after a moment's thought he rejected his own hypothesis. "I guess not. The birds would have picked at it."

"Yes. Such a long time," Kunta sighed. They were silent again. With a resonant clatter, Khabug's wife poured the corn from her lap into the pan. She stood up and shook her skirt, picked up a handful of corncobs and thrust them into the fire. She stirred the bean soup with a wooden spoon, took the spoon out, blew on it, licked it, and laid it across the top of the pot, then sat down again.

"If he was wearing something iron—buttons, hooks—you might find them in the ashes," Khabug said.

Kunta shrugged and looked at Khabug with his pale faded eyes. "There's ashes up to your knees there."

Khabug's wife stopped shelling corn. "You could sift them through a sieve," she said.

"That's true too," Khabug agreed. "But first you should go to Kengur and get the bones. You have to bury them—it's shameful."

"At the police station, did you say?" Kunta inquired.

"At the police station. In the fireproof locker, if you can believe my no-good son."

"To hear you talk, everyone's a no-good but you," his wife put in. Angrily rasping at an ear of corn, she shelled a whole handful at once.

Khabug paid no attention to her.

"Will they give them to me?" Kunta asked hopefully.

"I think so," Khabug said. Then he added, "Take a pair of turkeys and a sack of nuts, just in case. But don't take them with you openly. These people don't like it done openly. Send them through our relatives."

"All right," Kunta said, standing up. "Should I take the kettle now?"

"Yes, of course," Khabug answered, and he too stood up.

"Wait," Khabug's wife said. Tossing aside a corncob, she poured the kernels with a clatter from her skirt into the pan.

She put several good slices of fresh honeycomb into the kettle for him (so as not to have to apologize for the unfilled volume).

"Oh, are you sure—," Kunta protested.

"Of course," Khabug joked gloomily. "These may be the descendants of the bees who stung your father to death."

"It's a strange world," Kunta said. He picked up the kettle and stumbled across the yard.

Khabug stood in the doorway for a long time, looking after him.

"All power to the people, they say—people like him," he said, nodding in the direction of the departing Kunta. "Just as I thought."

Khabug's wife pulled apart the half-burned logs and raked the coals nearer to the pot of bean soup. Then she turned from the fire and said, "All power to which people?"

"I meant Kunta," Khabug said, still standing in the doorway looking after him.

"He always was a sad one, with his hump, and he still is," his wife sighed, and she sat down again to shell corn. Khabug still stood in the doorway.

"Why do you just hang around," his wife said with a loud rasp as she took a shelled corncob and scraped the kernels from a full ear. "You should catch your mule and go visit your son."

"As if I didn't have anything better to do than go visit your dancing boy," Khabug said. He added, "I'm going to the mill, fix me something to eat."

"I'd rather send Kunta to the mill. You should go see your son," his wife repeated, but no longer with any conviction. She stood up again and reached down the little kitchen table from where it hung with its legs hooked over a rafter.

"Kunta will send people to the mill himself now, if he wants," Khabug grinned, sitting down at the table. "He's the boss . . ."

Incidentally, if old Khabug had heeded his wife, if he had really caught his mule and saddled it and gone to visit his son, he might have gotten a word in at the very beginning of the great controversy that unfolded in the pages of *Red Subtropics* on the subject of the mysterious bones of the unknown man found in the hollow of the Prayer Tree.

The first article I stumbled on when I looked through the newspaper files for those years was called "The End of the Prayer Tree." It told how the youth of the village of Chegem had gaily—with songs, so it said—committed to flame the famous Prayer Tree of the village of Chegem. No longer would the shepherds, on their way up to alpine meadows with the kolkhoz herds, stop near this tree to slaughter a goat and hold a feast under the guise of a pagan custom; they would advance purposefully toward their summer stations. At the end of the notice the correspondent pointed out that the Prayer Tree possessed a unique hollow, which stretched to the crown and had several apertures. The width of the hollow at the base of the tree made it possible for two horsemen to ride into it and ride out again without impeding each other. (By the way, I have noticed that wherever a unique hollow tree is mentioned, someone points out that a horseman, at least one, could ride into it without dismounting. One might think that the burning dream of every horseman since Don Quixote had been to find a hollow tree into which he could ride without dismounting, stand there a while, maybe do something—without dismounting—and ride back out.)

At the very end of the article the correspondent indicated obscurely that a skeleton "of prerevolutionary origin" had been found in the hollow. (I suspect that this phrase, with its covert polemic against the article in the *Kenguria News*, was secretly intended as a recommendation to the investigative agencies of the Kenguria district to leave Uncle Sandro alone.)

Here is the last sentence of the article, as I transcribed it in my notebook: "Apparently we shall never know to what poor plowman or downtrodden shepherd this skeleton belonged, but we are sure that this is yet another crime of the local prerevolutionary feudal lords."

After a while, about a week later, *Red Subtropics* carried an article by a scholar from Moscow, a Caucasist who was in Abkhazia just then with an archaeological expedition.

He was conducting excavations in the village of Eshery, twelve kilometers from Sukhum. The newspaper printed his article under what seemed to me a rather cold neutral title, "A Scholar's Opinion."

He advanced the hypothesis that the skeleton that had been found might not be the result of a murder but an example of a very interesting ancient custom, aerial interment of the dead, which Apollonius of Rhodes described with such lively interest in the second century B.C. It seemed the ancestors of present-day

Abkhazians considered it a sacrilege to bury men in the earth. They wrapped them in oxhides and hoisted them into trees by means of a grapevine. The same could not be said of women, whom they committed to the earth.

The ancestors of present-day Abkhazians had apparently had an ancient settlement in the Chegem region, and it would be fitting to make a careful study of the oldest trees in this locality.

For some reason this notice provoked an angry rebuke in the pages of *Red Subtropics*. The reply to the famous archaeologist's article was entitled "Scholarly Slowpoke."

When I stumbled on this rebuke in the yellowed files of *Red Subtropics*, I felt my eyes fill with tears of emotion. I detected in it—very faintly, but still I could detect them—the beginnings of the style that became so firmly entrenched in years to come.

The author began by calling the scholar's hypothesis an awkward and, to say the least, a strange attempt to shield a prerevolutionary murderer. After this, the author's glib pen pierced Apollonius of Rhodes himself and then our scholar, who was Apollonius's prisoner.

Reading the phrase about imprisonment, I was again filled with emotion. It struck me that this was just about the time when scholars and other public figures began to be taken prisoner.

As I recall, this expression was current when I first started school, and I had a rather picturesque image of these scholars who had been taken prisoner by the bourgeoisie. For some reason I imagined them as a convoy of bearded little old men with their hands tied behind them, shuffling despondently over to the bourgeois side. What I did not understand at the time was why, instead of merely cursing our men for being taken prisoner, we did not send the Partisans on a sudden raid to try and liberate them from the convoy and restore them to our side.

Anyway, after repudiating Apollonius of Rhodes, this article defended the tradition—generally accepted among Abkhazians and many other peoples—of burying the dead. It particularly mentioned the inadmissible license of the hypothesis that the bodies of men had been hoisted into the trees, whereas women were humiliatingly buried in the ground.

Abkhazians, the author observed, had always been noted for their chivalrous treatment of women, especially now, under Soviet rule, when men and women worked side by side with equal rights at construction sites and in kolkhoz fields.

"While Nestor Apollonovich is alive, no Apollonius of Rhodes will succeed in calumniating our national customs!" On this unexpectedly bombastic note the then still youthful journalist concluded his article, signing with the pseudonym Levan Golba.

Incidentally, as soon as Lakoba died, and the Abkhazians began to undergo artifical Georgification, that journalist began appearing in print under the pseudonym Levan Golbidze. At times—precisely those times when Mingrelians had the upper hand in the Georgian government—he varied it with the pseudonym

Levan Golbia. To do him justice, I must say that while he changed his pseudonymous last name, he always kept firmly to his original pseudonymous first name.

Having changed his own pseudonym so many times, it is no wonder that in 1948 he proved to be a past master at decoding the pseudonyms of others. Granted, he made a blunder early in 1953 when he wrote an article entitled "Pseudohighlanders of the Caucasus." The article was typeset but did not get printed, owing to the death of the Father of All Nations except those exiled to Siberia or Kazakhstan. The journalist found himself in disfavor for some time and was even forced to change jobs and work in an industrial cooperative. At present he has been restored to the press and for the time being is working under his original pseudonym.

Apropos of his original pseudonym, let us return to the era of his youth. We must give our young scholars, then still Abkhazian, their due: they rebuffed his devastatingly critical article. As we see, even in those times good sense occasionally found the light of day.

One of our scholars, whom I cannot now name, wrote in *Red Subtropics* that neither the Moscow scholar nor, especially, Apollonius of Rhodes, who lived in the second century B.C., had intended to calumniate our national customs or our present-day society.

As for the custom of aerial interment among the Colchians, ancestors of present-day Abkhazians, references to it could actually be found not only in Apollonius of Rhodes but also in Nicholas of Elis, who as late as the third century A.D. wrote that "the Colchians bury their dead in hides: they sew them up and hang them in trees." (I find nothing objectionable in the fact that the young scholar, as may be observed even in my retelling, was flirting a bit with erudition. Later on, scholars began to flirt with illiteracy and achieved in this regard a suspiciously natural effect.)

The common feature of these and all other sources, the young scholar continued, is that all of them state bluntly that they are speaking of the aerial interment of men, not women. Therefore, what we have here is no slander but the bitter scientific truth.

On the other hand, he added, references in antique and other sources are as yet uncorroborated by either ethnographic or archaeological findings, not counting the more-than-doubtful Chegem case.

In any event, he added unexpectedly at the end, whatever one's opinion of aerial interment among the Colchians, the excavations which are being conducted by the Moscow expedition in the region of the village of Eshery, and from which our scientific community expects so much, have no relation to the above-mentioned problem.

What did the excavations have to do with all this? Levan Golba's article had said nothing about them. We can only assume that after his attack the administration had undertaken to halt the excavations.

Unfortunately, it proved none too easy to ask the archaeologist about this. He now lives in Moscow, works in a history institute, and visits our parts only with archaeological expeditions.

On one of my trips to Moscow I finally managed to see him at his institute. He greeted me with truly Abkhazian cordiality, we chatted half an hour or so in his office, and, as always in such cases, the conversation turned to Vakhtang Bochua. That put us both in a good mood, and I soon found an opening to remind him of his long-ago article.

"Yes, yes," he beamed. "We did succeed in saving the excavations. You're not planning to write about that, are you?" His face had already clouded over.

"Yes," I said. "Why not?"

"It's not worth it," he advised, glancing at the telephone with a certain questioning anxiety. "Exaggerations . . . The distant past . . ."

It struck me that he addressed the last phrase not to me so much as to the telephone. When he caught me glancing at it too, or rather, when he realized from *my* glance that I understood the meaning of *his* glance at the telephone, he decided not to conceal his misgivings. Jabbing a finger at the instrument, he made a negative gesture and reinforced it by screwing up his face in disgust. The gesture left no doubt that the instrument enjoyed no trust from him; there was also a nuance of far-reaching friendliness that invited me to share his skepticism.

"Not you, too?" I asked, indicating the telephone.

He spread his hands in a gesture which meant that this issue had assumed a configuration of depressing confusion.

"Well, what do you hear, in general?" I asked, somehow sensing that the telephone was drawing me into the sphere of its own interests. It made me feel like toying with the Great Dumb One, feel like teasing it.

"How shall I put it," he murmured slowly, glancing again at the telephone.

"They sent Levan back to the newspaper," I said.

"Not a good sign," he said, and somehow he came alive. This small but precise bit of information instantaneously set in motion a well-tuned machine of historical prognosis, which had been stalled for lack of facts.

He made a ferocious face and with both hands twirled nonexistent mustaches. After that he gestured upward, as if indicating to a crane operator that he could lift his load.

"But they did send Levan back to the newspaper under his original pseudonym," I reminded him.

"That's actually not a bad sign," he said, and fell silent. The prognosis machine went into reverse and stopped, right where it had started from in the beginning.

"Joking aside," I asked, going back to his article, "what can it mean to you now, after thirty years? You're a professor, and besides, you live in Moscow."

"But the excavations?" he objected. "We're getting ready for an interesting expedition in the Tsebelda area. It's not worth ruining that. We'd never find another crazy young fool to write an article in my defense!"

We laughed and parted, moved by our mutual liberalism.

Here I break off the story of the Prayer Tree, stop myself with a gesture of mercy, to return to it later when I have gathered my courage and calm; and then—do not take offense, friends, for sad will be my tale.

BELSHAZZAR'S FEASTS

Uncle Sandro started living the good life after Nestor Apollonovich Lakoba brought him to the city, made him superintendent at the CEC, and got him appointed to Platon Pantsulaya's celebrated Abkhaz Song and Dance Ensemble. He quickly worked his way up to become one of the very best dancers, able to compete with Pata Pataraya himself.

Thirty rubles a month as superintendent at the CEC, and as much again as a member of the ensemble—not bad money for those times, downright decent money, by God!

As superintendent at the Central Executive Committee, Uncle Sandro kept after the maintenance staff, occasionally went to the post office to pick up Nestor Apollonovich's German hearing aids, and also saw to the garage, including Lakoba's personal Buick, which he called the "Bik," to simplify the foreign pronunciation.

Of course, Lakoba's personal Buick was at his disposal when Lakoba was away in Moscow or off some place at a conference.

At these times the people's commissars and other powerful officials used to ask Uncle Sandro for the Buick so that they could go to their village for some relative's funeral, celebrate a birth or a wedding or—if nothing else—their own arrival.

Barreling into one's native village in Lakoba's personal motorcar, which everyone knew by sight, was doubly pleasant—that is, politically pleasant and just plain pleasant. Everyone understood that if a man arrived in Nestor Apollonovich's car it meant he was on his way up. Maybe Nestor Apollonovich had let him into the inner circle and was always slapping him on the back. Maybe he had even given him a bear hug and personally seated him in the car: Go on now, you son of a bitch, wherever you have to go; just don't throw up on the seat on your way back.

Of course, there were also unpleasantnesses. Thus a certain not-so-powerful but nevertheless highly placed comrade once used the Buick to go home to his village. There, at table, to someone's question about the Buick, he gave a craftily evasive answer to the effect that although he had not yet been given Lakoba's job, the matter was being decided at the very top, and one thing he could say for sure was that the car had already been transferred to him.

He never got up from that festive table, or to be more precise, he sat there so long that a party of three—Lakoba's nephews or namesakes, I think—arrived from the neighboring village. Circumspectly, so as not to alarm the other people there, they dragged him away from the table, and in the yard they pounded the stuffing out of him.

To top it all off, they strapped him across the trunk of the Buick, planning to drive him through the village. In point of fact, the plan did not succeed, because they did not know how to drive the car themselves, and the chauffeur had fled to the cornpatch.

The plain truth is that the comrade should have known better. By his stupid remarks he had insulted not only Nestor Lakoba but his entire clan. In those days an insult to a clan was something that rarely went unpunished.

After this incident, decent people were long amazed that the comrade had so openly dared to indulge in blasphemy, and mendacious blasphemy at that.

He himself said that his head had been befuddled from drink. Since the owner of the house where the feast took place swore by all his forefathers that no one had left the table, he never has figured out who went to inform the neighboring village.

Fortunately, none of this story reached the ears of Nestor Apollonovich, or everyone would have really caught it—all the nephews or namesakes, and Uncle Sandro, and, for the second time around, the victimized blasphemer.

Uncle Sandro got something, of course, in return for these minor liberties with the Buick. Nothing flagrant, really, but he might need to get a relative into a good hospital, obtain some needed document in a hurry, have a friend's case reexamined . . . (That was a friend who seemed to think that czarist times were not over. He stole some horses and then at the trial, instead of denying it, turned to the audience and proudly told them all about it.)

In this golden era Uncle Sandro did a lot for his friends, but not all of them repaid kindness with kindness; many of them subsequently proved to be ingrates.

Sometimes Uncle Sandro would go out on the balcony of the CEC headquarters and look down along the street, and there at the very end he could see the sea; and if a ship was in port, its smokestacks and masts would be visible from the balcony. It made Uncle Sandro feel good to look over at the port; it was nice to think that he could get on a boat and sail away to Batum or Odessa. Uncle Sandro had no intention of going anywhere, because a bird in the hand is worth two in the bush, but still, it was nice to think that he could get on a boat and sail away.

If he stood on the balcony and looked in the other direction, there was nothing to see but mountains and forests, so that one might have thought there was no reason to look over there.

Only once in a while, when a yearning for home crept over him, would Uncle Sandro look at the mountains and heave a furtive sigh. He sighed furtively because he considered it improper to sigh loudly when he had such honorable work—in power. Because if a man sighs when he's in power, it looks as if he doesn't like being in power, which would be ungrateful and stupid. No; Uncle Sandro liked being in power, and naturally he wanted to remain there as long as possible.

What Uncle Sandro really enjoyed, however, was to stand on the CEC balcony on a nice day and just look down at the passing crowds, among whom there were many people he knew and many beautiful women.

Those who had known Uncle Sandro before and still liked him would look up and say hello, their cordial gaze indicating that they were glad he had been moved up. Those who had known Uncle Sandro before, but now envied him, walked on by, pretending not to notice him. But Uncle Sandro did not take offense: Let them go about their business, you can't please everyone by being moved up.

Those who had not known him before, but saw him now on the CEC balcony, thought he was a powerful official who had come out on the balcony for a breath of air. Uncle Sandro replied to their greetings with a polite nod, not because he was playing along with the involuntary deception, but simply because he knew how to forgive people their small human weaknesses.

Sometimes people he knew would stop under the balcony and ask in gestures, How is Lakoba? Uncle Sandro would clench his fist and shake it slightly to show that Nestor Apollonovich was solidly in place. His acquaintances would nod gladly in reply and stride onward with a certain extra briskness.

Sometimes, knowing that Lakoba was away somewhere, these acquaintances would ask in gestures, Where did he go? In reply, Uncle Sandro would point toward the east (which meant Tbilisi) or gesture more portentously to the north (which meant Moscow).

Sometimes they would ask—again, mostly through gestures—Well, has Lakoba gotten back yet? In these cases Uncle Sandro would nod affirmatively or shake his head negatively. Either way, the acquaintances would nod with satisfaction and walk on, glad to have shared, however transiently, in the affairs of state.

The fashion plates of Mukhus would click by on their high heels, and meeting their eyes, Uncle Sandro would twirl his mustache, hinting at mischievous intentions. Many an ingenious love affair was begun from this balcony, although he also struck up many new acquaintances from the stages of the theaters and clubs where the troupe performed.

There were a few women who snickered at his flirtatious posing on the balcony. Uncle Sandro did not take offense, he merely lost interest in them: Oh, you don't like me? Well, I don't like you either.

The ones he liked best were the women who blushed when their eyes met his, only to lower their heads and walk quickly on. Uncle Sandro believed that shame was the finest ornament a woman could wear. (Sometimes he said that shame was the most irritating ornament, but basically this meant the same thing.)

Occasionally, as he stood on the CEC balcony, Uncle Sandro would see his old buddy Kolya Zarhidis. He always greeted him heartily to show that he was not getting too big for his britches, that he still recognized and loved his old friends. From Kolya's eyes he could tell that Kolya felt neither spite nor envy over the fact that Uncle Sandro was playing host in his confiscated mansion, or that he was standing around on the balcony as he had in peaceful times.

"Try and get up there on a horse, why don't you?" Kolya would say, reminding him of the feat he had performed so long ago.

"Not any more, Kolya," Uncle Sandro would reply with a smile. "Times are quite different now."

"Mmmm," Kolya would say. As if he had received sad confirmation of the correctness of his own way of life, he would walk on toward the coffeehouse.

Uncle Sandro would look after him, somewhat sorry for him and somewhat envious, because sitting in a coffeehouse with a shot of cognac and a Turkish coffee was pleasant even under Soviet rule, maybe even pleasanter than before.

The Abkhaz Song and Dance Ensemble was already making a splash all over Transcaucasia, and later made a splash in Moscow. People say they even performed in London, although I don't know that they made a splash there.

In the era I am describing now, their fame—created mainly by Platon Pantsulaya, Pata Pataraya, and Uncle Sandro—was already on the upswing. On the anniversary of the Revolution, after the formal parts of the celebration, the ensemble would perform on the stage of the district theater. Moreover, they performed at Party conferences and at rallies for High Achievers in industry and agriculture; they were not too busy to travel to the outlying districts of the republic; and they also put on shows for the larger sanatoria and vacation hotels on the Transcaucasian coast.

After a performance for any of the more or less important organizations, the members of the ensemble would be invited to a banquet, where they did more singing and dancing in close proximity to the banquet table and the higher-ranking comrades.

Uncle Sandro, as I have already said, was virtually an equal of the best dancer in the troupe, Pata Pataraya. At any rate, he was the only person in the troupe who mastered Pata Pataraya's most celebrated trick: getting a running start backstage, falling to his knees, and sliding, sliding, all the way across the stage, his arms thrown back like the wings of a soaring bird.

Well, Uncle Sandro became so good at this celebrated *pas* that many people said they could not tell the one dancer from the other.

One member of the ensemble, a dancer and lead singer by the name of Makhaz, said one day that if the dancer performing this number were to pull his turban down over his face, there was no way you could tell who it was sliding across the stage—the celebrated Pata Pataraya or the new star, Sandro Chegemsky.

Maybe Makhaz wanted to flatter him a bit, since he was from Uncle Sandro's home district, because after all you really could tell them apart, especially if you had a dancer's experienced eye. But that is beside the point. The point is that Makhaz's chance remark gave Uncle Sandro the idea for a great improvement on an already rather elaborate number.

The very next day Uncle Sandro started training in secret. Taking advantage of his official position, he trained in the CEC conference hall, behind closed doors so that the cleaning lady could not spy.

Incidentally, this was the very hall where Uncle Sandro had once galloped around on his unforgettable skewbald charger, thereby saving his friend Kolya and bankrupting the Endursky cattle dealer.

Uncle Sandro practiced for about three months, and the day finally came that he determined to exhibit his new number. He did not feel it was sufficiently polished, but circumstances forced him to take the risk and play his secret trump on stage.

The better part of the ensemble, twenty of the members, had left for Gagra the previous day. The ensemble was to perform at one of the largest sanatoria, where a conference of the Secretaries of the District Committees of Western Georgia was currently taking place. Rumor had it that the meeting was being conducted by Stalin himself, who was vacationing in Gagra.

Apparently the idea of convening the district committee secretaries had come to him while he was here on vacation. But why he had called a conference of the secretaries of the district committees of only western Georgia, Uncle Sandro simply could not understand.

Apparently the district committee secretaries of eastern Georgia had committed some offense; or maybe he wanted to make them feel that they were not yet worthy of such a high-level conference, so that they would do better work in the future, competing with the district committee secretaries of western Georgia.

Or so thought Uncle Sandro, exerting his inquisitive mind—although strictly speaking this was not within his purview as superintendent at the CEC, or still less as a member of the ensemble.

So the better part of the ensemble had left, while Uncle Sandro stayed behind. The problem was that Uncle Sandro's daughter was very ill at the time. Everyone knew about it. Just before the group departed, Uncle Sandro had asked Pantsulaya to leave him behind, in view of his daughter's illness. He was sure that Pantsulaya would fly to pieces, would beg him to go with the group, and then, after being obstinate a while, Uncle Sandro would sadly accede.

This would have preserved the proprieties in relation to his family: he could say he wasn't all that eager to dance, himself, but he was forced to. Besides, the other dancers would have been made aware that while it was possible to go on without Sandro, the dance would not have been the same.

Quite unexpectedly, the director of the ensemble agreed right away, and there was nothing for Uncle Sandro to do but turn around and leave. That same day the manager of the CEC gave him an insulting reprimand.

"In my opinion, someone is stealing firewood from us," he said, pointing to the huge pile of logs that had been cut and stacked in the CEC yard back at the start of the summer.

"It's just settling," Uncle Sandro replied carelessly, aching with the dullness of his artistic isolation.

"I never heard of a woodpile settling," the manager said, with intentional innuendo, or so it seemed to Uncle Sandro.

"I'll bet you never heard about the forest fire around Chegem, either?" Uncle Sandro asked insinuatingly.

This was the notorious Chegem sarcasm, which not everyone can handle.

"What's the Chegem forest got to do with it?" the manager asked.

"Why, I've been taking the CEC wood home to the hills," Uncle Sandro said, and he walked away from the manager. The manager just threw up his hands.

They've already gone through Eshery, Uncle Sandro thought as he went up the stairs of the mansion; they're probably getting close to Afon now. A cool draft touching his face seemed to him a breath of disgrace. The manager must know something, Lakoba must be cutting me loose, Uncle Sandro thought, correlating the manager's insulting tone and the even more insulting ease with which Platon Pantsulaya had acceded to his request.

It was particularly regrettable because everyone presumed that Comrade Stalin himself would be at the banquet. True, no one knew for sure. But one wasn't supposed to know for sure; somehow it was even sweeter that no one knew anything for sure.

The next day Uncle Sandro sat by his daughter's bedside, dully watching his wife change the wet towel on her head from time to time.

The little girl had pneumonia. She was being treated by one of the best doctors in town. He had some doubt as to a favorable outcome, although he was relying, as he said, on her strong Chegem constitution.

Four Chegemians, distant relatives of Uncle Sandro's, were also sitting in the room, their hands warily on the table. In recent years they had started coming to town more and more often, and it must be admitted that Uncle Sandro found them a bit tiresome.

The historical development of the people of Chegem had been unnaturally accelerated. They managed this with a certain patriarchal clumsiness. On the one hand, at home, in complete accord with the march of history and the decisions of higher organs of government (in point of fact, the march of history was also determined by the decisions of these higher organs), they were building socialism—that is, engaging in collective farm agriculture. On the other hand, they came to town to sell things, engaging for the first time in capitalistic trade relations.

A double load like that could not pass without leaving its trace. Some of them, amazed that one could get money for such simple things as cheese, corn, and beans, went to the opposite extreme, piling on incredible prices, and they would stand in silence for days at a time beside their unbought produce. Sometimes, stung by the contempt of the customers, the Chegemians would cart their produce back: All right, then, we'll eat it ourselves. As time went on, however, there were fewer and fewer people so arrogant; the despotism of the marketplace did its work.

One thing the Chegemians could never get used to, that there was no fireplace fire in city houses. Without a real fire on the hearth, a house seemed unlived-in to the Chegemians, more like an office. It was hard to have a conversation in such a house, because they did not know where to look. A Chegemian was used to staring into the fire while he talked, or at least, if he had to look at his companion, he could spread his hands to the fire and feel the heat.

That is why the four Chegemians were silent and kept their hands warily on the table, which added to Uncle Sandro's irritation.

Today, Uncle Sandro thought, our troupe may be going to dance for Stalin himself—and I have to sit here and listen to the silence of Chegemians. At the bazaar they had been offered the chance to stay in the Kolkhoz Workers' Club, but they had indignantly rejected the offer on the grounds that their Uncle Sandro lived here in town, and as a relative he might take offense. It cannot be said that Uncle Sandro was particularly moved by such loyalty to family ties. Conceivably he would not have been the least offended.

"Thank God our Sandro has gotten in with the watchers-over," one of the Chegemians said, making an effort to overcome his discomfiture at the lack of a real fire in the house.

There was a long, thoughtful pause.

"Iron knees are valued more than ever by the powers that be," the second Chegemian said, explaining the reason for Uncle Sandro's success.

"I recall as how Prince Tatyr Khan valued good dancers too," the third Chegemian said, drawing a historical parallel.

"Still, not so much," the fourth Chegemian added after a long silence. He had thought for a long time because he wanted to say something of his own, but, unable to find anything of his own, he had decided he would make a small correction in what had been said by someone else.

The Chegemians went on with their meager discussion. The wife, sitting beside the sick little girl, slowly waved a fan over her. A fly buzzed and beat against the windowpane. Uncle Sandro tried to be patient.

Suddenly the door burst open, and in came the manager. Uncle Sandro jumped up, feeling that the stalled motor of time had started up again. Something had happened or the manager would not be here.

The manager greeted everyone, went over to the sick girl's bed, and said a few sympathetic words before getting down to business. Uncle Sandro listened distractedly, waiting impatiently for him to say why he had come.

"Easy come, easy go," Uncle Sandro replied to his sympathetic words—using the Turkish proverb not altogether felicitously.

"I didn't want to bother you," the manager said, sighing, as he pulled a piece of paper from his pocket, "but there's a telegram for you."

"From whom?" Uncle Sandro said, snatching the folded blank.

"From Lakoba," the manager said with respectful wonder.

"COME IF YOU CAN NESTOR," Uncle Sandro read, so happy that the words swam before his eyes.

" 'If you can'?" Uncle Sandro cried, and kissed the telegram with a smack. "Why, is there anything I wouldn't do for Nestor? Where's the Bik?" he added, turning imperiously to the manager.

"Waiting outside," the manager replied. "Don't forget to take your passport. They're really strict about that now."

"I know," Uncle Sandro nodded, and he snapped to his wife, "Get my cherkeska ready."

Twenty minutes later, standing at the door with his professional case in his hand, Uncle Sandro turned to those who were staying behind and said with prophetic certainty, "I swear by Nestor, the girl will get better."

"How do you know?" the Chegemians said, brightening. His wife said nothing; she just watched her husband contemptuously as she continued to fan the child.

"I can feel it," Uncle Sandro said, and he closed the door behind him.

"Not everyone is allowed to swear by the name of Nestor," Uncle Sandro heard from behind the door.

"Not more than one or two people in Abkhazia," another loyal Chegemian said, making it more specific, but Uncle Sandro was heading for his car and did not hear.

Incidentally, to jump ahead of my story, I can say that Uncle Sandro's prophecy—although based on nothing but shame for his hurried departure—did come true. The next morning, for the first time since she had been sick, the little girl asked for something to eat.

. . . After three hours of wild driving, the Buick stopped in Old Gagra at the gates of a sanatorium on one of the quiet green streets.

It was getting on toward evening. Uncle Sandro was nervous, suspecting he might be late. He ran into the gatehouse and went to a little lighted window, behind which a woman was sitting.

"A pass," he said, shoving his passport through the long tunnel of the bay window.

The woman looked at his passport, checked it against some sort of list, then glanced critically at Uncle Sandro several times, trying to detect alien features in his face.

Every time she looked at him Uncle Sandro froze, trying not to let any alien features materialize, setting his face in an expression of nonchalant likeness to himself.

The woman wrote out his pass. Uncle Sandro grew more and more agitated, sensing that this strict check-in process implied the nerve-racking exhilaration of an encounter with the Leader.

With the pass and his passport in one hand and his suitcase in the other, he quickly crossed the deserted courtyard of the sanatorium and halted at the entrance, where he was met by the policeman on duty. For some reason the latter stared long and hard at his pass, checking it against his passport.

"The Abkhazian ensemble," Uncle Sandro said, by implication stressing the peaceful nature of his visit. The policeman made no reply. Keeping the passport in his hand, he shifted his gaze to the suitcase.

Uncle Sandro nodded joyfully in response, to indicate that he fully understood how crucial the moment was. He briskly opened the suitcase and took out his cherkeska, his Asiatic boots, his riding breeches, his Caucasian belt and dagger, laying them all at his feet. As he took out each article Uncle Sandro honorably shook it, thus providing an opportunity for any ill-meant object that might be there to fall out.

When he got down to the belt and dagger, Uncle Sandro smiled and slid it out of the scabbard a little way, as if distantly suggesting its utter uselessness for regicide, even if such an insane idea were to arise in some insane mind.

The policeman followed his movements attentively and nodded curtly, as if acknowledging the fact of the dagger's uselessness and cutting off all possibility of discussion on this point.

Uncle Sandro put all the things back in the suitcase, closed it, and was on the point of reaching for his passport and pass—but the policeman stopped him again.

"Are you Sandro Chegemba?" he asked.

"Yes," Uncle Sandro said. With a flash of insight he added, "But on the posters I'm Sandro Chegemsky!"

"Posters don't interest me," the policeman said. Without inviting Uncle Sandro to pass, he took a shiny new telephone from the wall and started calling someone.

Uncle Sandro felt desperate. He remembered the telegram—the document was his last salvation—and started rummaging through his pockets.

"Bik, CEC, Lakoba . . ." In his nervousness he muttered the words like a magic spell, rummaging through his pockets with no success.

Suddenly Uncle Sandro spotted Makhaz, his fellow ensemble member, coming down the broad carpeted staircase. Uncle Sandro felt that fate itself had sent him this countryman and neighbor. He gesticulated desperately, beckoning him over, even though Makhaz was coming down toward them anyway, slightly outdistancing the flaring hems of his cherkeska.

"Ask him," Uncle Sandro said when Makhaz came to a stop beside them, puffing out his chest and swelling with involuntary pride. Paying no attention to Makhaz, the policeman went on listening to the receiver. Makhaz's neck started to turn red.

If Uncle Sandro had been listening to the telephone conversation, however, he would not have had to worry so much, and Makhaz would not have had to tire his chest muscles, which were essential for the singing to come.

The problem was that the woman at the gatehouse had first mistakenly written "Chegen" instead of "Chegem" and then corrected the letter. This correction of the letter—apparently outside the rules for such a place—was what aroused the policeman's suspicion. Now, straightening out the misunderstanding over the phone, he convinced himself that she and she alone had corrected it.

Although the telephone was new, perhaps installed only that day, it did not work very well, and the policeman had to keep repeating his questions.

When he finally hung up, Makhaz thrust his puffed-up chest forward and announced, "Member of the ensemble, the well-known Sandro Chegemsky."

"I know," the policeman said simply. "You may pass."

Uncle Sandro and Makhaz went up the red-carpeted stairs. It turned out that the director of the ensemble had already sent Makhaz out to meet him several times.

Uncle Sandro felt no enmity toward the policeman now. On the contrary, he felt that the strict precautions surrounding his passage into the sanatorium were a guarantee of the grandeur of the encounter that lay ahead. Uncle Sandro would probably have agreed to face even more obstacles, so long as he knew he would overcome them in the end.

"Will he be here?" Uncle Sandro asked quietly when they reached the third floor and started down the corridor.

"Why will be, when he already is?" Makhaz said confidently. He already felt at home here. Makhaz opened one of the doors off the corridor and stopped to let Uncle Sandro go ahead of him. Uncle Sandro heard the familiar backstage hubbub, and with his excitement at fever pitch, he entered a large, brightly lit room.

The members of the troupe, already dressed in their costumes, were walking around the room limbering up. A few sprawled limply in soft chairs, their long legs stretched in front of them.

"Sandro's here!" cried several joyful voices.

Uncle Sandro embraced and kissed his comrades and showed them the telegram from Lakoba, which he had finally found.

"The manager brought it," he said, waving the telegram.

"Hurry up and change!" Pantsulaya shouted.

Uncle Sandro went to a corner where the troupe's clothes were hanging over chairs, and started to change, listening to the director's final instructions.

"The main thing is," Pantsulaya said, "when you're invited, don't jump at the food and wine. Behave modestly, but you don't have to play hard to get either. If one of the leaders invites you to have a drink, drink it, and then go back to your comrades. Do *not*—especially if you're chewing—stand beside the Leader as if you'd stormed the Winter Palace with him."

As they listened to Pantsulaya, the dancers kept walking around the room, limbering up, bending at the waist. From time to time one of them would rise up on his toes, lift one leg buttoned into a glove-soft Asiatic boot, and suddenly—hop, hop, hop!—take several giant leaps, all the while listening to the even, soothing voice of the director.

Pata Pataraya took several trial runs, practicing for his famous number. He did not fall to his knees, merely slid, in order to get a good feel for the floor. After each slide he would stop, turn around carefully, and measure how far he had gone by putting the heel of one foot to the toe of the other.

Uncle Sandro did the same thing. By now he could regulate the force of his running start and the distance of his slide with an accuracy of the length of his foot. True, Pata Pataraya did it with an accuracy of the width of his hand, but Uncle Sandro had his secret number in reserve, and now his soul was seared with nervous exultation: Would it work?

"Remember, there isn't going to be any stage," Pantsulaya was saying, pacing back and forth among his charges in his white cherkeska. "You'll be dancing right on the floor, the floor in there is the same as here. The main thing is, don't get nervous! The leaders are people just like us, only much better—"

Just then the door opened and a middle-aged man wearing a tussah tunic appeared. It was the manager of the sanatorium. Ominously, and at the same time fearfully, as if anticipating some failure, he nodded to Pantsulaya.

"Follow me, one at a time," Pantsulaya said quietly. He slipped softly to the door behind the tussah tunic.

Pata Pataraya went next; after Pata, Uncle Sandro; and then the others, who reflexly made way for the best.

With the noiseless steps of court conspirators they went through the corridor and started into a room where a man in plainclothes stood at the door.

The sanatorium manager nodded to him. He nodded in reply and began letting them through, looking carefully at each one and counting with his eyes. The room turned out to be absolutely empty except for two men sitting at the far end by the window, wearing plainclothes like the one at the door. They were smoking, talking comfortably back and forth. On noticing the troupe members, one of them, without getting up, nodded to let them know they could pass.

The manager opened the next door and there was a roar of voices at table. Without going inside, he stopped at the doorway and silently, with a desperate gesture of his arm—Come on! come on! come on!—swept them all into the banquet hall.

Within a few seconds the troupe members had flitted into the hall and lined up in two rows, blinded by the bright lights, the plenteous table, and the vastness of the crowd.

The banquet was at its height. Everything had happened so fast that not everyone noticed they were in the hall. At first isolated claps, then a joyous squall of applause greeted the twenty cypresslike knights who had sprung up from nowhere, led by Platon Pantsulaya.

It was manifest that those who were applauding had eaten and drunk well and were now pleased to have their merriment prolonged by dint of art, in order that they might later return to fresh merriment at the table.

Regaining their wits, the troupe members tried to spot Comrade Stalin, but did not immediately locate him, because they were looking into the depths of the hall, whereas Comrade Stalin was sitting quite close to them, right at the end of the table. He was facing slightly away, toward his neighbor, who turned out to be the All-Union head man, Kalinin.

The applause continued, and Pantsulaya, his head bowed, stood before the cypress line like a marble image of gratitude. Then, sensing that the applause was not waning and that further silence from the troupe would therefore be immodest, he lifted his head, glanced sideways at the troupe members, and clapped his hands. In the same way, a horseman, after raising his quirt, looks back at his charger's croup before giving it a crack.

The troupe members began to applaud, the roar of their love forcing its way through to the very source of love, through the countering roar of governmental affection. Stalin suddenly got to his feet, and the whole hall rumblingly followed suit, everyone trying to catch up with him before he could straighten up.

It lasted for about a minute, this bloodless battle of mutual affection, like the friendly uproar of chums slapping each other on the back, a silly lovers' skirmish where the conquered thanked the conqueror and then lovingly conquered him, toppling his wave of roars with a new wave of roars.

The dancers continued to applaud while talking back and forth, as they were accustomed to do, without turning to each other.

"There's Comrade Stalin!"

"Where, where?"

"Talking to Kalinin!"

"Look, Voroshilov's short too!"

"And who's that?"

"Beria's wife!"

"The leaders are all short—Stalin, Voroshilov, Beria, Lakoba . . ."

"I wonder why?"

"Lenin was short—that's how it got started."

"They may be short, but they're pretty solid."

"Sandro, you should be the tamada at a table like that."

"Our Nestor's the tamada!"

"Or maybe Beria?"

"No, see, Nestor's sitting at the head of the table."

"Stalin always picks him. He's his favorite."

Gradually the mutual applause melted together and evened out, finding a common epicenter of love, its reason for being. And the fulcrum on which its being turned was Comrade Stalin. Now even the secretaries of the district committees, as if unable to resist the fascination exerted by the epicenter of love, turned their applause to Stalin. Gazing at him and raising their arms, they all clapped as if trying to throw their own personal sound wave to him. And he, understanding this, smiled a fatherly smile and applauded as if faintly apologetic for the treachery of his cohorts, who were applauding not with him but for him, which was why he was powerless by himself to answer their wave of applause with equal might.

He was gladdened by the sight of these well-built dancers, tightly buttoned into their black cherkeskas. At moments like this, he loved anything whose value was both obvious and irrelevant to politics, which sometimes wearied him. *Seemingly* irrelevant, that is, because subliminally he associated this obvious value and perfection with the cumbersome, crawly thing that metamorphosed from his every political act, and he interpreted it as a material, if small, proof of the thing's innocence.

Thus the twenty well-built dancers metamorphosed into flourishing delegates for his ethnic policy, just as the children who ran to the Mausoleum where he stood on holidays metamorphosed into the heralds of the future, its rosy kisses. And he could appreciate these things as no one else could, stunning those who surrounded him by his unparalleled range—from demonic mercilessness down to tenderness over what were, in point of fact, very small joys. Noticing that those who surrounded him were stunned by his unparalleled range, he more keenly appreciated his own ability to appreciate the small joys of life that lay outside history.

As it happened, one of the rejoicing delegates for his ethnic policy—Uncle Sandro, to be precise—had finished feasting his eyes on the leaders. Still applauding, he shifted his gaze to the table.

The table, or rather tables, traversed the banquet hall and at the end forked into two fruit-laden branches. The platters of food stood out in pleasant contrast to the cool whiteness of white tablecloths.

Gibbous turkeys lay in rich brown nut sauce, roast chickens presented their bare rumps with a certain appetizing indecency. Vases bloomed with fruit, candy, cookies, pastries. Split pomegranates, as if cracked by inner fire, opened a glimpse of their sinful caverns crammed with precious stones.

Beds of salad greens glistened as if they had just been rained on. Young lambs, cooked in milk in the ancient Abkhazian manner, mildly evoked a lost innocence, while the roast suckling pigs, by contrast, clenched the crimson radishes in their bared teeth with a sort of devilish glee.

Alongside every bottle of wine, like vigilant hospital orderlies, stood bottles of Borzhom mineral water. The wine bottles were without labels, obviously from local cellars. By the smell Uncle Sandro determined that the wine was an Isabella from the village of Lykhny.

Most of the food was still untouched. Some had long since gone cold—the roast quails had congealed in their own fat. Stalin did not like to have waiters and other superfluous people flitting around at the table. Everything was served at once, in a heap, although the kitchen was kept ready in case of any sudden desires.

At the table everyone ate what he pleased and as he pleased, but God forbid he should cheat and omit the required glass. That the Leader did not like. The democracy of food at his table was balanced by the despotism of drink.

At the head of the table sat Nestor Lakoba. A large, dark horn with a slight scorch mark lay beside him—the scepter of power at table.

To his right sat Stalin, then Kalinin. To Lakoba's left sat his wife, the dusky Sarya; beside her the beautiful Nina, Beria's wife; and then Nina's husband, with his pince-nez flashing energetically. Beyond Beria sat Voroshilov, who stood out because of his snow-white service jacket, his sword belt, and the revolver at his waist. Beyond Voroshilov and Kalinin, on either side of the table, sat secondary leaders, ones who were not known to Uncle Sandro by their portraits.

The rest of the room was taken up by the secretaries of the district committees of western Georgia, with their eyebrows raised as if frozen in surprise. Scattered among them here and there were comrades from the local secret service. Uncle Sandro recognized them immediately, because unlike the district committee secretaries they were not surprised by anything and did not have their eyebrows raised.

Nestor Lakoba, sitting at the head of the table, now turned abruptly to look at the ensemble. As the host, observing the proprieties, he applauded with much more reserve than the others.

When Stalin lowered his hands and sat down, the applause ceased. But not all at once, because the people sitting farthest off could not see him. It ceased the way the wind drops, rustling in the foliage of a large tree.

"Our beloved Leader and dear guests!" Pantsulaya began. "Our humble Abkhazian ensemble, organized at the personal initiative of Nestor Apollonovich Lakoba . . ."

Uncle Sandro observed that at this moment Stalin looked at Lakoba and smiled roguishly in his mustache, to which Lakoba replied with a bashful shrug.

". . . will perform for you several Abkhazian songs and dances, as well as songs and dances of the friendly family of Caucasian peoples."

Pantsulaya bowed his head low, as if apologizing in advance that he must now turn his back on his lofty guests. Without raising his head—in one smooth movement, striving to avoid any offensive suddenness in the pose he was about to take (since the pose itself was now inevitable), all the while wearing an expression of grief at having to turn his back—he completed his polysemantic turn, raised his head, waved his arms in the winged sleeves of the white cherkeska, and froze in mid-wave.

"*O-rayda, siua-rayda, hey*," Makhaz intoned, as if from deep in a narrow ravine.

And then, at a wave of the winged sleeves, the chorus took up the ancient song. Not everyone will return from the raid, the song says in sparing words.

Not everyone is fated to see again the flame on his family hearth. And when the youth lying dead across his saddle rides into the yard of his father's house, the steed shudders, and the corpse moves, at the mother's scream.

But the father does not cry out and the brother does not weep, because only when he has taken revenge does a man gain the right to tears.

Such is the will of fate and the fate of man.
Woman ripens to give birth to a man.
Man ripens to give birth to courage.
The grape ripens to give birth to wine.
Wine ripens to summon up courage.
And the song ripens into dance to summon up the raid.

Gradually the energy shifts from the melody into the rhythm. The song tightens up, throws off excess clothes, as a warrior throws off his before entering the fray.

Uncle Sandro feels the approaching intoxication, feels the song pouring into his blood, and now he wants to become the dance, a fulfillment of the oath embedded in it.

The members of the ensemble are already clapping their hands, though all are still humming the tune, which is compressed to a minimum. Now all of the energy is in the rhythm of the clapping hands, but the dance must ripen, build to the right point, and therefore they go on warming it at the tiny fire of melody.

"*O-rayda, siua-rayda!*" the chorus repeats.

Tash-tush! Tash-tush!—clap the hands, continuing the process of drawing the dance out of the song.

Some of the spectators cannot resist, and they too start clapping their hands, trying to hasten the onset of the dance. Everyone in the hall, along with Comrade Stalin, is clapping his hands.

Tash-tush! Tash-tush! And at this point Pata Pataraya breaks forward. The mad dash of a steed breaking loose from its tether, and suddenly—he stops dead! He reaches high, up on his toes, arched taut, illustrating his readiness to fly like an arrow, to slice into enemy ranks, but at the last moment he changes his decision, and in a mad spin he quenches the insatiable thirst of the warrior to break through somewhere and slice into something.

Sandro Chegemsky throws himself into the circle! And now all the dancers soar in the black whirlwinds of their cherkeskas, illustrating man's ancient readiness to become a warrior, and the warrior's to slice, to fly, to break through . . . But at the last second it turns out that the order to slice, to fly, to break through has not yet been given.

"Oh, so it's like that?" the dancers seem to say, and ominously stamping their feet, they begin to whirl around. A moment later they stop spinning, only to learn that the order is again late in coming.

"Oh, so it's like that?" And again, stamping their feet, they whirl around.

"Like that? Oh, not yet?" And again.

"Like that? Like that? Like that?"

Circling and whirling they become thin, stratified, and finally semitransparent, like a propellor. It seems that by spinning around they can quench the insatiable thirst for battle.

"*O-rayda, siua-rayda!*" Tash-tush! Tash-tush!

Skillfully, and with perfect timing, the dancers replace one another, flying into the circle, and now it seems that the carousel of the dance is moving of its own accord, by some ancient plan whose essence is the desire to stupefy the invisible enemy (in olden days, when the princes invited one another to feasts, the enemy was visible), stupefy him with the inexhaustibility of their fierce energy.

With brief intervals for songs, the ensemble dances Abkhazian, Georgian, Mingrelian, and Adzharian dances.

And now, the climax—a wedding dance. The long-awaited moment has come. With an abrupt shout, Pata Pataraya takes a flying start, tucks up his legs in mid-leap, thuds to his knees, and with arms outflung slides to a halt near the feet of Comrade Stalin.

This was so unexpected that some of the guests, especially those sitting farthest away, jumped to their feet, not understanding what had happened. Beria was the first one up. The lenses of his pince-nez flashing, he froze in a warlike posture over the table.

But there was no malicious intent, and Comrade Stalin smiled. A storm of applause broke, and Pata Pataraya, as if blown away by the storm, straightened up and flew back into the moving circle of dancers.

Now it was Uncle Sandro's turn. Catching just the right point in the music, he leaped whooping out from behind the backs of the clapping dancers and repeated Pata Pataraya's celebrated number, but stopped much closer, right at Comrade Stalin's feet. Uncle Sandro slid his eyes up from the Leader's well-cleaned and polished boots to his face, and was struck by the similarity between the oily glitter of his boots and the resplendent, oily glitter of his dark eyes.

Again applause.

"They're competing!" Lakoba shouted to Stalin, trying to shout over the roar and his own deafness. Stalin nodded and smiled his approval.

Again Pata Pataraya, crying out as if he had been stung, plopped to his knees, slid, and froze with arms outflung in a posture of audacious devotion, at Comrade Stalin's very toes.

Beria shook his head. "Out of bounds."

"Well, I think it's great!" Kalinin exclaimed, peering over Comrade Stalin's shoulder.

A storm of applause, and Pata Pataraya fell back into the whirlwind of dancers. The fact that he had succeeded in stopping a mere handbreadth from the Leader's feet had virtually assured his victory.

But a man from Chegem is not one to surrender without a fight! Now the fate of the best dancer was to be decided, and Uncle Sandro had something saved up for this occasion. Keeping a sharp eye on the distance from Comrade Stalin's feet to the spot where he was standing, he tried to intuit a moment when Stalin and Lakoba would not change their position. With the gesture of a knight covering his face with his visor, he jammed his turban down over his eyes, whooped a Chegem whoop, and charged straight for Comrade Stalin.

Even the other dancers did not expect anything like this. The chorus suddenly stopped clapping and all the dancers halted, with the exception of one who had been dancing at the opposite end of the room. A few more futile stomps and the dancer's feet fell quiet in terror.

In the silence, his face concealed by the turban, his arms thrown wide, Uncle Sandro flew crackling across the dance floor on his knees and came to a halt at Comrade Stalin's feet.

Stalin frowned in surprise. The pipe he gripped in one hand jerked slightly. But Uncle Sandro's pose, which expressed an audacious devotion—the poignant defenselessness of the outflung arms, the blindness of the proudly thrown-back head, and, paradoxically, a mysterious urgent stubbornness about the whole figure, as if to tell the Leader, "I won't get up until you give me your blessing" —made him smile.

Still smiling, indeed, he laid his pipe on the table, and with the expression of curiosity that one has at a masquerade, he started to untie the turban on Uncle Sandro's head.

When the tie-end of the turban slipped from Uncle Sandro's face and everyone saw it illumined with the blessing of the Leader, a hurricane of unprecedented applause broke out, and the secretaries of the district committees of western Georgia raised their eyebrows even higher in surprise, although it had seemed that their eyebrows were already raised as high as they could go.

Still holding Uncle Sandro's turban in one hand, Stalin displayed it to everyone with a smile, as if to let them see for themselves that the number had been done honestly, without any tricks. With a gesture he invited Uncle Sandro to stand up. Uncle Sandro stood up, and Kalinin took the turban from Stalin's hands and started examining it. All of a sudden Voroshilov leaned across the table and deftly snatched the turban out of Kalinin's hands. To the laughter of those around him, he held the turban to his eyes, showing that he really could not see through it.

Stalin looked at Uncle Sandro with his radiant eyes and asked, "Who are you, abrek?"

"I am Sandro of Chegem," Uncle Sandro replied, lowering his eyes. The leader's gaze was too resplendent. But that was not the only reason. An uneasy shadow had flitted through those eyes, and an alarm echoed in Uncle Sandro's soul.

"Chegem," the Leader repeated pensively. His mind seemed to be elsewhere.

"Come here," Lakoba said in Abkhazian. He thrust Uncle Sandro's turban into his hands. Uncle Sandro walked away.

"What precision," he heard Kalinin say. Stroking his beard, Kalinin looked affectionately in Uncle Sandro's direction.

"You can see the sun even through a turban," Voroshilov observed pompously as he cut off the ear of a suckling pig. While he was working on the ear, the pig released the radish that had been stuffed in its mouth, and it rolled across the table, much to Voroshilov's surprise. He was so startled that he left his fork in the half-severed ear of the pig and started hunting down the radish in among the dishes and bottles.

Only now did Uncle Sandro turn his attention to the fact that those sitting at the table had had a great deal to drink. Now he trained his experienced eye on them and determined that they had already consumed twelve to thirteen glasses apiece.

Uncle Sandro used to say that from the appearance of men at table he could determine to within one glass how much they had drunk. He explained that the more people there were at the table, and the more they had drunk, the more precisely he could determine their consumption. But that was not all. It seemed that the precision of the estimate did not increase indefinitely with the amount of wine drunk. After three liters, Uncle Sandro said, the precision of the estimate decreased again.

. . . Platon Pantsulaya stood before the doubled cypress ranks of his charges. Now they were to sing "*Keraz*," a song about the Red Partisan guerrillas. Everything was going as well as possible, and so Pantsulaya took his time, giving the dancers a chance to catch their breath.

"Good going," said Makhaz, the one from Uncle Sandro's home district. "Now you're set for life."

"Oh, come on, Makhaz." Uncle Sandro tried to be modest.

"And why not?" Makhaz said hotly, without looking at him. "Sliding right up to Stalin himself, and with your turban over your face, too! Even the Germans couldn't think up anything like that!"

Yes, Uncle Sandro understood perfectly well that this brilliant trick not only made him number one in the ensemble, but permanently established his authority at headquarters. Now, of course, the manager wouldn't dare bother him with stupid questions about the firewood.

When they started singing the Partisan song "*Keraz*," Uncle Sandro just pretended to sing, opening and closing his mouth slightly in time with the melody. This was a first small reward for his feat.

While they were singing, Lakoba leaned over to tell Stalin something, and from the fact that he and Stalin glanced in his direction several times, Uncle Sandro sensed, with sweetly fluttering stomach, that they were talking about him.

When Nestor Apollonovich clenched his fist and swung his arm to illustrate something, Uncle Sandro surmised that he was telling Stalin about the Prayer Tree: his gesture meant that one had to strike the tree with something to make it sing "*Kum-khoz . . .*" In any case Stalin leaned back and burst out laughing at this point in the story, and Kalinin nudged him to indicate that he was interfering with the singers. Stalin stopped laughing, leaned over to Kalinin, and, as Uncle Sandro surmised, began retelling the same story. When he reached the point where he had to illustrate how the tree was struck, he made several energetic gestures with the hand that clutched his pipe. At this, Kalinin could not restrain himself, and his little beard bounced as he went off in a fit of laughter, whereupon Stalin shook a finger at him, indicating that his laughter was interfering with the singers.

Taking the horn in one hand and a bottle of wine in the other, Stalin stood up and walked over to the dancers.

Nestor Apollonovich whispered something to his wife, and she seized a chicken platter from the table and hurried after Stalin. Before Stalin could reach the dancers, the sanatorium manager appeared and tried to assist him. Stalin shouldered him aside and himself poured a full horn of wine and served it to Makhaz.

Makhaz put one hand on his heart, accepted the horn with the other, and carefully raised it to his lips. As he applied himself to the horn and drank, Stalin watched him with satisfaction.

"Drink, drink, drink," he said methodically, chopping the air with his small puffy hand.

It was a one-liter horn. Taking the empty bottle from Stalin, the manager put it on the table and ran for a fresh one. He took the platter from Sarya and held it for her to cut up the chicken. Either from embarrassment or because the platter shook in the manager's hands, Sarya was clumsy with the knife and fork. A blush appeared on her dark cheeks, and the manager began to gasp for breath.

Meanwhile Makhaz drained the horn, turned it upside down to show his honesty, and handed it to Uncle Sandro. Stalin, noticing that the food was late in coming, gave up on Sarya. Decisively, using both hands, he took the chicken by the legs and—with enjoyment, Uncle Sandro noted—ripped it in half. Then he ripped each half again. The fat dripped down his fingers, but he paid no attention to it.

It struck Uncle Sandro that the Leader's left hand was not entirely dextrous in its movements. Wonder if he has a withered arm, Uncle Sandro thought. Discreetly examining it, he decided yes, a little bit. I should get him together with Bad Hand, he thought for no apparent reason. Uncle Sandro felt that on the whole this slight impairment somehow diminished the leader's image. Just a bit, but still . . .

Taking a chicken leg with his wet hand, Stalin gave it to Makhaz. The latter bowed again, accepted the leg, and took a decorous bite.

The manager was about to try and fill the horn, but Stalin again took the bottle away from him. Grasping it in fingers slippery with chicken fat, he filled the horn and gave the empty bottle to the manager. The latter ran for another.

"Drink, drink, drink," Uncle Sandro heard, as soon as he raised the horn.

Uncle Sandro drank, smoothly tilting the horn with the nonchalant artistry of the true tamada—not drinking, but pouring the precious liquid from one vessel into another.

"You drink the way you dance," Stalin said. Proffering him a chicken leg, he looked into his eyes with his resplendent feminine gaze. "Have I seen you somewhere before, abrek?"

Stalin's hand, proffering the chicken leg, suddenly stopped motionless, and an expression of menacing alertness appeared in his eyes. Uncle Sandro had a sensation of mortal danger, although he could not imagine why. He knew that Stalin was wrong, that he, Sandro, would remember it if he had ever seen Stalin anywhere.

The ensemble, which was silent anyway, turned to stone. Uncle Sandro heard Makhaz's jaws stop chewing the chicken. He had to answer. He could not deny that Stalin had seen him, and at the same time it was still more terrifying to agree that he had, not only because Uncle Sandro did not remember it, but mainly because Stalin was inviting him to be part of some disagreeable memory. He sensed this immediately.

A mighty engine of self-preservation, developed through many dangers, turned over all the possible answers in a second or two and cast up to the surface the least dangerous one.

"They made a movie about us," Uncle Sandro said, to his own surprise. "You might have seen me in it, Comrade Stalin."

"Ah-h, a movie," the Leader said slowly, and the light in his eyes went out. He handed him the chicken leg. "Here, you deserve it."

Again came the gurgle of wine being poured into the horn.

"Drink, drink, drink," echoed beside him.

Uncle Sandro took a bite of the chicken leg and made a slight movement with his neck, feeling that it had gone numb, and recognizing by the numbness what a weight had fallen from him. Well, well, Uncle Sandro thought, how did I remember that we had been in a movie? Hi-ho, Sandro, thought Uncle Sandro, intoxicated with joy and pride. No sir, it's not so easy to nip a Chegemian! Can we really have met somewhere? He must have confused me with someone else. I wouldn't want to be in the shoes of the man he confused me with, Uncle Sandro thought, glad that he was Sandro of Chegem and not the man the Leader had confused him with.

Stalin was already giving the horn to the last dancer in the front row when Nestor Apollonovich came over to him.

"Maybe we should invite them to the table?" he asked.

"Whatever you say, my dear Nestor; I'm only a guest," Stalin replied. Accepting a napkin from Sarya, he began wiping his hands, slowly and significantly, like a mechanic who has finished a job. Throwing the napkin on the ravaged platter, he walked to the table beside Lakoba, at a springy gait that carried his strength easily.

The members of the ensemble were seated around the banquet table, the best performers among the leaders, the more ordinary ones among the secretaries of the district committees of western Georgia. A rather considerable amount of noise now rose over the banquet table. Heterogeneous islets of conversation began to take on independent life.

Suddenly Comrade Stalin stood up with his wineglass raised. A thundering silence fell, and in an instant the air was cleansed of the rubbish of noise.

"I raise this glass," he began in a quietly impressive voice, "to this medal-bearing republic and its permanent leader . . ."

He stood motionless for a long moment, as if for the last time attempting to weigh this leader's lofty qualities, for which he himself had rewarded him by making his position permanent. Although everyone understood that he could now name no one but Lakoba, still, the lengthy pause engendered a fever of anxious curiosity: What if—?

". . . my best friend, Nestor Lakoba," Stalin concluded, and his hand made an affirmative gesture, somewhat abbreviated by the weight of the wineglass.

" 'Best,' he said the 'best,' " buzzed the district committee secretaries, pondering how this remark would hit Party leadership in Tbilisi, and whether from there it might ricochet to hit each and every one of them. The eyebrows of every one of them were still fixedly raised in surprise.

". . . In this republic you know how to work and how to make merry . . ."

"Long live Comrade Stalin!" one of the district committee secretaries shouted suddenly, jumping to his feet. Stalin swiftly turned toward him with an expression of menacing contempt, whereupon the secretary, a tall and mountainous man, slowly started to sag. As though satisfied of the certainty that the man would complete his slump, Stalin looked away from him.

"Some comrades . . ." he continued slowly, and in his voice one could hear distant rumbles of irritation. Everyone realized that he was angry at the district committee secretary for his inappropriate glorification of Stalin.

Beria fidgeted in his seat. Removing his pince-nez for a moment, he threw the man one of his notorious murky green glances. The district committee secretary recoiled as from a blow.

The district committee secretaries sitting beside him imperceptibly moved away, forming between themselves and him a gap that had an ideological nuance. All the district committee secretaries looked at him with their eyebrows raised in surprise, as if trying to see who he was and where the devil he'd come from.

Bracing his hands on the table, staring at Beria, he continued to sag slowly, trying to ease his way into the company at the table unnoticed, and at the same time holding himself back in case he should be ordered to leave.

". . . some scholars, there in Moscow . . ." Stalin continued, after an even longer pause, and the note of menace and irritation sounded still more distinctly in his voice. It was immediately clear to everyone that he was deciding something very important in his mind and had long since forgotten the clumsy district committee secretary.

Beria removed his gaze from the man, and he seemed to collapse beneath his own broken backbone, tumble joyously down—it had passed!

"Bukharin." Uncle Sandro heard the whisper from one of the secondary leaders not known to him by their portraits.

"Bukharin, Bukharin, Bukharin." The whispers buzzed through the ranks of the district committee secretaries.

It was known in Party circles that Stalin did in fact call Bukharin that. In the days of their friendship, "our scholar." Now, "that scholar."

". . . think that governing by Lenin's way," Stalin continued, "means holding endless discussions, timorously avoiding decisive measures . . ."

Stalin again lapsed into a reverie. He seemed to be listening to the buzz with the estranged interest of an outsider, and enjoying it. He loved this kind of vague innuendo. His listeners' imaginations inevitably widened the meaning of it, owing to the ill-defined margins of the contaminated area. They would all retreat farther than necessary, and later he could make political hay by accusing those who had retreated too far of vacillation.

". . . but governing by Lenin's way means, first, not fearing decisive measures, and second, finding specialized personnel and adeptly placing them where they belong. A little example."

Suddenly Stalin looked at Uncle Sandro, and the latter felt his heart plunge straight down while he returned the Leader's gaze unblinkingly.

". . . Nestor found this abrek in a remote mountain village, and made his talent universally accessible," Stalin continued. "Before, he danced for a narrow circle of friends, but now he dances for the enjoyment of the whole republic and for your enjoyment and mine, comrades.

". . . So let us drink to my dear friend, the host of this table, Nestor Lakoba," Comrade Stalin concluded. Still standing, he drained his glass and added, "*Allaverdy*, Lavrenty."

He knew perfectly well that Beria and Lakoba did not like each other, and he was amusing himself by making Beria be the first to drink to Lakoba.

With the tip of his knife, Stalin took a dollop of *ajika* from the relish dish and transferred it to his plate. Slathering a chunk of lamb with the purple condiment, he put it in his mouth and crunched the milky gristle.

"Not too hot?" Kalinin asked warily, watching Stalin smear the meat with *ajika*.

"No," Stalin said, shaking his head, "I think this Abkhazian *ajika* has a great future."

Many of those who heard Stalin's remark reached for the *ajika*. Subsequently this prediction of the Leader's, unlike many of his others, did in fact come true: *ajika* spread far beyond the borders of Abkhazia.

Meanwhile, in no way betraying his feelings, Beria offered a toast and drank to Lakoba. Lakoba, who had listened to the Leader's toast on his hearing aid, now took it off and listened to Beria with his hand cupped to his ear. In no way did he betray his feelings, either; from time to time he nodded to show his gratitude and that he had heard the words.

After Beria, Kalinin took the floor and drank to Lakoba, saying a few words about scholars who had long been out of touch with the common people. Stalin liked his toast and reached over to kiss him. Kalinin unexpectedly ducked the kiss.

Stalin frowned. Uncle Sandro was again amazed at how quickly his mood changed. His eyes had just been shining resplendently at Kalinin, and suddenly they were opaque, withdrawn. Beria's pince-nez flashed animatedly, and the district committee secretaries stared at Kalinin, eyebrows raised in surprise.

That means he's with them, not with me, Stalin thought in fright, how could I have missed it? He was frightened not by Kalinin's betrayal itself—it would take nothing to crush him—but by the fact that his own sensitivity to danger, a sensitivity he trusted, had betrayed him. This was terrifying.

"Who wants to kiss a pockmarked fellow like you?" Kalinin said, looking at Stalin with an impertinent grin. "Now if you were a sixteen-year-old girl [he carefully cupped his right hand and gave it a slight shake, as if hearkening to the sweet bell of youth], that would be another matter."

Stalin's face lit up, and a sigh of relief whispered through the hall. No, my sensitivity didn't betray me, Stalin thought.

"Oh, you—my All-Union goat," he said, hugging and kissing Kalinin, in reality hugging and kissing his own sensitivity.

"Ha, ha, ha, ha!" laughed the district committee secretaries, rejoicing in the leaders' mutual joke. Lakoba joined in a little belatedly, after Uncle Sandro, who was now sitting beside him, explained the joke, which he had not quite heard. Lakoba's belated laughter sounded rather strange, and Beria, unable to restrain himself, guffawed ambiguously, although his guffaw might have been taken for an echo of Lakoba's laugh.

But Stalin perceived the mockery in Beria's laughter. Just now he found it disagreeable. He looked over at Beria and said, "Lavrenty, ask your wife to dance for us."

"Of course, Comrade Stalin," Beria said, looking at his wife.

"But I can't, Comrade Stalin," she said, flushing.

Stalin knew she could not dance.

"The Leader wants you," Beria whispered threateningly.

"Why 'the Leader'—we all do," Stalin said. Encompassing the members of the ensemble in his gaze, he added, "Come on, fellows."

Clapping and humming as they went, the members of the ensemble formed a semicircle, the open side toward the head of the table.

"I'm not being coy, I really don't know how," Beria's wife said, trying to make herself heard over the clapping. But now everyone was calling for her. Urged on by her husband, balking timidly, she walked into the circle. At a moment when Beria turned his back to the table, Uncle Sandro noticed that his distorted lips were whispering obscenities to his wife. Spreading her arms, she took a couple of awkward turns and stopped, not knowing what to do next. It was clear that she really did not know how to dance.

"Good girl," Stalin said, smiling and applauding her. Everyone applauded Beria's wife.

"Sarya, we want Sarya," called some voices. Sarya was sitting between Uncle Sandro and Lakoba. Her dark eyes flashed and she looked at her husband.

"Go on," Lakoba said in Abkhazian. She glanced at Stalin. He smiled back affectionately. Everything was going the way he wanted.

Sarya entered the circle. Her head somewhat tilted back by her heavy knot of hair, the dusky beauty took a few smooth turns and suddenly stopped beside Pata Pataraya, inviting him to dance. Smiling modestly, Pata glided alongside her.

Beria sat at the table without looking at the dancers, his head resting heavily in his hand. His wife, distraught, stood beside the ensemble, apparently unable to decide whether to resume her place.

"Lavrenty," Stalin said softly. Beria straightened up and looked at the Leader. "It looks like specialized personnel aren't the only thing the Deaf One knows best."

Beria shrugged his shoulders as if to say, There's nothing to be done about it—it's fate. This made Uncle Sandro uncomfortable, he sensed danger lurking here for Lakoba. Oh no, the Leader shouldn't provoke him that way, Uncle Sandro thought.

At this point Sarya ran out of the circle, embraced Beria's wife, and kissed her on the eyes. Everyone felt a secret nobility in this impulse of hers, a desire to soften Nina's failure, to turn it all into a joke. Everyone clapped joyfully, and the women, their arms around each other, returned to the table.

"Tell me later what they said," Lakoba whispered to Uncle Sandro during the final burst of applause, while everyone was watching Sarya embrace Beria's wife. Lakoba had noticed Stalin saying something to Beria, and the latter shrugging his shoulders. He must have sensed that they were talking about him.

Almost as Lakoba spoke, three pistol shots rang out. Uncle Sandro leaped to his feet. Voroshilov returned a smoking pistol to his holster. Stirred by Sarya's dance, and especially by her noble impulse, he could not restrain himself from making this little salute. Everyone buzzed gleefully and started looking at the ceiling, where beside the chandelier there were three little black holes joined by a jagged crack.

The plaster that rained down after the shots had covered a cooling turkey with a white deposit. Stalin looked at the powdered turkey, looked up at the black holes in the ceiling, and then shifted his gaze to Voroshilov and said, "You missed."

Voroshilov flushed darkly and hung his head.

"We have among us," Stalin said, "a genuine first-class sniper. Let's get him up here."

He looked at Lakoba, laid his pipe on the table, and began to applaud. Everyone amiably took up the applause, joining the Leader, although almost nobody actually knew what was going on.

Lakoba understood what was being asked of him. He ducked his head and shrugged in embarrassment.

"Maybe it's not worth the bother?" he said, glancing at Stalin. The latter held a match to his pipe.

"No, it is, it is!" voices cried all around. Stalin stopped in the middle of lighting up and nodded at the cries as if to say, The voice of the people—what can you do.

Embarrassed at the pleasure that lay ahead, Nestor Apollonovich gestured helplessly. He started looking around for the sanatorium manager, but the manager was already trotting toward him.

"Call him," Lakoba said as the manager bent down to him.

"Should he change his clothes?" the manager asked, still bending down.

"Why?" Lakoba frowned. "Let's keep it simple."

Nestor Apollonovich poured himself a glass of wine and gestured to indicate that everyone should follow suit. Everyone filled his glass.

"I want to raise this glass," he began in his splintery voice, "not to the Leader, but to the Leader's modesty."

Apropos, Nestor Apollonovich told the following anecdote. It seemed that last year he had received a note from Comrade Stalin in which the latter had asked him to send him some mandarin oranges, giving strict orders for the parcel to be accompanied by a bill, which the Leader would pay out of his very next paycheck.

Stalin pensively puffed on his pipe as he listened to Nestor's story. This is all true, he was thinking, the Deaf One is not flattering me. And I did send the money out of my next paycheck. A good lesson to all these secretaries, who don't know how to do anything but crane their eyebrows all evening long.

It pleased him that everything Nestor was saying was true, but, looking deeper within himself, he found another source of a more secret but also a more subtle joy. The source of this joy, he remembered, was that even as he was writing that note, he knew that sooner or later it would crop up and play its little historical role, just this way. So, who knew how to look into the future—he or those "scholars"?

". . . One might wonder, would it really impoverish our republic to send this miserable bunch of mandarins to Comrade Stalin?" Nestor Lakoba continued.

"It wasn't you and I who put the mandarins in, my dear Nestor." Stalin jabbed his pipe in his direction. "The people put them in."

"The people put them in," buzzed through the ranks.

The people put them in, Stalin repeated to himself, still dimly groping after the explosive play on words imprisoned in this innocent expression. Later on, when his magnificent formula "Enemy of the People" was worked out and issued, there were those who tried to attribute its origin to the French Revolution. Maybe the French did have something of the sort, but *he* knew that he had nursed it to life himself, right here in Russia.

(Like a poet, for whom a sudden combination of words is a flare illuminating the contours of a future poem, he found in these chance words the embryo of a future formula.

It is terrifying to think that the mechanism for crystallizing an idea is the same for a hangman and a poet, just as the stomachs of a cannibal and a normal man accept food with the same good conscience. But if we think about it, what seems to be the indifference of human nature may be a result of the highest wisdom of man's moral nature.

Man is given the choice of becoming a hangman, just as he is given the choice of not becoming one. In the final analysis, the choice is ours.

And if the cannibal's stomach simply would not accept human flesh, this would be an oversimplified and dangerous way of humanizing the cannibal. No one knows where his proclivity might lead him next.

There is no humanity without triumph over baseness and there is no baseness without triumph over humanity. Every time, the choice is ours, and the responsibility for that choice as well. If we say that we have no choice, it means the choice has already been made. We talk about having no choice only because we are burdened by guilt for the choice we have made. If there were in fact no choice, we would feel no burden of guilt.)

. . . To the thunder of applause, Lakoba drained his glass. Before this thundering glorification of the Leader's modesty had stopped, the cook came through the door in his white apron, and behind him the sanatorium manager carrying a plate.

On hearing the applause, the cook tried to back out, but the manager gave him a little shove and drew him away from the door.

He was a plumpish, middle-aged man of average height, with the pasty complexion that cooks often have and a head of thick curly hair.

Gesturing for him to wait there, the manager, trying to hold the plate motionless, went over to Lakoba.

"Nestor Apollonovich, the cook is here," he said, bending down to show him what was on the plate. On the plate, rolling around a little, lay a half-dozen eggs.

"Good," Lakoba said. He looked frowningly at the plate.

Only at this point did Uncle Sandro guess that Nestor Apollonovich was going to shoot at the eggs. He had never seen this.

"Turkey eggs?" Beria asked suddenly. He reached over and took an egg from the plate.

"Chicken, Lavrenty Pavlovich," the manager supplied, holding the plate closer to him.

"Then why so big?" Beria asked, examining an egg curiously. The eggs really were quite large.

"I chose them myself," the manager giggled, nodding in the direction of the cook, trying to direct Beria's attention to the latent humor of the situation. But, paying no attention to the latent humor of the situation, Beria continued to examine the egg. The manager grew anxious.

"Maybe I should change them, Lavrenty Pavlovich?" he asked.

Beria collected himself and hastily put the egg back on the plate. "No, it was just a comment."

"He's jealous of the Deaf One," Stalin whispered to Kalinin, and laughed soundlessly into his mustache. Kalinin's little beard bounced in reply.

"I think that corner would be better," Lakoba said, examining the chandelier and nodding toward the corner opposite to where the cook stood. In the same way, a photographer tries to choose the best lighting effect before he starts shooting.

"Quite right," the manager agreed.

"Is he nervous?" Lakoba asked, indicating the cook.

"A little," the manager said, bending low over Lakoba's ear.

"Calm him down," Nestor Apollonovich said, pulling away from the manager, whose posture somewhat too insistently called attention to his deafness.

The cook was still standing in the doorway with the apathetic expression of a test subject. Only now did Uncle Sandro notice that he was gripping his tall white cap in one hand. The fingers of that hand were in constant motion.

The manager went over and whispered something to the cook, and they started for the opposite corner. The manager solemnly carried the plate of eggs in front of him.

It grew quiet. By now everyone clearly saw the meaning of all this. His starched apron creaking, the cook stopped in the corner and turned to face the hall.

"If you only knew how I hate this," Sarya whispered, turning to Nina. Nina did not respond: she was staring wide-eyed at the corner. From then on Sarya did not once look in the direction that everyone else was looking.

The cook stood tightly pressed against the wall. The manager was talking to him nonstop, and he was nodding. His face had turned the color of flour. The manager selected an egg from the plate and the cook watched his gesture—no longer moving his head, just his white eyes, which seemed to be floating detached from his face. The manager started trying to set the egg on his head, but either he was nervous himself or the egg was not a steady one, because it simply did not want to stay put.

Nestor Apollonovich frowned. Suddenly, still standing motionless, the cook raised his hand, felt for the egg, squinted his white, floating, detached eyes, found the balance point, and smoothly lowered his arm.

The egg perched on his head. Now he stood erect and immobile in the corner, and had it not been for the expression in his eyes, he would have looked like a draftee having his height measured.

The manager quickly glanced around, without finding anywhere to put the plate of eggs. Suddenly, as if afraid that the shooting would start before he could get away, he shoved the plate into the cook's hands and rapidly moved away toward the door.

Lakoba pulled his revolver from its holster and cocked it, taking care to point the barrel down. He looked back at Stalin and Kalinin, trying to stand in such a way that they could see everything. Uncle Sandro had to leave his place. He stood behind Sarya's chair, gripping the back with his hands. Uncle Sandro was very agitated.

Lakoba extended his arm with the pistol raised and started slowly lowering his hand. The arm remained steady, and suddenly Uncle Sandro saw Lakoba's pale face turn to a slab of stone.

All of a sudden the cook went white, and in the dead silence one could clearly hear the eggs rattling on the plate he held in one hand. Suddenly Uncle Sandro saw something yellow splatter on the cook's face, and only afterward did he hear the shot.

"Bravo, Nestor!" Stalin cried. He began to clap. Applause thundered like an electric discharge of relief. The manager ran to the cook, grabbed the cap from his hand, wiped off his yolk-covered cheek, and stuck the cap in his apron pocket.

He looked back at Lakoba, the way a firing-range attendant looks back to tell the marksman where his shot hit or to inquire whether the target is to be readied for the next shot.

"Go ahead," Lakoba nodded. This time the manager quickly stood the egg on the cook's head and went back to the doorway, crunching the shell of the broken egg underfoot. Again Lakoba's face turned to a slab of stone, the outstretched arm went rigid, and only the wrist moved, slowly and mechanically lowering the gun barrel like a blunt clock hand.

And again this time Uncle Sandro saw the yellow fountain of egg splash up first, and only afterward heard the shot.

"Bravo!" Explosions of applause shook the banquet hall. Smiling a pale happy smile, Lakoba put away the pistol. The cook still stood in the corner, slowly coming back to life.

"Seat him at the table," Lakoba snapped to his wife in Abkhazian.

Sarya picked up a napkin and ran over to the cook. The manager followed her, and the cook angrily pushed the plate of eggs at him. Sarya stood in front of him, wiping off his face with the napkin, and said something to him. The cook nodded with dignity. The manager squatted down, set the plate of eggs on the floor, and picked up the shells of the broken ones.

Sarya started to lead the cook away, but he suddenly stopped to take off his apron and fling it to the manager. Evidently, what had happened gave him such rights for a little while, and he was showing the audience that he was not one to risk his life just for nothing, but had quite a bit to gain by it.

While the manager was hastily walking to the door with the apron slung over his shoulder and the plate in his hand, Uncle Sandro thought with amazement that the cook and the manager might well have traded places, because much in this life is decided by chance.

Sarya seated the cook between the last of the secondary leaders whom Uncle Sandro did not know from portraits and the first of the district committee secretaries.

Sarya poured the cook a glass of cognac, pulled over a plate for him, and put a splash of walnut sauce and a piece of turkey on it. The cook immediately drank off the cognac. Now, looking around the table, he was nodding importantly to whatever it was Sarya was saying to him.

Poor Sarya, Uncle Sandro thought. She was trying to atone for the sin of this shooting, which she so disliked and which, incidentally, had once ended in trouble.

It happened in an Abkhazian village. After a long session at table, the guests had turned to target practice. For some reason—perhaps precisely because they were shooting at targets and Lakoba was not being very careful—he wounded a villager who had been running back and forth looking at the targets. The wound was not serious, and the man was immediately shipped off to the district hospital in Lakoba's Buick.

Lakoba rode back with the other members of the government in a second car. And on the way one of the members of the government had a real quarrel with Lakoba and even made him get out of the car in the middle of the road.

"I'm sick of your guerrilla games," he is said to have told him. It is difficult now to determine why Lakoba agreed to get out of the car. He himself may have been so crushed by what had happened that he found it impossible to resist this insulting measure. I think the man who cussed him out was most likely older than he was. If the man said something like, "Either you're getting out or I am," then Lakoba, as a true Abkhazian, could not allow it and probably decided to get out of the car himself.

. . . When Nestor Apollonovich put away his pistol and turned toward the table, Stalin was on his feet with open arms. Smiling shyly, Nestor Apollonovich went over to him. Stalin embraced him and kissed his forehead.

"My William Tell," he said. Suddenly remembering, he turned to Voroshilov: "And who are you?"

"I am Voroshilov," Voroshilov said, quite firmly.

"I ask you, which of you is a Voroshilov Medalist in marksmanship?" Stalin asked, and Uncle Sandro again felt uncomfortable. Oh no, he thought, he shouldn't provoke Voroshilov against our Lakoba.

"He's the better shot, of course," Voroshilov said in a conciliatory manner.

"Then why do you go showing off like a Voroshilov Marksman?" Stalin asked. He sat down, anticipating the pleasure of a long string of casuistical taunts.

The district committee secretaries, with difficulty raising their now-heavy eyebrows, began listening in surprise. Lakoba stole away and sat down at his place.

"Now, that's enough, Iosif," Voroshilov said, breaking out in crimson blotches and looking pleadingly at Stalin.

"That's enough, Iosif," Stalin said, gazing reproachfully at Voroshilov. "Opportunists all over the world say that. Are you going to start in too?"

Voroshilov, hanging his head, flushed red and began to sulk.

"Tell them to start his favorite song," Nestor whispered to his wife. Sarya quietly got up and went to the middle of the table, where Makhaz was sitting. Lakoba knew that this was one way to abort the Leader's sudden gloomy caprices.

Makhaz struck up the ancient Georgian drinking song, *"Gaprindi shavo mertskhalo"*—"Fly, Black Swallow." Voroshilov looked up and tried to say something to Stalin. But the latter suddenly raised his hand in an imploring gesture, as if to say, Leave me alone, let me listen to the song.

Stalin sat with his head resting heavily on one hand. In the other hand he clutched his extinguished pipe.

Nothing else—neither power, nor the blood of an enemy, nor wine—gave him such enjoyment. With an all-dissolving tenderness, with an all-submissive courage that he had never in his life experienced, this song, as always, liberated his soul from the burden of being eternally on his guard. It did not liberate him in the same way that the excitement of passion or struggle did, because as soon as the excitement of passion ended in the death of his enemy, a hangover set in: victory started a putrid toxin flowing from the corpse of the vanquished.

No, the song liberated his soul in a different way. It colored his whole life with the fantastical light of fate, in which his personal concerns became the concern of Fate, where there were neither hangmen nor victims, there was only the movement of Fate, History, and the funereal necessity for him to take his place in this procession. And what did it matter that he was destined to occupy in this procession the most terrible and therefore the most magnificent place?

Fly, black swallow, fly . . .

But Fate's funereal procession gradually moves on, becomes the distant backdrop for a fairy-tale scene . . .

He sees a warm fall day, the day of the grape harvest. He is driving out of the vineyard on a cart laden with baskets of grapes. He is taking the grapes home, to the winepress. The cart creaks, the sun is bright. From back in the vineyard he can hear the voices of his family, the shouts and laughter of children.

On the village street a horseman has stopped by a wattle fence. He has never seen the man before but for some reason recognizes him as a visitor from Kakhetia. The horseman is drinking water from a mug that a local peasant has offered him over the fence. The well is right by the fence, that is why the horseman has stopped here.

As he passes the horseman and his fellow villager, he nods cordially to them, smiles fleetingly at the horseman, who peers at him. Although he looks like a modest winegrower, the horseman correctly guesses his essential greatness. His fleeting smile is a response to the horseman's guess, to show the horseman that he himself does not attach much significance to his own essential greatness.

He rides on by and senses that the horseman from Kakhetia is still looking after him. He even hears the conversation between his neighbor and the visitor from Kakhetia.

"Listen, who's that man?" the horseman says, splashing the last of the water out of the mug and handing it back to its owner.

"That's Dzhugashvili himself," the owner says happily.

"Not *the* Dzhugashvili?" the visitor from Kakhetia says in amazement. "I thought it looked like him, but it can't be."

"One and the same," the owner confirms. "The very Dzhugashvili who did not want to become the sovereign of Russia under the name of Stalin."

"I wonder why not?" the visitor from Kakhetia says in amazement.

"Too much trouble, he says," the owner explains, "and he says he'd have to spill a lot of blood."

"Tch, tch," clucks the visitor from Kakhetia. "I can't pass up a single grapevine root, but he passed up Russia."

"Why does he need Russia?" the owner comments. "He has a fine farm, a fine family, fine children."

The visitor from Kakhetia continues to cluck. "What a man!" he says, looking after the cart, which is now turning off toward a house. "He passed up a whole country . . ."

"Yes, passed it up," the owner confirms, "because he's sorry for the peasants, he says. He'd have had to unite them all. Let them all live for themselves, he says, let each one have his bit of bread and his glass of wine."

"God grant him health!" the horseman exclaims. "But how does he know what would happen to the peasants?"

"He's that kind of man, foresees everything," the owner says.

"God grant him health!" the visitor from Kakhetia clucks. "God grant . . ."

Iosif Dzhugashvili, who did not want to become Stalin, just sits on his cart, hums a little song about a black swallow. The sun warms his face, the cart creaks, he listens with a quiet smile to his neighbor's naive but essentially true story.

And now he drives through the open gate of his yard, where a peasant has been waiting for him in the shade of the apple tree. The peasant, who has evidently come to him for advice, stands up and bows to him respectfully. Well, he'll have to take the time to chat with him, give him some sensible advice. A lot of them come to him. Maybe it would have been better after all, to take power into his own hands, so as to help all of them at once with his advice?

Chickens drunk on grape pressings wander around the yard hearkening to their odd condition; the peasant bows respectfully as he waits for him; his mother, on hearing the creak of the cart, glances out of the kitchen and smiles at her son. His kind old mother with her wrinkled face. Only in old age have respect and plenty come to her at last . . . His kind old . . . Damn her to hell!

Here, as always, the vision broke off. He could never carry it further, always got stuck at this point, because the blood of an old insult rushed to his head.

There was no forgiving her, none. How stricken he had been that time, how stricken, when, playing with the other boys on the village green, he had suddenly heard (tear up the green!) two grown men start to talk about her, chortling obscenely.

They sat within ten paces of him in the shade of a cherry-plum tree (ax the cherry-plum, may it wither!) and talked about her. And then one of them suddenly stopped and nodded in his direction, told the other to lower his voice, because he thought it was her boy playing over there.

They lowered their voices and went on talking. Crushed with humiliation, he had to carry on with his game so that his comrades would notice nothing and guess nothing. How he had hated them, how he dreamed of taking revenge on them, especially, for some reason, the second one, who had told the first to lower his voice. There was no forgiving her for her extreme shameful poverty, or for anything else . . .

Fly, black swallow, fly . . .

He raised his head, and as he looked around now at the singing district committee secretaries, he gradually regained his calm. With every wave of melody, the song was washing from their faces those pathetic raised-eyebrow masks of surprise, and under the masks, ever more distinctly, more independently, were revealed (never mind, it's all right so long as they're singing) the faces of winegrowers, hunters, shepherds.

Fly, black swallow, fly . . .

They think power is honey, Stalin reflected. No; power is the impossibility of loving anyone, that's what power is. A man can live his whole life without loving anyone, but he becomes an unhappy prisoner if he knows that he *must* not love.

Here I've grown fond of the Deaf One, and I know Beria's going to gobble him up, but there's no way I can help him, because I like him. Power is when you must not love anyone. Because the minute you love a man you begin to trust him, but once you begin to trust, sooner or later you get a knife in the back. Yes; yes, he knew this. And they loved him, and they got the knife for it, sooner or later. Damn life, damn human nature! If only you could love and not trust at the same time. But that is impossible.

But if you have to kill the ones you love, fairness demands that you make short work of the ones you don't love, the enemies of the cause.

Yes, the Cause, he thought. Of course, the Cause. Everything is done for the sake of the Cause, he thought, listening with attentive surprise to the hollow, empty sound of the idea. That's because of the song, he thought. I ought to prohibit that song altogether, it's dangerous, because I love it too much. Nonsense, he thought, it would be dangerous if others could feel it as deeply as I. But no one can feel it so deeply . . .

Continuing to listen to the song, he poured himself a glass of wine and silently drank it off without looking at anyone. After setting down the glass, he took his long-since extinguished pipe from the table and made several unsuccessful attempts to pull on it. Noticing that the pipe had gone out, he now pulled on it purposely, as if he were still deep in his reverie. The matches lay beside him on the table but he waited: Would someone think to give him a light, or not?

So there—you could be dying and they wouldn't give you a drink of water, he thought, pitying himself, but at this point Kalinin lit a match and held it to the pipe. Deep in his reverie, he waited until the match flame burned down to Kalinin's fingers, and only then bent for a light. As he lit up, he watched the bright flame touch Kalinin's trembling fingers. Never mind, he thought, I don't have to suffer alone.

He inhaled with pleasure and leaned back in his chair. His glance fell on Voroshilov. He was still sitting at the table hanging his head and knitting his brows, with the hurt expression of a child. Stalin was suddenly stabbed with pity for him. He too has a burden on his conscience, Stalin thought.

"Klim," he said, his voice thick with emotion, "where's Tsaritsyn, where are we, Klim?"

Voroshilov raised his head and gazed at Stalin with bitter, devoted eyes. "Why did you hurt me, Iosif?"

"Forgive me, Klim, if I hurt you," Stalin said, repenting and admiring his own repentance, "but they're hurting you and me even worse."

"Never mind, Iosif!" Voroshilov exclaimed, electrified by the fact that the Leader not only understood his hurt feelings but placed them on a level with his own. "You'll show them a thing or two."

"I think I will," Stalin said modestly. He puffed on his pipe. The song ended, and the swarm of dim, unsteady thoughts cleared from his sobered mind.

How could I be angry at him, Voroshilov thought, cheering up and looking discreetly around at the leaders to be sure they had heard Stalin elevate him just now. And how precisely he understood, Voroshilov thought triumphantly, that my enemies among the top brass of the army are a continuation of the anti-Stalinist line within the top echelons of the government.

"Comrade Stalin, what should we do with this Tsulukidze?" asked Beria, who had been listening attentively to Stalin's remarks. He had been wanting to ask about this for a long time and had decided that this was an opportune moment.

The problem was that this old Bolshevik, who was still respected as one of Lenin's cohorts although he had long since been relieved of any practical responsibility, continued to heckle and grumble at every opportunity. In his time he had dropped a remark, since picked up by the Georgian Communists, that Beria was trying to break into the Party leadership in Transcaucasia with a Mauser in his hand. ("You swine, how was I supposed to break into the leadership—

with the Erfurt Program? Wouldn't you have ended up in the shitpile along with it?")

Any other man he would long since have strung up by the tongue for such a remark (now that he had broken into the leadership), but this one he was afraid to touch. The issue was not clear-cut. Stalin himself had annihilated many old Bolsheviks, but certain ones, for some reason, he supported and honored with decorations.

"What has he done?" Stalin asked. He looked point-blank at Beria.

"He blabs too much, he's gotten senile," Beria said, trying to guess what Stalin thought of this before he could express an opinion.

"Lavrenty," Stalin said, his face clouding because he could not hit on the right answer, "I came here to take my rightful vacation. Why must you hand me a question like that?"

"No, Comrade Stalin, I merely wanted some advice," Beria replied hastily, fleeing ahead of Stalin's gathering gloom. His tone indicated that he was apologizing and did not himself attach any great importance to the question. Good thing I didn't liquidate him, he thought with a flash of joy and fright.

". . . Lenin hated blabbermouths, too," Stalin said pensively.

"Maybe we should throw him out of the Party?" Beria asked, reviving. Maybe Stalin was not averse to punishing the son of a bitch somehow after all.

"Can't oust him from the Party," Stalin said, and he added impressively, "We didn't admit him, Lenin did."

"What should we do?" Beria asked, utterly bewildered.

"He had a brother, I believe," Stalin said. "I wonder where he is now?"

"He's alive, Comrade Stalin," Beria said, breaking out in a cold sweat. "He manages a soft-drink factory in Batum."

Stalin lapsed into reverie. Beria was in a cold sweat because he had not known of the existence of Tsulukidze's brother until just this past year, when he was gathering evidence against the formerly prominent Bolshevik and happened to learn about the brother. The dossier on the brother, requisitioned from Batum, contained nothing useful; he hadn't even been caught embezzling at his soft-drink factory. But the fact that Beria knew of the man's existence, knew what he was doing and how he was getting along, now worked to his advantage. Stalin liked it.

"How is his work?" Stalin asked severely.

"Good," Beria said firmly, showing that his enmity for the blabbermouth in no way extended to his relatives, and that his knowledge of the soft-drink factory manager's business qualifications was the simple consequence of his being a Party-minded leader who knew his specialized personnel.

"Let this blabbermouth"—Stalin jabbed his pipe at the unseen blabbermouth—"regret all his life that he destroyed his brother."

"Brilliant!" Beria exclaimed.

"You people in the Caucasus are too strong on family ties," Stalin said, to explain his train of thought. "Let this be a lesson to other blabbermouths on the dialectics of punishment."

Realizing that by this remark Stalin had set himself apart from the Caucasus, several district committee secretaries began looking at him with melancholy reproach, as if to ask, Why have you abandoned us?

"Live and learn," Beria said, spreading his hands.

"But not at the expense of my vacation, Lavrenty," Stalin admonished severely, a joke that gladdened Lakoba. He considered it tactless of Beria, here at a festive table in Abkhazia, to get Stalin to sanction reprisals against his own enemies. This Beria's always trying to worm his way up, and I have only myself to blame for introducing him to Stalin, thought Lakoba. This was the right time to raise a toast to elder brother, to the great Russian People. Not without reason had Stalin said, "You people in the Caucasus . . ." It meant he already thought of himself as a Russian.

He signaled to the other end of the table for everyone to pour another drink.

"I want to raise this toast," he said, getting up from his seat, pale, stubbornly fighting off an early-morning drunkenness, "to our elder brother."

The festive night caught second wind. Again they drank, ate, danced, and by now even Uncle Sandro, the greatest tamada of all times and nations, found his head spinning. It was a little too much even for him, to see in one night so many ominous and wonderful things.

Lakoba, as tamada, relaxed the reins a little, sensing that the strict ritual of the Caucasian table was beginning to weary the Leader.

"We want Sarya, beautiful Sarya!" Kalinin shouted, clapping his hands and tilting his bearded chin affectionately.

" *'Mravaldzhamie,'* we want *'Mravaldzhamie'!*" called some people at the other end of the table. They struck up the song.

" 'Many Summers'!" shouted others. They struck up the Abkhazian drinking song.

"Now you're off and away," Makhaz shouted from the other end of the table, his eyes meeting Uncle Sandro's. "Bliss has descended on you—bliss!"

"My hair is curly, like a fern," the cook was telling one of the district committee secretaries, letting him feel his hair. "The egg lies there like it's in a little nest."

"All the same it's a risk," the secretary said, dourly feeling the cook's hair.

"Some men's wives," Beria muttered, resting his head heavily on his hands.

"But, Lavrik, try to understand . . . I was ashamed to, and he didn't even get angry."

"We'll talk when we get home—"

"But, Lavrik—"

"I'm not Lavrik to you any more—"

"But, Lavrik—"

"Some men's wives . . ."

"Where's the risk, my dear fellow? My hair is three fingers deep," the cook said enthusiastically, trying to outargue the district committee secretary, who was touching his head mistrustfully.

"He didn't hit your head?"

"Of course not," the cook said, gleeful at his naiveté. "There's a lot of fear, but little risk."

The district committee secretary dourly held to his own interpretation. "All the same, it's a risk, the man is drunk."

" 'You people in the Caucasus,' he says," another secretary was saying, shaking his head. "What have we done to him?"

"Shota, I ask you as a brother, don't take offense at the Leader—"

"I'd lay down my life for him, but my heart aches," Shota replied, casting a bereaved glance at the far end of the table.

"Shota, I ask you as a brother, don't take offense at the Leader . . ."

"Lucky stiff! Lucky stiff!" Makhaz shouted drunkenly, meeting Uncle Sandro's eyes. "Now you've got all Abkhazia in your pocket!"

Uncle Sandro shook his head reproachfully, intimating that such shouts were indecent, especially when aimed into the thick of the government. But Makhaz did not understand his signal.

"Don't pretend it's not in your pocket!" he shouted. "Don't pretend, you lucky stiff!"

"What's he shouting?" Even Lakoba had noticed Makhaz.

"Just nonsense," Uncle Sandro said, and he thought to himself, It's a good thing he's shouting in Abkhazian, not Russian.

"Now here's something!" The cook was trying to amuse the dour secretary. "I started out as an apprentice cook here in Gagra back in Prince Oldenburgsky's time. The prince used to carry a cane, like Peter. He sampled the workers' dinner himself. Sometimes he used to beat the cooks with his cane, but always for cause."

"All the same, it's a risk." The secretary shook his head dourly. He felt overwhelmed and could not get the egg-shooting out of his mind.

"Here's something!" the cook went on, trying to distract him with his remarkable memories. "His Majesty the Emperor came here—"

"Why make things up," the secretary said, distracted against his will.

"I swear by the cross—on a cruiser! The cruiser dropped anchor out at the roadstead. His Majesty came in on a motor launch; but Her Majesty didn't want to come ashore, which offended the prince," the cook said.

"Court intrigues," the secretary interrupted dourly.

. . . Early in the morning, when at Lakoba's order the sanatorium manager opened the heavy curtains and a soft pink August dawn peeped into the banquet hall, it (the soft pink dawn) saw many district committee secretaries asleep at the tables—some sprawled back in their chairs, and some with their faces right on the table.

One of the ones sprawled back in his chair held a radish in his mouth, stuck there by his friends. This could only have perplexed the soft pink dawn, because the suckling pigs, each holding a radish in its bared teeth, were no longer on the table, and the humorous analogy was intelligible only to the initiated.

The troupe members approached Stalin one by one. Stalin shoveled up candy, cookies, chunks of meat, roast chickens, *khachapuri*, and other eatables from the table. Holding up the hem of their cherkeskas or holding out their turbans, they accepted the gifts, said thank you, and walked away from the Leader.

"Off you go!" Stalin said as he threw a batch of presents to each dancer in turn. He tried to give everyone equal shares, looked closely at the chunks of meat, at the roast chickens, and if he gave less of one thing he tried to pile on more of another. In the same way, a village patriarch, the Eldest in the House, hands out shares for his neighbors and for guests who will be traveling home after a great feast.

"All the same they'll chalk it up to Stalin," the Leader joked, piling eatables into the widespread skirt of a cherkeska. "All the same they'll say Stalin ate it all."

That being the case, several troupe members exchanged winks and grabbed bottles of wine to take with them.

The ensemble returned to Mukhus in three overcrowded motorcars. When they were getting into the cars, a curious mix-up occurred. Platon Pantsulaya, the director of the ensemble, got in next to the chauffeur of the first car, of course. Pata Pataraya, as usual, was supposed to sit next to the chauffeur of the second car. He was about to stick his head in the open door but then pulled it out and offered his place to Uncle Sandro, who happened (let us suppose) to be right beside him.

Uncle Sandro tried to refuse, but after some polite wrangling he was forced to yield to Pata Pataraya's urging and sit next to the chauffeur in the second car.

It had been decided to drive as far as the Gumista River and find a picturesque spot to have a picnic. They sang boisterously as they rode. Frequently they encountered children on the road and threw candy and cookies to them out of the car. The children rushed to gather this manna from heaven.

The dancers smiled wearily. "If they knew where it came from!"

Beyond Eshery, at a point where the road passed among thickets of ferns, blackberries, and hazelnuts, their way was suddenly blocked by a small flock of goats. The cars braked, and the goats proceeded across the road, tossing their beards and snorting. The goatherd was nowhere to be seen, but his voice carried from the thicket; he was in there driving out a goat that had lagged behind.

"*Kheyt! Kheyt!*" the boyish voice shouted, awakening a strange alarm in Uncle Sandro. From time to time the boy threw stones, and they crashed through the tightly woven branches to land dully, at intervals, on the ground. When one stone hit the unseen goat, Uncle Sandro had a sudden feeling that he had known, the moment before, that this was the one that would hit her. And when the goat ran grunting out of the bushes, and after her the youth, who halted shyly when he saw the cars, Uncle Sandro went cold from agitation and remembered everything.

Yes; it had happened almost the same way back then. The boy had been herding the goats into Sabid's Hollow. And one goat had gotten stuck this same way in the bushes, and the boy had thrown rocks the same way and shouted. Just this same way, the goat grunted and jumped out of the bushes when the rock hit her, and the boy jumped out after her and halted in surprise.

A few steps away, a man was walking along the path, driving ahead of him some heavily laden pack horses. Hearing the branches snap, the man started and looked at the blue-eyed youth. Never in his life had anyone looked at him with such malice.

At the first instant the boy thought the man's fury was due to the unexpectedness of the encounter, but after he perceived that it was only a boy and a goat, the man threw him another look, as if he were considering for a fraction of a second what to do with him: kill him or leave him. He went on without bothering to decide, merely jerked an elbow to hitch up the carbine that had slipped off his sloping shoulder.

The man walked unusually fast, and it was plain to the boy that he had left him alive only to save time. There was neither a stick nor a quirt in the man's hands, and it struck the boy as strange that the horses moved so fast without any kind of goading.

After several seconds the path led into a grove, and the man and his horses disappeared. But at the very last moment—one more step and he would be hidden behind a bush—he hitched up the carbine that had slipped off his sloping shoulder again, turned around, and caught the boy's eye. The boy thought he heard a distinct whisper, right in his ear: "You tell, and I'll come back and kill you."

His flock was already far below, and the boy ran down the green mountainside, driving the goat ahead of him. He knew that the grove the man had entered with his horses would soon end, and the path would lead them out to an open slope on the far side of Sabid's Hollow.

When he caught up with the flock and looked up, he saw the heavily packed horses begin to appear, one after another, there on the green slope. Eight horses and the man, distinct against the green background of the grassy slope, quickly crossed the open expanse and disappeared into the woods. Even from here, at a distance of about a kilometer, it was noticeable that the horses and the man were walking very fast. And now the boy surmised that this man needed no stick or whip, he was one of those whom horses feared even without any kind of goading.

Before disappearing into the woods, the man again glanced back and jerked his sloping shoulder to adjust the slipping carbine. Although his expression was now impossible to make out, the boy was sure that he had looked back very angrily.

A day later rumors reached Chegem that some men had robbed a steamboat going from Poti to Odessa. The robbers had operated precisely and ruthlessly. Not only did they have a man waiting for them near Kengursk with horses bought beforehand, they had also been able to win over four of the sailors to participate in the robbery. By night, they bound the captain, the helmsman, and several sailors and locked them in the captain's cabin. They lowered the lifeboats, into which they had loaded their loot, and rowed to shore.

Late the next day the bodies of the four sailors were found in a marsh near the hamlet of Tamysh. A day later two more bodies were found, eaten away by jackals, beyond recognition. It was decided that the robbers had quarreled among themselves, and the two that survived had taken their cargo to some unknown place or maybe even perished in the marshes. After another few days, this time quite close to Chegem, they found the body of still another man. He had been killed by a shot in the back and thrown off the steep Atary road, almost onto the heads of the residents of the village of Naa, who had stubbornly settled below these precipitous slopes. The body was well preserved, and it was recognized as that of a man who had bought horses a month ago in the village of Dzhgerdy.

The Chegemians took the whole incident rather calmly, because it was a lowland affair—someone else's, especially since it had to do with steamboats. Only the boy, with terror, guessed that he had seen that other man, in Sabid's Hollow.

About ten days after that encounter, a horseman rode up to their house wearing an Abkhazian burka but an official service cap, which indicated from afar that he was an important man, paid by the authorities.

The horseman, without dismounting, stopped by the wattle fence and waited for the boy's father to approach him. Then he pulled his foot from the stirrup and rested it on the fence while he conversed with the boy's father. Shooing away the dogs, the boy hovered near the fence to hear what the grown-ups said.

"Have any of your folks," the horseman asked his father, "seen anyone go by with heavy-packed horses on the upper Chegem road?"

"I heard about that," his father replied, "but I haven't seen the man."

"Not the upper—the lower!" the boy almost blurted, but he bit his tongue in time.

The man, still talking, found the stirrup with his foot and then rode on.

"Who's that, Pa?" the boy asked his father.

"The sergeant major," the father replied. He went into the house without saying anything more.

Only in late fall, when he and his father, after packing a donkey with sacks of chestnuts and climbing up from Sabid's Hollow, sat down to rest on that same lower Chegem path, almost at that same spot—only then could he no longer restrain himself, and he told his father everything.

"So that's why you stopped bringing the goats here?" His father grinned.

"That's not true!" the boy flared: his father had struck home.

"Why didn't you say anything before now?" the father asked.

"You should have seen the way he looked at me," the boy confessed. "I keep thinking he might come back . . ."

"By now you couldn't drag him back on a rope," his father said, standing up and urging on the donkey with a switch. "But if you'd told right away, they still could have caught him."

"How do you know, Pa?" the boy asked, trying not to lag behind his father. Since meeting that man he did not like this place, did not trust it.

"A man with heavy-packed horses can't get farther than one day's journey," his father said. He flicked the switch; the donkey kept wanting to stop, the grade was steep.

"But you know how fast he was walking!" the boy said.

"But no faster than his horses," his father objected. After a moment's thought he added, "And he killed that last man because he knew he had only one day's march left."

"Why, Pa?" the boy asked, still trying not to lag behind his father.

"He probably left him alive," his father said, still thinking aloud, "so that the man could help him pack the horses for the last day's march. And then he got rid of him."

"How do you know all this?" the boy asked, no longer trying to keep up with his father, because they had come out on a slope from which their house was visible.

"I know their infidel ways," his father said. "They'd just as soon not work. I don't even want to think about them."

"I don't either," the boy said, "but for some reason I keep remembering about this all the time."

"It will pass," his father said.

It did indeed pass, and with the years receded so far that Uncle Sandro, remembering it once in a while, questioned whether it had all really happened or whether he, the little boy, had imagined it after people started talking about the steamboat robbery near Kengursk.

But then, after the never-to-be-forgotten banquet that took place on an August night in 1935 or the year before, but certainly no later, it all came back to him with uncommon clarity. Superstitiously marveling at the Leader's menacing memory, he thanked God for his own quick-wittedness.

Uncle Sandro often told his friends—and even, after the Twentieth Congress, people who were merely acquaintances—about this festive night, appending to the story his own youthful imaginings or recollections.

"I can still see it now," Uncle Sandro would say. "His carbine kept slipping off his shoulder, and he kept jerking it up as he went, hitching at it without looking. A very sloping shoulder, That One had . . ."

So saying, Uncle Sandro would gaze at his companion, his big eyes tinged with mysticism. His gaze made it plain that had he told his father soon enough about the man who passed on the lower Chegem road, the whole of world history would have taken a different path, in any case not the lower Chegem path.

All the same, it was not exactly clear whether he regretted his long-ago silence or expected a reward from the none-too-grateful younger generation. Most likely his gaze meant that while he regretted he had not told, he would not be averse to receiving a reward.

Then again, this ambiguity in his gaze implied a dose of demonic irony, which seemed to reflect the confusion and vacillation of earthly judges in appraising Stalin.

The very fact that he died a natural death—if, of course, he did die a natural death—prompts me personally to the religious thought that God requisitioned the dossier on his deeds in order that He Himself might judge him in the highest court and Himself punish him with the highest punishment.

THE TALE OF OLD KHABUG'S MULE

I WAS EATING GRASS in Sabid's Hollow that morning when my old man appeared on the crest of the ridge that divides the hollow into two parts. Several horses and donkeys were grazing alongside me, the cows were grazing a little way off. A horse belonging to one of our neighbors, the cranky old forest warden Omar, was there with her colt, and of course I was trying to keep near him. We mules in general, and I in particular, adore colts. Especially since I had saved this one from the wolves forty days before. But I'll tell that story another time, although in case I forget to later, I'll give the gist of it here too.

That time we were grazing the same way in Sabid's Hollow, only much farther down. As always, I was trying to keep near the colt, because I go out of my mind with tenderness when I catch the scent of a colt or see his awkward long-legged figure.

Two wolves suddenly sprang out of an alder thicket, and all the horses and donkeys took to their heels. I started to run too, of course, but in spite of my terror, I didn't forget the colt. When he began to fall behind on the steep grade, I slowed down myself. I knew that the two wolves were trying to cut the colt off from the rest of the horses and donkeys. Oh no, I decided, you won't snap his delicate neck as long as *I'm* around.

The horses and donkeys were all way ahead now, and the wolves were closing in on the colt from either side. I was running alongside, and one wolf was already between us. His hackles were up, his teeth were bared, I sensed he was just waiting for the right moment to leap on the colt's neck.

But as it happened, he was not paying any attention to me at all. I took advantage of this. Just as he got set for his leap, I drew even with him, turned slightly, and kicked him with my right hind hoof. After that kind of a blow you don't have to look back. I had the pleasure of feeling the wolf's skull crunch under my hoof.

Yes, I'll tell you, that was a good sound blow. The wolf fell down dead, and the shepherd Harlampo picked him up later that day.

After I kicked that first wolf, I went for the second without a backward glance. I caught up with the colt again and passed him on the side where the second wolf was. But the wolf either saw what I'd done to his comrade or else he took fright at the incredible fury of my charge—anyway, he lost his nerve and vanished into a green thicket of rhododendron.

All the other horses and donkeys, including the colt's dam, by the way, were way ahead on the top of the ridge. I might have been there too but the colt had fallen badly behind on the steep grade, I couldn't leave him to the wolves. It's true what people say: your mother is not the one who bore you, but the one who raised you.

We mules are generally notable for the fact that we love foals. Oh, the fact that we're the most intelligent of all animals has been well known for a long time. But not everyone knows that we adore foals. And wouldn't you know, we're the ones that can't have them. This is very unfair. True, I've sometimes heard rumors of female mules giving birth. But I've never seen it myself. And then it's not clear who the stud is, a mule or a stallion.

Personally, I am notable even among mules for my special love of colts. I also like donkey colts and human children, though of course you can't compare them with horse colts.

So, if I sense that something is threatening a colt, I become incredibly savage. In my lifetime, to save colts, I have killed two wolves and four foxes and trampled eight snakes. I don't even count the rabbits. People might object that a fox wouldn't attack a colt. True; in a tranquil mood I understand that myself. But when I'm grazing beside a sweet, defenseless colt, and suddenly a fox darts between us, I lose my head from fury. If I'm grazing beside a colt—you just move over! What's the matter, not enough room for you?

I also kick big mean dogs when they attack me. But never people. True, there was one fool I did kick, but for cause. I was just standing there, tied to the mill, and he came up behind me and lifted my tail, for no reason at all. To this day I don't know why he had to lift my tail. It's one thing when my old man is washing me in the stream and lifts my tail to splash water there, get rid of the damn flies. It's another thing when somebody you don't know comes over and pulls up your tail for no reason at all. An awful lot of people, by the way, are fools.

In general, according to my long observation, the mind of the average mule is far superior to that of the average man. And it's easy to see why. Man, as a beast of prey, makes his own flesh out of flesh. But a mule makes his flesh from grass. Any fool can make flesh from flesh. But just try to make flesh out of grass—that, brother, is a lot harder.

That's the way things are. But I have to be completely fair. And fairness bids me confess that although the mind of the average mule is far superior to that of the average man, still, the mind of the most intelligent men is superior to that of the most intelligent mules. I see this when I honestly compare my own mind with my master's. Yes, my old man is basically more intelligent than I am, though sometimes even he does foolish things.

It bothers me that I'm rarely able to correct my old man when he says or does something stupid. I understand Abkhazian perfectly well, but I can't say a thing, because the mule is a dumb animal.

Some dull-witted people may say, as if taking me at my word, "How come you're telling all these stories if you're a dumb animal?"

For the benefit of the dull-witted, let me explain how this happens. Everything that I say I mentally tell to the angels, and they'll make one of our boys see and hear it all in a dream. And he in his turn will tell the rest of the people about it. Never mind now, don't worry, he'll do it right. It's a fact that he's more literate than your scribes in tussah tunics.

Now that everyone's clear on how it works, let me change the subject and talk about dogs, so that I don't forget later. The thing is, many people have the illusion that the dog is the most intelligent animal.

That's only because people like to think their property is being guarded by a very intelligent animal. They're more relaxed that way. I mention this not because dogs often attack us, though that too says something about their dull-wittedness. I don't deny, for example, that dogs are devoted to their masters. This really is true. But the way they always cast this devotion in your teeth, forgetting their own dignity, is no sign of intelligence either.

But that's not the main thing. If you calmly weigh and consider all the reasons a dog barks in the course of one day, you can't help wondering: Is there something the matter with his brains?

Let's suppose a dog barks a hundred times a day, though they usually bark much more often. If you sort through the reasons he barked a hundred times, it will turn out there was only one time he really had to bark. The other times he should have sat there quietly or slept. Now imagine a mule that goes to the mill a hundred times in order to bring home one sack of meal, and it will immediately become clear what a dog's mind is worth. I think everyone's clear on this question now, and to say any more about it would be the same as imitating the dog's senseless barking.

So, my old man appeared on the slope of Sabid's Hollow, where I was eating grass with the other horses and donkeys. He began coming down toward me, shouting loudly, "Blackamoor! Blackamoor!"

That's what he calls me, though I'm not all that black. But I don't mind, a name doesn't mean anything in itself. By the way, he also calls his donkey Blackamoor. But it's one thing for me, a mule, to be Blackamoor, and it's another thing for him, a donkey, to be Blackamoor. Same name, but it has a completely different ring to it.

So, then, my old man came toward me, loudly calling me by name so that I'd pay attention to him. At first I pretended not to hear him. I always do that at first, because if he's looking for me he's not going to walk right by.

Finally I raised my head and looked at him. In one hand he held a handful of salt, to entice me with, and in the other a bridle. I realized that a long trip lay ahead. I could tell this from the fact that his face was cleared of stubble. Whenever there's a long trip ahead, he always clears his face of stubble with this special little sharp knife. When we have to go to the village soviet or to the mill or to visit close neighbors, he doesn't clear his face of stubble. When the trip is to another village or to the city, he always does. So I could tell that a long trip lay ahead.

My old man came up to me warily, as if I might run away somewhere. Where would I run from you, you nut? I'm not about to run anywhere, because you're my master, and I don't want to have any other.

He came up to me, and I waited—raising my head, but without displaying excessive eagerness—for him to hold out the palm with the handful of coarse salt. He held out his palm and I took from it the most delicious salt in the world, and when I had chewed and swallowed it all, he put the bit in my mouth, threw the bridle over my withers, and climbed on my back.

We set off for the house. I looked back at the colt for the last time; when we started off he raised his head and watched me go. Oh, if only I had seen in his eyes any regret that I was abandoning him! But no, the sweet little long-legged chestnut lowered his head indifferently and began calmly nibbling grass. Ingrate—I saved you from death, I'd lay down my life for you, and you understand nothing of this. But who knows, maybe he loves me anyway and just can't show it outwardly. Why, twice he's allowed me to approach him and lay my head on the mane of his quivering little neck. The utter sweetness of those moments! Against my neck I felt the warm blood pulsing under the tender hide of his neck. This warmth lent warmth to my body, and I felt an unparalleled bliss flow over him. True, all this didn't last very long. The little fool suddenly cut short what I considered to be our mutual bliss and ran snorting away from me.

The second time we stood like that he didn't interrupt our bliss, I think he felt the sweetness of our intimacy, but then his mother came over and chased me away. So as not to offend the colt, I didn't put up any resistance; otherwise, I might have bitten her so she'd howl to all of Sabid's Hollow. You jealous old fool! If you love your colt so much, why were you the first to run away and leave him to the wolves!

We came to my old man's house. He bent down to push the gate, and we entered the yard. Near the kitchen my old man dismounted, pulled the bit from my mouth, and tied me to the veranda railing. I began to feel very anxious. Usually, before a big trip, they bring me ears of corn in a pan, for me to fortify myself with.

But sometimes they don't, because they just forget. That's the thing that really hurts. If they didn't bring the corn because they begrudged it, I wouldn't mind so much. But it hurts a lot that they sometimes simply forget to do it.

My old man went into the kitchen and began talking to his old woman. From their conversation I understood that we were going to visit his son in the city, where he lives now. This son of his, Sandro, lives in the city and earns his living dancing. I never in my life heard of anyone feeding and watering a man and keeping a roof over his head for dancing. I can't understand it at all. What if everyone takes a notion to dance? Who will plow, sow, and reap the harvest?

From my old man's conversation with the old woman I understood that Sandro was planning to buy a house but wanted his father's advice before doing it. So the old man was getting ready to go to the city. The old woman kept trying to persuade my old man to talk his son into returning to Chegem, because terrible things were happening in the city.

I had heard about this many times—when I was tethered by the village soviet and when we went to a funeral feast in the next village, and at the mill they talked about the same thing, and I heard it despite the racket of the millstones.

Down there, in the city, some people are seizing other people and sending them off to a cold country, I forget the name of it. And sometimes they just kill them. No one knows what for. Maybe they think they're poisoning the wells. But somehow I don't believe it. I've been on many long trips with my old man, and we've drunk from wells along the way and haven't been poisoned once.

One thing I'll never understand is why all those people don't run away somewhere before they get caught. What are they, hobbled? If that's the way things are—run to the hills, to the woods, who'll find you there? Even I, in my time, once ran away from a bad master to come to my old man. And nothing happened—it turned out all right.

So, then, the old woman began pushing my old man to persuade his son to return to Chegem, and the old man began assuring her that a lazybones like Sandro would never want to change his freeloading city life for life in the village. Then they really started to squabble, and I got depressed, deciding that now of course they'd forget to give me my corn.

"Enough," my old man barked finally. "Pack me something to eat on the way and give my mule his corn."

Good for my old man, he didn't forget. The old woman, though she continued to rail on about her son dying because of him, brought me a whole pan full of corn. Ten ears, no less. I began gnawing the tasty golden kernels off the cobs. Now, as always, the hens and roosters came around, waiting for individual kernels to pop off the ears. Of course I tried to gnaw the kernels so accurately that none of them would pop off. Well, you can't keep track of them all. From time to time the kernels would pop off to the side, and those empty-headed hens and roosters immediately snapped them up.

I ate all the corn, so that only the bare cobs were left in the pan. My old man ate, too, and came out on the veranda to wash his hands and mouth. For some reason he always rinses his mouth after eating, so as to wash out the last bits of food. A strange practice. With me it's the opposite—I like to have little pieces of food left in my mouth after a tasty meal, then you remember the pleasure longer. Evidently he likes to forget what he's eaten. I'm the opposite, I like to remember what I've eaten. Like the corn just now, for example.

After washing his hands and rinsing his mouth, my old man saddled me. As always, when he began to tighten the saddle girths, I inflated my belly, and as always, he punched me to make me let out the air so he could cinch up the saddle girths properly. The interesting thing is, I never forget to inflate my belly, and he never forgets to punch me. I keep waiting for him to forget that I've inflated my belly some time, but so far it's no good. He always notices.

After saddling me, my old man took one last look around the yard to see whether everything was in its place, whether he needed to put anything right or give any orders to his family. After convincing himself that everything here was as it should be, he looked across at the hillside where the house of his son the hunter Isa stood. Having surveyed Isa's house and his yard without finding any signs of mismanagement, he looked downhill, where not far from the spring stood the house of his son the shepherd Makhaz. And here he discovered something amiss.

The thing is that my old man can't bear to have the kitchen door closed in his own house or in his sons' houses. He feels that if the owners are home, the kitchen door must stand open all day, in keeping with Abkhazian custom.

A wide-open kitchen door signifies that the owners are always ready to receive a passing horseman or foot traveler if he should want something to eat or drink. A closed kitchen door, especially if smoke is rising over the roof, signifies that this is the home of niggardly hosts who fear a chance guest.

So when he's home, my old man tirelessly watches his sons' kitchens to see that they're open all the time, lest anyone think—God forbid—that he has inhospitable sons.

But all sorts of things can happen. If the mistress goes for water, or to the garden to get some greens or weed the vegetables, she closes the kitchen door so that the chickens or dogs don't come in. But the minute he sees a closed kitchen door, my old man starts to shout.

And now he noticed that Masha, his son Makhaz's wife, had her kitchen door closed.

"Hey, you there at Masha's," he shouted down, "who are you locking out of your kitchen?"

"Mama's taking a bath, Grandpa," one of Masha's daughters shouted back. "That's why it's shut!"

"May a water sprite get her," my old man muttered. "Did you ever hear tell of a woman splashing herself for days on end."

No, of course Masha doesn't make it a habit to bathe for days on end. The old man just can't stand to have the door of any kitchen closed.

Finally he clambered up on me and we started off.

"Bring back my son!" the old woman shouted after him.

"May your tongue dry up," my old man muttered. He bent down to open the gate and we went out of the yard.

Just before the steep slope that goes down to the River Kodor, my old man stopped me by his friend's house. The friend was hoeing corn in his private plot. His name was Daur. This Daur has proved to be even more stubborn than my old man. In all of Chegem he's the only one that hasn't joined the kolkhoz yet. My old man keeps jealously scrutinizing him, still can't figure out whether he did the right thing by joining the kolkhoz or whether he'd have done better to hold out, like this Daur.

"Good labors to you!" my old man called.

"Well be you, Khabug," Daur replied. Dropping his hoe, he started in our direction. He climbed over the fence and came up to us to shake hands with my old man.

"Dismount, let's have a glass," Daur said.

"No, no," my old man replied, "I'm just passing by."

"Where are you headed?" Daur asked.

"I'm going to visit my son in the city," my old man replied.

"Still on your mule," Daur said suddenly. "I should think you'd switch to a horse, now that you're a kumkhoz man."

They're obsessed with this horse business. Everyone we meet wonders why my old man rides on me and not on a horse. The numskulls won't understand that the reason he rides me is that I'm more comfortable and pleasant than a horse in all respects.

"I'll ride my mule till the day I die," my old man said. He sighed and added, "As for the kumkhoz, what can you do, the times forced it on me."

"Yes, the times," Daur sighed in reply.

"Well, and what about you, they aren't bothering you?" my old man asked.

"They summoned me to the village soviet again," Daur said. "It seems they thought up a new tax."

"No—they won't leave you alone," my old man said.

"Hey, you!" Daur shouted in the direction of the house. "Bring us something to wet our gullets!"

I realized that they were about to have a long conversation and began quietly nibbling grass near the farmer's fence.

"Well, what's happening at your kumkhoz?" Daur asked.

"The numskulls," my old man said, "they've thought up a piece of folly called a plan. The tobacco isn't tall enough yet, but they've ordered it to be cut according to the plan. No matter what I say they don't listen. Mark my words—this is bad business. In the spring I told them: You mustn't be in a hurry to sow the low-lying field, you have to let the ground dry out. They didn't listen that time either. Now the corn there is no higher than my hand."

"At least for the time being, thank God, I'm master on my own land," Daur said gloomily.

Just then his old woman brought a decanter of *chacha* and some shelled nuts on a plate. They drank and ate. My old man drained his glass and graphically tipped it over, pronouncing his usual dictum: "May the kumkhoz be overturned like this wineglass."

"Allah heed thy words," Daur seconded him.

They drank three glasses apiece, and the farmer entreated my old man to have another, but my old man flatly refused, saying that he had dallied too long as it was.

In truth, the sun had already risen as high as the trees, and we'd only gotten as far as the end of our own village. I myself couldn't wait to get going, because I'd nibbled all the grass by the fence, and when I tried to reach a corn leaf sticking out between the stakes of the fence, this independent farmer rapped my head with his hand. It didn't hurt much, it just offended me. What does he care about a corn leaf? They're greedy anyhow, independent farmers.

To tell the truth, I like the kolkhoz better in this respect. Let's take an example. Once a neighbor's buffalo broke through a hedge belonging to a certain peasant, and we followed the buffalo into the field. There were three cows, two donkeys, and myself. We had a very short time to enjoy the cornstalks. We ate quite a small part of the field—well, no bigger than what a peasant's house usually occupies. And suddenly the farmer discovered us. What a scene! He almost killed us! He thrashed us with such a big staff that I almost passed out. Oddly enough he hit everyone he could get his hands on, even though it was easy to guess that only the buffalo could have broken through that hedge.

But another day we had a glorious time trampling a kolkhoz field. Incidentally, this same buffalo broke through the board fence. It was a habit of his; if he raised his head and his eye happened to light on some juicy cornstalks, he simply bore down on them, and no fence would hold him. Well, so we had a glorious feast there, for maybe an hour, maybe longer. Only then did a kolkhoz worker notice us. True, he did drive us out, but he didn't beat us. He just threw clods of dirt at us to make us leave. Now where, I ask, is the kinder, more cordial attitude to animals? In the kolkhoz field, of course, not on the private plot. To tell the truth, a lot of foolishness goes on in the kolkhoz, and in general my old man is right. But they do have their good points, and we have to be fair to them.

My old man took his leave of Daur and we started down the steep slope to the Kodor. I moved my feet very carefully so as not to stumble or, God forbid, throw my old man downhill. Fine pebbles cascaded from under my feet and I had to be on my guard to find solid footing at every step.

To the right and the left of this very steep descent there were peasant houses, and big and little dogs barked at us constantly from both sides. Though I paid absolutely no attention to them, this incessant malicious barking irritated me. If only there was some sense to it! After all, we're not turning off into your yard, brainless creatures, we're only going by, going by! You ought to know that when you live on a road like this a lot of pedestrians and riders go by! But no;

every time, they pretend to their masters that after great difficulty they've succeeded in driving robbers away from their house.

Despite the difficult road and this irritating barking, I managed to scan the front yards in hopes of glimpsing a colt somewhere. But I didn't see a single one. Such neglect of colts, I think, is not only criminal, it's stupid. You may not love colts, but after all, they grow up to be horses, did you ever think of that? What are you going to ride on a few years from now, if this attitude toward colts keeps up?

Halfway down to the River Kodor we encountered a wandering Jew named Samuel. He was riding on one donkey and driving ahead of him another one carrying a pack. This wandering Jew from Mukhus brings various city wares to Chegem and exchanges them for money or village products.

When we drew alongside of Samuel my old man stopped. Samuel also stopped his donkey.

"Well be you," my old man said.

"Well be you, too, Khabug," Samuel replied cordially.

"What are you bringing us?" my old man asked.

"Yard goods for women's dresses and men's shirts," Samuel said, "galoshes with turned-up toes of the kind Abkhazians adore, lamp chimneys, sewing-machine needles, thread, buttons, plague, cholera, and other sundries."

"Drop in at our place, maybe they'll take something," my old man said after a moment's thought.

"I'll be sure to do that," Samuel said.

"And what do you hear in the city, which is where I'm going?" my old man asked.

"Better not ask, Khabug," Samuel said, wringing his hands. "In the city, where you're going, they're taking people every night and sometimes even by day."

"Which nationality are they taking more of now than others, Samuel?" my old man asked.

"What are you saying, Khabug," Samuel said, wringing his hands again. "Is there any nationality they're taking less of now? If there were such a nationality, I'd buy a document and join it. But right now I'd like to hide with my family in Chegem."

"Things are bad, Samuel," my old man said, "if a commercial traveler like you wants to hide in Chegem."

"Things are even worse than you and I think, Khabug," Samuel said.

"What do you think," my old man asked, "what's the Big Mustache trying to accomplish?"

"Not one man in the world knows what he's trying to accomplish by this," Samuel replied. "Learned men are racking their brains to understand it, but no one can."

"Learned men don't know," my old man said, "but I do."

"I know what you're going to say," Samuel exclaimed. "Some people say he's out of his mind. That's not what I say, some people say it."

"No," my old man said firmly, "he's not out of his mind."

"I know what you're thinking, Khabug," Samuel exclaimed, "but I beg you, don't tell anyone! Especially in the city, where you're going! You mustn't confide in anyone now. Don't even confide your thoughts to your own mule!"

Now, I never expected to hear such foolishness from Samuel. I not only wouldn't betray my master, but would lay down my life for him. If you want to know the truth—animals never betray anyone. Only people betray.

"I know," my old man said calmly. "Not only in the city; I can't say it anywhere the other side of the Kodor, because informers have already turned up among the lowland Abkhazians."

They talked like that a while longer and went their separate ways. Samuel went up. We went down. This Samuel had me very upset. I even began to fear for my old man. After the Kodor he usually holds his tongue, but he's altogether too sure that the informers haven't gotten over to this side of the river.

This wandering Jew Samuel first showed up in Chegem five years ago. Before that there had never been even one Jew in Chegem, and many Chegemians hadn't even suspected that such a nationality existed. They began coming to the Big House to gawk at Samuel, talk to him, marvel at his knowledge of the Abkhazian language.

Only that cranky fool, the forest warden Omar, didn't come to look at Samuel; he tried to dissuade the others from coming to look at him. During Nicholas's war with Germany, Omar served in the Wild Division, and he loved to tell how over there in the Wild Division they used to slice men from the shoulder to the saddle. But the Chegemians had long since grown tired of his stories and no one wanted to listen to him. Now he was offended that everyone was running to the Big House to listen to Samuel and look at him.

"Where are you going, where, where!" he shouted to the Chegemians from the veranda of his house when they were going over to meet Samuel. "You people were still wading in goat shit when I saw Jews!

"In Poland! In Poland!" he called hysterically. "It's that kind of country! I saw them there! Nothing special! Like an Armenian! In Poland! In Poland!"

But the Chegemians, wanting nothing to do with the cranky forest warden, wordlessly walked by his house. One of them did turn around and ask, "Did you see any Endurskies there?"

"Didn't see Endurskies," Omar replied. "I won't lie."

"They have it good without Endurskies," the Chegemian said, and he walked on.

The Abkhazians have a very complicated attitude toward the Endurskies. The main thing is that no one knows exactly how they got to Abkhazia, but everyone is sure they're here to gradually destroy the Abkhazians. At first the hypothesis was advanced that the Turks were sending them down on the Abkhazians. It was thought that the Turks sailed over by night in their feluccas, put the Endurskies ashore in the region of Poti, and said, "Now, go!"

"Go where?" the Endurskies asked.

"Over there," the Turks told them, waving a hand toward Abkhazia.

And ever since, the Endurskies go on and on in Abkhazia, there's no end to them. But some Abkhazians dispute this story. They cite the fact that Endurskies don't know Turkish, and if they were from Turkey, even for all their devilish guile, at least one of them would have let slip a Turkish word.

The Chegemians put forward a different version of the story. Their version was that somewhere deep in the dense forest between Georgia and Abkhazia, the Endurskies had been spontaneously generated from wood mold. Very likely that was possible in czarist times. And later they grew into a whole tribe, multiplying much faster than the Abkhazians would have liked. Several very old Chegemians say they remember a time when Endurskies did not live in Abkhazia, merely showed up occasionally in small bands, hiring themselves out to Abkhazians to build a house or hoe a field.

"That's when they sized up where, how, and what we had," the younger Chegemians replied. "And you thought they were just hoeing the field."

To be honest, I don't know myself who's right, but it seems to me there's some exaggeration in all this. But here I've digressed from the wandering Samuel. The thing that most impressed the Chegemians was that he spoke Abkhazian.

"Are you an Abkhazian Jew," the Chegemians asked him, "or a Jewish Abkhaz?"

"Neither," Samuel answered. "I'm a Jewish Jew."

"Then how do you know our language?" the Chegemians asked in wonder.

"I traded for twenty years in Abkhazian lowland villages," Samuel said, "but now they've forbidden me to trade there. Because the Bolsheviks have opened stores there and want people to come to the stores and buy things that the people don't want to buy. And the stores don't have the things they do want to buy."

"This we know," the Chegemians said. "But Samuel, explain to us, where is your people's homeland?"

"Our homeland is wherever we live," Samuel replied.

This reply of Samuel's struck the Chegemians as too simpleminded, and they undertook to correct him.

"My dear Samuel," the Chegemians told him, "you're our respected guest, but we must correct your mistake. A homeland can't be just any place a man happens to live. A homeland, in our understanding, is where the people of your tribe settle on the land and obtain their bread through the land."

Then (as the Chegemians tell it) Samuel said, "Oh-oh-oh," and began rocking back and forth in his chair. "We did have a homeland like that, but they took it away from us."

"Who took it," the Chegemians asked, "the Russians or the Turks?"

"Neither," Samuel replied, "not the Russians and not the Turks. Another nation entirely. It happened in an age long forgotten. And it's all described in our holy book, the Talmud. This book describes all that has ever been on earth and all that ever will be."

The Chegemians had never imagined there was such a book. They became very excited when they found out about it. They immediately undertook to find out from Samuel about their future fate.

"Then don't torture us, Samuel," the Chegemians implored. "Tell us what the book says about the Endurskies. Will they subjugate us in the end, or not?"

"I haven't read it," Samuel said. "I'm a traveling Jew, but there are learned Jews, you'll have to ask them."

At this the Chegemians were a little crestfallen, realizing that it was highly unlikely a learned Jew would ever reach Chegem. They began putting other questions to Samuel.

"Answer this question for us, Samuel," the Chegemians said. "Does a Jew who is born among alien people know by himself, from birth, that he's a Jew, or does he find it out from the nations around him?"

"Mainly from the nations around him," Samuel said. Looking around at the Chegemians in surprise, he added, "Then you're by no means so simple as I thought?"

"No." The Chegemians shook their heads. "We're not so simple. It's the Endurskies who think we're simpletons and don't know anything about their plots."

The Chegemians asked Samuel a host of different questions, and he finally grew tired. He said to them, "Are you going to buy anything from me, maybe, or are you going to ask questions the whole time?"

"We'll buy everything you brought, since you've come all the way up here," the Chegemians replied. "To our way of thinking, it would be disgraceful not to buy anything from you."

They did buy everything he'd brought, and Samuel was well pleased with the Chegemians. But on the way back he had a misadventure. Samuel, the great expert on commerce, knew nothing about how the wealth of the Chegem mountains and forests was distributed. And Sandro, who accompanied him from the village, took advantage of his ignorance.

It was fall, and Samuel said he would like to lay in a stock of Chegem chestnuts and sell them in the city.

"Certainly," Sandro said. He pointed to the chestnut grove in Sabid's Hollow. "This grove is mine, as far as the little river at the bottom of the hollow, and beyond the river it belongs to somebody else. I'll sell you my grove. You can hire some Greeks in the village of Anastasovka, and they'll come over with their donkeys, gather the chestnuts for you, and carry them right to the bus that goes to the city."

Then they began to haggle, but Sandro outwitted him here too.

"Why haggle with me," he said to Samuel. "For that price, not only will I sell you the grove, I'll guard it till you come back. Besides, this is the height of the season. Any minute the Greeks and Armenians will descend on it, and there'll be nothing left of your chestnuts."

"Done," said Samuel. "Guard my chestnuts, and I'll be back in ten days."

"Rest easy," Sandro replied. "I won't let anyone into your grove, not even a wild boar."

"Don't let them in," Samuel said. "And I'll hire the Greeks with their donkeys and come back."

"Just don't tell a soul that I sold you the chestnut grove," Sandro requested, "because folks up here dislike it terribly when anyone sells a chestnut grove to an outsider."

"What do you take me for, Sandro?" Samuel said in surprise. "A commercial traveler knows how to keep a secret."

Ten days later Samuel came back with the Greeks. They began gathering chestnuts for him, and he paid them for every sackful. When they had picked the whole grove, down as far as the little river, Samuel asked them whether they knew where he might find the owner of the chestnuts that grew on the other side of the river.

When the Greeks heard him ask about the owner of the chestnuts, they dropped their sacks and began to laugh at Samuel. Samuel was very displeased.

"I'm surprised to hear you laugh," Samuel said. "I wonder, did you hire me to work, or did I hire you?"

"Master," the Greeks said, when they finally stopped laughing, "of course you hired us to work and you'll pay us money for it. But it struck us funny to hear that the chestnuts on the other side of the river belong to someone. Around here this is considered forest—forest! Whatever a man gathers in the forest belongs to him."

"And the chestnuts on this side of the river," Samuel said anxiously, "don't belong to anyone either?"

"No," the Greeks affirmed gleefully, "the chestnuts on this side of the river don't belong to anyone either, and the river itself doesn't belong to anyone. Put a mill on it, if you want."

"I'd have no reason to put a mill on it, especially in such a wild place," Samuel said pensively. "But I figured the chestnuts belonged to someone, since they sell them at the bazaar."

So Sandro deceived him that once, but Samuel forgave him the deception, because he made a good profit on the chestnuts even so, and besides, he was accustomed to stay at my old man's house when he came to Chegem.

Anyway, we parted from Samuel and continued our descent to the River Kodor. Finally, when I was getting good and tired of the steep slope, we came out on a level place where we could hear the roar of the river quite clearly. But just then we came to the house of a Georgian, another friend of my old man's. My old man stopped me and peered into the yard. I peered in too, in hopes of spotting a colt, but there wasn't a one. The yard was full of turkeys and piglets. A Georgian has no use for a colt, all he wants is turkeys and suckling pigs.

My old man's friend was lying on a cowhide in the shade of a cherry-laurel. When he saw us he got up with a loud hello and started over to us. I realized that the conversation would begin all over again; I wasted no time getting started on the grass at the side of the road. The master opened the wicket gate and came up to my old man to shake hands. After that he inspected me rather mockingly, and I knew he was going to say something about me. And so he did.

"The world has turned topsy-turvy," the master of the house said with a smile, "but you sit on your mule as you've always sat, Khabug."

"As I have sat, so I shall continue to sit," my old man answered in a firm voice.

Good for my old man. What I like is that no one can muddle him. Once he's made up his mind to something, even if the whole village puts pressure on him, he'll still do it his own way. The main thing is, everyone knows that he's the most intelligent old man in Chegem, everyone knows that with his own hands he built up the largest farm, everyone knows that he had a dozen horses but he chose me.

So, isn't it clear to all of you that if a man is more intelligent than you in every respect, it means his intelligence is revealed even in the fact that he chose a mule over a horse? These numskulls think that an Abkhazian is degrading himself if he sits on a mule and not on a horse. But my old man knows better than anyone else what each animal is worth. Another man in his place, if people had said so many things against his mule, would have listened to them; he would have parted with me, and shaken up his liver on some jolting horse.

Well, anyway. My old man's friend invited him to dismount and come sit in his house at the table. My old man refused again, saying that he was in a hurry to get to the city. Then our host called to his wife, and she brought a teapot full of wine, two glasses, and *churkhcheli* for a snack.

And of course they began to drink and snack. To be honest, my old man also has quite a few amusing quirks. Both at this place and the last, he flatly refused to go into the house, saying he was in a hurry, and then he drinks and snacks sitting astride me. He calls this hurrying. If you must have a snack, then get down off me, let me take a break, too.

"How are things on your kumkhoz?" my old man asked.

"Oh, we keep putting in eucalyptuses," his host replied.

"What's a eucalyptus?" my old man asked in surprise.

"It's some kind of tree from overseas," his host replied. "It's no good for firewood, and it doesn't bear any more fruit than your mule."

Another dig.

"Then why plant them?" my old man asked.

"Orders," his host answered. "They say eucalyptus will scare off the mosquitoes."

"But why scare them off?" my old man asked.

"They think people catch malaria from mosquito bites."

"The sheepheads," my old man said in surprise. "Don't they know it's the damp fog that brings on malaria?"

"They don't know," his host said, pouring them each another glass of wine, "but you can't go against them: authority . . ."

"No, you can't," my old man agreed. He drank off the wine and graphically overturned the glass.

"May the kumkhoz be overturned the way I overturned this glass," my old man said.

"God grant it to you," his host agreed, and he poured wine in the glasses again.

All right, I thought, unburden your soul, talk till we get to the Kodor, if you're sure the informers haven't got up the nerve to cross the river yet. But suppose the informers are already on this side of the Kodor, it's terrible to think my old man is still blabbing whatever comes to his tongue.

On the other side of the Kodor he behaves more quietly. Yes, even there he turns his glass over, but he doesn't say it in so many words, only by innuendo. But I know that he has the same thing in mind.

They drank another two glasses apiece and his host asked my old man how things were going on his kolkhoz. Here, so that his friend could understand better, my old man switched to Georgian, which I don't really understand. Even so it was clear to me what he was going to talk about.

By the way, besides Abkhazian, my old man also knows Georgian, Turkish, Greek, and Endurian. With Armenians he speaks Turkish. The only one he doesn't know is Russian, because the Russians live in the city, and we don't go there very often. He knows just one word in Russian: *durrak*. In translation this word means a no-good, pathetic excuse for a man. Sometimes when my old man is angry with someone, he puts in this word; the people quarreling with him are flustered and don't know how to answer him.

Finally they said good-bye, and we went on.

"Eucalyptus," my old man muttered, remembering the strange word. "They think they know better than God where what tree is supposed to grow."

My old man spat in indignation and even let some excess air out his rear. It's interesting that when I let out excess air he always grumbles crossly, but when he does it, I don't mind at all. I don't even understand what offends him about it. Why am I supposed to hold the excess air inside, doesn't he want me to breathe? My old man has a hell of a lot of funny quirks.

We were getting close to the river. With every instant the roar of it grew louder, and I felt myself getting nervous. The problem is that I can't bear to cross docks and bridges and what have you, or stand on the planking in the ferry, when I know that the furious water is rushing by under the planks.

If they let me choose whether to cross over icy water by a bridge or a ford, I would choose the ford, unless the water was too high, of course. So far as I know, horses and donkeys are made the same way. We always like to feel solid ground under our feet. And when it's not there, I have a disagreeable sensation. My soul feels faint and my body resists; it doesn't trust things that sit on the water or hang in the air.

When we came to the river, a peasant with a heavily packed donkey and two other men were already standing there. One of the men was a hunter with a dog. But this dog didn't bother me, because hunting dogs are rather wise creatures: they don't bark much and they don't bite at all.

I was somewhat relieved to find the donkey with the pack standing on the bank. Somehow it's always easier when you don't have to climb up on the ferry alone. My throat had gone dry from agitation, and I leaned toward the water for a drink. My old man slackened the reins, and I purposely moved a little farther away from the people waiting for the ferry. I was afraid my old man would take advantage of his last chance to talk to someone on this shore and start wagging his tongue about the kolkhoz. What if one of them was an informer from the other side and was only pretending that he was about to cross over? In order to keep my old man distracted, I drank a long, long time from the cold, turbid water of the Kodor. When the donkey saw me drink, he remembered that he felt like drinking too, and leaned toward the water. But his master didn't let him. I understood that the donkey was nervous, like me, but his stupid master didn't.

Meanwhile, the ferry was already drawing near from the other side of the river. By the way, no matter how hard I strain my mind, and thank God I do have a mind to strain, I cannot understand what force moves the ferry across the river. The water is pushing it downstream, after all, but it goes against the current. This is a very amazing mystery, in my opinion. I don't think people understand why the ferry moves against the current either, but they pretend that they've always known. And another thing I've noticed—in the middle of the river, where the current pushes it hardest of all, that's right where it moves fastest against the current.

The ferry kept getting nearer and nearer, and the fact that we would have to cross on it was not the only thing that upset me. I was also worrying about who would get on the ferry first, me or the donkey. I didn't want to go first, of course. In all fairness, since the donkey got here first, he should get on the ferry first.

What I feared most of all was whether the little dock that led from the bank out to the ferry would hold. I'm heavier than a donkey, of course. But with his pack the donkey would be about two hundred pounds heavier than me. I decided that if the dock would hold the donkey and his pack, then it would hold me too.

I was disturbed about something else, too. I noticed that one board in the dock had cracked, right where a nail had been driven into the joist. So the nail wouldn't hold it at all on one side. While someone was crossing onto the ferry this board could perfectly well slip off the joist, and then the donkey or I would be sure to break a leg. Oddly enough, here were all these men standing waiting for the ferry, and not one of them paid any attention to this. In the end, of course, it was my sharp-eyed old man who, as always, noticed something amiss. My old man got down off me, took a good big stone, moved the cracked board aside, pulled the nail out of the joist, straightened it, put the board in place, and, where he found solid wood, hit the nail right on the head.

But now came the grating sound of the iron rope on the special little wheel, sliding along the other iron rope stretched over the river, and the side of the ferry bumped against the dock. There were about eight people on it and not one animal, so that it wasn't clear whether the dock would hold me or not.

As I hoped, the donkey was sent first. But the donkey's master upset all my calculations. First he took both sacks off the donkey and dragged them onto the ferry. The dock sagged slightly under him, but it held. Unfortunately, he dragged the sacks across one at a time. If he had dragged both sacks across at once, I would have been less worried. After all, a solid well-fed mule like me weighs much more than a man with one sack.

After dragging the sacks across, the man took his donkey by the bridle and started to pull him onto the dock. The donkey dug his heels in as hard as he could, he wanted very badly not to go. But you have to go anyway, there's nowhere to hide. His master pulled him stubbornly, and the hunter also fetched him a few blows with the butt of his rifle. At last the poor thing stepped warily up on the dock and then jumped onto the ferry.

Now it was my turn. I plucked up all my courage. When my old man got up on the dock and lightly pulled the reins, I set my foot on the board. Without waiting for any stray hunter to hit me from behind with his rifle butt, I stepped up on the dock and quietly jumped onto the ferry. Everyone began praising me for my intelligence and daring. That was nice to hear, of course. Well, nature herself gave me intelligence, I don't deserve any special credit for that, but in order to behave bravely, I did have to harness all my willpower.

The ferryman pushed off with the boat hook, and slowly, then faster and faster, our old tub started for the other bank. I stood in the bottom of the ferry, trying not to stir and not to shift my weight, lest the boards of the bottom break under me. My old man paid the ferryman, somehow we made it to the bank and went on.

We came to the village of Anastasovka. At the village soviet stood an iron cart called a bus. Many people use it to ride to the city and back. Before, I couldn't understand at all what force moved these buses. But then I guessed. Once my old man and I were passing through the village of Dzhgerdy. There I saw a bus standing on the street by a brook. Its master took a pailful of water from the brook and poured it into the bus. Then he got in and drove on. I realized that these machines move on water power, like a mill wheel.

When we passed the bus, my old man glanced at it and said, "You'll have a lot of iron, but then where will you get meat, I'd like to know."

That's a sore point with my old man. He used to be the best stockbreeder in

Chegem. He still has some livestock, but he used to have a great deal. In his best days, the Chegemians say, my old man had so many goats and sheep that when they were being driven to summer pastures, the ones in the lead were already three kilometers up the Chegem crest while the ones in the rear were still stamping in the pen. That's how much livestock he had.

And after all, he began with one single goat. No one was living in Chegem then. He was the first to arrive; he sampled the local water and liked it so much that he decided to settle here.

At that time he had just returned from Turkey, where many Abkhazians had been driven, some by force, some by trickery. He had nothing. Only a young wife, one child, and the goat. A relative had lent it to him so that he would be able to give the child milk to drink.

In his very first year on the rich Chegem soil, he reaped such a harvest of corn that he was able to buy a small flock of sheep and goats. And after twenty years of unrelenting labor my old man had it all—children, a farm, and a huge pen of stock. His was a house of plenty, and guests used to fill the yard, so that his wife and five daughters could hardly take care of them. There was so much milk that they didn't have time to make it into cheese and poured it out for the dogs.

Yes, he did keep shepherds! And what of it? For three years' work a shepherd received thirty goats, after which he could leave and start his own farm. With you people, a man who works on a kolkhoz for three years won't earn even three goats. That's the truth!

Sometimes I see my master as a young man, when he's just taken a sip from the icy cup of the Chegem spring, wiping his mouth with his hand and deciding: Here's where I'll live! That's how he stands before me: not too tall, broad-shouldered, hooknosed, stubborn, with a mighty, indomitable dream in his eyes.

And now what? Now they don't have as much stock in the whole kolkhoz as he alone had then. Big talk, but they've thrown it all to the winds! That's what hurts my old man. Sometimes now there's such sorrow on my old man's face that my heart bursts with pity for him. The sorrow on his face means: The peasant way of life has ended. Nevertheless, he sometimes hopes that these madmen will come to their senses, and every peasant will begin to live on his own again.

We continued to walk along the road. I kept glancing to either side, wherever I saw green little yards, in hopes of spotting a colt. There were calves, pigs, chickens, and turkeys grazing in the yards, but not a colt to be seen.

Mark my words. If things keep on this way with colts, Abkhazia will be left without horses. Or do they plan to import them ready-made from Russia? Somehow I can't believe it. Besides, the cumbersome Russian horses are no good on our mountains. Nevertheless, I have hope that somewhere on a long trip like this we'll come across a little colt.

Suddenly a horseman came out of a side road onto the street. He stopped and inspected us, shading his eyes with his hand, as if trying to figure out who we were, though I could swear by all the colts I've loved in my life that he recognized us immediately. It was the well-known horse lover from the village of Ankhara, known by the nickname Bad Hand.

My old man drew even with him, they said hello and rode on side by side. I expected no good from Bad Hand, and I was right.

"What's your kumkhoz reduced you to," Bad Hand shouted, though we were only two feet away and my old man, thank God, has excellent hearing, "that you've started riding around on a mule."

He said that on purpose, though he knows perfectly well that my old man always rides a mule.

"Even before the kumkhoz I sat on a mule," my old man replied calmly, "and, God willing, I'll be sitting on my mule after the kumkhoz."

"I know, I know," Bad Hand laughed. "I was just kidding."

"That's a nice-riding horse," my old man blurted suddenly, for no reason at all.

"Of course," Bad Hand replied boastfully. "I still know a good horse when I see one; they haven't driven me that crazy."

As soon as I heard my old man's remark about that horse, I felt my gorge rise. What's good about him, I ask! Keeps twisting his head, keeps trying to trot off to the side somewhere, as if from an excess of energy and impatience. That's an outright sham and deception! Let him walk from Chegem to Mukhus like me, stand there starving all night, and come back the next day. Then you'd see whether he'd trot sideways from impatience or sway like a scarecrow in the wind!

It's a bitter pill. If you behave like a reliable wise mule and don't worry your master with jerking and twisting, they figure you don't have much mettle. But there's nothing you can do, that's the way the world is set up—wisdom is always doomed to be thankless.

"Well, and how are things with you at the kumkhoz?" my old man asked. "They aren't planting eucalyptuses yet?"

"No," Bad Hand said. "What's a eucalyptus?"

"It's some kind of tree from overseas," my old man replied. "They're planting them everywhere now to scare away mosquitoes."

"Why scare away mosquitoes?" Bad Hand asked in surprise. "They'd do better to scare off the flies, my horse is getting bitten to death."

"They figure mosquitoes cause malaria," my old man said, "although anybody knows malaria is caused by a damp fog. In low-lying villages, where there's a damp fog, that's where people get malaria. We have lots of mosquitoes in the mountains too, and no one gets malaria. They can't comprehend a simple thing like that, and they're taking it on themselves to turn our whole life upside down."

"Even a child can see that," Bad Hand agreed. "No, we're not planting eucalyptuses yet. We've gone crazy over tea. They're raising tea everywhere."

"Tea?" my old man asked in surprise. "Our fathers and grandfathers never drank tea in their lives. The Russians drink tea. Let them raise it themselves."

"They say the Russians don't have any soil that's good for tea," Bad Hand replied, "so they decided to use our soil for tea."

"Where did they get it before?" my old man asked. "After all, the Russians can't live even a day without tea."

"Don't you know?" Bad Hand replied. "They bought it from the Chinese."

"So have the Chinese died out, or what?" my old man asked.

"No, the Chinese haven't died out," Bad Hand replied, "but that's another story. That's all right, I'll tell it to you, because you're a man devoted to our people, even if you do ride a mule."

Again Bad Hand tried to wound me. But my old man wasn't at all put off.

"By all means," he said. "Tell it, and we'll while away the road listening to you."

"Well, so the Chinese haven't died out," Bad Hand repeated. "The whole world will die out before the Chinese do, they're so hardy. But the Chinese czar informed our Big Mustache that he wouldn't give the Russians any more tea to drink because they killed Czar Nicholas along with his wife and children."

"What's the matter with the Chinese czar," my old man asked in surprise, "did he just wake up? The Russian czar was killed ages and ages ago."

"What, don't you know the evil wiles of the Big Mustache? He had the Chinese czar fooled the whole time. He told him the Russian czar and his family were living with him in the Kremlin and receiving a people's commissar's pension. Sometimes he lives at the Kremlin, sometimes at a health resort. And he doesn't live anywhere else.

"But then the English butted in. They told the Chinese czar, 'What, don't you see that Stalin is deceiving you? Send an agent to Russia, and if the Russian czar is alive, let them show him to the agent.'

"Then the Chinese czar wrote the Big Mustache that he was sending him an agent. And if the agent saw Czar Nicholas alive, then he, the Chinese czar, would send tea to the Russians again—let them drink it till they burst.

" 'All right,' the Big Mustache replied to the Chinese czar, 'send an agent, though I'm hurt that you don't believe me.'

"So a Chinese agent arrives and they lead him to the Kremlin, where Czar Nicholas's house supposedly stands next to the Big Mustache's house. And Nicholas supposedly tells the Big Mustache how the former authorities governed people, and the Big Mustache tells him how the present authorities govern people. And supposedly they've gotten to be such good friends that their children play together and run around in the Kremlin day in and day out. They keep getting mixed up themselves where whose child is. Things have gotten to the point that when the Big Mustache is in a good mood, he calls over his child to give him candy; and the child turns around and turns out to be Czar Nicholas's son. But he gives him the candy anyway.

" 'Come here,' the Big Mustache says to him, 'don't be afraid, it's not poisoned.'

"That's how close-knit they've gotten to be. So they bring this Chinaman into a house in the Kremlin and point out a man who's the spitting image of Czar Nicholas. And next to him, supposedly, sit his wife and children.

"The Chinaman looks at them a long time and they look at him. And the Big Mustache's aides wait to hear what the Chinaman will say.

" 'You're Czar Nicholas?' the Chinaman asks this man.

" 'Yes, I'm Czar Nicholas,' the man answers, brightly enough.

" 'And this is your wife?' the Chinaman asks, pointing to the woman.

" 'Yes,' the man answers, just as brightly, 'she is indeed my wife.'

" 'And these are your children?' the Chinaman asks, and for some reason he stares at the children.

" 'Yes,' the man answers confidently, 'these are my children.'

" 'You know for sure that these are your children?' the Chinaman asks again, and again he stares at the children.

" 'What, don't I know my own children?' the man who's the spitting image of Czar Nicholas says, offended.

"Then the Chinaman looks at the Big Mustache's aides and says, 'The fact that Czar Nicholas hasn't aged in fifteen years you might explain by saying that Stalin has set him up in a good life. But how do you explain the fact that in fifteen years the czar's children haven't grown up?'

"The Big Mustache's aides were flustered, they turned red, turned white, didn't know what to say. Now they caught on that in their hurry they'd made a blunder, they'd forgotten that children grow; but it was too late—the damage was done.

" 'We're surprised ourselves,' they say. 'We feed them, water them, but for some reason they don't grow.'

" 'It seems that the czar's children,' says the Chinaman, 'don't grow under Soviet authority?'

" 'So it seems,' the Big Mustache's aides agree.

" 'It seems they've turned into Lilliputians?'

" 'So it seems,' the Big Mustache's aides affirm.

" 'No,' says the Chinaman, 'it does not. You are bad. You are swindlers. You killed Czar Nicholas and his children.'

" 'How can that be,' the Big Mustache's aides say indignantly. 'We don't understand. Then explain to us, who is that man, and those children?'

" 'That's not the czar,' says the Chinaman, 'that's a Chekist in disguise. And those aren't the czar's children, they're the Chekist's children.'

"Then the Big Mustache's aides tell the Chinaman, 'Well, all right. Maybe there's been a mistake. You sit in the next room for a while, and we'll consult on what to do.'

"They led the Chinaman into the next room and began to consult among themselves. And here's what they decided. They decided to give the Chinaman a thousand of Nicholas's gold ten-ruble notes so that he would tell his czar that he had seen the real Czar Nicholas. And they went into the room where the Chinaman was sitting and told him about this.

" 'You are fools,' the Chinaman told them. 'Even to this day you don't know that Chinamen don't take bribes.' "

At this point my old man interrupted Bad Hand. "They really don't?"

"No," Bad Hand said. "It seems that Chinamen don't take bribes."

"How do they get things done?" my old man asked in surprise.

"No one can understand it," Bad Hand replied. "It's just the way they are, the Chinese. Stubborn!"

"Well, what happened next?" my old man asked.

"Here's what happened next. The Big Mustache's aides went out again and began consulting among themselves. Now, I don't know whether they called up the Big Mustache or just decided on their own. The man who told me the story didn't know about that himself, and I don't want to add anything. So then they went to the Chinaman in the room and said, 'If you won't tell the Chinese czar that you've seen the real Russian czar, we'll kill you. And we'll send our own Soviet Chinaman to your czar, and he'll tell him anything we want. And the Chinese czar will believe him, because all Chinamen look alike.'

" 'It won't work,' the Chinaman answers with a smile, 'because my wise Chinese czar foresaw it all. When he sent me to you, he told me a secret word, which I must repeat when I get back to the palace. And no torture can force me to tell you this word. Therefore my czar will expose your false Chinaman.'

"The Big Mustache's aides were very depressed to hear that, and they had to tell their master all about it. The Big Mustache went into an incredible rage, but there was nothing he could do. Because he couldn't kill the Chinese agent—that would lead to war with China. And he couldn't have a war, because it turns out there are even more Chinese than Russians."

"Are there really more of them than Russians?" my old man marveled.

"Yes," Bad Hand said confidently. "The Russians themselves admit this."

"But what do they live on?" my old man said.

"They use everything," Bad Hand said. "Beetles, spiders, worms. They eat everything. Doesn't matter, they wash it all down with tea."

"So how did the story of the Chinaman come out?" my old man asked.

"Here's how it came out," Bad Hand replied. "The Big Mustache called this Chinese agent and told him, 'My country is large, and you don't always know at one end of it what's going on at the other. And my aides are foolish, whatever you tell them they get it all mixed up. I told them, "Protect the czar and his family," and they got it all mixed up and shot them.'

" 'They showed me a false czar,' the Chinaman said.

" 'Don't worry about the false czar,' the Big Mustache told him, 'I'll order him to be shot along with his false wife. You can tell your czar.'

" 'That's good,' the Chinaman said, 'but my czar won't give the Russians any more tea to drink, because he will grieve for the Russian czar and his family.'

"With that the Chinese agent went away. Ever since then the Big Mustache has decided to raise tea on our soil so as not to be dependent on the Chinese any more."

"That's all politics," my old man said.

"Yes, yes—politics," Bad Hand agreed.

At that, Bad Hand went to turn off on a side road and was very surprised that we weren't turning there.

"What, aren't you going?" Bad Hand asked.

"I'm going to the city," my old man replied. "Where are you going?"

"I'm going to Karaman's wake," Bad Hand replied. "I thought you were going there too."

"What, evil-ass Karaman died?" my old man asked in surprise. *Evil-ass* is our Abkhazian term for lascivious people.

"Yes, he died," Bad Hand replied, "and he died because of his evil ass."

"Probably took one last Russian girl into his house?" my old man said.

"Exactly," Bad Hand replied. "He died right on top of her."

"How would you know?" my old man asked in surprise. "She didn't tell?"

"No," Bad Hand replied, "she just ran to the sons at night and said their father had died. The sons live next door. They came into the house and saw their father lying face down on the bed in such a way that it was clear what he'd been doing in his last moments."

"Pah!" My old man spat. "To die face down like a mad dog killed by a bullet! It may be all right among other peoples to die face down, but not among us. A true Abkhazian old man never dies lying face down. A true Abkhazian old man dies lying on his back, in a clean shirt, surrounded by his loved ones. That man lived like a dog and died like a dog. Why didn't the messengers of woe inform me?"

"They must not have had time," Bad Hand replied. "He's not being buried till the day after tomorrow."

"I'll mourn him anyway," my old man decided, "even though he was a bad man."

My old man turned me onto the cart-track, and we started for this Karaman's house. I didn't like this business at all. If my old man was going to keep stopping the whole way, we'd never get to the city.

"Let me tell you, Bad Hand," my old man continued, "after seventy a man ought to forget about women. Very wise men forget even sooner. After seventy a man is considered old by our standards. And an old man ought to observe cleanliness. He oughtn't to dirty his bed with a woman. An old man's business is to watch over the honor of the family, the honor of the clan, the honor of the village, and the honor of his tribe. Especially in our day, when dishonor hangs over our house and plagues us with the threat of shame. Among the lowland Abkhazians, they say, informers have already appeared who tell the authorities what we say in our home, in our field, in our assembly. What's happened to Abkhazian men, I ask you, why aren't they out following our glorious ancient custom, cutting off the informers' ears and tongues?"

"O-ho-ho," Bad Hand said, "there'd be too many left without tongue and ears. But, Khabug, you're saying that after seventy a man dirties his bed with a woman. After all, now, everything depends on nature. Sometimes it's just in his old age that a man becomes especially evil-assed. What's he supposed to do if he can't stand it?"

"Fiddlesticks!" my old man said, and he spat again. "Let him take an ax or a hoe in his hand and he'll forget about women soon enough. Some old men's brains go to rot, their blood doesn't move in their bodies right, and it gets stuck in the groin, and the old fool thinks his youth has come back.

"And besides—it's a sin. A sin to pour an old man's soured seed into a woman, a sin against the future child. If a sickly stalk of corn grows from bad seed in the field, you cut it down with the hoe. But you can't kill a child. Incidentally did they have any, or not?"

"A son, they say," Bad Hand replied, "but I haven't seen him myself. He picked up this young woman five years ago, when they had the famine in Kuban and people were pouring out of there to escape starvation. That was when he lured her into his house for a couple of tomatoes and a piece of *churek*. Later on, when she was fattened up and cleaned up, he took such a fancy to her that he made her his wife. His sons tried to shame him and dissuade him from the marriage. They even threatened him, they said she was a woman without a clan, without a tribe, she might poison him to get her hands on the farm. As if anyone could stop evil-ass Karaman! 'Shut up, you bastards,' he told them, 'I've buried three wives, and I'll bury this one!'

"Far from it. This Russian woman, as soon as she put on some weight, turned out to be such an evil-ass herself that she buried him instead. He lasted five years, and now he's turned up his toes."

"Lived like an animal and died like an animal," my old man said.

It's a surprising thing. My old man scorns this Karaman, but still he goes to his wake. That's how he is. He has a great respect for custom. But, thank God, this Karaman's house turned out to be nearby. We soon came to it. The gate was wide open, and a great many people were crowded into the yard. The coffin with the deceased stood near the house under a small canopy. His nearest female relatives and the women hired to mourn him peered out from the far side of the coffin. On the right stood a pavilion shaded by a huge tarpaulin. The funeral supper was being set up there, for people who came to mourn the deceased.

We were met by a young fellow, evidently one of this Karaman's sons. He led us to the hitching rack. My old man and Bad Hand dismounted. The fellow wanted to take the reins from my old man, but my old man didn't give them to him; he took the bit from my mouth and fastened the reins to the saddle, saying, "Let my mule graze a bit. I have a long way to go."

"All right," the fellow said. He tied Bad Hand's horse and led him and my old man to the wake.

Near the coffin stood a little table, on which people were leaving their caps, fur hats, and turbans. My old man and Bad Hand laid their caps on the table and stood near it waiting their turn. Among our people it's the custom that you can't mourn the deceased wearing a cap—as if the deceased cared whether you wore a cap or not. But that's the custom, and everyone observes it.

After waiting for the man who was mourning at the coffin to be led aside, my old man moved toward the deceased, beating his brow with his hands. From behind him, a man specially appointed to this task kept a light, steadying grip on his side. As I understand it, the general idea of accompanying the mourner this way is to restrain him from excessively tumultuous and life-threatening manifestations of grief. Well, for example, so that he doesn't beat his head against the coffin. This is understandable, of course, when a good man dies and his loved ones are mourning him. But the odd thing is that there's a man to accompany every mourner to every deceased. Including such a disreputable deceased as this Karaman. And knowing all that my old man had said about him, wasn't it comical to suppose my old man might maim himself in a fit of despair at the sight of Karaman's body?

"Oh! Oh! Oh!" my old man groaned, continuing to beat his brow as he stood at the coffin. "Why have you left us, Karaman?"

The women, the deceased's relatives—their heads sticking up from behind the coffin—responded to my old man's words with a friendly sobbing, just as sincere, I think, as my old man's sobbing. No, my old man is not a deceiver. He had said what he thought of Karaman, and now he was merely fulfilling the ritual of mourning. That's the way he is—honors custom.

"You see, Karaman," the hired mourners said, sobbing, "old Khabug has come to bid you farewell, without even waiting for the messenger of woe."

"Oh! Oh! Oh! Poor Karaman," my old man repeated rather foolishly, evidently unable to come up with anything else, "why have you left us?"

You don't know why he left us? Have you forgotten that he turned up his toes because of his evil ass?

My old man cried for about a minute, without bruising himself too badly, and then was led over to his cap by the man who had been assigned to him. From there, after jamming the cap on his head, he briskly set off for the funeral pavilion to drink his several glasses and have a bite to eat.

I was afraid. What if he went and turned over his glass to show what would happen to the kolkhoz, forgetting that we were already on this side of the Kodor?

I was eating grass, of course, taking advantage of the fact that they hadn't tied me. A dozen horses standing at the hitching rack looked askance at me, dying of envy. Not a one of them was allowed to graze freely in this corner of the yard. My old man trusts me, and for good reason. I, after all, in contrast to certain stupid horses, won't go wandering around among the people or walk out the gate. I'll graze here, nibbling at every clump of grass, until my old man comes for me.

While I was eating grass, a big house dog walked right by me, but I didn't bother to watch him, because when there are a lot of people and animals gathered in a yard, dogs lose heart and can't bring themselves to bark or to bite either. I myself am never muddled by swarms of people. But on the other hand, I have no such stupid obligation as to bark at living creatures. My duties are much more complex and honorable, thank God.

A white-haired little boy about four years old appeared beside me with a big piece of *khachapuri* in his hand. I surmised that this was Karaman's son by the Russian girl. Abkhazian children don't have white hair like that. The Russian's blood must have been stronger than Karaman's, because the little boy favored her.

A girl of about twelve, obviously one of ours, was looking after the little boy. I realized that this was probably Karaman's granddaughter looking after his son. Isn't that comical? It turns out the granddaughter is three times as old as the son. Let me tell you, there isn't one single animal that can muddle the laws of nature like man. This funny little boy watched long and hard while I ate grass. Evidently it was the first time he'd seen a mule. But why feast your eyes on a mule, white-haired little Russian, I thought, when you're a little mule yourself? After all, you're the son of an Abkhazian jackass and a Russian filly. That makes you a little mule.

The child continued to watch me in silence. And then—he must have liked me a lot—he came up to me and held out his piece of *khachapuri*. I didn't spurn him, I carefully took the piece from his hand and ate it up. It turned out to be delicious, and I was grateful to the little boy from the bottom of my heart. I had seen *khachapuri* before, but never tried it. Who would have guessed that I'd sample Abkhazian cheese bread for the first time in evil-ass Karaman's yard from the hands of a Russian boy. As they say, you never know where you'll find, where you'll lose.

By the way, I scrutinized the boy attentively after that and didn't notice any sickliness or deformity. Just a little boy, only his little head was white. Either my old man got too worked up about an old man's seed turning sour, or the effect will show up later. Let's hope my old man was wrong this time. I should mention that I didn't spot the little boy's mother anywhere. I suppose Karaman's sons, ashamed because of her youth, had hidden her somewhere for the duration of the wake and the funeral.

Finally, his spirits greatly improved by funeral libations, my old man came over, freed the reins, and clambered up on me. We went out the gate. People were still arriving, and from the funeral pavilion came the clamor of excited voices, loud to the point of indecency, to our way of thinking. I don't know, maybe among other peoples it's common practice to sing and dance at a funeral supper, but not here. Our folks drink the funeral glass in silence, listening to words of wisdom from the one who has been called upon to speak. But these people were shouting their heads off. On the other hand, come to think of it, did this dirty old man really deserve a respectful funeral supper?

We went back over the cart-track, came out to the street, and started on. We walked along the street for a long time. Several times buses and trucks came toward us, and some passed us from behind, covering us with clouds of dust. I kept looking from side to side, trying to spy out a colt in the street or in a yard somewhere. But no colts turned up. Grazing along the street there were donkeys, pigs in great numbers, sometimes cows and buffaloes, but no colts.

Several times men on horseback came toward us, and to my great satisfaction not one of them proved to be an acquaintance of my old man's, and he didn't stop me once. There could be no question of any horseman passing us from behind; I'd never allow it. My old man loves me not only for my smooth gait but also for my very brisk pace. Well, of course, if someone starts off at a gallop, he'll leave us behind. But that doesn't count. A saddle animal is valued for a brisk and smooth pace. But running—that's a pastime for people, and a rather vulgar one at that. I've seen races, I've been to them with my old man. Crazy young people, they rush around in a circle on their horses. Wildness, that's all it is.

We passed through a village called Estonka. A nationality called Estonians lives here, and no one really knows who they are. But they live quietly, don't bother our folks. In general, there's not much to say about them.

One thing you can say, they raise enormous cows that give twenty liters of milk a day. But our Abkhazians have no use for such cows. An Abkhazian finds it disagreeable to fuss with a cow like that. She humiliates him with her dependency. These Estonian cows can't walk on the mountains and don't feed themselves. You're always having to feed them, wash them, keep them in a clean dry place.

No, our folks have no use for such cows. The Abkhazian takes a completely different approach. Let's say one Estonian cow gives twenty liters of milk and an Abkhazian cow, let's say, two liters—although in actual fact she may give as much as four. But let's figure two, it will show more clearly the folly of the other concept of profit. The Estonian has twenty liters from one cow, and the Abkhazian keeps ten cows and has the same twenty liters. The Estonian fusses around with his cow the whole day long, and all the Abkhazian has to do is open the barnyard gate and let them out in the morning and let them in again when they come back at night.

So which is more profitable—to spend all day fussing with one cow and have twenty liters, or to get the same milk from ten cows and not have to fuss with them at all? And now let's take the question of meat. Clearly, slaughtering a calf is easier for someone who has ten cows than for someone who has one.

But now the kolkhoz has arrived, and Abkhazians aren't allowed to keep more than three cows. Well, our folks can be pretty wily, of course, out where they live a little farther from the authorities. But no matter how wily you are, the authorities will outwit you all the same; that's why they're the authorities. Nobody can understand who's bothered by the cattle, why folks aren't allowed to raise them. After all, anybody can see that the more cattle the peasants have, the more meat ends up in the city. They're the ones who profit, but for some reason they don't understand this. That's why my old man says, "You'll have a lot of iron, and then where will you get meat, I'd like to know."

It was getting hot. The sun was up toward the middle of the sky. I knew this without even raising my head because my shadow tramped along underneath me. In one place, by a big, spreading blackberry patch, my old man dismounted and went behind the bush. I realized that the wine had gone through him and he needed to make water. I made water too, taking advantage of the fact that he had walked away. For some reason he doesn't usually like me to make water as we go along. So I try to hold it when we're walking, if it isn't killing me. He doesn't like me to relieve myself of dung as we go along, either, but for another reason altogether.

The thing is that people value our dung very highly. No, not just mule dung, though mules of course have better dung, but other animals' too. For people, it's practically gold. The earth grows rich from our dung and transmits its richness to the plants of the fields and vegetable gardens. The peasants would be happy if we relieved ourselves of dung only at night, in the barnyard. But then, you can't always manage it so that you only need to go in the barnyard, though we do leave quite a bit of loot for them there too.

In one place a loathsome little dog jumped out of a gate and ran after me for a long time, barking shrilly. She badly wanted to bite my left hind leg, but she couldn't make up her mind either to bite or to drop back, the base creature. Of course I could have flung her aside with one blow of my hoof, but that would have meant admitting that she was driving me out of my wits. And that would have been degrading for such a reliable mule, carrying such a rider as my old man.

It took all I had to keep my temper until the wretched dog dropped back. I could feel my nerves straining and my heart pounding. It just goes to show how a no-account creature can discombobulate you. When a real dog, a big one, goes after you, it may be disagreeable but it's a battle. But this is a no-win situation. She comes too close—I'll clobber her with my hoof. She knows it and I know it. She nags, nags, nags, and it's degrading to deal with her and impossible to put up with her.

The Lord God must have decided to reward me for my sufferings. We'd hardly gone a hundred paces from the little dog when out of a side road came a wagon harnessed to a mare, and beside her ran a colt of blinding beauty. He was white as a cloud, with long flailing legs and a marvelous mane, which I had an urge to nibble and tousle—not so as to hurt, of course.

The wagon turned onto the road ahead of us, and I discreetly quickened my pace so that I could keep near the colt. I tried to be discreet about it so that my old man wouldn't suspect anything. He knows about my passion for colts, of course, but I try not to call it to his attention. He's probably hurt to think that I love anyone else besides him. Doesn't the old nut understand that this is a different kind of love? I take pride in my old man, but I experience an insane rush of tenderness for colts. I am bathed in delight when my eyes look upon them, and my nostrils filter out all other smells, carrying their fragrance to the very bottom of my soul.

This wondrous, this amusing, colt now walked next to his mother, now lagged behind to sniff something unfamiliar on the road. Then, suddenly recollecting himself and bucking at a nonexistent enemy, he would run ahead, his tail streaming, and outstrip the wagon.

One time when he ran ahead of the wagon there was a flock of geese crossing the street. The colt stopped dead in astonishment when he saw them. It must have been the first time he had seen geese. One goose passed quite near him and he bent his head, wanting to examine her more closely, perhaps even sniff what she smelled of. The little fool—what he didn't know was that a goose can't smell of anything good. There was one gander who was greatly displeased that the colt bent down to the goose. Stretching its neck like a snake, the gander charged at the colt. The poor thing took such a fright that he leapt up with all four feet off the ground, and then turned and bolted for his mother. Well, what were you so scared of, silly dope!

When he fled from the gander, the colt ran up to his mother on the side toward us, so that I saw him close up now, and the smell of him simply enveloped me. Whether out of fright or for some other reason, he began nuzzling at the mare's teats. He couldn't quite catch them in his lips—he was too upset, probably, or else the wagon was in his way—though he tried very hard, craning his long neck. The mare, of course, was hard pressed to give him the teats (I don't blame her at all), she kept trying not to kick his little muzzle, and he kept nuzzling. In the end she stumbled. At that point the man sitting in the wagon barked, "Go to hell!"

With that, he lashed the colt as hard as he could with his whip! I saw with my own eyes the fine little stripe, the trace of the whip on the colt's tender back. He yelped with pain and sprang ahead. The distraught mare also broke into a gallop. And I was so angry I lost my head and took off after them to bite and trample that flayflint.

"What are you, gone berserk?" my old man shouted, and he fetched me a blow on the back with his whip.

I didn't feel the pain, but I recollected myself, and I was suddenly ashamed that I had lost my head. I could never have gotten my teeth into the bastard anyway.

"You old mule," my old man muttered, "are you going to run after colts till the day you die?"

I felt the blood rush to my head from shame. I was ashamed of my passion; but then, I don't ask anything of these colts. Only to admire them, only to catch their smell. If that flayflint hadn't struck the colt with his whip, my old man would never have suspected that I had my eye on someone in secret delight.

In a cloud of dust up ahead, the wagon turned off on a side road again, and I caught one last glimpse of the little white colt. I sighed and looked away. No, of course such passion was unbecoming at my age. A mule of my age—and, I make bold to add, of my intellect—must of course behave more reliably. I promised myself to oblige my old man by never looking at another colt again, even if any turned up in our path. If I have the strength, that is. Anyhow, I'll try.

The way I took off after that bastard on an angry impulse reminded me of another impulse I had once. In contrast to this one, thoughtless but kind, that was one of wild fear, which led me to the blackest days of my life.

On that fine fall day, my old man and I were returning from the mill. Out of love and respect for my wisdom, my old man never used me as a pack animal. So the donkey was tromping ahead of us packing the sacks of meal; my old man rode on me and drove the donkey from behind.

We had already made the very exhausting climb up from Napskal and were walking along a level path, passing through the chestnut grove. Now and then, by bending my head, I managed to grab a chestnut or two. I tried to do it without slowing down, in order not to irritate my old man. It was partly because of those chestnuts that the whole thing happened. Because of them and because of the donkey, though I don't mean to put the blame on anyone but myself.

The donkey was walking ahead, and he picked up the best chestnuts and the ones lying nearest to the path. As a matter of fact, he picked up almost all the chestnuts, and only an occasional one was left for me. That provoked me to an ugly fever of envy. I forgot myself, all I could think of was not to miss any chestnuts.

Suddenly, off to our left, I heard a loud crack in the blueberry bushes. For some reason I instantly decided it was a bear. Bears are very fond of blueberries. Terrified, I started down the path at breakneck speed. My old man was so surprised he let out a yell and fell right off me. At this I completely lost my head and ran and ran and ran. I ran about a kilometer before I finally recollected myself and stopped. Only then did I realize what I'd done.

Remembering what had happened, I shuddered with shame, repentance, and disgrace. A bear? What bear! How could I have seen a bear! Old numskull that I am, how could I forget that there weren't any berries at this time of year, and the bear had no business in the blueberry bushes. Maybe someone's cow had gone astray; at the worst, a roebuck had snapped the branch. But I had run, throwing my old man. Dreadful! Dreadful! And the final searing humiliation was that it had all happened within sight of the donkey, who had not succumbed to fear and had not run away.

I started back in a very black frame of mind, not knowing what had happened to my old man. I decided that if I found my old man dead, I would throw myself off a cliff and smash myself. Right nearby was the Napskal downgrade and a precipice about a hundred meters high. But if he was still alive, I thought, let him beat me with a stick for three days, let me never lay eyes on a colt for the rest of my life.

When I got back I saw my old man sitting on the ground, and the donkey

(Shame! Shame! He saw it all!) calmly strolling around near him. Cautiously, so as not to stick himself on the prickly bolls, he was pulling out chestnuts that had not yet popped and eating them.

"Ah-h-h, you're back, wolfbait," my old man said when he saw me.

Hanging my head, I went over and stood beside him. He got up with great difficulty, and I realized that he had injured his leg. Cursing a blue streak, he somehow got up on me, drove the donkey back to the path, and we started for home. I felt horribly guilty before my old man and was ready to endure any retribution. It worried me that my old man hadn't hit me even once.

And now we were home. My old man stopped me right by the kitchen. Grunting, he slid down from me and shouted to the family, "Unsaddle this wolfbait!"

Limping badly, he went into the kitchen. They took the sacks off the donkey, unsaddled him, and then unsaddled me too. They turned us loose to graze in the yard, but I could hardly swallow, the grass stuck in my throat, and I just ate it out of habit.

The next morning they let the donkey out of the yard and he went with the other animals to graze in Sabid's Hollow, but they left me in the yard. I sensed that this was a sign of some punishment to come, but what it would be I did not know. This made me very miserable. If my old man had beaten me, or shut me in the barn with nothing to eat, I wouldn't have been so miserable.

I spent three days mooning around the yard in complete ignorance. My old man didn't come near me. Only his grandchildren, a little boy and girl, the children of his son Kyazym, tried to comfort me sometimes. But I was in such a bad mood that there was no way I could respond to their kindness and affection.

On the fourth day an acquaintance of my old man's rode into our yard on an ugly mare. He lived in a completely different village. I was gripped with a most ominous premonition. I vividly recalled the acquaintance encountering my old man last year and asking him to sell me. At the time, of course, my old man had refused outright.

And now, for some reason, this very man had come to see us. He dismounted, tied his horse, and he and my old man went into the kitchen. Nevertheless, I still had a sliver of hope that the man had arrived by chance. I hadn't heard my old man send anyone to fetch him. They stayed in the kitchen a long time, and the uncertainty made me violently nervous.

But now they came out of the kitchen and started over to me, and my heart stood still. They came up and stopped beside me. My old man said that I was a magnificent mule in all respects. My gait was even and fast, and my endurance was beyond all praise. And he said that he was selling me only because he was very angry at me for throwing him on the way home from the mill.

Bitter as it was for me to hear this, I couldn't help marveling at his pride. He could easily have hidden the fact that I'd thrown him, but he didn't want to. Proud. It was his damn pride that made him decide to sell me, I think: how could it happen that he fell off his mule, and within sight of a donkey at that.

Maybe if the rotten donkey hadn't been there he wouldn't have given me such a terrible punishment.

I don't know how much they settled on, but my old man sold me. They tied a rope around my neck, the man took the end of it and mounted his mare.

The whole family came out to see me off, and the old woman, my old man's wife, who had fed me my corn so many times, lamented over me as she would over a dead man: "Poor Blackamoor, poor Blackamoor."

The wife of Kyazym, my old man's son, said, "Poor Blackamoor, can it be that we'll never see you again?"

Her children, sweet children, hugged me, kissed me, and cried. Only my old man didn't look at me, and I tried not to look in his direction, because my heart was breaking with grief and hurt.

They opened the gate for my new master, and he rode out on his mare, leading me behind him on the rope. It took us a long time to walk to his house. I knew there would never be any happiness in my life again. But a living creature, as long as it lives, whether it's a man or an animal, seeks some sort of comfort. As I walked behind this jolty, low-rumped mare, I was thinking she might have a colt at home. And that colt, I thought, would be the last consolation of my sorrowful fate.

Ten hours later we entered my new master's yard. He untied the rope from my neck and turned me loose to graze. I took a quick look around the yard. There were lots of chickens, a pair of grazing calves, but no colt. I secretly watched the mare to see whether she was looking around for anyone, but the mare wasn't looking for anyone, and it was unclear whether she had a colt or not. But still I didn't lose hope. I thought the colt might be grazing in the pasture with the rest of the family's livestock.

They unsaddled the mare and turned her out to pasture. They left me in the yard. I grazed in the yard until evening, expecting that when the cattle returned home at dusk the colt would arrive along with his mother.

But dusk fell, the cows came to the barnyard gate and mooed, asking for the calves to be let out to them. The calves mooed back. Standing alongside the cows at the gate was the mare, without any colt, and my heart was consumed with anguish. Lord, whatever made me hope for such a thing! How could I have thought that any stallion would ever cover this droopy-rumped freak of a mare!

The next morning the mistress brought out some ears of corn and threw them in front of me on the dirty ground. Why, my old man's wife always brought my corn in a nice little pan. I ate the ears, of course, though I knew perfectly well that they weren't giving me this treat out of any great generosity. They were planning to send me out to graze with the local herd, so that at dusk I would remember the corn and come back to my new master's house.

Well, what of it, I wasn't planning to run away. Where can you run, if your master himself has renounced you. You can't run into the forest, to the bears. They turned me loose with the master's cattle and the mare, whose belly was incapable of producing anything but dung. We went out to the pasture and I looked around. There were about a dozen of the neighbors' cows here, about as many donkeys and horses, and not one colt.

A black cloud of despair settled over my soul. Outwardly I was alive, but inwardly I felt myself to be a corpse. After several days, the master saddled me, and we set out for the next village. Everything about him was disagreeable to me—his smell, and his weight, and his habit of coarsely tugging on the reins. I tried to walk as badly as possible. No matter how hard I tried, of course, no amount of wishing could make me walk worse than his mare.

Nevertheless, he was very surprised. Several times he got down from me, examined my hooves and pasterns, and simply couldn't understand what was the matter with me. He was very dissatisfied and kept muttering curses at my old man for having supposedly deceived him.

Five or six times he rode me to neighboring villages, and I tried to shake him up so badly that his spleen and his liver would trade places. The upshot was that he ceased to ride me and switched back to his droopy-rumped mare.

They used me now only for carrying sacks to the mill or to the bazaar in the city. My old man had used me only to ride on. Now the used me as a beast of burden, but it didn't humiliate me in the least. As I say, I was alive only outwardly, inwardly I was dead. And a dead mule has nothing to be ashamed of. Once I had lost my old man, nothing mattered to me any more.

People may ask me, "Well, wasn't there anything you liked in the new place?"

I answer, "Nothing!"

Neither the house nor the yard nor the master nor his wife nor the children nor the cattle nor the pasture. This low-lying village was deeply disgusting to me in itself, with its swarms of flies, its wretched swamps full of turtles, its everlasting nocturnal howl of jackals.

Once, at dawn, I jumped out of the barnyard over the wattle fence and completely trampled the corn in my master's private plot. I ate as many cornstalks as I could, and what I couldn't eat I trampled underfoot. I didn't care what they did to me. I even wanted them to beat me.

In the morning, of course, they discovered me in the corn. They raised a cry, the master drove me into the barn, put a strong rope on my neck, and tied it to the wall. Then he went out of the barn and brought back a mallet that they use to thresh corn. Gripping it in both hands, he began to beat me.

He beat me with all his might, he beat me grunting, he beat me stopping only to spit on his hands now and then. He beat me for more than an hour, perhaps, because he was completely soaked, and he stopped beating me only after the mallet broke on my back. My hatred, fury, and despair were so great that I didn't groan once while he beat me. I didn't afford him this satisfaction, and this was what enraged him most of all. And, of course, he felt bad about his broken mallet, too.

"You goddamned animal, you're going to gnaw the boards," he said as he left the barn.

I realized that they were not going to give me anything to eat. Let me die, I thought, but I'll never stoop so far as to remind them of me by my pitiful cries, much less gnaw on the wallboards. Three days I stood in the barn without a drop of water, without a clump of grass, and the master came every day to look at me. Evidently he was waiting for me to give him pitiful groans and guilty glances, begging for mercy.

Having waited in vain, on the fourth day he led me out of the barn, took the rope off my neck, and turned me loose. I recovered in a week. People noticed long ago how hardy a mule is, but not everyone knows that a mule has his pride and his sense of dignity.

I continued to live with the local farm animals, and my master and his family didn't touch me again. In the morning I went out to pasture along with the master's animals, and at dusk I came back with them to his hateful house. I was no longer allowed into the barnyard, by the way. During the winter, the rest of the animals received their bundle of corn straw in there. As I say, I stood all night at the gate, next to the stinking pigsty. But by now nothing could humiliate me. I was dead inside.

Nevertheless, as I think I've already said, as long as a living creature breathes, hope comes to him sooner or later. Hope came even to me that spring. And it came very simply. Out on the pasture I saw a magnificent local stallion cover the master's no-good droopy-rumped mare. I had thought this mare would be unable to attract even an ordinary donkey, let alone such a mighty stallion. She did, however, and I saw it all with my own eyes. You never can tell about these things, I guess, they're pretty obscure.

And then it occurred to me that if the master's mare had been bred, she would surely throw a foal. And I would be beside him, I would delight in his nearness, would love him and protect him from all possible enemies.

I settled down to wait, and I felt my soul, which had been bleeding with anguish and despair, slowly, slowly, begin to heal.

Yes, I did and I do love that old man, I thought. But what can you do! That happiness is ended, and the sooner I forget him the better. A foal is going to be born, whom I will love more than life, and for the sake of this foal I must reconcile myself with my new master's house and with all its inhabitants.

Then I thought soberly: What have they done to me that was so bad? What made me hate them all? Nothing special. Yes, the master beat me unmercifully and kept me three days without food. But after all, not only had I trampled and destroyed his corn, I had annoyed him thoroughly even before that. I had purposely distorted my gait to teach him not to ride me. So was he to blame, the poor man, that his smell was not so comfortable as my old man's, his voice not so pleasant, his habits not so wise?

And what made me hate the mistress? Imagine, she threw my corn on the ground. After all, she didn't mean to offend me. And I told myself, "Blackamoor, be tolerant. It's not everywhere that people live as wisely and elaborately as in the house of your old man. These people may not know plates themselves, yet you're offended that they didn't give you your corn in a pan."

My soul began to warm toward my new master and his family—not to mention the mare, who was plainly with foal. I sensed this in her subdued behavior. She even stopped shaking her rump so much. Now I tried to eat grass next to her on the pasture, so that no one would accidentally frighten her and harm the foal in her belly.

By now I myself wanted my new master to saddle me once more; at last I would show him my true gait. Besides, I didn't want the pregnant mare hauling him around to neighboring villages. Anything could happen—something could frighten her, she'd slip, and the foal in her belly might suffer. But he didn't bridle me. I waited patiently, with my soul warming toward him and all his family, while the foal, it must be supposed, kept on growing in the mare's belly.

It's an amazing thing, the way your attitude toward what a man has done changes when you change your attitude toward the man himself. Now, when I remembered what had happened in the barn, I felt neither the bitterness nor the insult. I couldn't even recall the sensation of pain. What kept coming to mind, over and over, was the same picture, which struck me rather funny: the expression on the master's face when his mallet broke, and he was so surprised he got flustered and took the two broken pieces in his hands, trying to stick them together, as if the graft would take. A sort of childish hurt appeared on his face, he seemed to say, "I wanted to punish the mule, but I punished myself."

Then one day my master came to the pasture, caught me, and put the bridle on me. He led me to the house. I walked at a prancing gait, rejoicing that I was needed at last. No, I thought, no longer will I hide my famous, my brisk and smooth pace from him.

He led me into the yard, tied me to the fence, and then a man I didn't know at all came up to him. The master began praising me highly to this man—my good character, my wonderful gait and unparalleled endurance. Though it was all true, I was ashamed to hear it. After all, my master himself hadn't had a chance to enjoy my peaceable character and magnificent gait. The only thing he could have been sure of was my endurance.

Suddenly they started talking about money, and I realized that he was planning to sell me. All his praises were shameless lies, which he himself did not believe.

He told the man that he used to ride on mules, but then, when his mule died, he was forced to switch to a horse, though he continued to hanker after a mule. And now he had acquired a wonderful mule from no less reliable a man than Khabug of Chegem. But it turned out that he was already out of the habit of riding a mule and had now decided not to get off his horse till the day he died.

An unbearable pain once more seared my soul. What about my foal, who had not yet been born and whom I had already managed to fall in love with? Would I never see him, ever in my life? Oh, God, and I had been ready to forgive this man all!

Once more my soul went numb. My new master put his bridle on me. Mounted on my unsaddled back, he took me to his village. We walked for a whole day, arriving at his house only toward evening. I was so stunned with grief that I walked along without noticing the road and without trying to spoil my gait.

We entered his yard. So as not to rub salt on my wounded soul, I gave no thought to the possibility of encountering a colt in this new place. But I couldn't close my eyes and keep from noticing that there wasn't even a smell of a colt in the yard. In the morning they turned me out to pasture with the rest of their animals, and I gave no thought at all to the possibility of meeting any colt. I had decided not to love anyone ever again in my life. However, there was no colt in the pasture anyway.

I won't say the new master treated me well, I won't say he treated me badly. It's simply that crude manners prevailed in this village, both among people and among animals. Here's an example.

One time my master led me to the mill, after packing me with three huge sacks. This was the usual thing around here, no one adjusted the weight of the pack to the animal's capabilities. When my master split shingle in the forest, he used to force me to carry such incredible bundles of shingles that I survived only thanks to my great endurance. But the animals in this village were just as crude, and that's the point I'm getting to.

So we arrived at the mill; the master unpacked me and tied me at the back of the mill. One she-donkey and one horse were tied in the same place. Then another peasant arrived, bringing some huge sacks of corn on a donkey. He unpacked the donkey, tied him next to the she-donkey, and carried the sacks into the mill.

I thought it would take a while for the donkey to catch his breath after those sacks. But far from it! As soon as his master went away, he began displaying obvious signs of a desire to master the she-donkey standing next to him. His incredible genital organ came out of him like a wild animal from its burrow. When it reached the ground, it quivered as if sniffing the dust.

I realized that something awful was about to happen. In his effort to get at the she-donkey, this monstrous lewd creature broke his bridle. He clambered on, and she let out a bellow of horror and pain.

At this point people began to come out of the mill. They laughed to see the donkey's games, thereby demonstrating their own penchant for these games. The donkey's master came out too, and at first he laughed along with everyone else, perhaps proud of his animal's might. He must not have suspected at first that his donkey had broken the bridle. He probably thought the donkey had simply pulled it off. Because when he noticed the torn bridle, he went into an indescribable rage and seized a log that was lying there. Holding his donkey by the torn bridle, he began to club him on the back with all his might. Finally the master stopped beating the donkey, mended the bridle somehow, and tied his animal farther from the she-donkey. I realized that this was not the first time the donkey's master had delivered him from his lust. What crude passions, and what crude means of deliverance from them.

Neither animals nor people behave this way at home in Chegem. How many times have I stood at our mill, tied along with horses and donkeys, but never seen anything like that. In the field, in the forest—go right ahead, to your heart's content. Chegem animals try to do it nicely, not within sight of people. Not at the mill, in any case, and not at the village soviet hitching rack, where there are lots of people. But such were the crude people and crude animals I had to live with for nearly a year.

One time my master saddled me and went to visit a distant village. Within half an hour I felt my back burning unbearably. The numskull hadn't even taken the time to saddle me properly. The saddle blanket was chafing my back, causing me incredible pain. It's our misfortune that we mules understand human language but can't say a word.

The pain drove me into a frenzy. Several times I tried to grab his leg with my teeth, and one time I succeeded. But he didn't even pull his leg away very fast. The local animals and people weren't too sensitive to pain, which was yet another proof of the coarseness of their nature.

His response to my bite was to hit my head as hard as he could with the whip handle. He simply had no idea, of course, why I was misbehaving. Several times, unable to bear the pain, I bucked, kicked the air with my hind feet, then bolted, but the dolt simply didn't understand.

Any master in Chegem, in such circumstances, would have sensed that something was wrong; he'd have gotten down from his horse or mule, examined him, resaddled him. But this one just kept on going.

It goes without saying that I gave him a most outrageous gait. I think I pulverized his innards, if they weren't made of stone. But what was the use! I had ended up in a land of crude, underdeveloped people who had no more sensitivity than a log.

Anyway, when we returned from the other village and he unsaddled me, it turned out that my back was chafed raw.

"Look at that," my master said. "Turns out he's got a saddle sore."

And you, blunderhead, had no idea why I was out of my mind the whole trip. He didn't lift a finger to treat my wound in any way. All night long my back burned, and I couldn't stand still. In the morning a swarm of flies clustered around my wound, and an unbearable itching was added to the unbearable burning pain.

I made a desperate decision. I decided to swallow my pride, run away from this monster, and return to my old man; I'd take my chances there. My mad resolve contained a modicum of shrewd conjecture. I hadn't lost my intelligence, despite my long association with underdeveloped people and animals.

My old man had always understood animals and could not bear to see them clumsily mistreated. This is what I was counting on. I couldn't tell him how they had beat me, how I had stood in the barn for three days without food or water, that they hadn't thrown me even a bundle of corn straw all winter long, but he could see with his own eyes that my back was rubbed raw, and he would understand all.

As soon as they turned me out to the pasture, I left. I didn't know the exact way to Chegem, but I clearly remembered that from Chegem to the first village we had traveled toward the sunrise, and from that village to this one we had again traveled toward the sunrise. It didn't take much to see that on the way back I would have to head toward the sunset.

I set out on my journey. Some places by the road, some places through forests and mountains, some places through thickets of edible and inedible plants—on the third day I arrived in Chegem, covered with burrs, sunken, wild, with a swarm of flies on my bleeding back.

I butted the wicket gate of the Big House and went into the yard. The kitchen door was shut, and I was very surprised. Could the old man have changed his ways during my wanderings? He never could bear to have the kitchen door shut. Then I realized that it was raining and a strong gusty wind was blowing toward the Big House. They had shut the door against the wind.

The dog began to bark when he saw me, but then recognized me and began to wag his tail. No, dogs aren't completely bereft of wisdom, I thought in passing. Everything that I had suffered rose up to choke me, and in desperation I crossed the yard, went up on the veranda, and flung the kitchen door open with my head, stopping in the doorway.

The sweetest smell in the world struck my nostrils, the smell of my home kitchen, from which corn and other tasty things had been brought out to me so many times. The kitchen hearth was all ablaze, my old man was sitting on the big bench beside it, staring into the fire, and I saw his dear, hooknosed face. Next to him sat his son, a good soul, the hunter Isa. Right by the fire, bending over a kettle of cornmeal mush and stirring it with a spatula, stood Kyazym's wife. And across from the door, on the couch, sat the old woman with her spindle, and Kyazym's children romping by her side, the little boy and girl, whom I had more than once taken for a ride.

"Blackamoor's back! Blackie!" The children, the first to see me, jumped up from the couch and ran over to me.

"What do I see!" cried Kyazym's wife. She dropped her spatula and ran over too. "Strike me blind if it isn't Blackamoor!"

The old woman dropped her spindle and came to me too. And Isa, dear Isa, simple soul, tears came to his eyes when he saw me.

"How did he ever find the way!" Isa said.

My way was far longer than you think, Isa. I will never forget your tears, Isa. You are grateful, you remember that when you killed a bear in the woods, two horses and two donkeys refused to bring it home. They wheezed and backed away from that frightful burden in terror. And only I, gathering all my strength and overcoming my repugnance, was willing to pull its body to the house.

Yes, they all gathered around me, and only my old man continued to sit by the fire. He merely turned his head to cast a stern look in my direction. No, no, I didn't believe that he was indifferent, I didn't believe that he hadn't been thinking about me all this time, hadn't missed me. But that's my old man. Not another man in the world has the self-control that he has.

"Blackamoor's back! Blackie!" was all that I heard around me. Yes, I said to myself, your Blackamoor has come back to you, come home after incalculable sufferings, as loving and devoted to his master as ever.

"Grandpa! Grandpa!" the children shouted suddenly, looking at my back. "He has a wound on his back!"

At that my old man stood up, everyone made way, and he came over to me. Silently and carefully he examined the wound. Yes, yes, I thought, look what they did to me.

"Turns out the infidel can't even saddle a mule," my old man said with quiet hatred. "Isa, ride over and return his money to him. I'll take Blackamoor back, since he can't stand to live there."

Then the old woman brought out some corn and served it to me in a pan, as decent people are supposed to, instead of throwing it in the dirt. Lord, I thought, everything's the way it was before, as if there had been no long separation and unbearable sufferings. And again, as before, the hens and roosters surrounded me in hopes of pecking up a stray kernel. Peck away, my dears, peck away, I thought, Blackamoor's kind, he's home again, he's happy again.

My old man got some burning water called kerosene from the lamp, poured it on a clean rag, and wiped the wound on my back. At first it stung badly, but then it felt much better, because the flies stopped pestering me.

That same day Isa went to my first master with money. I was very worried that my old man's money would be lost. I couldn't tell him that that master had already sold me to another place, because I may understand Abkhazian but I can't speak a word.

But, thank God, the next day Isa came into the yard and told my old man that that master had sold me a long time ago and didn't even want to hear about this obscene mule. The swindler, evidently he didn't catch on at first that he could get money for me twice, and when he did it was already too late, he had let the cat out of the bag. I didn't listen to sa in order to hear that flayflint's opinion of me. No. I listened to Isa to find out whether he had happened to notice a mare with a colt. Evidently he hadn't. Strange; how could he not notice a colt, if in fact the mare did foal.

After about a month, when the wound on my back had healed completely, my old man saddled me and went to the village of Atary. He and I have been inseparable ever since, and I remember the time he sold me only as a bad dream.

We live in perfect harmony. Well, of course, we have our little skirmishes. Sometimes he's not entirely satisfied with me, sometimes I insist on my own rightness. Sometimes he grumbles at me, sometimes I turn obstinate, defending the dignity of a reliable mule who knows his own worth. That's how we've lived ever since, and I wish no other life for myself.

But enough of reminiscing. Back to our journey. My old man and I were still walking briskly onward when suddenly we heard the terrible squealing of a pig. It was a rasping, heartrending squeal. Before long I saw a pig being dragged out of a wicket gate, fifty paces ahead of us. Two men were holding her by the legs, a third held her by the ears, and a fourth walked alongside. They were obviously planning to slaughter the pig, and she knew it. She was squealing incredibly loud.

They laid the pig down on the grass near the gate. The two men continued to hold her by the legs, one by the forelegs, the other by the hind legs, and the third man, who was still holding her by the ears, pulled her head all the way back. The fourth man took out a large knife and bent over her. For some reason he did not plunge the knife in, but discussed something with the others. The pig, realizing that death was imminent, continued to squeal at the top of her lungs. I sensed that my old man was beginning to get irritated. He can't bear it when a thing isn't done cleanly.

The men obviously couldn't cope with the pig, they were either drunk or simply incompetent. Finally, as we drew even with them, the one that held the knife plunged it into the pig, and she fell silent. The ones that had been holding her let go and walked off, satisfied with what they had done.

Suddenly my old man and I saw a terrible sight. The pig, which had seemed dead, got to her feet with the knife handle sticking out of her chest and started staggering away. Evidently, the man who did the killing had not struck her heart.

"Rastak your mother, you bums!" my old man shouted, jumping to the ground. "How can you torture an animal, even if it's only a pig!"

With that he ran after the pig with unusual agility, caught her, seized her by one ear, bent back her head, pulled out the knife planted in her chest, and forcefully stuck it back in. And, of course, he struck her right in the heart. The pig fell dead on the grass.

Good for my old man. What's especially interesting is that while he'd slaughtered all sorts of animals and birds, of course, this was the first time he had slaughtered a pig. It's only in recent years that he's begun to raise and sell pigs, anyway; he himself has never butchered them or eaten pork.

Throwing warlike glances at the now-silent men and muttering something about weak eyes and weak arms, my old man clambered up on me and we started off. The men continued to stand there, shifting from one foot to the other in embarrassment, looking now at the dead pig, now at my old man, as if still stunned by the pig's unexpected resurrection and the butcher who had turned up from nowhere.

Ahead of us the Kodor came into view again. But here it was spanned by a huge iron bridge. Crossing it was unpleasant, and I was glad when the bridge ended.

An airplane flew overhead with a roar. My old man stopped and watched it for a long time, shading his eyes with his hand.

"You've taught iron to fly," he muttered, starting me forward, "let's see you teach meat to fly, so that all you have to do is catch it and hurl it into a kettle."

The amazing thing about my old man is that you can't impress him with anything: neither airplanes nor trucks nor offices nor big city houses. He's always sure there's something within him that's a thousand times more important than all these airplanes, trucks, and offices. He does have such a force within him, but I can't explain it. I only feel it. And I'm not the only one. Everyone feels it. Even our Chegem authorities feel it, and they try not to have much to do with my old man. They even turn a blind eye to the fact that he still keeps the shepherd Harlampo.

More and more often we began to come across Endurskies. In fact, there were nothing but Endurskies around here. We entered a big Endursky village. My old man looked around calmly and gave no sign that such a big concentration of Endurskies in one place had any effect on his nerves. Never in this world will you find another man with the self-control that he has.

The funniest thing is that my old man rode calmly through the Endursky village, and when we came to an Abkhazian village he had a nervous breakdown over our own Abkhazians. We were passing a big cornfield, which ten kolkhoz workers were hoeing. My old man stopped, evidently out of an urge to rinse his throat with his native language. He began talking with the peasants about this and that. Of course he asked them about eucalyptuses, and they replied that all was quiet there regarding eucalyptuses.

As they talked with my old man they went on hoeing the corn, looking up from time to time to ask him about things in Chegem. At first my old man talked eagerly, but then he began to get angry; I realized this because he began to pull on the reins as if I were trying to go and he wanted to stop me. But I was plainly standing still, and he was the one who was beginning to rage.

"Listen here," my old man shouted, "what kind of a hoeing job is that?"

"What kind of a hoeing job?" one of the men asked, straightening up over his hoe. "The right kind, that's what!"

"You're not hoeing like decent people!" my old man shouted. "You're hoeing like infidels!"

"You just ride on, old man, wherever you were going," the man said, taking up his hoe again. "Teaching me a lesson . . . and on a mule at that . . ."

This was the wrong thing to say to my old man. The problem wasn't that he made a stupid reference to me. But he was much younger than my old man, and in Abkhazia you can't talk that way to an old man.

"*Dur-rak!*" my old man shouted in Russian, and I realized that he was in a great rage. "What's my mule got to do with you turning into swine?"

With these words he leaped down from me like a boy, climbed the wattle fence, jumped into the field, and bent down to the cornstalks to rake the dirt out from around them. As he went along he pulled up the stalks that were growing too close together, which should have been cut out by the hoe before.

"Have you turned into absolute swine?" he repeated, continuing to rake the

I realized that she was the children's mother. It wasn't hard to guess that she was the wife of the old black's son. And I thought: Here she's a white Abkhazian, and her children are all black, without a single white spot. What's going on here, I wondered. At this house black blood proved stronger than Abkhazian, and each child turned out blacker than the last, while at the other house Russian blood proved stronger than Abkhazian, and the child turned out too white. If Abkhazian blood gets any weaker, the Endurskies will take over completely.

But what do the Endurskies have to do with it, I thought suddenly. I sensed that I had been infected by our Abkhazians, and I was ready to dump the blame for all our misfortunes on the Endurskies. Today I had heard a pureblooded Abkhazian insult my old man by saying, There's nothing you can teach us, sitting astride your mule. If you told another Abkhazian about that incident he'd say, The Endurskies taught him to talk like that.

But I say there's no call to blame your own folly on the Endurskies! Obey wise old men like mine in everything and you'll never be lost. Otherwise the Endurskies will hobble you, bind you hand and foot . . . Damn! Well, if not the Endurskies, somebody else!

My old man was invited into the kitchen, but, citing the heat, he said he would sit out on the veranda. He sat down at the table with the old blackamoor, and the white Abkhazian woman and the old black woman began bringing refreshments for them from the kitchen and putting them on the table.

I ate grass, from time to time glancing at them and listening to their talk. Seeing the blackness of the old blackamoor and hearing his Abkhazian speech, I couldn't make any connection between the two. I kept thinking there was a white Abkhazian sitting inside this blackamoor and speaking for him. Gradually I got used to the odd combination of Abkhazian speech and Moorish blackness, however, and began to listen more calmly to what they were talking about.

My old man, of course, began by asking the Abkhazian blackamoor about kolkhoz affairs. First off he asked whether they were making them plant eucalyptuses. The old black replied that they had made them plant eucalyptuses last year, but this year they were making them plant tung.

"What's tung?" my old man wondered.

"It's a plant that has terribly poisonous juice," the old black replied. "Man or beast, you die instantly."

"What do they want with this poisonous juice?" my old man asked anxiously. "Whom are they planning to poison?"

"No," the old black soothed him, "they're not planning to poison anyone, neither men nor beasts. They need the juice for airplanes. Airplanes can't fly without it, they can only run along the ground like trucks."

"Things are going from bad to worse," my old man said.

They drank off their wine, and my old man turned over his emptied glass, hinting that their enemies' affairs should be overturned just like the glass. They went on eating and drinking, and my old man began to tell about the affairs of the Chegem kolkhoz. He told about the low-lying field, and about the tobacco, and also about the kolkhoz livestock farm, which a worthless man had been appointed to run. He told about the farm with great bitterness, and I alone knew the reason. My old man had hoped that they would ask him, as the best Chegem stockbreeder, to run the farm. But no one had asked him, and out of pride he wouldn't suggest it himself for anything.

"Even under Nicholas," my old man said, "this fellow couldn't breed a pair of sheep. What will he be able to do now? He'll destroy all the livestock!"

"He surely will," the old blackamoor agreed.

"If things keep on like this," my old man said, "the only four-legged animals left in the villages will be the dogs."

"The dogs will be left," the old blackamoor agreed, "because the authorities have no interest in dogs."

"Mark my words," my old man said, "there'll be lots of iron and little meat."

"That's for sure," the old blackamoor agreed again. "They brought a tractor to our place recently. It was all iron, from head to tail."

They talked for another half-hour, drank several glasses of wine apiece, and my old man began getting ready to leave. The old blackamoor and his little blackamoors accompanied us to the gate. My old man said good-bye to the master of the house, mounted me, and we went on.

I had managed to have a good rest, fortify myself, and my pace was light and brisk. We hadn't gone even one kilometer from the blackamoor's house when suddenly, on a little meadow near the street, I saw a chestnut colt standing by his mother. How about that! The meeting with the blackamoor must have been a good omen. I'll have to remember that for the future.

I simply melted with tenderness. But I told myself, "Hold on, Blackamoor, don't shame yourself in front of your old man, watch your step, don't betray the quivering in your legs."

I walked on, trying not to look toward the colt. But I couldn't purposely close my eyes to keep from noticing him. That would have been plain stupid. When we walked past him, he was standing with his wobbly legs amusingly splayed out and his neck twisted, biting himself under the shoulder blade. Oh, these colts will be the death of me, I feel it, they will.

When we had passed him, I had a terrible desire to look back. But I controlled myself and didn't turn my head. True, just at that moment an insolent fly sat on my eyelid, and I was forced to shake my head with might and main. I caught sight of him again for a brief instant. Now he had stopped scratching, and the white star on his forehead gleamed as he looked amazedly in my direction. Something about me must have interested him. Pleased with this encounter and my own self-control, I walked and walked along the road.

Two hours later, crossing yet another bridge over a river I didn't know, we entered the city. Large and small vehicles passed us constantly, and against my will I began to get used to their disagreeable smell. Now the whole road was spread with black tar. It was worse to walk on than dirt, but nicer than stones.

A multitude of people walked to and fro, and now and then I heard words in different languages. From occasional familiar words I recognized Georgian, Endurian, Armenian, Turkish, and Greek. When I didn't encounter even a single familiar word, I knew people were speaking Russian. Like my old man, I don't understand even a word of Russian, because Russian is spoken only in the cities, and we very rarely go there.

We came to the big house where Sandro lived. The house was big to look at, but I knew that Sandro had only one little room in it. My old man dismounted, led me into the yard, and tied me to a fence picket. I settled down to wait. The little city boys playing in the yard surrounded me, admiring me and taking me for a horse in their naiveté. Actually, I'm often taken for a horse, but never for a donkey.

Soon Sandro came out of the house with my old man and a golden, long-legged little girl, Sandro's daughter. My old man was holding her hand. I knew he worshiped this granddaughter of his, and besides, I couldn't take my eyes off her myself. Of all the human children I've seen, she's probably the only one that I'd compare with a colt for beauty.

"Grandpa's little horse!" the little girl cried, and ran up to me.

My old man set her in the saddle, then took me by the bridle and led me out to the street. I realized that we were going to inspect the house that Sandro planned to buy. Incidentally, I sensed right away that he was embarrassed about something and had something to hide from my old man. Of course I was sure he was planning to ask him for the money to buy the house. I think my old man was sure of that, too. I knew he'd be a little stubborn at first and then give it to him.

But that's the thing, Sandro's embarrassment wasn't connected with that at all. As if he hadn't wangled plenty of money from his father in his life! No, I sensed that it was something else. May a bear strip the hide off me, I thought, if there isn't something hidden here.

I don't know whether my old man sensed what I did. After all, he's not easy to see through; there isn't one man in the world with the self-control that he has. Still, I don't think my old man suspected anything this time. Sometimes my mind works faster than his.

We went down several streets and came to the gate of a house. Sandro opened the gate and let us into the yard. It was a very small yard with very juicy grass, several well-tended fruit trees, and flowers by the steps. The house was small but well tended.

I sensed that my old man liked the house. He especially liked it because it came with a piece of land. That's what I think.

"It's a good house," my old man said with a nod. "Call out the owner, let's talk, let's drive a bargain."

"There isn't any owner," Sandro said. "The city soviet is selling the house."

"What, did the owner die?" my old man asked. Taking the bit out of my mouth, he fastened the reins to the saddle so that I could graze on this rich grass that had never known livestock. By now I was utterly convinced that my old man hadn't noticed anything special in Sandro's face. He just thought Sandro was going to try and wangle the money out of him, he hadn't thought beyond that.

"It's not that he died," Sandro said. Hesitating, he added, "A Greek lived here. He and his wife were arrested and sent to Siberia."

"So that's it," my old man said, and fell silent. Sandro was also silent. I knew there was something wrong here!

"Didn't he have any children?" my old man asked, breaking his silence. He threw me a distracted glance, and I sensed that he regretted having taken the bit from my mouth. He needn't have worried, I couldn't eat the grass anyway, knowing what a hurricane was approaching.

I looked at Sandro, and although he was a little embarrassed, he didn't understand what hung over him.

"There were two," Sandro answered. "Their relatives took them away to Russia."

"Is that so," my old man said, still controlling himself. "Then they exiled the parents to Siberia, took the children away to Russia, and they're selling the house to you. What have you done to deserve it, I wonder?"

"I'm the best dancer in the troupe now," Sandro said. "They're arresting a lot of people now and selling their houses to the most deserving people in the city. I understand you, Father. But *we* didn't arrest them. If I don't buy it, somebody else will—"

"I don't think you do understand," my old man replied, still controlling himself. "And how much do they want from you for the house and land?"

He looked around the premises again. In passing he glanced at me too, and it seemed to me he was pleased that I was standing motionless and not eating that graveyard grass. It wouldn't have gone down my throat now. I knew what a hurricane was going to break from my old man's breast, but he was still restraining himself.

"Two thousand rubles!" Sandro exclaimed, trying to cheer my old man with the bargain price.

"Two thousand rubles," my old man grinned. "These days that's the price of two good pigs. This is fantastic, if a man can buy a decent house for the price of two pigs."

"The city soviet set the price," Sandro explained. "Why should I raise it?"

And now my old man spoke.

"My son," he began in a quiet and terrible voice, "before, if a blood avenger killed his enemy, he touched not a button on his clothes. He took the body to the enemy's house, laid it on the ground, and called to his family for them to take in their dead man clean, undefiled by the touch of an animal. That's the way it was. These men, now, kill innocent people and tear their clothes off them to sell cheap to their lackeys. You can buy this house, but I will never set foot in it, nor will you ever cross the threshold of my house!"

With these words my old man came over to me, rammed the bit into my mouth with such force that he almost knocked my teeth out (*I* didn't do anything!), swept the little girl from the saddle in order to mount me and leave the city.

At that, Sandro came to himself and ran to his father.

"Father!" he cried. "Don't be angry, please! That's why I sent for you, to get your advice. I sensed myself that there was something dishonorable here. What did you think, that I couldn't get the two thousand rubles? My friends would have lent it to me!"

"Ah-h-h," my old man said, hesitating, and once more set the little girl on me. "To get my advice. Then this is my advice: come back to the village. Your mother's made holes in my head with her lamentations. The way times are, they may even take you. Or are their dancers immune?"

"Oh sure, immune," Sandro replied, sighing. "They've already taken Platon Pantsulaya—"

"Then what are you waiting for?" my old man asked.

"That's the problem, Father," Sandro answered, his face darkening. "I'm terrified to stay and terrified to leave. If I leave they'll say I got scared because I was Lakoba's favorite. And you know what they did to Lakoba . . ."

"You can't just leave," my old man said after thinking a moment. "I'll fix it up for you. I'll hire a good doctor, he'll wreck your knee temporarily, they'll discard you, and you'll come home."

At that we abandoned the escheated house and went to Sandro's. My old man was obviously relieved. He was pleased that he hadn't lost his son and hadn't sullied his conscience either. My old man spent the night with Sandro, and in the morning we started back.

My old man did as he had promised. He hired a good, trustworthy doctor from the village of Atary; the doctor wrecked Sandro's knee a little, so that he was still limping two months after they discarded him and sent him back to the village.

That fall my old man hired four Greeks, and they built Sandro a house so that it stood in plain view, and my old man could see from his yard whether the kitchen door was always open, and if it wasn't, then shout down to remind him or his wife that such forgetfulness was shameful.

Now, after all that I've told you, I'd like to ask: Have you ever known another old man like mine? If you have—show me. That's the thing, you haven't anyone to show.

Now I'll tell the story of Sandro's famous cucumbers. The next year Sandro undertook to raise cucumbers near his house for the kolkhoz. And he had an unparalleled crop. No matter how often the cucumber patch was rifled by passing kolkhoz workers, countless multitudes of cucumbers remained. Word of these cucumbers spread through the whole district, and commission after commission came from Kengursk, and they all sampled the cucumbers and carried them off by the sackful, and there were still cucumbers all over the place.

The authorities who came to sample the cucumbers said that Sandro had bred a new variety, which ought to be made available first throughout the district and then throughout the whole country. And Sandro himself, the authorities said, would be put up for deputy.

"Numskulls!" my old man shouted at them. "I used to have my goat pen there. It's a half-meter deep in dung!"

All the same, no one listened to him. In the middle of the summer they plucked a cucumber vine, on which they counted as many as a hundred cucumbers, and assigned four Chegemians to take it to Mukhus to the agricultural fair. Sandro wanted to go with them, but they told him that he was practically a deputy now, and they could use more ordinary people to transport a cucumber vine.

At first the four Chegemians carried the vine carefully, reaching Anastasovka without shedding any cucumbers. But when they got on the bus, the passengers began marveling at their unusual burden, and they began treating everyone, boasting of the unparalleled cucumber crop. True, they cut the cucumbers from the vine with a knife—very cleverly as they saw it—instead of tearing them off. That way, a stub was left where the fruit had been cut, so that people could see that a cucumber had in fact grown there.

Moreover, one of the passengers on the bus turned out to have a big bottle of *chacha*. He began treating them all to *chacha*, and our boys kept slipping them cucumbers, neatly cutting them from the vine so that the stubs remained. When they arrived in Mukhus, there were about twenty whole cucumbers left on the vine and a great number of stubs.

The envoys from Chegem arrived at the fair with their vine, but it wasn't accepted. The fair supervisor said there were too few cucumbers on the vine.

"But you can see how many there were," the Chegemians replied, pointing out the stubs.

"That could mean anything," the supervisor said. "People will think that I or my assistants ate the cucumbers."

"Let them think what they want," the Chegemians exhorted him. "The main thing is, you can see how many cucumbers grew on it."

"No, no." The supervisor refused point-blank, pushing away the vine, which the Chegemians were trying to spread out on his desk. "It would look like sabotage."

Despondent over the supervisor's stubbornness, the envoys from Chegem left the fairgrounds and began considering what action to take and what to do with the remaining cucumbers. One of them conceived a suspicion that the fair supervisor was probably an Endursky disguised as an Armenian.

"Ah-h-h," the others said, "that explains everything. Could an Endursky ever promote our fame?"

Then they dropped into a wine shop and began drinking wine, snacking on the remaining cucumbers.

When the Chegemians learned of the debacle at the fair, they were so vexed at the supervisor that they completely cleaned out Sandro's cucumber patch. The district center, by the way, heard nothing about all this. In the fall a new commission arrived from the district center to take cucumbers for seeds for other

in the secret luminary of the "Treatment Commission," as the big shots call their restricted-access polyclinic.

Later Tengiz said that he had had to rustle two nice new twenty-five ruble bills between his palms for fifteen minutes before the restrictive doors of the polyclinic cautiously opened. The celebrated doctor stuck his head out, and Tengiz, presumably still rustling, drove him to Uncle Sandro's.

A few hours after his fall, Uncle Sandro came to and saw the face of the secret luminary bending over him.

"No offense, but I don't know you," Uncle Sandro said, after peering at him for rather a long time, with eyes that had already seen the next world. His loved ones rejoiced at the judiciousness of his words and the correctness of his surmise.

"You're not supposed to know him," Tengiz responded. "We're keeping you under the veil, like a bride."

This joke totally restored Uncle Sandro to life. He immediately made it a point to explain to the gathering that he had fallen, not because he was drunk, but because he had tripped over a root that protruded from the ground by his gate.

"Well, if that's the culprit, I'll cut it out right now," Tengiz said, and he left the room. He got the ax from the kitchen, went down to the gate, and soon returned with a gnarled length of root like a severed dragon foot.

In the days that followed, as he lay in his bed, Uncle Sandro kept hold of this root, slightly washed and trimmed, to show to visitors as material evidence that his fall had been caused by external forces rather than alcohol.

When I visited him two days later, he was lying in bed, his hands on top of the covers, holding this knotty, twisted piece of root, the size of a hefty boomerang.

Uncle Sandro silently pointed it at a chair, and when I sat down by the head of his bed, he repeated for my benefit, over Aunt Katya's protests, the story of his fall, adding that there had been a downpour that night and a lot of earth had been washed away from around the root. Giving it to me to sniff, he suddenly asked with a crafty smile whether the root didn't smell like mulberry.

"Sort of," I said. "Why?"

"Think about it," he said, taking back the root and sniffing it.

"There you go again with your foolishness," Aunt Katya responded. Thrusting a broken match into a vial of valerian, she began to measure drops into a wineglass for him, counting silently with her lips.

"I don't have a mulberry tree on my land," he said, shooting me a crafty glance from the pillow. "The nearest one is across the road at my neighbor's . . . Get it?"

"No," I said. "What?"

"An Endursky lives there," Uncle Sandro pronounced. He nodded meaningfully from his pillow: he could not say all in his wife's presence.

I burst out laughing.

"The old sot has completely left his senses," Aunt Katya remarked in a level voice, trying not to lose count or spill the medicine drops. She came over and carefully handed him the glass.

"Look, she's dripped me some first-shot," Uncle Sandro said. Sitting partway up on the pillow, he took the glass, frowned, swallowed, frowned again, leaned back on the pillow, and sighed, "If anyone's going to kill me, it's her . . . But I'll have the last laugh, wait till spring and we'll see . . ."

"Why spring?" I said blankly.

"We'll see the tree begin to wither." Lifting the root in one hand, he closed his other hand around it at its thickest point. "A tree that's lost a root this big can't help but wither, at least half of it. Then all you scatterbrains will understand that the Endurskies have spread their roots everywhere."

I realized that Uncle Sandro—ashamed of this disagreeable incident and, what was more important, trying to deflect Aunt Katya's long-standing efforts to part him from his beloved social obligations—had attributed to this root the significance of a mystical bugaboo (the way they used to frighten us with the Colorado potato beetle).

"Come over next Sunday," he said to me in farewell. "People want to celebrate my recovery."

"I swear to God I'm not making a single move to help with this shameless plan," Aunt Katya said, sitting sorrowfully immobile in her chair by his feet. She said this without changing her posture.

"So don't make a move, other people will do it all," Uncle Sandro said. Moving around under the blanket himself, he found a more comfortable position and sniffed the root, as if the smell would help him detect the degree of danger in the Endursky intrigues.

On Sunday, at sunset of a warm fall day, I climbed up to Uncle Sandro's house again. The chopped-out root had left its mark by the gate in the form of a deep excavation. Where the remainder of the root led was hard to tell, because it ran along the fence and went deep into the ground in both directions. Of course, if you dug up the street you might track it down, but for the time being no one had thought of doing that.

While still at the foot of the path I heard the polite murmur of voices—the guests had assembled. I went on up.

In front of the house rose a pavilion covered with a tarpaulin, where the celebratory banquet was to be held.

By the front door stood Uncle Sandro's brother Makhaz, the same old man who had once commissioned me to take his brother a jug of honey. Next to him, leaning on a staff, stood the old hunter Tendel, who still peered at the world with piercing hawklike eyes.

Makhaz recognized me immediately. Shaking my hand, he thanked me for not refusing to come and mark this joyful occasion.

"You too, in your time, have gone to some trouble for him," he said, alluding to the jug of honey, delivered intact to its addressee. "You too did what you could, like the rest of us," he continued, including me in the ranks of those who had honorably fulfilled their obligation to Uncle Sandro, as if Uncle Sandro had become a symbol of military duty or some other generally accepted obligation.

"Sorry, but I don't recognize you!" Tendel shouted at me, drilling into me with his hawklike eyes.

Makhaz explained my Chegemian origins to him and gave him to understand that I was here in the city on duty, one of the watchers-over.

"I bet you wipe yourself with money!" he shouted, gleefully drilling me with his yellow hawk eyes.

I laughed.

"You do," he repeated confidently. Unexpectedly he added, "And the way you toppled the Big Mustache, that was pretty clever."

I shrugged, feeling that it would be hard to explain to him what an incredible distance lay between me and those who had in fact toppled him. On the other hand, Tendel was right about the main thing. The watchers-over had toppled the Big Mustache, and the distance between one or another of the watchers-over (or, as they still say, Those Admitted to the Table) and those who did in fact overthrow him has in truth no meaning. The important thing is that it was not he, the hunter Tendel, not he, the shepherd Makhaz, nor any of them, the Chegemians or people like the Chegemians, who did it. People of a completely different sort, that is, the watchers-over, toppled the watcher-over-all-watchers-over. Everyone seems to feel better now (that is why we speak of it so lightly), but the ones who stood to gain the most by it were the watchers-over; otherwise, it could not have been, that was the point of the undertaking. Or so I understood from Tendel's words, in combination with his stentorian voice and piercing hawk eyes.

. . . In front of the house, a little to the left of the pavilion, a fire had been built, over which, in a huge medieval kettle, the cornmeal mush was coming to a boil. Some men were busy around the fire. Tethered next to a fig tree was a rather well-fed calf.

A few steps away from it a young fellow, evidently one of the neighbors, was sharpening a large hunting knife on a whetstone. He tested it from time to time by lifting his shirt sleeve and shaving the hair from his arm. The steer looked gloomily askance at him, as if it divined the purpose of the knife. The steer, of course, had been brought by Uncle Sandro's brother.

I joined the men who were calmly and happily awaiting supper, picturesquely seated on logs.

In our part of the world there is a sort of special gusto in the nocturnal vigil at a sickbed, or even in the anticipation of a funeral feast (knock on wood!), when the feast is occasioned by the death of a man who has lived long enough. Nowhere will you hear such gay and spicy stories, about everything under the sun, as at these gatherings. Apparently, the imminence of death or of mortal danger sharpens people's interest in vivid impressions of life.

In the same way, probably, lovers find it especially sweet to kiss in a graveyard among the sepulchers. I myself have never tried this, unless one equates with sepulchers the sepulchral gas stoves of a communal kitchen. In such kitchens, in my student days, during exam periods, I used to sit up late at night over the textbooks with my girl friend, the sweetness of our embraces heightened by our dim terror before the commandant-like steps of her papa in the corridor, or, conversely, the soft ghostly steps of an inquisitive neighbor-woman.

In either case, I was always stunned by the hurricane swiftness and efficiency with which the sweet face was transformed, leaving no evidence except for blazing lips and glazed eyes, now focused on her book.

But I have let my tongue run away with me; by today, there was no question of any mortal danger. Uncle Sandro had been forbidden to get up, but he insisted on being among the celebrants, and after a small conference among his closest friends it was decided to carry him out of the house and into the tent.

For this purpose, several people suggested that the bed, in view of its cumbersomeness, should be replaced by a folding cot. Once he was out there, he could be transferred back to the bed if he insisted.

Aunt Katya agreed to this, and the proponents of the folding cot, perhaps fearing that she would change her mind, hastily began dragging Uncle Sandro from his bed to the cot. The proponents of whole-bed transport watched the actions of the folding cot's proponents somewhat distractedly, now and then shifting their lackluster gaze to the bed, which was considerably devalued by Uncle Sandro's absence.

During the conference on the method of transporting Uncle Sandro, Aunt Katya had had time to put a clean shirt on him and give him a pair of pants, which he himself put on, under the covers. But now, when they transferred him to the cot and flung a camel's hair blanket over him, and the already impatient proponents of the cot seized him and started to carry him off, Uncle Sandro's big bare feet were discovered sticking out from under the blanket.

"How can you just lie there like a corpse," Aunt Katya said, wringing her hands. "You might have told me if I forgot."

She ordered the cot to be put down—much to the displeasure of those who intended to carry it, incidentally—and fussed around in search of socks. She found the socks and began to pull them over Uncle Sandro's stubbornly unbending feet, which may have signified both his dissatisfaction at her forgetfulness and his wish to encourage the proponents of whole-bed transport, give them an opportunity to gain time.

When Uncle Sandro's bare feet were discovered and the cot had to be set down, the proponents of the bed came to life and decided that they should at least emerge from the house ahead of the folding cot, so as not to make themselves a laughingstock by descending the front steps with an empty bed after Uncle Sandro had already been carried out in the cot.

They made a dash with the bed while Aunt Katya put the socks, which she had at last found, on Uncle Sandro's unbending feet. To get to the veranda they had to go through three doors. This proved to be no easy matter, considering the bulk of this nickel-plated contraption and the relative narrowness of the doors, not to mention the rather deficient structural sense of those doing the carrying—a deficiency compounded by their anxiety that those following with the cot would ask them to make way and would go out ahead of them.

All this could not help but affect their handling of the bed itself, especially its latticed nickel-plated headboard, which emitted strident complaints, accompanied by the creak of the jouncing springs.

Poor Aunt Katya responded immediately to these sounds by abandoning the cot and Uncle Sandro. Joining the men carrying the bed, she cried out and lamented at its every painful contact with the doorposts. Her lamentations finally provoked Uncle Sandro, who was being borne along behind her, to a jealous annoyance. He muttered something to the effect that he was not made of iron, yet no one was worrying whether he was carried carefully.

"Keep that in mind when you're drinking," Aunt Katya replied, without looking back.

It was a funny sight. They carried him down the steps while he solemnly lay under the picturesquely draped blanket, solemnly hearkened to his body's undesirable tendency to slide down, and, evincing no personal involvement in the matter, gave trivial orders to the four men carrying him.

"Well, don't disgrace yourselves at the last minute here," he said when the men got halfway down the steps and the slant of the cot took on a character threatening its upper, most fruitful stratum with a landslide.

"Good Lord, you might at least have left your root behind," Aunt Katya said. She had stopped following the men carrying the bed and was now observing from below as Uncle Sandro was lowered down the steps. He lay with his hands on top of the covers, clutching his root like a steering wheel.

Uncle Sandro was carried into the middle of the tent, where the bed already stood. At the bed Aunt Katya bent down and plumped up his pillow. Reproving her for doing this here where people would eat, instead of before, he allowed his body to be transferred to the bed. Then he ordered the cot to be folded and leaned against the headboard of the bed, where it stood like a dinghy tied to a large ship in case it was needed in shallow waters.

We sat down on long benches, or, more precisely, on ordinary boards supported by bricks. Wider boards, hastily nailed to supports, served as tables.

The women began to hand out plates of hot cornmeal mush, distribute chunks of steaming meat from big bowls, pour out cherry-plum sauce.

A tall, slender young man, paying no attention to the commotion, although supper was just about ready, stood on a stool, completing the electrification of the tent. This was Tengiz.

During the ten or fifteen minutes it took us to get seated, he stretched a cable, wired a lamp socket to it, and finally screwed in the last light bulb.

Next to him, by the stool, stood a pretty, black-haired girl with a bright flush on her cheeks, caused, as presently became clear, by her embarrassment. From time to time Tengiz took from her hands a tool that she got from the box lying at his feet, or handed down to her the one he was holding in his hand.

It was manifest that he was teasing her the whole time, all the while doing his job easily, with artistic nonchalance. His words were inaudible, but the atmosphere was palpable. When he handed down the pliers or the wire cutters or the hammer, he smiled at her as insinuatingly, held her hand as significantly, as if he were slipping her a none-too-decent postcard, or as if the instrument he handed her represented a ubiquitous Freudian symbol.

Incidentally, as I watched him, I remembered hearing a stupid rumor that he was Uncle Sandro's illegitimate son. Like any man who does not believe gossip, I went ahead and mentally compared this man's appearance with Uncle Sandro's.

Naturally, they had nothing in common except their height. This lad was dark, thin, even had a somewhat childish build, whereas Uncle Sandro's appearance combined good proportions with a gentle might.

At last Tengiz screwed a bulb into the socket, and it lighted up. He threw the screwdriver into the box himself, without flirtation, as if at the flip of the switch the energy of his flirtation had become electric energy and had lost its intimate meaning, now that it was public property. He jumped down from the stool and was immediately hailed from all sides.

"Tengo, over here!"

"Tengiz, sit with us!"

Tengiz spread his hands helplessly and turned to Uncle Sandro, who was reclining on his bed, gazing beneficently around the table. With a slight smile, he extended the hand with the root and pointed Tengiz to a place next to the young women, where he could easily see and hear him.

My place was not far from his, and I watched him with curiosity, trying to hear what he said.

I soon learned that he had a television in his house—the First in the neighborhood. He had recently installed a telephone for himself—also the First in the neighborhood.

Apropos of the television, he said that the neighbors' children had fixed his house up like a movie theater, so that there was no room to turn around. Pretty soon he intended to start selling admission tickets, especially when a spy movie was on, or a soccer match with the Tbilisi Dynamos. Of course he said it jokingly, as if adding his home's appeal as a place of entertainment to its other appealing qualities. Apropos of nothing, so far as I could see, he also reported that he had planted his plot in laurel trees.

"A hundred laurel roots," he reported. "Hope they grow . . ."

Addressing a wider circle of guests, Tengiz also told the story of how he had become acquainted with Uncle Sandro.

It was seven years ago, he said. From the district police, where he had worked until then, he had moved to Mukhus to work as manager of the NKVD garage. At first he did not have an apartment, and he tried to rent one in this neighborhood with the idea that he would later wangle an allotment for himself and build his own house here. As he told it, however, the homeowners, on learning where he worked, politely refused him. At last he happened on Uncle Sandro. Uncle Sandro also asked him where he worked. Tengiz told him that he worked at a garage, but he did not say to whom the garage belonged. Or rather, he did not even have time to say.

"Wish I had someone to truck in a little firewood for me," Uncle Sandro said when he heard mention of the garage.

"That could be arranged," Tengiz said. This answer pleased Uncle Sandro so much that he gave him a room on the spot, without asking about anything else.

In the first few days Uncle Sandro told him about many stormy events of his life, some of which he obviously would not have shared had he known where Tengiz worked, garage or no garage.

In any case, when Tengiz came out of his room one day wearing what might be mildly described as a military uniform, Uncle Sandro was so disconcerted that he jumped up from his chair and saluted. However, when he saw that Tengiz meant him no harm, he made friends with him for good.

While Tengiz was telling this story, Uncle Sandro lay smiling, benevolently listening to him. From time to time he lifted the root to his nose, sniffed it, and then dropped his arm along the blanket.

Everyone laughed at the good-humored anecdote, and Tengiz poured himself some wine. Ordering everyone to pour, he turned serious and rose to offer a toast in Uncle Sandro's honor.

With epic leisureliness, his toast first addressed Uncle Sandro's life as a whole and then, as the trunk of a tree naturally branches out into living greenery, was enlivened with many particular details.

According to Tengiz, Uncle Sandro walked through life striving to ornament festive tables, if they turned up in his path; and if the tortuous path of life led him to a funeral banquet, for all sorts of things happen in life, he did not turn aside here either, but fulfilled his public duty with the propriety, the sad dignity, that was bequeathed to us by our grandfathers. So here, too, he made both the deceased's relatives happy, and the neighbors, and the deceased himself, if he is allowed to see from over there what is going on back here.

At this point Tengiz paused for a moment to resolve this dualistic problem. His solution was that the dead are most likely allowed to see much, though by no means all, of what goes on here.

His listeners, with nods and supportive exclamations, expressed their agreement with his point of view, but there was one skeptic.

"God grant that my enemies may see the way the deceased do," he said. Looking around the table—as if to ask, Who'd like to check that out?—he dipped a chunk of meat in the sauce.

"That's true too," sighed some of those sitting nearby, partly to reject even the most remote possibility of this kind of experiment being tried out on them.

"What a fine mind he must have," Tengiz continued, "in order to get by in our difficult times without working for a living, devoting his life wholly to your interests and mine. No, he hasn't worked a day in his life, unless you count that miserable orchard he's guarded for three years, if I'm not mistaken?"

Here he turned his gaze to Aunt Katya, she being Uncle Sandro's life companion, able to testify to the veracity of his toast. She was standing by Uncle Sandro's bed; the other women waiting on table had gently pushed her over there when Tengiz began his toast.

"He agreed to guard that miserable orchard only because of the cow," she put in, blushing like a schoolgirl. She seemed to want to stress that this small aberration from his life principles was not a personal caprice or frivolity, merely the consequence of extreme necessity.

"All the more, then," Tengiz said, graciously accepting this information. Concluding his toast, he suggested that the guests follow his example. They did, roaring their approval.

While he spoke, Uncle Sandro listened to him mildly, his head resting on one arm. From time to time, at the more florid passages in the toast, he opened his eyelids a little, as if softly leaving the tent and coming back again. His lips were slightly parted in an attentive smile, which might have been interpreted thus: I wonder if he'll remember this virtue of mine? See, he did . . . Good for him. And now let's see . . . So he remembers this one too . . . And now . . .

All through this comradely supper Tengiz kept up a running banter with the women sitting next to him, who obviously found him good company. Sometimes he exchanged gibes with Uncle Sandro, sometimes interjected remarks in the conversations around him.

He drank and ate very little, I noticed. He had a small penknife in his hand and worked all evening over a not very meaty joint, cutting off tiny scraps of meat and indifferently directing them to his mouth as he made humorous remarks to the people around him.

"Dimwit," he said to one of his neighbors who was planning a trip to the country to check on a sick relative, "why go, when I have a telephone? I'll call the village soviet tomorrow and find out all about it."

He seemed to feel bad that no one was using his telephone, in contrast to the television. People in this neighborhood, mainly emigrants from Abkhazian mountain villages, get along fine without a telephone, preferring to shout back and forth, since the terrain here is hilly and sound carries well in all directions.

He did not let that inexhaustible bone out of his hands all evening. He seemed to be preoccupied with giving it a definitive sculptural form, putting the meat in his mouth only to avoid making a mess. He worked like an expert bone carver making scrimshaw. Later I was convinced that he might be an expert bone setter, too.

I must admit that without noticing it I fell under the spell of his offhand charm. His boasting was so frank that it was even becoming to him. He may have liked me too, because before supper was over we ended up beside each other. On learning that I was interested in alpine hunting, he said that hunting was his favorite pastime; he had some Svanian friends who would take us to places where there was so much game you could just kill it with a stick.

"Be ready, I'll let you know when we can go," he said, still working over his bone, occasionally licking a scrap from the blade of the penknife.

Then he told the story of an alpine fishing trip in which he had happened to take part, along with Uncle Sandro. The remarkable thing about this fishing trip was that it had been arranged for Comrade Stalin and conducted with the aid of explosives.

When I expressed doubt about that, Uncle Sandro nodded from the bed as if to say, It's all true, that's the way it was.

"Where would the Leader find the time to sit around with a fishing rod, like a pensioner?" Tengiz explained. Cutting a thin sliver of meat from his bone, he tossed it into his mouth and said, "And do you know that's typical?"

He looked at me, and having made sure that I did not know, he added, "It turns out they did the same thing in the ocean. They used to stun fish from a torpedo boat, with depth charges. But I didn't see that myself, our boys told me."

According to Tengiz, one fine day the chief of the NKVD of Abkhazia was informed that Comrade Stalin, then vacationing here in Sinop, had expressed a desire to go fishing in a mountain stream. The chief was ordered to select from among his secret police a fisherman who could be trusted with dynamite in the presence of the Leader. The chief panicked, because, although he had quite a few secret police in his department, none of them knew how to stun fish. Then he recalled that Tengiz had boasted many times of being a good hunter. He decided that a hunter must certainly be a fisherman, and a fisherman must obviously be a poacher, which was untrue. He summoned Tengiz and ordered him to head up the fishing trip for Comrade Stalin.

"Comrade Chief," Tengiz said, "I'd love to do it, but I've never held a fishing rod in my life."

"You won't have to hold a fishing rod," the chief replied. "You'll stun them with explosives."

"I've specially never held explosives," Tengiz replied, and realized that this greatly displeased the chief.

"We'll ruin the Leader's vacation," the chief pronounced sadly. Then Tengiz, frightened, recalled that Uncle Sandro had told him how under the Mensheviks he had stunned fish on the Kodor. But in his fright he got it all mixed up. Uncle Sandro had not said that. Uncle Sandro had said that under the Mensheviks the Mensheviks themselves had stunned fish. But now, getting it all mixed up in his fright, he told the chief that the owner of the house he lived in, a man respected by all, was very good at stunning fish.

"This is Sandro?" the chief asked frowningly.

"Yes," Tengiz said, "and there's no man better than he at table."

"Can you vouch for him?"

"I can," Tengiz replied, "especially since he's already performed in Stalin's presence as a member of the song and dance ensemble."

"Dancing is one thing, holding explosives is another," the chief replied, thinking back over his career.

"Comrade Chief," Tengiz reminded him, "the ensemble dances with daggers—"

"Cold steel is one thing, explosives are another," the chief objected, but evidently there was nothing else to do. "All right, we'll send him to Tkvarcheli, let him practice with the powder men. And we'll assign you to him during the fishing trip. Anything happens—shoot without warning."

"Comrade Chief," Tengiz tried to soothe him, "I give my word I won't have to shoot, he's tried and true."

Thus Uncle Sandro, at government expense, in a government car, was sent to Tkvarcheli, where he was assigned to the best powder man in Comrade Stalin Coal Mine No. 1, who spent three days in the Galizga River teaching him to stun fish. So after three days Uncle Sandro came home an expert poacher.

And after another three days, Uncle Sandro, with Tengiz and two other secret service men, in a black ZIM with closed curtains, drove up to a government villa, from which four other ZIMs with closed curtains then drove away. In accordance with instructions, they followed these four cars to the region of one of the mountain lakes, but exactly which lake was not revealed until the last moment.

At this point Uncle Sandro interrupted Tengiz to say that he had immediately guessed the fishing trip would be somewhere near Ritsa, because not even one of the other mountain lakes had a highway leading to it.

Tengiz smiled at Uncle Sandro's remark and added that he had known too, especially since all those days the secret service had been stationed the whole length of the road. That was not easy to accomplish, because, for one thing, they had to be disguised from criminals, and for another, Comrade Stalin must not notice them.

Suddenly Tengiz turned to me. "Suppose you're vacationing in Gagra. Suddenly you have an urge to go to Sochi. What do you do? If you have money, you take a taxi. If you don't, you take the train, right?"

"I suppose so," I agreed.

"But Comrade Stalin couldn't," Tengiz said. "He had to inform the secret service three days ahead so they'd have time to station their men. But over those three days he'd either lose the desire or the weather would turn bad. And some people think the leaders have it easy! They think you go where you want, eat what you want . . . All free . . ."

With these words he rapped a finger on the back of his head as he stared around at the guests. The finger rapping the back of his head hinted at the mental backwardness of those who thought such a thing; at the same time, it let us know that the job of a leader demands and devours such a quantity of intellectual energy that it drives you out of your mind, makes you see stars. Both these points were understood and appreciated as he intended them.

"Oh no, Tengiz!" some of the guests exclaimed, as if superstitiously retreating from the job. "There's nothing worse than being a leader! It's enough to make your head burst!"

"Chiang Kai-shek's been having his brains treated for years!"

"What are you talking about? I can't even manage my wife, but he controlled the whole country. And built up the socialist camp besides."

"Admittedly, Tito got away . . ."

"But about the wife," came the skeptic's voice again, "you were wrong. Stalin couldn't manage his wife, either."

Tengiz heard out these exclamations calmly, and then, taking his penknife, cut another shred of meat from the joint and dispatched it to his mouth.

"Tell them about the man with the hoe," Uncle Sandro said comfortably from his bed, looking at Tengiz, his tone indicating that he was not hurrying him, simply reminding him of something interesting.

Tengiz looked at Uncle Sandro. "What man with a hoe?"

Uncle Sandro was now lying on his side, with one hand tucked under his pillow, from time to time lazily swinging the other hand, which held the root. It was the same way that one swings a quirt, not touching the horse, but letting him know that he must not slacken his pace.

"Why, the one who was standing by the river when the Big Mustache got out of the car."

"Ah-h," Tengo remembered. "That one had a shovel."

"What's the difference," Uncle Sandro said. "So it was a shovel."

"A big difference," Tengo said, unexpectedly quibbling with him. "In the secret service they can issue a shovel, but they can't issue a hoe. You might as well say a plow or a harrow."

"Okay." Uncle Sandro waved his root. "We know . . . You people have plenty of shovels. Go on with the story."

"You stinker," Tengiz said after a pause, looking at Uncle Sandro with suppressed delight. Then he went on with his story.

Up in the mountains, where the road ran now by the river, now through golden beech groves, Comrade Stalin took a notion to get out of the car at one point to look at a huge, half-kilometer cliff that hung over the river. He got out of the car and stood in the road admiring the cliff for some time, shading his eyes with his hand. Then he suddenly went down to the river and began to wash his hands.

Just at that moment, less than thirty meters away, a man with a nice new shovel peered out from behind the bushes.

Evidently he was so thrilled that Comrade Stalin had suddenly appeared so close to him that he forgot all his instructions and stared at him openly, all eyes.

Meanwhile, when Stalin got out of the car, everyone but the chauffeur had also left his seat. Along with Stalin were his secretary, Poskrebyshev; the head of the Kremlin secret service, whose name Tengiz had forgotten; and a doctor, whose name Tengiz said he didn't know even at the time. All the rest were secret service men or officials of the secret service.

They all saw that Comrade Stalin's eye was about to light on the inexperienced agent, and that this could lead to much unpleasantness for all. To prevent this from happening, they all signaled him to get back in the bushes, where he had been before.

"But that was the interesting thing, my friends," Tengiz said, interrupting his story. "He didn't see them, although there were a lot of them; he saw only Comrade Stalin, because he was looking only at him."

Comrade Stalin washed his hands, got a handkerchief from his pocket, and had just begun to wipe his hands when he noticed this comrade. And of course he didn't like it. It seemed suspicious to him. Here in the mountains, where there was no sign of habitation, not even a little village soviet, a man pops up from behind the bushes and gawks at him, not even ashamed of his shovel.

Stalin turned swiftly and went back, frowning. It seems he said something to Poskrebyshev when he got into the car, and to judge by the reply he had asked about the man.

"They say he's a local resident," Poskrebyshev replied. "He's digging worms to fish with."

As he spoke he took out a notebook and wrote something down. The cars went on, and Comrade Stalin did not get out anywhere else until they got to the place where they were to fish.

On a green meadow, near the base of a huge chestnut tree, they set up camp, started a fire, and brought out a folding chair. They seated Comrade Stalin near the fire, setting at his feet a bottle of Armenian cognac.

Here Tengiz interrupted his story and turned to Uncle Sandro, saying, "Now I'll let you take over. You fished with Stalin, you drank cognac with him, you tell it."

Uncle Sandro thought for a moment, sniffed his root, and. convinced that the Endurskies were behaving tolerably well, went on with the story.

"The day was fine and sunny, but getting into the mountain water at the end of October is no easy matter," Uncle Sandro began.

After each explosion, ten or fifteen trout floated up. Uncle Sandro, with his long johns rolled up, went into the water and threw the fish up on the bank. There the boys from the secret service picked them up and carried them to the cook, who was bustling around by the fire.

Every time Uncle Sandro got out on the bank, rigid from the icy water, Comrade Stalin called him over and poured a wineglass full of cognac for him.

"No need, Comrade Stalin, I'm not cold," Uncle Sandro replied, his teeth chattering, because he was ashamed to approach the Leader wet, in his rolled-up drawers. But the Leader silently beckoned him over, and there was nothing Uncle Sandro could do but approach him and accept the life-giving glass.

This happened four or five times, and then Uncle Sandro threw a charge into a small but deep pool. Along with the trout an enormous salmon floated up, and everyone standing on the shore raised a joyful shout. Comrade Stalin, laying his pipe on the chair, walked over to the bank and into the water.

. . . "What was he wearing?" I asked.

"Sort of a military uniform," Uncle Sandro said, and glanced at Tengiz.

"A regulation marshal's uniform," Tengiz said. Shaving off a long thin shred of meat, he licked it from the blade of the penknife and added, "Only without epaulettes."

. . . So, to everyone's surprise, when he saw this big salmon float up and lodge against a rock, Comrade Stalin walked into the water. Then the Kremlin doctor started shouting, "Comrade Stalin, don't forget, it's the end of October!"

But Comrade Stalin, without turning around, waved at him with his left arm, the withered one, and kept walking into the water.

Now the chief of the Kremlin secret service started to shout, "Comrade Stalin, I categorically forbid you!"

Comrade Stalin waved him off, too, with his withered arm and went in deeper, trying not to get water in his boots. He was still walking along the shallows. At this point his personal secretary, Poskrebyshev, was running along the bank like a hen that has hatched out a duckling, and he kept clucking, "I'll complain to the Politburo! I'll complain to the Politburo!"

Comrade Stalin bent down and reached for the salmon, which had lodged against a rock on a small shoal. But his arm did not reach; he took another step and got water in his boot. Then he waved his withered arm one last time—no point shouting when I've already got a bootful of water—and took one more step. Wet to the pockets of his marshal's riding breeches, he grabbed the salmon, lifted it, and turned around. Holding it in his arms with a smile—well, exactly like he held that little girl Mamlakat in the picture—he carried it out of the water and handed it to the men who came running.

. . . At this point Uncle Sandro was forced to break off his story, because several of the guests had completely forgotten who Mamlakat was, whereas others, on the contrary, began saying that they well remembered this photograph of the little cotton picker embracing Comrade Stalin, because huge enlargements of it had hung everywhere before the war.

Some of the listeners, once they got the point, recalled their own long-ago resentment at Comrade Stalin because he had put his arm around this little girl from Central Asia, who wasn't even pretty, whereas he could have put his arm around one of our own little tea pickers, pretty as a little doll. But for some reason he didn't want to. Others immediately entered into argument with them, justifying the Leader by pointing out that at the time there were political reasons why he had to put his arm around a little girl from Central Asia, so that the Indians would notice and think of themselves.

Uncle Sandro listened indulgently to all these points of view and went on with his story.

In a word, he continued, before the Big Mustache could get up on the bank they all dashed over—Poskrebyshev, and the Kremlin doctor, and the head of the secret service, carrying a towel, extra long johns, extra riding breeches, boots, and various other unmentionable bits of clothing.

They surrounded him and led him to the car, while Uncle Sandro took his own trousers, socks, and shoes and went upstream, where he saw a blackberry patch about fifty meters away.

He went into the thicket, took off his long johns, and was wringing them out when suddenly he heard something moving in the depths of the bushes. Uncle Sandro was frightened, thinking it might be a berserk bear and he would have to run from it naked, which for him, as an Abkhazian, would have been a great shame.

"*Kheyt!*" he shouted, thinking that if it was a bird it would flutter up, and if a wild animal, it would run.

"Don't worry—secret service!" a voice said suddenly in the bushes.

Uncle Sandro was again discomfited, because for him, as an Abkhazian, it was very shameful to show himself naked even before a secret service man. He turned his back on the voice and, silently marveling at the way you couldn't go anywhere without running into them, began to pull on his wet long johns. He had just stuck one foot in when steps sounded from the direction of the camp. Someone approached the bushes and stopped.

"Where is Comrade Sandro?" a voice asked.

"What's the matter, are you out of your mind?" Uncle Sandro shouted. "Let a man get dressed!"

"I have a pair of long johns for you, a present from Comrade Stalin," the man said. Uncle Sandro pulled his foot out of his long johns, covered himself with them, and peered out of the bushes. There stood a young fellow from the secret service, holding in his hand a pair of gray woolen long johns.

"Stalin's?" Uncle Sandro asked.

"Yes," the secret service man said. "You can wear them."

Uncle Sandro took the long johns, marveling at their fluffy lightness. Forgetting to thank the departing secret service man, he began to pull them on, feeling the unusual lightness and warmth of the wool.

"You can think what you like, but the fate of the Abkhazians was decided at that moment," Uncle Sandro said suddenly. He looked around the silenced table.

Tengiz grinned and continued to work on his bone without looking up.

"Why is that?" Tendel asked from his corner.

"Do you know that at that time there were special trains waiting in Eshery and in Kelasuri?" Uncle Sandro asked.

"We do know," a young store manager said. "When I heard the Rukhadze case—"

"What does the Rukhadze case have to do with this?" Tengiz raised his head over his bone and looked severely at the store manager.

The store manager fell silent in embarrassment. He was one of Uncle Sandro's neighbors, and the store where he worked was right at the exit from the highway, at the foot of the hill where Uncle Sandro lived. After Beria's arrest, when the chiefs of the Georgian NKVD were being tried, the store manager happened to be in Tbilisi and got into the theater for one day of the trial. Evidently some friends had used influence to arrange a one-day pass for him. He was forever bringing it up, whether it was relevant or not.

"There were trains waiting in Ochamchiry and Tamyshy," someone added.

"You know, of course, that they were planning to deport us from Abkhazia, as they had deported many other peoples?" Uncle Sandro said, solemnly gazing around the tables.

"They say that's true," people responded on all sides.

"Tengiz must know," one of the guests said. "He was working in the system then."

"In the first place, I don't know," Tengiz said, raising his head and looking significantly around the tables. "And in the second place, even if I did know, I wouldn't have the right to say."

"My, aren't you strict!" someone said in surprise.

"Tengiz," came a voice from the other end of the table, "I don't understand, are you in the system or have you left the system?"

"I left the system a long time ago. I'm in the motor vehicle inspectorate," Tengiz replied.

"I know. But I didn't think they let you out of the system that easy."

"They let *me* out," Tengiz said with dignity, indicating that he was he, but there was no reason to go on about it.

"Uncle Sandro," the young store manager asked, "what's the connection here anyway—the Leader's long johns and the deportation of the Abkhazians?"

"Why listen to him?" Aunt Katya said. "He'll go to jail for his tongue in his old age, and take you all with him."

"By way of this gift," Uncle Sandro said, after waiting out Aunt Katya like the roar of the elements, "he wanted to show that he was canceling the deportation of the Abkhazians. Either he liked me a lot or there was some other reason. He couldn't say it straight out, so he used this way of letting me know: Live in peace, I won't touch your people."

"You read too much into it, Sandro," the skeptic said. "He was capable of giving you the long johns and deporting you too."

"Exactly," someone added. "A buffalo plows the field and then he tramples it!"

"You'd better go on with the story," Tengiz said. "We'll never know now why Stalin gave you his long johns."

Somewhat disgruntled that no one supported his hunch, Uncle Sandro went on, gradually recovering his animation in the process of telling the story.

In brief, having put on his pants, he came out of the bushes carrying the old army long johns that he had been given, back during the war, by a soldier from the Destroyer Battalion, in exchange for a basket of pears.

These old long johns now struck him as dreadful, and he felt ashamed that he had dared to approach Comrade Stalin in them, although he tried to gain comfort from the thought that they had been rolled up.

Uncle Sandro decided he did not need them now, and besides he felt awkward approaching the campfire with his old drawers in hand. He looked around. Noticing a big stone near his feet, he moved it aside and put the twisted wad of long johns under it.

"What did you hide there?" Tengiz asked him in Abkhazian when he came over to the others.

"My old long johns," Uncle Sandro answered. "Why?"

"They've already informed us here that you hid something over there," he told him severely, and warned him never to do things like that.

According to Uncle Sandro, Tengiz said it as if he, Sandro, planned to stun fish for Stalin all his life, and Stalin in return planned to keep giving him long johns all his life, and Uncle Sandro, accepting the gift, would keep on trying to dispose of his old long johns under the first stone he found.

This amusing assumption made the guests laugh. Tengiz, scraping at his already bare bone, smiled and shrugged without looking up: "That's how times were then."

"What amazes me," Uncle Sandro went on, "I've been wearing these long johns ever since, and they're still like new. They must be a special kind of wool."

"Secret sheep," Tengiz remarked, without raising his head or tearing himself away from his bone.

"Lord! Maybe that's enough about underwear, there are young women here," Aunt Katya said, addressing her husband. She was now sitting on the foot of his bed.

Uncle Sandro threw her a distracted glance and continued his story, in no way revealing his attitude toward her words.

. . . By the campfire they spread a big Persian carpet, on which they laid a tablecloth, and on that they set out all kinds of good food, with especially large quantities of roast young chicken.

At Stalin's feet, right on the rug, sat the retinue of officials, headed by Poskrebyshev. Comrade Stalin called over all the boys from the secret service. Although they hung back, he made them sit down on the rug and take part in this dinner under the open sky.

"Have a chicken before they grow up," Comrade Stalin said to the boys from the secret service, who were very shy about eating in the Leader's presence.

When Uncle Sandro mentioned this joke, Tengiz nodded joyfully. Tearing himself away from his bone, he added, "But how could they grow up when they were already roasted?"

By stressing the absurdity of the Leader's remark about the chickens, Tengiz, as if to prevent false rumors, gave his listeners to understand that this retort was merely a joke, a rather ingenious one, but still merely a joke. The Leader had joked to encourage the boys from the secret service, and no other significance need be attached to his words.

Uncle Sandro went on. It seems that during dinner Comrade Stalin repeatedly made fun of his retinue, giving Poskrebyshev an especially hard time. He mocked him for not being able to sit cross-legged on the carpet in the Turkish manner, and later, when they started on the champagne, he caught Poskrebyshev trying to put his lips to his glass quickly, before the foam settled, so that they wouldn't fill it quite full.

According to Uncle Sandro, this was a subtle and correct observation, which proved that Stalin too might have become a pretty fair tamada if he had not been so busy with politics. Here Uncle Sandro stopped and looked slyly around from his high pillow, as if trying to see whether his far-reaching innuendo had reached his listeners.

Whether it had or not is hard to say because at that point Tengiz tore himself away from his bone and gave Uncle Sandro a scornful look, asking, "So if you hadn't spent so much time at the table you might have become a leader?"

"I wouldn't have wanted to," Uncle Sandro said, "especially after the Twentieth Congress."

The conversation switched to the Twentieth Congress, and many people began to express various thoughts regarding Khrushchev's criticism of Stalin.

I asked Tengiz what he personally thought about it.

"You mean me?" he asked, and looked me in the eyes.

"I mean you," I repeated.

"Khrushchev was right about a lot of things, of course," Tengiz said. "He was right about the kolkhozes. He was right about the evacuation of the ethnic groups and right about the arrests. But if you want my personal impression, I'll tell you."

"Yes, your personal impression," I repeated.

"No one treated the boys from the secret service better than he did. This I saw with my own eyes."

Here we were unexpectedly interrupted by Tendel, still sitting in the corner next to Uncle Sandro's brother, who, incidentally, had sprawled back in his chair and gone to sleep.

"Sandro!" Tendel cried. "You should've thrown a charge into the campfire, Khrushchit would've given you a medal!"

Everyone burst out laughing, and Uncle Sandro's brother woke up and looked around wildly, hiccuping.

"Posthumously," Tengiz added, continuing to work on his bone, which suddenly began to look like one of the two crossed bones under the skull (the drumsticks of fate!) in the familiar symbol.

"Posthumously," he repeated, this time in Russian. He added, "The boys would've been right on you—you couldn't have moved."

"What did he say?" Tendel asked, but they didn't have time to explain, because Uncle Sandro went on with his thought.

"How could I throw a charge," Uncle Sandro said thoughtfully, as if he had studied the possibility but rejected it as impracticable. "How could I, when they wouldn't even let me put my long johns under a stone—"

"Must you keep on about that?" Aunt Katya looked at him with reproach.

Uncle Sandro did not dwell on his long johns, however, but continued the story. As he told it, he sat opposite the Leader and observed him covertly, trying not to let him see the flash of his eyes, which, although not so bright as in his youth, were still bright.

He still feared that Stalin would recognize him, although more than fifty years had passed since the time of that first meeting.

As Uncle Sandro observed, Stalin had changed a great deal, even compared to the way he had been twenty years before, not to mention the first meeting. He had gone completely gray, and his withered arm was noticeable even when he was not moving it. But his eyes remained just as bright and radiant as at the first meeting. And when he stood up and went to get the salmon, he moved very lightly and rapidly.

Yet he did remember Uncle Sandro again, and again Uncle Sandro was able to outwit the Leader! (In speaking of this, he smacked his lips with a satisfaction that he would not put into words.)

As Uncle Sandro told it, toward the end of dinner the Big Mustache sensed something and began to look closely at him. Uncle Sandro became alarmed and tried to avoid raising his eyes, but even without raising his eyes he could feel Stalin looking at him from time to time.

Suddenly he heard Stalin's voice. "I've seen you somewhere, fisherman."

"Me?" Uncle Sandro asked, and raised his eyes.

"Yes, you, fisherman," the Big Mustache said, peering at him with his radiant eyes.

"I used to dance in Pantsulaya's chorus," Uncle Sandro replied, using the line he had thought up ahead of time, "and we performed for you in Gagra—"

"And before that?" the Big Mustache asked, without taking his radiant eyes off Uncle Sandro. Suddenly everyone at the table froze. Poskrebyshev, trying not to make any noise, wiped his hands on a napkin and reached into a pocket, ready to pull out his notebook at the first sign.

"Before that you might have seen me in a movie," Uncle Sandro said, looking him right in the eye.

"In a movie?" Stalin asked in surprise.

"They made a movie about our ensemble," Uncle Sandro said briskly. Again he looked the Leader in the eye.

"Ah-h-h," said Stalin, the light in his eyes going out. "And where is Platon Pantsulaya now?"

He drenched a chicken leg in *satsivi* and took a languid bite. Then he raised his eyes again to Uncle Sandro.

"He was arrested in '37," Uncle Sandro said. He spread his hands, implying that the man was unlucky, he got hit by an avalanche. (Telling about it now, that was how he explained his gesture.)

Stalin looked at Poskrebyshev as if he wanted to say something. Poskrebyshev swallowed what he had in his mouth and wiped his hands on his napkin again, then sat motionless in expectation. According to Uncle Sandro, he looked at Stalin as if he wanted to say, "By all means, give the order and we'll set him free."

Or so it seemed to Uncle Sandro. In any case, Uncle Sandro felt a rush of excitement and joy at the thought that they could free Platon Pantsulaya. It occurred to him that it would be nice to put in a request for Pata Pataraya, too, and for Lakoba's son Rauf, arrested in '37 as a boy of fourteen. But then the thought flashed through his mind that it was still dangerous to request anything for Lakoba's son, and he honestly confessed that he had mentally abstained from that mental request.

Here several people interrupted Uncle Sandro to remind him that Lakoba's son had been killed in 1941, when he wrote a letter to Beria asking to be sent to the front. Surprised that he was still alive, Beria had ordered him killed.

"Evidently they couldn't kill him in '37 because he was a minor, and later they forgot about him, and when the poor boy applied for the front in '41 it reminded them of his existence," one of Uncle Sandro's guests suggested, quite judiciously, it seemed to me. According to rumor, the letter Rauf managed to forward from prison had included a request to be sent to the front.

"Poor boy," Aunt Katya sighed. "He'd be free now."

"But do you know what Attorney General Rudenko said at Rukhadze's trial?" the young store manager from whom Uncle Sandro got credit suddenly put in.

"No, what did he say?" Tengiz asked scornfully, sure that he was going to say something irrelevant again.

"Rudenko said they should put up a monument to Sarya, Lakoba's wife, because no matter how they tortured her she wouldn't betray her husband," he said, gazing triumphantly around the table.

"So they should—who's stopping them?" said the man who had spoken about Rauf.

"Poor Sarya," Uncle Sandro sighed. "Back then I saw her every day, the way I see you all now—"

"You'd better tell us how it came out, with you and the Big Mustache," one of the guests prompted. "What did he say when he looked at Poskrebyshev?"

"That's just it, he didn't say anything," Uncle Sandro replied. "Or rather, he said Poskrebyshev was sitting the wrong way again, had his feet turned out from under him—"

"Yes, yes," Tengiz nodded, smiling, "he never could sit cross-legged. Stalin taunted him for that—"

"You'd better tell us," Tendel shouted from his corner, "did you lay a load in your pants when the Big Mustache looked at you?"

"I was good and scared, but not that bad," Uncle Sandro answered seriously.

"Too bad he didn't remember the lower Chegem road, or you'd have had a whole pants-load!" Tendel shouted, to general laughter. Everyone knew the story of Uncle Sandro's encounter with Stalin, or the man he took for Stalin, on the lower Chegem road.

"Maybe you would've laid a load in those long johns if they hadn't been Stalin's," Tengiz shouted over the general laughter. "As it was, you were afraid it would make things even worse."

"Go ahead and laugh, you shitheads, but I saved you from deportation!" Uncle Sandro shouted, barely able to keep from laughing himself.

Late that night, when the supper was over, Tengiz and I said good-bye to Uncle Sandro and walked down the lane leading to the highway.

"A terrific old man," he said, slamming the gate. "I really love him."

"He loves you, too," I replied, and noticed that Tengiz nodded his head in agreement. The night was crisp, starry. The smell of overripe Isabellas and drying corn hung in the air.

When we came to his house, he tried to persuade me to spend the night with him. I thanked him but refused, explaining that I was expected at home.

"Call up from my place," he suggested, and added as an enticement, "I'll tell you how I went hunting with Marshal Grechko when he vacationed in Abkhazia."

"We don't have a phone," I said, feeling that I'd had enough for today. We said good-bye and I started down to the highway. Ahead and behind me, Uncle Sandro's guests were walking home, loudly talking and calling to one another.

Three weeks later Uncle Sandro came to see me at the newspaper office. He was already fully recovered, and I had encountered him briefly several times in the coffeehouses. At the moment he looked upset.

"What happened?" I asked, standing up and showing him to a chair.

"They've outraged my wife," he said. He remained standing.

"Who, where?" I asked uncomprehendingly.

"The director of the polyclinic, at the polyclinic," he said, and laid out the details.

It seemed that at the newly opened commercial polyclinic where Aunt Katya had gone to have her teeth cared for, they had promised to put in gold crowns for her and then refused to at the last moment, citing a lack of gold.

The worst of it was that they themselves had suggested putting in six crowns instead of four, although Uncle Sandro and Aunt Katya had inquired about four teeth. And now, as Uncle Sandro told it, having filed down two extra teeth for greater convenience in putting on the crowns, they said they'd run out of gold for this quarter; she was to wait another month, then maybe they'd have the gold.

But how could the poor woman wait when she couldn't talk and couldn't eat?

Well, her not being able to talk wasn't all bad, but not being able to eat, that was too much.

"But what could have happened over there?"

"Let's go, you'll find out," he said. I shut the door of my office and left the building with him.

"I think," he continued as we walked, "they were expecting an audit, and in order to demonstrate that they weren't selling gold to speculators but were even installing it in the populace, they made this promise and took two extra teeth besides, to meet their plan. And now either they've found a common language with the auditor or the audit has been postponed."

We turned the corner, walked two blocks, and came to the polyclinic. On the sidewalk in the shade of a plane tree stood Aunt Katya, dolefully covering her mouth with the end of the black shawl that was tied on her head. At the sight of me her face wrinkled into a grimace, in the center of which, evidently hidden under the shawl, there must have been an embarrassed smile. Then she looked reproachfully at Uncle Sandro, as if he were the culprit in the outrage.

"What did I do?" Uncle Sandro said with a shrug.

"It was your idea," she said through the shawl. "I would have pulled out the aching one and that would have been the end of it."

She spoke in a soft, level voice, evidently trying not to aggravate the pain.

"Does it hurt?" I asked.

"They don't hurt by themselves, but when the air strikes them, it just goes right through me," she said. After a silence she added, as if the moral suffering intensified the physical, "I can't talk."

"So don't talk," Uncle Sandro said.

"That's all you wanted," she pronounced mournfully through the shawl.

"Never mind, Aunt Katya, we're here now," I said briskly, in order to get myself into a positive mood.

"Wait for us here," Uncle Sandro said, and we started for the entrance.

"As if I'd fly away," she sighed after us.

"The interesting thing is," Uncle Sandro remarked as we went into the polyclinic, "now that the pain keeps her from talking, she talks more than ever."

We walked down the corridor, where here and there on benches sat people with faces twisted by toothache or petrified in bleak anticipation of an encounter with the drill.

We came to the director's office. I opened the door a crack and saw a small man in a white coat seated at the desk, talking with another man in a white coat.

When I opened the door, they both looked in our direction. The one sitting at the director's desk thought for several seconds, trying to figure out whether I had turned up at the door with Uncle Sandro by chance or whether we represented a single united force. Evidently he decided that we were together.

"Just a moment," he said, flashing his gold teeth. "I'm almost through."

I closed the door.

"There's no gold," Uncle Sandro grumbled, "but he's been working here two months and his mouth is already full of it."

We stood for half a minute listening to the muffled voices from the office. The director's voice became louder; evidently he was making a phone call. Suddenly Uncle Sandro bent his head to the door. I became uncomfortable. I walked away and sat down on a bench beside some gloomy patients awaiting their turn. Uncle Sandro continued to listen to what was going on in the office. No one paid any attention to him.

I peered down the corridor, where nurses and doctors in white coats appeared in the distance from time to time, each carrying sheafs of papers or folders filled with patient records. I was afraid that one of them would come to the director's office. But no one approached or noticed Uncle Sandro. Everyone was busy with his own job.

Finally Uncle Sandro pulled himself away from the door and came over to me.

"He was talking about you," he said, nodding toward the office.

"About me?" I repeated, for some reason sure that this promised me no good.

"He was asking someone over the telephone," Uncle Sandro explained. "They told him your job is shaky."

"Why?" I asked, although I already knew why.

"They suspect that you informed Moscow about the goatibex," Uncle Sandro said. He looked into my eyes with curiosity. "They say that the editor is just trying to think of a way to get rid of you."

My mood was ruined. I was getting fed up with this base rumor. The worst of it was, why would anyone inform, when the stuff on the goatibex had been published in the local papers, and one of the articles had even been reprinted in Moscow?

The door of the director's office opened, and the man who had been sitting with his back to us came out. He too carried a thick record. As he walked by, he shot me an evil glance, as if he knew some disagreeable secret about me.

"Threaten him with a satirical article," Uncle Sandro whispered as we went into the office.

"Please have a seat," the director said, nodding at some chairs. His tone had the benevolence of a man who is sure of his cards.

We remained standing.

"I've already told Comrade Sandro," he continued, "we aren't to blame for the way it turned out. They've refused us the material for this quarter."

He spread his hands: Circumstances have overpowered our good intentions.

"But what a position you've put the woman in," I said. "You filed down her teeth, she can't eat, she can't speak—"

"I told Comrade Sandro," he said, energetically waving a hand in Uncle Sandro's direction, "we can put in metal crowns for her. Incidentally, they're more durable and hygienic."

I turned to Uncle Sandro.

"My wife," he said, "is supposed to go around with an iron jaw like a witch?"

"That's a superstition, Comrade Sandro," the director said, bowing jauntily in Uncle Sandro's direction. "Metal crowns are more becoming in an old woman."

"So put them in your own old woman," Uncle Sandro said.

"Comrade Sandro, please don't be rude." He displayed his palms like little signs telling the penalty for rudeness.

"For my wife it's okay, but for your wife it's being rude!"

"Your wife is our patient. And my wife has nothing to do with it." He lowered his signboard palms to the table, but metal appeared in his voice—perhaps the durable, hygienic metal from which crowns were made.

"You told me yourself that she needed six instead of four, and now she doesn't get even one?"

"I told you," he began again, "they aren't giving us enough gold, because the country is short of currency . . ."

He stopped, goggle-eyed, as if amazed that Uncle Sandro was still demanding gold from him instead of grieving with him over the currency shortage.

We left.

"You should have threatened him with a satirical article," Uncle Sandro said as we went down the corridor. "No, it's plain to see, you'll never be any use. I'll have to ask my Tengo again."

We emerged from the polyclinic and walked over to Aunt Katya, who was still standing there in the shade of the plane tree, her mouth covered with the end of the black shawl.

"Well, what did he say?" she asked through the shawl, in the voice of a person who expects no good.

"The same thing he said before," Uncle Sandro replied. "It turns out this poor fool is barely holding on himself, never mind helping us. I'll go see Tengiz now, he'll show them. Don't you go away. Sit over there on the bench and wait." He indicated the public garden across the street. "If anyone starts talking to you, don't answer, pretend to be dumb."

Uncle Sandro turned away without saying good-bye to me and set off decisively toward the bus stop. I was annoyed at the undistinguished role I had played and sorry for Aunt Katya, who was still standing there with her mouth covered by the end of the black shawl.

"Go along, sonny," she said through the shawl, "it can't be helped. You've got your own troubles."

Hanging my head, I went back to the newspaper. Just before the end of the workday Uncle Sandro walked into my office.

"We're going out," he said in the authoritative tone of a man who is giving you a lesson in life. I trailed along after him.

We started down the steps. Aunt Katya was standing by the newspaper building. She was still covering her mouth with the end of the shawl, but now she did it quite differently—the way a young woman who has put on lipstick for the first time hides her lips from acquaintances.

"Come on, smile!" Uncle Sandro said as he came down toward her.

"Don't!" Aunt Katya said, trying to hide her embarrassment, unable to bring herself to pull the shawl away from her lips.

"Have you turned into a complete ninny?" Uncle Sandro asked severely, from above.

"What's got into you?" Aunt Katya said. Pulling back the shawl, she smiled a shy golden smile. "You talk as if everyone looks at my mouth."

"Well, how about it?" Uncle Sandro said, turning to me. "Did they do a good job on my old woman?"

"Wonderful," I said, watching Aunt Katya raise the shawl again and carefully hide her gold.

"Now you understand what kind of a man my Tengo is?"

"But where did he get the gold?" I asked.

"Ha!" Uncle Sandro exclaimed scornfully. "Where did he get it? You should ask *how* he got it!"

"How did he get it?" I asked, and he told me how.

"When we came roaring up to the polyclinic on the motorcycle, all the windows flew open, and they realized: this meant trouble. Tengiz left the engine running and we went inside. As we walked down the corridor, the doors opened a crack and the swindlers poked their noses out; and as soon as we drew even and Tengiz looked in, the doors went slam! slam! slam!

"Tengiz opened the door to the director's office—no one there. He had managed to get away. Now I ask you, what would you have done in Tengo's place? You'd have stood in the doorway like a poor pensioner and waited for him to come back. What did Tengiz do? Tengiz walked into the office and sat down in the director's chair. Just as he sat down, the phone rang. He picked up the receiver.

" 'Hello,' he says, and he looks at me. The other party evidently asked who was speaking.

" 'Tengiz speaking,' he answered, 'Chief of Vehicle Inspection on the Enduria Road.'

"The other party evidently asked where the director was.

" 'The director's in hiding,' he says, 'we're looking for him right now. He's suspected of absconding with government gold. The roads have been closed.'

"The other party evidently took fright and hung up without answering Tengiz. Tengiz calmly dialed a number and had a conversation with his acquaintances. And what do you think? In five minutes the director walks into his office like a beaten dog, and Tengiz (ah, my Tengo!) goes on talking on the telephone, only now he's looking not at me but at the director. He signals him with his hand—sit down!—but the director doesn't sit down, because he wants to sit in his own chair. Finally Tengo hangs up and looks at the director.

" 'What do you say?' Tengo asks.

" 'I've already said it all,' the director says, as if he's angry, but actually he's scared.

" 'But I haven't said it all yet,' Tengiz answers, 'because I can't stand it when people insult old women, especially nice shy old women like our Aunt Katya. And she's an upright old woman, too. If she's got nothing in the house but beans,' he says, 'she'll fix you a *lobio* that'll leave you licking your fingers. And now, when people insult old women like this one, when they deceive them and file off their teeth like Beria's executioners and then offer iron instead of gold,' he says, 'I leave the Enduria Road and come to the defense. At this very moment, crooked truckers are bringing in uninvoiced black-market goods from underground Endursk manufacturers.'

"Tengiz practically had me in tears with his speech. But the director had the opposite reaction. Evidently he decided that Tengiz was revealing a weak point by talking about nice shy old women. But the poor jerk was wrong, because Tengiz never reveals a weak point, he always has something up his sleeve.

" 'Why are you lecturing me?' the director says loudly so that his colleagues can hear how brave he is. 'We don't have any gold, and you can just get up from my chair.'

" 'You do have gold,' Tengiz answered, and he calmly went to open the drawer, as if he hoped the gold was lying there.

" 'Don't touch that drawer!' the director shouted, and he ran over to him.

"It turned out this was just what Tengiz wanted. Like a hawk after a chicken, Tengiz grabbed him by the beard! To tell the truth, I didn't like it. To hell with him, I thought, my old woman had better go around with an iron jaw.

"The director's mouth was wide open, he couldn't say a word, he turned black. Tengo kept hold of his beard and gave his head a shake.

" 'You've got enough gold in your mouth for two old women,' he says, 'and I will prove it to you completely officially, as senior motor vehicle inspector on the Enduria Road.'

"With these words he let him go, I swear by the bones of my father, he dusted off his hands, and we left.

" 'Bring Aunt Katya in,' he said at the door, 'and in the meantime he'll remember where the gold is.'

"To make a long story short, they both found the gold and fixed my old woman, as you see, and they didn't take a kopeck for it."

"Not a kopeck?"

"We paid the tax to the government," Aunt Katya added, "but we didn't give them anything."

"And we had planned to give them fifty rubles," Uncle Sandro added.

"A mighty man!" I said, utterly sincere.

"Of course!" Uncle Sandro concluded. "They don't assign just any old simpleton to the Enduria Road."

They left. I stood a while longer, looking after them: the neat little old lady in a black shawl and the tall trim old man beside her. Right at the corner they stopped, having encountered some acquaintance. Uncle Sandro gestured toward Aunt Katya, and I knew that he was going through the story again. I went back to the newspaper.

I don't know whether it happened exactly as Uncle Sandro told it, but about a month later I had occasion to see for myself that Tengiz was a man of the most decisive character, and that quite a few dangers lurked on the Enduria Road.

That Sunday, Tengiz and I had agreed that he would take me on his motorcycle as far as the turnoff to the village of Atary, where I was going to visit relatives. This was not too burdensome for him, because he himself went to the country every Sunday to visit his own relatives, who lived farther out; it was right on his way.

He pulled up at my house, I got into the sidecar, and we drove out of the city. It was a fine sunny day, and we rolled swiftly along the Enduria highway, beside the sea. Ten kilometers outside of the city, Tengiz suddenly jammed on the brakes and the motorcycle stopped.

"What happened?" I asked.

"I have to check something," he said, jerking his head toward the road behind us and tossing his gladiator gloves on my knees. "Endursky speculators."

I looked back and saw, far behind us, an ordinary light van. It overtook us, and now it was passing us. Tengiz raised a hand and waved carelessly to it. I noticed that there were two men in the cab. After traveling another twenty meters the truck stopped—reluctantly, it seemed to me.

To this day I do not understand how he recognized the truck, because he had not looked back once the whole time we were driving out of the city. Either he recognized it by the sound of the motor, or he saw it in his mirror, or perhaps by some complex calculation known only to motor vehicle inspectors he determined that it had to appear here precisely at this time, the way astronomers predict the approach of heavenly bodies.

Whatever the case, the truck stopped, and Tengiz walked over to it, his gait lazy and relaxed.

Sitting in the sidecar, I watched him approach the cab and rest his foot on the running board to converse with the driver. I caught only an occasional word or two, from which little could be understood, and besides, I was not trying to make sense of what they said.

Having nothing better to do, I pulled on his gloves. They were heavy, and I felt myself plunged up to the elbows into the Middle Ages. I felt the center of gravity of my being shift toward my weighted hands. I felt a mild desire to close the grip of these tournament gloves on a knightly spear or sword.

After a moment, apparently, the lack of other knightly appurtenances returned me to my usual peaceable frame of mind, and I dozed off, feeling the warm autumn sun on my face and hearing the roar of the sea beyond a eucalyptus grove. I was drowsily aware of words carrying to me from the truck. They talked for five or ten minutes.

Then I opened my eyes and saw the driver's thick red arm sticking out, his sleeve rolled up to the elbow. He was offering some sort of paper to Tengiz. Perhaps it was a bill of lading. Tengiz's face changed. His hooknosed profile took on a scornful expression, like that of Mephistopheles when someone tries to palm a sham indulgence off on him: he knows the price of a real indulgence, and this one's a sham. Tengiz threw just one glance at it and with mild annoyance drawled into the window, "Show . . . grandmother . . ."

They talked a while longer. Tengiz was still standing in the same relaxed pose, his foot resting on the running board of the truck, and the driver was evidently trying to prove something to him. I confess I was surprised at Tengiz's patience, and what was more, his conscientiousness. It was his day off, after all, and he could have given himself a break.

But here's what happened next. The hand from the cab passed him some sort of document, evidently a driver's license, and Tengiz, without looking, thrust it in his pocket and walked toward the motorcycle. Now the door of the cab opened on the opposite side, and the driver swiftly overtook him.

He was a man of about thirty, not too tall, very stocky, with an unshaven face and eyelids red as if from lack of sleep. He walked beside Tengiz saying something to him, and I noticed his broad shoulders and the incredibly thick arms sticking out from the rolled-up sleeves of his cowboy shirt.

Suddenly I saw the driver reach into his pocket, take something out, and, as he brushed against Tengiz for an instant, thrust something into his pants pocket.

At this point I snapped out of my drowsiness and stared at them. I could not understand: had the driver really thrust something in his pocket, or had I just imagined it? Neither his expression nor Tengiz's had changed. The driver continued to talk, and Tengiz took the document out of his pocket—now I was sure it was a driver's license—and gave it back to him, after waving it under his nose.

The driver nodded his tousled head, and now it was especially noticeable what hefty shoulders and arms he had, especially in comparison with Tengiz, tall and slim like a stage dancer.

The driver turned his broad back and walked quickly to the truck. Tengiz came over to the motorcycle at his relaxed gait. As he approached I simply could not tell whether he knew the driver had thrust something into his pocket, or whether I had dreamed the whole thing. Only when he got back could I tell, by his thievish, self-satisfied smile, that he knew.

At that moment the truck shot away, roaring to high speed almost instantly. Tengiz went on smiling, but it struck me that a shadow of alarm crossed his face. Slowly he stuck his hand in his pocket and pulled out a pre-reform three-ruble bill.

The next instant he threw the three-ruble bill away and looked down the road, his face distorted in anger. The truck was raising dust far ahead.

"Get out!" he barked.

Instantly, not knowing what I was doing, I tumbled out of the sidecar. I think he shook me out of it like a bean from an overripe pod.

The motorcycle revved up like an airplane taking off, enveloping me in a whirlwind of hot air and dust, and disappeared into the distance. Needless to say, I was good and mad at that point—most likely because of the stupidly awkward way I had tumbled out of the sidecar. Besides, I still had his tournament gloves on, which was especially inappropriate. I stood up, took off the gloves, and slapped one of them on my pants to dust myself off. Then I tossed the gloves on the side of the road and began to wait. I did not know what to make of all this, but I had the clear sensation that the air smelled of false witness.

For thirty minutes the motorcycle did not reappear, and I stared into the cabs of oncoming trucks, trying to guess from people's expressions whether they knew anything about what had happened up ahead, but no one appeared to know anything, and besides there weren't all that many trucks.

Finally the motorcycle appeared. It was traveling at low speed, like the winner of a heat making the lap of honor. When he drew even with me, Tengiz stopped and wearily dropped his hands from the handlebars. His dusty face shone with the triumphant satiety of a blood avenger who has taken the head of his enemy.

"What happened?" I asked him, handing him his gloves.

"What happened was what had to happen," he said, wiping his face with one of them.

Here is the story he told, glancing into the cabs of passing trucks and sometimes nodding to drivers he knew.

"I caught up to him in about fifteen minutes. I saw he wasn't going to let me pass. I veer right—he veers right. I try the left—he swings left too. Son of a bitch, I thought, we'll see who buys whom. I didn't pull in close, I knew he'd slam on the brakes and I'd plow into him. An old Endursky trick. Well, all right, I thought, next time an oncoming truck passes him, I'll give it the gas and spurt between them. But he's no fool either. Next time an oncoming truck passes, he pulls over just enough so the other guy barely gets by, leaving me no room to get through.

"Well, never mind, I thought, we'll see who blinks first. I stuck to him like a burr. He speeds up, I speed up—he slows down, I slow down. He wants me to come in just a little closer so he can slam on the brakes. I speed up just barely, he thinks I want to shoot by, I slow down again. Finally his nerves gave out. He braked and swung to the right, and I spurted past on the left, I dropped the bike and pulled out my pistol. He knew he'd had it. He stopped the truck. I walked over. They were sitting there like corpses. The fat one didn't say anything. The other one says, 'Sorry, Tengiz! I swear by my mother, we were joking around.'

" 'I want to joke around, too,' I say. 'Get out!'

"I hold the gun on them, because the fat one's such a speculator, he'll do anything.

" 'Turn your back,' I say. They turn.

" 'Take three steps,' I say to the driver. He does. I frisk his pal, his pockets are empty. I frisk Tubby. Just looking at the back of his neck I can tell he's got something in his pocket. Correct. A roll of bills in his pocket. I put it in my pocket without counting.

" 'Three hundred?' I ask.

" 'Yes,' he grumbles, 'three hundred.'

" 'Correct,' I say. 'Tax on transport of uninvoiced nylon blouses from Endursk to Mukhus. Now go and tell them in Endursk how you mocked Tengiz with a pre-Khrushchev three-ruble bill.'

"They didn't say anything. Tubby breathed heavily. I could tell he wanted to eat me alive, but he was afraid of choking on a bullet. They got into the truck, and I kept the gun on them until they drove off, because this Tubby is the number one speculator in Endursk."

At that Tengiz pulled out a roll of ten-ruble bills from his pocket and counted them.

"Is it really three hundred?" I asked.

"Yes, but that's not the point," he said, slipping the money into his wallet and putting it away in his jacket pocket.

"What is it, then?" I asked.

"Imagine how he could have shamed me!" Tengiz exclaimed. Biting his lip, he shook his head. "Well, now let him tell who shamed whom."

"Would you really have fired if they hadn't stopped?" I asked.

"Why else would that speculator stop?" he asked, putting on his gloves and starting the motor.

"But you could go to jail for this!"

"Of course," he agreed, and then loudly, shouting over the motor, "Wound a man's honor and he'll do anything! Get in, let's go!"

I got into the sidecar.

"He wanted to shame me, the bastard!" he remembered again as he turned around.

We set off. After a while Tengiz slowed down and shouted something to me, nodding at the road. I saw on the highway the dark tire marks laid down by a sharply braking truck. The marks veered off to the right, as if the truck had been swept away. Tengiz gave it the gas again, leaving behind the scene of his duel with the Endursky driver.

"Shame me!" His voice carried over the roar of the motor, and I saw his back shudder. It was the way people shudder from a sense of loathing when they remember some miraculous escape from degradation.

He delivered me successfully to the Atary turnoff, and he himself drove on. It seemed to me that he had already regained his calm. In any case, his posture on the motorcycle expressed his usual lazy relaxation.

Since that time, needless to say, I have made no great effort to go on motorcycle excursions with Tengiz.

. . . About a year later I learned that he had been fired from his job. I met him one day on the street.

"You already know?" he asked, looking me in the eye.

"I heard," I said.

"What do you think?"

"You know what I think," I said. "You got off easy."

"Foolishness." He brushed me aside in annoyance. "That wasn't the problem."

"What was it?"

"Intrigues," he said significantly. "I had a good job, many people envied me. But I won't leave it at that, I'm going to complain to the Central Committee."

As we talked, he kept glancing at the road in expectation, as I could tell, of an approaching vehicle. At last he raised a hand, and a private Volga stopped near us. Evidently he had not yet lost the magic of power.

"Give me a lift to Kashtak," he said to the owner of the car. The man nodded his head in bleak submission.

"Intrigues," he repeated, getting in next to the driver, and he nodded significantly, as if there was some powerful corporation which was planning to destroy him, but with which he intended to keep on struggling.

Evidently he did keep on, and the struggle was not easy. In any case, the corporation gained the upper hand at first. I saw him a few months later behind the wheel of a taxi near the bazaar. He was sprawled back in the seat while he waited with lazy condescension for several clamoring women to get in back with their shopping bags. One of them had thrust her arm out of the window and was holding a peeping bouquet of chickens by the feet.

His whole pose, expressing a condescending indifference to the present, for some reason reminded me (so I imagined) of a monarchical émigré in an alien land, forced to engage in a humiliating business, but confident of his rightness and awaiting his hour.

In contrast to monarchical émigrés, Tengiz lived to see his hour. After another six months he was restored—admittedly, as an ordinary inspector—to the same Enduria Road. Perhaps his experience was needed.

The reason was that at that time, among the peaceful underground factories of Endursk, there had appeared a supersecret knitting mill which turned out articles made of jersey and used Japanese machines. This fact was established, unfortunately, only upon examination of samples of the final product by the experts of Mukhus, Sochi, Krasnodar, and other cities of our land.

Irritated by the successes of the new factory, the old manufacturers of Endursk, through an irony of history already noted by Marx, entered into class-alien contact with agents of the DCESPS (Department for Combating the Embezzlement of Socialist Property and Speculation), to help the department find and destroy their successful competitors.

But this proved none too easy. The struggle lasted for several years, and the new—without ever coming out from underground, incidentally—conquered the old. The jersey mill's stockholders, in spite of their Japanese machines, used an old cottage-industry ploy. One fine day the underground warehouse in Endursk burned down, and with it a huge stock of nylon blouses.

And again, the irony of history went to work, admittedly in reverse. Soviet firemen (and Endursky firemen may confidently be called Soviet) were called upon to extinguish this class-alien fire.

It turned out that the house in which the goods were stored had formerly belonged to a Georgian Jew named David Arakishvili, who had gone to Israel, presenting his house, as it developed after the fire, to his fictitious nephew. One refinement of this Zionist mockery of David Arakishvili's was that while he left his house in the name of a nonexistent nephew, he took all his existent nephews with him.

Why the passport, why the residence permit, why the house register, one may well ask, if in Endursk a whole house can be sold to underground manufacturers under the pretext of a melancholy gift to a nephew left behind by an uncle disenchanted with the possibilities of socialism!

But, as they say, there is no great loss without some small gain. Ever since, the lecturers of Endursk and Mukhus have used this story with considerable success as a graphic example supporting the proposition that the development of private ownership is rapacious in character, a fact repeatedly noted in the best classic works of both Marx and Engels.

TALI, MIRACLE OF CHEGEM

ON THAT UNFORGETTABLE summer day, a contest was under way between the tobacco stringers of the two tobacco brigades in the village of Chegem. The rivals—one of them Uncle Sandro's fifteen-year-old daughter Tali, or Taliko, or Talikoshka; the other the hunter Tendel's nineteen-year-old granddaughter Tsitsa—were competing between themselves for Chegem's first phonograph and a complete set of records, "Report of Comrade I. V. Stalin to the Special All-Union Congress of Soviets, 25 November 1936, on the Draft Constitution of the U.S.S.R."

He who had not seen Tali had lost much in life, but anyone who saw and truly discerned her had lost all. The moist shadow of her image had lodged forever in his soul, and sometimes, remembering her many years later, the man would suddenly sigh with a sort of bitter gratitude to fate.

At fifteen she was a long-armed and long-legged adolescent, with a childish neck, dark golden eyes, eyebrows of chestnut down, and tidy hair with thick bangs that slapped against her forehead when she ran.

Only the unusually well-defined line of her chin, a lunar line, hinted at the heavenly design in her aspect. At the same time it evoked an immediate, entirely earthly desire to touch this chin, test its feel: Was it as smooth and defined as it seemed in profile?

But there were plenty of nice-looking and even downright beautiful girls in Chegem. What was it that made her stand out among them?

Her face *breathed*—that was how she differed from them all. Her eyes breathed, blazing up as the bottom of a spring blazes up in a jet of golden sand grains; the pouches under her eyes breathed languidly, her neck breathed so that the pulse rate of the throbbing vein could be counted from five paces away. Her large, fresh mouth breathed, or rather, the corners of her lips breathed, not so much concealing the secret of her marvelous smile as tirelessly preparing the smile long before her lips opened. The corners of her lips seemed always to be testing and sampling the air around her, extracting from it some sunny substance, so that they might respond with the thankful radiance of a smile to the radiance of the day, the noise of life.

Later on it would take a whole mountain of immense baseness and cruelty to finally glue her lips shut in anxious immobility. Even then, her vanished—no, almost vanished—smile would suddenly break through, and at the sight of it those who had known her in the time of her youth wanted to bite their knuckles in pain or wring the neck of Fate herself for having allowed all this.

But back then, all this was still a long way off.

Almost from the day she was born the little girl was marked by a sign, or more precisely by signs, of heaven's grace.

Once, when she was four or five months old, her mother was holding her on one arm as she took down the laundry from the line strung up on the veranda. Suddenly the little girl threw out her arms toward the apple branches hanging over the veranda and began to shout "Moon! Moon!"

Peering in the direction of her daughter's uplifted pink hands, the mother gasped and almost dropped her. The pale silver disk of the moon was shining through the branches of the apple tree, in the quiet sunset sky.

When the Chegemians learned of this unusual phenomenon, they kept coming for several days to see it. Miraculously, they had only to direct the baby's glance to the sky, and she would lift up her hands with extraordinary glee and say brightly, "Moon!"

Some Chegemians offered to keep watch in order not to miss the moment the baby pronounced her second word, so that by putting the two words together they could learn what she meant by commencing her vocabulary with so lofty an object as the moon.

The local teacher, incidentally, listened to the report of this miracle with a smile (which immediately displeased the Chegemians) and then, still with a smile, refuted it.

He said that science took an entirely different view of this issue. He said that most likely someone holding a big red apple in his hand had compared it to the moon; the baby had heard this, and it had simply been stored in her head. And now, when she saw on the tree fruits similar to that apple, she mistakenly named them by the familiar sound, and even if the full moon was visible through the branches of the apple tree, it had nothing to do with this at all. Thus was the miracle explained by the teacher of the Incomplete Secondary School that had opened in Chegem in the early twenties.

The Chegemians, out of their native hospitality (science, they felt, was a guest in Chegem), did not try to argue with science. They invited the teacher to come over and see for himself that the baby was giving the name "moon" to the moon, not an apple.

The next day, toward evening, the teacher came to Uncle Sandro's house and conducted an experiment in the presence of a considerable crowd of people. The verification of the miracle took place under conditions precluding any element of chance. The mother carried the baby into the yard and stopped in a spot where the full moon shone in the sky in complete isolation, not through the branches of the apple tree. The teacher took up a stand beside the mother and then, to the Chegemians' surprise, pulled from his pocket a ruddy apple. He jabbed his other hand at it and asked with sly naiveté, "Moon?"

The baby immediately threw back her head, found the moon with her eyes, and stretched her arms toward it. Smiling a toothless smile, she mildly corrected the teacher: "Moon! Moon!"

The teacher was undaunted. Several more times he pointed impressively at his apple and asked with patiently feigned obtuseness (the Chegemians felt that he needn't have feigned it), "Moon?"

Each time, the little girl pulled away from the apple. Almost leaping out of her mother's arms, she pointed to the sky and with satisfaction pronounced the heavenly body's name, which had caught her fancy.

Finally she must have guessed that the teacher wanted to confuse her. She suddenly leaned out of her mother's arms and smacked his cheek quite hard with her hand. The teacher dropped the apple in surprise, and it rolled away from him down the sloping yard. The Chegemians hooted gaily. The teacher began looking around in a distraught manner, which the baby mistook for an attempt to find his apple. Evidently taking pity on him, she hung over her mother's arms and began pointing out to him where it had gone, this time making not the slightest attempt to call it a moon.

The discomfited teacher left the yard, hastily remarking to the Chegemians as he went that it was three hundred thousand kilometers to the moon. At another time this news might have made a great impression on the Chegemians, but not just now.

"Now you'll find something else to say," the Chegemians laughed. They nodded after the departing teacher as if to say, He wants to get back at us.

Before a thin crescent could replace the full moon, a second miracle occurred, and it was on the same veranda. Aunt Katya had left the baby there, asleep in her cradle, while she herself went off to putter in the garden for a couple of hours.

Returning from the garden with her apron full of lima beans, which she planned to cook for dinner, Aunt Katya went up on the veranda and suddenly saw that the cradle was rocking violently and the baby was singing—admittedly without words—the drinking song "Many Summers."

Her hands fell to her sides, the lima beans spilled, and the mother stared dumbstruck at her only daughter. Noticing her mama, the little girl stopped singing and stared back. The cradle rocked a few more times and stopped . . .

Aunt Katya said later that it looked as if the Invisible One—whoever was rocking the cradle—had become ashamed or frightened at the mother's arrival and had quietly stepped aside to see what would happen next. Coming to her senses, Aunt Katya rushed to the cradle and uncovered the little girl. Alternately kissing and slapping her (an experiment in contrary stimuli), she convinced herself that the baby was safe and sound.

Such an event could not pass unnoticed. It was urgently necessary to ascertain who had visited the child—an envoy of Allah or of Satan. That day, toward evening, Khabug brought in a mullah from a neighboring village.

The mullah read a prayer of deliverance over the child's pillow, taking rather a long time about it in order to produce an impression of genuine labor. On closing the Koran, he prepared an amulet, into which Aunt Katya put, by way of supplement, a paid tax receipt and a government bond ("It can't hurt, anyway"). Then she fastened the triangular amulet to a silken thread and hung it on the baby's neck. The mullah pretended not to notice the extraneous papers Aunt Katya placed in the amulet—there was nothing he could do, he had to reconcile himself to the superstitions of social life.

Aunt Katya asked the mullah whether they shouldn't rebuild the veranda, since this had happened on it.

"Why just the veranda, let's rebuild the whole house," Uncle Sandro corrected, with a somewhat peevish grin.

The mullah, taking no note of Uncle Sandro's peevish grin, remarked that for the time being there was no need to rebuild the veranda, much less the house, because to all appearances it was an envoy of Allah who had visited the child. Obviously, the instant the little girl first said "Moon!" he had taken off from the moon, and today, after a ten-day flight, he had appeared at her pillow. What were the signs that this was an angel and not one of Satan's devils?

In the first place, as you yourselves say, when the little girl pointed at the moon she rejoiced, laughed and smiled the whole time, and this is quite typical of a visit from a celestial being. In the second place, when the Invisible One began rocking her cradle, she struck up "Many Summers," a fact which speaks for itself. And in the third place (here the mullah smiled cunningly and pointed to the swallows' nests under the eaves of the veranda), the swallows would surely have scented any envoy of Satan's and pursued him with their cries, the way they pursue a hawk, a crow, or, let's say, a jay.

So said the mullah, the only man in the Kenguria district who possessed and read the holy book, the Koran. The relatives and neighbors who had gathered to hear the mullah rejoiced at his words and began trying to guess what direction Allah's envoy might have come from, so as not to brush against the fruit trees as he flew into the yard.

The possibility that Allah's messenger could have come straight down from heaven like a stone was immediately rejected, because it sounded predatory.

One of the Chegemians recalled the teacher's remark about the distance between the earth and the moon and promptly calculated the angel's average speed, which, as he said, must have been thirty thousand kilometers a day.

"If he didn't land anywhere during that time," several people specified.

"Where would he land?" others added, alluding to the absence of any landing point in the heavens.

"You can say that again," the rest of the Chegemians agreed, impressed less by the angel's rate of speed in the heavenly expanses than by his unusual endurance, which enabled him to make a ten-day trip without landing.

In spite of the plain-as-day explanation of this benign miracle, the mullah took no chances. He ordered them to parch some cornmeal, mix it with finely ground salt, and scatter it around the cradle whenever the cradle was out on the veranda—if the baby was in it, of course.

If the angel took a notion to approach the baby again, there would be no tracks in the scattered meal, because our Muslim angel would rather be reduced to ashes than step on bread and salt, the symbol of our Muslim hospitality.

And if it was a devil (which was improbable), and if he managed to overcome the talisman's power to repel (which was still more improbable) and took a notion to approach the cradle again—then his swinish hooves would certainly leave tracks in the scattered meal. Because Satan's kind have no greater satisfaction than to trample on our bread and salt, symbol of our ancient hospitality.

So said the mullah, a man respected by the Chegemians because under all regimes (czarist, Menshevik, Bolshevik) he had read one and the same holy book, the Koran, in contrast to up-to-date scholars, who under the one regime manage to change books practically every year.

Incidentally, the mullah gave very strict orders that after they had scattered the meal mixed with salt they were not to spy, because, he explained, they wouldn't see the spirit anyway but they might make it angry, especially if it was a devil.

These additional instructions were issued by the mullah when he was already seated at the table, dipping crispy pieces of spit-roasted chicken into the aromatic cherry-plum *satsivi*. Incidentally, before he got up from the table, he asked Aunt Katya for the recipe for her cherry-plum sauce, which he liked very much.

Flushing with pleasure, Aunt Katya said that her cherry-plum sauce wasn't anything special, except it had two or three little-known herbs that she raised in her garden. She ran to the storeroom and brought out a little bag containing three kinds of seeds tied in separate bundles.

Aunt Katya was indeed an excellent gardener. Not only did she raise the familiar garden vegetables of Abkhazia, but she herself found new ones in the woods, including medicinal herbs, and raised them at home. Evil-tongued Chegemians said that she followed sick dogs to see what kinds of herbs they ate, and then raised them in her garden.

In any case, the mullah pocketed the little bag of aromatic herb seeds, mounted his horse, and rode out of the yard, dragging on a rope the goat he had earned.

From out on the road he shouted that they should send for him if they discovered any tracks left by Satan's kind. Urging the balky goat along and loudly expressing the suspicion that Satan's kind had taken up their abode in it, his voice resounded over the Big House a while longer and then faded away. Aunt Katya stood at the gate and listened to his voice with a blissful smile.

"May your diseases be on my head," Aunt Katya said. She returned to the house as if touched by grace.

The next morning she ground the salt, parched the meal, and scattered this pacific mixture around her daughter's cradle, having first dragged the cradle out on the veranda. After that she went as usual to her garden to do some weeding, as she said. About an hour later she suddenly heard the screams of disturbed swallows coming from the yard. Aunt Katya tried to hold out, but her motherly heart could not endure it. The screams became so piercing and sharp ("Why, it was enough to split your head") that she started running toward the house.

She had just vaulted over the stile into the yard when with her own eyes she saw the screaming swallows flash like lightning over the cornfield, obviously chasing something. Later she swore that she saw the tops of the cornstalks shake before the oncoming swallows. It was clear that an envoy of the devil, not having had time to gain altitude, was skimming along low (although invisible), brushing the cornstalks with his heathen wings.

"Blackie! Blackie! Sic 'em, sic 'em!" Aunt Katya shouted to the dog, and cursed him for disappearing somewhere.

Running up on the veranda, she saw that the cradle was rocking again. The baby had worked her hands free and was clutching the amulet with all her might. Aunt Katya snatched the little girl from the cradle and felt her. Reassured that she was safe and sound, she put her back in the cradle and only then noticed that the thin layer of meal scattered around it had disappeared.

Here, as she told it, she experienced a slight confusion in her mind. On one hand, the swallows were obviously chasing Satan's envoy; on the other hand, the cradle could be rocked only by Allah's envoy. On one hand, there were no tracks of any blasphemer who had trampled the symbol of hospitality; on the other hand, the symbol itself had disappeared somewhere. Could it be that both forces were operating at once, was the battle of the other-worldly forces being enacted at the cradle of her only daughter?

Four days in a row the same thing happened, and nobody knew what was coming to the infant's cradle. Only one thing was clear: that this being had worked up an awful appetite on its long trip to Earth—the parched meal and finely ground salt disappeared every time. Just in case, Aunt Katya began spreading the meal deeper and deeper every day, although she did not know exactly who would eat it, Satan's envoy or Allah's. But she reasoned this way: an envoy of Satan, being a shameless person, would feed wherever he could, but an envoy of Allah might go hungry because of his conscientiousness—he wouldn't steal, wouldn't beg.

All the same, on the fifth day she broke down; she was either fed up with parching meal every morning or fed up with the uncertainty. She told Uncle Sandro that if he would not fetch the mullah she would go for him herself.

"All right," Uncle Sandro said, "feed them one last time, and I'll go."

But Uncle Sandro did not go for the mullah. He felt bad about the prospect of losing yet another goat. Without saying anything to anyone, he went out of the house and then furtively went in again by the back porch. He loaded his shotgun and concealed himself at the window, where he had a good view of both the cradle, and the meal scattered around it, and the swallows darting in and out under the eaves.

Suddenly everything changed, all at once: the cradle began jiggling, the swallows wheeled madly, and Uncle Sandro heard the cautious click of claws coming across the floor of the veranda from the direction of the kitchen.

So it has claws, not hooves—the mullah's mistake flashed through Uncle Sandro's mind. With pounding heart he raised his shotgun, deciding to fire from both barrels at once, and then—come what may!

One more moment and he would have killed, to the amusement of the Chegemians, his own dog. Yes, it was Blackie. To the accompaniment of the infant's howls of joy, the rumble of the rocking cradle, and the screams of the diving swallows, the dog approached the cradle, carefully licked up all the meal around it, licked the baby's outstretched hand in passing, and left the veranda, looking around mischievously.

Once he was down in the grassy yard, the swallows were even bolder, having room to maneuver—they attacked and almost struck him as he made his ambling escape. He trotted off toward the cornfield, making a mighty effort to maintain his dignity and keep from running.

Right at the fence his nerves gave out. He turned and clacked his teeth at a swallow that had grazed his ear. The whole flock exploded in chirping irritation: "And he's snapping, too?" Mingled with the explosion of chirping irritation was Aunt Katya's wail from the vegetable garden. The dog leaped heavily over the wattle fence and took off through the cornfield, still accompanied by the agitated racket of the swallows.

That night, sitting around the flaming hearth in a circle of his closest relatives, Uncle Sandro kept chuckling and nodding toward his wife—who was sitting there too on a separate bench—as he recounted what he had seen that day.

(Incidentally, the nods in his wife's direction had a dual meaning: on the one hand, he invited his listeners to laugh at her superstitions, and on the other hand, he directed their attention to the fact that she kept nodding off to sleep.)

This was a fairly usual scene. Worn out from her long day, Aunt Katya would settle down like this after supper with a flock of wool and a spindle, and a great struggle between waking and drowsiness would begin. No one knew which was the victor, because her waking was filled with recollections of her dreams, and her dozing did not interrupt her work.

Giving the spindle a twirl and drawing a thread from the cloud of wool, she would go to sleep for the time it took the spindle to reach the floor. In these few seconds she managed not only to fall asleep, but also to have a dream. The odd thing was that the action-packed dreams she had in this interval did not fit at all with either the brevity of her sleep or the mildness of her disposition.

"If only you were this pert when you're awake," Uncle Sandro would say when she woke up and launched into an account of her dream.

"Go on, look and see what happens next," a neighbor or relative would tell her sometimes, if the dream seemed interesting and incomplete. Giving the spindle a twirl, she obediently fell asleep. Not right away, but usually on the fifth or sixth try, she would get back on the track of the desired dream after all and see it through to the end.

It was amusing to watch her prepare herself to settle into the track. She would sit with her arm upraised and her eyes screwed up as if scrutinizing the outlines of the twilit land of dreams. Then, as if trying to divine the spot where her dream had taken place, mentally measuring in order not to miss it, she twirled the spindle. Sometimes she was quick to get back on the track of the required dream, but sometimes the process was very long, or didn't succeed at all.

"Leave me alone, mind your own business," she would say at these times to impatient listeners, as if partly attributing her own failures to their too-fidgety pestering. Sometimes people were already occupied with other topics—as a matter of fact, had even forgotten what had been the appeal in continuing her dream—by the time she extracted it again from the shadowy chaos of the other world.

"I was there again," she would explain as she woke up, winding on the spindle the length of yarn produced during her dream.

"Go along with you!" Uncle Sandro would say with a derisive nod in her direction; but even he would listen.

Aunt Katya would tell a dream as fresh as a just-opened grave. Her dreams usually represented quasi-legal encounters with near and distant relatives and fellow villagers who had left this world. In any case, the locality in which her dreams took place was equally accessible to the inhabitants of this world and the other. Those who were already over there, when they encountered those who were still here, were forever expressing their dissatisfaction, presenting their sad, sometimes very tangled claims. Oddly enough, although they knew beforehand that no one would pay their claim or discharge it, they tried to state it as exactly as possible, which must have laid additional reproach on the consciences of those who met with them. They behaved much like a peasant who is stuck in the hospital for a long time, perhaps forever; on meeting with his loved ones he gives them instructions for the house and farm, sensing that they will do everything wrong, and yet unable to refrain from the bitter sweetness of reproachful advice.

(Here your modest historian would like to take the floor and share his observations on the nature of sleep, which are by no means an attempt to belittle the value of the discoveries made in this realm by Aunt Katya or even by Uncle Freud.

However we interpret a dream that has made a strong impression on us, its true meaning lies in the fact that it has opened before us the shroud of daily routine, if only for an instant, and made us aware of the tragic distance of life. In this lies its destined power to revive. However absurd or muddled the plot of the dream, its hidden meaning is never trivial: an unacknowledged, or more often an unrequited, love; perfidy, horror, shame, mercy, pity, treachery.

The plot of a dream may be likened to a monkey with a movie camera on its neck, running through the jungles of our subconscious; and perhaps the subconscious is the flotsam and jetsam of life, cast up by the surf on a desert shore. And suddenly, among hundreds of meaningless movie frames, we find several that reveal the true meaning of what we have seen in the flotsam on the shore: some useless scrap has weighted our sleep with dull pain, and on awakening, or still in our sleep, we guess that it has reminded us of a dress worn by a woman we loved long ago—and we had thought all was forgotten . . .

And now we begin to understand that hundreds of absurd frames were needed in order to make the two or three that revealed the meaning persuasive to us. After all, if all the frames led us more or less logically to the meaning, we might suspect that someone had slipped us a moral fable. The more authentic the trash from which we pull it out, the more searingly persuasive the discovery is . . .)

Naturally, when Aunt Katya went deeper into her dreams she did not always reach the meaning, more often simply got stuck in the trashy shadows. Or, if she simply could not get back on the track of the interesting dream all evening, she would put away the spindle, then seize a half-burned log and rake up the ashes to cover the coals—the way people bury a seed in the ground—so that the hearth would bloom again tomorrow with friendly shoots of fruitful fire.

"Nothing's going right today, somehow. Time to go to sleep," she would say, yawning luxuriously.

"You might think she'd been doing something else all evening," Uncle Sandro invariably answered, his habitual grin hiding his vexation that they had not succeeded in learning how her current dream ended.

This evening, however, when Uncle Sandro was chuckling and telling about what he had seen that day, something completely different happened. The little girl was lying right there in the cradle, rocking it herself in token of the general joy and her own unusual liveliness. Suddenly, looking at her father, who was just demonstrating how he had come within an ace of shooting his own dog, the little girl smiled and said, "Papa!"

Now the relatives and neighbors correlated the sequence of the preceding miracles and arrived at the incontrovertible conclusion that all this time, beginning with her unexpected recognition and naming of the moon, her singing of the drinking song (even though without words), and rocking herself in the cradle, the child had been moving toward saying "Papa!"—thereby prophetically alluding to his great and eternal vocation as tamada.

The moon signified the time of his activities; the rocking in the cradle and the singing of the drinking song, the result of his activities. (For some reason it did not occur to anyone that the child could have memorized this melody because it was sung rather often during nocturnal feasts in Uncle Sandro's house.)

"See, even the baby condemns you," Aunt Katya said, not very appropriately, but single-mindedly, utilizing every opportunity to try and deter Uncle Sandro from his aspirations to a career at the table. Giving the spindle a twirl, she dropped off to sleep.

"On the contrary," Uncle Sandro replied, laughing at her unsuccessful reproof. "She called me by name first, that means she approves of me."

She grew to be an unusually high-spirited girl. Even before she could walk, she would try to dance to any sound from which she could extract, if not a melody, then at least a rhythm. She would cut loose and rock herself in her cradle whenever she heard the ringing of cowbells, the rapping of hail on the roof, the clapping of hands on a sieve, or even the clucking of the hens.

At eight she learned to play the guitar and was forever dragging it along the road between the Big House and the neighbors.

At twelve she played all the melodies that had ever been heard in Chegem. She could play in any position—sitting, standing, lying down, running, and even riding on her grandfather's mule, who danced lightly along, the Chegemians observed, when he heard above him the strumming of the strings.

But best of all she loved to play sitting at the top of her grandfather's apple tree. On a summer's day, rattling the nuts she had poured inside her guitar, she would climb up in the apple tree, and there at the very top, at a fork in the branches intertwined in grapevines, she had a comfortable perch where she could sit for hours, observing Chegem and its environs.

Sometimes when a traveler was walking by on the upper Chegem road, a lively melody would suddenly pour down from above, from the heavens. He would stop and dart his eyes around for a long time, trying to figure out where the melody came from. Once he determined that it was coming from the apple tree, he would continue on his way, still trying to discover who was concealed there, and often he would trip or even fall on the rocky upper Chegem road. At that the melody would end abruptly in laughter.

Some travelers were very angry and swore by the bones of all the dead that the evil eye, the plague, and Siberian anthrax must have descended on this house, if its daughters roamed the trees with guitars, like witches.

"Why stir up the bones of your dead? You'd do better to join them!" the little girl would shout after the angry traveler, purposely twanging the strings as hard as she could.

And the way she met guests!

"Grandpa, someone's coming to our house!" she would shout joyfully from above. Rattling the guitar, she would slide down the tree.

"Maybe not to our house?" Aunt Katya would repeat hopefully. She was sick and tired of guests.

"To our house! To our house!" Tali shouted in midair. Landing on the ground, she ran to the gate.

Aunt Katya, grumbling at people who found the best way to go broke—by settling beside a main road—went into the house, only to reemerge a moment later in a new role, that is, in the role of a genial hostess, smilingly welcoming her guests.

Tali was already racing out the gate, way ahead of the dog, rushing to hug them and drag them into the house—relatives, acquaintances, or people who had merely been overtaken by night on the upper Chegem road.

Sometimes she would stand over the table until dawn, pouring wine for the guests, setting out food, and listening with greedy, grateful curiosity to everything they said. Then she would even put all the guests to bed, help them undress, with a disarming boldness and purity pull up the covers over the ones who were tipsy, wish them all a good night, and carry out the lamp, her pellucid face shining—the lamp illumined her face, or perhaps her face the lamp . . .

What the hell's going on, the guest would think in his luxurious drowsiness, and he would fall asleep without ever understanding, only to remember the evening years and years later and savor its every detail with bitter sweetness.

In winter, when the deep Chegem snows fell, the little girl would be out on her grandfather's mule, ahead of all the children in the neighborhood, trampling smooth the road to the village soviet school. In these moments her little voice, which rang especially clear over the snow, used to carry to half of Chegem, and everyone who heard her—shouting at the mule, encouraging the little ones, forever quarreling with her cousins, and calling them twice-spoiled milk or thrice-soured cream—involuntarily smiled at her impassioned voice over the snow, her indomitable energy.

And everyone who met her at this moment on the upper Chegem road and saw how, on the steep grade, red in the face, she shouted now at her companions and now at the mule, smacking him with a foot encased in a thick homespun wool stocking and shod in a rawhide moccasin with a few protruding wisps of a special grass, which had been stuffed in for softness and warmth—and which was evidently very tasty, too, because at every opportune moment the mule tried to nibble off at least a tuft, at least a few blades of grass—everyone who saw how she turned around on the very steepest slope, never falling silent for a second, and invited some children to grab her mule's tail, while driving away others who tried to seize the tail without having earned the honor, in her opinion, and those who had already grabbed hold argued that they had earned it, or at least they would earn it in the very near future, and finally, the whole gang burst tumbling out onto the crest of the hill, only to go sliding down the other side—everyone who saw this scene would remember it later, many years afterward, as a vision of piercing freshness, youth, happiness.

On the way home from school, walking through the beech and chestnut groves, the children chose the steepest slopes and sat on their briefcases and schoolbags to slide down them. If they succeeded in scraping away the snow cover, then on the exposed, almost dry ground, hidden by the frozen flame of fallen leaves, they would suddenly find a store of chestnuts or beechnuts untouched by the wild boars and squirrels. If there were enough of them, the mule, too, got a share of the treat. Old Khabug's mule, incidentally, according to many signs which may confidently be equated with a direct declaration, counted Tali's school years the most enchanting years of his life. It seems that like all the other animals around her, he loved her and understood her almost before she spoke.

In any case, from childhood on the little girl was endowed with a gift for accepting the world, so to speak, the gift of charity and benevolence. Besides, her grandfather's extraordinary love for her gave her a feeling of omnipotence, and in her childhood years she frequently behaved with the scatterbrained wastefulness of a little princess.

One time she gave away Uncle Sandro's horse to some geologists, who were climbing up to their camp from the city and had halted near the Big House. Tali brought them something to slake their thirst. One of them, the youngest, after drinking his fill, looked at the horse, which was grazing in the yard: "Could we hire her?"

"Why hire her?" Tali replied. "Just take her."

The young man—a student intern, as it later turned out—was slightly taken aback. "But what about you?"

"Oh, we have the mule too," Tali said. She herself dragged a saddle out of the house, caught the horse, and helped saddle her.

When Uncle Sandro came home that night and found out what she had been up to, he said not a word but, for the first time in his life, gathered a bunch of nettles. He did not allow for the friskiness of her feet, however, and besides he was being too careful picking the nettles. She escaped from him into the cornfield and from there made her way to Aunt Masha, who put her to bed among her five daughters.

To save bed linen, Aunt Masha's daughters slept right on goatskins on the floor of their room. They made space for her next to the wall, so that if Uncle Sandro took a notion to come after her he would have to overcome the fire-breathing barrier formed by the young giantesses' bodies.

Perhaps because these girls had used few covers since childhood, owing to their poverty, or perhaps it was a consequence of their vigorous good health, or most likely both, but anyway their bodies were characterized by a sort of special heat exchange, an elevated heat output. If you looked closely at any one of them, you could observe the soft shimmer of heat waves over her, especially noticeable in the shade. The Chegemians had noted that their dog, which slept under the house in winter, chose a spot directly under the room where the girls slept. In the Chegemians' opinion, they warmed up the floor so much that even under the house the dog felt the heat radiated by their vigorous circulation.

It is not known whether Uncle Sandro would have risked stirring up these embers smoldering with secret fire in order to get at his daughter, because that night the young man came riding back on his horse. The chief of the geological expedition proved wise enough not to accept a gift from a little girl.

Uncle Sandro, who had strongly suspected that Endursky horse thieves disguised as geologists had swindled the horse away from his foolish little girl, was now overjoyed. He invited two or three neighbors in and staged a modest carouse for the fellow.

"Where's my girl?" came Katya's voice that night in Aunt Masha's daughters' room. "Get up, they've brought the horse back, you can be the cupbearer!"

The student, though young, proved to be a hard drinker. He had no wish to ease up before morning, even though people hinted that it was not a good idea to get into a drinking match with Uncle Sandro.

"Never," the lad boasted, to the laughter of the company, "will this dried-up skinny Abkhaz outdrink me!"

He himself had a powerful build, but in the opinion of a majority of those present, he was somewhat pudgy and wet behind the ears, which would get him into trouble in the end. Others objected that he was pudgy by our Chegemian standards, but maybe not by Russian standards. To this the first speakers objected that it was still our wine that he was drinking, not Russian vodka, and therefore he could still be considered a wet-head.

"That's true too," agreed the ones who did not think the hard-drinking young rake was such a wet-head. "Let's see what happens."

When he saw Tali the student boasted even more swaggeringly, because he liked her very much and, more importantly, thought she was a lot older than she was. The more he drank, the older she looked to him.

In vain did one of the neighbors try to explain to him, in Russian, that "dry earth drink much water [a nod in Uncle Sandro's direction], wet earth drink little water [a nod toward the student]." The student flew into a rage.

"Never," he shouted, to the laughter of the company, construing their laughter as a consequence of his own wit, "will this dried-up skinny Abkhaz outdrink me!"

With the first rays of morning, they set before the student a tray with eight glasses of wine, like a fantastic flower with blood-red petals of alcohol. Uncle Sandro had just lapped up the nectar from the same kind of flower and was now watching the student with a certain mischievous curiosity, smacking his lips. The student stood up and easily drank off two glasses, one after another.

"A wet-head, huh?" one of the guests said, as the student lifted the third glass with the same ease and put it to his lips. Then something unexpected happened. The third glass crashed down on the remaining five glasses, and the student leaped out of the house as if scalded.

"Can't hold it," said Uncle Sandro, the first to guess. He looked after the fleeing student with a fatherly smile. "Now if he can just get unbuttoned . . ."

The student wasn't even halfway across the yard when a fountain gushed from him, and he kept right on running, bearing the fountain in front of him until he scrambled up the fence and jumped over into the cornfield. One of the people at the table was struck that the source of the fountain was located somewhat higher than it should have been.

"Maybe his belly button burst," he hypothesized, somewhat fancifully. Naturally the student did not come back to the table, although they sent someone after him. They should have known—he had liked the cupbearer too much.

Subsequently Uncle Sandro was often asked how he had known that the student couldn't hold it in precisely this sense, and not, for example, in the sense that the wine was coming back up his throat.

"Very simple," Uncle Sandro would reply. "When the belly gives out, a man turns pale first and sweats, but when the bladder gives out, you don't see anything."

"Is there anything this Sandro doesn't notice," the Chegemians said, and they clucked their tongues, meaning that you live and learn.

Another, much sadder incident reveals some of the mental traits that later blossomed with such mighty force when she grew to be a woman.

In order to tell this story, we must go back several years. One of Khabug's sons, Isa, was a passionate hunter. He often hunted with Tendel, and during one of their protracted winter expeditions he came down with a bad cold, or more likely pleurisy, which in the end led to tuberculosis.

"That winter," Tendel later recalled, "he'd be coughing on the trail and he'd spit up a red spot on the snow. You'd say to him, 'How come you're spitting blood, old buddy?' 'It's nothing,' he says, 'I guess I've picked up a cold.' He thought he had a cold, but it turned out much worse."

That was how Tendel told it, usually sitting by the flaming hearth, and with the closing words he hawked and spat into the fire, perhaps to reassure the company that he himself was coughing up the healthy phlegm of an old smoker.

Poor Isa coughed for two years and then died. His wife caught the disease from him, and two years later she also died. From his wife it passed to the eldest daughter, Katusha, who had looked after her, and she died. And that spring, when the disease was discovered in Isa's son—the fiery-eyed Adgur, twenty years old, in the flower of manhood—the relatives living in the immediate vicinity quietly decided among themselves not to let the children into this house of plague. Only two people were left in the house, Adgur and his younger sister Zarifa, an eighteen-year-old girl who seemed petrified with the horror of awaiting her turn.

Up to this point, ever since the unfortunate Isa had fallen ill, all the relatives, and old Khabug in particular, had done everything in their power to help his family. Now, after the hospital, Adgur spent a month at the sanatorium, and of course his grandfather provided the money for that.

Nevertheless, the decision was made not to let the children into Isa's house. People bound by tradition are slow to accept the idea that a disease can jump from one man to another like a flea, but after they become convinced that it is possible to catch the disease, they go to the opposite extreme and become too suspicious.

So Adgur arrived home and suddenly sensed that all his hopes for recovery had stumbled against the alienation of his relatives, who had quietly closed ranks against him. For about a week Tali watched him wander around the village, lonely and restless, and her heart contracted with pity for him. For the first time in her life she became aware that in this world, which for her shone with the expectation of infinite happiness and to which she responded with a smile of gratitude for the happiness of expecting happiness—she became aware that in this world there was a cruelty and villainy which nothing could explain. Why must her cousin, in whom she had divined with delight the beauty and strength of flowering manhood, die from this dread disease? And how could she abandon him at such a time? After all, some survived—didn't the grown-ups say so themselves? And how could he survive if he saw that they had all abandoned him because they did not believe that he could be saved?

Such thoughts flashed through her mind, but it was not her thoughts so much as a sense of shame that showed her the right thing to do: she broke the ban and came to the house to see her cousin.

She came at noon, when his sister had returned from the kolkhoz field and was in the kitchen making the cornmeal mush. He was sitting by the fireplace fire, hunched over with a chill, his freezing hands stretched to the flame.

"Tali," he asked when he saw her, "did they send you for something?"

His eyes brightened. It was as if a wind had breathed life into dying coals.

"No," she said, "I just came."

She walked in. With a rush of shame (just don't let him think I'm afraid), she plunked herself down beside him on the bench. In his hoarse voice he began telling her how he had seen bear tracks in Sabid's Hollow, he would have to set a trap there, but it was hard for him alone now, and he couldn't find anyone to work with him. He had inherited his father's passion for hunting.

When he began telling about the bear, his sister, who was stirring the mush in the kettle, suddenly glanced at him with a caustic amazement that horrified Tali—as if to say, "Good Lord, he's still talking as if he were alive!"

Adgur did not notice her look, or perhaps he was used to it and paid no attention. Tali noticed that the kettle, which hung on a chain over the fire, was stretched way over to the far side of the hearth, where Zarifa stood. She sensed that Adgur's sister tried to have as little contact with her brother as possible and did not even hide the fact.

While he talked on about the bear tracks, she remembered a certain bright winter day when a shot had rung out near her cousin's house, then another and another. Then after a while, from Sabid's Hollow, they heard Adgur's voice. he was shouting that he had killed a roebuck, someone should help him bring it home.

None of the men were around, so that only the women and children went to meet him, and Tali was among them. He was climbing up the path, flushed, his coat thrown open, his eyes shining, with the roebuck lying across his shoulders and its marvelous head hanging against his chest. Holding it by its stiffened legs, he climbed up, so tall and lithe, unable to conceal his delight and triumph, calling out some sort of details and shouting at the dogs that were running around him. Sinking into the snow and bounding up out of it, the dogs were licking the dripping blood, swirling around him, and sometimes yelping with delight, trying to reach now his face, now his kill.

"Get away! What are you doing!" he shouted at them. He was trying to make his voice express an angry surprise, but he could not pull it off; what came through was the delight, the ecstasy which he was experiencing with all his being and which the dogs sensed—that was why they ignored his shouts and went on raving, bounding up from the snowdrifts, yelping and wreathing around him.

That was how Tali saw him as she stood in the crowd of women and children at the brim of Sabid's Hollow, where he was climbing up to them, plowing through the deep snow, all disheveled, wet with snow, his coat wide open, with streams of sweat running down his face, his eyes blazing with a hot blue fire, his hand now and again scooping up snow and in the same motion stuffing it, greedily jamming it, into his mouth.

Later, here in this very kitchen, by a roaring fire, as he dressed the carcass, which was suspended from a beam by a rope, he told how he happened to spot the roebuck from the yard. So happy he couldn't believe it—they had never come so close to the house before—he brought it down with one shot.

Then he ran down into the hollow, and when he got there and seized it by the foot, it suddenly jerked with such force that he was thrown back several meters. The roebuck, despite its serious wound, jumped to its feet and started to run. Even so he had time to take aim and fire (he seemed to insist on the fact that he had had time to take aim, that is, it was no accident that he had hit it the second time, too), and it fell again, and again he ran to it, this time convinced that it was killed. Yet when he seized its foot again, it jerked with incredible force, but he managed to catch hold of the same foot with his other hand. Even so, in spite of the two bullets it had taken, it dragged him ten meters through the deep snow, but then its strength gave out and it crashed to the ground. But even after that, they went on floundering for several minutes in the snow until he contrived to sink a knife in its throat, and then at last it fell quiet.

The huge fire roared, the great kettle hung over it ready to boil the meat, and as he told his story he dressed the carcass, now pulling off the hide, which separated from the carcass with a ripping sound, now—carefully, so as not to spoil it—making an incision, still with the same knife, in the tenacious membrane that held the hide to the carcass, sometimes pulling away the wet elastic hide with one hand and shoving the other fist under the hide from time to time to make it easier to separate.

The fire roared, the hide ripped, and all his wet clothes steamed; it was easy to guess the lithe strength of the healthy young body underneath them. Then, at the long low table, the children ate the boiled meat with cornmeal mush, and they had shares to carry home, too, along with the story of how their cousin had killed a roebuck. So could it really be he who sat here now, with his wasted body all hunched over and his cold hands stretched to the fire in the middle of summer?

After a few minutes the sister silently put a low table before Adgur and served him a helping of cornmeal mush from the kettle. With a nod toward the far side of the fire, where she had put a table for herself, she asked Tali, "Will you eat with me?"

"I'll eat here," Tali said.

Making no reply and showing no surprise at her words, Zarifa took another helping of cornmeal mush from the kettle and laid it out next to her brother's—not too far, not too near.

Still in silence, she set between them a little plate of sliced cheese and two dishes of lima beans, then laid several slices of wet pickled cabbage right on the table. After that she set a jar of some sort of medicinal fat on the corner next to her brother.

By doing all this in silence, she was saying to Tali, "You can play at being noble, that's your own business. But I know what this is, and I'm going to do everything I can to keep from dying."

Adgur began taking gobs of fat from the jar. He did this with an unpleasant clanking of the metal spoon, which Tali perceived as a sort of hospital instrument. Chegemians used only spoons made of wood or bone.

Having served everything at once—Tali realized she had done it this way to avoid being near the table any more than she had to—Zarifa silently left the kitchen. She called the dog away from the open door and sat down on the railing of the kitchen veranda, silently and indifferently watched them from out there.

She sat on the veranda railing, a strong young woman illuminated by the sun, and made no secret of the fact that she intended to survive, whatever the cost.

Sometimes clouds of smoke from the fire drifted to the doorway, and the girl sitting on the railing would disappear for an instant. But then she appeared there again in the same pose, and the changelessness of her immobile pose seemed to underscore the decisiveness of her intention to survive.

Tali did not condemn her for intending to survive, but she sensed that the crude frankness of Zarifa's desire meant that she was certain her brother must die. And it was this certainty that Tali could not reconcile herself to . . .

With his dreadful metal spoon he made a well in the cornmeal mush, put into it pieces of the fat from the jar; the fat melted and flowed over the mush. He ate the beans, dipped cornmeal mush into the melting fat, and sank his teeth with a crunch into the squeaky, dripping cabbage.

The energy with which he ate, Tali sensed, spoke not so much for his appetite as for his furious unwillingness to give up. He was sending reinforcements to his weakening reserves. Every time a mouthful went down his dreadfully emaciated throat, she saw it with her peripheral vision, and every nerve in her body felt the effort of will with which he pushed down each swallow, as if repeating, "Help me . . . help me . . . and *you* help me . . ."

The little girl did not feel like eating. Nevertheless, she tried to eat as usual, without betraying her feelings. Unexpectedly, Adgur started to cough and could not stop for a long time. Still coughing, he began making some sort of signal with his hand, and at first Tali could not understand what he meant. Suddenly she understood, and he immediately understood that she understood, because she nodded in agreement, and he beamed through his coughing, rejoiced at her understanding. Tali had guessed that the hand signals he was making meant that he had started to cough, not because of his disease, but because the fire was very smoky.

He continued to cough. Something kept making excruciating squelching sounds in his throat, and she suddenly felt a droplet of spit spatter from his gurgling throat and strike her face, just above her upper lip. Turning cold with horror, the little girl thought that this was the end, that now of course she would die. At the same time, she felt so keenly the shame and even disgrace that would be hers if she were so fainthearted as to let him see her horror that she kept herself under control. Not until some moments later did she wipe her sleeve across the spot where the droplet of his spit had struck, which for some reason itched agonizingly.

His sister continued to sit on the railing. The whole time he was coughing she changed neither her motionless pose nor the expression of stony indifference on her face.

They finished eating and got up from the table. Tali ladled water from the bucket and poured it for him when they went out on the veranda. He washed his hands and rinsed his mouth with special care, using his finger to scrub his strong squeaky teeth. He seemed especially fond of his teeth, because this was the only part of his body that had not suffered at all during his illness. But to an outsider's eye, there was no more terrible reminder of the horrible ravages of the disease than his strong, healthy teeth, in involuntary contrast to the emaciated face, convulsively working neck, and sagging shoulders.

While he rinsed his mouth, the chickens came over warily and pecked up the crumbs that he spat out.

As soon as they came out to wash their hands, his sister tied over her mouth and nose a black scarf that had probably been set aside for the purpose: it hung on the veranda like an emblem of mourning. With the scarf on her face, she brought out the little table at which they had eaten. Lifting it by one end, she shook off the scraps of food, which the dog snapped up and ate, growling at the chickens. Then she poured boiling water over the table from a pitcher which had stood by the fire all this time, then washed off the plates with more water from the pitcher, put away the table, took off the scarf and hung it on a nail, then carefully washed her hands and went into the kitchen.

There she had her dinner in solitude, from time to time glancing at them expressionlessly through the open kitchen door. Tali was sitting with him on the kitchen veranda, and he was telling her about some miracle drug made by a certain woman who lived in the Donbass, where he planned to go as soon as he got a little stronger, if his callous relatives didn't have the sense to go there themselves. This was the quite usual grumbling, the usual story, of people who have been sick a long time.

The attention with which Tali listened to his story made his words about the miracle drug more convincing, as if some detached observer had corroborated that it was all true. Aroused by his hopes for recovery, which were corroborated partly by the attention with which his young cousin listened, partly by the very fact of her coming here, he really did feel encouraged and cheered.

He watched her go—barefoot, well-proportioned, her movements still angular but already softened by a hint of womanhood—and thought with some tenderness, "She's getting to be quite a girl!" For the first time since his illness, it seemed, he had thought of, and taken pleasure in, something that had no direct bearing on his own health. This observation, with its feeling of freshness, of irrelevance to his own interests, made him rejoice, although it brought him back to thoughts of his illness. It occurred to him that his good mood must mean he was beginning to get well. And he had the further thought that illness had made him too suspicious: here he had decided that his relatives had forbidden the children to visit him, but Tali had come and even had dinner with him.

That evening, at home in the kitchen, the little girl was sitting in front of the fire, washing her feet in a basin, when she had a coughing fit.

"You shouldn't run barefoot in the wet grass!" Aunt Katya scolded, knowing nothing of her visit to her tubercular cousin's house. Tali felt her insides go numb: it meant she had caught the disease.

After she was in bed the cough came over her again several times, and she was utterly convinced that nothing would save her now. With a sort of sweet pity she pictured herself dying and even dead, and felt terribly sorry for her grandfather. And yet, remembering this day and the visit to her cousin, she felt that even now she had no regrets. She could not say why, she only knew that it was impossible to leave a person alone with such grief; this was stronger than any kind of argument, and she herself could not explain it. She dimly felt that her trust in the world and in people, her happy ability to draw constant ease and joy from the breath of life itself, were somehow linked to the fact that at the back of her soul she had not a single motive that enclosed or concealed her own self-interest, her own gain. And since this openness, frankness, benevolence toward everything around her constituted the security for her inspired happy state, she knew unconsciously beforehand that there was no way she could close herself off, even if her openness should some day prove mortally dangerous.

. . . In the morning when she woke up, she took stock of herself and realized with joyful surprise that she was well and that nothing could ever happen to her.

The sun had already risen and was slanting in the window through the branches of the apple tree. The shadow of a swallow, flickering around the nest on the veranda, now flickered on the curtain of the window under which Tali slept.

Tali playfully began to swing the curtain back and forth; she was surprised that the swallow's flickering shadow did not go away.

Silly me, thought Tali, now completely awake. The swallow doesn't see me rocking her shadow, why should she be frightened? And if the swallow isn't frightened, then her shadow will just keep on flickering on the curtain. Laughing at her own naiveté, she jumped out of bed and started to get dressed, feeling within her that sweetly insatiable hunger for the golden, still untasted summer day, that appetite for life at the beginning of life, which is true happiness.

Tali was twelve years old when the miller's son, still wearing the mop of curls with which he had evidently won her heart—in brief, a lad not a lot older than she, though a lot sillier—persuaded her to run away from home with him.

Taking advantage of the fact that her grandfather had gone to the city to sell his pigs, she consented. She grabbed her guitar and went to the Prayer Tree, where they had agreed to meet.

Fortunately, they were dogged by failure right from the start. The first failure was that the miller's son obtained—and that with great difficulty—only one horse, which a neighbor lent him.

Since Tali did not consent to sit in the same saddle with him, he had to put her in the saddle while he himself sat behind her on the horse's back, which the horse disliked right from the start. In addition, the horse disliked the look of the strange object the little girl held in one hand, sometimes laying it across the horse's croup, sometimes holding it over her head.

Before they could begin to feel like fugitive lovers, the horse turned off the intended path and set off toward her own home at an irritated trot. Tali simply could not hold the animal's strong head, and the horse raced faster and faster for home, an event that had not figured in the fugitives' calculations—after all, an abductor never takes his captive bride straight home.

Meanwhile, thoroughly irritated by the guitar—which Tali was now holding up high, afraid of breaking it over the horse's croup—the horse had started racing at top speed.

"Drop the guitar!" the miller's son shouted. Gripping the rear saddle bow with one hand, he tried to reach the guitar with the other.

"Never!" Tali replied, jerking the guitar away. The horse rolled a maddened eye at that plangent object and raced on with still greater speed.

They covered about three kilometers before the miller's son fell off the horse in one of his attempts to reach the guitar. As soon as he fell, the horse stopped, as if she had decided to reconcile herself to one of the inconveniences on condition that they deliver her from the other.

After making sure that the miller's son was in one piece, Tali set about proving to him that the guitar had had nothing to do with it: here she was, sitting on the horse with the guitar, and the horse was just standing still.

Rubbing his bruised hip, the miller's son came over and seized the horse by the bridle. In response to Tali's remark he began bawling her out, saying that her grandfather's mule might let her twiddle the guitar right in his ears, but that didn't mean a good horse would put up with it.

Tali, sparing no words, began to state her opinion of Napskal horses and their mop-haired jockeys. At this point, Khabug appeared on the path where they stood arguing. He was climbing up the path leading his mule, which was laden with purchases from the city.

If they had both been sitting on the horse, or if Tali had been without her guitar, or at least if they had not been chewing each other out, the old man might have guessed something was up. As it was, he was merely surprised.

"Where are you off to with your guitar so near bedtime?" Halting his mule beside the horse, he took in both the horse and the boy holding it in one instantaneous glance (which did not confer on them any difference in species).

"To the mill," Tali said, already disenchanted with her bridegroom and perhaps utterly undone by that glance.

"There's enough racket at the mill, they don't need you," her grandfather said. Paying no attention to the miller's son, who stood there sulkily holding the horse by the bridle, he dropped the mule's reins and stretched out his arms to his granddaughter.

Tali put her arms out to him out of habit, and he seized her. Throwing her arms around his neck and banging the guitar on his back, she hung on him as she had hung on him hundreds of times before, when, after washing her feet in the kitchen and tucking her feet up on the bench, she would cling to his neck and he would carry her out of the kitchen, down the long veranda to the clean part of the house.

"What's the matter, anyway, Grandpa?" was all she said. Lowering herself between a sack and pannier, she straightened her skirt and laid the guitar across her knees.

"Give me that dingbat," Khabug said. He took the guitar from her and shouldered it like an ax, then picked up the reins and started off. Tali looked back at her unlucky bridegroom. He was still holding the horse by the bridle. Sulkier than ever, he was now staring after Tali, his gaze reproaching her for great treachery. Tali shrugged her shoulders to indicate that she wasn't exactly to blame for what had happened. Pouting even more sulkily, he let her know that he considered the whole thing to be her fault.

Tali took offense at this. "And why did you have to fall off?" she replied. With one last shrug she turned her back on him.

It was their exchange of glances, or perhaps Tali's last remark, that aroused dim suspicions in old Khabug. The more he thought about it as he walked along in front of his mule, the more immobile the back of his neck became. His gait took on a savage swiftness.

The mule could barely keep up with his master by the time they reached the house.

"What the devil!" old Khabug shouted at last, turning to his granddaughter as he opened the gate. By now, evidently, his suspicions were fully ripened.

"Why were you—?" The mule entered the yard, and now Tali turned back to look at her grandfather.

"What the devil! There on a horse?" the old man said, losing the gift of speech in his agitation. He dragged up the gate and slammed it with all his might.

"Why, what do you mean, Grandpa," Tali said. With an open smile she put her arms out to him. And just as she had flung her arms around his neck out of habit when he reached up toward the horse, so now, when he saw her outstretched arms, he picked his granddaughter up, even though he was angry at her, and set her down from the mule.

Nevertheless, rumors began to spread among the Chegemians that Tali had tried to run away with the miller's son, and had failed only thanks to the fact that old Khabug's mule caught up with the fugitives; or, according to another version, the mule himself, on whom they were allegedly fleeing, had chosen a convenient spot and thrown the abductor, so that the latter had rolled right down the steep slope to the mill.

Tali's mother tirelessly denied these rumors, as did the miller's wife.

While they were at it, the two mothers exchanged compliments behind each other's backs. Aunt Katya said that Tali was no poor orphan, to have to marry the miller's son, who was so deaf he had cobwebs sprouting in his ears.

That, of course, was not quite true, because even though the miller's son was not noted for great intellect, he had tolerably good hearing. Admittedly, his father was indeed somewhat deaf from working so long at the mill, but the son's hearing was good, although out of stupidity he did sometimes ask people to repeat things. That was why Aunt Katya had decided they had hereditary deafness.

Considering that she herself, as Uncle Sandro put it, although a good woman, did not have much of a reputation for outstanding intellect either, so that she might easily confuse one thing with another; and bearing in mind the fact that she was insulted by all these rumors; and besides, people speak louder than usual with both the stupid and the deaf—then no wonder she decided that the lad had had flour packed in his ears since the day he was born.

The miller's wife, in her turn, said that her son had never meant to marry Tali. Why marry Tali, she said, he'd've done better to marry her guitar—at least he'd have something to tweak. She went on to explain that if her son had in fact courted Tali, it was only in order to make a roundabout approach to her cousin Firuza, the eldest of Aunt Masha's many daughters.

Indeed, the miller's son promptly married the mighty Firuza. Apropos of this, the Chegemians said that the miller's wife had decided to go to any lengths to prove that her son was quite worthy of a Chegem girl.

(Like the Moscow police, who consider that humanity is divided into two parts—that which has already registered to live in Moscow and that which still dreams of doing so—the Chegemians were sure that all Abkhazia dreamed of becoming related to them. Not to mention the Endurskies, who dreamed not so much of becoming related to the Chegemians as of subjugating them, or not even subjugating but simply destroying the flourishing village, turning it to a wasteland, and then taking off for home, so that they could go around saying that there had never been any Chegem, frankly speaking, it was a fabrication, a mirage of the tired shepherds who had camped around there on their way to the alpine meadows.

The several Endurian families who had lived in Chegem from time immemorial were kept under constant secret surveillance by the Chegemians. When there were alarming rumors or elemental catastrophes, the Chegemians invariably turned their gaze to the Endurskies in order to ascertain their position on the matter.

"I wonder what They're saying?" they would ask one another in such cases. Any response from the Endurskies was perceived as a crafty, but also a stupid, attempt to conceal their true, allegedly most often malicious, attitude toward everything that alarmed the Chegemians.

None of this prevented them from maintaining quite friendly relations with their Endursky aliens in normal times, but in a difficult moment the Chegemians would begin to suspect the Endurskies of secret intrigues.

Let's say it's summer, there's a drought. One of the local Endurskies walks past a cornfield where a Chegemian is hoeing.

"What do you say, countryman," calls the man hoeing the corn, "is it going to rain?"

"Who knows?" the Endursky replies, shooting a glance at the sky, and he goes his way. The Chegemian takes up his hoe again and works in silence for a while. Suddenly he grins and says to himself—from which it follows that he has been tensely mulling over the Endursky's reply the whole time—" 'Who knows,' " he says, repeating the Endursky's reply with a sort of meek irony. "May God grant us as much good in life as there is evil in what you hide from us . . .")

One way or another, however, the miller's son did marry Aunt Masha's daughter. Tali presented her cousin with the dress material that their grandfather had brought home on the day of her own ill-starred flight. On the day of the bride's departure she threw herself into the festivities so energetically that it would never have occurred to anyone that six months ago she herself had been planning to run away from home with him.

"He's nice," she said with satisfaction, combing her cousin's hair in front of the mirror, "and it doesn't matter that he fell off the horse does it, Aunt Masha?"

"A clever boy," Aunt Masha agreed. With the sweeping gestures she used in everything she did, she was sewing a simple dress for her daughter. "The main thing is, with a miller's son you'll never go hungry . . . Well, come here, shorty, let's try it on," she added, biting off the thread and surveying her work.

Wherever Tali went, she introduced the excess of vitality that nature had conferred on her. Even at the funeral of some great-great-aunt, whom she had never laid eyes on even when she was alive, she suddenly burst into such loud sobs that the closer relatives began to comfort her, saying that there was no help for it, the old woman had lived her time.

"All the same it's sad," she said through her sobs, bathed in tears.

Half an hour later, her breathing face aflame, she was telling something to some other girls her own age. All around her, eyes began to sparkle and giggles rang out, especially gleeful because they were suppressed.

"Tali! You're not at a wedding!" came the voice of one of the close relatives.

What Tali disliked above all in those years was sluggishness, gloominess, moroseness. She used to fly into the tobacco shed, where tired, depressed women were silently stringing tobacco, and shout, "Lift up your twice-spoiled, thrice-soured faces!"

She would flop down near her mother or one of her cousins, snatch the needle from her, and clap on the tobacco leaves. The women would revive and rouse themselves, their refreshed minds would suddenly recall that there was someone they had completely forgotten to gossip about.

At fourteen she had her working papers and was considered one of the best stringers in Chegem, and a year later (at last we have reached the day with which we began this story) she became the only rival of the other best tobacco stringer, a young woman named Tsitsa.

The chairman of the kolkhoz was disagreeably surprised to learn that Uncle Sandro's daughter was one of the two best stringers.

"That's not the little minx who comes to school in winter on the mule?" he asked Mikha as he looked over the reports.

"The very one," Mikha nodded with satisfaction. "She's not human, she's like lightning."

"All right," the chairman assented gloomily. He set aside the report and sank into a reverie.

More and more often, lately, he felt this sense of gloom at what he saw as the malicious inconsistency between the course of life and the clear precepts of the proletarian science of Marx.

Now, why did the best kolkhoz tobacco stringer have to be the granddaughter of the former rich kulak Khabug? Well, and who, at least, would stand up to her? Tsitsa? And who was she? The granddaughter of that old no-good, the reactionary hunter Tendel!

Later on, when Chairman Timur Zhvanba took up the life of an outright swindler, he stilled the none-too-loud reproaches of his conscience with the malicious reply that there were some inconsistencies in Marx, too—as if Marxian doctrine had been devised, not by Marx, but by his own poor conscience.

His conscience, which had already been harassed and impoverished anyway by rumors about its class origin, was silenced for good and took no sides in the feuding among his passions—like a poor female relative, an extra mouth to feed, who fixes herself up in some out-of-the-way corner lest she invite too much attention, lest her s[illegible]ual uselessness irritate the head of the Marxist spiritual family, a hairy male animal by the name of Hatred.

And so, it was announced that the phonograph would be competed for by the two girls, Tsitsa and Tali, who had strung more tobacco than anyone else to date.

The phonograph itself, along with the records, was at Aunt Masha's, because she was considered the leading activist among the women of Chegem. Before, her house had been reminiscent of a young people's club, owing partly to the abundance of daughters (five girls and not a single boy), partly to her own sociable character. Now, after the appearance of the phonograph, middle-aged and elderly Chegemians began to drop in, too, to listen to the Leader speaking in his somewhat toneless (in the Chegemians' language—somewhat "rotten") voice.

The Chegemians knew that other records were sold in the city, records of Russian, Georgian, and even Abkhazian songs; but these had not yet reached Chegem, because up to now no one had had a record player. Everyone was waiting for someone else—especially one of the local Endurskies—to buy one, so that they could see whether a man's voice, when detached from the man himself, would make the cattle waste away or the grapevines lose their leaves.

So when the prize phonograph appeared, the Chegemians had only these records to amuse themselves with. But then, they came to know them very well, the peculiarities in the modulation of the voice, the stammerings, exactly where there would be applause. What especially impressed the Chegemians in this historic speech was where the Leader poured himself some water, drank it, and then knocked the glass against the table on which, as the Chegemians quite correctly supposed, he was setting it down.

Irrepressible Tali had the idea of accompanying the Leader's speech on the guitar, with pauses timed to coincide with the applause or the distinct gurgle of Borzhom water being poured into the glass.

"Listen, he's drinking water," the Chegemians said when they heard that sound. Its mysterious naturalness stunned them every time.

"You could lay him out now," Tendel added suddenly once, having decided for some reason that the point where he drank the water was the most convenient for an evil deed of this sort. Surmising that the old hunter's remark was based on his long-standing habit of lying in wait at a water hole, the Chegemians began to laugh at his ignorance. They said that if the Leader wanted a drink he wouldn't go down to a water hole like some old shepherd, he'd just wink, and they'd bring him the best lemon fizz in the country. "But I know how he drinks there," the old hunter answered good-naturedly.

The Chegemians—except for Uncle Sandro, who had heard applause as a way of showing approval for oratorical speeches back in the time of revolutionary meetings in the cities and the lowland villages—had heard people clap, and they themselves clapped, only during the dances at banquets; it was a long time before they understood why no one jumped up on stage during the applause and began to dance.

Well, of course, the Leader wouldn't jump out on stage and start whirling in the *lezginka*, precisely because he's the Leader. Well, the Russians don't even know how to dance, the Chegemians reasoned, precisely because they're Russians. Well, but why is Mikoyan being shy? He's an Armenian, he grew up on our soil, he knows the taste of our bread and salt!

Gradually the Chegemians got used to the fact that nothing would happen after the applause. If a novice appeared and joyfully pricked up his ears at the familiar sound of clapping, the initiates would wave carelessly in the direction of the record and say, "Nah, nothing comes of it when *they* clap."

In short, it was an especially large crowd of villagers that gathered in Aunt Masha's green little yard in those days.

Aunt Masha herself, who was a bit portly (a build rare and therefore highly valued in a mountain woman), sat in the shade of a cherry-laurel tree on a large ibex skin, evenly cranking the handle of the phonograph. With a half-eaten peach sticking out of her mouth, she would wind up the spring of the phonograph and put the record on the spinning turntable, after which she would break off a bite of peach with her strong teeth and look around at the company, allowing them to enjoy the Leader's voice and all the sound effects accompanying his speech.

Her company, too, peeled and ate peaches, which one of Aunt Masha's daughters brought over from time to time in her apron hem and scattered right on the grass in the shade of the cherry-laurel. Aunt Masha's whole yard was planted in peach trees, but she could have sworn that not a man alive had ever tasted them ripe—they were completely finished off by the numerous visitors to her house before the peaches ever ripened.

Aunt Masha's husband, whom she viewed with some scorn because of his inability to beget a son, was rarely home, because he worked at the kolkhoz livestock farm as a shepherd. He spent almost all summer in the alpine meadows to which he drove the stock, and was rarely home the rest of the time either, because the stock farm was situated several kilometers from the house. Besides, over many years of being a shepherd he had become so unused to people that, as he himself confessed, his head began to spin when he saw five or six people together, especially if they showed any tendency to excessive gesticulation when they talked. He preferred to remain at the farm with his goats.

When he did come home for a few days, he would take care of some masculine chores: oh, he'd prop up the wattle fence and repair it, plane some beanpoles, fell a tree for firewood, that sort of thing. He usually came home with a dreadful growth of beard, but Aunt Masha would heat up a kettle of water that very day and shave him with her own hands. After the shave his face seemed to express an agonized irritation at its shameful nakedness, and the expression never left his face during the several days that he busied himself with his domestic chores, shouting at his daughters and occasionally getting their names mixed up.

"Hey, Firuza, or whatever your name is," he would shout from somewhere up on the roof of the barn.

"Papa, I'm not Firuza, I'm Tata," the daughter would answer. "Firuza got married last year—"

"I don't need you to tell me!" he would snap. Pounding away with his ax, he would add something like, "I'm supposed to have a big nail lying back there behind the house, near the whetstone. So bring it here, if your mama's pals haven't made off with it."

After a few days, having done all the masculine chores (to his own way of thinking, as Aunt Masha caustically noted), he would start back to his goats with evident relief—with secret exultation, as a matter of fact. As the Chegemians had observed, each time he came home after a long absence he had built up a morose, savage dream of begetting a son, and when he went back to his goats, he would seem to be listening from afar with a mistrustful moroseness, a premonition of evil, to the progress of his wife's pregnancy.

In due course his wife would bear him a baby girl, with unheard-of ease, and everything would begin all over again. The Chegemians maintained that this was how she bore them: She would be hoeing corn along with the kolkhoz women, or out in the field priming tobacco. Suddenly she would straighten up, raise her head, open her mouth, and listen, listen to something.

"Hush, girls!" she would shout to the young people, so that they would not interfere with her listening.

"What is it, Aunt Masha?" the stupidest ones would ask.

"I think the baby's coming," she would say. She would drop the hoe and go into the bushes. "Keep the men away."

They had no time to collect their wits, let alone send for the midwife. Not only that, those who were out of earshot did not catch on; she'd drop her hoe and go into the bushes, they said, and the next thing they knew, they'd hear the wail of the new baby.

Although Aunt Masha did have her babies easily, the Chegemians were exaggerating, of course. They have sharp tongues, thanks to the freedom of their imaginations, and are apt to stretch the truth. Thus they say that a certain person, on learning that Aunt Masha's husband had arrived after a long absence, purposely hid under their house and eavesdropped.

"But why? But why? It still won't be a boy," Aunt Masha's voice kept saying all night, according to this mysterious person.

It was both interesting and easily observable, even without the Chegemians' pointing it out, that all the girls were born pretty and even somewhat inclined to plumpness, like Aunt Masha; but that was not the main thing. The main thing was that each girl was born sturdier than the last. Beginning with the third, they resembled good-natured giantesses, and the youngest, while still just a baby, when they forgot her in her cradle—and that happened rather often, given Aunt Masha's sociable inclinations—well, when they put the baby in the cradle and forgot her in the shade of the cherry-laurel, and the shade moved off, then the baby got up out of the cradle with a grunt and dragged it into the shade herself. Then she lay down in the cradle again, if she felt like lying down.

In the Chegemians' opinion, the increasing might of Makhaz's daughters was the consequence of his efforts to have a boy; but since his wife had only one progenitive form operating in her—that is, the form of a woman—then even though Makhaz's efforts were reflected in the increasingly mighty masculine strength of his daughters, there was no way he could alter the single progenitive form given her by God.

The Chegemians believed that a woman's progenitive forms were given her at birth. Most women were given both forms, a male and a female, but some were given only one, and then no matter how hard you tried, nothing happened. You might as well pour wine into a carafe and require the wine to take the form of a bottle.

Whether because Aunt Masha's husband was an unsociable person, or because it was a trait of her own nature, Aunt Masha loved to be among people. And nothing, especially for an Abkhazian woman, provided such a natural opportunity to be among people as the kolkhoz. For this reason Aunt Masha was one of the best kolkhoz workers, and she was always held up as an example by the leadership.

In those days she was practically the only woman who attended the kolkhoz meetings, and entirely of her own free will at that.

She used to get dressed up, go out on the upper Chegem road, and pause to wait for the men walking behind her or, conversely, call loudly to those walking ahead and ask them to wait up. Other Chegem women would look at her from their yards and mutter, "Go on, go on. They'll make you a boy over there."

Thus Aunt Masha lived with her herculean daughters—poor, free, and slovenly. The children, and she herself, lived from hand to mouth, but mighty nature had its way and all of them looked rosy, strong, and content.

Every day, during the protracted noonday break, especially in bad weather, they had the phonograph playing in the yard. They ate up the last of the peaches and began on the first roast corn.

The shepherd's wolfhound, which had been left at home by his master to serve as male protector, was bewildered by the crowds of people coming and going after the phonograph appeared. He ceased to bark at all. For days on end he sat under the house, which was built on high pilings, and kept a miserable eye on what was happening in the yard.

Incidentally, that dog never did get used to the phonograph. The first time he heard the Big Mustache's voice, he let out a growl and crept over to the shade of the cherry-laurel where the phonograph stood. He barked uncertainly a few times. Then, as if he had realized whose voice it was, he suddenly put his tail between his legs and within full view of everyone turned and fled to the cornpatch, snapping as he went. There he continued to bark for a long time and returned home only toward evening, when everyone had dispersed.

"He knows whom to fear, he can feel the time we stand in," the Chegemians clucked. They exchanged knowing glances over the animal's powers of prophecy.

("Oh, the time we stand in," the Chegemians like to say, apropos of anything. This expression, depending on how it is uttered, has a multitude of nuances, expressing varying degrees of hopelessness. In all these nuances, time itself is invariably viewed, or I should say felt, as an element that flows but is not subject to us. It is not within our will to enter it or leave it; we can only stand and wait in it, as in a stream—the stream may get stronger and roll over our heads, or it may suddenly disappear beneath the soles of our feet.)

Eventually the dog became accustomed to the phonograph's voice and no longer bothered to bark or snarl at it. If it caught him in the yard, all he did was get quietly to his feet and go away under the house.

An amusing subtlety of his behavior (which naturally did not go unobserved by the Chegemians) was that he went away, not when they brought the phonograph out of the house and settled down with it in the shade of the cherry-laurel, not even when they put the record on, but only after they had put the record on and begun to turn the crank. Then he lazily stood up, wandered under the house, and fell heavily in the cool dust, there to watch with sleepy sorrow what was happening under the cherry-laurel.

That summer a young man from a neighboring village began coming to Aunt Masha's house. His name was Bagrat. He was by origin half Laz, half Abkhazian. It was noted by many Chegemians that this young man with the deep-sunken eyes and the big Kirov watch on his thick wrist (he wore the watch over his shirtsleeve) created quite a stir among the neighborhood girls.

No one in Chegem had timepieces then, neither clocks (the sun took the place of clocks) nor watches. Only the chairmen of the kolkhoz and the village soviet had wristwatches. During a protracted meeting they would suddenly begin winding their watches, setting the hands forward or back, exchanging remarks—for some reason always in Russian, which lent their words and actions a certain cabalistic aura and once more convinced the Chegemians that these people did indeed hold in their hands the very time in which we stand.

Incidentally, besides watches, another item that began to come into fashion in those years as a mark of power was the tussah tunic of military cut. Some Chegemians, like inhabitants of other villages, began to have these tan silk tunics made for themselves, so that at weddings or funerals in other villages, among people they did not know, they could pass for unknown big shots and thus occupy the best places at wedding and funeral tables. In the early days, when these impostor-tunics with their sham ideological linings first began to appear, the true big shots occasionally surveyed them with a look of perplexed suspicion, which was soon replaced by a look of scorn; but the tussah impostors were not embarrassed in the least. Indeed, they could not be outlawed, because tussah tunics were only an unofficial symbol of official position.

In the end, as they say, life teaches everything. The true big shots in true tussah tunics got the idea of arriving at funeral and holiday feasts only after a goodly delay. By this ploy—a solid pause, a purifying hiatus in time—they dissociated themselves from their intolerable doubles.

Admittedly, in our own day, when the authorities arrive at funeral and holiday feasts without fanfare, in official cars, these damned imitators have again adapted to circumstances. For example, some store manager who has his own Volga: if he's invited to such a feast, do you think he just gets in his car and comes? Hell, no! He hires a chauffeur, you see, most often an off-duty taxi driver, and arrives sitting solid and bored beside his chauffeur. Just try and figure out whether he's a store manager or an official, if there are hundreds or even thousands of people there. Sometimes at the height of the feast this store manager posing as an official suddenly calls over some of the people waiting on table and asks, ostensibly in an undertone, "You haven't forgotten to give my chauffeur something to eat?"

"Oh, no, of course not," they answer him. "He's sitting over there in the corner, next to the district committee secretary's chauffeur."

"All right," he nods, "only for goodness sake don't give him any wine . . ."

The people sitting around him listen in, trying to learn something about their mysterious neighbor from this little dialogue, and of course they learn exactly as much as the neighbor wants them to.

But we seem to have strayed too far from the young man whose deep-set eyes and Kirov watch evoked pleasantly confused dreams in the Chegem girls. No, he really was good-looking even without the watch. Of average height, broad-shouldered and well-proportioned, he possessed extraordinary physical strength, to the respectful surprise of the Chegemians.

The first time they had noticed him was that spring, when he appeared at Aunt Masha's and offered to plow her private field for seventy-five pounds of corn. Aunt Masha gladly agreed. She sent one of her daughters to Khabug to ask for the loan of his oxen. The oxen were brought over and the young man plowed her field in two days, working from dawn to dark.

Having received his sack of corn, he put his watch on, slung the sack over his shoulder, and silently departed to his own village, accompanied by the affectionate gratitude of Aunt Masha.

"Son of a bitch," old Khabug said, driving the oxen home after surveying his work. "He's overworked my oxen."

For about a week after the young plowman's departure, the powerful smell of masculine sweat lingered in Aunt Masha's house. She and all her daughters sniffed it with pleasure.

"Ah, what a fine young man," Aunt Masha recalled, sighing. "Wish I had one like that."

It was not absolutely clear what she had in mind: husband, son, or son-in-law. The relatives and neighbors, puzzling over why he had taken it into his head to plow her field for such a laughable fee, came to the conclusion that he had conceived a liking for one of her pretty giantesses, specifically Lena. It was she to whom he had entrusted the watch while he worked, and when he took a break he taught her to tell time without looking at the sun. She did learn to tell time by the watch, but then she forgot again and switched back to the sun. The hypothesis was agreeable to Aunt Masha, although Lena seemed to her too statuesque for this fellow. She was a head taller than he, and to all appearances did not plan to stop growing—after all, she was only eighteen.

Now he began showing up at Aunt Masha's. Sometimes he would drop in on his own; sometimes they would hail him from below when he was walking along the upper Chegem road, and he would take a shortcut and come crashing straight down the scree of the mountainside.

In all the games the Chegem children organized, whether it was lifting stones, playing "ball" (Abkhazian football) or wrestling, he always came out on top. Somehow everyone immediately accepted the fact that it was impossible to compete with him. The only one who could not reconcile himself to this was Tali's cousin Chunka, a young giant madly envious of this outsider's successes.

Occasionally he did manage to even the score with Bagrat in something. One time he succeeded in stopping Bagrat when the latter, scattering people left and right, was racing to the opposing goal with the ball. Chunka made a flying tackle, plowed up Aunt Masha's green yard with his dragging toes, and finally brought him down.

Another time he managed to lift the two-hundred-pound shepherd Harlampo, whom Khabug kept at his house. At that season Harlampo roamed the environs of Chegem with his goats and ate an incalculable number of ripening walnuts, adding a full forty pounds to his weight; usually by this time of year no one could thrust him straight overhead. There were many Chegem boys who could lift him at the beginning of the summer, but not now, when he had been gobbling walnuts for days on end and gained a full forty pounds.

This is how the Chegemians usually perform the lifting of a live weight: A man who is preparing to lift another man lies down on the grass. The one who is to be lifted squats next to him, wraps his arms around his own thighs, and clasps his hands tightly. The one doing the lifting passes his own hand under the liftee's arms and grips his other arm with all his strength. Then, using the other arm to help himself, he hoists the liftee onto his chest and straightens out the arm holding the weight. From this moment on, he must not assist that arm in any way. The task is to get to his feet without touching the load again and without help from anyone else.

For some reason the shepherd Harlampo was the one most often used for this purpose. Perhaps this was because he was small and compact, a convenient size to lift; or because he never complained if the one doing the lifting was unable to bear up under the strain and unexpectedly dropped him.

Harlampo clearly took a certain pride in being more convenient to lift than anyone else. With some aspiring athletes, he could immediately tell that they would not be able to lift him, and he said so; but if they insisted, he sat down and clasped his arms around his thighs. As he was lifted up in the air he waited with doomed earnestness for the athlete to give out and drop him on the ground. If the athlete did not drop him on the ground but lifted him over his head, then Harlampo, after he was safely landed, shrugged his shoulders and admitted his mistake.

So that day, driven perhaps by jealousy, perhaps by something else, Chunka lifted Harlampo, who had attained his classic August weight. It was a titanic spectacle. First Chunka raised himself up little by little, his free hand convulsively groping for support, clutching at the grass. Soon he was sitting up. Slowly transferring the weight to one leg, he poised himself on the other leg. Bracing his free hand on the knee of that leg—all this time not letting the live weight out of his sight (the live weight for some reason did not let him out of sight, either, and even bared his teeth in a tense grimace as if trying with all his might to make himself lighter)—with a slow, heroic effort Chunka straightened up to his full impressive height and stood up like a monument to a Red Army soldier who has bound up an enemy and is about to hurl him back to his own territory.

After him, Bagrat did the same thing. He lifted the shepherd with such humiliating ease that when he mildly lowered him to the ground and began to put his watch on, many people thought, Why bother to take it off?

Chunka got two nosebleeds that day and came to hate Bagrat thoroughly.

Incidentally, Bagrat introduced a new game to Chegem, "snap the rope."

This game enjoyed a modest vogue for a while and then was quickly forgotten. For one thing, it was very hard to break the rope, and for another—this was more important than the first—they begrudged the rope.

The point of this strange game was to take a meter-long piece of rope and tie the ends of it, forming a loop, then thrust one's wrists through it and forcibly jerk them apart. Some Chegem boys succeeded in snapping the rope once or twice, but no one managed to outdo Bagrat. He broke the rope and tied it and broke it again, until it was so much shorter that they could no longer jerk their hands apart but could only unclench them.

Once, when Bagrat had littered Aunt Masha's yard with snapped ropes, Bad Hand happened to ride by on the upper Chegem road. Without stopping he shouted down, "I'm afraid the Chegem girls are going to lose the drawstrings from their underpants when this fellow runs out of ropes!"

When they heard that, the Chegem girls laughed in a friendly way, their laughter indicating that the threat did not strike them as too terrifying.

Aunt Masha decided that Bagrat had set his sights on Lena, but although she dropped all kinds of hints to everyone else, by Chegemian standards it would have been supremely tactless to ask him about this directly. Bagrat would be consulting Lena about something or joking with her, and Aunt Masha would nudge someone sitting near her as if to say, You can't fool us, we know what you're up to. For example, Bagrat asked for something to drink. Aunt Masha meaningfully picked up on his request.

"Give him to drink, child," she keened sweetly, "give him to drink of our spring, pure and untasted."

"Look here," the Chegemians joked with Bagrat, nodding toward the young giantess, "how are you going to kiss her?"

"On the bounce," Bagrat joked back.

It should be noted that by Chegemian custom all such remarks are considered the height of shamelessness, if made seriously. For example, if a young man declares to a girl's parents or other relatives that he likes her, from that moment on, regardless of how they feel about him, he is deprived of the right to visit not only their house, but any house that is near enough to serve as a meeting place.

A joke is something else again. Anything can be said in the form of a joke. In the form of a joke the Chegemians can circumvent all the taboos of the old pagan domestic order. I even think that when God (or another no less responsible person) put into effect the harsh pagan customs of the Chegemians, he was actually employing pedagogical subtlety in order to develop a sense of humor in his favorites (the Chegemians had no doubt that they were his favorites).

Thus the Chegemians, as if in jest, tried to find out from Bagrat what he was after at Aunt Masha's; but since Bagrat joked back as if agreeing with them, everything remained obscure, as before. And only one person, with sweet anxiety, guessed why he was here. It was Tali.

They had met for the first time the year before. Tali, with a brood of cousins (the younger children always tagged along after her, although she sometimes lashed out at them), was standing on the road not far from her house. She was knocking down green walnuts with a stick, and the indignant little bell of her voice kept chiming at the children, because they ran to gather the nuts she knocked down before her stick could fall to the ground.

Before he even saw her he smiled at her voice, and then, when just around a bend in the road the canopy of a huge walnut tree came into view, and under it half a dozen small children with their heads greedily thrown back, their faces smeared from ear to ear with juice from the green husk of the nuts, and next to them a long-legged young teenager in a loose, short-sleeved dress of apple-green cotton, her face upturned too and her whole slim and obviously strong figure arched backwards in a threatening gesture, with a stick in her still farther outstretched hand, in the peculiar maidenly gesture that cannot be confused with anything else, natural in its unnaturalness, that is, a gesture that tries to introduce smoothness into a throw, that is, to introduce smoothness into what by nature must be abrupt—he suddenly found something touching in this whole scene, and stopped opposite the girl on the path. Absorbed in the throw she was about to make, she and the children simply did not notice him. This struck him funny, especially since the girl silently and tensely continued to take aim, arching backwards and stretching her arm ever farther behind her back until the tip of the faintly quivering stick bumped against his stomach.

"Watch out, don't kill me!" he said.

Tali dropped the stick and spun around. The children also turned to look. On seeing the stranger two steps away, a fellow with deep-set eyes, a broad chest, an empty sack slung over his shoulder, she was suddenly ashamed of her stained hands and swiftly hid them behind her back.

"Where will you hide your mouth?" he asked.

The girl tried to wipe her mouth with the back of her hand, remembered that you couldn't wipe off the walnut's strong juice that way, was ashamed at her shame, and flared up: "Go on, wherever you're going!"

This time her angry voice came out unexpectedly low. Bagrat grinned, threw his sack off his shoulder, picked up the stick the girl had dropped, shook it to make sure it would not break in mid-flight, drove the children away from the tree with a glance, set his sights on a high branch thickly studded with walnuts, and hurled the stick at it with such force that a green torrent of nuts rained to the ground.

"Halloo!!!" the children howled gleefully, and dashed to gather the green pebbles that bounced over the rocks. Some of them, the ripest, hit the ground so hard they burst from the husk and disappeared in the grass with a flash of their golden shells. The children darted after those with special glee.

Bagrat noticed the large stone on which they were smashing the nuts that had husks. The stone was all wet with the savage freshness of the juice from the flattened and husked nuts. Bagrat suddenly felt a childish appetite for green walnuts. Scooping up a couple of handfuls, he thrust them in his pocket, picked up his sack, and went his way.

Tali, watching him go, saw him feel for the knife at his hip and unsheathe it. Then, taking one nut at a time from his pocket, he slit them in half, picked out the meat, and threw the empty hemispheres on the road.

Bagrat said later that that was when the thought flashed through his mind—and was promptly forgotten—that it would be nice to take this little girl home, give her a good scrubbing, have her graze a while without letting her out of the yard so that she'd fatten up a bit, and then marry her. This thought flashed and disappeared when he had eaten the last nut, putting the knife away in the sheath that hung at his hip.

Half an hour later, after driving the children away, Tali was walking toward her grandfather's with a sense of joy and the dim understanding that her joy was connected with the fact that she liked this grown-up stranger. She walked quickly along the path, an obscure tenderness filling her as her eyes sought out (there's one! and another one!) the precisely slit and neatly scraped-out hemispheres of the walnuts. Suddenly it struck her that these freshly scraped-out hemispheres in some way recalled the stranger himself. She was very surprised at this obscure similarity. How could the shell of an eaten nut, with a green husk at that, be similar to a man? But it was, and that was all there was to it! Perhaps his deep-set eyes recalled the hollows of the scraped-out hemispheres, perhaps the thick green husk somehow recalled his sturdiness. Suddenly, for some reason, she picked up one of these halves and sniffed it, inhaling the bitter, delicate aroma of the underripe nut with pleasure, as if she were smelling it for the first time, although she herself was steeped in the smell. Suddenly ashamed that someone might catch her doing this, she threw away the green half-shell, jumped up, and burst out laughing: somehow she was amused, pleased, and ashamed . . .

Now she remembered that she had seen an ear of corn in their field that morning that was ready to pick. This was how you could tell: After you spotted an ear that was more or less well filled, you used your nails to spread open the jacket of husks that covered it; the outer jacket was always thick and coarse, and the under layer fine and delicate. You had to spread it open, right down to the ear, and when you got down to it, you crushed a swollen kernel. If a colorless juice came out, that meant it had to ripen some more, but if milk spurted out, you could roast it.

In general, Grandpa did not like people to test the corn for ripeness this way. Although the tested ears continued to fill and ripen, it was easy for the birds, especially the jays, to thrust their beaks through the already opened jacket (try as you might, you couldn't hide it) and gradually peck the whole ear away.

But could he forbid his pet anything? And Tali recognized the ripe ears almost unerringly, because these were the ones that had been first to let down their tresses of flax, rose, and gold, and she had braided them, long before they dried out . . .

Ten minutes later, bounding up to the threshold of her grandfather's kitchen, Tali suddenly froze—the stranger was there.

It turned out he had come to buy piglets. By this time Khabug had learned to raise pigs of a special long-snouted and vigorous breed. When these pigs were crossed with wild boars, they produced hardy offspring which, thanks to their unusual speed, easily escaped from any predator and sometimes switched from flight to pursuit if provoked, forcing not only jackals but also full-grown wolves to take to their heels in panic.

Bagrat had already selected three speckled piglets in the barn, and he and the owner were back in the kitchen haggling. Now and again they slapped palms, each trying to convey the impression that he was taking a loss, but—agreed! The old man brought the full weight of his mighty authority to bear on Bagrat, but the fellow proved to be unusually tough, almost as tight about coming up in price as the old man was about coming down.

Now Tali suddenly bounded up to the kitchen and froze at the threshold, not having expected to see this fellow again here. And he saw her—all excited, her neck throbbing, her childish face breathing, an unchildish curiosity in her eyes and an expression of passionate devotion to the future, her lips still smeared with walnut juice. In her hands she held a large ear of corn, tightly swaddled in its green jacket, which had been brusquely turned down to reveal the sparse, shining, delicate, moist hairs, and, showing through them, corn kernels swollen with milk.

"Well, what is it?" old Khabug said, frowning. Tali had interrupted the high-pressure atmosphere of the bargaining process, the air of psychic superiority that he had been creating in order to break this stubborn fellow. Now, he thought, he would have to begin all over.

"It's ripe, Grandpa!" Tali exclaimed, and was at his side in one bound. She stuck her thumbnail into a kernel to make it spurt milk. "See?"

"Look at you, Tali!" her grandmother exclaimed, coming into the kitchen from the storeroom and trying to ameliorate the dreadful impression that her hands and face had made on the stranger. "It's those wretched nuts!"

"He knows!" Tali shouted with a laugh. She ran out on the veranda, where the washtank Uncle Sandro had brought from the city hung.

"She thinks she's still a child!" Khabug said frowningly. He was about to put on his gloomy face again, in order to show that he was losing out in this transaction and thereby create an atmosphere of psychic superiority; but at this point, for some reason, the young man suddenly surrendered.

"All right, have it your way!" he said, and slapped Khabug's palm.

"Bring us a glass," Khabug said, turning to his wife.

"What a neck," the old woman said, looking at Bagrat's back. She went into the storeroom, where dried snack foods and *chacha* were kept.

Bagrat sat beside Khabug at the flaming hearth. Almost without hearing what Khabug was saying to him, he listened against his will to what was going on on the veranda. By the sound of the plug stem of the washtank, he determined that she was washing; then, from her voice driving away the dog, he understood that she had dropped the soap, and the dog had run over to see what it was.

Then he heard the rasp as she tore the husk from the ear of corn, and this sound, with its creaking freshness, recalled his long-ago inexhaustible childish joy in the succession of the fruits—wild strawberries, cherries, blueberries, cherry-plums, sweet plums, hazelnuts, corn, walnuts, grapes, apples, pears, quince, and finally chestnuts.

Strange, he thought; why did the fresh rasp of the husks that she was stripping from the corn remind him so sweetly of this cycle of fruits, this childish joy?

At that point Khabug's wife brought a carafe of pink *chacha* into the kitchen. She sliced some cheese, broke up some *churkhchely*, and moved a low table over to the hearth to put the food on. Old Khabug poured the *chacha*.

Through the open kitchen door Bagrat saw Khabug's mule coming across the yard to the veranda, tossing his mane—listening, just as Bagrat was, to the juicy sound of husks being stripped from the corn.

A moment later the mule started crunching the corn husks.

"Oh, no you don't!" he heard her say, and he vividly imagined the mule reaching for the shucked ear of corn.

". . . let not God empty our cup!" he heard the end of old Khabug's toast. Tali flew into the kitchen with the shucked ear of corn.

They drank, and he felt the stream of fire roll down his throat, and on down almost to his waist.

"Mmmh!" He was sincere, this time, in saying what the laws of hospitality required him to say. "It packs a real wallop!"

"It's not bad," old Khabug agreed. He splashed the end of his drink into the fire, which instantly flared in a blue flame.

Tali sat down on a low bench right beside the fire. Pulling the burning logs apart, she raked out some coals and stood her ear of corn close to them, leaning it against a log.

The bench was so low that she sat with her chin resting on her knee. She kept glancing at Bagrat with a curiosity that disturbed him. When she raised her head from her knee and turned to the fire, her face was delicately translucent, and he involuntarily rested his gaze on her.

After a while the irresistible smell of roast corn tickled the nostrils of everyone sitting in the kitchen. Tali snatched up the corn but could not hold on to it, it was too hot. The corn plopped by the hearth. She seized it again and rapped it against her bench to knock the ashes off of it, constantly shifting her grip so as not to burn herself. Forgetting that there was a stranger in the kitchen, she submitted to long habit and hastily wrapped the corn in the hem of her dress, baring her leg above the knee, while her grandmother exclaimed, "Shame on you, Tali!"

Even as her grandmother spoke, Tali managed (bang! bang!) to break the ear into four parts. She took one, admittedly the thickest, for herself, straightened her dress with a lightning-swift, scornful movement (imagine!), and began to eat, nibbling off several kernels at a time and noisily sucking in air to cool them in her mouth. All the while she kept tossing the ear of corn from hand to hand, and by her noisy inhalation of air seemed to answer her grandmother: "See, it's too hot for me, what's the shame in it?"

"She may look full-grown, but everything goes in one ear and out the other," Khabug said. He took a fragrant golden piece of the corn in his own hardened hand.

"A marvelous little girl!" Bagrat said, trying to say it in an indifferent voice and marveling at the effort it required. He too took a piece of the ear of corn.

"*Mash-Allah!*" Bagrat said. He nibbled off a handful of kernels and put them in his mouth.

"*Mash-Allah!*" Khabug repeated after him, pleased that this half-breed Abkhazian remembered our ancient formula, which blesses flowering, ripening, abundance. They drank another glass apiece.

"To look at you, I'd've thought you were a full-blooded Abkhazian," Khabug told his guest. He was satisfied with both the successful sale of the piglets and the comeliness of this deferential young man.

"You mean I could be an Abkhazian son-in-law?" Bagrat asked. He was mocking Khabug, but Khabug did not notice.

"No doubt about it," Khabug replied firmly, pouring pink *chacha*.

Tali sat by the fire and her face shone, illumined perhaps by the heat of the fire, perhaps by its own heat. Now she gnawed calmly at her corn, and from time to time her eyes rested on Bagrat with a curiosity that disturbed him strangely.

Even so, when he left for his own house that day with the piglets squealing in his sack, Bagrat did not know how dearly he had paid for them. He did not know that the little girl for whom he had knocked down green walnuts would force him to return to this house again and again, and make narrowing circles around it until he chose Aunt Masha's yard as the launching field for his project.

But that happened a year later, and back then he could not believe that he had fallen in love with this little girl, whose stemlike neck, damn it, you could span with the fingers of one hand, and so loosely that she could twist and turn her throbbing neck within your hand—if, of course, you let her.

Yes, it all came about somehow strangely and unexpectedly. Here he was, a twenty-six-year-old man. The girls had long since been stealing glances at him, trying to make their swift glances a small fraction of a long glance; he was aware of this and knew it even before he acquired the Kirov watch. After he bought the watch they began to ask him the time, even girls to whom the time mattered about as much, let's say, as the age of the earth. And the girls who used to steal glances at him, passing off their swift glances as a small fraction of a long glance, were now emboldened to cast long glances at him—admittedly, passing them off as short glances, lengthened out of absent-mindedness.

And suddenly he was losing sleep over this little girl? True, her smile was like a sunny break in a cloudy sky. But good Lord, how thin she was!

Yet he was not angry with himself in the arid hours of sleeplessness; he found it pleasant to remember her voice, so ringing that it had made him smile before he even caught sight of her, and then suddenly so low and chesty when she flew into a rage and said, "Go on, wherever you're going!"

Remember the swift and stubborn movement with which she hid her hands behind her back, remember how she flew into the kitchen with the ear of corn and suddenly froze on the threshold when he was bargaining there with her grandfather! Strange as it may seem, everything he remembered about her struck him as either amusing or ridiculous, but in no way worthy of delight. Nevertheless, the amusing and the ridiculous tormented him and would not let him sleep.

Once when he went to the mill he saw her grandfather's mule tied there. He felt so frightened that he wanted to turn right back, but then, ashamed of his timidity, he decided to go into the mill. The mule, which had turned at his footstep, looked at him as if it knew something about his secret.

There was no one in the mill but the miller Gerago, who was drying tobacco leaves over the open fire.

"Whose mule is that?" Bagrat gestured outdoors, inquiring which of them had come with corn.

"Khabug left them," Gerago said, indicating the plank shelving near the mill wheels, where the sacks of corn stood waiting their turn. Khabug always combined his trip to the mill with any business he had in the village of Napskal, which was very near the mill.

Bagrat looked at the shelves. Immediately, with a sort of feral infallibility, he recognized Khabug's goatskin sacks, although there were others like them there as well. For some reason they reminded him of her (by their fluffiness, perhaps, he thought fleetingly). As if testing his intuition, he nodded toward them: "Those?"

"Yes," Gerago nodded, slowly turning his palm with the tobacco leaf spread on it, right over the flame. Without saying another word, Bagrat left the mill.

With the calculated cunning of a madman he began watching the Big House as he went by on the upper Chegem road. Whenever he saw her, he felt disenchanted with her appearance and was soothed for a while. Her appearance had yielded to the image that love's imaginings had created, and each time he was glad to prove his passion guilty of laughable exaggerations. His passion, as if shamed by the obviousness of the shortcomings in her appearance, would be silenced for some hours, but then it would always begin again. He himself was surprised at the avidity with which he sought and found shortcomings in her. One time she was walking around with her legs all blotchy; that happens if one stands barelegged by the fire, too close and too often. The search for shortcomings soothed his self-esteem a little, gave him the feeling that he was busily resisting the passion, not sitting on his hands while it closed in on him. He did not even suspect that it was not he who told his passion, "Let's go have a look at her, you'll see she doesn't amount to much," but his passion itself that inspired him to go and seek out shortcomings in her. Taking advantage of this harmless pastime, his passion could gawk at her, timidly admire her, rejoice that she was alive.

Once he went to the tobacco shed where the women of their brigade were working. He had come in the vague hope of meeting her here.

She was in fact sitting beside her mother, stringing tobacco. When she caught sight of him, she lowered her eyes with lightning swiftness, and as long as he stood there did not raise them even once. Inwardly he was agitated and did not know what to do, but then Aunt Masha asked him to help roll the tobacco frames into the shed, because a thunderstorm was coming up. This gave him an opportunity to master himself and leave with dignity.

But he was greatly disturbed. It seemed to him that she guessed his feeling, was angry at him! How quickly she had lowered her eyes! What he did not know was that only the rising star of a yet-unacknowledged love was capable of this lightning swiftness, this swallowlike alertness.

Sometimes, when old Khabug took his shepherd to do other farm chores, she grazed her grandfather's goats. Above Khabug's house rose a hill covered with lush grass, thickets of hazelnut, dogwood, blackberry. It was there she grazed her grandfather's goats. Just above began an unbroken pampas of fern, where he hid and watched her.

She was always singing something or calling back and forth to her cousins, Aunt Masha's daughters, or playing with the goats—now with one, now with another, putting a garland of flowers on their necks for some obscure service, and for some still more obscure offense taking it off, if they themselves did not manage to throw it off, which they tried to do as soon as she let go of them.

Sometimes she badgered the flock's huge leader, with his long beard yellowed by time and his huge horns, the tips of which came together as if forming a triumphal arch, the gateway to folly. The old fool waited with solemn calm for her to plait his respectable beard into an unrespectable braid, and still she shouted at him to stop chewing his cud while she was busy with his beard.

Once (evidently she wanted a drink but was too lazy to go down to the spring), she caught a nanny goat, lay down beside her, and shamelessly began squirting a stream of milk right from the udder into her open mouth.

Bagrat was especially impressed, for some reason, by the goat, who during what struck him as an indecent milking stood stock-still with her head turned toward the girl, with an expression of secret amusement or, at any rate, gracious bewilderment.

He sensed that he had no business being here and quietly abandoned his ambush, without waiting for her to slake her thirst. That night he experienced an onslaught of such fierce longing—perhaps this scene with the goat had done him in—that he decided to wait his chance and meet her face to face, whatever the cost. A week later he learned that her grandfather and Harlampo had gone down into Sabid's Hollow for several days to split shingle, and he realized that she would be with the goats again. He decided to lure her into the ferns, and there leave everything to the will of chance.

That day he got out of bed at daybreak, took from his cupboard several chunks of lick-salt (a low grade used for cattle), carefully crushed it, shook it into his pockets, and set out on his way. Before the sun had risen he was on the hill near Khabug's house. Choosing a spot where the goats most often grazed, he began scattering salt as he moved toward the fern thickets, and went as deep into them as his salt supply allowed. Having thus salted a green salad for Khabug's goats, he hid in the ferns and settled down to wait.

His mad cunning—considering that he was relying on goats, that is, on creatures who are quite mad—was fully vindicated. At about ten in the morning some of the goats hit on the trail of his salt and stubbornly headed into the ferns, despite Tali's cries.

He remembered forever the moment when she started to make her way into the ferns and he realized that now she would not go away, and his heart suddenly began beating in his chest with slow jolts, and each one seared his body with an anxious, sweetly thickening flame . . .

As soon as she entered the ferns he lost sight of her, but he heard her now with redoubled keenness. He heard the crunch and rustle of her bare feet on the dry stalks of last year's ferns, and the soft swish of live fern fronds parted by her hands. These sounds, which agitated him more and more violently, sometimes fell silent, sometimes went off to one side, and yet turned invariably toward him, as if obeying the unseen pull of his passion.

All around him, now here, now there, came a crunching, an occasional snort or a bleat, and the clink of bells, as the goats wandered in the ferns; but through all these sounds he clearly distinguished her footsteps. From time to time he heard her voice, scolding the goats—"May the wolves get you!"—and again the rustle of footsteps and the swish of fronds being parted. When she stopped to figure out where to go next, he suddenly heard high in the sky the song of larks, which filled him with a strange, inappropriate sadness.

Suddenly her footsteps ceased. The silence this time lasted much longer than necessary to look around and see where to go next in order to get ahead of the goats and turn them back. He could not understand what had happened, and went toward her himself, for some reason trying to step as quietly as possible.

He walked about fifteen paces, parted the tall fern stalks, and saw her about where he had expected to.

She was sitting on the grass, twisting her right leg up and gripping her foot as hard as she could with both hands. Baring her teeth and even growling a little, she was gnawing her big toe. The little witch, he thought, before he realized that she was trying to pull a splinter out of her foot.

Suddenly she raised her head and looked at him from under her brows. Not at all frightened of him and not even surprised (she was so irritated by the splinter), she slowly lowered her foot, spat, and pinched something from the tip of her tongue. Looking up again, she said simply, "Is that you? I thought it was a goat."

"It's me," he said with a blank smile, and began to walk toward her.

She hastily stood up. He stopped.

"What are you looking for in here?" she asked, at the same time looking around and listening for the invisible goats—helping him, with intuitive insight, to find some simple explanation for having turned up here.

"You," he said. He took one more step and stopped. Now she was three steps away, and if he had had the courage he might have seized her before she could cry out or jump away from him.

"Why, yes," she said slowly, and her eyes blazed with such spontaneous joy that he had a sense of ease, of clarity, as of a complete understanding which could not have been otherwise.

"Yes," he said, feeling that he was gaining control of himself. "I want to marry you."

"Right now?" she asked, and it struck him that for a fraction of a second her eyes scanned the terrain in search of a nesting place. Suddenly she added, "But what about the goats?"

He burst out laughing, because this did sound funny and incomprehensible: either she meant that it would be shameful to get married with the goats watching, or she meant, "How can I leave the goats, if we're getting married right now?"

When she saw that he was laughing, and realized that at least she had not said anything he found disagreeable, she too smiled—as if cautiously spreading her wings—and then laughed.

Her laughter resounded with such childish spontaneity that he suddenly had the thought, Does she really know what it means to get married, or does she think a husband is someone who'll hang around his whole life just to knock down walnuts for her?

She stood before him, looking at him with her golden eyes, sometimes squinting at the rustlings in the ferns; the corners of her lips quivered slightly, and her face, as always, breathed, and her little stem of a neck throbbed; her right foot fidgeted cautiously, and he realized that she was rubbing her big toe on the ground to check whether the tip of the splinter was still there or not.

The sun was already quite hot, and from the fern thickets rose the singular scent of warmed fern, the melancholy spirit of earth's creation, the spirit of uncertainty and easy repentance.

In this still-fresh heat, in this quiet, monotonous swishing of ferns, you can just see the Creator, who, having created this Earth with its simplistic vegetation and its equally simplistic, and therefore ultimately mistaken, concepts of the ultimate fate of its future inhabitants—you can just see the Creator, who is making His way through the ferns to yonder green hill, from which, it must be supposed, He hopes to glide down into outer space.

But there is something strange in the Creator's gait, and besides, He is not cutting directly across to the hill, but somehow moving on a tangent: maybe going to the hill, maybe bypassing it . . .

Aha, now it comes clear to us: He is trying to forestall the guess, ripening behind His back, that He is fleeing; He is afraid that He is about to hear behind His back the howl of the abandoned world, His unfinished project: "What! Is this all?"

"Why, no, I'm not leaving yet," His gait seems to say. "I still have quite a few improvements to make."

There He goes, smiling the distracted smile of a failure, and His wings trail limply at His back. Incidentally, the distracted smile of a failure is intended precisely to distract bystanders from the impact of his failures. The smile says: "Should you bother to stare so fixedly at my failures? Let's spread them around over my whole life; if you like, we can even put them on the map of my life in the form of a chain of islands, on the generally accepted scale: one man to 1,000 villains."

To the distracted smile of the failure—which seems to say, "Should you bother?"—we, that is, his colleagues, friends, neighbors, have a direct answer: "Yes, we should." We are not such fools as to let a failure slur over his failure by means of a distracted smile—reduce it to nought, dissolve it, so to speak, in the sea of collectivity. Because the failure of a close or a distant acquaintance (better, of course, a close one) is an inexhaustible source of optimism for us, and we have never, as they say, denied our material interest in failures.

Even in the most extreme case, if you are an out-and-out dawdler, ditherer, scatterbrain, and there's no way you can take advantage of your close friend's failure—even then, you can come up to him and shake your head, saying, "What did I tell you?"

. . . But these are all details of the distant future. While our Creator goes His way, smiling the distracted smile of the failure, His wings trail limply at His back, as if to stroke the curly tops of the fern clumps, which toss off those limply trailing wings and straighten up angrily every time. Incidentally, just the same way, in the future, some millions of years hence, a childish little head will toss away the hand of a parent who is about to go to the tavern and who for this reason, reflexly and with a sense of secret guilt, is fluttering over his little one's head, all the while trying to pick a convenient moment to slip away from the house; and the childish little head—understanding that there's no help for it, Father will leave anyhow—angrily shakes off his hand: "Well, go on then!"

But again, these are all details of the distant future, and our Creator, naturally having no suspicion of all this, is moving toward His hill, still at the same evasive gait. Yet now, not only do we notice in His slack evasiveness the desire to conceal His desertion (the first in the world), we also see some hint of a touching human hope: If only He'll have time to do something, think of something, before He reaches His hill.

But nothing is thought of, nor will it ever be, because what's done is done, the Earth has been set to spinning. Every instant of its existence will infinitely complicate His calculations, because every instant gives rise to a new alignment of things; and no final scene will ever be the final scene, because even the instant spent in becoming aware of it will be enough to make the latest information the next-to-latest. After all, you can't say to life, to history, and whatever else is whirling past, washing over us and washing everything away from us—hopes, thoughts, and then even our very flesh, down to our very skeletons—after all, you can't say to all this: "Stop! Where are you going? Earth is closed to take stock of ideas!"

That is why He walks away toward His hill at such an uncertain, such an intellectual, gait, and His whole figure bears the stamp of dire forebodings (distant ones, of course), shamefacedly balanced by the still more distant Russian hope, "Things will probably turn out all right . . ."

The sun really was quite hot, and from the fern thickets rose the singular scent of warmed fern, the melancholy spirit of earth's creation.

Strong fern stalks, reddish at the base, rose above earth carpeted with the remains of last year's generation of ferns, through which penetrated the emerald green of grass and the brand-new, stout, leafless little pink stalks of ferns with tightly coiled tops.

One that had been accidentally snapped by her foot stuck up beside her, and from its fleshy stalk dripped a thick liquid, not quite blood, not quite sap, as if from those far-off times when no differentiation had yet been made between the blood of the warm-blooded and the sap of plants, between the thirst of the soul and the thirst of the body.

He felt anew the passion that chained his consciousness, and took a step. She did not move away, did not take fright, but put out her hand and suddenly caressed, or rather touched, his eye with a rough palm. Her touch held more the sober curiosity of a child than the timid tenderness of a maiden. He put one arm around her hard childish back, hot from the sun.

"What do you see in me, I'm thin," she said, half in warning, half in surprise at the force of enchantment that was stored in her and had broken out in spite of her thinness and youth.

If I'd only known, he thought. He pulled her to him and was instantly aware of the smoky, milky smell of her body, her hands lying on his shoulders and scorching him through his shirt, her near face breathing a fresh sultry heat, and the irresistible curiosity of her eyes. Ready for everything now, he nevertheless could not bring himself to kiss her, as if the light of consciousness still illumined too brightly the childishness and chastity of her face, yet his body pressed closer and closer to her, as if the current of passion had covered them to the throat and there was no reason to be ashamed of what was done within this current, which seemed to be whirling past consciousness.

"Ssh!" she hissed suddenly. Her hands slid quickly from his shoulders and made fists against his chest.

"What?" he asked blankly, looking at her suddenly remote face.

"Someone's coming," she whispered, and nodded over his shoulder.

He looked back. Through the fern fronds, about thirty paces away, he could see the rocky crest of the hill, which was traversed by a little path. He scanned the barren crest—covered with sparse blackberry bushes and shining with sad white rocks like the skulls of some sort of prehistoric animals—and thought that she had made it up on purpose to distract him; but at that moment there appeared on the crest of the hill the slightly stooped figure of her consumptive cousin.

Clearly visible from here, he was climbing to the crest, his hands clasped behind his back, with a soft, listless step, a sort of hollow-stemmed gait—indifferent to everything in the world, and alienated from everyone by the expression of bitter resentment frozen on his thin face and stooped figure, which shivered even in this heat.

"He doesn't see us," Bagrat whispered. When he looked back at her face he was stunned by its expression of sorrow and remoteness.

"Is he really going to die?" she whispered, and somehow she reached out after the cousin disappearing on the far side of the hill. Bagrat felt a stab of jealousy.

"We're all going to die," he said, and sensed that his words had dropped into a void.

Still looking over his shoulder at the crest of the hill behind which her cousin had disappeared, she shook her head. He suddenly felt like a naughty child to whom someone has revealed the cruel point of his joke. She raised her eyes and looked at him with melancholy surprise, as if to ask, "How could we be happy, with something like that nearby?"

He made no reply to her look, he was utterly disconcerted. He sensed some sort of force standing behind her and was disconcerted because he could not explain to himself where the force in this little girl came from.

"You know," she said to him, relaxing her watchfulness, looking down, "I'd better finish school and then, if you don't change your mind, you'll take me. But Grandpa . . ."

"Grandpa what?"

"Well, you know yourself, he won't like it," she said, as if imploring him not to specify what, exactly, Grandpa wouldn't like and why. He was sure that Grandpa would never agree to give away his favorite granddaughter to him, a half-breed.

"What about your father?" he asked, surprised that she spoke only of her grandfather. He had a feeling that in the future it would be better to deal with her father than her grandfather, who was stubborn as his mule.

"Oh, Papa." She smiled the smile of an older person thinking of someone younger. "He'll survive."

In the spring of the next year, Bagrat suddenly showed up in Chegem and undertook to plow Aunt Masha's field for a sack of corn.

Two days before Tali's contest with Tsitsa, Bagrat showed up in Aunt Masha's yard again. This time he brought a stack of phonograph records, wrapped in burlap and layered between enormous pumpkin leaves. Extracting them from the burlap as carefully as eggs, he played all the records, one after another. They were recordings of Russian, Georgian, and Abkhazian songs. The last one was a recording of the Abkhaz Song and Dance Ensemble under the direction of Platon Pantsulaya, although his name had been carefully erased from the record label.

After playing all the records, he layered them between the pumpkin leaves again and wrapped them up in the burlap.

"You could leave them," Aunt Masha said. "Don't worry, we won't ruin them."

"I'll give them to the one that wins the phonograph," Bagrat replied. Tucking his fragile musical load carefully under his arm, he left the yard.

Taliko, who was sitting there on an ibex skin, flopped on her back when she heard these words, grabbed her guitar, and played, lying down, "The Death of the Chelyuskinians"—a tune much in vogue at that time in Chegem. No one knows where this melancholy tune came from and whether it was really dedicated to the Chelyuskinians or whether that was a figment of the Chegem girls' imagination, but that was what they called it, and Tali played it best of all.

Now the crucial day was upon them. Since the night before, heaps of primed green tobacco leaves had been lying in the cool of the shed, which in honor of the occasion had been spread with fresh fern, to make it softer and more festive for the women to sit there and work that day.

About a dozen women and girls of the local brigade, nearly all of them related, or if not related then very close neighbors—all of them, led by Aunt Masha, zealously strung tobacco and still more zealously discussed the possibilities and consequences of this kind of contest.

Tali was especially pretty that day. With her lively, breathing face bent over the long tobacco needle that stuck out from under her arm, she strung with lightning speed, biting her tongue in effort.

Clack! Clack! Clack! The leaves crunched like a bitten cucumber as they were strung on the needle.

"Don't get too excited, you'll bite off your tongue," Aunt Masha told her from time to time, glancing at her. "The phonograph is ours—"

"Yes, Aunt Masha," Tali answered her. "It's fine for you to talk . . ."

After filling the needle with tobacco leaves, she pressed it to her breast (pulling in her tongue for an instant); then, in the gesture of a spirited accordion player, she jerked the creaking needleful onto the string with three or four tugs (snap! snap! snap!); and now, pressing it (the needleful) to her breast, she swished the free part of the string through it, guided it almost to the end of the string, and with swift slaps of her palm spaced the tightly packed leaves the right distance apart—the string having first been wound around her big toe, which, incidentally, was enchanting, and in itself worthy of a small lyric poem.

Uncle Sandro and Kunta put yesterday's strings of tobacco on the drying frames. They each took an end of the four-meter string, which sagged heavily under the raw leaves; they lifted it, shook it lightly so that any leaves which had a poor hold would fall off right away, and then fastened it to a frame standing on wooden tracks. When the frame was filled they rolled it away down the tracks until it rested against the other frames on which tobacco was drying.

At noon, when the women—their clothes creaking, permeated with glossy black tobacco oil, or *zefir*, as the Chegemians called it—went to the spring to wash and have a bite to eat, Tali remained in the shed. Without interrupting her work, she drank the traditional cold vegetable soup, made with yogurt and cornmeal, which Uncle Sandro brought her from the house.

"Don't work yourself to death, Daughter," Uncle Sandro told her, not too loudly, just in case. "Your grandfather's had a pretty good life even without a phonograph."

"All the same, I'd feel bad," Tali replied. She scraped the bottom of the bowl and licked the bone spoon. "I *can* string faster than anyone . . ."

"You know whose daughter you are," Uncle Sandro agreed with sudden pride, although he had never in his life threaded a tobacco needle.

Uncle Sandro counted up her work. It turned out that before noon Tali had done sixteen strings of tobacco—about a day's work for a diligent, strong woman.

Tearing off a clump of fern leaves, Tali wiped her hands and reached for her guitar (like the rifle of a good guerrilla, her guitar was always with her). She lay down on her back to rest her numb spine a little and played "The Death of the Chelyuskinians."

A ten-year-old boy, Kunta's adopted son, had been hanging around the barn all day, his eyes glued to Tali. Now, when she began to play "The Death of the Chelyuskinians," he felt his eyes stinging treacherously from the sweet melancholy of the foreign melody. The boy was afraid that his tears would arouse Uncle Sandro's scorn, or more especially, Tali's, and he did not know what to do—run away, or master his tears and listen to the end of "The Death of the Chelyuskinians." Trying to make his brimming tears flow back in, he tipped his head back and pretended that he had gotten interested in something up high. At this point Uncle Sandro hailed him and ordered him to go to the tobacco shed where Tsitsa was working and find out how many strings she had done since morning. If they should hide this information, he ordered him to look and see roughly how big the heap of strung tobacco was beside her.

"See here," he said, showing him the tobacco Tali had strung. "There are sixteen strings here, and about ten over here, and no more than eight over here."

"All right," the boy said, and ran out of the shed.

"Wait!" Uncle Sandro called. "If they ask who sent you, say, 'No one! I was out walking and just dropped by.' "

"All right!" the boy said, and ran off again.

"Wait!" Uncle Sandro stopped him again. "And if they ask about Tali, do you know what to answer?"

"Sishteen," the boy said.

"Dumbbell," Uncle Sandro corrected him. "You mustn't say anything. Say, 'I don't know, I haven't been over there.' Got it?"

"Yes," the boy said, and dashed off like a shot, afraid of being stopped again and utterly confused with further details of this interesting, but, it turned out, too complicated game.

"You'd have done better to go yourself," Tali said, putting away the guitar and taking up the needle again.

"What!" Uncle Sandro replied. "The minute I leave, they'll have a spy over here!"

Soon all the women returned, sat down in their places, and got back to work. About an hour later the little boy came into the shed and said that Tsitsa had nineteen strings.

"Impossible!" all the women exclaimed in unison, abruptly raising their heads, their needles bristling.

"Wait!" Uncle Sandro exclaimed angrily. "What does it look like? Does she have a big heap beside her?"

"It's not much of a heap, it's nothing," the boy said, disconcerted by the general indignation.

"Lie! Lie! Lie!" Tali exclaimed. "That twice-soured, thrice-rotten girl, string faster than me? They're helping her!"

With that she hurled away her needle and started toward the house, sobbing loudly, interspersing her sobs with curses aimed at her rival and the whole hunting clan.

"May I tear your lying heart out of your breast!" Tali sobbed. "May I skewer it on a tobacco needle and roast it—"

The women in the shed fell silent, listening with alert amazement to the novel details of her curses, so as to memorize them and apply them when the occasion arose. Their alert faces expressed with amusing frankness the split in their attention: written on their faces were both a general expression of pity for the deceived Tali and an individual curiosity about the theme of her curses—the individual curiosity quite unsuspecting that in the given instance it was indecent or contradicted the general pity.

". . . And may I!" Tali continued meanwhile, having finished a mighty chord of sobs, "Feed it to our dogs! And may they!"—here she rose to yet another completely unexpected note—"Champ! Champ! And eat it up!"

At this point the women in the shed who were most highly skilled in the art of popular oaths exchanged glances. The unexpected verb, used by Tali with billboard boldness, evoked a close-up view of the muzzle of a dog, vengefully champing on the lying heart of her rival.

"Not bad," one of them said, and looked at the other.

"She squashed her, no question about it," the other agreed.

"Why are you sitting here like sheep!" Uncle Sandro roared at the women. "Come on, get her back here! God forbid they should hear her over there, too."

Tali was brought back to the shed, and they had hardly sat down when a voice rang out from the other side.

"Who was that crying at your place?" a woman's voice asked from the rival shed.

"What did I tell you!" Uncle Sandro said. Leaning out of the shed, he shouted in his resonant voice, "It was Lena crying, Lena! What's it to you?"

With that he quickly raised his binoculars and trained them on the neighboring brigade's shed, as if he wanted to be sure what impression his words had made on the woman who had shouted.

"Makrina, maybe?" they asked from the shed.

"Yes, it's Makrina," Uncle Sandro said. "Quiet, she's shouting again."

Without removing the binoculars from his eyes, as if they helped him hear (and they did in fact help him listen), he listened hard.

"We thought we heard . . . Tali's voice, Tali's!" Makrina's voice carried from afar.

"Ha! I knew it!" Uncle Sandro grinned.

"Tali's got no reason to cry! No reason!" he shouted, looking at his daughter's eyes, which were swollen with weeping. "Tali's singing and laughing!"

Uncle Sandro looked through the binoculars again and saw the woman turn toward the shed, evidently relaying his words to the others. Then Makrina's face appeared in the binoculars, and Uncle Sandro knew by her bright, mischievous expression that she meant to say something disagreeable.

"We heard her sing, we heard!" Uncle Sandro made out.

"We have to get back to work! Work! Eh-oooee!" Uncle Sandro shouted, and he went into the shed, demonstrating that he did not want to waste time on idle conversation.

"I can always tell what she's strung and what they've palmed off as hers," Tali said, without tearing herself away from her work.

As a matter of fact, Tali was right. Every stringer has her signature. One pierces the stem of the tobacco leaf higher, another lower, a third this way and that; a fourth cracks the stalk when she pierces it; and so on. But to read these signatures, of course, is exacting and disagreeable. It is better to get by without doing it.

Uncle Sandro decided to send the little boy to the other brigade's shed again. For camouflage he persuaded Kunta, too, to look in after a while, ostensibly in search of the boy.

The boy set out on his way, and after a while Kunta stumbled off after him. When the road began to climb uphill, Kunta, out of long habit, took a shortcut, which bothered Uncle Sandro greatly.

"What a goathead," he muttered, watching them through the binoculars. "See if he doesn't show up there before the boy."

Without waiting for the news from the other side, Uncle Sandro went into the shed. Now he noticed that the mound of tobacco by his daughter was greatly depleted, and evening was still a long way off. With the tacit consent of all the other women, Uncle Sandro began bringing over to her armfuls of tobacco leaves that had been primed by other women. As he did this he chose the biggest leaves, because the bigger the leaf, the easier it was to string, and in addition it filled the needle more rapidly. This was an infraction of the rules of the contest, but a comparatively minor one. She did string them herself, after all.

Uncle Sandro went out of the shed from time to time and looked through the binoculars. Finally Kunta appeared.

"Well?" the impatient women began asking. Uncle Sandro did not like the way Kunta looked.

"Gloomy as his own hump," Uncle Sandro said, lowering the binoculars.

Kunta's gloom proved fully justified. When he arrived at the shed he announced that Tsitsa had done thirty-two strings.

"Is that so!" Aunt Masha exclaimed. Jerking a last needleful onto her filled string, she took it by both ends and, without standing up, tossed the heavy green garland to Tali, sitting beside her.

"Me too! Me too!" the other women all shouted. Jumping up from their places, they began dragging and throwing to her pile the tobacco they had strung. In one instant, fourteen strings of tobacco were added to Tali's total, and she went ahead again.

Tali laughed through her tears and reciprocated by playing "The Death of the Chelyuskinians" at an unexpected bravura tempo, as if to sprinkle the women with a revivifying cheerfulness.

A couple of hours later Uncle Sandro noticed through the binoculars that Makhty, the chairman of the village soviet, had entered the rival tobacco shed.

"Well, with him there they won't cheat," he said, lowering the binoculars.

"No question about it, with him there they won't dare," the women agreed, and from then till evening each worked only for herself. Uncle Sandro kept an eye on the rival tobacco shed and the upper Chegem road, to be sure and spot the village soviet chairman if he should leave the neighboring brigade before the end of the workday.

It was already dusk when Tali finished her sixty-sixth string of tobacco. By strict agreement, during a contest one was allowed to string tobacco for any stretch of time in the twenty-four hours, but without the use of artificial illumination.

When she had strung sixty-six strings, Tali seized her guitar and ran home. She still had to wash, change, and appear in her holiday best to receive the prize she deserved. She was sure of her prize; according to preliminary intelligence data, it was clear that there was no way Tsitsa could rise above fifty strings, in spite of her relatives' help.

Just as people trying to make sense of life's most confused phenomena will suddenly ask the opinion of children or notorious fools, as if sensing that in the given instance they cannot approach the truth by the path of logic but may be able to pluck it from the darkness through the instantaneous glance of a chance observer—so Uncle Sandro, as he lighted a lamp to begin the task of recounting the tobacco strung that day and piling it all in one row, asked Kunta, who was helping him, "What do you think of this contest?"

Kunta lifted the other end of the string and shook it. When they had stretched it and laid it out separately, he said as he straightened up, as far as his hump permitted him to straighten up, "I think a contest is sort of like a blood feud. Whoever has more relatives wins."

Before Uncle Sandro could appreciate the aptness of his definition, Makhty's brisk voice resounded near the shed: "Artificial illumination is forbidden!"

Uncle Sandro recognized in his voice the familiar intonations of someone slightly high on a daydream, as sometimes happens with the true alcoholic who has an imminent and absolutely guaranteed prospect of a few drinks.

It had been decided (earlier in the day) to have a friendly supper at Aunt Masha's house for a narrow circle of about seventy or eighty people, the best workers of both brigades, where Tali would be presented with the phonograph and the record album. Accordingly, they had already set up tables in Aunt Masha's yard, slaughtered chickens, and collected lamps from neighboring houses.

"Artificial illumination constitutes a flagrant violation of socialist competition!" Makhty continued to declaim loftily as he came into the shed and shook hands, not only with Uncle Sandro but also with Kunta.

"Look here, my friend," Uncle Sandro answered. He held up the lamp to demonstrate that, while there remained in the tobacco shed incalculable treasures wrought by the people's labors, there were no actual people violating the conditions of socialist competition.

"I know," Makhty said. He surveyed the dark drifts of tobacco that had not been tidied up, and moved toward the exit. "Our girls are great, just great!"

From his enthusiastic voice Uncle Sandro understood what Makhty meant: he meant that no matter how many toasts you made to girls like these, you could never say enough. And now Uncle Sandro caught his mood.

"Come on, hurry up," he said to Kunta, and grabbed the end of a string.

Just then his wife's cry resounded from the house. Uncle Sandro dropped the string and straightened up.

"Eh-hey, you!" she shouted to her husband, through her sobs. "Is Tali there?"

"Hell, no!" Uncle Sandro shouted in reply. "She went to wash with you!"

"She isn't anywhere!" Aunt Katya shouted in despair, and her voice choked up with funereal sobs.

"What do you mean, she isn't anywhere?" Uncle Sandro said, and the lamp trembled in his hand. "Well, hold on!"

He handed the lamp to Kunta and raced toward the house.

When he got there, Aunt Katya was sitting on the steps, sorrowfully shaking her head, with her hands lying helplessly in her lap.

This is the story she told him, and later on told many times over. Her recollections did not grow dim with the years; on the contrary, they kept sprouting fresh and novel details, which at this hour she could not recall, or even considered inappropriate to recall.

It seems that when her work was done the girl grabbed some fresh clothes and went to the spring with her mother. There they started a fire and heated the water. After throwing off her dress, which was permeated with *zefir*, the girl washed as usual in the green hut made of alder branches. All the women usually washed here.

Aunt Katya did not notice anything special about her. All she observed was that Tali was in a great hurry and that she had the imprint of a fern frond on her left leg, above the knee. (Interestingly enough, according to the old-timers of Chegem, when Aunt Katya first told about this she would artlessly bare her leg and point to the spot where the mark had been. Your modest historian has never observed this, but not because he turned away at this point out of his characteristic modesty. By the time Aunt Katya told the story in my presence, as she has on several occasions, she simply pointed to the spot where, in her opinion, the symbolic mark had been imprinted. And besides, it would be quite odd to expect such abrupt, bizarre gestures from a serene, softhearted old woman.)

Anyway, Aunt Katya noticed this mark while her daughter bathed. At first she attached no significance to it—Well, what do you know, her leg is numb from sitting—although, with her characteristic natural inconsistency, she added that this fern mark on her little daughter's tender leg had immediately displeased her, and she made a point of rubbing at it with a loofa, but there was no way to wash it off.

"Yes, it was obviously the imprint of fate," Aunt Katya used to say with a sigh. "You can't rub that off with any loofa, but I didn't know."

Then, according to her mother, the girl hastily dried off with the towel. Here the unfortunate mother (according to the same unfortunate mother) again noticed that the mark of the fern frond still clung to her daughter's innocent leg, but evidently it was already too late to do anything, fate was picking up speed like a bus leaving town.

"Although who knows," she would add, sighing thoughtfully, "maybe if I'd steamed it off her leg, things would have turned out all right."

In short, there's nothing to say . . . Tali put on a crepe de chine dress (almost like new), a red wool sweater, and red shoes (never worn even once) that poor Khabug had brought from the city, and dashed for Masha's without even drying her hair.

"Where are you going with your hair down, there are other people there!" Aunt Katya shouted after her. But the girl had already jumped over the stile and disappeared among the tall cornstalks.

"I forgot my comb!" Tali shouted over the rustle of the corn, and then Aunt Katya could not hear her voice any more.

Now Aunt Katya turned back to the fire and saw that her daughter's work clothes, thrown off too close to the fire, were quietly smoldering and smoking. Before she could get to them the dress burst into flames, enveloping her in the stinking breath of an old smoker, and turned to ash.

"One thing after another," Aunt Katya would say, returning to the theme of fate, as if viewing from afar that evening, that little bathhouse, that campfire. "She tossed her clothes out of the hut without looking, but why didn't I pick her dress up right away?"

Aunt Katya did not know what to make of all this, although by now she felt vaguely alarmed. She put out the fire, filled a pitcher with water, and shouted up the hill for Tali to come back. Masha's voice rang out from above; she said that Tali had not yet come by. Now Aunt Katya was thoroughly scared. Even so, she supposed that the girl had run to Aunt Masha's yard, and, when she saw that there were a lot of people there, had in fact become ashamed of her wet, uncombed hair and then headed straight home, taking a shortcut through the corn. What was there to do? Her unfortunate mother, with the heavy pitcher on her shoulder, with her daughter's underwear but without her work dress—which, as she had already said, had turned to ashes—climbed up to the house without stopping once.

"Tali!" she called as she entered the yard, but no one answered her. Now her knees buckled, but even so she lugged the pitcher to the kitchen and then rushed to the girl's room. She looked—the guitar was hanging over the bed. She bent down—the suitcase was under the bed.

The girl couldn't have run off with anyone, Aunt Katya thought, without taking a change of underwear! Still, she did not feel right, her mind kept going back to the accursed mark from the fern frond on he .e girl's tender leg, above the knee.

She went out on the veranda. Seeing that a light glimmered in the tobacco shed, she decided maybe they had called the girl over there for some reason. She shouted to her husband, and when she heard his answer, she completely lost heart.

Of course she told the whole story in such detail only later. When Uncle Sandro ran up she gave it to him in a nutshell, and did not even mention the mark of the fern frond.

"You're a fool!" Uncle Sandro shouted at her. "That place is full of people! She's probably hiding somewhere with the girls, making faces in the mirror!"

With that he hastily set out for Aunt Masha's house. Almost everyone was already there, the tables had been arranged, and the women kept carrying food out of the kitchen and putting it on the tables. Uncle Sandro looked around, reflexly appraised the food, and determined the epicenter of the feast—that is, the tamada's place, that is, his own place. Heaving a sigh, he called Aunt Masha over.

Aunt Masha came out of the kitchen, flushed from the heat of the fire and preoccupied with the merrymaking that lay ahead. Uncle Sandro told her about how Tali had disappeared.

"Well, she's here somewhere," Aunt Masha replied, surveying the tables and trying to think what was missing where.

"Bring me a lamp!" Uncle Sandro shouted. One of the young men, who had been listening to their conversation, ran to the kitchen and brought out a lamp. Within moments everyone knew that Tali had disappeared.

Half a dozen young men, led by Uncle Sandro, went down to the stile. From there they climbed up the trampled path and quickly found the spot where Tali had left it. Her feet sinking deep in the soft tilth, she had set off across the field, here and there tearing the bean and cucumber vines.

Suddenly one of the young men whistled and bent down to pick up the stump of a half-eaten cucumber.

"It's her!" they all exclaimed in unison, because the stump looked very fresh.

"Either they've stolen her or nothing has happened!" exclaimed a young Chegemian, who was nicknamed Quickdraw because of the haste and frivolity with which his mind worked.

"If she picked a cucumber, it means she didn't know they were going to steal her," he said, to elucidate his hypothesis, which did not strike Uncle Sandro as very convincing.

Several people agreed with the hypothesis that a maiden who had decided to elope with her lover wouldn't go grabbing cucumbers along the way, but several others stopped and began arguing that anything could happen in this world. Especially since she had been through a lot that day and might be very thirsty.

Uncle Sandro moved on, not letting his daughter's tracks out of the lamplight. Two minutes later her tracks led to the back porch of Aunt Masha's house. Uncle Sandro was mightily cheered, deciding that this was one of his daughter's childish pranks.

"She's hiding here somewhere!" he exclaimed. Handing the lamp to his most warlike nephew, Chunka, he ran into the house.

They turned all the rooms inside out, even climbed up to the attic, but she was nowhere to be found. Uncle Sandro's desire to sit calmly at the festive table, where he and only he would have been chosen as tamada, was so great that it kept generating new hope that nothing had happened to his daughter, the whole thing was about to be cleared up, and they would all head for the tables in a friendly swarm. Uncle Sandro recalled that under the house there was a trough used for pressing grapes. She's probably climbed into that, he thought. He jumped down from the porch and stooped to crawl under the house. Approaching the trough, he jerked an old cowhide off of it and said menacingly, "Come on out, you minx!"

At that instant the dog came clambering out of the trough. Showering him with rotted wood dust, he ran howling into the cornpatch.

"May you . . . !" Uncle Sandro cursed. He climbed dolefully up to the house, where they not only had not found Tali, but, on the contrary, had discovered that the phonograph was gone, although the records were all there, except that one of them had gotten broken in the hubbub.

By now it was clear to everyone that this was bad business. They began hunting for her return tracks, and of course they quickly discovered them. With the phonograph in hand she had leaped from the porch and landed three meters away in a hill of pumpkin vines. Her footprints (deeper now, because of the phonograph, as the Chegem detectives joyfully explained) led to the most remote corner of the farm.

Now a dreadful noise went up in Aunt Masha's yard. The women wailed; the men shouted to be turned loose, they'd wipe out the lousy half-breed's whole clan. As soon as someone began shouting to be turned loose, three or four men instantly hung on him so as to make clear to everyone that they would not turn the fellow loose, or he'd make trouble. Interestingly, while they were subduing and extinguishing this angry hot spot, one of the hot spots already extinguished would suddenly flare up again, as if the spark from this one had flown into him. Now everyone rushed to subdue him, and the newly extinguished hot spot lapsed into a shamefaced silence and stepped aside, as if to say, Well, that's the way it goes, leave the revenge to the man who is more enraged and therefore more worthy. This did not always prevent him, after a slight respite, from catching fire again and making another dash to wreak revenge on the offender. When the men who were subduing people seized him, their astonished gaze seemed to say to him, Why, we already subdued you! He would continue to rage and shout, and his eyes would reply, It's not my fault, there was still some fire left, you didn't totally extinguish me.

Chunka raged with special fervor. He rent his shirt and twice shot his Colt in the air, thereby waking all the jackals in the vicinity. They did not quit howling and exchanging barks with the Chegem dogs until morning.

When she heard this racket, Aunt Katya understood all. With loud sobs, from time to time calling her daughter, she started over to Aunt Masha's house.

"Ta-li!" she shouted, casting up her daughter's name from a wave of sobs.

"A-a-ah," the women sobbed in reply from Aunt Masha's yard, as if to tell her: We too grieve with you, and as you see, we're not sitting on our hands.

In a word, everything was done right. In a case like this, the younger clan members, men the same age as the stolen maiden, must display unspeakable fury, whereas the elder clan members must grieve and try to guide the fury into the reasonable framework of the blood feud.

Great sorrow, as often happens, was compounded by vexing trifles—in this case the ludicrous claims of the hunting clan. As the drama of the abduction heated up, the clan members began grumbling more and more loudly and confidently over the fact that Taliko had eloped with a man from another village and had no right to take the phonograph with her.

"But she won it!" Tali's relatives said in surprise. "She belongs to our kolkhoz!"

"No," the stubborn hunting clan answered, "her flight was obviously planned before the contest, that means she was already over there, mentally."

"Why argue," the girl's relatives said, feigning a sigh. "We'll never get the phonograph back now. But here, you can take the records, the ones that aren't broken yet."

Such malice struck the hunting clan as intolerable, and they sought help from Tendel himself; after all, Tsitsa was his granddaughter. But Tendel unexpectedly brushed them aside. The opportunity to go hunting for the live abductor of a maiden roused him to such unselfish fervor that he remained completely cold to the opportunity to acquire a phonograph. He even appeared to misunderstand the legal catch found by the other members of the hunting clan.

"To hell with your phonograph!" he even shouted at them. "Don't you see what's happening?"

Finally, with shouts and pistol shots, the pursuers surged out of Aunt Masha's yard, headed by Tendel. From the veranda the village soviet chairman shouted after them in parting, "Forward, men! Just don't shoot my Stakhanovite champion!"

Trampling down the innocent corn, the pursuers ran to the wattle fence over which the fugitive had jumped. Just beyond the fence flowed a little stream, one of the Kodor's small tributaries. Everyone crossed the stream, and here on the clayey bank they discovered the tracks of maidenly feet, unexpectedly transformed into a horse's hooves.

"Here's where he pulled her up on his saddle," Tendel said, and the young clan members gnashed their teeth to show their hatred for the abductor. Judging by the tracks, however, there had been two horses here, so that Bagrat had no need to pull the girl up on his saddle. They began to study where the tracks led, and discovered that the horses, after stamping around on the bank for a while, had gone into the water.

"To hide their tracks!" Tendel exclaimed. He divided the posse into two groups, one to go upstream and the other down. He himself headed the group that went downstream, the fugitives' most probable direction. Not surprisingly, his was the group that ended up with Chunka, who could not stop reminding them how he had always hated Bagrat, and with Uncle Sandro, who would have been satisfied to go upstream but feared that these overexcited youths would make a mess of things.

The sound of the chase faded away, the pursuers withdrawing into the distance as if going deeper into the meaning of their destiny. The people left behind in the yard marked time aimlessly within sight of the supper tables, now illumined not only by the lamps but by the full moon, which had appeared from behind the hill. At last the village soviet chairman made a speech.

"My friends," he said, "those who have gone are gone, and as for us, let us take our places at these tables. If they bring our girl back safe and sound—the feast will be just the thing. If they don't—we'll count this as the funeral table."

With these words he came down from the veranda and took his seat under the biggest lamp, right at the foot of the cherry-laurel. The rest of the men came rushing after him, as if rejoicing that they too had finally been allowed to go deeper into their own meaning, and at the same time marveling at the agreeable wisdom of the village soviet chairman.

Everyone speedily sat down at the tables, except that the closest relatives ate and drank in the kitchen. In a case like this, although custom does not directly forbid a session at table, the Chegemians feel that there is no particular reason for the closest relatives to go letting their belts out.

Only poor Aunt Katya kept a silent vigil by the wattle fence, staring out where the posse had gone. She wept quietly, now and then switching to motifs from funeral chants. People were ordered not to touch her, but, out of respect for family and clan, to watch from a distance lest she lay hands on herself. No one believed that she would just up and commit suicide, of course, but this was considered the most tactful expression of sympathy for a mother's sorrow. By this custom, as it were, the Chegemians told Aunt Katya: So great is your grief that it would not be surprising if you tried to end your life in suicide. But you are not doing this, only because you know that we are watching you and will not let you lay hands on yourself.

Meanwhile, the mood of the diners quickly improved. Moths circled around the lamps and also around the glowing pink Isabella in the glasses, confusing the metaphysical light of wine with the direct source of light.

Once in a while, those at the table would suddenly remember. Calling for silence, they listened to the night noises, as if they had caught some arcane detail of the chase: a shout, or the neigh of a horse, or shots. After listening a moment, they felt convinced they had dreamed it, but at least they were not just sitting and drinking, they were anxiously keeping watch at the same time, in spiritual sympathy with the posse.

The toasts became longer and longer, so that the drinkers had to interrupt themselves from time to time in order to fish the absolutely demoniacal moths out of their glasses and then shake them off their fingers.

The moths especially harassed the chairman of the village soviet, Makhty, because he was sitting by the biggest lamp and talked longer than anyone else with his glass raised.

"What do they see in me," he muttered, brushing off the moths and repeatedly fishing them out of his glass.

"You're the light of our world," Aunt Masha said, perhaps explaining the reason for the abundance of moths around the village soviet chairman, perhaps joking. In any case, she ordered one of her herculean daughters, Mayana, to stand behind Makhty with a homespun towel and wave the moths away from him. For a while the simple-hearted Mayana did a good job waving the moths away, but then her mind wandered and she swept the lamp, a roast turkey, several bottles of wine, and a plate of *khachapuri* off the table along with the moths.

"Better the moths," said the village soviet chairman, frozen in injured immobility, while people around him picked up the scattered food and dishes. The young giantess had to be sent home, and she went away grumbling, "But what did I do?"

Watching her go, with her powerful back and lofty neck of an ancient Greek statue, the guests really did understand that she might just as reasonably have overturned the pushed-together tables.

"My friends," Makhty began, after order had somehow been restored to his portion of the table and the supper had taken on an air of completely legitimate optimism . . .

"My friends," he repeated, in order to dampen the roar of this optimism a bit, "regardless of the outcome of the courageous pursuit our men have undertaken"—at this point came a sob from Aunt Katya, who was still standing by the fence—"no one will ever abduct the record set by this wonderful girl of ours, it will be with us forever!"

After this toast no one interrupted the strong, even current of the merrymaking. Incidentally, someone glanced at the high, mirrorlike moon and suddenly remembered that it was with this word that the little girl had begun her verbal communication with people; and now, under just such a full moon, she had run off to be married; from which it followed that Providence had dropped a hint back then of what would happen fifteen years later.

But then someone objected that all this might not be quite true, because she had already made one attempt to run away with the miller's son, so they might bring her back now, too, and the moon probably had nothing to do with it.

The memory of the miller's son prompted another, no less mysterious observation, namely, that every time she ran away she took along her music: that time the guitar, this time the phonograph. What instrument, the guests speculated gaily, would she take when she ran away a third time, if they brought her back now?

This question occupied the table a very long time, although as regards musical instruments, it must be plainly stated that Chegem did not have a great variety—the Abkhazian *chamguri*, the Greek *kementzes* played by some of the local Greek families, and the international guitar. So it is no wonder that one of the Chegemians finally offered the bold hypothesis that the next time Tali would probably go after the district piano, which stood in the Kenguria House of Culture.

In short, those who sat at the table whiled the night away in gaiety. But all night Aunt Katya wept softly, standing by the fence and staring out where the posse had gone; silently the herculean maiden Lena wept, covering her head with a sheepskin so as not to hear the din from the table; and all night the shepherd Harlampo groaned, because his night was full of voluptuous visions—alas, inaccessible even in dreams.

The pursuers headed by Tendel walked down the river, consoling themselves with the thought that the horses could not have gone far on such a stony riverbed.

About fifteen kilometers from Chegem, the little river crashed down through the rapids with sudden fury and flowed into a narrow canyon. In Tendel's opinion, they must have ridden up on shore at this point and moved on, leaving their tracks on the ground to give them away.

But, alas, when they came to the roaring waterfall, they were convinced that no tracks led to the bank. Some of the pursuers, especially Chunka, kept trying to peer down into the misty, roaring, twenty-meter-deep abyss, as if the madman could have taken his young captive and the phonograph and glided down there on the widespread skirts of his burka.

Perhaps Chunka—the fiercest of the pursuers—peered down in the secret hope of seeing the loose end of the drowned kidnapper's turban spinning around far below in the whirlpool. But there were no traces of any successful or unsuccessful flight into the abyss, and the pursuers turned back.

"We missed the trail somewhere!" Tendel shouted over the roar of the water. Not a bit embarrassed by the failure—on the contrary, with still greater enthusiasm—he led the pursuers back.

On the way back he did find the spot where Bagrat had taken the risk of coming out of the water and climbing straight up a very steep bank overgrown with boxwood. Now everyone but Chunka began to affirm in unison that the horses could never have climbed this bank, it was so steep and wild that they themselves were reluctant to try it. But Tendel found hoofprints, and there was nothing for the pursuers to do but cross the stream and scramble after their leader.

"With that damned strength of his," Tendel said, hauling himself up and forcing his way through the brushy boxwood, "he could have portaged them."

Meanwhile, the climb became harder and harder.

Cold with fatigue, the pursuers had soon spent all their fury in the fruitless struggle with rhododendron and cherry-laurel branches that unexpectedly lashed their faces, thorny blackberry canes and liana vines that tore at their clothes.

"Look!" Tendel shouted suddenly, turning back to his comrades. He was triumphantly clutching a red tuft from Taliko's sweater. The tuft was handed to Uncle Sandro for him to acknowledge, although it was plain as day that this was her sweater. There was nothing for Uncle Sandro but to acknowledge the sweater. Not knowing what to do with this strange trophy, he put it in his pocket.

After a while, several more tufts from the sweater were handed to Uncle Sandro. Each time, full of the hunter's zeal, Tendel handed him these shreds of clothing with a look of triumph, as if sure that they could bring the girl back—if not whole, at least in parts.

"The dress has started to go!" Tendel shouted. He handed back a strip of fabric that looked as if it had been ripped out with a strong, precise motion.

"Probably the horse shied suddenly," the pursuers speculated, marveling at the ribbonlike form of the torn scrap.

"If it keeps up like this," someone said cautiously, "he'll get her there stark naked."

No one knows how far the tired pursuers would have carried this joke if Tendel, who was in the lead, had not signaled for them to stand still and be quiet. Everyone stopped and watched the old hunter. Although they tried to peer beyond him, they could see nothing but chestnut trees.

Tendel, meanwhile, kept turning around to signal that he saw something very important—perhaps even the kidnapper himself, trying to take advantage of a poor girl's trust.

Then why, the pursuers wondered with increasing agitation, didn't the old hunter interrupt the bastard's villainous caresses with a good shot, or at least let *them* have a look at what was happening?

That was what they said, addressing the hunter in impatient sign language. Finally Tendel allowed them to approach. Before them lay a small glade encircled by chestnut trees, carpeted with thick grass, and strewn with last year's chestnut leaves.

In the middle of the glade stood a young cedar, with a clump of blueberry bushes nearby. It was toward this young cedar that Tendel pointed, explaining in sign language that if anything had happened, it had happened right there. After that he signaled for them all to stay put while he himself cautiously approached the young cedar. As Tendel told it, he had noticed right away that horses had been tied to the cedar; and then, when he parted the blueberry bushes, he saw a green space cleared of fallen leaves, or rather, swept clean by a whirlwind of love. Two bushes were so mangled that even old Tendel could imagine what strength it must have required to hold on to them to keep from flying up into the sky.

Tendel turned around and walked thoughtfully back to his party, no longer muffling his footsteps.

"What happened there? Are you going to tell us, finally, or not?" Chunka asked, losing patience.

And Tendel told. Foolish old hunter though he was, in this hour he pronounced words filled with dignity and beauty, even in the opinion of the fussy rhetoricians of Chegem.

"My friends," he said, "we wanted to shed the blood of our girl's kidnapper, but not that of her husband . . ."

"Ah-h-h," the pursuers said, as if casting off their weapons with relief, "then he succeeded?"

"Don't even ask!" Tendel confirmed, and everyone started down the mountain.

Accepting the fact that the lovers had been too quick for them, the pursuers returned home with a clear conscience. (Incidentally, many years later, Bagrat confessed to one of his friends that the noise raised by the posse that night had served them as an excellent safety indicator.)

Anyway, the pursuers made their way back to the river, tranquilized by fatigue. Chunka was the only one who could not simmer down.

"They might at least have had some shame before the horses!" he said, finding fault with both of them now as he fought his way through the cherry-laurel bushes.

"That's a quibble!" old Tendel defended the lovers. "There's nothing to be ashamed of—husband and wife!"

"Yes, but they could have tied the horses a little farther off," Chunka said, unable to quell his darkly stormy imagination.

"The cossack hosts are after them, so to speak," Tendel argued loudly, "and he's supposed to think where to tie the horses?"

When they got down to the river, an eagle suddenly flew up over their heads, evidently startled from sleep. Chunka seized his Colt and killed the mighty bird with a single shot. Somehow this cheered him up immediately and he stopped grumbling. He draped the slain eagle over his shoulders, hooked the bird's claws at his throat like iron buckles, and, drawing the enormous wings around him like a military cloak, walked at the head of the procession.

When they drew near Aunt Masha's house, the sun was already rising from behind the mountain. Aunt Katya still stood waiting by the fence. The guests had departed at dawn, done in by wine and fatigue; only the closest neighbors and relatives were still there.

The young giantesses were clearing the tables, now putting scraps of last night's meal in their mouths, now tossing them to an assemblage of neighborhood dogs. One of the giantesses was milking the cow. Irritated by the cow's switching tail, she clamped her teeth on it and went on with her milking, looking around with a mustachioed face at the people on the veranda, who were watching the return of the pursuers.

When she saw that her daughter was not among those returning, Aunt Katya shrieked as one shrieks over the deceased. Aunt Masha ran to her and began trying to calm her, stroking her back and summoning her to steadfastness in an affectionate voice. The rest of the Chegemians, those who had stayed at Aunt Masha's, were violently curious to learn what it was that Chunka had hanging from his shoulders.

"Strike me dead if it isn't an eagle," one of them said finally.

"It's the wrong eagle," a member of the hunting clan said caustically, looking at the bronzing dazzle of the morning sun as it played on the wings of the slain bird.

That morning poor Harlampo, out of grief, ate too many walnuts. He ate without stopping from morning to noon. At noon the potent walnut oil went to his head, and he charged after one of the goats—the one that was Tali's pet and had a red ribbon tied around her neck, or rather, not around her neck but to the wire collar on which hung her little bell.

Many people said later that he might have gotten over it if it hadn't been for the red ribbon on the goat's neck. But his glance lighted on that red ribbon, and the walnut-oil vapors exploded in his skull.

He charged after the goat, who, being no fool, also took to her heels. First they ran through the village, attracting the dogs after them, but then either he drove her onto the path leading to the mill or she turned off there herself—no one knows—but anyway, the goat, Harlampo, and the pack of dogs at their heels went plunging down the steep, spiraling path.

Despite the clatter of the mill wheels, the men who were at the mill heard the chase long before they realized what was happening. They all poured out the door to listen to the ever-nearer yelping and baying of the dogs. They decided that the dogs had accidentally raised a boar in the forest and driven it to the path, and the whole pack were now dashing after it full speed, just on the verge of popping out from around the cliff in front of the mill.

No one was carrying a gun, although some had axes or sticks. The heroic might of Gerago, however, would suffice to toss the boar into the air with one kick.

Everyone was utterly bewildered when an ordinary goat with a little bell tinkling fearfully at her throat came popping out from around the cliff. She ran past the men, darted into the mill, scattered the logs in the open fire, got burned, and unexpectedly leaped into the hopper from which the grain was funneled under the millstones.

A moment later, Harlampo came running around the cliff with the pack of dogs at his heels. Now everyone realized that something terrible had happened. Some, recognizing their dogs, began calling to them and soothing them in an effort to get at least a little information out of them.

But neither the shepherd nor the agitated dogs could make any sensible report to the men gathered at the mill.

"What are you doing?" Gerago shouted, gripping the shepherd in his mighty embrace.

"Let me go!" Harlampo cried, trying to break away. His mad eyes stared in through the doorway, where, in response, the goat's head poked out of the hopper from time to time. The hopper, its inner walls polished by the years, had the shape of an inverted pyramid; the goat's hind legs were buried in corn, and her front legs kept slipping down the steep planks.

The hind legs, rapping out a bony drumbeat, helped the goat scramble up far enough to stick her head out, but then she would slip back down. Splashing out golden fountains of corn, she would begin madly running in place again in order to finally thrust her head out of the hopper, catch sight of Harlampo, and crash down again. Harlampo saw all this, peering through the doorway with his blood-shot eyes.

"What did she do to you?" Gerago persisted, clasping the shepherd to him in a tighter and tighter grip.

Unable to make any intelligible reply to the miller's question, the shepherd kept up a furious flailing in his arms. The goat also kept up her mad running in place, her feet pounding on the wall of the hopper, sometimes with the speed of machine-gun fire, her hind legs constantly churning out golden streams of corn, which sometimes even flew out the door of the mill. That, in the end, was what provoked even the levelheaded miller.

"Ropes!" Gerago barked. He laid poor Harlampo right down on the ground and bound him tightly from head to foot, seeing as there were always plenty of ropes at the mill with which to secure burdens on the animals' backs.

All of a sudden an old peasant bent swiftly down and sniffed Harlampo.

"Ha!" he said. "Now I know—he's gone rabid on walnuts!"

They all took turns bending down to sniff poor Harlampo, convincing themselves that he stank of walnut like a freshly split walnut trunk. On the advice of the same peasant who had thought to sniff him, and who turned out to be a pretty good authority on Walnut Rabies in general, they carried Harlampo over and lowered him into the icy water of the stream that fed the mill. With the peasant's approval, Gerago laid on the shepherd's groin—carefully, so as not to harm his internal organs—a spare two-hundred-pound millstone, the more firmly to ground the lightning of madness, for one thing, and for another, to keep Harlampo from being washed away by the current. Rocks were piled around Harlampo's head so that even if he wanted to he could not drown.

The shepherd lay in the water in this position for twenty-four hours, and everyone who saw him there was astounded that the millstone lying on his groin continued to vibrate, betraying the internal workings of madness. Only toward the end of the next day did the millstone cease to vibrate. Then Gerago carefully thrust a hand through it and lifted it a little. Seeing at a glance that the shepherd's bound body was floating calmly, he grabbed the ropes with his other hand and simply heaved both the millstone and the shepherd up the bank simultaneously.

Later on, any time one of the Chegemians began boasting of the miller's strength—the miller was not a Chegemian, but since he served his own village and Chegem at the same time it was as though he belonged partly to the Chegemians too—well, when the Chegemians told of his strength, they often gave as an example the way he had simply heaved the two-hundred-pound shepherd and the two-hundred-pound millstone out of the water simultaneously. In telling the story they never forgot to point out how steep the bank was where the miller had to climb up with his four-hundred-pound load.

Admittedly, the listener usually turned a deaf ear to the remark about the steepness of the bank. That was not entirely fair. But, on the other hand, the listener should be forgiven, because he could not make head nor tail of it—how the devil did the millstone end up lying on the shepherd, and the shepherd lying in the water?

That was all the storyteller needed, of course, and he would tell the whole story over from the very beginning, which we do not plan to do in this case; we will simply pick it up at the point where we left off.

So, after the millstone ceased to vibrate, they pulled poor Harlampo out of the water, unbound him, and warmed him all night at a well-laid fire in the mill. Toward morning he warmed up.

"My heart is broken," he said, for some reason in Turkish. It was as if the icy water of the stream, in washing his brain of the walnut madness, had accidentally washed out along with it his knowledge of the Abkhazian language, which admittedly was rather scanty, but for a shepherd, especially for a Greek, was quite adequate. The Chegemians know Turkish pretty well, however, so they had no trouble communicating with the silenced Harlampo.

In the morning they sent Harlampo back, putting into his hands a rope to which they had tied the goat, who had also calmed down, incidentally. Not only had she calmed down, but during this time she, too, had overeaten: since there was no one to graze her, and Gerago had to keep her tied up, he fed her on pure corn.

Just in case, a little while later, a Chegemian who had had his corn ground climbed up the path behind them. As he told it, he followed the shepherd and his goat at a distance, now urging his donkey on, now holding it back slightly, but did not notice anything special in the behavior of either the shepherd or the goat.

The only point worth remarking, as he told it, was that the goat occasionally looked around at Harlampo, gave a snort, and ran on. The shepherd paid no attention to her.

Incidentally, when they decided to send Harlampo off with the goat, Gerago—displaying a surprising sensitivity, which might have seemed unnecessary in a man of such mighty build—not only thought to take the red ribbon off the collar on the goat's neck, but also stuffed the bell tightly with a clump of grass, lest its ringing awaken bitter memories in Harlampo.

There were five goats with bells on their necks in old Khabug's flock. Following Gerago's wise example, Uncle Sandro stopped the clappers of the other goats' bells with clumps of grass, just in case.

On top of everything else that had happened in the house, the family awaited with dread the arrival of old Khabug, who had been away in the mountains all this time; he was taking the waters at Kislovodsk. On the eighth day after Tali's flight (Aunt Katya still called it an abduction, despite the obvious), old Khabug rode into the yard on his mule. The family simply could not bring themselves to report what had happened, and no one knew whether he had found out about it yet.

Her lips compressed in sorrow, Aunt Katya went out to meet him. Harlampo was just driving a flock of goats with ominously soundless bells across the yard.

"What's this?" Khabug asked, indicating the flock.

"Something terrible has happened," Aunt Katya sighed, still unable to bring herself to say anything more definite.

"What have the goats got to do with it?" the old man asked.

"Our poor fellow . . . ah . . ." She gave a slight nod in Harlampo's direction to indicate that the presence of the shepherd himself prevented her from speaking more definitely.

Old Khabug dismounted in silence and flung the reins to his daughter-in-law. As the flock rushed in through the open gate, he began plucking from it the goats with bells on their necks and freeing the bells from the grass gags. Showing no surprise that the flock had begun to tinkle again, Harlampo followed his goats past old Khabug.

"Never mind, he'll survive. He's not Prince Shervashidze," old Khabug said as he straightened up. He threw Aunt Katya an expressive glance, from which she immediately understood that the old man knew all.

Without taking time to sit down, old Khabug packed two sacks of walnuts and ten smoked cheeses on his mule, took his granddaughter's birth certificate and report cards, and set off for Kengur. The old man knew that the Soviet authorities very much disliked it when girls were given in marriage before they came of age. Therefore he hoped to win his granddaughter back through the courts and, if he was lucky, get the seducer arrested.

By evening he was at the gates of the Kenguria investigating magistrate's house. The magistrate personally walked out of the house and came over to the gate.

"What brings you here?" he asked, after greeting him and opening the gate. While he let the heavily laden mule into the yard, he studied the shape of its burden in an effort to guess the content of old Khabug's request.

"Is it true," old Khabug asked, entering the yard with his mule but stopping just inside the gate, "that They don't like girls to rush into marriage before they fill out?"

"Don't doubt it for even a second," the magistrate replied. He looked pityingly at the overworked mule, as if trying to lighten its burden by his glance.

"Then help me," Khabug said, and he and the magistrate together unpacked the mule.

When they went into the house, old Khabug displayed his granddaughter's birth certificate, issued by the Chegem village soviet, and the report cards, on each of which was inscribed Lavrenty Beria's aphorism: "In a schoolboy, heroism and daring means being an *A* student." (Incidentally, this aphorism gave no clue as to what the all-powerful minister thought about heroism and daring in schoolgirls. Many years later, after his arrest, it became clear that he had a very peculiar view of the nature of heroism and daring in schoolgirls—in some of them, anyway.)

The little girl's report cards did not interest the magistrate much, but he examined her birth certificate for a long time. He even held it up to check it against the light.

"The girl's as good as in your pocket," he said, handing back the report cards and snaffling off the birth certificate as a worthwhile document which he would keep for the battle.

"Come back as soon as I send word," the magistrate said as he saw old Khabug out.

Khabug mounted his mule and returned home the same night.

After all that had happened, the attempt to win his granddaughter back was uncommonly bold for those times. But Khabug so loved his granddaughter that he was sure her flight was the consequence of her trustfulness and goodness, that is, a mistake which must be corrected; he so believed in the uniqueness of her virtues (in this he was right) that he had not the least doubt of her happy future if he should succeed in winning her back. The notion that she might be happy with the man she had run away with was crowded out, flung out of his consciousness by the very force of his love, his bitter resentment that all this had happened too early and without his knowledge.

For ten days running, Aunt Katya wept by her daughter's bed, where she had spread out her things, some photographs, the records of Comrade Stalin's speeches. The broken record lay near the rest like a symbol of catastrophe, along with the red scraps of the sweater and the ribbonlike strip from the crepe de chine dress.

The dominant motif in Aunt Katya's funeral recitative was that of prematurely interrupted childhood. ("Not yet have they dried, the tassels that you braided on the ears of corn. Not yet have they ceased to suckle, the kids that you first put to suck at their mothers' teats . . . Oh, let your own mother's teats dry up, though they've long since dried up as it is . . . Oh, and not yet has the ink dried in your inkstand, your pen still wants to clack like a little beak on the bottom of the inkstand, yet you have abandoned it . . . Like a hawk with a chick, the evil Laz has torn you apart, only the feathers have floated down to your poor mother . . .")

At this point she usually took in her hands the scraps from Tali's last clothes. After holding them thoughtfully for a while, she would move them to another spot, as if to give the whole dramatic exhibit a slightly new design, although without changing its basic tone.

On the fifth day Uncle Sandro noticed a new motif creeping into the funeral recitative with a certain mischievous persistence (evidently Aunt Katya herself felt that she was overstepping the limit, but the hypnosis of creation sucked her in)—the motif of the poor, prematurely bereft Leader, who in the goodness of his heart had sent her his voice, yet she had abandoned him, as she had abandoned her poor mother.

"Leave him out of it, for God's sake!" Uncle Sandro thundered when he caught her at this motif. "What do you mean, poor! Did you want to go to Siberia?"

Without interrupting the recitative, she backed off from this motif when she heard her husband's voice, but, as Uncle Sandro realized, she continued to circle dangerously close to it.

In the next few days the funeral chant became more and more saturated with the prosaic thought that the little girl had ended up in a foreign land practically naked and barefoot, without a change of underwear. This motif so weighted her chant that in the end the melody thudded to the ground. Beginning with the rhetorical question "Are you really a father?" Aunt Katya's voice shifted into the everyday rhythm of the domestic nag.

The situation being what it was, Uncle Sandro was quite ready to send over a suitcase with his daughter's things, but he really had no idea where she was. Relatives in all the villages had been informed that if they heard anything they were to tell the parents where Tali was. But no one knew a thing.

A month went by before it became known where Bagrat had hidden with his beloved. He had taken her to the village of Chlou. Although Tali had not once left the house where he had taken her, they discovered her by a certain amusing bit of evidence.

While she herself did not leave the house, of course, the local young people, as is customary, came to visit the newlyweds. Soon all the evening parties in the village of Chlou began to resound with the sobbing strains of "The Death of the Chelyuskinians," a fact that could not help but reach Chegem.

One night a suitcase with her things was delivered to the village of Chlou, and a week later the young couple moved home. It was Kunta, of course, who delivered the suitcase. Incidentally, as payment for delivering the suitcase he asked Aunt Katya for the pieces of the broken record, saying that he needed them for something, although he did not say what for. Later it turned out that he had tried to melt the record pieces in a frying pan and pour the molten mass over the holes in his old rubber boots.

Poor Kunta had decided for some reason that rubber boots and phonograph records were made of the same material. But it turned out that the material of which the records were made, although it softened up nicely over the fire, would not stick to rubber at all. Kunta was greatly vexed by this failure. Wondering where he might use the broken record pieces, he thought of taking advantage of the smell of the scorched record, which was unique in Chegem experience.

The thing was that a wild boar was wreaking havoc in his cornpatch. At two or three places in the wattle fence that faced the forest, the boar would work the twigs apart, crawl into the field, and gobble the corn, using its snout to dig up the stalks with the biggest ears. Kunta calculated correctly that if the smell of burned record was completely unfamiliar to the inhabitants of Chegem, then it must be all the more unfamiliar to the animal world roundabout and would arouse all the more apprehension.

Kunta built a fire by the fence, softened the pieces of the record, and spread them on the places in the fence that the boar usually headed for. Believe it or not, his calculation proved correct—the boar did not disturb his field any more that year. And in succeeding years Uncle Sandro traded him records for various household services. One record was enough for a whole year. Breaking the record into two parts, he smeared them on the dangerous places in his cornpatch twice: the first time when the ears of corn were putting out tassels, and the second time when the ears were getting ripe but had not yet dried enough to harvest.

While Tali was running away with Bagrat and hiding in the village of Chlou, her fame as one of the best tobacco stringers had come out of hiding, for no two things in nature are more incompatible than fame and the underground. So her fame came out of hiding and spread through all Abkhazia, in the form of a large news photo in the republic's newspaper, *Red Subtropics*.

She was already living in her husband's house in the village of Naa when she was invited to Mukhus to a rally for all the High Achievers in Agriculture, where, in recounting her successes, she named Aunt Masha as the one who had taught her to string tobacco.

Incidentally, the photograph was uncommonly good. It is preserved under glass in Uncle Sandro's house to this day, and even on the yellowed surface of the cheap newsprint you can still see how her face quivers, how it breathes.

She is shown as a laughing amazon with a tobacco needle sticking out from under her arm like a spear, and on the spear she is stringing heart-shaped tobacco leaves. With a little imagination you might see these tobacco leaves as the flattened hearts of her worshipers being strung on her spear. This fantasy is all the more permissible in that the tobacco leaves, just between us, were sham. When they took the picture, the tobacco was already gone, so the unflustered news photographer handed her a bunch of plane leaves. That, incidentally, was what provoked her unrestrained laughter in the picture.

After the newspaper photo came out, Uncle Sandro was unexpectedly elevated to be foreman of the work brigade in which Taliko had so gloriously shown her worth. Aunt Katya obtained a copy of the newspaper that had the photo and included it in her funeral exhibit, unembarrassed that her daughter's laughing face, next to the red (slightly bloody-looking) shreds of her sweater, canceled out the ominous symbolism of these latter substantive proofs of her abduction.

She stubbornly continued to assert that her daughter had been taken by force, that the scraps from the sweater and dress were the best proof of her heroic resistance to the barbaric onslaught of the Laz.

Now she seldom took up her funeral lament, only about once a week. Her lament was most often addressed to the newspaper photo, as the freshest, least lamented-over object. Sometimes her lament would come to an abrupt halt with the completely inappropriate phrase "Poor baby, I think you've lost weight . . ."

She would hold the newspaper up close to her eyes and study her daughter's picture by the hour. But sometimes her gaze would shift to the photo of a soldier full of courage and valor, who was in the International Brigade then fighting in Spain. It was on the same page of the paper.

With a certain maternal jealousy she studied it, too, by the hour. Without understanding who he was, she sensed that this man, to judge by his appearance, could stand up for himself and his loved ones. He had obviously performed many heroic deeds, since they had put him in the paper with his grenades and his rifle.

"If you'd only married someone like that, silly girl," she said with a certain sorrow, and added, after a little thought, "but who would give us one like that . . ."

It was old Khabug who was most restored when the picture came out in the paper. Without waiting for a summons from the Kenguria magistrate, he saddled his mule and went to see him. This time he carried no burden, merely put the newspaper with his granddaughter's portrait in his pocket.

Now that his granddaughter was famous, he thought, it would be easy for him to get her back. But it turned out to be the other way around. When he rode up to the gate of the house, the magistrate's wife came out to meet him. Writhing in shame ("writhing in shamelessness," the old man said later, telling about it), she assured him that the magistrate was not home, that he would be in his office tomorrow, and that nowadays he generally discussed business only in his office.

Old Khabug realized that this meant trouble, but he decided to wait until the next day. The magistrate did receive old Khabug the next day in his office and explained to him that now that the girl had become so famous, he could not take anyone to court, because They disliked that even more than when a no-good abducted underage girls. Besides, he added, it wasn't an abduction, either.

"Why not?" the old man asked, barely restraining his fury. He could not see how his granddaughter's fame as a worker strengthened the position of this outsider, and not that of the girl's relatives, who had raised her.

"The phonograph," the magistrate said with feigned regret. "If she hadn't taken the phonograph to where he was waiting for her with the horse . . ."

As he talked with Khabug, the magistrate occasionally tore his eyes from the newspaper photo—which the old man had laid before him—and then went back to studying it, a pastime which obviously was not facilitating matters and which exasperated the old man worse than ever.

"You're all obsessed with that phonograph!" old Khabug said through his teeth. He tried once more to turn the magistrate's thoughts in the right direction. "It could have been this way: she was carrying it home, and halfway there this fellow seized her and the phonograph. There'll be witnesses—"

"No," the magistrate said, this time not even tearing himself away from the photo.

"The birth certificate!" the old man barked. He snatched the newspaper away from the magistrate and folded it up.

"Here you are," the magistrate said, taking the birth certificate from his desk drawer and offering it to the old man. "I'd be glad to, myself, but it's impossible now."

"I'll send our hunchback, you'll return everything you took," Khabug said. Without looking back he walked heavily to the door.

"That goes without saying!" The magistrate caught up with him at the doorway. "I don't take a kopeck if I can't deliver."

A few days later Kunta did indeed bring back from the magistrate's house two sacks of walnuts and nine cheeses, for the tenth, as they explained to him, had already been eaten. Uncle Sandro figured that the tenth cheese had been retained in consideration of legal consultation. To avoid enraging the stubborn Khabug, he ordered Aunt Katya and Kunta not to tell anyone that the magistrate had shorted them the tenth cheese. Aunt Katya, in her turn, when she opened the sacks of walnuts and saw that these were not the high-grade Chegem nuts but a coarser lowland nut from the village of Atara, did not tell Uncle Sandro about it, to avoid irritating him. It is quite possible that the magistrate's wife, who returned the tribute, had simply mixed up the geography of the offerings.

The days passed. Gradually the wound inflicted by Bagrat healed in Aunt Katya's soul. In any case, one fine day she put her entire funeral exhibit away in the bureau. She cut her daughter's portrait out of the newspaper and put it in a frame under glass.

Perhaps it was old Khabug who suffered most of all, although he never once complained of his hurt to anyone. The one thing everyone noticed was that he could not bear the sight of the knotty ropes from Aunt Masha's house. Indeed, for several years after, the farm chores at Aunt Masha's were done with ropes that were lumpy with numerous knots: the last souvenir of Bagrat's perfidious games.

The next year, one summer day when the whole family was sitting in the kitchen having dinner, two shots suddenly rang out at the gate of the house. Everyone froze.

The first to guess what it meant was Aunt Katya.

"Go out there," she said to her husband, and her face freshened with inspired curiosity.

Uncle Sandro ran out to the gate, where a horseman from the village of Naa was putting his pistol back in its holster, at the same time trying to calm his frightened horse.

"Our Tali's given birth to two boys!" he shouted. Making his horse rear, he wheeled around and raced back along the upper Chegem road.

Uncle Sandro stood stock-still, his hand frozen in a gesture of hospitality: Come into the yard and we'll have a talk. The gesture was really just a reflex, of course: without an adequately complex ritual of reconciliation, no relative of Bagrat's could cross the threshold of the Big House. Besides, Uncle Sandro did not care for this particular messenger. His Dzhigit-style riding tricks, coming right after his boastful announcement of the safe and lavish delivery, hinted distantly at some special virtue in his clan: Horses sport under us the way we want, and our women are best at giving birth.

Uncle Sandro was glad, of course, that his little daughter had safely delivered. But why put on airs before him, the great Tamada? If I got you at a good table, Uncle Sandro thought, I'd make you drink your own vomit.

"Well?" Aunt Katya met him impatiently at the threshold. Uncle Sandro entered the kitchen in silence. The situation was complicated. On one hand, there was the joyful news; on the other hand, who knew what his father would say, having suffered most of all over his granddaughter's elopement.

"She has two boys," Uncle Sandro said brightly as he came into the kitchen and sat down by the fire. "Not bad for a start."

"The poor little girl," the grandmother and Aunt Katya keened softly. Old Khabug was silent. Obviously he did not find Uncle Sandro's joke funny at all. When he had finished eating, he sat silently by the hearth for a while longer. Then he went out on the veranda, shouldered his ax, and started for the woods, where he was chopping stakes for beanpoles.

"Where are you going?" the grandmother asked him, although she knew perfectly well. Like everyone else in the house, she simply had to find out what to do with this news, how to behave from now on in relation to Tali.

"That Naa is a malarial hole," the old man said without turning around, and he went out of the gate.

The old woman went into the kitchen and relayed old Khabug's words. Everyone understood that this was the beginning of forgiveness. His words could be—even, in part, had to be—understood as implying an invitation to his granddaughter to bring the children to the Big House for the summer.

When the Chegemians, who always seek additional meaning in everything, learned that a girl as young as Tali had borne two boys, they decided that it was no accident; the place where she spent her wedding night had obviously had some effect. A truly popular trail was blazed that summer to the young cedar under which Bagrat had spread his impatient burka.

The cedar turned out to be so rich in secretions of succulent, fire-loving resin (some said it got that way after the lovers camped by it) that its every little branch, when you lighted one end of it and stuck the other in the ground or in the crack of a board wall, would burn like a candle, a lamp, or a torch, depending on its thickness.

Incidentally, shepherds are well aware of the existence of such trees—conifers especially rich in resin—and often use them for illumination in the alpine meadows.

But everyone, especially the women, wanted to think that this cedar was quite singular. In the end, some of them went so far as to begin secretly drinking a broth decocted from the fragrant branches of this cedar; they gave off a strong odor of turpentine, but many people did not guess where the odor came from at the time. Only after a year, when Aunt Masha gave birth to twins—girls again, to her great regret—did she confess that she had drunk a little of that same decoction.

The Chegemians gathered as before in Aunt Masha's yard. When they saw the twins, they considered it their duty to remind her of the tried-and-true Chegem theory of women's progenitive forms, a theory which she was trying in vain to outwit.

Surprised that she was so dull, they explained to her again and again that no decoction could change the progenitive form given by God or by nature (here the Chegemians saw no difference, in principle). At best, they said, a decoction could only clean out, put in working order, the form that existed. Incidentally, that was what had happened, they said, alluding to the twins: All you accomplished by fortifying your progenitive form was that it immediately provided you with two little girls.

"That's probably it," Aunt Masha answered. Unloosing her mighty breasts, she pressed the babies to them. The twins simultaneously nestled up to her breasts, each fixing on the other a greedy eye, as if dimly remembering her companion from preterrestrial life, but not expressing any joy on that account, and, most important, in no way planning to share with her the good things of this life.

The way the babies exchanged these one-eyed glares while sucking milk from their mother's breasts sent Aunt Masha's good-hearted daughters into raptures.

But some Chegemians had the opposite reaction. "Oh, the time we stand in!" they said, associating the babies' greedy stares with the fratricidal doings that had already begun in the lowlands and might reach Chegem any day now.

"Don't worry, there's enough for everyone," Aunt Masha said, missing the point completely and looking down at the babies. And then, turning to one of her daughters, she would add, out of habit, "If you could bring me a little something to eat . . ."

Here we leave the Chegemians, especially since they are getting along very well without us; but in the right place, we shall return to them again, if, as they say, God grants us the strength and no one else takes it away.

And now we forsake Chegem, for even our beloved Chegem seems deserted without Tali, without her lively voice, without her soul-satisfying smile. May my readers forgive me this senseless sorrow, for even a court historian has the right to a momentary weakness, if, of course, he finds in that weakness the strength to affirm—if only from afar, if only with a barely perceptible nod—his confidence in the ultimate triumph of the proletariat. And we do, with a nod (in the presence of witnesses), affirm our confidence, reserving to ourselves a demitasse of Turkish coffee and the modest right to personal sorrow.

TRANSLATOR'S NOTE

Although Abkhazia is a very ancient land, its language had no alphabet until this century. Iskander grew up speaking Abkhazian and Russian; he writes in Russian.

Abkhazia is familiar to his Russian readers as a seacoast resort area, ringed by dramatic mountains whose inhabitants live very long lives; as a source of tea, silk, fruit, and tobacco; and as a part of the romantic and valorous history of the Caucasus. For the last two hundred years, Caucasian history has been inextricably entwined with that of Russia.

You may not feel the need of any information beyond what Iskander provides in the novel. Just in case, however, since very little has been written about Abkhazia in English except for studies on longevity, I have appended a short historical outline, as well as a glossary of foreign words, miscellaneous terms, and the names of historical figures—bits and pieces of information that are part of the Russian reader's general background of awareness.

The Abkazians share many traditions with other Caucasian peoples. Many of the justly celebrated Abkhazian foods, for example, are known throughout the region; for historical reasons the name is often or Turkish, Arabic, or Persian origin. Exept where otherwise noted in the glossary, therefore, foreign words should be understood as common to several Caucasian or Middle Eastern languages.

The various ethnic groups living in Abkhazia can be recognized by their surnames, which have distinctive endings. The common endings are:

Abkhazian	*-ba*
Armenian	*-ian, -yan*
Georgian	*-dze, -iani, -shvili*
Mingrelian	*-aya, -ia, -ua*
Russian	*-in, -ov, -sky*

When speaking Russian, an Abkhazian may find it convenient to russianize his surname: Sandro Chegemba (Sandro of Chegem) becomes Sandro Chegemsky. In an official context he will acquire a patronymic devised on the Russian pattern: Sandro, son of Khabug, is politely addressed as Sandro Khabugovich.

Although place names have been omitted from the glossary, the places mentioned are real. The only exceptions are the districts of Kenguria and Enduria, with their respective central cities, Kengursk and Endursk. The latter name derives from the Russian root *dur-*, "fool." The name Mukhus is an anagram for Sukhum, the capital of Abkhazia.

I would like to acknowledge my great debt to Carl Proffer of Ardis Publishers, who turned the project of translating *Sandro* over to me after making a good beginning on it himself. Substantial portions of the chapters entitled "Sandro of Chegem" and "Belshazzar's Feasts" are based on his initial draft.

I am also grateful beyond words to my friend Rima Zolina and all the many others who have been kind enough to comment on my manuscript or answer questions about the text.

—SUSAN BROWNSBERGER

ABKHAZIA: A SELECTIVE HISTORICAL OUTLINE

Sixth century B.C.	The Greeks colonize Abkhazia, a Caucasian land then known as Colchis, at the eastern end of the Black Sea. Their cities—especially Dioscurias, modern Sukhum—grow to be prosperous trade centers.
First century B.C.	The Romans build fortifications at Sukhum. Roman writers comment on the longevity of the indigenous hunters and shepherds.
Third century A.D.	Abkhazia begins to develop a form of feudalism based on the patriarchal clan system.
523 A.D.	Abkhazia becomes a vassal of the Byzantine Empire, accepts Christianity.
780–978	The independent Kingdom of Abkhazia enjoys a brief flowering before it is absorbed by its powerful neighbor to the east, Georgia.
1578	Abkhazia falls to the Ottoman Empire and accepts Islam, although traces of Christianity and paganism endure. The country enters a period of economic decay, since the Turks use it primarily as a source of cattle and slaves.
Eighteenth century	In alliance with Georgia, Abkhazia makes repeated efforts to drive out the Turks.

1810	The prince of Abkhazia seeks and receives formal Russian protection, although the highland tribesmen resist "infidel" czarist rule.
1840s	After a series of revolts Abkhazian peasants begin emigrating, deluded by promises of wealth and religious tolerance in Turkey.
1859	Imam Shamyl, the great leader of Caucasia's highland tribes, surrenders to Russian forces.
1860s	Abkhazia is annexed outright by the Russian Empire; a major rebellion is crushed; the old fortress at Sukhum is converted to a prison. Mass emigrations reach their peak.
1903	Lenin's underground paper *The Spark* attacks Prince Oldenburgsky's plan for making Gagra into a Russian health resort.
1905	The abortive revolution in Russia sparks a wave of violence in the Caucasus; many socialists are imprisoned at Sukhum.
February 1917	Noy Zhordania, a Menshevik, becomes head of the new Communist government in Transcaucasia (the area including Abkhazia, Georgia, Azerbaidzhan, and Armenia).
October 1917	The Bolsheviks storm the Winter Palace in Leningrad and take over the Soviet government.
April 1918	Zhordania declares the Federation of Transcaucasian Republics independent from the Soviet Union. His Menshevik government has wide popular support, although the federation is threatened by internal dissension.
May 1918	The Battle of the Kodor ends in victory for the Mensheviks, a major success in their struggle for control of Transcaucasia.
1921	The Red Army regains Transcaucasia after heavy fighting; Abkhazia is now a republic of the U.S.S.R., headed by Nestor Lakoba.
1921–28	Lenin's New Economic Policy, a blend of capitalism and communism, is successful as an interim measure to restore the Russian economy to its prewar level.
1924	Lenin dies, Stalin begins his power grab.
1929	The collectivization of agriculture begins, over widespread resistance in Abkhazia.
1931	Abkhazia is reduced to the status of an administrative unit within Georgia, although Lakoba remains president of its Central Executive Committee until his death in 1936.

1936–38	Stalin's purges are carried out in Georgia by Beria (a Mingrelian).
1942–43	The Germans invade Abkhazia, aiming for the North Caucasian oil fields.
1948	Tito's revolt against Stalin and a rise in nationalist sentiments among other ethnic groups lead to a renewed period of terror in the U.S.S.R.
1953	Stalin dies, Khrushchev takes over.
1956	At the Twentieth Party Congress, Khrushchev denounces the cult of personality surrounding Stalin and inaugurates a period of liberalization.
1964	Khrushchev is ousted, succeeded by Brezhnev and Kosygin.

GLOSSARY

ABREK A rebel outlaw; originally, a member of one of the guerrilla bands formed by Caucasian highlanders to resist the rule of Czarist Russia in the nineteenth century.

ADYGEANS The people of the Adygei Region, in Northern Caucasia.

AJIKA A very hot condiment made of ground walnuts, garlic, red pepper, and other spices.

ALEXANDER III (1845–1894) Emperor of Russia 1881–1894.

ALLAVERDY "To your health!"

AVARIANS A people of Dagestan, in the northeastern Caucasus.

AZRAEL The angel of death in Islam.

"BAD HAND" A short story by Iskander, translated by Marcia Satin under the title "Kolcheruky" (*Ardis Anthology of Recent Russian Prose*, Ann Arbor, 1973).

BERIA, LAVRENTY (1899–1953) A Mingrelian, born in Georgia; became head of the Soviet secret police in 1938; lost out in the power struggle after Stalin's death; executed for conspiracy in 1953.

BISMILLAH IRRAHMANI IRRAHIM! "In the name of Allah, the Compassionate, the Merciful!" (Arabic formula, used at the beginning of chapters of the Koran.)

BOLSHEVIKS After 1903, the majority wing of the Russian Communist Party, led by Lenin.

BORZHOM Sparkling mineral water from Borzhomi, in Georgia.

BORSCH Russian beet and cabbage soup.

BUKHARIN, N.I. (1888–1938) Communist theoretician; editor of *Pravda*; wanted to move slowly on collectivization; expelled from the Party, 1929; readmitted, 1934; suspected of Trotskyism; executed, 1938.

BURKA The Russian name for the long felt cloak traditionally worn by Caucasian men. The Abkhazian version is usually black, very full, with broad boxy shoulders.

CATHERINE II (the Great, 1729–96) Empress of Russia, 1762–96.

CHACHA A strong liquor distilled from grape pressings.

CHACHBA The royal house of Abkhazia, c. 780–1864.

CHAMGURI A small, harplike Abkhazian folk instrument.

CHARU-SE Roll of the dice: 4,3.

CHEKA (Russian) Acronym for a notorious special unit of the Soviet secret police, 1917–1922.

CHEKIST (Russian) An official of the Cheka (q.v.); colloquially, any secret police agent.

CHERKESKA The Russian name for the coat traditionally worn by Caucasian highlanders. It is usually calf-length, collarless, closely fitted to the waist, with a row of polished cartridge cases stitched across the chest.

CHUREK Unleavened bread, baked in flat rounds.

CHURKHCHELI A snack made by stringing walnut meats, candying them in grape syrup,and hanging them to dry.

COLCHIANS The Greek name for the Abkhazians' ancestors.

CENTRAL EXECUTIVE COMMITTEE Until 1936, the executive organ of the Congresses of Soviets, which were the highest elective bodies of the several Soviet republics.

COUNCIL OF PEOPLE'S COMMISSARS From 1917 to 1946, the government of the U.S.S.R. or one of its member republics.

DADIANI The medieval princely family of Mingrelia, in Georgia.

DEPUTY An elected representative of the people to a Soviet of Workers' Deputies, the local governmental unit of the U.S.S.R.

DESTROYER BATTALION A civilian militia raised to help repel the German invasion of Abkhazia during World War II.

DIABOLOS (Greek) Devil.

DORT-CHAR Roll of the dice: double 4.

DU-BARA Roll of the dice: double 2.

DUR-RAK (Russian; properly, *durak*) Fool.

DU-SE Roll of the dice: double 3.

DU-YAK Roll of the dice: double 1.

DZHIGIT A type of Caucasian horseman, noted for a daring, showy riding style.

ERFURT PROGRAM Marxist program adopted in 1891 by the German Socialist Labor Party.

ERTOBA (Georgian) Unity. Around 1905, the word came into use as the name of the Georgian revolutionary movement.

GREAT SNOW, THE A seven-foot snowfall in Abkhazia in 1910.

GREAT WALL OF ABKHAZIA Built in the sixth century A.D. to keep out marauding northern tribes.

GRECHKO, A.A. (1903–76) Commander in chief of Soviet armed forces, 1960–67; minister of defense, 1967–76.

HALVA A sweet made of nuts or sesame seeds and honey.

JEZVE A small, narrow-necked, long-handled Turkish coffeepot made of brass or enamel.

KALININ, M.I. (1875–1946) President of the U.S.S.R., 1923–46.

KEMENTZES A lyrelike Greek folk instrument.

KERAZ Originally, an Abkhazian mutual aid organization for peasants. In 1917, the word was used as the name of a peasant army, led by Lakoba (q.v.), which helped take Sukhum for the Bolsheviks.

KHABAR (Arabic) Rumor, inside information.

KHACHAPURI Caucasian cheese-filled pastry made for special occasions.

KHASH A spicy soup based on lamb broth.

KHRUSHCHEV, N.S. (1894–1971) First secretary of the Communist Party, 1953–64; premier of the U.S.S.R., 1958–64; presided over a period of liberalization in internal politics; ousted in 1964.

KHURJIN A Middle Eastern saddlebag.

KOLKHOZ (Russian) Collective farm.

KOMSOMOL (Russian) Young Communists' League, for ages fourteen to twenty-five.

KOZINAKI Brittle candy made of almonds or walnuts and honey.

KULAK (Russian) A wealthy peasant farmer, especially one who used hired hands.

KUMKHOZ Local Abkhazian pronunciation of *kolkhoz* (q.v.).

LAKOBA, NESTOR APOLLONOVICH (1893–1936) Active in the early Bolshevik movement in the Caucasus; president of the Abkhazian Council of People's Commissars from 1922, president of Abkhazian Central Executive Committee 1930–36.

LAZ An ancient Caucasian tribe, eastern neighbors of Abkhazia.

LEZGINKA A Caucasian dance.

LOBIO A spicy bean dish.

MARS A gammon, the loss of a double game in *nard* (q.v.).

MASH-ALLAH! (Arabic) A Muslim blessing; literally, "That which God has given."

MENSHEVIKS After 1903, the minority wing of the Russian Communist Party, opposed to Lenin. They held power in Transcaucasia, 1917–21.

MIKOYAN, A.I. (1895–1978) Soviet statesman of Armenian descent; held positions of power under both Stalin and Khrushchev.

MINGRELIANS An ethnic group living in Abkhazia and western Georgia.

"MRAVALDZHAMIE" (Georgian) "Long life."

NARD The ancient form of backgammon played throughout the Middle East. The jargon used is a mixture of Turkish and Persian.

NEW ECONOMIC POLICY A policy encouraging a mixture of socialism and capitalism, introduced as an emergency measure by Lenin in 1921. In 1928, when the war-ravaged economy had recuperated to its 1913 level, strict communism was reintroduced and private trade was outlawed.

NICHOLAS II (1868–1918) Emperor of Russia, 1894–1917; executed with his family in 1918.

NKVD People's Commissariat of Internal Affairs, the Soviet security agency, 1934–41; responsible for Stalin's purges of 1936–38.

OIN A "single" in *nard* (q.v.).

OLDENBURGSKY, ALEXANDER PETROVICH A scion of the Holstein-Gottorp line of the German house of Oldenburg; related to the Romanov czars; opened a health resort at Gagra on the Black Sea coast in 1903.

O-RAYDA, SIUA-RAYDA A standard refrain in Abkhazian folk songs.

PARTISANS Communist guerrilla bands, especially those active in the Revolution of 1917 and in German-occupied territories during World War II.

PETER I (the Great, 1672–1725) Czar of Russia from 1682, emperor 1721–25; famous for his attempts to westernize Russian government and culture.

PETER III (1728–62) Grandson of Peter the Great; son of Charles Frederick of Holstein-Gottorp. Emperor of Russia 1761–62; deposed with connivance of his wife, who succeeded him as Catherine II (q.v.).

POTEMKIN A Russian battleship on which sailors mutinied in 1905.

PREOBRAZHENSKY REGIMENT A guard unit formed by Peter the Great, disbanded in 1917.

RASTAK (Russian) Euphemism for "fuck" or "fuck over."

RUDENKO, R.A. (b. 1907) Attorney general of the U.S.S.R. since 1953.

RUKHADZE, N. Georgian minister of state security, 1952–53; installed at the behest of Beria (q.v.) to effect a purge of "nationalists" in the Georgian government; imprisoned after Stalin's death, executed in 1955.

SATSIVI A spicy walnut sauce.

SHAKHSEY-VAKHSEY Ritual of mourning.

SHAMYL (c. 1790–1871) Imam of Dagestan, 1834–59; led the highland tribes of the Caucasus in a long, spectacular holy war against czarist rule. He was captured in 1859, received with honor by the czar, and died in the holy city of Medina.

SHASH-BESH Roll of the dice: 6–5.

SHERVASHIDZE The Georgian name taken by the Chachbas (q.v.) after Abkhazia came under the sway of Georgia.

SOVIET (Russian) An elected council.

STAKHANOVITE A title awarded to prolific workers (Stakhanov was a prodigious coal miner of the 1930s).

STALIN (Iosif V. Dzhugashvili, 1879–1953) A Georgian, active in revolutionary politics from the 1890s; seized power after Lenin's death in 1924.

SVANS An isolated tribe of the high mountain valleys of the Caucasus. Formerly they lived in tower-houses, the better to watch for enemies; their language is still unwritten.

TAMADA Head of the table, toastmaster. Always a skillful speaker, a master of ritual, an indefatigable drinker, and an expert in human nature.

TITO (Josip Broz, 1892–1980) Led Yugoslavia to independence from the Soviet bloc in 1948.

TOVARISH (Russian) Comrade.

TROTSKY, LEON (1897–1940) Russian revolutionary, active from 1890s; banished in 1929 for "anti-Party activities"; assassinated in Mexico.

TSARITSYN Russian city on the Volga, taken by the Bolsheviks in 1917, defended by Stalin and Voroshilov in 1918–19. (Later renamed Stalingrad, now Volgograd.)

TWENTIETH CONGRESS The 1956 Party congress at which Khrushchev gave his "secret speech" denouncing Stalin and the cult of personality.

VOROSHILOV, KLIMENTY (1881–1969) Early supporter of Lenin; fought in revolution; people's commissar for defense, 1925–1940; commanded Leningrad front in World War II; president of the U.S.S.R., 1953–60.

WILD DIVISION World War I Russian army unit drawn from warlike southern tribesmen.

WINTER PALACE The imperial residence in Leningrad, taken over by the Communists as a government building in February 1917; stormed by the Bolsheviks in October 1917. Now the Hermitage Museum.

YAT An archaic letter of the Cyrillic alphabet, retained by aristocratic writers until the reforms of 1917 abolished it.

ZHORDANIA, NOY (1870–1953) Georgian socialist, active from the 1890s; leader of the Menshevik faction in the Caucasus; after the 1917 revolution, sought to establish an independent federation of Transcaucasian republics, with aid from European powers; finally fled in defeat in 1921.

ZIM A large Soviet car produced in the 1940s, used mainly by high officials.